PAT CONROY'S
THE LORDS OF DISCIPLINE

THE
LORDS
OF
DISCIPLINE

Pat Conroy

BANTAM BOOKS

TORONTO • NEW YORK • LONDON • SYDNEY • AUCKLAND

*This low-priced Bantam Book
has been completely reset in a type face
designed for easy reading, and was printed
from new plates. It contains the complete
text of the original hard-cover edition.*
NOT ONE WORD HAS BEEN OMITTED.

THE LORDS OF DISCIPLINE

*A Bantam Book / published by arrangement with
Houghton Mifflin Company*

PRINTING HISTORY

*Bantam edition / February 1982
2nd printing . . . February 1983*

ISBN 0-553-23396-3

Published simultaneously in the United States and Canada

PRINTED IN THE UNITED STATES OF AMERICA

H   11 10 9 8 7

This book is dedicated with love and gratitude to Lt. Col. Thomas Nugent Courvoisie, U.S.A. (ret.), the finest military officer I have ever known. And to Joseph Michael Devito and Robert D. Marks, friends and brothers.

And to James T. Roe III and John C. Warley. And to my friends, teachers, classmates, and teammates at The Citadel from 1963 to 1967. And to the boys who did not make it.

Special thanks to these five remarkable people from Houghton Mifflin: Norman Berg, Shannon Ravenel Purves, Jonathan and Susan Galassi, and to Anne Barrett, whose retirement was a great loss to publishing and to the writers who loved her.

With heart at rest I climbed the citadel's
steep height, and saw the city as from a tower,
hospital, brothel, prison, and such hells,
where evil comes up softly like a flower.

BAUDELAIRE'S EPILOGUE

Contents

THE
LORDS
OF
DISCIPLINE

Prologue

I wear the ring.

I wear the ring and I return often to the city of Charleston, South Carolina, to study the history of my becoming a man. My approach to Charleston is always silent and distracted, but I come under full sail, with hissing silk and memories a-wing above me in the shapes of the birds I love best: old brown pelicans, Great Blue herons, cowbirds, falcons lost at sea, ospreys lean from dives, and eagles over schools of mullet. I am a lowcountry boy. My entrance to this marsh-haunted city is always filled with troubled meditations on both my education and my solitude during a four-year residence at the Institute.

The city of Charleston, in the green feathery modesty of its palms, in the certitude of its style, in the economy and stringency of its lines, and the serenity of its mansions South of Broad Street, is a feast for the human eye. But to me, Charleston is a dark city, a melancholy city, whose severe covenants and secrets are as powerful and beguiling as its elegance, whose demons dance their alley dances and compose their malign hymns to the side of the moon I cannot see. I studied those demons closely once, and they helped kill off the boy in me.

I am not a son of Charleston. Nor could I be if I wanted to. I am always a visitor, and my allegiance lies with other visitors, sons and daughters of accident and circumstance. Edgar Allan Poe was a son by visitation. It was no surprise to me when I was a freshman at the Institute to discover that Poe was once stationed at Fort Moultrie and that he wrote "The Gold Bug" about one of the sea islands near Charleston. I like to think of him walking the streets of Charleston as I walked them, and it pleases me to think that the city watched him, felt the shimmer of his madness and genius in his slouching promenades along Meeting Street. I like to think of the city shaping this agitated, misplaced soldier, keening his passion for shade, trimming the soft edges of his nightmare, harshening his poisons and his metaphors, deepening his intimacy with the sunless wastes that issued forth from his kingdom of nightmare in blazing islands, still inchoate and unformed, of the English language. Whenever I go back to Charleston, I think of Poe. I remember that Poe spent a single year attending West Point before dropping out in disgrace and beginning his life among words. I wonder how that year in the barracks marked him; I wonder if our markings were similar.

Osceola was another visitor to Charleston. The Seminole chieftain, betrayed by white flags and white man's honor and brought to prison in Fort Moultrie, died there after a month's internment, dreaming of tannic-stained creeks flowing through mangrove, flowing north from Florida, through the salt-rusted bars, bringing the heat of council fires, the cries of betrayed warriors, and the shiver of a man returning to the serenity of cypress and safety of otters. Osceola's bones rested in a grave on Sullivan's Island until they were stolen in the spring of my sophomore year. I remember hoping that the thief was a full-blooded Seminole who knew where the greatest of his tribe should be put to rest. Shortly after the theft of Osceola's remains, I found myself in H. R. Rabun's bar on King Street, surrounded by a group of cadets from R Company, toasting the escape of the chief. In the midst of this, I indulged myself with a vision. I saw myself cutting through the bars of Osceola's cell, and together we made it back to the swamps, the Indian teaching me the ways of the forest as we traveled southward, giddy with the star-blaze of freedom. My God, it was a beautiful thing to see the Everglades through the eyes of Osceola. But in this vision I had one regret: I would have liked first to have shown him Charleston through my eyes, through the eyes of Will McLean. I, too, had my Charleston cell, and I, too, would have some bones to show him.

Though I will always be a visitor to Charleston, I will always remain one with a passionate belief that it is the most beautiful city in America and that to walk the old section of the city at night is to step into the bloodstream of a history extravagantly lived by a people born to a fierce and unshakable advocacy of their past. To walk in the spire-proud shade of Church Street is to experience the chronicle of a mythology that is particular to this city and this city alone, a trinitarian mythology with equal parts of the sublime, the mysterious, and the grotesque. But there is nothing to warn you of Charleston's refined cruelty. That knowledge must be earned. No gargoyles hang from the sides of St. Philip's or St. Michael's. No messages are in the iron scrollwork of its gates to warn visitors like Poe, Osceola, me, and you.

The city of Charleston burns like a flame of purest memory. It is a city distorted by its own self-worship. I do not believe there is another city like it on earth, nor do I believe there is another college like the Institute. Nor can I imagine the Institute in any other city. The school has adopted many of the odd, quirky mannerisms of Charleston itself, an osmotic, subterranean effect, and each has shaped the other, magnified the other's flaws, reinforced the other's strengths. If the Institute existed in San Francisco, Chicago, Dallas, or Phoenix, it would be a vastly different school, and I would be a vastly different man. The city, river-girt, has a tyrannical need for order and symmetry. It is not a city of outlaws, not a landscape for renegades. There is no ambiance of hazard here, but something so tightly repressed, so rigidly ordered, so consecrated to the adoration of restraint that you sometimes want to scream out for excess, for a single knee bent toward bad taste, for the cleansing roar of pandemonium to establish a foothold somewhere in the city. But, of course, the charm of the city lies in this adherence to a severity of form. Entering Charleston is like walking through the brilliant carbon forest of a diamond with the light dazzling you in a thousand ways, an assault of light and shadow caused by light. The sun and the city have struck up an irreversible alliance. The city turns inward upon itself, faces away from visitors, alluringly contained in its own mystery. The city has a smell, a fecund musk of aristocracy, with the wine and the history of the lowcountry aging beneath the verandahs, the sweetly decadent odors of lost causes. Around you, in late August, beauty is reduced at last to beauty at the confluence of two rivers. But I know what the late August smell of the city is; I know it well. It is the awful fear of boys entering the Institute to begin their plebe year. That is what I smell when I cross the Ashley River on my return to Charleston.

*　*　*

I define myself in this way: I am the son of Thomas Patrick McLean of Savannah, Georgia, a volatile, brawling man who attended Benedictine High School and Carolina Military Institute, and as a Marine captain won a Navy Cross for his valor under fire during the invasion of Iwo Jima. He returned to Savannah as a wounded hero in 1944, went to work for Belk's department store, and married a girl from Dahlonega, Georgia, who worked in the perfume department after a brief stint in notions. I liked neither the Corps nor Belk's nor my father, but grew up worshiping the black-haired woman from the perfume department. My mother blamed my father's temper on Iwo Jima, but I entertained the heretical thought that he was a son of a bitch long before the Japanese invaded Pearl Harbor. When he was dying of cancer, he made me promise to attend and graduate from Carolina Military Institute, and through tears, I promised. He told me to stop crying and act like a man and I did. Then he made me promise I would be a pilot when I entered the service, that he didn't want any son of his getting killed on some godforsaken beach like Iwo Jima, especially a son he loved as much as he did me. Eight hours after he told me he loved me for the first time, he died of melanoma and left me a prisoner of his memory. At age fourteen, I was the man of the house.

My mother is a different case. As lovely a woman as I have ever seen, bred and nurtured like a gardenia, she has always seemed somehow odorless and sexless to me, yet viscerally seductive in the manner of Southern women, that taloned species who speak with restrained and self-effacing drawls, fill a room with elegance and vulnerability, move with the grace of wind-tilted cane, and rule their families with a secret pact of steel. The sweetness of Southern women often conceals the secret deadliness of snakes. It has helped them survive the impervious tyranny of Southern men more comfortable with a myth than a flesh-and-blood woman.

It took me years to spot the howitzers in my mother's eyes and many more to understand why they were there. Because of my father, my childhood was a long march of fear; my mother's dispassionate assent to his authority took me longer to discover. She won my everlasting love by wading fearlessly into battle with my father whenever he abused me. For years I looked at her uncritically. But I learned something in my long earnest study of my mother. The adversary who is truly formidable is the one who works within the fortress walls, singing pleasant songs while licking honey off knives. It was my mother who encouraged me to keep my promise to attend the Institute. It was my mother who made me stay. Because she was a Southern wife, my domination by things totalitarian did not end when my father

4

died, weighing one hundred pounds less than he had in his prime. Her severity was soft, but severity nonetheless, for she was a product of the South as much as I was. My father's discipline was harsh and unmistakable; the discipline of my mother disguised itself in love and tenderness and often held far greater terrors. I am always writing revisionist histories of my mother. But because I needed to love her and love her deeply, her strafing runs against me brought on surrender almost immediately. I was all white flags and trembling fingers signing treaties and giving up territories to her. She, a Southern lady, had raised me to be a Southern gentleman, and that made us both foreigners in my father's house. In the lock step of my nineteenth year I entered Carolina Military Institute. I did it because of my mother. She and I agreed it was because of my father. A lifetime of practice had taught us to blame everything on him. My father had become the manager of Belk's, but he never could lure me from behind the perfume counter.

But in the end, the Institute was my choice and my responsibility. It, too, became part of my definition. My instincts were those of sheep, lemmings, and herring. I trundled along with the herd on the course of least resistance. My parents had trained me exquisitely in the fine art of obedience. Because I was Southern, the military school seemed like the place for a final honing, the polishing of the rough spots. I would emerge glossy and shiny from the Institute as a man to serve my country in any way I could, but with absolute devotion and forthrightness. A Southern man is incomplete without a tenure under military rule. I am not an incomplete Southern man. I am simply damaged goods, like all the rest of them.

At first, I thought I had wasted my college years, but I was wrong. The Institute was the most valuable experience I have ever had or will have. I believe it did bring me into manhood: The Institute taught me about the kind of man I did not want to be. Through rigorous harshness, I became soft and learned to trust that softness. Through the distorted vision of that long schizophrenia, I became clear-sighted. Under its system, a guerrilla was born inside me, and when the other boys rushed to embrace the canons of the Institute, I took to the hills.

Whenever I look at photographs of myself in the cadet days, I stare into the immobile face of a stranger. His name is mine and his face seems distantly related, but I cannot reconcile the look of him. The frozen, unconvincing smile is an expression of almost incomprehensible melancholy. I feel compassion and unspeakable love for this thin, fearful ancestor. I honor the courage he did not know he possessed. For four years he was afraid. Yet he remained. A lifetime in a Southern family negated any possibility that he could resign from the school under any conditions other than unequivocal disgrace. Yet I know what he did and what he said, how he felt and how he survived. I relive his journey in dreams and nightmares and in returns to the city of Charleston. He haunts me and remains a stranger. Once while they were doing pushups on a shower-room floor, a classmate, too exhausted to turn his head, threw up on him. The upperclassmen made all the freshmen roll in the vomit of their classmate until nothing was left on the fetid tiles. He remembered the moment often, not because of his disgust or humiliation, but because it was then that he had the first premonition that someday he would tell his story, tell what it was like to be at the Institute, an eyewitness report on the contours and lineaments of discipline. Amidst the dark hearts of the boys around him, he felt a magnificent radiance. He would roll in vomit again, but the next time the symbolism of the act would be clear to him. This was the story he would tell: At the Institute the making of men was a kind of grotesque artistry.

Yet I am a product of this artistry. And I have a need to bear witness to what I saw there. I want to tell you how it was. I want precision. I want a murderous, stunning truthfulness. I want to find my own singular voice for the first time. I want you to understand why I hate the school with all my power and passion. Then I want you to forgive me for loving the school. Some of the boys of the Institute and the men who are her sons will hate me for the rest of their lives. But that will be all right. You see, I wear the ring.

PART I

THE CADRE

September 1966

1

When I crossed the Ashley River my senior year in my gray 1959 Chevrolet, I was returning with confidence and even joy. I'm a senior now, I thought, looking to my right and seeing the restrained chaste skyline of Charleston again. The gentleness and purity of that skyline had always pleased me. A fleet of small sailboats struggled toward a buoy in the windless river, trapped like pale moths in the clear amber of late afternoon. Then I looked to my left and saw, upriver, the white battlements and parapets of Carolina Military Institute, as stolid and immovable in reality as in memory. The view to the left no longer caused me to shudder involuntarily as it had the first year. No longer was I returning to the cold, inimical eyes of the cadre. Now the cold eyes were mine and those of my classmates, and I felt only the approaching freedom that would come when I graduated in June. After a long childhood with an unbenign father and four years at the Institute, I was looking forward to that day of release when I would no longer be subject to the fixed, irresistible tenets of martial law, that hour when I would be presented with my discharge papers and could walk without cadences for the first time.

I was returning early with the training cadre in the third week of August. It was 1966, the war in Vietnam was gradually escalating, and Charleston had never looked so beautiful, so untouchable, or so completely mine. Yet there was an oddity about my presence on campus at this early date. I would be the only cadet private in the barracks during that week when the cadre would prepare to train the incoming freshmen. The cadre was composed of the highest-ranking cadet officers and non-coms in the corps of cadets. To them fell the serious responsibility of teaching the freshmen the cheerless rudiments of the fourth-class system during plebe

9

week. The cadre was a diminutive regiment of the elite, chosen for their leadership, their military sharpness, their devotion to duty, their ambition, and their unquestioning, uncomplicated belief in the system.

I had not done well militarily at the Institute. As an embodiment of conscious slovenliness, I had been a private for four consecutive years, and my classmates, demonstrating remarkable powers of discrimination, had consistently placed me near the bottom of my class. I was barely cadet material, and no one, including me, ever considered the possibility of my inclusion on the cadre.

But in my junior year, the cadets of fourth battalion had surprised both me and the Commandant's Department by selecting me as a member of the honor court, a tribunal of twenty-one cadets known for their integrity, sobriety, and honesty. I may not have worn a uniform well, but I was chock full of all that other stuff. It was the grim, excruciating duty of the honor court to judge the guilt or innocence of their peers accused of lying, stealing, cheating, or of tolerating those who did. Those found guilty of an honor violation were drummed out of the Corps in a dark ceremony of expatriation that had a remorseless medieval splendor about it. Once I had seen my first drumming-out, it removed any temptation I might have had to challenge the laws of the honor code. The members of the court further complicated my life by selecting me as its vice chairman, a singularly indecipherable act that caused me a great deal of consternation, since I did not even understand my election to that cold jury whose specialty was the killing off of a boy's college career. By a process of unnatural selection, I had become one of those who could summon the Corps and that fearful squad of drummers for the ceremony of exile. Since I was vice chairman of the court, the Commandant's Department had ordered me to report two weeks before the arrival of the regular Corps. In my senior year, irony had once again gained a foothold in my life, and I was a member of the training cadre. Traditionally, the chairman and vice chairman explained the rules and nuances of the honor system to the regiment's newest recruits. Traditionally, the vice chairman had always been a cadet officer, but even at the Institute tradition could not always be served. Both tradition and irony have their own system of circulation, their own sense of mystery and surprise.

I did not mind coming back for cadre. Since my only job was to introduce the freshmen to the pitfalls and intricacies

10

of honor, I was going to provide the freshmen with their link to the family of man. Piety comes easily to me. I planned to make them laugh during the hour they were marched into my presence, to crack a few jokes, tell them about my own plebe year, let them relax, and if any of them wanted to, catch up on the sleep they were missing in the barracks. The residue of that long, sanctioned nightmare was still with me, and I wanted to tell these freshmen truthfully that no matter how much time had elapsed since that first day at the Institute, the one truth the system had taught me was this: A part of me would always be a plebe.

I pulled my car through the Gates of Legrand and waited for the sergeant of the guard to wave me through. He was conferring with the Cadet Officer of the Guard, who looked up and recognized me.

"McLean, you load," Cain Gilbreath said, his eighteen-inch neck protruding from his gray cotton uniform shirt.

"Excuse me, sir," I said, "but aren't you a full-fledged Institute man? My, but you're a handsome, stalwart fellow. My country will always be safe with men such as you."

Cain walked up to my car, put his gloved hand against the car, and said, "There was a rumor you'd been killed in an auto wreck. The whole campus is celebrating. How was your summer, Will?"

"Fine, Cain. How'd you pull guard duty so early?"

"Just lucky. Do you have religious beliefs against washing this car?" he asked, withdrawing his white glove from the hood. "By the way, the Bear's looking for you."

"What for?"

"I think he wants to make you regimental commander. How in the hell would I know? What do you think about the big news?"

"What big news?"

"The nigger."

"That's old news, and you know what I think about it."

"Let's have a debate."

"Not now, Cain," I said, "but let's go out for a beer later on in the week."

"I'm a varsity football player," he said with a grin, his blue eyes flashing. "I'm not allowed to drink during the season."

"How about next Thursday?"

"Fine. Good to see you, Will. I've missed trading insults with you." I drove the car through the Gates of Legrand for

11

my fourth and final year. I realized that the Institute was now a part of my identity. I was nine months away from being a native of this land.

Before I unloaded my luggage in the barracks, I took a leisurely ride down the Avenue of Remembrance, which ran past the library, the chapel, and Durrell Hall on the west side of the parade ground. The Avenue was named in honor of the epigram from Ecclesiastes that appeared above the chapel door: "Remember Now Thy Creator in the Days of Thy Youth." When I first saw the unadorned architecture of the Institute, I thought it was unrelievedly ugly. But it had slowly grown on me. The beauty of the campus, an acquired taste, certainly, lay in its stalwart understatement, its unapologetic capitulation to the supremacy of line over color, to the artistry of repetition, and the lyrics of a scrupulous unsentimental vision. The four barracks and all the main academic buildings on campus faced inward toward the parade ground, a vast luxurious greensward trimmed like the fairway of an exclusive golf course. The perfume of freshly mown grass hung over the campus throughout much of the year. Instruments of war decorated the four corners of the parade ground: a Sherman tank, a Marine landing craft, a Jupiter missile, and an Air Force Sabre jet. Significantly, all of these pretty decorations were obsolete and anachronistic when placed in reverent perpetuity on campus. The campus looked as though a squad of thin, humorless colonels had designed it. At the Institute, there was no ostentation of curve, no vagueness of definition, no blurring of order. There was a perfect, almost heartbreaking, congruence to its furious orthodoxy. To an unromantic eye, the Institute had the look of a Spanish prison or a fortress beleaguered not by an invading force but by the more threatening anarchy of the twentieth century buzzing insensately outside the Gates of Legrand.

It always struck me as odd that the Institute was one of the leading tourist attractions in Charleston. Every Friday afternoon, the two thousand members of the Corps of Cadets would march in a full-dress parade for the edification of both the tourists and the natives. There was always something imponderably beautiful in the anachronism, in the synchronization of the regiment, in the flashing gold passage of the Corps past the reviewing stand in a ceremony that was a direct throwback to the times when Napoleonic troops strutted for their emperor. Ever since the school had been founded in 1842, after a slave insurrection, the Corps had marched on Fridays in Charleston, except on the Friday

12

following that celebrated moment when cadets from the Institute had opened fire on the Star of the East, a Northern supply ship trying to deliver supplies to the beleaguered garrison at Fort Sumter. Historians credited those cadets with the first shots in the War Between the States. It was the proudest moment in the history of the school, endlessly appreciated and extolled as the definitive existential moment in its past. Patriotism was an alexin of the blood at the Institute, and we, her sons, would march singing and eager into every battle with the name of the Institute on our lips. There was something lyric and terrible in the fey mindlessness of Southern boys, something dreary and exquisite in the barbaric innocence of all things military in the South. The Institute, romantic and bizarre, was the city of Charleston's shrine to Southern masculinity. It was one of the last state-supported military schools in America, and the boys who formed her ranks were the last of a breed. I had always liked the sound of that: McLean, last of a breed.

I pulled my car up to the front of Number Four barracks. In my loafers, Bermuda shorts, and a T-shirt, I savored my last moments out of uniform. I was lifting my luggage out of the trunk when I was frozen into absolute stillness by the roar of a powerful voice behind me.

"Halt, Bubba."

I had jumped when he let loose with his scream. I always jumped when he yelled at me. He knew it and enjoyed the fact immensely. I did not turn around to face him but merely stood at attention beside my car.

"Good afternoon, Colonel," I said to Colonel Thomas Berrineau, the Commandant of Cadets.

"How did you know it was me, Bubba?" he asked, coming into my field of vision.

"I'd recognize that high-pitched castrato voice anywhere, Colonel. How was your summer, sir?"

"My summer was fine, Bubba. I could relax. You weren't on campus. I didn't have to worry about my niece's virtue or plots against the Institute. Where did you spend your summer, McLean? The Kremlin? Peking? Hanoi?"

"I stayed home knitting mufflers for our boys in Vietnam, Colonel," I said. "It was the least I could do."

"You son of a Bolshevik," he whispered softly as he drew his face nearer to mine. A cigar hung from his pendulous lower lip, and its ash glowed brightly inches away from my right cornea. I had never seen the Bear without a cigar in his mouth. I could more easily have imagined him without a nose or ears. You could often smell his approach before you saw him. Your nose would warn you of the Bear's quiet scrutiny before he unleashed that voice so famous among cadets.

"McLean, I bet you were plotting the overthrow of this country, the assassination of all the members of the Senate and the House, and the imprisonment of all military officers."

"You're absolutely right, Colonel. I was lying. I spent a jolly summer in the Kremlin studying germ warfare with Doctor Zhivago. But one thing you got wrong. I would have nothing to do with the imprisonment of all military officers. I voted to line them all up against the wall and let them have it with Yugoslav-made flame throwers."

"Who would be the first American officer to meet such a fate, lamb?" the Bear asked rhetorically. The cigar ash was on the move toward the eye again.

"Why, the most fierce fighting man in the history of the United States Army, sir. The man with the soul of a lion, the heart of a dinosaur, the brain of a paramecium, and the sexual organs of a Girl Scout. The first to be executed would be you, sir."

"You god-blessed fellow traveler Leninist," he roared, smiling. "I've got one more year to make a man out of you, McLean."

"In June, I'll be a full-fledged alumnus, Colonel. A bona fide, dyed-in-the-wool, legitimate Institute man. How does that make you feel?"

"Ashamed, Bubba. Sick to my stomach. You've got to give me one good shot at getting you kicked out of here. Promise to do something, lamb, anything. We have an international reputation, and you could be the undoing of a hundred years of pride and tradition."

"I'll make the school proud, Colonel," I said, backing away from him slightly. "I'm going to have an operation and have the ring surgically implanted in my nose."

The Bear threw his head back and bellowed out a laugh. He had an extravagant, pulpy nose, stiff, white-thatched hair, sad but cunning brown eyes the color of his cigars, and a great shovel of a mouth with dark uneven teeth that looked as though he could strip-mine a valley or graze in a field of quartz.

"It's good to see you back, Bubba. Good to see you and all the lambs. This place doesn't seem natural when the Corps is gone for the summer. But I need to see you sometime tomorrow and it'll be serious, no pootin' around like we're doing today. Meet me at Henry's down on Market Street at 1200 mañana. That's español, McLean, and it means the day after today."

"A man at home in many languages, Colonel. You should try English."

"Like you little girls down in the English Department. Tell me the truth, Bubba, is it really true what they say about English majors in the Corps? And this is confidential. I wouldn't breathe a word of it to higher authorities."

"Well, Colonel," I whispered conspiratorially, "if you promise not to tell. We go to class wearing panties and bras and Kotex underneath our uniforms. We discuss literature, giggle a lot, then sit around mincing, bending our wrists, and blowing each other. It's a very friendly department."

"No wonder you love it down there, Bubba. You've found yourself a niche. I never want to see you in the same latrine as me when I go in to take a whizz. You understand me, lamb?"

"I couldn't stand that kind of temptation, Colonel. No English major could."

"I'm nervous about taking you to lunch."

"Colonel, you've nothing to fear from me. I'll be very gentle."

"Remember. Tomorrow it's serious, Bubba. I have some business to discuss with you."

"Yes, sir."

He appraised me closely and said, "I don't know if you're more of a disgrace as a civilian or as a cadet. Carry on."

"Sir," I said.

"Yeh, Bubba."

"It's good seeing you, sir."

"Yeh, Bubba, yeh."

2

Early that evening I left the Gates of Legrand wearing my starched summer whites for my first general leave of the year. Humidity staggered the city throughout the summer. Walking the streets of Charleston in the late afternoons of

August was like walking through gauze or inhaling damaged silk.

I drove slowly through the city, past Hampton Park, down King Street, through the business district with its rows of antique shops and fine men's stores. For three years, I had felt the thumb of the city shaping me with a passion for marshes, for tidal creeks, for symmetry, and for the disciplined architecture of the eighteenth century. Charleston has a landscape that encourages intimacy and partisanship. I have heard that an early inoculation to the sights and smells of the Carolina lowcountry is an almost irreversible antidote to the charms of other landscapes, other alien geographies. You can be moved profoundly by other vistas, by other oceans, by soaring mountain ranges, but you cannot be seduced. You can even forsake the lowcountry, renounce it for other climates, but you can never completely escape the sensuous, semitropical pull of Charleston and her marshes. It is one of those cities where childhood is a pleasure and memory a flow of honey; one of those cities that never lets go, that insinuates its precedence by the insistent delicacy of its beauty.

Charleston is built on a peninsula located between two tidal rivers, the Ashley and the Cooper, which flow together to form Charleston Harbor. The peninsula has produced, oddly enough, a people with the siege mentality of islanders. Observers have described Charlestonians as vainglorious, obstinate, mercurial, verbose, xenophobic, and congenitally gracious. Most of all, they elude facile description, but they do possess a municipal character that has a lot to do with two centuries of scriptural belief that they are simply superior to other people of the earth. If you do not subscribe to this theory or are even offended by it, well, it simply means that you are from "away," that you are obviously not a Charlestonian. The entire mythology of the city is dependent on the existence of an ancient, beleaguered aristocracy who trace their heritage to the first stirrings of the Colony. They live—or would like to live—in the splendid mansions and townhouses South of Broad Street, or SOB, the rather mythical and whimsical Maginot Line of society. Each of these houses is a vessel of exquisite solitude and unrestricted privacy. Charlestonians have made an art out of living well, and the area South of Broad is arguably the most flawlessly preserved historical area in America.

The rest of South Carolina has a keenly developed inferiority complex about Charleston, a complex that Charlestonians feel is richly deserved. Unlike other cities in the region, including Savannah and Columbia, Charleston never had to endure the full fury of an assault by the armies of William Tecumseh Sherman. Charleston survived the Civil War with her architectural legacy intact and her collective unconscious simmering with aggravated memories of bombardment, reconstruction, and emancipation as she struggled to become whole again. The war succeeded in making an odd city odder, and it often seems as if Charleston still feels the presence of a phantom Armada holding the city under a perilous eternal siege. In Charleston, more than elsewhere, you get the feeling that the twentieth century is a vast, unconscionable mistake.

The mansions South of Broad Street form a magnificent archipelago of exclusion. It was not a matter of money that assured access to the charmed region; it was a matter of blood. The alloy of wealth and background was ideal, of course, but the century had proven testy and ungenerous in its treatment of some of the oldest, most celebrated families of Charleston. The descendants of planters often found themselves with the bank accounts of sewing machine salesmen. But a modest income alone never denied access to those haughty parlors; and wealth alone could never insure it. If you were crass, lowborn, or socially offensive, it would have made no difference to the proud inhabitants South of Broad that you owned France; they would not invite you to their homes. I knew girls my own age who would as soon be courted by a palmetto as by a boy denied access to South of Broad society. They were often blonde, long-stemmed girls, thin and clean and frail, who attended Ashley Hall for twelve years, went off to college in the hills of Virginia, then returned buffed and polished to marry princely fellows who were perfectly at home with all the stiffness and formality of the realm. But a casual inbreeding was beginning to have deleterious effects on some of the oldest families. During the day, the narrow streets filled up with ermine-headed children, with the eyes of Weimaraners, who were native to this land. Walking in their midst as they played games beneath the bored, distracted gazes of their nannies, I would look for chinless blonds or boys with nosebleeds. Aristocrats in Charleston, like aristocrats the world over, had proven the dangers of sipping from the genetic cup without a sense of recklessness or a gambler's eye for the proper stranger. Too many blue-eyed men had married their blue-eyed third cousins, and it was not uncommon to find husbands and wives who looked like brother and sister.

17

I was not immune to the pleasures and enchantments of Broad Street; I was not immune to pleasures and enchantments of any kind. I admired the elegiac understatement of its streets, the whole taut containment of the lower city, fragrant in its vines, disciplined in its stones. In the presence of the people who lived here, I had learned much about myself and the way I really was. My flat Irish features often shamed me as I walked in their midst. There was nothing understated or subtle about me, and my aura was one of energy, restlessness, and inadmissability. I bobbed precariously on the immigrant flood; I smelled of Kilkenny, the back seats of station wagons, and the chlorine of YMCA pools. It seemed that I had to dive down through the waters of history even to glimpse these brilliant gouramis and golden carp who dwelled so easily in the distilled fathoms of their heritage. I was more at home among the multitudes than the chosen, and the chosen knew it very well.

But I had come often to South of Broad, and I had learned that aristocracy was not a navigable river. My access to this civilization came about by accident; my instructors in the art of moving among the habitués of a charmed circle were surpassingly fine, and I owed them much. One of my roommates was born and reared on East Bay Street. His name, Tradd Prioleau St. Croix, paid tongue-twisting homage to two hundred years of Carolina history. Because of Tradd and his family, I had become familiar with the manners and customs of old Charleston. I found a parking space on East Bay and walked to the wrought iron gate of the St. Croix mansion. The house of my roommate was as splendid an edifice as I would ever enter without paying admission. Architects considered it among the five finest houses in the city of Charleston. The Tradd–St. Croix house evoked a mythic, possessive nostalgia from the reverent crowds who walked single file through its hushed, candle-lit interior each April during the annual spring tour of homes, for it was emblematic of the most remarkable instincts of that form-possessed society. All the strict and opulent criteria of taste that had once brought pleasure to the wealthiest merchants of Charleston could be studied at leisure once you crossed the threshold of Twenty-Five East Bay Street.

Abigail St. Croix was waiting for me on the lower piazza. She leaned against one of the severe, rounded Doric columns, a large-boned, awkwardly constructed woman, silent in her meditative repose, watching me climb the steps toward her. Her movements were slow and languorous, with-

18

out guile or stratagems, and as her large hands reached out to me I remembered how I had learned that there could be an immensely poignant beauty in the awkwardness of human beings from watching Abigail set a table or open a book or simply brush the hair from her eyes.

"Abigail," I said happily, running to her.

"Welcome home, Will. We missed you. I missed you the most.

"Will, I want you to see the garden before you go in to see Tradd and Commerce. I also want to have a serious talk with you before Commerce starts in on football and the seven seas."

We walked to the rear of the house toward her huge formal garden, designed and planted by her husband's great-great grandfather. Upstairs, Tradd was playing Mozart, the music spilling into the garden like snow out of season. Abigail talked as we drifted toward the bench in the rear of the garden.

"You knew my sister had a breast removed, didn't you, Will? I thought I wrote you that. It was such a grisly summer. Missy Rivers, the girl next door, you know the one, a perfectly charming girl but ugly as homemade sin, married a boy from a very nice family in Virginia. Mrs. Rivers was absolutely furious that Tradd was in England and missed the wedding. One of the children of the rector of St. Michael's drowned while sailing in the harbor. His wife is practically crazed with grief, and he's requested a transfer from Bishop Temple. . . . So much has happened, Will, and it's all so boring."

The garden was scrupulously manicured and trimmed. It extolled the virtues of discipline in its severe sculptured rows and regulated islands of green and bloom. In this garden, few flowers were allowed to die on the bush or the trellis; most of them died in stale water contained within fragile vases near the reflection of family silver.

"What are you thinking, you spectacle?" Abigail asked, interrupting her abridged version of the past summer's history.

"I've decided I want to live like this always, Abigail," I said, making a sweeping imperious gesture with my arm. "What must I do to become a Charleston aristocrat?"

"What do you think you have to do?" she said, as we navigated the brick pathways without haste.

"Let's see," I thought aloud. "Judging from the aristocrats I've met, first of all, I should have a frontal lobotomy.

19

Then I should become a hopeless alcoholic, chain a maiden aunt in an attic, engage in deviant sexual behavior with polo ponies, and talk like I was part British and part Negro."

"I had no idea that you've met *that* many of my relatives, spectacle," she said. "But please don't forget that I happen to be one of those awful people."

"I don't mean you, Abigail. You know that. I'd love to be chained in your attic."

"Hush, Will," she demanded. "I want to show you some roses."

It was in her garden that whatever physical grace Abigail St. Croix possessed asserted itself. She moved among her flowers with consummate natural fluidity, enjoying the incommunicable pleasures of growing things with the patience and concentration of a watchmaker. In this, her small, green country, surrounded by an embrasure of old Charleston brick, there were camellias of distinction, eight discrete varieties of azaleas, and a host of other flowers, but she directed her prime attention to the growing of roses. She had taught me to love flowers since I had known her; I had learned that each variety had its own special personality, its own distinctive and individual way of presenting itself to the world. She told me of the shyness of columbine, the aggression of ivy, and the diseases that affected gardenias. Some flowers were arrogant invaders and would overrun the entire garden if allowed too much freedom. Some were so diffident and fearful that in their fragile reticence often lived the truest, most infinitely prized beauty. She spoke to her flowers unconsciously as we made our way to the roses in the rear of the garden.

"You can learn a lot from raising roses, Will. I've always told you that."

"I've never raised a good weed, Abigail. I could kill kudzu."

"Then one part of your life is empty," she declared. "There's a part of the spirit that's not being fed."

"I feed the spirit with other things."

"Such as?"

"Basketball for me."

"Basketball?" she said, unable to purge the disdain from her voice. "You substitute basketball for roses? That's so dull and common, spectacle. There's too much sameness in the world, and sometimes there's too much sameness in you. That's what I love about flowers in general and roses in particular. Each one is different. Every rose that comes to this garden has its own inherent surprise, its own built-in miracle. And the world needs more roses far more than it needs more basketball players."

"Abigail, basketball *is* like that for me. I know you think I'm an idiot for saying that, and I know it sounds common to you. I understand what you're saying about roses. I really do. I'll probably never grow a black-eyed Susan in my life, much less a rose, but I think I understand how someone could become completely attached to flowers. When I play basketball, every shot is different, complicated; and each game is beautiful or ugly in its own special way. I think I look at basketball the way you look at roses or Tradd looks at Mozart or Commerce looks at his ships. All of us have been lucky. We're all passionate about something. I feel sorry for people who haven't found their passions. But, you know, Abigail, I don't think I've ever found sameness in anything in the world. Not if I looked hard enough. I used to think that the Corps represented sameness. We all dress the same, we look the same, we live by the same rules, everything. But each one of us is different. When I walk into this garden each rose looks about the same to me, and you go to a parade at the Institute and all two thousand cadets look exactly the same to you. But if you look at them carefully, Abigail, the same thing happens to those cadets as to your roses. Each one is different, with his own surprise, his own miracle."

"There's hope for my favorite jock," Abigail said.

"But there's something I want to ask you, Will," she said. "Then we'll go in and face the other men in my life." Her eyes left mine and traveled up the brick, ficus-covered walls to the window, through which the bright, lovely petals of Mozart dropped into the garden. "You and I have never talked about Tradd. We've always had this silent acquiescence between us that there were things we both knew but never discussed. There have been far too many taboos between us, Will."

"I'm not sure I know what you mean, Abigail."

"What do the boys in the barracks really think about Tradd? I'd like the truth."

"They like him a lot. They think he's a really good guy. They're always talking about how well he's fitted in since his plebe year."

"That sounds like what a courteous young man tells a mother to make her feel good about her son."

"You should feel good. And you should feel very proud," I said, somewhat defensively. "He had a terrible time his plebe year. But that's not unusual. I had a terrible time, too. But once you make it through that year at the Institute, they leave you pretty much alone. Tradd has adapted to the ways of the Corps. He's a first lieutenant, Abigail. He's doing a lot better than I am."

"Do they find him odd, Will? Do they find him effeminate?"

"He's an English major, Abigail!" I almost shouted. "An English major like me. The Corps thinks all English majors are queer as three-dollar bills. He's gentle and unathletic. He has a high-pitched voice, plays the piano, and refuses to use foul language, which is the only way to make yourself clearly understood in the barracks. That causes people to talk, but it's not important. It doesn't mean anything. I've tried to get him to show more interest in girls to quiet some of the talk. But you know what he says to me?"

"Of course not."

"He says that he goes out with girls at least as much as I do."

"And what do you say to that?"

"I don't say anything, because it's true."

"Be patient about girls, Will," Abigail said tenderly, touching my face with a large, hesitant hand. "Some fine girl will come along and appreciate you for all the right reasons. Young girls have an infinite capacity for being attracted to the wrong sort of men. I know about this. All about it."

"Commerce is a fine man, Abigail," I said, uncomfortable with the sudden turn of the conversation. "He's got one of those screwed-up Charleston first names, but so does Tradd. So does everybody in this sad, silly town."

"He was very handsome and charming and available when I met him. He was considerably older than I was, and there was as much pressure for him to get married as there was for me. I was gawky and big-footed and horse-faced and felt very lucky to get him. And we've made a life together, after a fashion. I think because he's away from Charleston so much, we are able to enjoy each other's company much of the time."

"Is that why you seem unhappy sometimes, Abigail? Because of your marriage?"

"I'm not unhappy, Will. I want you to know that, and I want you to remember it. I have more to be thankful for than most people who inhabit the earth. I have a lovely home, and I've raised a fine and sensitive son. And I have a husband who loves me despite his eccentricities and my ample faults."

I loved the face of Abigail St. Croix as I often love the faces of men and women who have an unshakable faith in their own homeliness. On this overcast late afternoon, her face, in the green, leaf-filtered gauze of light, was both classic and frozen in its demeanor and repose. Her face had integrity, an undefilable resignation. If it was handsome, it was all a cold, sedate handsomeness that gave off a somewhat disturbing aura of wisdom and pain, of having lived deeply, suffered, rallied, despaired, laughed at her despair until the face that survived all these countless darkening moods and transfigurements was lined with discernment, with a resolute sense of commitment to form, and the power to be amused slightly by the whole long journey. Long ago, her face had become beautiful to me.

We neared the house. Abigail was an unflaggingly dedicated student of her husband's ancestral place. It was an education she gladly shared with me, and though I had no abiding interest in interior or exterior design, her enthusiasm was catching. There was no antidote against one of Abigail's enthusiasms. In this extraordinary house I learned about the difference between Hepplewhite and Regency, and between Chippendale and Queen Anne. I could point out to tourists who happened by while I was reading on the wicker couch on the lower piazza, the enormous stone quoins at the entranceway, the exceptional stuccowork in those princely downstairs rooms, and the intricate delicacy of the woodwork. A passing knowledge of the Tradd–St. Croix mansion was a liberal education in itself.

It was impossible to study the history of South Carolina without encountering the venerable Huguenot name of St. Croix again and again. It was a name with an enviable, irreproachable past (unless one considered owning slaves reproachable, which, of course, the St. Croixs did not) but an uncertain future; it was a name ominously endangered by extinction. The rich and the well-born were not prodigious reproducers of their rare, thin-boned species, and my roommate Tradd had found himself in the unenviable position of bearing complete responsibility for carrying on the family name. He was the last St. Croix and the burden of extending the line weighed heavily upon him even though it was a subject he assiduously avoided. I had more first cousins than

23

a mink, or so it often seemed. If I died suddenly, the name of McLean would flourish prodigally for a thousand years; if Tradd died, the St. Croix name would survive only as a street name, a house name, and in distinguished references in history books. The grandeur and terror of extinction had formed the character of Tradd and had nearly ruined the life of his father, Commerce.

We found Commerce St. Croix where I usually found him when I came to this house—in the upstairs sitting room watching television.

"It took you long enough to come visit us, boy," he said formally as he rose to shake my hand. "I've been waiting around since morning for you to show up."

Unconsciously, he led me to a seat beside him, while his eyes returned to the television. Commerce never looked at the person he was talking to during a conversation. Nor did he ever seem to change expression. Fury or joy or grief, it did not matter; Commerce had one face and only one face to offer the world.

"I have many duties since I became regimental commander," I said, unbuttoning the bottom two buttons of my dress whites as I slumped into the chair.

"You were born a private, Will. My boy, Tradd, is a first lieutenant," Commerce said, addressing the television. If I did not watch myself, I would find myself speaking to the television, too.

"I know, Commerce. I room with your boy."

"Thank God you're back, Will," Commerce moaned. "Now I can talk to someone who knows a baseball score or two. Hell, Abigail and Tradd think the Boston Red Sox are a new clothing fad."

"I'm glad you're back too, Will," Abigail intervened quietly. "Now I can quit pretending that I'm interested in baseball scores. If you gentlemen will excuse me, I'll make us some tea." She slipped down the back stairway, once more the dutiful wife.

Staring fiercely at the screen, Commerce said, "Your last year, boy. You'll be an Institute man in June."

"Just like you, Commerce."

"What does it feel like? Tradd doesn't talk to me very much."

"It feels real different. My penis grew a foot and a half over the summer. That's how I could tell graduation was getting close."

"It'll have to grow larger than that if you expect to be a

24

real Institute man," he cackled, glancing nervously at the door.

"Where's Tradd?" I asked.

"He was practicing his goddam piano a minute ago. Don't call him down yet, Will," Commerce pleaded. "He doesn't approve of mantalk like this. At least, not from me." Then, leaning over toward the chair where I was sitting, his small, pale, ferret-like eyes still religiously affixed on the TV, he whispered, "Did you get any this summer, boy?"

"In the thousands, Commerce. The tens of thousands."

"You ought to ship out with me next time. The women in Brazil will do anything you want. Anything. At least, that's what the crew tell me. But don't tell Tradd," he said, putting a thin finger over his lips.

"You don't look like you're feeling very well, Commerce," I said. Commerce always seemed enshrouded in a nimbus of unhealthiness. He was a short, wiry, rodent-faced man who even in repose had a motor running somewhere, as though his heart was working for no particular reason. Though twenty years older than Abigail, he didn't have a single gray hair on his thin, nervously vigilant head.

"Boy, I can never feel good when I'm entombed in this city. You know that. I can never wait to get out of here, away from all of this. Charleston sickens me because I belong to it so entirely."

After a pause, "I ship out again next week," he said to the television.

"Where to, Captain?"

"South America again."

"When will you be back?" I asked.

"I hope for the Ring Hop."

"I hope so too, Father," Tradd said, entering the room. "It would be so common if you weren't there when I went through the ring."

"Roommate," I cried, leaping to my feet.

"Hello, William," Tradd answered with stiff, innate formality. The St. Croix family had mastered the art of placing distance between themselves and others, eschewing physicality as an activity practiced by the lower classes.

"You should have come to Europe with me, Will. We could have made the grand tour together."

"I've told you before, Tradd, but you seem to have a hard time grasping this concept: I'm a McLean, not a St. Croix. My family didn't inherit a billion dollars to spend on the entertainment of their eldest son."

"Excuses, excuses," he replied. "Did you improve your slovenly habits this summer, or do I still room with the biggest slob in the Carolinas?"

"Oh, yes, I became neurotically compulsive about cleanliness. You can eat dinner on my fat behind now."

Tradd winced. "Father, Will is a fine boy but he has a tongue that even soap couldn't clean."

"He's one of the guys, son. That's something you'll never be. Just one of the guys. That's what I love about being on a ship."

"Since I got back three days ago, Father has been lamenting nonstop that I'm not a weightlifter or something else he could be proud of. I brought you a present, Will."

"I hope it's outrageously expensive," I said.

Tradd handed me a small package wrapped in brown paper. I tore it quickly, opened a thin rectangular box, and lifted out a stubby, finger-worn fountain pen.

"It's thirty years old. I found an eccentric store in London run by an even more eccentric old man who repairs old fountain pens. I thought you could use it to write your senior essay."

I hugged Tradd before he could pull back. I kissed him on the cheek, and he blushed a deep scarlet and turned away from his father and me. His father, watching the television again, missed the gesture.

"Keep away from the sacred bod," Tradd stammered, but I knew he was pleased.

"This is beautiful, Tradd. Absolutely beautiful. And I can't think of anyone who deserves it more."

"You don't deserve anything nice until you learn to clean up your act. His corner of the room always looks as though it's part of the city dump, Father."

"And I bet your side of the room looks like the place little girls play dolls," Commerce said. "I thought you and the other boys were going to teach Tradd how to fit in like one of the guys. Even when you try to act like a man you mess it up, son."

Tradd adjusted the buttons on his blazer and walked over to the window, which looked out onto Charleston harbor and the Battery. Abigail entered the door on the opposite side of the room carrying glasses and a frosted pitcher of iced tea. She stared at her son by the window; she stared at her husband in his chair. I became suddenly invisible, the unassimilated motionless voyeur. It was experience, not clairvoyance, which brought Abigail instant recognition of the nature of the conflict. In the war for the soul of this one child, there had been no real battle. There had only been an occupation and three proud, dispirited casualties indissolubly linked by the bloodless yet passionate nature of the skirmish. No forces had ever taken to the field. Commerce had wanted his son to be an athlete, a companion, a drinking buddy. What he had produced instead was a slim, brilliant boy with a voice mannered and flutelike, a boy in love with architecture, painting, furniture, music, poetry: all the pursuits that would please Abigail and irritate Commerce. He had also produced one of the finest friends I had ever known.

Tradd had enrolled at the Institute to satisfy a dream of his father's, who thought that his son would not—could not—make it through the plebe system but that the process, no matter how brief or cataclysmic, would liberate him from the soft and victorious tyranny of his mother's rule. It had surprised and impressed Commerce that his son had survived that first year, but it also dismayed him that there had been no fundamental change in his son's nature. The Institute had not purged his son of his reserve and delicacy. Even the Institute was helpless in erasing the signature of chromosomes. But it had proven that there was a toughness at the very center of Tradd that neither his mother, his father, nor he himself had recognized. It had been the one time in his life he had presented his father a gift of incalculable value. Few had suffered as long or endured as much humiliation that year, but Tradd had taken it all, every bit of it. He walked through the Gates of Legrand on the first day of our freshman year not knowing how to do a pushup. At the end of the year he could pump out fifty without breaking a sweat. But he never did another pushup after that first year and vowed he would never do another for the rest of his life. Once during our freshman year, I asked Tradd why he just didn't quit and go to another college since his parents had enough pocket change to buy Yale. Tradd had explained to me, "I want to make my father glad that I'm his son for the first time in his and my lives. There isn't an upperclassman in the world who could make me leave." Many tried, but Tradd had been right, none of them could. In less than three months, he would wear the ring.

"When are Pig and Mark arriving?" Tradd asked, breaking the long silence in the room.

"They got permission not to report until Wednesday," I answered.

"General Durrell's letting me stay home until the plebes

27

arrive, Will. I hope you won't get too lonely in the room."

"Why don't you just stay here in the guest room, Will?" Abigail said, pouring tea into four glasses.

"There are no bugles here, Abigail. I can't sleep without bugles or the sound of plebes dying on the quadrangle."

"Tell General Durrell to kiss my fanny if you see him, boys," Commerce shouted to the television, trying to direct the subject far away from the remark that had wounded his son. "I saw the pompous son of a bitch on King Street the other day. I think he was buying elevator shoes. He isn't satisfied with being six-three. You would think he was somebody the way he carries on. My god, he's from Spartanburg. Spartanburg of all the pitiful places. The upcountry. The goddam, no-count upcountry.

"The first exhibition football game is on Saturday night, Will," he continued. "Why don't you and Pig and Mark plan to watch it with me?" Commerce asked, aware he was being tested again in a trial by silence.

"Tradd," Abigail sighed, but easily, and teasing again, "I'm thinking about having your father fed intravenously during football season this year. Hook up a couple of gallons of Cutty Sark and glucose beside his easy chair."

"You might try to find other pursuits, Father. Other avocations. Only vulgarians and Methodists watch football games with such fanaticism."

"Your poor old man *is* a vulgarian, Tradd. No doubt about it. A goddam one hundred percent unreconstructed vulgarian. Will, I don't know if I've ever told you this story, but about ten years ago I read in the paper that bowlers have the lowest IQ's of any athletes and were generally from a socially inferior class. Well, I ran right out and joined a bowling league in North Charleston. One sixty-four average. Met the greatest guys I've ever met on land."

"How come you never invited these greatest guys on land for dinner, Father?"

"They must have been from Spartanburg," Abigail teased. "The upcountry."

"Bowling is so sweaty and uncultured," Tradd sniffed, winking at me.

"Culture!" Commerce screamed at the television. "I've had culture shoved down my throat since I was born. Do you know I've been going to operas since I was six, Will? Six years old and I'm listening to fat broads belting out dago songs to bald-headed fags wearing silver pants. You can take all the culture in America, tow it out to the Sargasso Sea, and set it

28

on fire and I wouldn't even spit once to put it out. I'm embarrassed to tell you how often I wished my name were not St. Croix but something like John Smith or John Nigger. That's it. John Thicklipped Nigger. That's the name I'd have chosen."

"Father, you certainly do overstate your case," Tradd said, turning toward the window and facing Charleston harbor again.

"Who wants some more iced tea?" Abigail chirped brightly.

"I'm going to my room and let y'all literati get in some chi-chi cultural chit-chat before dinner. Will, could I see you upstairs for a minute? If you'll excuse me, dear," he said, rising and bowing to his wife in a quick, snapping motion like a blade returning to a jackknife.

By the time I followed Commerce upstairs, he was moving a potted palm outside of his study. Carefully unlocking the door, he then disappeared into this forbidden sanctum for a moment, leaving me to fidget in the hallway. No one was allowed in his private study, and according to Tradd and Abigail, no one entered the room, even when Commerce was out to sea. When he came out of the room, he led me by the arm to the third-story porch. We stared out at the garden, an aromatic black sea of vegetation that breathed in the salt from the river.

"Do you see it?" he asked.

"See what?"

"I put it on when I went into the room. On my hand, Will."

I looked down on his right hand and saw its dull shine.

"The ring," I said.

"I keep it in my room. Along with everything else."

"Gold, frankincense, and myrrh."

"Books and notes. Things I've collected in ports around the world that Abigail thinks are junk."

"Why don't you wear the ring all the time, Commerce?" I asked. "You're the only Institute man I know who doesn't treat the ring as if it were made from the nails of the True Cross."

"My years at the Institute were the happiest in my whole life, Will. But ever since Durrell came back to be president and changed the plebe system into that brutal mess, I haven't worn the ring. It was all his ego, too, Will. When I talked to him about it, he told me he was going to make sure that the Institute had the toughest plebe system in the world. According to you and Tradd, he succeeded admirably. But it wasn't that bad when he and I were knobs. In fact, it was kind of fun."

"You were in General Durrell's class, weren't you?"

"Yes, I know some things about him, too. I kept a diary when I was a cadet. It was good practice for when I went to sea and had to keep a log. I can look back and tell you everything I did since I was fifteen years old. I'm very disciplined about some things, Will."

"Discipline is the one gift the Institute has not bestowed upon me."

"You fought it, boy," Commerce said. "Discipline comes easy when you decide to go whole hog at something."

He stared at the ring for a full minute without speaking.

"Tell Tradd that I didn't mean to hurt his feelings, Will. It just slipped out."

"Why don't you tell him, Commerce? I'm sure it would mean a lot more coming from you than from me."

"If you don't tell him, Will, he'll never know how sorry I am when I say these things to him. Please tell him."

"I will, sir."

"I noticed something years ago, son. When I'm with the people I love most, I feel lonelier than at any other time on earth. Lonely, Will. Lonely. Lonely," he declared in an undermined voice. Suddenly he turned his eyes toward me for understanding, for affirmation.

He gave me a look that linked us as spiritual allies, resolute desperadoes in headlong flight from the false and sinister veneer of Charleston. I did not return the look with equal measure or with any measure of faith in his basic premise that we shared some immensely suggestive linkage of soul and temperament. All because I like to watch football games, I thought. Since I was born a McLean and not a St. Croix, I was not tormented by the formidable demons of the city that cried out in disengaged voices for conformity from its sons and daughters. I could not help or even sympathize with the agony of being too well born, too well bred, or too well named. Nor could I help but notice that Commerce, despite his objections to the city, had chosen to live out his life in the dead center of the tribe he professed to hate. The pull of Charleston was lunar and feminine and partisan and even affected those natives, like Commerce, who professed to loathe her extensive artifice and the carnivorous etiquette of its social structure. He could no more cease being a Charles-

30

tonian than I could cease being a Caucasian male. Charleston possessed his soul and there was nothing he or I could do about it.

But he seemed satisfied with the look I gave him. I have eyes that give people what they want, eyes that whore in order to please, commiserate, endorse, affirm. People take from my eyes anything and everything that they need. Usually, I am simply looking at someone as they tell me a story; I am later amazed to discover they have believed I was agreeing with them completely. I have the eyes of a ward politician or a priest on the make with choirboys. I have eyes I have learned to distrust completely.

"I'll tell Tradd what you said, Commerce," I said as he left the porch and disappeared into his room, which was lit only by a ship's lantern. I heard the door lock behind him.

* * *

When I left the house that evening, I turned to look back at the Tradd–St. Croix mansion and thought of the many accidents and distortions of fate that had occurred to make my history and the history of this splendid house commingle. Tradd had brought me home for dinner at the beginning of our freshman year, right after we had become roommates. When we left that night to return to the Institute, Abigail had taken me aside and thanked me for helping her son. I told her that I thought Tradd was incredibly brave and that he was enduring the full savage brutality of the plebe system without complaint. Later that year, on another of my visits, she had press something into my palm. It was a key to the Tradd–St. Croix mansion. "You have a home in Charleston now, Will," she had said. "You can use that key anytime you want to, whether we're here or not."

I had never used the key, but I always kept it with me and I always liked to think that I could enter the house whenever I pleased. I wondered what the builder of the house, the distinguished barrister, Rhett St. Croix, would say if he knew that Will McLean was walking the streets of Charleston with a key to his house.

3

It took a brief moment for my eyes to adjust to the darkness when I entered Henry's Restaurant at noon the next day. The August sun was dazzling at high noon in Charleston. I walked toward the smell of cigar smoke. The Bear was sitting in a corner booth with an unimpeded view of the door. He was eating a dozen raw oysters and had ordered a dozen for me. I saluted him before I took a seat across from him.

"I think I'll have oysters, Colonel."

"Don't eat the shells, Bubba. Just spit 'em out on the plate."

"I've never eaten oysters that taste like cigars," I said through a miasma of smoke.

"No joking around today, Bubba," Colonel Berrineau said, extinguishing his cigar. "You and Poppa Bear are going to have a serious heart to heart."

When I was a freshman, I had quickly learned the central underground law of the Corps. The law was unwritten and unpublicized and essential for survival in that militant, inflammatory zone entered through the Gates of Legrand. The law was this: If you are ever in trouble, no matter if it is related to the Institute or not, go see the Bear. You sought out the Bear when there was trouble or disaffection or grief. You looked for the Bear when the system turned mean. You found him when there was nowhere else to go. In my tenure at the Institute, I never saw a cadet in serious trouble who did not request an interview with the Bear as soon as possible. Often, he would yell at the cadet, berate him for negligence or stupidity, offer to pay his tuition to Clemson, burn him for unshined shoes, insult him in front of the secretaries in the commandant's office; but always, always, he would help him in any way he could. That was the last, indispensable codicil to the law. No one outside the barracks was aware of the law's secret unofficial existence, not even the Bear.

"Bubba, I know you've heard about Pearce coming to the Institute."

"The Negro?"

"Yeh. That's the one. We're a little behind the times, Bubba. Every other school in South Carolina integrated a good while ago and God knows we held out as long as we could, but Mr. Pearce is coming through these gates next Monday and he isn't coming to mow the lawn or fry chicken in the mess hall. He's entering the Long Gray Line. Now some very powerful alumni have tried for years to keep this school as white as a flounder's belly. We're one of the last holdouts in the South, if not the last. Now, several members of the Board of Visitors know that it's very important for this young lamb to make it through this school. Otherwise, there could be real trouble with Federal funds and every other damn thing. They also know that the General has hated everything black since a platoon of niggers he commanded in the Pacific broke and ran from the Japs. So they're just sweet-talking the General and keeping him out of it. The Board doesn't talk much to the General unless they want water changed into Burgundy or the Ashley River parted. He's the school's miracle man, Bubba, but he's a little too old to have much to do with the nuts and bolts of running the place. I asked you here today because we've got to keep Pearce in school. That means we've got to keep these Carolina white boys off his tail as much as we can."

"You'll have to put him in a cage for that, Colonel. And if you show him any favoritism at all, the whole Corps will run him out, and you and I know they can get rid of any freshman they want to if they're so inclined. They could run Samson and Hercules out of here the same night if they thought they didn't belong here."

"Bubba, thanks for the lecture about the Corps. But I've been watching it a lot longer than you have and I know what the Corps can and cannot do a lot better than you do. But you're right. They can run him out with the morning trash. The thing is we selected Pearce over five other black applicants. We lucked out—or at least we think we did. He's smart. Comes from a good family, wants to make a career out of the military, and is pretty good looking for a nigger. But most important, he's tough. He could eat any five other freshmen for breakfast. But God knows he's going to need to be tough. We want you to be his liaison, Bubba. You watch

33

over him when you can. Work out a system where he can contact you if things get out of control. He got a bunch of threatening letters this summer, and word is out that there's a group on campus that doesn't want him to make it, that has sworn to run out every nigger that the Federal government jams down our throat. It's up to you and me and the other authorities and good cadets to make sure they fail."

"What group, Colonel?" I said, puzzled.

"If I knew who it was, Bubba, I wouldn't be wasting my breath talking to you. They'd be walking so many tours on the second battalion quad that they'd have blood blisters where their toes used to be. All we know, Bubba—and this is just guessing—is that we think it's a secret group. One of the Board of Visitors thinks it might be The Ten."

"The Ten is a myth, Colonel. It's supposed to be a secret organization, but no one can tell me it's possible to keep a secret on this campus."

"Pearce got a letter from The Ten this summer," the Bear said, looking toward the door.

"He did?" I said. "What did it say?"

"It mainly warned him to keep his black ass out of the Corps of Cadets if he knew what was good for him. It also said that niggers were living proof that Indians did fuck buffalo."

"He'd better get used to that kind of stuff, Colonel. But how do you know the letter came from The Ten?"

"I'm a detective, Bubba. It was signed 'The Ten.' "

"It could have been anyone, Colonel. It could've been me. That's been a joke on campus since I was a knob."

"I know, Bubba, I know," he said, rolling his eyes at me and daintily picking the cigar stub out of the ashtray. He began to chew on it as he resumed speaking. "I've never seen one ounce of proof that it exists since I've been here. But there's a rumor in the Corps that someone's out to get Pearce and the Bear listens to rumors. Do you know why the Commandant's Department wants you as Pearce's liaison?"

"The editorial?" I ventured.

"Yeh, Bubba, you flaming Bolshevik, the editorial," he said, leaning across the table, his brown eyes twinkling. "I was against letting the school paper print your editorial. If we're going to have censorship, I think we ought to have real censorship, not the namby-pamby kind. But it did help spot the one bona fide nigger-lover in the Corps."

"Not everyone in the Corps is a racist, Colonel. There are a few holier-than-thou deviants among us."

"How about if I say that ninety-nine percent of the Corps is racist, Bubba?" he said, grinning.

"You're being too cautious, sir. It's a much higher percentage than that."

"Did you write that editorial because you wanted to piss off the authorities, or do you really get a hard-on when you think about niggers? Tell me the truth, bum."

"I knew you wouldn't sleep for a week, Colonel."

"Well, Pearce is going to make it, lamb. Pearce has got to make it. His time in history has come."

"And your time's over, eh, Colonel?"

"It may be, Bubba. But bums like you never had a time and, God willing, you never will."

"Colonel," I asked, finishing the last oyster on my platter, "are you a racist? Do you want Pearce in the school?"

"Yeh, I'm a racist. I liked the school when it was lily-white. Pearce is going to stand out like a raisin on a coconut cake during parade."

"Then why are you trying to protect him?"

"It's my duty, Bubba, my job. And when Pearce comes in on Monday, he becomes one of my lambs, and I like to make sure that all my lambs get an even break."

"I'll be glad to watch over Pearce, Colonel, but I had best be seen with him only once during the first week."

"Word will leak out that you're assigned to him. In fact, I've already leaked it. I want the Corps to know that the Bear is watching Mr. Pearce closely."

"Colonel, when did you graduate from the Institute?"

"Nineteen thirty-eight, Bubba."

"How do I know that you're not one of The Ten?" I said, teasing him.

"I was in the bottom five of my class academically," he answered before he swallowed an oyster.

"Does that mean anything?"

"It means I was stupid, Bubba. The Ten wouldn't touch someone stupid. That's stupid with books, Bubba. But I'm Beethoven when it comes to catching my lambs breaking the rules of the Institute. You keep in touch. If you need me, give a yell. Come to me. No one else. No one in the Corps. None of your friends. Me. Spelled B-E-A-R."

4

That evening as I awaited the arrival of my other two roommates, I meditated on the nature of friendship as I practiced the craft. My friends had always come from outside the mainstream. I had always been popular with the fifth column of my peers, those individuals who were princely in their solitude, lords of their own unpraised melancholy. Distrusting the approval of the chosen, I would take the applause of exiles anytime. My friends were all foreigners, and they wore their unbelongingness in their eyes. I hunted for that look; I saw it often, disarrayed and fragmentary and furious, and I approached every boy who invited me in.

I was sitting at my desk in the rear of the alcove shining my inspection shoes when I heard the door open and Mark Santoro come into the room. He did not see me at first, but I smiled as I saw his old fierce scowl when he heard me say, "Hey, Wop."

It was an old game between us and we could play it for hours without missing a beat. He put his luggage on the floor near his rack and walked toward me.

"You must be new in town, sir," Mark said respectfully. "It hurts my feelings when a very ugly human being like yourself casts aspersions on my heritage."

"Wop," I repeated. "Wop, Wop, Wop, Wop, Wop."

"Excuse me, sir, you must not have heard me. I asked you kindly to treat me with dignity and respect. So I would suggest that you look for another way to address me before I'm forced to perform radical surgery on that fat nose of yours that your mother stole from an Irish pig."

"Speaking of noses, yours grew a little bit over the summer, Mark. You could land a DC–8 on that schnozzola of yours."

"You couldn't land a fruit fly on that little sniffer of yours."

"Why don't you have a nose job, Mark?" I said. "No kidding. It would take a team of twenty-thirty surgeons chopping away like beavers, but they could have it down to normal size after a day or two."

He put a large finger on my nose. "I'm real sensitive about my nose. *Real* sensitive."

"How does it feel, Santoro, to come from a race of men who once ruled the earth, who brought order to the entire Mediterranean world, who redefined the meaning of empire, and who humbled countless warriors and civilizations? How does it really feel to be Italian, Mark, past masters of the universe who now spend all their time rolling dough and making pepperoni pizza?"

"Do you know, McLean, that I didn't have to take your shit all summer? No one had the balls to tease me this summer. And do you know what," he said, ominously looming above me, "I missed the hell out of your Irish ass."

He scooped me out of my chair, the left shoe and the can of polish flying off the table in opposite directions. He squeezed me until I gasped for oxygen. He kissed me on both cheeks. He picked me up again and threw me on my bunk. When finally I could speak, I was looking up at his strong, dark face, his white teeth flashing in a broad smile. After long separations, Mark's greetings were a form of martial art.

"Mark, it's so good to see you," I said.

"How'd you live without me, Will? And you start being nicer to us sweet Italian boys."

"Nice!" I yelped. "If it even looks Italian, I'm nice to it, man. I'm not stupid. I'm nice to grease bubbles, oil slicks, and lube jobs. They all remind me of two of my roommates. How's your mother and father?"

"Begged me to change roommates and sent their love. They want you and Tradd to crack down on my ass and make me study. By the way, where's Pig and Tradd?"

"Pig hasn't shown," I said, glancing at my watch.

"If I know muscle beach, he'll be rolling in two minutes after muster, wearing a track suit and a hard-on."

"You go on over to Tradd's house, Mark. Abigail's fixing dinner for all of us tonight. I'll wait for Pig and bring him over later. I think Commerce would like someone to watch the baseball game with him. He's been riding Tradd pretty hard again. But put your uniform on, son. You're a senior now."

37

Mark picked me up again and crushed me against his powerful, hirsute chest. He kissed me again on both cheeks and with no self-consciousness at all looked into my eyes with benign tenderness and said, "I love you, Will."

My answer was a lesson in history and sociology and you could derive some of the major differences between Ireland and Italy by the emotional diffidence of my response. Both of us were unassailable proof that each of the tribes of Europe had imported their own separate fevers, predilections, and reveries into the capricious, turbulent consciousness of America. Our Europes were different; our Americas were different. Mark was emotional and sentimental beneath his scowling, brooding visage. I feared emotion, dreaded any commitment of spirit, and was helpless to translate the murmurings of the inarticulate lover I felt screaming from within. In a laugh-it-off, pretend-it-isn't-serious, tight-assed parody of the Irish American, preserved like a scorpion in my emotional amber, I answered, "I think you're a gaping asshole." We had said the same thing and Mark left for dinner at the St. Croixs' as I continued to wait for Pig.

Pig. Dante Pignetti. I had heard upperclassmen say that there had never been a freshman like him in recent memory. He was the only member of my class who was not affected or scarred by the plebe system at all. In fact, throughout that first year, he gave intimations that he loved both its regularities and its aberrations. It was an act of orgasmic pleasure for him to do a pushup, a devotional of unutterable joy to do fifty. Once I had watched three juniors work on him for an hour, trying to break down his indefatigable stamina with a grueling, synchronized combination of running stairs, holding out an M-1 rifle, and pushups, but they never even began to crack Pig and eventually surrendered out of sheer boredom and a begrudging awe. But awe was not the right word. It was fear. If they had broken Dante Pignetti, I am sure that none of them would have slept soundly for the rest of the year, for he carried with him a legendary unpredictability and an awesome capacity for rage. His body was a work of art forged through arduous repetitive hours with weights. It was not the type of body I admired—the long fluid muscles of swimmers hold more esthetic appeal for me—but it had a magnetic, almost nuclear, tension. His upper torso was breathtaking, his chest muscles, his shoulders, all were simply extraordinary. He did not play football; his love affairs were with the weights, with boxing and wrestling, with karate, with all sports that hurt seriously.

38

In the first month of our plebe year, upperclassmen came from the other three battalions to see Pig, and the cadre would force him to strip off his shirt and stand braced as the obscene, uninvited eyes of upperclassmen examined his already famous physique. From my vantage point in the second platoon, I could see the entire ceremony, and I filled up with an immense pride for this freshman, so much a man that our inquisitors, our lean tormentors, were coming to the ranks of plebes to study the most magnificent body in the Corps. They would hit him in the stomach as hard as they could and he would take their best punches. I could not convey how beautiful Dante Pignetti looked to me then, exposed to sunlight, barechested, struck by them, admired by them, more than them. As I was witnessing the strangeness of this ceremony, I decided on the spot to make friends with him. Wisdom and a knack for survival told me that it was no foolish act to have the strongest man in the Corps tied up with my destiny. Because powerful men inspire fear, they usually have very few friends and almost never have developed the soft skills necessary to make friends; they have spent too much time developing their pectoral muscles. I also knew Pig would instinctively like me. As I watched him from a distance, I knew with absolute surety that Pig had isolated and imprisoned himself in his own physical invulnerability. He was lonely that first year, and he smiled foolishly, boyishly, when I asked him to walk downtown for a beer.

There was a disturbance outside on the gallery. The door shivered violently as someone was hurled against it. I heard shouts, profanity. Suddenly, the door was flung open and Gooch Fraser flew into the room and tumbled onto the floor. Pig was behind him and gave him a swift kick on the buttocks that sent Gooch sprawling into Mark's luggage.

"Over here, Toecheese," Pig ordered.

"Pig?" I said in a half-question, half-greeting.

"I can't say hello now, paisan," Pig answered, throwing his suitcase on the bed and snapping it open. "Toecheese has just insulted my girl."

"I didn't know you had a girl, Pig," Gooch whined. Gooch Fraser was a junior sergeant and as harmless and inoffensive as a gerbil.

"You call me Mr. Pignetti. I don't like the way you say 'Pig.'"

"Please, Mr. Pignetti. I didn't mean anything."

"I've got to teach you a lesson, Toecheese," Pig explained. "I've got to make sure it doesn't happen again. I'm

39

going to show you a picture of the girl you just insulted and you'll understand why I become a wild man when someone says something nasty about her."

"But, Pig . . . ," Gooch said, desperately trying to explain.

"Shut up," Pig yelled, slapping Gooch on the top of the head. "I'm Pignetti to you and you're Mr. Nothin' to me. I'd be doing myself a favor to strangle your scrawny, greasy neck. Now watch as I show you the girl you insulted."

He reverently slid the photograph out of his suitcase. I had seen the photograph for three straight years; it was as familiar to me as the face of Lincoln on a five-dollar bill.

"There," Pig said with obvious self-justification. "Now do you understand why I become a homicidal maniac when some nothin' makes a dirty remark about her? Did you ever see such a beautiful woman?"

Then he slapped Gooch on the back of the head again.

"Take your beady eyes off her!" he screamed. "You're not worthy to gaze upon such an exquisite sight. If you only knew how good she was, how kind she was, how humble, how quiet, how smart—you wouldn't blame me for throwing you to your death off fourth division. You'd beg me to kill you. That's how ashamed you'd be."

"I didn't know, Mr. Pignetti. I really didn't know."

"What did Gooch say, Pig?" I asked.

"I asked him if he got any pussy this summer," Gooch explained to me with penitent, uncomprehending eyes.

Pig slapped him on the back of the head and kicked his ribs until Gooch lay hunched in a fetal position on the floor.

"Did you hear him use that word in front of Theresa?" Pig said to me.

"That's not Theresa, Pig," I said. "That's a photograph of Theresa."

"It's the same thing to me, Will. You know that. It's like church. When I look at the statue of the Virgin, I fill up with love. I kiss the feet of the statue like it was the mother of God herself."

"Gooch," I said.

"Yes, Mr. McLean."

"It's Will, Gooch. Apologize to the photograph of Theresa and Pig might let you go sometime this week."

"I might rip your gall bladder out with my bare hands if you don't," Pig said.

"I'm sorry, Theresa," Gooch whined. "I'm so sorry."

Pig chopped him to the floor again with a rabbit punch

to the neck. Then looking up at me again for approval, he said, "He just doesn't learn, beloved roommate."

"What did I do wrong?" Gooch moaned.

"You mentioned her first name. I don't want Theresa's name ever mentioned by a scummy tongue like yours. It's all I can do right now to keep from tearing your tongue out of your head."

"Call her Miss Devito," I instructed.

"I'm sorry, Miss Devito. I apologize. I'll never do it again," Gooch said, nearing hysteria.

"That's better, Nothin'," Pig said, appeased as last.

But Gooch was swept away by the theatricality of remorse. He made a swift, fervent grab at the photograph and began planting wet, sorrowful kisses all over Theresa's dark, shining face.

A demonic howl rose from Pig's furious lips as he began to cuff Gooch's ears with stinging slaps that resounded throughout the room. I jumped on Pig's back and screamed at Gooch, "Run, man. I can only hold him for a second."

With speed born of terror, the normally phlegmatic Gooch Fraser sprinted from the room without a single wasted motion.

Pig did not move. I was wrapped around his back like a ludicrous, outsized papoose. I waited for him to separate our bodies with one of the fierce, hammering blows that he kept in his inexhaustible repertoire. But he remained motionless as though he had hibernated on the spot. Finally I spoke.

"Pig, we're late to Abigail's house. So let's get ready. I don't want to have to whip your behind before dinner."

"Will," he said.

"Yeh, Pig."

"You can't hold me for a second, beloved roommate. You can't even hold me for a nanosecond."

"I worked out this summer, Pig. My strength has become gorilla-like."

"Do you know what I learned over the summer?" he said in his low rumbling voice.

"No."

"I learned how to kill a man using only my thumb."

"Pig!" I screamed out so it could be heard throughout R Company.

"Oink," he screamed back.

"Pig."

"Oink."

"Pig."

"Oink, oink, oink, oink."

5

On Thursday, I received an invitation to meet with General Durrell in his office after lunch. I put on my full-dress salt-and-pepper uniform, shined my shoes and brass, and stood before the mirror as Mark expertly wrapped me in the scarlet sash required when a cadet had an audience with our remote and distinguished president. An invitation from the General was not an invitation at all. In the complex vernacular of military euphemism, it was an inescapable summons. I had sent back word through the orderly of the guard that I would be delighted and honored to accept the General's invitation.

Delighted, honored, and extremely agitated, I arrived at the General's office at precisely 1300 hours. Generals made me very nervous, and I avoided all encounters with them when humanly possible. But Bentley Durrell was not only a general, he was a sublime prototype of the species. On campus, General Durrell was known simply as "The Great Man." People actually referred to him in that grandiose way, even in his presence. He was the Institute's living memorial, their single, undeniable totem of distinction in international affairs. Seventeen nations had honored him; fourteen universities had granted him honorary degrees. The museum of the Institute on the third floor of the library overflowed with mementoes that traced the course of his exploits in the Second World War and the Korean conflict. Some considered him the greatest South Carolinian since John C. Calhoun. The Bear had once confided to me that Durrell's ego could fit snugly in the basilica of St. Peter's in Rome but in very few other public places. This runaway megalomania marked him as a blood member of the fraternity of generals.

If looks alone could make generals, Durrell would have been a cinch. He was built lean and slim and dark, like a Doberman. A man of breeding and refrigerated intelligence, he ordered his life like a table of logarithms. Normally, he spoke slowly and his modulation had an icy control to it, but

I had witnessed many times when he had caught fire and when he did, when he arrived at a subject that consumed him, then you could see the eyes change, not the color, but the light behind the eyes, which flared whenever an article of his unwavering faith arose in a speech or a conversation. During speeches to the Corps, the indisputable power of his own rhetoric would affect him so viscerally that he would dance along a thin, precarious edge of control in constant danger of plunging headlong into much darker and more radical passions. When praising the nation or the nobility of the founding fathers' vision, we had known him to break down almost completely, not to weep of course, but to falter, his voice breaking, his emotions poised unsteadily in a miraculous duet between virility and tears. It was the only hint that there was fury beneath the form.

Otherwise he possessed the markings of the military thoroughbred. His hair was a distinguished gray of that special silver that only seems to grow on the heads of powerful, supremely confident men. It was close-cropped and stayed in place even in high winds. His nose was long and finely shaped; generals are a long-nosed, strong-jawed race. He was bred to wear the stars. The Presidency of the Institute was a fitting destiny for a man who had received his grandfather's cavalry sword as a christening gift. He wore the sword whenever he reviewed the troops at Friday afternoon parade. He had kept it on his wall when he was a cadet officer at the Institute. Though he had had a congressional appointment to West Point, he had chosen to attend the Institute instead, in affirmation of his belief in the South and in Southern ways. By spurning the Point, he was following in the footsteps of both his father and grandfather. He had graduated from the Institute with extraordinary distinction and, crowning a brilliant Army career, became the first four-star general who had ever graduated from The College. As the most famous and successful of all graduates of the Institute, he offered an example to all of us of the hope and promise and possibility that life offered on the other side of graduation. And the administration constantly reminded us that Bentley Durrell had once entered the Gates of Legrand as a freshman, had once marched anonymously in the ranks of plebes, had once slept beneath the arches of second battalion. There had been a time when Bentley Durrell had been recognizably human before he walked off campus and into the history of his times. It was thought that after he returned from World War II, he would become either President of the Institute or President of the United States. He waited for his country and the Republican party to call him from his South Carolina plantation, but both decided to call Dwight David Eisenhower instead. General Durrell, it is said, never quite forgave either for their bad judgment or inferior taste. And when the Board of Visitors asked him to assume the Presidency of the Institute, he accepted with magnanimity and a certain desperation.

When I entered his office, I saluted him sharply, snapped my heels together in a satisfying, phony click, and fixed my expression in a fierce cadet's scowl that I hoped would pass for high seriousness. In my full dress, I looked like one of Napoleon's grenadiers, even though I felt like the king of the penguins.

The General waved me into my seat with a magisterial sweep of his long slender arm. Then he studied me at his leisure. He settled back into his chair behind his vast mahogany desk without his eyes ever leaving mine. From the intensity of his gaze, it was apparent that he was accustomed to staring other men into submission. He was an athlete of the stare; he enjoyed the sport. I did not and I diverted my eyes about the room. There was a cold symmetry to General Durrell's office, a rigorous attention to detail that was both fastidious and obsessive.

"Do you think we can go all the way this year, Mr. McLean?" the General said, his soft, lethargic voice brushed by the sweet cadences and slurred elisions of the upcountry.

"All the way, sir?" I asked.

"Yes, I want to know if we can go all the way, if we can grab the brass ring."

"All the way to what, sir? I don't understand what you mean, sir."

"That's perfectly obvious, Mr. McLean," he said, smiling and folding his hands neatly on his desk like a schoolboy. "I want to know if our basketball team can go all the way and win the Southern Conference championship."

"I hope so, sir. I think we'll have a pretty good team, sir," I answered, relieved that the subject was basketball.

"A pretty good team is not good enough and neither is your answer. I suggest that you answer, 'We'll have a great team, sir, and there's no reason why we shouldn't win the national championship.' "

"We'll have a great team, sir, and there's no reason why we shouldn't win the national championship," I replied with

44

the required brio, although I could think of a hundred reasons why we wouldn't win that championship.

"Splendid! Splendid!" he cried out. "It's all in the mind, Mr. McLean. The mind is an intricate mechanism that can be run on the fuels of both victory and defeatism. I saw it when I led troops into battle. I never lost a single battle in my career as a field commander, because the word 'retreat' was not a part of my vocabulary. I didn't know what it meant and neither did my men. The exact same thing applies to athletics. So do you think we can go all the way this year?"

"There's no reason why we shouldn't win the national championship, sir," I repeated, feeling even more idiotic.

"That's the spirit, Mr. McLean. You said it with even more enthusiasm the second time. Keep repeating it over and over again, and it will become an article of faith to you and your teammates. I want that kind of enthusiasm to infect the Corps this year and every year. I despise negativism, don't you, Mr. McLean?"

"Yes, sir."

"Yet you are rather well known on campus for your negative attitude, Mr. McLean. If you despise negativism as you just professed to do, what do you think inspired this reputation?"

"I have a reputation for being a little sarcastic, General. I didn't know I had a reputation for being negative."

"Sarcasm might be even more insidious and dangerous than negativism. Now I would like to get to the point of your visit with me this afternoon. I want you to tell me what you know about honor, Mr. McLean. I want you to define honor in your own terms. I want to ascertain if our concepts of honor are significantly different."

"May I ask you why, sir?" I asked.

"You may not ask anything, Mr. McLean," the General said pleasantly. "You may simply define honor for me."

"I'm not sure I can define it in my own words, General."

"And yet you expect to speak to the freshmen for an hour next Wednesday about the honor system."

"Sir, I can define honor as the dictionary defines it or the honor manual. I know all those words and all those definitions. I just can't define honor in my own words yet. The words were all written by someone else."

"Then you are not certain what honor is?"

"No, sir, I'm not certain what honor is. I've been

thinking about it all summer, but I'm not absolutely sure what it is or who of my friends has or does not have it."

"That is a major difference between you and me, Mr. McLean. A major difference. I have never had to look up a definition of honor. I knew instinctively what it was. It is something I had the day I was born, and I never had to question where it came from or by what right it was mine. If I was stripped of my honor, I would choose death as certainly and unemotionally as I clean my shoes in the morning. Honor is the presence of God in man. It distresses me deeply that you are having a problem. It gives me cause to wonder about your ability to infuse the freshmen with the necessary zeal required for them to become exemplary graduates of the Institute. You must remember that the goal of the Institute is to produce 'the Whole Man.' The Whole Man, Mr. McLean. It is a noble concept. But the man without honor cannot be the Whole Man. He is not a man at all."

"Sir, I do know this," I replied, meeting his gaze directly for the first time. "When I was elected to the honor court, I made a vow to myself, to uphold the honor system as it is written. That is what the cadets of fourth battalion elected me to do, and I'm going to represent them to the best of my ability. I admit to being confused about honor and I admit to not liking some parts of the system. But if a cadet is tried before me this year and the prosecution proves to me that the cadet is a liar, a thief, or a cheat, or one who tolerates lying, stealing, or cheating, then I am going to vote guilty. I'm going to vote to have him removed from the Corps of Cadets."

"I hope you don't expect me to applaud this decision, Mr. McLean. You are merely doing your duty and I've never had any difficulty in the performance of duty. And I would like you to specify which parts of the honor system you do not happen to like."

I hesitated a moment, then said, "I don't like the Walk of Shame, sir."

He gave a short laugh and responded, "You know, of course, that I instituted the Walk of Shame when I returned as President."

Blushing, I answered, "Yes, sir, I know that."

"And you are also aware that the number of honor violations has decreased by sixty percent since my return to the Institute."

"Yes, sir," I said as he rose and walked to the rear door of his office. From what appeared to be a small, well-appointed anteroom, he ushered two cadets into the office:

46

John Alexander, the second battalion commander, and his exec, a spaniel-eyed boy named Wayne Braselton, whose identity was irretrievably fastened to the destiny of the fiercer, more charismatic Alexander. John Alexander was a splendid looking cadet, erect and arrogant, with an instinct for survival in the Corps that was as uncanny as it was disingenuous. They walked to the two leather chairs on the right side of the General's desk and sat facing me, not the General. Their faces were austere, inquisitorial. Then I heard the General's voice again: "Mr. McLean, you know your classmates, Cadet Alexander and Cadet Braselton, I'm sure. They asked to meet with you in my presence. These two cadets are concerned about the efficacy of allowing a senior private to address the incoming freshmen. They feel strongly that a cadet officer would make a much better impression on the freshmen. Is this not correct, gentlemen?"

"Yes, sir," Alexander answered forcefully, with Braselton nodding his vigorous assent. "We feel that the training cadre is composed of specially selected elite men whose personal appearance and devotion to military excellence provide a high standard for the plebes to emulate. Mr. McLean is well known in the Corps for not taking the military part of the Institute seriously. We feel that this attitude could only harm the freshmen and undermine the plebe system. We feel that a substitution for Mr. McLean should be made for the good of all concerned. If necessary, Mr. Braselton or I will assume Mr. McLean's responsibilities of helping to indoctrinate the freshmen in the honor system."

"Gee, thanks a lot, John," I said, trying to control my anger. "What a grand, selfless gesture on your part. But I think the freshmen will survive a single hour's exposure to my grossness."

"There's a principle involved here, Mr. McLean," the General replied. "One that I do not think you are grasping. If we allow a private to influence the thinking of the recruits, then a precedent has been set. But if we continue to uphold our standards, the highest standards of any military college in the world, I cannot help but think that our system is growing stronger and that our vigilance will be rewarded. I agree that our cadre should be composed only of the most select cadets in the Corps. I owe that to the freshmen, to their parents, to the men of the line."

"That was very well put, sir, if you don't mind my saying so," Alexander said with Braselton nodding passionately.

The General did not mind Alexander's saying so; in fact,

he was radiant and positively enchanted by Alexander's oily compliment. If I ever attend a convention of generals, I hope to control the Chapstick concession to offer some small relief to the obsequious legions of asskissers who spend their days pandering to the egos of generals. Every general I had ever known required the presence and the gentle, insincere strokes of these self-serving acolytes of flattery and I simply could not understand it.

"Sir," I spoke directly to the General, "Cadet Alexander and I are not friends."

"That is true, sir," Alexander replied. "I do not like what Mr. McLean represents in the Corps of Cadets."

"What exactly does Mr. McLean represent?" the General asked, leaning toward Alexander and cupping his hand over his right ear.

"He represents the negative attitude, sir. He makes fun of the traditions of the school . . . sacred traditions like the ring and the uniform and even the cadet prayer. I myself heard him give a profane and disgusting rendition of the cadet prayer while R Company was forming up to march to chapel."

"A profane rendition of the cadet prayer?" the General said with a gasp.

"It wasn't that profane, General," I whined.

Braselton, sensing the kill, suddenly burst out, "And his appearance is a disgrace, sir. That is how I would put it after careful thought. He goes out of his way to wear a uniform that is wrinkled and brass that's scratched. And his shoes are a joke throughout the Corps. That's how I would put it, sir. After careful thought. His shoes are a joke."

"What do you say in your defense, Mr. McLean?" the General asked.

"Sir, you and all my classmates know that I have not performed splendidly in the military part of Institute life. This is my fourth straight year as a private. But I have heard you say before, General, that the ideal cadet excels militarily, academically, and athletically. I have a better academic record than these two cadets, and I'm captain of this year's basketball team. So using your own criteria for measuring the model cadet, I have done well in two areas of achievement and these two have excelled in only one. Therefore, I feel I'm just as well qualified to address the freshmen as they are."

"It is Mr. McLean's attitude that we object to, General," Alexander interjected. "I think you can see from the way he tries to attack Mr. Braselton and me personally that his attitude leaves much to be desired. We question his love of the Institute and his devotion to the Corps. This is not a personal attack on Mr. McLean, and we think it is immature of him to consider it such."

"Sir," I answered, looking at the General. "The members of fourth battalion selected me as their honor representative. Me, Will McLean. The cadets could have selected Mr. Alexander or Mr. Braselton. For whatever reasons, they chose to select me instead. The members of the honor court then chose me to be vice chairman of the court. I have never taken the military seriously. But I'm taking my position in the honor court very seriously. The Corps entrusted me with the responsibility of serving on the honor committee without conferring with these two gentlemen. It appears presumptuous to me for these two gentlemen to try to interfere with the will of the Corps."

"I believe we *are* acting in the best interest of the Corps, General," Alexander said.

"I appreciate your concern, Mr. Alexander, and I will take what you say under consideration."

"I resent Mr. McLean's implication that he is more honorable because he happened to win a popularity contest among cadets, General."

"I'm sure Mr. McLean was not impugning your honor, Mr. Alexander. Good day, sir. And thank you for sharing your views so openly. It takes courage to criticize one of your classmates man to man."

The two cadets saluted and left the room. It struck me as both odd and symbolic that we should be ushered in and out of the General's presence through different doors. Before he left, Alexander shot me a languid, supercilious look. I grinned at him, and with the General's back to me as he escorted them to the door, I shot Alexander the bird. It might have been the first finger thrown in the august confines of that room.

The General returned to his seat, smiling, folded his hands beneath his chin, and immobilized me with the withering crossfire of his eyes again. Then the smile vanished and the voice, husky and controlled, filled the room again. My anger had passed when the two cadets departed and my instinctive fear of the General returned to fill up the void.

"Do you think you won that little skirmish, Mr. McLean?" the General asked.

"I didn't need to win it, General. I received my orders this summer that I was to report back to the cadre and be prepared to lecture the freshmen on the honor system."

"You are wrong, Mr. McLean. You did need to win it. If I had known that a senior private was to be a member of the 1966 cadre, I would have put a stop to it myself. Your presence on campus was a bit of a surprise to me, but I think you will perform your duties adequately."

"Thank you, sir."

"Let me tell you a little story, Mr. McLean. I hope you have the time. Ten years ago I was watching a swim meet when I watched our star swimmer stop competing in the middle of the race and climb out of the pool. I heard him tell the swimming coach that he had just choked up, that he simply could not go on. I called him to my office the next day and told him I was taking away his Army contract, that I did not want a person like him in the Armed Forces, someone who might choke up and quit during the middle of a battle. I told him I did not tolerate quitters. To me, a quitter is not only dishonorable, he is immoral. Do you agree, Mr. McLean?"

"I guess so, sir."

"I think you are like me, one of those men who would rather die than quit. I've watched you play basketball for three years, McLean. You won't quit out there either. Men are born with that instinct or they are not. It's an absolute necessity for a professional soldier. I would not know how to lead an army in retreat, Mr. McLean."

The General had never retreated in his entire career nor had he lost a single battle in which his troops engaged the enemy. But his splendid military reputation had been ventilated slightly by revisionist innuendoes that Bentley Durrell had sacrificed too many men in his encounters with the enemy, that he had traded too much American blood for too little Japanese real estate. Once, when ordering the capture of a heavily fortified Japanese position, he had screamed to his staff that he didn't care if it took a shipload of dog tags to do it. General Durrell won that battle while incurring extraordinarily heavy losses and picked up a battlefield nickname in the process. "Shipload" Durrell was more popular with the American public than he was with the infantrymen who cleared the way for his triumphal push toward the Japanese mainland.

"The gentleman who did not finish the swimming race became one of our most successful alumni, Mr. McLean. He is a lawyer in Nashville, Tennessee, and I hear from him every year. He thanks me now for giving him such a valuable lesson so early in life. He has never quit at anything since. The reason I am letting you address the freshmen is because you fought back when I confronted you with Alexander and Braselton. I love a competitive spirit. Now, just what is the nature of your enmity with Cadet Alexander?"

"I think he's a jerk, sir."

"You are talking to the President of this college, Mr. McLean," the General snapped harshly at me. "You will mind your mouth and manners."

"I'm sorry, sir. It began with a disagreement our plebe year."

"I happen to think Cadet Alexander is one of the most impressive cadets ever to go through the Long Gray Line. A born leader."

"Yes, sir. He thinks that too, sir. I just don't agree, sir."

"Do you think you are potentially as fine a leader as Cadet Alexander?"

"No, sir. I don't think I'm much of a leader at all. Sir, Alexander and I had a fight when we were knobs. Not much of a fight, really, more of a shoving match. It happened after another freshman left the Institute. Since then, we've kept out of each other's way. We usually don't even talk to each other on campus unless it's to exchange unpleasantries. It's nothing serious, sir. There's always going to be a couple of people you don't like out of two thousand."

"Well, that will be all, Mr. McLean. Do your duty with the freshmen. Good day."

"Good day, sir, and thank you, sir," I said, saluting.

Before I got to the door, I heard the General ask, "Who won the fight between you and Cadet Alexander, McLean? I'm curious."

"I did, sir," I answered. Then smiling, I added, "He quit."

6

After a fine dinner at the St. Croixs' on Sunday night, Abigail invited me to join her on a walk along the Battery. My roommates all returned early to the barracks. With the rest of the cadre, they would rise early to greet the freshmen as they arrived on campus. I had no assignments until the honor code speech on Wednesday morning.

Our pace was unhurried as Abigail and I left the house. We walked down East Bay Street, crossed South Battery, and continued under the grove of wind-hewn oaks to the seawall that separated the aristocracy from the Ashley River. The tide was high and almost perfectly still, with the moon's image graven into the water's surface in a silvery imperfect coinage. Abigail drifted ahead of me, her head thrown back, looking at the stars. I did not try to catch up to her. Instead, I watched her as she danced awkwardly up the steps of the seawall, pausing against the railing to study the soft lights of houses strung along the shore of James Island. This walk was ritual with her. She knew this promenade well enough to give her undivided attention to stars and water and the lights of the familiar, marvelous harbor. The tide was reversing slowly, almost imperceptibly. The Atlantic was inhaling, and the two rivers that sketched the shape of Charleston began to feel the immense, light-inspirited authority of the lunar flux. To me, there was always a severe magnificence in this recall of rivers, especially on these clear, humming nights in the lowcountry when the air was sweet breathed and starry. I loved these salt rivers more than I loved the sea; I loved the movement of tides more than I loved the fury of surf. Something in me was congruent with this land, something affirmed when I witnessed the startled, piping rush of shrimp or the flash of starlight on the scales of mullet. I could feel myself relax and change whenever I returned to the lowcountry and saw the vast green expanses of marsh, feminine as lace, delicate as calligraphy. The lowcountry had its own special ache and sting. In Charleston I had found the flawless city rising splendidly, economically, out of a ripe, immaculate landscape. But it was also the city of the Institute and I never could quite forgive her for that single indiscretion.

Abigail slowed her walk and turned to wait for me to catch up. The wind caught her hair, honey-colored and sensibly cut, but she brushed it back with a charming, distracted sweep of her hand. She was smiling and her face was younger, even girlish, in the darkness. She took my hand, and we skipped down the seawall for twenty yards. Then she stopped and walked to the railing. With her eyes closed, she began inhaling the warm, fragrant air in large breaths. The wind was rising slowly.

"There is an old Charleston joke, Will," she said with her eyes tightly shut. "Someone asked an old Charleston woman why she never traveled anywhere and she replied, 'Why should I travel, sir? I am already here.' That's the way I feel about this city."

"That's not how I feel about Charleston. It's not that I don't like the city. I do like it. I love the way this city looks. But sometimes I don't like the way this city feels. It feels dead to me and sometimes it feels mean. I don't know whether it's the city itself or because of the Institute. Maybe if I hadn't gone to the Institute I'd feel the same way about the city you do."

"All the boys complain about the Institute while they're there, Will. You know that. Then as soon as they graduate they become crazed fanatics about the place, lunatic alumni who think the place was designed by God on the first day he rested. You'll be just like all the rest of them when you graduate, mark my words."

"I'll never be like that, Abigail."

"Hush, you simpleton. I'm telling you gospel stuff and you're not even listening. Now I want you to tell me something else, and I've got a good reason for asking. Who is the girl creature in your life? You've never brought a girl to the house a single time since you've been rooming with Tradd and I demand a plausible explanation."

"There is no girl creature, Abigail."

"Pourquoi, monsieur?"

"I don't have time," I lied.

"Nonsense, monsieur."

"Girls have this funny habit. They turn green when I

come in sight. I don't know what's really the problem. I've never learned to talk with girls. I don't know how to say the things I hear other boys say to them, and I feel stupid trying. I'm not comfortable around them and, God knows, they're not comfortable around me."

"Confidence, Will. Confidence," she said soothingly. "You've got to start realizing that you're adorable and eligible and desirable. You're twenty-one and composed of fresh, juicy, tender, delectable man-flesh. We'll find a girl for you this year."

"I don't like South of Broad girls, Abigail," I said. "You know that, don't you? You set me up with that one girl when I was a sophomore. What was her name? Buffy or Missy or Punkin or something. I'd have done the world a favor if I'd drop-kicked her off the Cooper River Bridge at low tide. She was the biggest snob I've ever met."

Abigail giggled with pleasure. "I admit it was not a match made in heaven, Will, but Suki was a darling-looking girl and I thought you two might get along just famously. Stranger things have happened between men and women. But you certainly must try to get over this prejudice you have against snobs. I came from a long, distinguished family of snobs, and you absolutely adore me."

Clumsily, she leaned forward and kissed me on the lips. She held the kiss for several seconds; it was chaste, motherly, the way women always kissed me. Her eyes were invisible in the shadows cast by the streetlight.

"How does that make you feel, Will?" Abigail asked softly. "Does that make you feel better?"

"It makes me feel hopeful that Commerce isn't watching, that your friends don't see us, that nobody sees us," I said blushing.

"Oh, Commerce wouldn't care what I did. He hasn't cared about things like that for years. For decades. It was a friendly gesture, Will. You're like a son to me and I'm trying to build up your confidence. I hope I didn't embarrass you. I don't pull off things like that very well."

"I'm glad you did it, Abigail," I said, and now I could see that she was embarrassed, too.

I did not know if Abigail could really gauge the extent of my inexperience with women, my absolute lack of confidence around them, my fear of them. But I suspected she knew it instinctively. My virginity was settling in hard on me. It seemed both silly and rather affectingly pitiful that a twenty-one-year-old male with awesome enthusiasm and all his parts intact had not managed to make love to a single woman. Though I had taken no vows of chastity, women responded to me as though I were an affable rural curate with no thunder in my pants. It was not that I lacked the desire, the necessary heat: There was something almost nuclear about the lust. Sex had become the central, consuming obsession in my life. It charged the cells of my blood with energy, jewel-fire light, and the sweet forbidden glucose of sin. Restless and on the prowl, I had entered my young manhood tired and desperate to be done with these sexless days, though sexless is not completely accurate. Cadets become clandestine but brilliantly imaginative masturbators of a very high order. Show me a product of a military school and I will show you a man who can beat off without moving a muscle, without rustling a sheet.

I had once read in a book that traced the natural history of blue whales that the great creatures often had to travel thousands of miles through the dark waters of the Pacific Ocean to find a mate. They conducted their search with the fever and furious attention of beasts aware of the imminence of extinction. As the whaling fleets depleted their numbers, scientists conjectured that there were whales who would exhaust themselves in fruitless wandering and never connect with any mate at all. When I read about those solitary leviathans, I feared I had stumbled on an allegory of my own life, that I would spend my life unable to make a connection, unable to find someone attracted by the beauty and urgency of my song. Sometimes I felt like an endangered species.

Holding hands, Abigail and I walked for thirty minutes through those charmed, lovely streets South of Broad. It was 11:30 when I left her house to return to the barracks. As I opened my car door, I saw a note stuck in the windshield wiper.

I read it beneath the streetlight, my eyes straining to decipher the feathery, feminine script. The note was brief but to the point: "You have no right to park here. Tourists and cadets are ruining Charleston. Please park your car somewhere else or I will call the police." There was no signature.

I looked around in the darkness. There was nothing illegal or impertinent about where I had parked, nothing at all. Before I got into the car, however, I saw a girl watching me from the unlit entrance to Stoll's Alley, twenty yards away. She was wearing a scarf, a raincoat, and a pair of sunglasses.

When she realized I had seen her, she turned and began walking quickly down the narrow alleyway. I sprinted after her. She had not gotten very far. It was difficult navigating a tree-shaded Charleston lane wearing sunglasses as the hour approached midnight.

She stopped suddenly and wheeled toward me as I approached.

"Did you leave this note on my car?" I asked.

"You have no right to park your car on this street," she said in a harsh, strident whisper.

"When did you inherit it?"

"What?" she asked.

"The street."

"Cadets think they are so funny. I've always hated cadets," she said.

"At least we have something in common."

"I've got to go," the girl said furtively, glancing over her shoulder. "My mother would kill me if she knew I was out here talking to you. What's your name, cadet? You've got a funny looking nose. Hurry up now. I don't have much time. I want to know your name."

"Take back what you said about my nose."

"I will not. You have a perfectly ludicrous nose. I would try to cover it up with something if I were you. Now tell me your name so you can take your tacky car and your silly nose back to the barracks."

"My name is Will."

She laughed and said, "I knew it. I knew your name would be silly, too."

"You've been in Charleston too long. You think it's normal for a boy's first name to be Prioleau or Pinckney or Cathedral or Seawall or any of those other stupid family names they stick on kids."

"Those are aristocratic names," she explained with infuriating haughtiness. " 'Will' is not aristocratic. What's your last name?"

"Aristocratic. Will Aristocratic. I'm Greek."

"You're not a comedian and I'm not very amused."

"McLean. Will McLean," I said, trying to invest abundant dignity in that modest but comfortable moniker.

"An ethnic," she giggled. "A Hibernian. The Irish drink too much and they are never serious. They also beat their children and ignore their wives."

"That's me, OK. What's your name?"

"I wouldn't tell you if I wanted to. That's none of your

business. And I couldn't tell you if I wanted to," she said, involuntarily looking backward over her shoulder again.

"Why not?"

"Because I'm not supposed to be in Charleston. I am studying Spanish at the University of California at Santa Barbara. I'm very good at languages, and I've always refused to date cadets from the Institute. They are such animals and do not know how to behave as gentlemen. And there are far too many ethnics among them. Do you know that once upon a time they would only let Southerners into the Institute? It used to be a fine school."

"How do you like Santa Barbara?" I asked.

"I think you are a very cruel person," she said behind her sunglasses. "I don't think I want to talk to you any longer. You have no cause to try to embarrass me or to hurt my feelings."

"Can I ask you another question? Two questions, really. Why are you wearing a raincoat when it's not raining and why are you wearing sunglasses twenty minutes before midnight?"

"It's none of your business how I dress, Mr. McLean. A gentleman would never think to ask such personal questions. But ethnics are taught to be blunt when they grow up in tract housing, aren't they?"

I turned and began walking back down Stoll's Alley, saying as I went, "I hope you pass your next Spanish test." But I stopped when I heard her say in a voice that was half reconciliation and half plea, "I just wanted to be friendly. I just wanted to talk to someone. You looked like you might be friendly, but that's just because of your silly nose. And you smile all the time."

"Someone once told me," I said, returning to her, "that I was the only person in the world who thought it was a military duty to appear to be in a good mood."

"Do you have a girl friend, Will McLean?"

"Last time I checked three hundred girls from Sweet Briar had carnal designs on my body."

"Please don't make fun of me," she said in an estranged, helpless voice that made me feel like an insensitive bully. "Please don't."

"I'm not. I'm making fun of myself. I've never had a girl friend. Girls look upon me as their big brother, their father confessor, their friend, and good buddy. They like to kiss me on the forehead when I take them home at night."

"Do you think I'm pretty?" she asked suddenly.

"I don't know," I said, staring at her face in the darkness.

"Just yes or no."

"You're the prettiest girl I've ever seen in sunglasses and a raincoat and a scarf on a perfect Charleston night."

"Who told you that you were on stage? Who told you that you were a great comedian? Is that how people with your background make it out of the ghetto?"

"Sometimes we luck out and get to drive garbage trucks. By the way, raincoat, I don't like Charleston snobs."

"I've hurt your feelings," she said coyly. "A sensitive ethnic."

"This is fun, but I have important things to do," I said, checking my watch.

"Like what? How could a cadet from the Institute possibly have something important to do?"

"I've got to get back to the barracks and wash my socks."

"All cadets are exactly the same. All cut from the same cookie cutter."

"Just like Charleston girls."

"Who were you seeing in this neighborhood? This neighborhood does not cotton to ethnics."

"It's none of your business, but Tradd St. Croix is my roommate."

She cleared her throat, stepped back as if she were leaving, and said, "And I thought you didn't like Charleston snobs."

"Do you live South of Broad? Where do you live?" I asked.

"That's none of your business."

"Your name is none of my business. Where you live is none of my business. It doesn't look like we have any business together. Besides it's getting toward midnight, that magic hour when cadets turn into pumpkins. I've got to be going."

"I'm not sorry one single bit. I wish you had gone ten minutes ago."

"Well, good night, raincoat."

"Good night, cadet," she said, touching my arm, gently. "Maybe I'll come talk to you again if I feel like it."

"My heart leaps like a gazelle just thinking about it. Do you know that I think you're crazy? I've met a lot of Southern girls in my life, but I've never met anyone so obviously stark raving mad. I've never . . ."

Then another voice sounded through the darkness, a controlled, peremptory voice that could have come from either a man or a woman. The girl made a high animal noise of surprise or fear or a combination of both.

"Get to the house, Annie Kate," the voice ordered.

The voice came from a slightly wizened, diminutive woman who scowled at me from behind a cigarette ash.

"Mother," Annie Kate said, her answer more supplicating than responsive.

"You know better than to go out like this," the woman said, approaching us slowly. She passed the girl and walked directly up to me, appraising me with clear, angry eyes.

"Good night, young man. My daughter is only visiting for the weekend. She will be gone tomorrow."

"I was just leaving, ma'am," I said.

"Splendid," she answered. "Do not let us keep you."

"Good night, Will McLean," Annie Kate said.

"Good night, Annie Kate. Now, at last, I know your name."

"Don't forget that I'm stark raving mad."

"Shut up, Annie Kate," her mother commanded.

"It was a pleasure meeting both of you, ma'am."

"Yes, it was such an extraordinary pleasure, young man. It is too bad we will never see each other again. Do I make myself absolutely clear? No one even knows she's here. As a gentleman, I ask you to tell no one you saw her."

"There's no one I could tell who would even know her, ma'am."

"I am asking you as a gentleman not to tell anyone, Mr. McLean."

"I won't tell anyone."

"Thank you. I'll hold you to your word. Good night, sir."

They turned and walked down Stoll's Alley together. They were not going to let me know if they lived in a house adjacent to the lane, but I had no time to find out. I had seven minutes to get to the barracks or receive confinements for breaking curfew. The midnight hour was a perilous time on the streets and highways of Charleston for cadets broke all existing speed records returning from general leave. But now I knew the fastest routes through the narrow streets of the old town. As a cadet, I had learned the Charleston streets by rote and was always refining my knowledge of shortcuts on the peninsula.

When I entered the barracks, a few seconds to spare before midnight, I heard a voice from the guardroom shouting my name in the barracks. My name reverberated off the four barracks walls with an astonishing resonance. "Will McLean. Telephone call for Will McLean."

"Hello," I said picking up the receiver in the guardroom.

"Hi, ethnic."

"Annie Kate."

"Surprise," she said. "I have to talk low so my mother won't hear me. I wanted to tell you that I enjoyed talking to you even if you try to act like a stand-up comic sometimes."

"I'm nervous when I meet people at first. Especially girls. I always think they'll like me if I can only make them laugh. It's never worked, not once in my life, but I still do it. I just don't know what to say to them."

"You certainly don't," she agreed, a bit too quickly I thought. "Are you shy?"

"No, I'm catatonic. Once I didn't move for four years. My mother put me on a hanger and hung me in a closet until I started showing vital signs."

"There you go again. You don't have to be nervous talking to me, Will. Why don't you try to relax and be yourself? I'm not going to bite you."

"Bite me. Please bite me. No, that's not why I'm nervous now, Annie Kate. In a minute, some guy is going to knock on my door and say, 'All in.' The Institute kind of likes it if I'm there for bed-check."

"So you don't want to talk to me," she pouted. "No wonder you don't have any girl friends."

"I told you. Three hundred girls from Sweet Briar."

"I'm in love with a boy," she said suddenly.

"Congratulations."

"He doesn't love me, though I still love him. Very much. I'll always love him."

"That's great."

"You can be my friend if you want, Will."

"Sure, I'll look you up in California the next time I'm out there."

"Do you ever get lonely, Will?" she responded, ignoring my sarcasm.

"No, I'm surrounded by two thousand other fabulous guys."

"You were the first person I've talked to in a month besides my mother."

"I didn't think people were that unfriendly in Santa Barbara."

"Good night, Will," she said angrily.

"Wait a minute. Please wait a minute," I shouted in the phone, attracting the curiosity of the OG. "Tell me what this is all about. I don't understand any of this, Annie Kate. None of it. I'll be your friend. I'll be happy to be your friend. Anybody's friend. But you're leaving tomorrow and I'm in Charleston and your mother told me that I would never see you again. She told me to forget that I ever met you in the first place. You heard her say that. Look, Annie Kate, I'll write you. I write funny letters. Girls love me when I write them letters. They love me all the way up to the time they meet me. If you're lonely, I can help that. I've never been anything but."

"You don't know anything about loneliness," she said in a pitiless voice. "There's a garden behind my house on Church Street, Will. You can get to it by walking down an alley that cuts beside the second house on Stoll's Alley. There's a wooden gate at the end of the alley. In the garden, we can meet on the wrought iron bench behind the carriage house. Mother will never see us, and she always goes visiting on Sundays anyway. Can you come then?"

"As soon as mass is over, I'll be there."

There was a groan and she said, "Oh, dear, you're not a Catholic, are you, ethnic? Oh, of course, you are. How tiresome. How predictable."

"And you're an Anglican. Right?" I answered.

"Yes."

"And you belong to St. Michael's."

"Yes."

"And you have a Huguenot last name."

"Yes."

"And your family belongs to the Yacht Club and the St. Cecilia Society and your mother was in the Junior League and your grandfather fought for the Confederacy."

"Yes. Yes. Yes. Yes."

"Don't talk to me about being tiresome and predictable."

"Be nice to me next Sunday, Will. I need a nice ethnic at this time in my life."

"I'll be nice," I answered. "Good night, Annie Kate."

"And, Will. One more thing. You're right about me

being a little crazy. But it's a temporary thing. It will only last a little while. I promise you that. Will you promise me one thing?"

"Sure."

"Don't wear that silly nose next week."

"I promise," I said, and we both hung up laughing.

7

The plebes arrived on the following day. They came from forty states and seven foreign countries. Seven hundred freshmen, most of them accompanied by their parents, entered through the Gates of Legrand on a day of astonishing clearness, a sweltering, bone-rusting day beneath a blue sky that made the heat seem all the more potent and dazzling. The campus was weightless and tense.

This was the day officially set aside for the swift business of transformation; a day when civilians would become recruits and boys would be reduced to something less than boys. The cadre was brisk, efficient, and courteous. The courtesy would vanish when the parents departed from campus that afternoon.

I spent the morning walking among the freshmen and their parents. Outside the four barracks, I witnessed scenes of unbearable tenderness in the awkward charades of sons leaving their families for the first time. I saw women kissing their sons again and again and the sons pull back blushing and moved. Fathers shook hands stiffly with their sons as they attempted to address them as men for the first time. The cadre watched, their eyes invisible beneath the oiled brims of their field caps. They joked and laughed with both the parents and the recruits. The laughter would cease when the parents left through the Gates of Legrand.

The plebes were fine-looking boys for the most part, but their eyes were lusterless and fearful. You could see in their faces the need to survive this one day, this one hour, so that they then could be about the business of surviving the year. You could feel their need to escape the soft, worried eyes of their families. They wanted to make it as easy as possible on their families and on themselves. Most of all, they wanted it to begin. At last, they wanted to measure for themselves the mystique and cunning weight of the plebe system. They wanted to test themselves in its landscape. But the landscape would not present itself until the parents left the city of Charleston.

Parents took a last measure of their sons, so that at the end of this year they could calculate how far their sons had traveled.

As the morning deepened, more and more freshmen took leave of their families and entered the main sally port of Number Two barracks to face the icefield of the cadre's eyes. Inside the barracks, cadre members sat at card tables with file boxes and name tags, their black field hats pulled low over the eyes and noses giving each of them the appearance of a monstrous, carnivorous species of bird. Once you entered the barracks, you surrendered to the plebe system, renounced the world outside the Gates of Legrand, and submitted to the laws of the Corps.

By 1000 hours, sophomore corporals swollen with the joy of calling cadence for the first time expertly marched squads of freshmen to Durrell Hall for the ritual haircuts. Other long lines of freshmen queued up outside of Alumni Hall being fitted for uniforms. I walked across the parade ground to Durrell Hall, where I watched the ceremony of Institute barbers render new heads bald with several athletic sweeps of their humming razors. A black janitor swept the immense piles of hair toward the back door. Each movement of his broom brought forth a new creature with its own perverse shape. After their haircuts, the freshmen, transformed now into plebes, moved back across the parade ground with their heads shiny as light bulbs. The air filled up with the rhythm of cadence. There was a decorous, efficient simplicity in this transfiguration from civilian to military, and the cadre performed its tasks with extraordinary precision and dispatch.

I enjoyed watching the fear and anxiety of the plebes. I had to admit that. It made me feel infinitely superior to these trembling, perspiring newcomers. I, along with every member of the cadre, had experienced my own first day. I had known the terror of this day but now found I enjoyed seeing the terror in others. The Institute had changed me as it changed all its sons. I knew that anyone who aspired to become an Institute man had to tolerate the solitary astonishment of that first day. All had to know and endure the awful violence of separation. I had all the markings of an upperclassman: There was something instinctive and primal in me that wanted all plebes to suffer as I had suffered. That and that alone gave any kind of certification to the fear and solitude of my own plebe year.

On the second floor of Durrell Hall at 1100 hours I listened to the General address the parents on what to expect from the Institute and what to expect from their sons in the coming weeks. Clearly, some of the parents were nervous (and, brother, did they have a right to be, I thought), but the vast majority of them believed that the Institute offered their sons the very finest education in the country. But apprehension was loose in the room; it created a tremulous, undirected energy that danced above the crowd like phosphorous on a night sea. They had come to be reassured, comforted, even praised. They rose when the General entered and gave him an emotional standing ovation that lasted for minutes. Imperially, he faced them, tall, slim, and imposing, as if he had been fashioned and whittled down from the barrel of a howitzer. When the applause subsided, his voice broke through the hall.

"Because of you, the parents of the Class of 1970, we have been able to assemble the finest incoming class of freshmen in the history of Carolina Military Institute. They will be trained by the finest cadre in the school's history. They have chosen the finest school in the United States of America."

The parents, hearing what they needed to hear, applauded wildly. With an upraised hand, he silenced them and continued: "Today, your sons are alone. They are frightened and they are leaving home for the first time. I promise you this: We will not strip your son of his individuality; we will enhance it. Today, you hand us a new recruit. In June, I will hand you back a cadet. Four Junes from now, I will hand you back an Institute man, and I can promise all of you parents that it will be one of the proudest days in his and your lives. He will wear the ring of the Institute, the tangible symbol of his worth and sacrifice, a symbol that is recognized all over the world by the men who belong to the brotherhood, to the proud intrepid fraternity of Institute men."

A reverent silence gripped the hall as the Great Man spoke. His voice controlled the audience by the power and conviction of his fervent, undistilled belief.

"Now," he said, his mood lightening. "I will tell you parents something that I know is a fact. In the next month you will be receiving a frantic phone call from your son. Mothers, you will be especially vulnerable to this call. In fact, your sons will probably call when they are sure their fathers are not home. When this call comes, brace yourself. Your son will be asking you, possibly begging you, to let him come home. Tell him no. Emphatically, tell him no. Tell him that under no circumstances will you allow him to quit before the completion of his freshman year. Tell him that you did not raise him to be a quitter, a man who ran away the first time he faced adversity.

"The first year is hard, ladies and gentlemen; make no mistake about it. It was hard when I was a freshman; it will be hard one hundred years from now. I will let you in on a little secret. As President of this college, I have done everything in my power to make the system harder. But the system is also effective. It has produced an extraordinary breed of Americans, and your son is about to embark on a journey that will make him equal to that breed. As you were, it will make him better than that breed. We are producing a higher quality of Institute man now than ever before. That is because America requires more than ever the kind of man produced by the Institute."

He paused, drew a deep breath, and, with a slow magisterial gaze, swept his eyes from the right side of the hall to the left. The pause was prelude. He always ended his speeches with grand, symphonic statements. I always waited for his exultant finishes; I always enjoyed them.

"Ladies and gentlemen, I will tell you why I chose not to go into politics after my military career was over. I came to the Institute not simply because I believe in the greatness of this college. No. I came here because I was and am appalled at the weakness and vulnerability of America. It has always been my dream that the Institute and her sons would be at the vanguard of a moral revolution, a resurgence of the American dream itself. It is my most heartfelt desire that the American spirit be rejuvenated from its weakness and degeneracy by the disciplined, patriotic bands of men we produce at the Institute each year. I am asking you this favor. Give your sons to me and let me keep them for this first year. I want them to know the satisfaction of submitting themselves fully to a system of discipline that has been tried and tested as effective again and again. I want each of them to know the pleasure of walking up to his parents four years from now, strong, proud, clear-eyed, and erect, and thanking you for giving him the strength and fortitude to endure the rigors of the plebe system. America is fat, ladies and gentlemen. America is fat and sloppy and amoral. We need men of iron to get her on the right path again. We need Institute men. We need your sons. Help us not to lose them in the difficult but rewarding days ahead. Help us make them submit to the will of the cadre, the shapers and molders of our strong creed. Help us turn them from the frightened boys you have brought us today into men of iron, men of the Institute."

General Durrell walked off the stage quickly and down the aisle to the exit. He did not acknowledge the deafening cheers. As he disappeared, I thought that he had neglected to tell the parents some important and vital statistics. Of the seven hundred boys who arrived on campus this August morning, one hundred would not survive plebe week, three hundred would not survive plebe year. Only men of iron would remain. Men like me, I thought.

8

So the fearful order lived again. From reveille to taps, the barracks filled with the screams of the cadre. During plebe week, laryngitis was a mark of vocational honor among sergeants and corporals and an almost universal condition among the freshmen. With the coming of the plebes, the barracks seemed normal again. It was difficult to relate to that environment without freshmen loping along the galleries with their zombie-like gaits and their chins tucked into fierce braces. It required the presence of human fear for normality to be restored after the long silent emptiness of summer. When the plebes arrived and the cadre was in full cry, the barracks came into a stunned and violent life again, full-blooded and lusty with the aphrodisiacs of duty and cruelty.

But now in my senior year the plebe system no longer seemed serious to me. For the most part, I was aloof to this inconsequential suffering. Some of the plebes would leave and some would stay. They had chosen the Institute, and their misery affected me only occasionally. My vision had acquired a longer range; it had deepened and broadened in my tenure at the school. Many of the boys who suffered most grievously would turn into the cruelest guidon corporals, the most sadistic platoon leaders. That was the way it was with the system; that was the way it was with the human race. These same bereft and frightened boys would populate the nightmares of future freshmen. I had seen it happen over and over and over again. I would not get involved with them, I promised myself. It was not my fault they were here and I had business with only one of them.

I waited for two days before I went to see the black freshman, Pearce; I knew it would be impolitic to make contact with him too early. An early rendezvous would arouse suspicion among the cadre of E Company, and Pearce would have enough on his mind during Hell Night without worrying about assignations and plots hatched in secrecy against him.

But on Wednesday morning, I entered the E Company area in second battalion to introduce myself to Pearce in my newly appointed role as his lord high protector. The E Company freshmen were on the quadrangle learning the rudiments and intricacies of the manual of arms. The steel-plated bottoms of the M–1 stocks smacked against the cement squares in unison. In the history of the Institute, there had never been an easier freshman to spot among the ranks. For several moments, I studied Pearce's physique with an admiring eye. He had the squat muscled body of a middle-weight wrestler, and he would have little difficulty in surviving the physical rigors of the system. His coloring was remarkable, a deep glistening ebony like a spit-shined shoe. His very blackness surprised me: Southern colleges traditionally began their experiments in integration with the lightest-skinned Negroes available on the planet. As I watched the E Company freshmen practice going from right shoulder to port arms, Alexander and Braselton walked up and stood beside me in the shadow that the second division cast over the first.

"This the first time you've seen the nigger, McLean?" Braselton asked.

"Hi, Wayne," I answered. "Yeh. This is my first glimpse of the young smackhead. They weren't lying, were they? He certainly does not appear to be white."

"Blackest son of a bitch that ever lived. You better see him quick, McLean," Braselton continued, looking toward Alexander. "We'll be running him out of here in a day or two."

"Maybe. Maybe not," I said, in my Gary Cooper voice.

"I heard John here say that he'd turn in his rank if he hasn't run that nigger out of South Carolina by Christmas."

I looked at John Alexander, who was gazing at me with what I know he considered to be unbearable menace. "I'd pay for his transportation if he took John here with him," I said.

"What are you doing in my battalion, McLean?" Alexander demanded, staring down at my comfortable but unshined shoes.

"I'm thinking about buying it, John. My quarters are so small."

"Fuck you, McLean," Alexander said. "Beat it."

"But, John, we haven't really had a chance to talk except for last week in the General's office. Our friendship is too beautiful a thing to wither from neglect. Let's spend the night, put our hair up in curlers, giggle a lot, and I'll stick my prick in your mouth so you won't have to use your thumb."

"Get out of my battalion, McLean," Alexander ordered.

"It's not yours, your highness."

"I think you ought to go, Will," Braselton said officiously.

"I don't like stool pigeons in my battalion, McLean, and you have no business over here during plebe week. Unless the rumor is true and you're over here to kiss the nigger's black ass," Alexander said, moving in closer to me.

"You're wasting your time with the nigger, McLean," Braselton insisted. "If John says he's gone, that means he's long gone. John eats knobs for breakfast."

"I bet Pearce makes it through the year, Wayne. I bet ten bucks he watches us graduate in June."

"I don't want to steal your money, McLean." Braselton laughed. "You're my classmate. And you don't seem to hear what I'm telling you. John here says that he's going to run him out or turn in his rank."

"Alexander would rather turn in his pubic hair than his rank," I said. "But he's not going to run that kid out, Wayne. That's no ordinary knob. That there boy has been carefully selected from the whole black race in these degenerate Deep South states to represent his people in this shithole we call a military college."

"If it's such a shithole, why didn't you leave three years ago, McLean?" Alexander asked.

"I couldn't stand the idea of missing parade on Friday."

"Don't you ever get serious about anything, McLean?" Braselton said angrily. "Or do you just enjoy being a professional wiseass?"

"Sometimes I do get serious, Wayne. But only with people I take seriously. But let's do cut the bullshit. I've already heard that you've sworn to run the nigger out, Alexander. But that doesn't exactly make you unique. So have five hundred other guys in the Corps. The Bear has given me the assignment of making sure the nigger gets an even break. No favors, just an even break."

"He'll be treated like every other knob in my battalion," Alexander declared huffily.

"That's all I want."

"Then why doesn't the Bear assign some asshole like you to every goddam dumbhead in the Corps?"

"The Bear has this strange idea, Alexander," I said. "He feels that some of you Deep South white boys look upon our black brother with something less than a tolerant eye. Word from the Bear to Cadet Lieutenant Colonel Alexander. As Pearce goes, so goes Alexander."

"There's been a lot of talk about the Bear among the alumni, McLean," Braselton said. "A lot of people think he's done a poor job handling discipline."

"Run the nigger out and you'll get a chance to see how he handles discipline," I answered, turning back to watch the E Company freshmen.

"I'm going to find a way to get you this year, McLean," Alexander said as he and Braselton moved toward the front sally port. "That's a promise, stool pigeon."

"Gosh, it was nice talking to you boys," I replied.

Watching Alexander leave, I decided you could write a fairly accurate biography of him just by observing him crossing a street. There was a swaggering cockiness to his walk, and he strutted like an imperfect cross between a pit bull and a bird of paradise.

I drifted into the harsh sunlight over toward Pearce's platoon and waited for the first sergeant to give the order for the drill period to end. When the freshmen broke for their rooms, I screamed at Pearce who was ten feet away from me.

"Halt, dumbhead. Rack it in, Pearce," I yelled.

Approaching him slowly, I stared into Pearce's dark brown eyes. He returned my stare measure for measure. For a plebe, his stare was too intense and bellicose. He had eyes that issued challenges. For several moments, I just looked at him and watched the sweat pour from his brow. I was studying a part of history. For one hundred twenty-five years the Institute had been an enterprise of Caucasians until this squat dark boy who stood before me made a decision to reverse history in his own small way.

"Pearce," I said at last.

"Yes, sir," he screamed.

"Talk quietly. I'm the guy they told you about."

"Yes, sir," he said in a softer voice, but one dangerously strained and undermined by the pressure of his first two days.

"You've got great taste in colleges, my friend. Heinrich Himmler must have been your guidance counselor in high school. But that's your business, not mine. Here's what I want to tell you. You can make it through here. You've got a good company commander and he's going to help. A lot of other guys are going to help, too. A lot of guys are pulling for you as much as they pull for any other poor dumbhead who comes here. Now hand me your rifle and give me ten pushups just for show, so these poor white boys will think I'm doing my level best to make your life hell."

I could feel the eyes of the barracks studying us at leisure. Pearce was astonishingly visible, and I could not hold a conversation with him without attracting the curiosity of everyone in sight. I returned his rifle to him after he had counted out his ten pushups and jumped up again to attention.

"Wasn't that fun?" I inquired.

"Yes, sir," he said.

"Sure it was, Pearce. So is cancer," I said. "Now here's our main problem, Pearce. Everyone's going to know by this afternoon that I'm your liaison on campus. So if anyone on campus ever sees us talking, they're going to think you're a stool pigeon, and they'll run you out of here for sure. This is going to be the last time you and I are ever seen together on campus. Here's how we're going to communicate. If you ever need to tell me something, if there's ever a time when you have any names to give or if anyone looks like they're taking an extreme dislike to you for reasons pertaining, how should I say it, to your unusual racial makeup . . . then you write me a note on a piece of paper and place it between pages three hundred eight and nine of *The Decline of the West* by Oswald Spengler in the philosophy section of the library. The book hasn't been checked out in the history of the Institute.

70

Can you remember that, Pearce? It's very important and I'll be going to the library twice a day."

"Three hundred eight and nine, *Decline of the West* by Spangler."

"Spengler, Pearce. Now I know all this sounds like a spy movie, but some people think there may be a secret group on campus that does not want you to enjoy the fruits of education at this grand institution. I belong to a group that does. Any questions?"

"Sir?" he asked.

"Speak freely, Pearce."

"What group do you belong to, sir?"

"We are called the nigger-lovers, Pearce."

He smiled.

"Glad you've got a sense of humor, dumbhead. You're going to need it. Good luck and welcome to the most miserable year in your entire life. Just do what they tell you and show lots of enthusiasm. If they're killing you and you show lots of enthusiasm, they think it's a sign of a wonderful attitude. You've got to change the expression in your eyes, Pearce. That's going to hurt you. It's the guys who looked pissed off that they try to break. I speak from experience, friend. Be hearing from you."

"I hope not, sir."

"Me, too, Pearce. By the way, how does it feel to be the dumbest fucking nigger in the world?"

"Not so good right now, sir."

"That's how I felt my knob year. Like the dumbest white boy, like the stupidest goddam cracker that ever lived. The funny thing was, Pearce, I was right. Absolutely right. Now I'm going to scream at you and order you up to your room. We've got to make this look official. Get ready for McLean, the assracker. You better fly to your room, dumbhead," I screamed into Pearce's ear.

Pearce turned and sprinted for the E Company stairwell on the first division. "I said move, boy, move. Move. Move. Move," I chanted as he moved rapidly up the stairs, the sweat staining his gray cotton field shirt from his underarm to his waist.

9

That afternoon I sat on the auditorium stage of Durrell Hall watching the plebes filing down the long rows of folding chairs minutes before I would address them on the Institute's honor system. The shouts of cadremen rang through the hall, and the plebes, bovine and disoriented, moved without animation in a blind, stunned herd toward their seats. The smell of them was overpowering. It was easy to loathe a group that smelled so horrible.

Gauldin Grace, the chairman of the honor committee, rose to deliver a brief synoptic history of the honor system at the Institute. His voice, fervent and evangelical, carried with it an absolute conviction of the rectitude and efficacy of a society ruled by honor; it quavered slightly and conveyed the earnestness and gentle decency of the speaker. In his simplicity and radiant faith in all systems of order, Gauldin represented to me the embodiment of the Institute man. Unimaginative but virtuous, unflamboyant but solid, he was good in the religious sense of that oft-abused word. He embraced the honor code as his personal catechism, and there was nothing ironic or incredulous in his solemn devotions to its service. When he introduced me to the freshmen, he listed my credentials and accomplishments at the Institute. It was an embarrassingly short introduction.

I rose and walked to the podium. Power flowed through my veins like a quicksilver intake of oxygen. When I spoke, my voice, magnified by the microphone, boomed out godlike over the hall. It was the phony, insincere voice I always use when I address assemblies. Today I was princely; today I was cadre.

"Good morning, gentlemen."

"Good morning, sir," they roared back.

"Gentlemen, my name is Will McLean and I'm a senior

72

private in Romeo Company. This is my fourth year as a private at the Institute. You and I are the same rank. When the rest of the Corps returns next week, you'll see other privates like me, but I'm your first glimpse of this strange, maligned breed of cadet life. Today, I would like to talk to you about honor.

"There are some wonderful things about this school, although it's very hard for you to notice them right now. You are thinking, quite naturally, that you screwed up badly when you selected the Institute as your college. But the Institute has promised to make a man out of you and this Institute will do it.

"Gentlemen, I too entered the Institute as a spindly freshman. Like you, the cadre tortured, humiliated, beat, and otherwise abused me during my plebe year. They made me do pushups until I dropped, run the stairs until I couldn't feel my legs, and hold my M–1 straight out until I couldn't feel my arms. But at the end of the year when I looked into the mirror, I saw what the plebe system was all about. I had become an Institute man. I had a twenty-inch neck, legs like redwood trees, the temper of a piranha, and my IQ had dropped a hundred points. In other words, gentlemen, I had become the rock who stands confidently before you today."

I could feel Gauldin's rising disapproval blaze into life behind me as the laughter grew in volume. It made Gauldin ill to see a freshman smile. He had always opposed my militant flippancy about the plebe system, and I knew it would offend him deeply to see it directed at newly ordained aspirants to the invigorating rituals of that system. Laughter was the one unassailable survival technique of the plebe year, and one you would never learn from the cadre.

"Gentlemen," I continued, "you do not understand what you've been going through in the past couple of days. It is as though the world has gone suddenly berserk, completely unraveled, taken leave of its senses, and someone has thrown you like meat to the wolves. I remember sitting as a freshman listening to the chairman and vice chairman of the honor court intoning very solemnly and pompously about the importance of honor and how you would be kicked out of school if you did not have it. I remember how the two cadets who spoke to me about honor that day seemed as mean and inhuman as all the rest of the cadre. I came away from plebe week with a very distorted view of honor. The men who told me about honor brutalized me in the barracks, and they did not seem to be honorable men to me.

"I later found out that they were men of high integrity. But I was confused by the relationship of honor to the plebe system. I never quite separated honor from the first traumatic week of life at the Institute. Honor was a concept of fear. This is how my cadre failed me during plebe week."

I then told them in the clearest, simplest language possible the rules and pitfalls of the honor system as written and practiced by cadets of the Institute. I praised the uncompromising simplicity of the system. The cadet cannot lie, steal, or cheat, or tolerate anyone who does. I cited cases and gave illustrative examples from the past. Briefly, I recited the history of the honor system and compared it to the systems of other military academies. As I spoke, I began to feel rather foolish as I faced the inert artillery of their stunned, botanized gazes. Over and over again I repeated the word "honor," until it became like a pulse beat of my speech. The abstraction defeated me, strangled me in its maddening inexpressibility. It was like describing the hierarchy of the Trinity or the language of phalaropes. I could feel myself struggle with a game and ardent inarticulateness as I tried to explain the concept of honor to the staggered, uncomprehending mass of boys who shivered in the air conditioning below me. I sounded like a minor character in a flawed and cheaply produced operetta who delivers charmingly absurd recitations that have no meaning.

The freshmen now listened to me with resolute grimness. They listened because they feared me as the moment's appointed embodiment of the system. They had laughed at my jokes at the beginning of the speech, but their laughter was so joyless and forced that it depressed rather than elated me. They laughed because I was a member of the cadre, not because they thought I was a hoot. That hurt. I had made a minor career out of being a hoot. It was an odd feeling to be feared. And it was an even odder one to like it.

I ended my turgid, rambling, and painfully well-meaning address to the freshmen with a discussion of the final and most troubling aspect of the honor system.

"Gentlemen," I said, and I must have used that word fifty times in that single hour, making it a strong runner-up to "honor" itself, "the last part of the code is the most difficult to live by. To turn in a friend, a classmate, a roommate, or an upperclassman for an honor violation is the most demanding and crucial part of the code. It is also the severest test of its efficacy, its credibility. But for this part of the code, the honor system would not work. I have often wondered if I were put to the test whether I could actually turn in a good friend of mine. I honestly don't know. I have never been tested and hope I never am.

"But I will tell you a story that reminded me of the honor system. Several years ago in New York City a woman by the name of Kitty Genovese was beaten, raped, and stabbed to death in the New York City streets. It was later proven that at least thirty-eight people heard her cries for help, her screams, heard her begging the killer to spare her life. Not one of those thirty-eight people went to help her. Not one of those thirty-eight people called the police. Not one of them shouted at the murderer from their windows. Not one of them did anything. Anything at all. Kitty Genovese might as well have been raped and killed in the Gobi Desert for all the help she received from her fellow man. The most common excuse given by each of those thirty-eight people when they were later interviewed was that they did not want to get involved. A woman bled to death because no one wanted to get involved.

"The word *involved* caused me to think of the honor system. The Institute is a special environment that requires involvement. It's not enough that you do not steal. The Institute demands that you do not tolerate other thieves in your midst. It says that the Corps is responsible for the administration of the code. It says that you are responsible for the actions not only of yourself, but also your neighbor. Because of your living under the code, we hope that other men and women can put their trust in you. If the Institute, indeed, is something special, then the code is the central fact of that specialness. The Institute does not give you a choice about whether you wish to be honorable or not. The code is imposed upon you for your four years at the Institute. It is the written moral manifesto of how you'll behave. When you graduate, the code goes with you and the code lives as long as you live.

"You have chosen a strange school, gentlemen," I said to the plebes but I no longer saw them and had the strange sensation of talking only to myself. "There is much good and much bad in this college. I think the honor system is good. It is the one thing I believe in with all my heart. I think the integrity of the Corps is good. And I know this: If Kitty Genovese had screamed outside of Number Four barracks instead of that street in New York City, she might have been seriously hurt in the stampede to murder her attacker. Gentlemen, from this moment until you withdraw or graduate from the Institute, you are subject to the Code."

10

Before I came to Carolina Military Institute, I had never once heard of the obscure and thinly elongated country of Vietnam. But long before my senior year I became acutely aware of the distinct and extraordinary possibility that I might die in Vietnam for reasons that were rather unclear to me. Since I had never seen a Vietnamese in my life, it amazed me that somewhere, on the planet's largest continent, lived an Oriental man, perhaps plowing with a team of oxen or digging an irrigation ditch on the green fringes of an impenetrable jungle, who might one day kill me.

The thought did not altogether displease me. It would have been odd indeed if I had not fallen victim to some of the more lurid fantasies of the military mythology. I even had moments of wanting to die heroically in battle to fulfill my father's legacy or to prove the Institute wrong about my fitness as a cadet. When I was eighteen and nineteen there was some awful gravitational or lunar force within me that embraced the notion of a valiant death by fire. In my freshman year, I was so impressed and overwhelmed by a unit of Green Berets who came to the Institute to demonstrate the newest counterinsurgency techniques that I tried to enlist in their ranks that very day. A lantern-jawed sergeant talked me into staying until I graduated from the Institute because the Green Berets needed qualified officers and the pay was much better. The reprieve gave me three more years to consider myself in light of Asia, North America, duty to my country, duty to myself, and war. It gave me time to think, study, and ask questions; in other words, it gave me the time to obtain that most fascinating and life-changing of commodities—a college education. But I never forgot that I had once tried to sign up with the Green Berets. War is a religious conviction to an eighteen-year-old boy, and though it later became hard for me to relate to that boy, I had at least to acknowledge

76

the sincerity of his passionate, blazing idealism and his total willingness to sacrifice his life for his country.

But the Institute changed me, slowly, imperceptibly, as any good college would. There was a lot of time to think in the barracks and to talk with classmates, a lot of time to change one's mind. I did not view myself as the dangerous sort. I viewed myself quite artlessly as a prince among men, a real sweetheart, and my entrance into the masculine province of the Corps had only served to strengthen my conviction that I was at least as virtuous as the majority of my fellow human beings. I looked upon the Corps as a captive microcosm of the entire human race and thought if I could study them properly and learn all the secret rites and neuroses of the cadets, then in some profoundly inclusive way I could discover the most illuminating sanctities, dilemmas, and mysteries of the human spirit. As a soldier I would have learned much more about an aggrieved and singularly bewildered species, but by then due to the strangeness of our times, ol' Will McLean, born and bred to be a military man, had decided he would never be a military man. He had also resolved in his own mind, through beginning to believe in his own convictions, through his own slow unravelings of the great questions of his time, his own readings and interpretations of those readings, and his own colloquies and interrogations with his secret self, that he had no quarrel, absolutely none, with the Vietnamese.

I had originally planned to come to the Institute because I had wanted to become a fighter pilot. I wanted to be winged and silver and unseen in the dizzying heights of the stratosphere, where I would drop from the safety of cumulus and prey on enemy fleets and cities whose surprised citizens would speak not a single word I could comprehend. Nor would I even hear their cries of pain and death. Pilots are granted the luxury of not witnessing the results of their terrible passage, their rapacious encounters with earth; they are far removed from the carnage, grief, and destruction that their visitation inevitably brings to the targeted population. I wonder how many humans have died because sons wanted to prove themselves worthy of their fathers? I used to dream constantly of diving toward the earth, machine guns blazing, rockets streaking from beneath my wings, companies of enemy soldiers falling on their bellies in fearful adoration of my swift approach. This was the cyclical dream of the future aviator when the only wars I won were fought at night.

Yet even before I came to the Institute I knew I could

not be an aviator, despite my promise to my father. The vision in my right eye began to go bad in my final year in high school, and aviators have perfect eyes. It was the first absolute proof that I saw the world differently from my father, and by extension, from all aviators and Marines. When I took another eye test at the Institute, hoping to get a waiver on the requirement for 20/20 vision, the doctors found an additional flaw: color blindness of the red-green variety. It was further proof that I looked upon the world differently from others.

Later I would think of this myopia and color blindness as my salvation from a predestined course. The black, horn-rimmed glasses that I wore for driving were the first signal that my destiny was not inalterably preordained. It was the beginning of a long, convoluted crystallization that would prevent me from serving in Vietnam. At first it had nothing to do with the war itself; I thought it had to do with my not being able to fly. Because of my father's legendary heroism on Iwo Jima, I did not want to be a grunt. Nor did I want to die in a country of whose troubled existence I had only so recently learned. But in the committed, engaged milieu of the Institute, my decision not to enter the military was looked upon with alarm by both cadets and the administration. Because there was a war going on and because the Institute was losing a number of its graduates each month, my refusal to sign an Army contract my junior year was seen as a betrayal of the Institute and an act of minor sedition against my country.

The Institute took a remarkably proprietary attitude about the war. At first, the war stimulated enrollment and conferred a sense of mission on the school, a stature and an eminence it did not enjoy during those rare times when the United States was not trading the blood of its sons for the blood of other, darker, sons. Nothing made the college prouder than the death of a graduate in combat. We kept a tally of those fallen heroes and felt that we were in direct competition with the service academies as to who would have the most graduates killed in Vietnam. Careful records were kept, and when Captain David Foxworth Johnson was killed while leading a night patrol in October of 1966, we pulled ahead of West Point for the first time. When the Regimental Adjutant announced this fact, the mess hall ignited in a spontaneous chant from the Corps, "We're Number One. We're Number One. We're Number One." It was done with the highly oxygenated, disingenuous, high-humored esprit of boys still young enough to laugh at death. The black, grisly humor of the barracks even viewed the death of heroes with a gruff and vigorous irreverence. Until we began to recognize the names of the graduates killed, until we began to hear the names of our friends included on the fatality lists. Then the war became ugly and serious; then, and only then, did it become real.

Yet even then humor remained the one legitimate response to diffuse the horror of those weekly reports from the front. Often it would appear as graffiti on latrine walls. One could trace the political and sociological history of the Institute by collecting the most representative and angrily comic examples of graffiti from its latrines.

In 1966 most of the graffiti were partisan editorials about the war in Vietnam. One grouping was a series of suggestions for ways to end the war: train packs of piranhas to swim up North Vietnamese rivers and chow down on anything with slanty eyes and a rice base; invite the leaders of North Vietnam, China, and Russia to America for peace talks and make them eat in the Institute mess hall—they'd all be dead in forty-eight hours; parachute the Bear into Hanoi alone—give him a day or two to rack ass and shape the place up; parachute John Alexander into Hanoi—he'd be such a pain in the ass the North Vietnamese would voluntarily leave Hanoi.

Beneath this series of proposals scribbled in an angry, almost illegible prose was this sentence: *You chicken shit fucks, how dare you make fun of the war when our boys are getting it every fucking day.*

But even this was not the final word. Even this furious anonymous cadet had merited a response: *Big deal, hero—I'm getting it from Third Battalion Mary every fucking day.*

The latrine walls became a battleground between cadets who wanted the war treated with reverence and those who insisted on treating it with skepticism, with the Corps's supernatural gift for reducing sacred topics to absurdity. In the Corps that often was an act of reverence in itself.

In 1964 they began to hang the portraits of graduates killed in Vietnam in the library. This was a commendable idea in the early stages of the war, but by 1966 the bottom floor of the library was a depressing gallery of toothy, clean-cut young men cut down in various horrible ways before they had reached their twenty-fifth birthdays. The librarian discovered that the cadets had begun to gravitate to the second floor, so as to study in an area not haunted by

79

those sweet doomed faces who had left the Corps only a brief time ago. The cadets began calling the library's first floor "the body bag." When the librarian asked the General for funds to build a special addition on the library to house the portraits, word was in the barracks that afternoon that the librarian had requested a building the size of a gymnasium as the only structure large enough to handle the number of projected fatalities from the war. The Institute was doing its job well and preparing its two thousand sons in the barracks to die prettily for their country. And there was this splendid reward for dying: You got your portrait in the library.

During those four years in Charleston we wore the outline of Vietnam etched indelibly on our consciousness. In military science class, we followed battles, skirmishes, and troop movements; we planned imaginary landings of assault troops near Haiphong, envelopments of Hanoi, the mining of rivers, and the limited use of nuclear warheads. So often did I study the map of Vietnam that I retained the image of its shape while dreaming. But I did not dream of maps. I saw myself in a twisted coffin shaped like Vietnam. My body was broken and fitted into the grotesque shape of the coffin, and there were maggots swarming beneath the lids of my decomposing eyeballs as an artist made a preliminary sketch for my portrait that would hang in the Institute's library. Almost all cadets, no matter how irreverently they referred to the war, were looking forward to leading troops into battle—it was the *grand guignol* of our generation, the testing ground of valor —and the collective eyes of the Corps were turned in an eager gaze toward Asia with all the blind irrational instincts of rutting boys, as new portraits began to arrive at the library each month, and as we began to recognize the faces in the portraits. I do not remember a single day of my college career when we did not discuss the war. But because we were at a military college, the war became an article of religious faith and to question it was an unforgivable blasphemy. We did not receive a college education at the Institute, we received an indoctrination, and all our courses were designed to make us malleable, unimaginative, uninquisitive citizens of the republic, impregnable to ideas—or thought—unsanctioned by authority. We learned to be safe; we learned to be Americans. Many of us learned too much and many too little, and far too many of us ended up on the walls of the library.

The entire design of our education at the Institute was the creation of the citizen soldier, a moral amphibian who could navigate both the civilian and the military worlds with equal facility. It demanded a limitless conformity from its sons, and we concurred blindly. We spent our four years as passionate true believers, catechists of our harsh and spiritually arctic milieu, studying, drilling, arguing in the barracks, cleaning our rooms, shining our shoes, writing on the latrine walls, writing papers, breaking down our rifles, and missing the point. The Institute was making us stupid; irretrievably, tragically, and infinitely stupid.

I did not know this when I was a cadet; this is the accumulated bitterness of an older man obsessed by memory. At that time I only had a glimmer of this intuition. At that time I only knew that I did not see things exactly as my classmates did. Something was different about me, and I suffered because of that difference. But I did know this: In my senior year I was beginning to learn how to discriminate between an idea that was for me and one that was for all the rest. And I was beginning to understand in a visceral inchoate way that every single thing I had been taught or had learned on my own since I was a child contained the elements of a lie. The whole construct of my universe was a cunning, entangled network of lies. I had to start over again. I knew that. And I had to begin by ceasing to loathe myself for my difference from the rest.

I was reading the *News and Courier* on the Thursday morning before our first basketball game with Auburn. I had just read Lord Ashley Cooper's column about his hatred of okra in any form, fried, boiled, baked, or in a gumbo, when I came across a small article about the Institute. General Durrell had announced that the Institute, attuned to the needs of the military, would begin teaching courses in the Vietnamese language and the history of Southeast Asia the following semester. I read one of the General's quotes to my roommates. "We will need alumni who can interrogate enemy prisoners with dispatch," the General had said.

"Can you see me interrogating some Vietcong bastard after I take that course?" I asked my roommates while putting the paper down on my desk.

"I wouldn't interrogate nobody," Pig said matter-of-factly. "I'd just cut their fucking balls off. It's an international language."

"Pig, why don't you go out and organize an International Committee for Idjits?" Mark said.

"You almost flunked French, Will," Tradd said. "So you know you aren't going to take any silly course in the Vietnamese language."

"Man, I'm a born interrogator," I disagreed. "I'll prove it to you. Tradd, you sit in that chair and pretend you're the meanest fucking Vietcong who ever lived. Good. Put your hands behind your back like you were tied up. Now, here's the scene," I said, speaking directly to Pig and Mark, ignoring the prisoner. "This important Vietcong prisoner is brought to my tent. He's a tiny little fucker. He's been wounded in a fire fight and he knows Ho Chi Minh personally. We've got to extract information from him. So the brass calls for the best master of the Vietnamese language in the whole fucking army, Colonel Will McLean, who has risen in the ranks faster than anyone in the history of the American military."

"Oh, sure, Will," Tradd groaned.

"Fat chance, Toecheese," Pig chimed in.

"Riii–gght," Mark added.

I ignored them and continued, "Will is a changed man after graduating from the Institute and spending two years in the jungle fighting gooks and acting with incredible courage. Who wouldn't be changed after winning two Congressional Medals of Honor and having personally captured General Giap after a firefight on the outskirts of Hanoi? The men in his outfit look upon Will as his roommates in college did, not as simply the greatest man who ever lived . . . no, that does not adequately describe their adoration of him. They look upon him quite simply as a god, a god among men. They affectionately refer to him as Colonel Will, that fighting fucking fool."

Tradd said, "They affectionately refer to him as that poor boy who lost his mind and his marbles soon after he graduated from the Institute."

"They call him Colonel Toecheese," Pig muttered, looking at me strangely.

"The Vietcong captive thinks he has been led before a torturer. He looks into McLean's cold steely eyes and is completely cowed. Though he has fought with the Cong for twenty years, has faced platoons of Green Berets, has endured the terror of napalm and B–52 raids, he has never known the true meaning of fear until he stares trembling into McLean's eyes. McLean looks at him like he is looking at a urine sample," I said, leaning forward and staring malignantly into Tradd's eyes.

"Trained by professors at the Institute," I continued, my nose now an inch from Tradd's, "in the secret nuances of the

Vietnamese language, McLean leans down close to the prisoner and begins the interrogation with these subtle, well-chosen words: 'Fuck you, Cong.' Naturally, the prisoner is taken aback. But McLean relentlessly presses ahead with the questioning. 'Have you ever eaten a Hershey bar? Have you ever owned a Chrysler or a Chevrolet? Have you ever seen *Gone with the Wind*? Have you ever got a hard-on looking at pictures of Marilyn Monroe?' I'm confusing him with this line of questioning. My accent is so perfect he thinks I was born next door to him in Hué. I've got him off guard—then, quick as a flash, I show him my Institute ring and he panics, he flips out, he goes fucking bimbo. He realizes that he is not being questioned by any ordinary man. He's being questioned by a full-fledged Institute Man, a goddam bona fide, Grade-A, government-inspected, sterling-silver Whole Man. He breaks down completely when I tell him that we've enrolled him as a knob at the Institute and he's going to have to go through the plebe system. Colonel Will, that fightin' fuckin' fool, has done it again. The prisoner gives me the telephone number of Ho Chi Minh's daughter. I call her up for a date. When we go out, she goes wild with lust at the sight of an Institute man's body. We get married and a peace treaty is signed. All because the Institute offered a course in the Vietnamese language."

"Are you really going to take that course, Will?" Tradd asked.

"Hell no," I answered. "I'm not going to have anything to do with that goddam country."

"You didn't hear the news this morning, did you, Will?" Pig said.

"What news?"

"Rodney Harris got killed in Vietnam last week."

"Hey, I'm sorry, Pig. I know you two were good friends."

"He was on the wrestling team with me. We used to work out together, get in shape together. I don't feel like joking about Nam the day I hear about my buddy getting wasted. OK?"

"You should have stopped me, Pig," I said. "I didn't know about Rodney. There are so many casualties over there now that you need a slide rule to keep up with them."

"Will," Pig said, "I want to talk seriously to you, paisan. I want to make a new rule in the room. No more jokes about Nam. OK? Not when we got friends of ours getting killed over there. You've got to earn the right to joke about something that serious. You got a big mouth and you can laugh about anything else you want to. But not the war."

For a moment the room was silent, but it was the silence of agreement, and I saw Mark and Tradd looking at me as though I were an outsider, a stranger in the clubhouse.

Finally Tradd spoke, "Pig, I can hardly believe my ears. But that's a remarkably intelligent thought and very moving, too. I'm afraid that I agree with Pig completely, Will. There are certain subjects far too serious for humor. You've never known where to stop. I've meant to talk to you about this before, but I was afraid of your ridicule. All of us are afraid of your tongue."

"Mark?" I asked, sitting in my chair and facing the interrogation of my roommates. "What do you think?"

"We might be dying there next year, Will," Mark said. "Have you ever thought about that? I don't give a shit if you joke about Nam or not. But are you going to laugh then? How are you going to find a way to laugh when they're burying one of your roommates?"

"No! No!" I said, despairing at the thought. "I won't laugh then. I won't know what to do."

"Well, Tradd, Pig, and I will all be over there about this time next year. So it might be good for all of us if we put the war off limits."

"Do you know what they're doing to us, boys?" I said, trying to find the exact words for what I was thinking for the very first time, in the face of the hostility of my best friends. "Do you know what this school is setting us up for? It's setting us all up to be killed."

"I couldn't disagree with you more, Will," Tradd responded angrily. "That's simply cynical of you to talk like that. And pure nonsense. Trashy talk. The Institute simply believes that her sons owe a great debt to their country. An immeasurable debt. It trains us to be both good citizens and good soldiers, just as it promised to do when we were dumbheads. In times of war, good citizens come to the aid of their country and there's a reason for it, Will. This country is simply better than most other countries. It has values and ideals like freedom and democracy, ideals that I'm sure you would joke about, but which have been won with the blood of patriots. I'm waiting for you to laugh. I'm waiting for you to make fun of what I'm saying, but it's what most of us believe at this school and none of us is ashamed of it."

"That was beautiful, Tradd," Pig said proudly. "Fucking poetry. Fucking Keats shit. Keats shit all the way, man."

"Why do you want to go to Vietnam, Pig?" I asked, realizing that the question had never once arisen in the room. "And you, Mark? Tradd just told us why he's going, and I accept that."

"I'm going to win medals and kill gooks," Pig said, his voice angry and explosive. "I hate gooks."

"You've never seen a gook, Pig," I said.

"I hate gooks for what they did to Rodney Harris."

"They killed Rodney Harris, Pig," I said. "I grant you that. But let us put it in perspective. Rodney was out in the jungle trying to kill them. They didn't have anything against Rodney Harris any more than they have anything against you. They won't even know your name, Pig. They won't even know how nice a guy you are. You won't know their names. Do you guys understand what I'm trying to say?"

Tradd walked over to where I was sitting and said, "Why are you against everything, Will? If someone holds a belief sacred why do you have to set yourself up as the grand judge to ridicule it and make it sound foolish and base? What do you hold sacred, Will? And do you have a single belief you'd die for? You ridicule religion. You ridicule patriotism. You ridicule the Institute. You ridicule Charleston and the people who are so proud of her history. You ridicule the South even though you're Southern. You ridicule General Durrell and all the tactical officers. Why are you against absolutely everything? I want to know, Will. What's troubling you about the war and our duty to our country?"

"I don't know, Tradd," I said truthfully. "Something's wrong with the war. Something's wrong in all of us walking out of here without asking any questions. No one's asking any fucking questions."

"But your three best friends in the world believe in the war, Will," Tradd insisted. "All of us are committed to going to Vietnam. All of us are going to put our lives on the line for our belief in this country."

"When did I start rooming with Sergeant York, Tradd? I could put those same words in the mouth of General Durrell or Major Mudge or any of the others in this school. Those are the same goddam words every goddam cretin in this school uses when talking about that fucking war. This is a college for parrots, not patriots.

Even smart guys like you, Tradd, truly intelligent guys sound like dimwits when they explain why they want to go to Vietnam."

"You're nothing but a fucking coward, Will," Pig shouted at me, approaching me with the veins in his forehead protruding, "so be a *quiet* fucking coward. Don't open your mouth about the war unless you want me to shut your mouth for good."

"I will always fight for the merits of cowardice, Pig," I said, trying to lighten the situation somewhat.

"You're so touchy and melodramatic, Pig," Tradd said. "This is simply a debate among men of good will. This is an intellectual exercise."

"It's like kicking the teeth out of dead men, paisan," Pig muttered, nearly out of control and hovering above me, "so shut up. Just shut your goddam mouth."

"I'll talk about anything I want to, Pig. If I can't, I'll find some new roommates. But you can't make me shut up about a single thing," I said angrily.

He put his hands suddenly around my throat, and with a certain unnerving quality of grieving, almost gentle violence, he lifted me off my feet, the huge muscles of his arms beautiful in their full definition, as he held me against the wall like a man lynched from below. His grip tightened and I squeezed his wrists frantically—and felt the urgency of his pulse; oxygen to my lungs and blood to my brain were cut simultaneously, and Pig's face, distorted and crazed, stared up at me and my own eyes strained to focus on his, but the trapped blood that burned behind the retina blossomed with indistinct images and formless movements in the room around me. I heard Tradd pleading with Pig to put me down; his voice was shrill and unhinged. I heard the sound of my own gagging, a terrible strangling noise that barely managed to escape from my throat. I did not see Mark. More significantly, neither did Pig.

It was easy to forget about Mark Santoro's speed. The strength you never forgot about: that was a given. But the speed was always a surprise in such a large man. Mark's fist caught Pig in the left temple, and the blow sent him spinning wildly into one of the steel presses near the alcove. I dropped from Pig's hands and lay on the floor gagging and fighting for breath. I tried to speak and choked; I tried to breathe and couldn't.

When I finally could look up and my eyes could

focus, Pig had entered that first sinister position of karate, and Mark stood facing him, resolute and dangerous, in a boxer's stance of at least equal formidability. Mark's eyes were wild and I had never seen Pig angrier. I didn't just fear they would hurt each other; I feared they would kill each other. Each of them had the strength, the capacity, and the occasional inclination to kill a man with either hand. Heavyweights can harm each other grievously and permanently, and that was what was always so fearful about strong and well-shaped men locked in mortal combat. I grew nauseated when I saw them about to fight, and I tried to rise.

But Tradd had already sprung between Mark and Pig. He looked thin, inconsequential, and fragile as he moved into the dangerous land between them.

"Enough," he cried. "Enough of this silliness."

"Get out of the way, Tradd." Mark spoke through grimly tightened lips.

"He's the only thing between you and a broken jaw, Toecheese," Pig said.

"I will not have this in my room." Tradd spoke again, with conviction and with a determined look on his face. "I will not tolerate this among us."

"You ever touch Will again," Mark snarled at Pig, "the nicest thing I do to you is throw you off the fourth division."

"I want to touch *you*, Mark," Pig answered. "I'm gonna touch you like you've never been touched before. Your body's gonna be broke up in a hundred places when I finish kicking you."

"You've never fought a man in your life, Pig. You always pick on guys who've never fought a single fight in their whole lives. For four years I've watched you pick fights with guys who were afraid of you."

"I refuse to allow you to fight. I simply will not tolerate violence among my roommates," Tradd shouted at the combatants.

Rising, my throat bruised and aching, I staggered across the room and stood between Mark and Pig, locking my arm with Tradd's, leaning on him for support. Mark stared fiercely over our heads, his eyes full of contempt and challenge.

"Pig," I said, my voice almost recognizable, "I'm sorry I made you mad about the war. I won't mention the war in this room again. I love the goddam war, if that's what you want. I was trying to make a point about the school, not the war."

"I didn't get the point," Pig said.

"That's because you've got four pounds of provolone where most people got brains," Mark shouted, shaking his fist. "This is college, you dumb bastard. This is a place where you're supposed to argue and learn and get pissed off. You don't go around choking your buddies just because they don't happen to believe what you believe."

"I don't care if you believe everything I do or not, paisan," Pig said to me, softening. "I just want you to believe the important things."

"Then you believe this, motherfucker," Mark said, pointing his finger at Pig's face, "if you ever lay a fucking hand on William or if you so much as touch Tradd with one of your fat pinkies, you're going to think a platoon of Marines staged a landing on your ass. They're off limits. They're to me what Theresa is to you."

"Hey," Pig said, uneasily feeling the hostile solidarity of the room directed against him now, "I feel the same way, Mark. You know I do. All of you know that. Will, you know it more than anybody. I lost my head. I really did. I'd rather die than to hurt you, Will. I'd kill myself if you were hurt. I'd never forgive myself."

"I hate bullies," I said to him, my own damaged voice almost breaking as I said it. "I've hated bullies all my life. And that's the part of you I hate. You make people afraid of you; then you use that fear against them."

"You do the same thing with your tongue, Will," Tradd said. "You sometimes use your tongue to hurt and bully people. Both of you can learn something from this silliness. Pig, you've simply got to learn to rely on your wits," Tradd continued in a gentle, conciliatory tone.

"Ha!" Mark snorted. "That's like asking a fish to rely on its legs."

"Don't piss me off, Santoro," Pig warned, the veins reappearing in his forehead, the physical roadmap of his emotions. "I said I was sorry. What do you want me to do? Kiss everybody's ass?"

"Yeh," Mark answered resolutely, "I want you to kiss everybody's ass. Everybody's in the room. Then I'll know you're really sorry."

Tradd and I looked at Mark, waiting for some external sign that he was joking, but his eyes were mirthless and his tone unmistakably serious.

"That's the grossest thing I've ever heard of, Mark," Tradd declared. "His word is good enough. He's an Institute man like the rest of us. You don't humiliate a man who's going to wear the ring for the rest of his life."

But Pig was beyond humiliation, and he had a touching need to perform a public act of contrition and expiation. He fell to his knees, pulled Tradd toward him and planted a wet, fervent kiss on his struggling behind. It was a far more unsettling ordeal for Tradd than for Pig, and I laughed out loud when I saw the appalled look cross Tradd's face.

"I bet that's the first St. Croix in the history of America that's ever been kissed on the ass," I said as the tension in the room dissipated.

"When Pig is wrong, he's man enough to say he's wrong. Come here, Will, I got to plant a big wet one on your backside."

I leaned down and grabbed my ankles. Pig, laughing again and enjoying the success of his performance, kissed my ass reverently, deliciously, moaning with exaggerated pleasure, as though he were a leading man kissing a lovely woman in the last frame of a film. Then he bit my ass and purred licentiously.

"I've always been an ass man, boys. Come here, Santoro. I'm going to kiss your ass instead of kicking it."

"Naw, I've changed my mind. I don't want you to kiss my ass. At least not yet," Mark said, walking to the window at the end of the room and staring out to the deserted tennis courts.

"I don't have forever, paisan. I'm in an ass-kissing mood now, and it ain't often I feel like kissing the hard hairy asses of my roommates."

"Just wait a minute," Mark said, smiling, and I knew by the smile, the old Santoro smile of mischief and deviltry, that he was up to no good.

"I want to kiss your ass, son," Pig begged. "I've got to kiss it or it will mean you haven't forgiven me."

"OK, Pig. Kiss my handsome ass now. I want to feel those lips through my pants."

Pig went down behind Mark and kissed him firmly on the behind, and Mark, with perfect timing, loudly and triumphantly farted.

Mark wheeled and sprinted out the door laughing maniacally, almost helplessly, as Pig, spitting on the floor and swearing, raced to the sink and began brushing his teeth furiously, brushing his teeth over and over again, brushing his teeth and coughing, as Tradd and I rolled on the floor of our alcove room, laughing until tears rolled down both our faces.

* * *

That night Pig wrapped my throat in a hot steaming towel before I went to bed. He gave me some vitamins, which he swore would remove the bruises caused by his hands within two days. Pig's real apologies always involved a dispensing of vitamins and a soft laying-on of the powerful hands.

I did not speak of Vietnam in that room again. But I used to worry and dream about Pig being killed in Vietnam.

I wish he had been. I only wish he had.

11

In the 1960s, to be liberal was one infallible way for a Southern boy to attract the attention of his family and friends. Since my father was a conservative of a particularly fevered strain, it was natural for me to study carefully every creed or doctrine to which he was irrationally and diametrically opposed. Rebellion came naturally to me. It is the tyrant's most valuable and life-enhancing gift. Very early I discovered that my father could control my behavior but not what I thought, though God knows he tried. Liberalism—and I use that term imprecisely and in the abstract, meaning only what I thought at a particular time in reaction against my environment—gave me the opportunity to sharpen my rather charming, naïve political and social views. I spoke often about politics and knew nothing. But there was an immense power in my sanctimony that lent a certain trembling credence to my outbursts. My blood told me what to think, not my brain. Facts only confused me and got in the way. My ideas were gaseous emanations rising out of a natural, inexhaustible wellspring of piety. Approaching the age of twenty-one, I was the most preachy, self-righteous, lip-worshiping, goody-goody person I have ever known. I had seen others who approached my level of righteousness but none of them was really in my league. This is why the incident with my roommates upset me so much. They had figured me out.

I had been called sanctimonious by every person who had ever known me well and for good reason. I am a member-in-good-standing of that contemptible race and I cannot help it. On my deathbed, I will be grandly dispensing good to my last breath, and my friends and loved ones will be despising that part of me to the very end. My goodness is my vanity, my evil. It does not well up naturally out of me but is calculated and plotted as carefully as a mariner studies the approach to an unfamiliar harbor. Sometimes I will reveal this to friends so they will like me and praise my honesty, but in actuality, I am presenting them with a mariner's chart of my character.

Anyone who knows me well must understand and be sympathetic to my genuine need to be my own greatest hero. It is not a flaw of character; it is a catastrophe. I have always been for the underdog and I've pretended it was because I was sensitive and empathetic, but that's not it at all. It was because I wanted the adoration of the underdog, the blind approval that the downtrodden so gratefully bestow on their liberators. It was all paternalism, my insatiable desire to be the benevolent tyrant dispensing tawdry gifts and moldy foodstuffs to the subjects who stumbled into the spiritual famine of my sad kingdom. When I bestowed my friendship on Tradd, Mark, and Pig, I was doing them a favor, liking them when other people ignored or feared them. I was a natural to take care of Pearce, not because of my radiant humanity (although that is what I wanted to believe) but because he would be indebted to me and I could rule him and own him and even loathe him because I had made him a captive of my goodness. I had the need to be the good master, but definitely the master, no matter what the cost. I did not like it that the three unpopular boys I had honored with my friendship had thoughts and ideas that differed from my own. It both surprised and angered me that my roommates had reached a consensus of agreement against me. The way I looked at the world, enemies criticized and friends affirmed. I granted my friends freedom of expression only when I was certain that the ideas expressed would be congruent with mine. It was but one of the reasons for my loneliness at the Institute; it was but one of the things that made friendship with me an ambivalent enterprise.

When my roommates asked me to go to a movie at Durrell Hall that Friday night, I told them I had some letters to write. It would take a few days for my petulance to subside. An infuriating piety reinforced even my anger. Knowing me well, they left for the movie arm in arm, and in ten minutes I was wishing I had gone with them. But as I look back on the events of that first week, I was not meant to see a movie that Friday night. It was my destiny to take an early shower.

It was nine o'clock and I was thinking all these thoughts about piety and friendship when I left my room, dressed in a light blue Institute bathrobe and my flip-flops. Pausing on the gallery I leaned against the iron railing and looked out into the checkered quadrangle far below me, my eye following the rows of perfectly congruent arches as they flowed across the opposite side of the barracks. The Institute was constructed as symmetrically as a rose, I thought. There was a quality of immense repose in the silent flow of stone. Then I heard a boy crying hard. The sounds came from the shower room.

I entered the room and found two members of the R Company cadre, a sophomore and a junior, surrounding an overweight freshman shaped like a yam, enjoying the spectacle of his weeping. The junior was Cecil Snipes. He turned to spot me coming through the door, and the demons of a long fine enmity flapped their leathery wings as we faced each other in the damp atmosphere of that room.

I did not wish to have words with Snipes on this night. Too much had already happened during this first week that I needed time to understand, to think out, and to plan for. Yet at the moment Snipes and I met head-on, there was the undeniable sense of confrontation.

"Easy, boys, easy. The lad looks like he's had about enough for today," I said in what I hoped was an affable, rather benign voice.

"Hi, Will," Matt Ledbetter said. He was the sophomore guidon corporal and like most sophomores had gone overboard in his zeal to inflict on plebes punishment as intolerable as he had endured the year before. Sophomores were dangerous in their vengeance.

"Hello, Matt. The young smackhead looks like he needs to call it a day to me."

"He's really a waste, Will," Matt said in disgust. "He couldn't have made it five minutes in the old Corps."

Snipes said nothing but turned from me wordlessly and faced the freshman. Clearly, he was relieved that I had not been a tactical officer on a reconnaisance foray through the barracks.

"You fucking pussy," he screamed into the boy's ear. "I want to see you cry some more, you fucking pussy. Bawl, little baby. Bawl, you fucking cunt-eyed baby."

The freshman had lost control long before I had entered the room. He was sweating profusely, and his face was flushed an unhealthy, overextended crimson. Tears had troweled out two ugly trenches beneath his eyes. His eyes were hideously swollen. He began sobbing uncontrollably as soon as Snipes screamed at him.

"Such language, Snipes," I said. "It makes me wonder if cadets are indeed gentlemen and scholars."

Snipes ignored me. He concentrated on watching the freshman, staring at the boy with intense, malevolent eyes. "What did you come here for, pussy? A fat little vagina like you ain't never going to make it in the Corps. Jesus, it's got snot running out of its nose. Spit running out of its mouth. Tears running out of its eyes. You make me sick, maggot-load. Why did you come here, wad-waste? Pop off!"

"Sir," the boy blubbered, his words barely coherent. "Sir, my father graduated from the Institute. I've always wanted to go here, sir."

"Well, you're here now, douchebag. How do you like it?" Snipes's voice was edged with menace.

"I love it, sir," the freshman replied.

"Bullshit, young innocent freshman," I butted in. "You think it sucks. Now why don't you tough, mean cadre boys run along while this young knoblet comes to my room for a long talk on the jolly art of how to survive the plebe system?"

"It looks like you were about to take a shower, Will," Snipes said. "Would you like me to run your water?"

"No, thanks, Cecil. I would like you to get off this dumbhead's ass."

"You're interfering with the system again, McLean," he answered, trying to control himself. "You almost got in trouble last year for interfering when I was trying to discipline a knob."

"It's not discipline, sweet Cecil. It's called hazing."

"Will, you have no right to butt in," Ledbetter said, not easily. It was no simple matter for a sophomore to challenge a senior at the Institute; it took considerable nerve, especially for someone as openly ambitious as Matt Ledbetter. "This knob is our responsibility, not yours."

"He's crying, Matt. I think you've convinced him that you're the big tough son of a bitch you think you are. Can you see that he's crying?"

"He's a fucking pussy," Snipes said.

"He may be, Cecil, but why don't you let him go to his room and figure that out for himself? You've cracked him, and now it's beginning to look a little more serious than just the game."

"You're interfering with the system, McLean," Snipes said, taking the freshman by the collar and shoving him brutally against the tiled wall.

"I'm interfering with an asshole, Snipes," I answered, then turning to the freshman, I screamed, "Get to your room, dumbhead."

The freshman took two steps for the shower room door before he braced to attention again when Snipes shouted, "Halt, smack. You stay where the fuck you are."

Snipes turned to face me and said, "I outrank you, McLean. I'm a platoon sergeant and you're nothing but a fucking private."

"Gee, a platoon sergeant. Jeepers-creepers, you must be something very special, Mr. Snipes. You must be a leader of men. Let me remind you of something, you fucking creep. I'm a senior and you're a junior. It's not rank that counts in this school and both you and Matt know it. It's the class system."

Matt spoke up nervously from the corner where he had retreated. "I don't think the dumbhead should hear this, Will."

"You can't talk like that in front of a knob, McLean," Snipes warned. "He's going to lose respect for me."

I walked over and stood directly in front of the

94

freshman. He was still crying but had regained a measure of control over himself.

"What's your name, dumbhead?" I asked.

"Sir, my name is cadet recruit Poteete, J. M., sir."

"Have you lost respect for Mr. Snipes, Poteete?"

"No, sir."

"Well, I have, dumbhead. I lost all respect for him two years ago when he was standing beneath the stairwell on first division."

"McLean!" Snipes said.

"He started crying when three seniors jumped him coming back from mess. They weren't even getting on him bad, Poteete. They were just racking his ass lightly. A little warm-up variety. Well, ol' Snipes cried like a goddam baby. I got him out of the rack line and into my room with the three seniors right behind me, screaming at me that they were going to jack it up my ass for interfering with the plebe system. They did, too, Poteete. Served confinements for one whole semester. Little Cecil cried in my room for half an hour. This same tough guy who's making you cry right now. I want you to remember that story. I want you to know about this sick fucking sadist who has you crying tonight. He cried his way through plebe year. Now you get to your room, Poteete. In an hour, I want you to come to my room for a little powwow. I'm in the alcove room on fourth division."

"Yes, sir," Poteete said, slipping on the wet tiles as he left.

"Don't you ever interfere when I'm disciplining a knob again, McLean," Snipes said, "or so help me, I'll report your ass."

"I'm so scared. I think I'm getting sick to my stomach. Fear does that to me."

"You interfered with me last year."

"Sadism repels me, Snipes. It's a quirk of mine."

"It's the system, McLean," he replied.

"It's an aberration of the system."

Matt Ledbetter cleared his throat and spoke to me in a voice trembling with emotion. "Will, that freshman doesn't belong in this school. We've got to run him out of here. We can't help it if he cries. He cries every time we look at him. He simply doesn't belong here. It'll be better for him and the other knobs when he goes."

"Last year, you were a freshman, Matt. This year you're God."

"He doesn't belong here, Will. It's our duty to run him out. We owe it to the Institute. We owe it to the line."

"Your duty?" I asked him.

"Our duty," Matt replied.

12

It was dangerous to have a sadist in the barracks, especially one who justified his excesses by religiously invoking the sacrosanct authority of the plebe system. The system contained its own high quotient of natural cruelty, and there was a very thin line between devotion to duty, that is, being serious about the plebe system, which was an exemplary virtue in the barracks, and genuine sadism, which was not. But I had noticed that in the actual hierarchy of values at the Institute, the sadist like Snipes rated higher than someone who took no interest in the freshmen and entertained no belief in the system at all. In the Law of the Corps it was better to carry your beliefs to an extreme than to be faithless. For the majority of the Corps, the only sin of the sadist was that he believed in the system too passionately and applied his belief with an overabundant zeal. Because of this, the barracks at all times provided a safe regency for the sadist and almost all of them earned rank. My sin was harder to figure. I did not participate at all in the rituals of the plebe system. Cruelty was easier to forgive than apostasy.

I placed a very high premium on my enmity with Snipes. He personified the Institute's capacity for deviance. He had the face of a young wolf—thin, carnivorous, and rapacious. His complexion was oily and barnacled with pimples, as though his very flesh was marked with his cunning debasement. Leanly, he moved along the galleries ferreting out plebes. I was glad he was not handsome; it was far easier to have ugly enemies.

As I waited for Poteete's knock on my door, I thought about my relationship with Cecil Snipes. In some deep instinctive way, I needed there always to be a Snipes at the Institute, perhaps throughout my entire life. I required always the hostility of the announced enemy, the devout and certified adversary. I needed the symbol of something worthy of encounter on the road, to test the resonance and mettle of my own humanity. If I could always be waging war against a Snipes, I would never have to turn a cold eye inward to discover the subtle and unexamined evil in myself.

The screen door slammed twice against the doorjamb, the signal of a freshman seeking entry into the room of an upperclassman.

"Drive in, dumbhead," I called out.

Poteete appeared in the entranceway, still sweating liberally. You could almost watch him losing weight. His face spoke eloquently of the day's rigors. His eyes, piglike and the color of tobacco leaf, were hideously swollen.

"Good evening, Mr. Poteete."

"Cadet recruit Poteete reporting as ordered, sir," he said.

"Not bad, Poteete," I said admiringly. "It's amazing how quickly you learn the little tricks they teach by torture this first week. Remove your cap when you come into an upperclassman's room. I forgot once during my plebe week and the first sergeant almost tore my head off. That's good. Now. At ease. Sit down and relax."

He stood before me bracing as earnestly as when he entered the room. It was almost impossible to relax in front of an upperclassman in the first months of school. The brace became a method of defense, a natural reflex like a turtle withdrawing into its shell.

"Relax your chin, Poteete," I ordered. "Quit bracing and sit down. You're making me nervous. You had a tough day, didn't you?"

"No, sir."

"Please try to remember that I'm not Snipes or any of those other assholes."

"Yes, sir."

"I'm a senior private, Poteete. I have no rank and no authority except that which comes naturally to any senior in this school. There aren't any privates around now, but there'll be a lot of them when the Corps gets back next week. We got where we are, to our incredibly unprestigious positions, by basically not giving a shit. Do you understand?"

"Yes, sir."

"You've got a great personality, kid. You're going to do well here," I said.

"Sir, permission to make a statement, sir."

"My god, Poteete, what do I have to do, get the General to sign a piece of paper that I just want to talk to you?"

"Sir," he said, and his voice was whining and rasping, "sir, I was the most popular boy in my high school. People liked me there."

"Ha! Wonderful, young dumbhead. Be sure to tell the cadre that. They'd hate to know they'd been abusing the most popular boy in his high school class. Let me do you a favor, Poteete, and suggest you keep that piece of information between us. They pick up on that kind of stuff and go for the groin. By the way, Poteete, are you sure you want to stay in this school?"

"Yes, sir," he answered. "More than anything in the world. I've been planning to come to the Institute ever since I can remember."

"So you've been fucked up a long time, Poteete."

"Sir," he bristled. "My father was a battalion commander in the class of 1947. He was a legend here. Sam Poteete. Have you ever heard of him?"

"Naw, not a single time in my whole life."

"It would've killed him if I'd gone to Clemson or Carolina. But when I was a senior he told me I could go to any college in the country, that he wouldn't interfere with my decision at all."

"And you chose this place?" I asked.

"He did make one stipulation, sir. He said he would pay for my education at the Institute."

"A legend in his own time, huh?" I said. "He sounds like a flaming asshole in his own time to me."

"He loves this place, sir. I think he was happier here that he ever has been since."

"How do you feel about it, Poteete?"

"I didn't know it was going to be like this, sir. I didn't know about the cruelty."

"Oh, they're just getting warmed up," I said. "It's just plebe week. You've got a big nine months to go. You're merely seeing the birth of the ghouls this week. They're only truly fearsome when they reach maturity in January. Then and only then is their cruelty really formidable. But by that time, if you make it that long, you could withstand an assault by the whole Chinese army."

"Do you think I can make it, sir?" Poteete said pleadingly. "I mean, I've got to make it. I could never go home to Dad as a quitter."

"You've got to quit crying, Poteete."

"I can't, sir. I'm easily upset."

"They'll run you out of here in a couple of days if you don't. They already know that you cry easily, Poteete. They already know they can get to you. So now they're going to start singling you out the way they were doing in the shower room tonight. They'll cut you off from the herd, use you as an example, get the other freshmen to turn against you. If you don't learn to quit crying, Poteete, it's going to be a gang-bang every moment of your life."

"I can't help it, sir. It just comes."

"I know, Poteete. I cried myself to sleep every night for three months. I cried throughout my entire plebe year. Do you know what happened to me after that?"

"No, sir."

"I haven't cried since. Not once. I don't know if I'm capable of crying now."

"So the system really works?"

"Oh, the system works fine, Poteete."

"I hope that happens to me, sir."

"Cry at night, Poteete. Cry in the latrine or when you're taking a shower. But please don't cry in front of them or you'll be back with your father in . . . where's your hometown?"

"Sir, my hometown is Pickens, South Carolina, sir."

"Otherwise, you'll spend a long winter in Pickens with your father not talking to you."

"I'll never go back to Pickens if I quit."

"I wouldn't go back to Pickens if I stayed," I answered. "But I wanted to warn you, Poteete. They have you marked now. I'll do what I can to help you but I'm not much respected for my love of the plebe system and if they see me helping you too much, then they'll be even tougher on you. You've got to become invisible to them, blend in with the background. Do everything they tell you to do. Look like you love doing it whether it's washing down the quadrangle with a toothbrush or doing a hundred pushups. They've sent more than one freshman packing because of a nervous breakdown."

"If you hate it so much, sir, why did you stay?" Poteete asked.

"Fuck you, Poteete," I flared back. "You ain't my analyst. I stayed for the same reason you want to stay. The upholding of the McLean tradition. That kind of crap. And

99

do you know something else, Poteete? I was a coward. I couldn't face the shame of having quit this dump. I envied those kids who walked out of here and started new lives that had nothing to do with the Institute or the system or the Corps. The irony of it all, Poteete, the goddam hilarious irony is that the rest of the world, if they could only know about this place, would think everybody connected with it was stark raving mad."

Poteete looked at me suspiciously and asked, "You don't believe in the system, Mr. McLean?"

"That's right, dumbhead," I answered him back meeting his gaze directly. "I don't believe in the system."

"Then I don't think I should be around you, sir," he said. "I believe in the system, sir."

"Then I suggest you go find some members of the cadre, Poteete. They'll be glad to indoctrinate you fully in its glories and triumphs."

"I appreciate your trying to help, sir. I really do. But I want to be an Institute man more than anything in the world."

"Good. Then I'm going to tell Snipes that you think he's a zit-faced cocksucker. Then Snipes will help you to become a much better Institute man than you might have become talking to softies like me."

"You misunderstand me, Mr. McLean. Everyone misunderstands me here."

"I'm not going to talk to Snipes, Poteete. I break out into hives every time I see him draw a level breath."

"Will that be all, sir?" Poteete asked, bracing again.

I put my hand on his shoulder and walked him to the door.

"Just remember this, Poteete. For what it is worth. And this is coming from a guy who doesn't believe in the system. If you keep on crying, you won't make it. They'll run you out. Good luck. And come up here if you ever want the pressure off. I've got real nice roommates."

"Thank you, sir. I'll do my best, sir."

"I hope you make it, Poteete. I hope you make it for yourself and not that prick father from Pickens, South Carolina."

"Sir, don't you call my father a prick," Poteete warned.

"What will you do about it if I do, dumbhead?" I asked curiously.

"I'll have to fight you, sir," Poteete answered. He looked

utterly pathetic as he stood there bracing and issuing me a challenge at the same time.

"Very good. Your father is not a prick. I'm sorry. Your father is a gift of the Magi. You'd have to fight me. Goddam, Poteete, you might make it after all."

"I'll never quit, Mr. McLean. Good night, sir. Thanks for the advice. I know you were only trying to help me."

"Thanks for not kicking my ass, Poteete. My whole goddam life just flashed before me when you threatened physical harm. Remember, you've got to quit crying. Otherwise, you're gone, Poteete. Long gone."

13

On Sunday, I found the white gate on Stoll's Alley that led down a narrow brick path to the garden of Annie Kate's house on Church Street. There was a runaway luxuriance to the garden's ruined profusion that made it seem sinister instead of tranquil. It was a surprising touch of wilderness in the most ardently civilized acreage in South Carolina and a perfect place for a secret rendezvous.

I saw Annie Kate sitting on a small bench behind an unoccupied carriage house, watching me through her sunglasses. An arbor of vegetation enclosed her as she waited with her hands inside her raincoat pockets. Even in the middle of a late August day, it was cool in the untended shade. She smiled at me and motioned for me to come quickly to her side, and I realized that I was visible from at least two windows of the main house. Quickly, I made my way to her. We shone, she in her faded raincoat and I in my summer uniform, like two ivory chess pieces in the green tumult of her garden.

"You wore that silly nose again," she said.

"It breathes well and I decided to keep it."

"I do hope you reconsider your decision," she replied, adjusting her scarf.

"You're wearing a different scarf," I said.

"I'm glad you noticed. This is my favorite. The one I wore that night we met is such a tacky thing. I've always detested it. Tell me everything you did this week. Every single thing and don't leave out a single detail. I've been so bored I almost read a book. Why didn't you call me?"

"I don't have your number. I don't know your last name. And I didn't know you wanted me to call you."

"You can't call me. Mother would be furious. Did you think about calling me? Did you want to call me?"

"Yes, I wanted to call you."

"If you'd really wanted to call me, you'd have found a way. If you had a true romantic temperament, you'd have come here at night, climbed to my bedroom window on a ladder, and begged me to give you my telephone number," she whispered. Since I could not see her eyes, I didn't know if Annie Kate was teasing me or slightly out of her mind. I had never met a Southern girl who talked so boldly in my entire life and would have denied the existence of such a desperately forward creature had someone described her in accurate detail.

"That's all I need," I answered. "To be shot off a ladder while trying to break into a house South of Broad."

"I've been so lonely this week I could've killed myself and never given it a second thought," she said, speaking more to herself than to me. "When I'm alone all I can do is think and I absolutely hate to think. Especially now."

"You look like you've been thinking long, deep thoughts on this bench."

"People who go around thinking deep thoughts are usually pretentious, silly things who have no sense of who they are. I bet you sit around thinking all the time. Boys from good families are out to have good times. They detest deep thoughts as much as I do. But they're serious about the important things."

Taking a seat beside her, I asked, "Such as?"

"Such as preserving history, selling real estate, making a good living for their families, hiring a good staff, and sending their children to the proper schools. Charleston boys always give a good account of themselves."

"Speaking of hiring a good staff," I said, looking around the garden, "who's your gardener? Johnny Appleseed or the Jolly Green Giant?"

"I'm not going to let you make me mad today," she said. "Did you bring me a flower, Will, or a box of candy, or some other nice, thoughtful presentable?"

"No, I didn't bring you anything," I answered, mad at myself for not having thought of it.

"No wonder you don't have any girl friends," she pouted. "Not only do you have a funny nose, but I always expect that the dear sweet boys in my life will bring me a presentable when they come to my door."

"Maybe if I was coming to your door, it would be different," I said, my voice rising, "but I'm coming to your back yard garden. I'm not sitting in your drawing room nibbling on bennie wafers and sweets, I'm sitting beneath an eight-foot-high camellia bush and three palmetto trees. No, Annie Kate, I didn't bring you a goddam presentable."

She was smiling again, and her voice was teasing as she said in a flawless self-parody, "A gentleman would never, under any circumstance, use such language in front of a lady. Especially a lady of my delicate coloring and breathtaking beauty. We Charleston girls are fragile, Will. Profanity bruises us."

"Annie Kate, do you always talk and act like you're a complete idiot?"

"How dare you to insult me like that in my own house," she bristled. "If you don't understand what I'm doing, Will, then you shouldn't ever be around women at all. I've been around men long enough to know that all they want is a woman who'll make them feel smart and handsome and superior. I've watched women flirt with men all my life, and I've become goddam good at playing the coquette. In case you haven't noticed."

"Please," I said. "I'm a cadet. Profanity bruises me."

"No girl in her right mind would ever put up with someone like you. You might as well declare yourself to be a homosexual."

"That was a joke."

"Your calling me an idiot was not a joke."

"I didn't call you an idiot. I said that sometimes you talked and acted like you were an idiot."

"I'm brighter than anyone who goes to that second-rate college you go to. The Institute's a rinky-dink college for cretins who weren't smart enough to get into a military academy. A boy of intelligence wouldn't think of going there."

"You can't offend me by cutting down the Institute," I told her truthfully. "I'm impervious to all criticism of my alma mater."

"You ought to have more loyalty. I detest disloyal people. I'm very well known for my loyalty."

"What are you loyal to?" I asked.

"My family. My city. My heritage. My religious beliefs."

"And Santa Barbara, your college," I added.

She whirled on me furiously and said, "God don't like ugly, Will McLean. He doesn't like ugliness and he doesn't forgive ugliness and you're acting like just about the ugliest human being I've ever met. Most girls I know have too much pride to be seen with a crude, nasty cadet like you."

"You're not being seen with me. We're hiding in a garden behind a carriage house. You'd have to have a pack of bloodhounds to flush us out of this jungle."

"No one forced you to come, Will, and I certainly couldn't care less whether you stay or not," Annie Kate said. A freeze had entered her voice. I stood up and walked in front of her.

"I'm not very good at talking to girls, Annie Kate. I tried to tell you that. I don't know why it always ends up like this when we talk. I was really looking forward to seeing you. I was looking forward to it all week because ... because it was so strange and I thought something wonderful could come out of our meeting."

"Nothing wonderful can come from our meeting. I can promise you that. Nothing wonderful will ever happen to me again. I had a perfect childhood in Charleston, Will. An incredible childhood full of rope swings and summer nights in hammocks and August regattas and debutante parties and climbing over the seawall on the Battery. But that's all in the past now and will never happen again. That's all finished and those times are dead."

"Yeh, your life is over," I said. "You must be all of twenty."

"I'm nineteen. Don't you make me older than I am. I won't be twenty for three months."

"It's hard to tell how old you are when you always wear those sunglasses, that scarf, and that raincoat."

"Do I make snide remarks about your silly uniform?" she replied. "Cadets all look like ice cream salesmen in those tacky summer uniforms."

"I'm very sensitive about my uniform. It's my outlandish loyalty at work again. No, I can explain why I wear my uniform, but I don't understand why you wear yours."

"I wear it because I'm in prison," she answered.

"If you think this is a prison," I said, gesturing around the garden, "let me show you the Institute sometime. But that's not the point. I'm asking questions about the sunglasses, Annie Kate, for a very good reason. Someday before I get gouty and rheumatic and live in a nursing home, I'd like to see what your face looks like."

"I've got a very pretty face," she said simply.

"I'd like to see what color your eyes are and what color your hair is."

"My eyes are of a very light blue. Not as light as yours, but my eyes aren't as threatening as yours are. Not as empty. Your eyes don't look inhabited."

I laughed, a bit too loudly, for she put a finger to her lips and turned in the direction of the main house. All was silent in the garden when I spoke again. "You keep talking like that and I'm going to wear sunglasses. I've always been told I have very nice eyes. That's the only thing people can think of when they try to say something nice about my face."

"If I were you, Mr. McLean, I wouldn't just wear sunglasses," she said coyly. "I'd purchase a huge mask or perhaps a shopping bag."

"You have a sharp tongue beneath those sunglasses."

"I told you I was smart."

Before I could answer another voice in the garden said, "Not that smart, my dear."

The woman was smaller than I remembered her and much thinner. But it was not her diminutiveness that left the strongest impression on me; rather, it was a quality of beleaguered delicacy, as though her spirit had endured the same heedless inattention as her garden. There was something insufficient and untended about her. Her voice was troubled and defeated, all low sad tones like the scrupulous grief of cellos.

"Ma'am," I said in the silence that followed the shock of her noiseless onslaught, "you are indeed a quiet little person."

But her arrival held no real elements of surprise. The very artificiality of the secret meeting invited capture. The mother's face was flushed with triumph and disapproval. Annie Kate had not looked up since she heard the other woman's voice. The garden resonated with melancholy and shame, with betrayal and sin.

"You are on private property, young man, and if you don't depart from these grounds at once, I will call the police and have you thrown in the city jail by the river. The Charleston city jail is famous for the size of its rats."

105

"Mother, please," Annie Kate moaned.

"I demand to know why you're pursuing my daughter."

"Mother!"

"What I'm doing, Annie Kate, I'm doing for you. You know that. You know that I don't like it any better than you do, but you know that it's absolutely necessary. This young man was not my idea. Remember that," she said, turning her attention back to me. "Cadet, you are neither absolutely necessary nor even very desirable."

"Ma'am, I did not just trip on a crack in the sidewalk on Church Street and accidentally land in this garden. I was invited here by Annie Kate, who appears to be badly in need of someone to talk to. She told me she needs a friend. I can be a good friend. I can also be discreet and if Annie Kate robbed a bank or molested chickadees in a bird sanctuary, I don't care. If you don't want anyone in Charleston to know that Annie Kate's in town, then I won't tell anyone. If you don't want me to know why you're acting like Annie Kate's radioactive, then you don't have to tell me. You have my word that I won't tell another living soul that I've met either one of you."

The older woman eyed me for a long time then asked her daughter, "Do you think you can trust him, Annie Kate?"

"I don't know," she replied. "He's got Catholic eyes."

"My daughter is very lonely and very bored, Mr. McLean. That is partially my fault and partially hers."

"Ma'am, if she's leaving anonymous notes on cars of cadets, she's more than bored."

"I'm stark raving mad," Annie Kate said, slumping down on the garden bench.

"Quit being silly, Annie Kate. You decide what to tell Mr. McLean. I'll leave that all up to you. Since you've tried to prove what a grownup girl you are, you can decide if he comes back to this house or not. And Mr. McLean," she said, fixing me with both the intensity and sadness of her gaze, "I'm holding you to your word of honor to speak of this with no one, not even your closest friends."

"Yes, Ma'am. I promise."

She disappeared down the brick pathway that led to the main house. Her walk was stiff, formal, and painfully graceless. As she left I became aware of a deep wild perfume exhumed in the rising heat of the day, lifting invisibly from the untrimmed hedges and grottoes of ill-disciplined flowers.

The garden smelled like an abandoned florist's shop. Annie Kate read the drift of my thoughts as I sat back upon the bench.

"We used to have a gardener," she said. "Before my father died."

"It looks like the gardener died, too."

"Mother let him go several years ago. She said it was because of his drinking, but it was actually because we had no money."

"You won't be needing a gardener soon. They'll be leading safaris through your back yard."

"You have a very Irish face," she said, observing me closely.

"Why don't you say that I have a very sexy face?"

"You don't have a very sexy face. You have a funny, sad clown's face."

"Women go wild over this face. They're always knocking into each other trying to lay a pinkie on my face."

"I want to be honest about this relationship from the very beginning."

"Yeh, honesty's your long suit."

"Don't be cynical," she said. "I don't need a boy friend. I only need a friend."

"I need a girl friend, but I'll be glad to be your friend."

"You don't need me for a girl friend, Will. I promise you that."

"Why not?" I asked. "You look like a perfectly respectable girl to me. A little weird the way you dress, but a fine specimen of womanhood."

"It's over for me, Will. My whole life is over," she said as she rose from the bench and stood facing me.

She removed her scarf and her long blonde hair fell luxuriantly to her shoulders.

Carefully, she took off her sunglasses and I saw her eyes for the first time. They were blue, shining, and lovely. Tears were spilling out of them. She unbuttoned her raincoat, then flung it open with sudden violence, sudden liberation.

"My baby is due in February," she said. "Would you like to be the father, Will?"

14

Cain Gilbreath poked his head in my room the night before the regular class schedule began. A guard on the football team, Cain was a native of Richmond, Virginia, and carried with him all the opulent aromas of Tidewater gentry gone to seed. His family once had money and it was the obsession of Cain's life that they would have it again. Politically a conservative, he considered me a dangerous radical because I had supported Johnson in the 1964 election. At the Institute, being a Democrat was beginning to smack of sedition. Mostly Cain and I were friends for the single reason that both of us enjoyed the type of collegiate dialogue that began with insult and ended with threats on each other's life.

"God is love," Cain began. He always thought about his opening sally deep in advance. "Love is blind. Ray Charles is God. God's a blind nigger."

"Too much time on the football field, eh, Gilbreath? The brain is showing signs of softening."

"It's painful to be a genius, McLean." He sighed, walking across the room and reclining heavily on my bed.

"Good to see you, Cain. Sure, go ahead and lie down on my bed."

Cain had a massive torso and thick muscled shoulders and a neck that sloped imperceptibly into those shoulders. But his hands and feet were disproportionately small, delicate, and sensitively made. His legs were thin and hairless, like a girl's, and his arms were short and stubby, hardly formidable weapons to bludgeon the chins of charging defensive linemen. In his face, one could trace the proud lineage. And in his tiny oriental hands and feet. His total appearance was as unlikely and surprising as a wildebeest's.

"I said it's painful being a genius. Thinking deep

thoughts all the fucking time. There are times I consciously try to be shallow, to lower myself and frolic a bit with the herd, the banana-eating chimpanzees that make up the student body of this college, but it's hard, Will. Extremely hard. Speaking of chimpanzees, where are your roommates, the two gorillas and the harmless fag?"

"I'd like you to do me a favor and call Pig and Mark chimpanzees when they're present sometime, Cain. Or call Tradd a harmless fag when they're present. You'd be thinking deep thoughts as you were airborne off the fouth division."

"Let's have a debate," he said, rising up on one elbow and grinning at me. His finger unconsciously traced a long, ugly, centipede-shaped scar that resulted from surgery on his shoulder the year before. He was boyishly proud of the scar, and he walked shirtless around the barracks when the weather permitted.

"I don't want to debate," I said. "That's all we ever do when we see each other."

"Let's debate Vietnam again. I murdered you the last time."

I groaned and buried my head in my arms on the desk. "Everyone murders me when we talk about Vietnam."

"That's because you're the only one in the school without a military contract."

"Yeh, I'm a real asshole."

"Do you want to know what I think, McLean?"

"No."

"Well, I'll tell you anyway. I think you're against the war just because everyone else is for it. I think that you like to be different for no other reason than to be different."

"That's it, Gilbreath. Bingo. Bull's eye. You figured it out completely. You're giving me a rare new insight into my personality. Nothing I can say to that. You've defined me, boy. Wow!"

"About Vietnam, Will," he said, enjoying me. "You ought to think of the war as an extension of your basketball career. A place for testing yourself. Aren't you curious about how you'd react in battle? Don't you think that it's only in battle that a man really learns what he's made of? I don't care about Vietnam one way or the other, but I look upon it as my chance for the great test. My support of the war is simply an act of faith in America, and I'm delighted that my two years in the Army will be spent in battle and not in some dull stateside post where enlisted wives walk around commissaries in pin curlers. Tell me the truth, Will, aren't you just a bit worried about missing the only war of this generation?"

"No, Cain, I'm worried about missing the only balls I have in this generation. And I already know how I'd react in battle. I'd be scared shitless. I'd be even afraid to walk around because of the land mines. I don't care about the great test, and I hope this *is* the only war in our generation."

"You must be the first pacifist this college has produced."

"I didn't say I was a pacifist, Gilbreath. There are wars that I would fight in joyously. For instance, I'd lead a goddam rebellion in Shenandoah Valley if you're ever elected governor of Virginia. And I'd make a general out of the National Guardsman who brought your nuts to me in a Mason jar. But this just isn't my war, Cain, and I'm not going to fight in it."

"Surely, Will, you must be sympathetic to the cause of the South Vietnamese and their efforts to repel the spread of communism in Southeast Asia."

"You sound like Radio Free Europe. Sure I'm sympathetic. I'm also sympathetic to the North Vietnamese. In politics, I find myself sympathetic with everybody. Every side has points for and against them. I just get confused. Do you remember what Mudge said last year in military science class, Cain, when we were studying communism? You must know the enemy before you can hate him. Well, that class affected me. We spent half a semester studying what total shits communists are and how they kill babies with pitchforks and bayonet virgins in the vagina."

"They do those things, Will. These are simple facts," Cain said.

"That's not my point, Cain. I don't know if they do those things or not. But what I realized is that I have never seen a communist in my whole life except on television. I have despised a whole segment of the human race and I've never even seen one."

"Do you need to have the clap to know you don't want it?"

"Cain, do you remember the military science class where you got so fired up about going to Vietnam?"

"That was when Mahaffy, class of '64, came back to talk."

"Yeh, Mahaffy. You thought he gave a great talk, didn't you?"

"It was by far the most stirring and patriotic talk I've heard while I've been at the Institute. The General never matched that speech, even though he has come awfully close. Hell, half of the room was crying after his talk. Of course, I'm absolutely positive you were belly-laughing on the floor during the entire thing."

"Yeh. It was a great speech," I agreed, "but that's when I realized I was different from you guys."

"Amen and praise the Lord for that difference."

"When his speech was over everybody was talking about how keyed up they were to go to Vietnam."

"That's natural. Mahaffy believed passionately in the war and he was extraordinarily articulate in describing scenes of battles he had participated in."

"Do you know what I noticed about the speech, Cain?"

"No."

"Mahaffy didn't have any legs."

"So what? That had nothing to do with the speech."

"Mahaffy had legs when he left the Institute. When he came back after his tour in Vietnam, he didn't have them. I related the two events."

"It was a hand grenade."

"I don't care if it was from eating day-old rice. I didn't hear his speech. I just stared at the place where his legs used to be. He ran track and was a pretty good miler in his day. He had nice legs. I've got nice legs, too. I want to keep them attached to my body, not have them tossed into a garbage bag and thrown into a Dempster-Dumpster."

"He gave a great speech."

"He gave up a great set of legs."

"You can't sentimentalize over a lost pair of legs."

"I won't sentimentalize if you lose yours. I'd give a party and start a scholarship in their name."

"Are you a coward, Will?"

"Of the trembling, quivering, knees-knocking, teeth-chattering variety."

"There has never been a coward in the history of my family. My father traced it back for centuries."

"Speaking of your family, Gilbreath, I've always been too embarrassed to ask you this, and I know Southern families of distinction put some dreadful monickers on their offspring, but who named you Cain?"

"My mother was a Cain," he answered. "Cain of Virginia."

"That's real swell. I'm beginning to like the aristocracy. Cain of Virginia, huh?"

"How'd you get your name, big fella? How do the lower classes name their children?"

"Haphazardly, son, haphazardly."

Cain ignored me and strained to hear the voices of the cadre who were conducting a surreptitious "sweat party" in the fourth division shower room. Whenever the hazing was particularly barbaric, it was an intelligent command decision to conduct it far from the eyes of the Officer in Charge. I had become so accustomed to the shouts of the cadre that I no longer even heard them. But Cain was right in his perception that some innate change had taken place in the nature of the tumult down the gallery. Something had gone wrong. It was as if a wasps' nest had been set on fire and thrown into the ranks of the plebes. The noise was chaos, not discipline, not training, not the institutional fear that was the darker constant of the plebe system. Cain and I looked at each other for a single uncomprehending moment before John Kinnell, the R Company commander, burst into the room.

"Will. Will. Here quick. Get out here in a hurry."

"Why, John? What's going on?"

"Poteete is over the rail. He says he's going to jump."

I sprinted out the door and was met by a great surge of freshmen being herded to their rooms, away from the pandemonium, away from the lone plebe who had in one moment of anarchy stepped out of the control of the system. Six members of the cadre formed a loose, indecisive semicircle around Poteete, who was hanging off the railing with one hand and foot suspended over the hundred-foot drop to the concrete quadrangle. He was shouting for them to keep back or he would jump at that moment.

"Get back, you motherfuckers!" he screamed over and over again. With each scream, the cadre retreated. The plebe had become commander.

"He said he wanted to see you, Will," I heard John Kinnell say behind me.

On the quadrangle, upperclassmen ran out to get an unimpeded view of Poteete. Pandemonium cut loose in every square foot of the barracks; the Officer of the Guard tried to clear the quadrangle of cadets, but the surge of the crowd overwhelmed him. From every direction fingers pointed at Poteete. He was the single focus of a thousand eyes. Even the freshmen were peering out of their rooms for a glimpse of the plebe who had cracked.

"Get everybody out of sight, John," I said. "It's like a goddam circus down there."

"All R Company men report to your rooms," John called out. He had a marvelous voice for cadence, for the issuance of command. I heard the other company commanders ordering their men to the darkness beneath the galleries. Over the loudspeaker, I heard the voice of Jimmy Bull, the fourth battalion commander, say, "All members of fourth battalion report to your rooms immediately." But though the cadets of fourth battalion would disappear into the shadows, they would not relinquish their roles as spectators, as rabid fans of the new barracks sport of suicide.

"Stop him, Will. He'll listen to you," John whispered as he withdrew.

"The plebe system builds men," I whispered back, hoping that the sarcasm would help allay my trembling. The trembling increased as I faced Poteete and our eyes met. He was weeping. Tears and fury and despair had intermingled in a violent desperate trinity, and now he was hanging out over the quadrangle. He was the first freshman I had ever known to freeze the cadre into complete impotence. By this time, the chain of command had regained control, and a fearful, unnatural silence gripped the barracks. Beneath the galleries, I could see the glow of cigarettes betraying the presence of upperclassmen. Poteete had centered himself in an arch in the area between O and R companies. The sobs broke out of him in regular intervals, loud, and infinitely sad.

"Don't come any closer, Mr. McLean," he said.

I did not realize that I had been moving.

"Well, Poteete," I said, with absolutely no sense or instinct about how to begin this confrontation. "What's up in the old freshmen class?"

"You can shove this school up your ass, Mr. McLean!" The power of the system had not completely broken down. He was still addressing me as "mister."

"It wouldn't fit, Poteete."

"How can you always joke about this place?" he said between sobs. "How can you think anything here is funny?"

"It was the only way I could make it through here. If I couldn't have found this place hilarious then I would have done something silly like trying to jump off the fourth division. This is going to seriously hurt your chances for rank, Poteete."

I leaned up against the arch nearest him. His eyes

113

appraised my every movement. He had fixed a proper distance for me to remain, a zone of separation that he intended to honor.

"Don't move any closer, sir. I mean it. I'm going to jump. I promise you that. You can't do anything to stop me. I just wanted to talk to you. I wanted to find out how you could survive all of this. How could you survive such cruelty? You're just like me, Mr. McLean. I could never do this to other freshmen. I know I couldn't do this to anyone. I didn't know this was such a hateful place. My daddy never told me it was hateful."

"That's not his fault, Poteete. I've seen that over and over again. Grads only remember the good parts of their plebe year. They even laugh like hell when they do remember the bad parts. What seems horrible to you tonight will seem hilarious a year from now. That's the way it happens. That's the way the system works."

"Did it work that way for you?"

"No. The bad parts still seem bad to me."

"Were they like this to you, Mr. McLean? Were they as cruel to you as they've been to me?"

"Will. Call me Will, Poteete. What's your first name?"

"It doesn't make any difference. No one's called me by my first name since I've been here. Not even my roommate."

"They weren't as bad with me, Poteete. I told you that they would never let you alone if you cried."

"I can't help it, Will," he said, breaking down again. "I just can't help it. I've tried to stop. I've tried everything I know to stop. They scream at me all the time. They scream and scream and scream. They humiliate me. They humiliate me more than the other freshmen. My classmates want me to leave more than the cadre."

"I'd like you to leave, too, Poteete, but for entirely different reasons."

"You don't think I belong here either, Will?" Poteete asked gently. "You don't think I'm man enough to make it through the plebe system? Tell me how you made it. What was it like when you were a knob?"

"They were always comparing me to Douglas Mac-Arthur and the Duke of Wellington because of my incredible military bearing."

He smiled and looked down from the dizzying heights where he stood, this sudden prince of the fourth battalion. I could see the red and white squares illuminated by eight floodlights on the top of the barracks. In the silence of the barracks, Poteete was trying to decide what to do. He had narrowed his field of vision down to two choices and two choices only. He had reduced his life to the simplest common denominator. He was becoming extraordinarily calm, and I feared his calm as it settled over him more than I feared his hysteria. I had a thought that I should rush him now, while he was preoccupied with the casual study of the alien terrain where his spirit had broken up into irreversibly fragmented parts. I wondered how many boys had broken under the fearful pressures of the plebe system. I wondered if the grotesque phantoms of their damaged spirits haunted the alcoves of the barracks for all times, recruiting others into their defiled tormented ranks with howls of gratitude as they watched the others come apart at the soul. The ague of suffering raged unchecked in the eyes of the recruit. Behind Poteete's eyes, the hive of terror was loose on him and each cell in his brain had become wasp-winged and deadly, each cell was hourglass-shaped, and each cell, tremulous with the diminutive thunder of hornets, felt the power of flight and the invulnerability of the swarm. His eyes blazed in the glare of the floodlights. I did not rush him when I saw his eyes look at me. All was madness there, and loathing for me and what I represented. He meant to jump.

"What does your father do for a living, Poteete?" I said when he did not answer me. "You told me he graduated in 1947, but you never told me what he did for a living."

"He's a banker. President of the First National Bank of Pickens, South Carolina. I'm majoring in business administration here. He wants me to go back and work in the bank when I graduate."

"Sounds like you've got it made, man. Get out of college and walk into a bank you'll own someday. Is your mother from Pickens?"

"She's from Greenville. Her father owns a mill near Greenville. Greenville's got more mills than pine trees, my mother used to say. She used to say that all the time. I'd always thought I'd rather work in the mill than try to get along with Daddy in the bank. Daddy's a good man but I don't think we could work together."

"You've got it figured good, Poteete. Hell, I don't have any idea what I'm going to do after graduation and I'm a senior. You've got two fine jobs just waiting for you. You've got it made, man. You've got everything going for you."

"I've got nothing going for me," he said. "I don't have a

single thing going for me. When I left home, my daddy told me that I'd better finish the first year. He didn't care if I quit the Institute after I proved I was man enough to go through the plebe system. I can't even take it for two weeks."

"There are other companies in the Corps, Poteete. Lots of other companies. They can transfer you down to first battalion tonight. I promise. Not all the companies are like R Company. There are some companies that don't give a shit about anything. Man, it's easy living up in 'Gentlemen First,' Poteete. Knobs up there think they've died and gone to heaven."

Poteete turned and studied me carefully. Except for the trembling, I was motionless beside the column.

"Do you know that most of my classmates think you're really fucked up, Mr. McLean?" Poteete said.

"A lot of *my* classmates think that I'm really fucked up," I answered.

"They think you're fucked up because you're nice to them and don't scream at them and don't make them do pushups. What kind of school is it when you hate somebody who doesn't scream at you?"

"You don't understand this school yet, Poteete? America is in short supply of assholes so it needs military schools like this to replenish the ranks. But the place is getting better. I swear it is. You still have your Snipeses. But you'll always have bastards like that. When I was a knob they had guys that would parboil newborn babies for sport. There was a supply sergeant my freshman year who got his kicks by tying little hamsters to parachutes made out of handkerchiefs. Then he would come up to the fourth division here and throw the hamster high up in the air. The hamster would go up about one hundred fifty feet, then drop down about eighty feet before the parachute would pop open and the hamster would land safely on the quadrangle. Two guys on the cadre would be waiting on the quad and they would stomp the hamster to death with their boots if it made a safe landing. But the real sport—and why the supply sergeant loved it so much—was when there was a malfunction in the little parachute and one of them wouldn't open and the hamster would fall all the way, with the whole battalion screaming it down."

"Will they scream me down?" Poteete asked coldly. His voice had gone beyond emotion, into a place beyond redemption.

"Poteete, no one wants you to jump. There's not a single person in this barracks who wouldn't do anything to see you

116

come back over the rail. Not a single one. You made the mistake I did when I was a knob. You took it seriously. You didn't treat it as a game."

"I don't like the game, Will. It seems too serious. Some of the cadre meant everything they said to me. Some of them hate me because I'm fat and ugly and don't look good in the stinking uniform. I thought I could make it. I thought I was doing better until they took me to the house."

"What house?" I asked.

"You know what house," he said sharply. "The one where they take freshmen."

"You mean to someone's room?"

"I couldn't stand what they were doing to me. They treated me worse than if I was an animal."

"What house, Poteete? What are you talking about?"

In the shadows behind Poteete I saw the almost imperceptible movements of someone coming slowly along the rail, moving with infinite patience, silent as a lynx. Instantly, I looked away and pointed to a spot on the quadrangle.

"I spent the worst year of my life right there, Poteete, not too far from where you stand, in second platoon. I thought the year would never end. I thought it would last forever. Then when it was over, I thought it was the quickest year I had ever spent in my life. I learned something about time that year and how it works and what it means. Nothing lasts, Poteete. Whatever made you go over the rail tonight won't last either."

"I'm not going back with them."

"Who, Poteete?"

"I don't know who, McLean. Goddam, I don't know anything. But I can feel them watching me. I know some of them are down there and I can feel their hatred. Do you know what else I feel? I can feel my father's eyes watching me. I can hear him calling me a baby. I can hear my mother and father arguing about me. Him blaming her. Her blaming him. Who spoiled me? Who ruined me? Who did this and who did that? Who did too much and who didn't do enough? Whose side of the family I take after? What went wrong?"

"Your parents would both want you inside the rail."

"I can't now."

The barracks were silent. Stars spoke the language of light years, mutely, dimly above the barracks. Stars, arches, stone, cadre, Poteete, me, and death. I struggled for the right words, the life-preserving words to leap from my tongue. I was nauseated; I was afraid. The figure in the shadow moved

117

inexorably toward us. I followed his progress peripherally. When he was ten feet away, I saw that it was Pig. Behind him, keeping to the shadow of the arches, crept Mark.

"Why, Poteete? All you've got to do is come over the rail. Just give me your hand and I'll help you."

"They'll laugh at me if I don't jump. They think I'm a pussy because I cry easily. I've got to prove to them that I have courage, too."

"That's nonsense. That's bullshit, Poteete. You let them feed you with all that bullshit and you bought it all," I said, sweeping my hand around the barracks in a gesture of disgust. "None of this makes any difference at all."

"It makes a difference to me," he shouted back. "There's no way out of this, Will. There's no way out of this with honor. Think of an honorable way for me to come back over the rail and I'll do it."

"This has nothing to do with being brave or manly or honorable or anything. This has everything to do with being human and being scared and having your world turned upside down and being humiliated. This has everything to do with your being better than us, Poteete. You can't endure the life in the barracks because you are infinitely superior to all of us."

"I'm afraid," Poteete said. "I've been afraid ever since I came here."

"All the freshmen are afraid. They're supposed to be afraid. They're supposed to be afraid out of their minds."

"I'm that afraid, Will," he said. "I'm scared out of my mind. Tell me how to get out of this, Will. I want to walk away from this. But I want to do it honorably. I don't want them screaming at me or laughing at me."

"Pig, Mark, and I will walk you out of the barracks, Poteete. If anyone laughs I'll set my roommates on them. They'll want to help you. I promise that. We'll get you out of here. I'll get the Bear to telephone your father and say you're getting expelled from school for beating the hell out of half the cadre the first week and the other half the second week. We'll tell him you broke the first sergeant's jaw. That you're too goddam tough to live in the barracks, that they ought to buy you a cage in Pickens and feed you raw meat and live ammunition."

"He'd like that, wouldn't he?" Poteete said, smiling at the thought. "But then he'd hear from someone. I sometimes wish that I came from New York City instead of Pickens. My father doesn't understand why anyone would want to live in a city with eight million other people. I've always understood it."

"Poteete, come in off the rail. I'll buy you a goddam ticket to New York City. I'll rent you an apartment. I'll buy you furniture."

"I can't. I can't turn back now," he said, looking straight down toward the perfectly congruent geometry of the quadrangle.

At that moment, Pig was on him. He grabbed Poteete fully around the chest and jerked him backward, trying to lift him over the rail. Mark leaped over the rail and seized one of Poteete's legs. I got a hand on Poteete's belt and in the midst of the violent crazed thrashing we lifted him over the rail and pinned him against the cement gallery. There was a rush of footsteps on the stairway. A hundred cadets surrounded us in a matter of seconds.

"Pussy."

"Fucking pussy," some of them sneered.

"Shut up!" I screamed.

"Shut up!" Pig screamed and they shut up.

Two orderlies from the guardroom brought a stretcher and we strapped Poteete to it, kicking and screaming and delirious now. In his screams, all the demons and the implacable cruelty of the Institute were contained in their purest, most essential form. I went over to speak to him before they took him to the hospital. Above the tumult, loose now upon the barracks with upperclassmen pressing forward to get a glimpse of the freshman who had silenced the system for a full fifteen minutes, I tried to speak to Poteete.

"I'm sorry, Poteete. It was the only way."

He stopped screaming for a moment. He looked at me and he looked at the mob that surrounded him. He looked back at me. His eyes and the wildness of the secret hive again blazed in frenzied dissociation.

"McLean," he said, his voice filled with loathing.

Then he spit in my face.

* * *

The next morning when the nurse at the infirmary brought him his breakfast, she found Poteete hanging from one of the heating pipes that traversed the ceiling of his room. He had hanged himself with his own uniform belt. I saw Poteete's father when he came onto campus to identify and claim the body of his son. He was the classic Institute man, erect, lean, and successful. When I saw him he was coming out of the infirmary. He did not look to the left or the right. His wife was weeping inside their Lincoln Continental. I wanted to ask her how it was to be married to a member of the class of 1947, a legend in his own time. I tried to get up enough courage to talk to them, but I could summon up neither courage nor talk. And I saw something in his father's face that made me glad I would never talk to the man in my entire life. I saw shame. I saw naked embarrassment for the weakness of his son.

I read about the funeral in the newspaper. They did not mention how Poteete had died, but I learned that his first name was John, and that his friends had called him "Bucky."

15

Taps sounded over the barracks. The music of sleep, the music of death, the song that extinguished every light in every room at the Institute. It was light-killing music that brought the coming of the small night creatures with it. In the silence following taps, I went out onto fourth division and stared out over the quadrangle. I was standing in the same spot where Poteete had threatened to jump. In this repose, as cadets began their seven hours and fifteen minutes of officially sanctioned sleep, the insects cautiously came alive to begin their night rule of the barracks. There was the faint rustle of small wings, the secret transit of spiders, the waxy promenades of huge roaches down the concrete galleries, the sudden blaze of fireflies, and sometimes the brown speed of rats scuttling toward garbage. Though the barracks gave the appearance that it could support no animal life at all, the small things had adapted themselves to a frantic existence between taps and reveille. Taps sounded by moonlight, by starlight, when owls swept low over the barracks, when the barracks looked as though it was carved from glaciers and the galleries looked like tiered cakes of gauzy ice. When reveille broke through the sweltering film of morning, the insects and rodents had retired to their secret places and the cadets assumed primacy once again.

I thought about the first fifteen days of my senior year and tried to consider all that was contained and implied in that period. At the Institute, I had learned to be cautious, to distrust the insistence of my own convictions, to cover my tracks, to walk invisibly through the Corps, without drawing too much attention to myself. I had disobeyed my own commandment; I was feeling naked, exposed, and vulnerable. Events had dominated me, forced me into the open terrain, flushed me from the main body of the Corps. As I stood there alone in the darkness, I could not dispel a feeling that something was going to happen to me that I had not prepared for, that I had to ready myself for surprise, for an attack on my flanks. Swarming about me were the disembodied faces of Annie Kate, Pearce, the Bear, the General, Abigail, Poteete, Alexander—faces, faces, faces, too many of them at once. I could not concentrate on any one face. I could not tell which face contained the elements of danger or which redemption. I could not tell which face or faces had given birth to my sense of foreboding. So I returned to the pretty face of Annie Kate Gervais. Again and again and again.

I did not hear Mark come up behind me. I felt his hand on my shoulder and turned toward him to see his dark scowling eyes appraising me. He had the somber eyes of an assassin in love with a cause. His hand moved along my shoulder to my neck. Then he cuffed me playfully on the head.

"Talk!" he ordered.

"Talk about what?" I asked.

"When I worry about things, I talk to you. When you worry, you come out here and stare at the quadrangle. What you're telling me is that I trust you a lot more than you trust me."

"That's not true, Mark," I answered. "It's just that I don't know yet what's bothering me. I haven't figured it out yet. I never know what I really think about something until two months later. There's this delayed reaction for all my emotions."

"That's what you get for majoring in English. You ought to change your major to chemistry. There you get blown up with delayed reactions."

"My roommate with all the answers."

"Your roommate with some of the answers. I've got to get you laughing again. Rooming with you in the last couple of days has been like rooming with cold lasagne. I want you to join the human race again."

"I've been thinking about Poteete, Mark. Can you imagine how lonely he was when he hanged himself? Can you imagine how lonely it would feel to die your plebe year?"

"The knob was out of his gourd."

"He said something that I can't figure out. He said something that's really been bothering me."

There was the sound of footsteps coming up behind us. Pig and Tradd moved out of the shadows and into the dim frame of light where Mark and I talked. The four of us were silhouetted in the central arch of the upper south gallery.

"I hope the Officer in Charge doesn't catch us out here," Tradd said, looking toward the front sally port.

"If he does, I'll make like a commando, sneak down to the stairwell, and break his spine with a kick to his fat anus," Pig said.

"What are you two conspirators doing out here after taps? I think it's my duty to turn you in to the authorities," Tradd said.

"Will's got the wrinkled-brow look again," Mark said.

"It's the honor court," Tradd explained. "The poor lad has suddenly been seized with a sense of responsibility and duty since he was elected. I prefer the old Will McLean who used to pray to the gods to sink every building on campus to the bottom of the sea."

"You got to take some vitamin pills, Will," Pig said, offering his placebo for every illness, mental or physical, that could afflict a human being. "I got some protein tablets that will pep you right up. You also got to start doing some bench presses. Your pecs are deflated."

"What exercises do you do to build up those overdeveloped muscles in your brain, Pig?" Mark asked.

"What's eating you, Mark?" said Pig.

"I've listened to you brag about your body for three years and I'm getting sick of it."

"Easy, boys," I said, moving between them as I felt the fuel of tension ignite between them.

"We weren't going to fight, were we, paisan?" Pig said, unsmilingly examining Mark's face.

"No, we aren't going to fight, Pig," Mark said.

"Good," I said. "For a minute I thought I was going to have to whip both your asses."

"You'd have what was left after I punched them around for a while," Tradd said, slapping playfully at Pig's head.

122

Pig ducked and ran his fingers through his hair like a comb.

"Don't mess with my braids, man. Don't track up the Vitalis."

We all turned and looked out into the quadrangle. The four of us stood with our shoulders touching, leaning against the railing. Directly across from us, a T Company freshman shuffled down the gallery to the latrine. For two or three minutes we did not speak a word until Tradd broke the silence by saying, "I never thought I'd come to love a place as much as I love the Institute."

"It's the best goddam school in the country. No doubt about it," Pig agreed.

"How do you feel about it?" Mark asked me.

"I still don't know if I like it or hate it. I feel both ways about it sometimes."

Tradd spoke up quickly, "You're just upset about Poteete, Will. What you don't understand is that something like that could happen anywhere. Poteete was mentally unstable. Some people just don't belong here."

"They used to say that about you, Tradd," I snapped back. "Do you remember the cadre saying that about you every day of our freshman year?"

"But they were wrong, Will," Tradd said in a patient, conciliatory voice. "And I didn't go out and hang myself."

"I bet the kid didn't take any vitamins," Pig said. "I bet he had a deficiency."

"It's good to have an expert in deficiency rooming with us," Mark murmured almost inaudibly.

"What do you think about the Institute, Mark?" I said. "I mean what do you *really* think about it?"

"I could never have made it at any other school," he answered. "I'd have flunked out my first semester if they hadn't made me stay in every night and study."

"Best school in the goddam country," Pig said. "Harvard and Yale ain't shit compared to the Institute and that's a proven fact."

"I think the standards are a trifle higher at Harvard, Pig," Tradd interjected mildly.

"Bullshit," Pig exploded. "I can run faster, do more pushups, lift more weights, and kick more ass than anybody in the whole Ivy League."

"What a fucking dimwit," Mark whispered to me, nodding his head dejectedly.

"Guys at Harvard aren't taught what to do in case of

123

emergency. They'd shit all over themselves if the Indians were after them."

"So would I, Pig," I said.

"Do you know what I love about this school?" Tradd said to all of us. "I like the order and discipline of this school. Everything has a place. Everything is answered for. Tradition is honored and there is no room for chaos here, no tolerance for confusion. I think it's this sense of sublime order that offends you, Will."

"Will's thinking about Poteete," Mark said to Tradd. "So how about laying off his ass."

"I'm not on his ass, Mark," Tradd explained. "I'm trying to get him to see that it's not the Institute's fault that she sometimes attracts mentally disturbed knobs."

"Forget Poteete," I said turning to Tradd. "What do you think is the real function of this school? What in the hell is all this about?"

"It builds character, Will," Tradd said. "It breaks you down completely the first year, and then it spends the next three years putting you back together in the image of the Institute man, the whole man. You know that it broke me in ways that were really good for me. I've got confidence in my ability to survive anything, anywhere, and that confidence came directly from the plebe system. I think the Institute prepares you for the hardships of life better than any other school in the country."

"I like the school for a different reason," Mark said. "I like the school because I like you guys. You guys have been good to me. So have all the guys in R Company. I've never felt this close to a bunch of guys in my whole life."

"That's it. That's it," Pig agreed enthusiastically. "This is a family. We got two thousand brothers who will kick ass for any one of us. That's what the Institute's all about."

All four of us locked arms and stood for a moment without saying a word, feeling the pressure of each other's bodies. I would remember this scene on fourth division with my three roommates. I would remember the feeling of incredible tenderness, the unbearable, unspeakable fragility of the love that we could not call love even to each other. In the barracks, imprisoned for four years, boys would meet other boys and fall in love with them, but no one in the barracks could ever speak of the love they felt for each other. It was spoken of as friendship, loyalty, camaraderie, but that was not it. We loved each other in innocence. Though the barracks contained a high quotient of barbarism, it also preserved our innocence. It kept the world from storming the gates, from letting us make decisions on our own, from meeting those humans who functioned in the normal civilized world with its own customs of survival. We knew very little about the world outside the Gates of Legrand.

I later thought that at that moment, unknown to all of us, some power unknown to any of us, some arbiter of violence, was studying us surreptitiously, was opening up the barracks to the outside world, and all the beasts and centaurs and clumsy leviathans of that world, monster-eyed, deadly, impassioned, and famished for a chance to make a game of us, rushed invisibly to the center of the quadrangle for a glimpse of us, the four boys secretly in love with each other. They did not look at us disinterestedly, those beasts of our final year, those leering impatient harbingers. No, they eyed us with discrimination as if they were making their choices. I would look back on this night years later and decide that three of us would be chosen to be victims. And one of us would be prey.

Before we returned to our room, Mark asked me a question: "What did Poteete say that's been bothering you?"

"He said something about being taken to a house. There's no house he could be taken to that I know of. Knobs can't even leave campus during plebe week."

"There's no house," Tradd said. "That poor boy was insane."

PART II

THE TAMING

Plebe Year 1963–1964

16

*I will take you down my own avenue of remembrance,
which winds among the hazards and shadows of my single
year as a plebe. I cannot come to this story in full voice. I
want to speak for the boys who were violated by this school,
the ones who left ashamed and broken and dishonored, who
departed from the Institute with wounds and bitter grievances. I want also to speak for the triumphant boys who took
everything the system could throw at them, endured every
torment and excess, and survived the ordeal of the freshman
year with a feeling of transformation and achievement that
they had never felt before and would never know again with
such clarity and elation.*

*I will speak from memory—my memory—a memory
that is all refracting light slanting through prisms and dreams,
a shifting, troubled riot of electrons charged with pain and
wonder. My memory often seems like a city of exiled poets
afire with the astonishment of language, each believing in the
integrity of his own witness, each with a separate version of
culture and history, and the divine essential fire that is poetry
itself.*

*But I will try to isolate that one lonely singer who
gathered the fragments of my plebe year and set the screams
to music. For many years, I have refused to listen as his
obsessive voice narrated the malignant litany of crimes
against my boyhood. We isolate those poets who cause us the
greatest pain; we silence them in any way we can. I have
never allowed this furious dissident the courtesy of my full
attention. His poems are songs for the dead to me. Something
dies in me whenever I hear his low, courageous voice calling
to me from the solitude of his exile. He has always known
that someday I would have to listen to his story, that I would
have to deal with the truth or falsity of his witness. He has*

always known that someday I must take full responsibility for his creation and that, in finally listening to him, I would be sounding the darkest fathoms of myself. I will write down his stories now as he shouts them to me. I will listen to him and listen to myself. I will get it all down.

Yet the laws of recall are subject to distortion and alienation. Memory is a trick, and I have lied so often to myself about my own role and the role of others that I am not sure I can recognize the truth about those days. But I have come to believe in the unconscious integrity of lies. I want to record even them, every one of them. Somewhere in the immensity of the lie the truth gleams like the pure, light-glazed bones of an extinct angel. Hidden in the enormous falsity of my story is the truth for all of us who began at the Institute in 1963, and for all who survived to become her sons. I write my own truth, in my own time, in my own way, and take full responsibility for its mistakes and slanders. Even the lies are part of my truth.

I return to the city of memory, to the city of exiled poets. I approach the one poet whose back is turned to me. He is frail and timorous and angry. His head is shaved and he fears the judgment of regiments. He will always be a victim, always a plebe. I tap him on the shoulder.

"Begin," I command.

"It was the beginning of September in 1963," *he begins, and I know he will not stop until his story is ended.*

* * *

It was the beginning of September in 1963 when I entered second battalion and walked up to the cadre of Romeo Company. Four of them sat at the card table thumbing through small boxes of files and index cards. The rest of the cadre watched from behind the table, their eyes invisibly appraising me beneath the shade of their field caps. They looked sleek, crisp, and efficient, and they seemed immune from the fury of the climbing Charleston sun. I was eighteen.

"Hello," I said, resting both hands against the card table and leaning down in a gesture of intimacy to talk with the leader of the group. "My name's Will McLean and I was told to report to R Company."

The company commander, a slightly overweight youth, stared at my hands with an imperious demeanor and petulant, dissatisfied eyes. His nametag read "Blasingame." I could smell Aqua Velva steaming off his face. His brown eyes met mine for an instant before he yelled, "Get your fucking hands off my table, dumbhead."

"Sure," I answered, moving back a step. Two other members of the cadre swept around the table and stood on either side of me.

"Put a 'sir' on that, wad-waste."

"Yes, sir," I replied.

"Your name again, knob," the one on my right demanded.

"Will, Will McLean."

"You say, 'Sir, my name is cadet recruit McLean, W. P., sir.' Do you understand, scumbag?" the executive officer of R Company said, consulting a list of names on his clipboard. He was thin and blond and had a pleasant intelligent face. His name was Wentworth.

"Your I.D. number is 16407, dumbhead," Blasingame said. "Your room number is 4131. And you're nothing but shit to me. Do you understand? Pop off, dumb squat."

"Yes, sir."

The voice on my right whispered, "You aren't even shit to me, douchebag. You're lower than shit to me. You're whale shit and that sits on the bottom of the ocean. That's as low as you can get. Do you hear me, douchebag?"

"Yes, sir."

"Don't you say a word until I order you to pop off, knob. Do you understand me? Pop off."

"Yes, sir."

"We're gonna run you out of here in a week, McLean."

"He's the basketball jock," a voice at the table said. I turned in the direction of the voice.

"Get your eyes off me, scumbag," the voice ordered. "Do you want to get in my pants, scumbag? Pop off."

"No, sir."

"Then keep your beady eyes off my body, faggot."

"Sir," I said, keeping my eyes directly in front of me and addressing anyone who would listen, "I came here to play basketball for the Institute. I'm on scholarship. There must be some mistake. Coach Byrum told me that athletes received different treatment from regular cadets."

"Oh," several of them answered in mock surprise. "Oh, please excuse us, Mr. McLean," Blasingame mocked, his voice full of apology. "We simply made a mistake and thought you were like any ordinary knob. We didn't realize we had the honor of addressing a Varsity Athlete. My, oh my, but we do get confused on these first days. Did any of you boys realize we were yelling at a Varsity Athlete?"

131

"Oh, gracious, no," Wentworth, the exec, said. "I won't be able to sleep tonight."

"This is terrible. How can we make it up to you, Mr. McLean?" Blasingame asked.

"It's all right, fellas," I answered, smiling. "Y'all just didn't know. I should have told you right away. Everyone makes mistakes. I won't tell anyone, so don't worry about getting into trouble. If you would be so kind as to direct me to my room."

"Would any of you gentlemen be so kind as to direct Mr. McLean to his room?" Blasingame inquired of his cadre.

"I would consider it a personal honor, Mr. Blasingame," the voice on my right said. Then I felt his moist fetid breath on my ear as he said, "I'm gonna kill you, jock. I'm gonna eat your ass for breakfast, lunch, and dinner. I'm gonna make your life one long fucking nightmare, douchebag. I'm gonna tuck you into bed each night and pull your ass out of bed at reveille until you beg me to open up the gate so you can run home to your slut mother. I'm gonna be in your dreams, dumbhead. You're gonna see me in the mirror, douchebag. I may decide to run you out tonight. Tonight! What do you say to that, pussy? Tell me what you say to that. Pop off."

"No, sir," I answered. "You won't run me out."

"Are you telling me I can't run you out, scumbag?" he screamed directly in my ear. "Pop off!"

"You can't run me out, sir."

"He's mine. This fucker belongs to me," a boy said, stepping in front of me, memorizing my features as I memorized his. He was my height, but leaner, more angular, with a long rather handsome face disfigured by a cruel, lipless mouth and narrow eyes.

"He's an English major," Wentworth said, reading from his clipboard.

"An English major!" several voices said at once.

The boy in front of me was named Fox.

"An English major," he said disgustedly. "Do you want to suck my dick, boy? Pop off."

"No sir."

"Shit, dumbhead, everyone knows English majors love to suck and blow on dicks."

"I wouldn't say that, Fox," Wentworth said, still studying the clipboard. "I'm an English major."

"What's my name, douchebag? Pop off," Fox said.

"Your name is Fox, sir," I said.

"Put a 'mister' on that."

"Your name is Mister Fox, sir," I said.

"What am I, idiot?" he yelled, pointing to the insignia on his collar. "Look at my uniform and tell me what I am."

I stared at his uniform, at the unfamiliar insignia, at his nametag, at his face. I was confused, disoriented, and I did not know what he wanted me to say.

"You better tell me what I am, idiot. Now, douchebag. Now. Say something. Anything. But you better answer me, smackhead. Now, boy. Now. Now. Now."

I looked at his nametag and said, "Sir, you are a small carnivorous animal kin to the dog."

The punch came from behind me, delivered by an invisible assailant, a perfect blow to the kidney. I staggered forward, fell to one knee, and almost knocked Fox and the card table over.

"Not here, Newman, you stupid bastard," the company commander said. "Wait until you get him to his room. If a tac officer sees you, we'll all be walking tours. If the Bear sees you, we'll be lucky to graduate."

"I don't like a smartass knob," a deep voice said from behind me.

"Get up, douchebag," Fox commanded. "You make any more remarks like that and we'll send you home with your nuts in your pocket. And for your information, I'm your platoon sergeant."

* * *

Late that afternoon, before evening formation, I studied my shaved head in the mirror. I did not recognize the boy in the mirror who stared accusingly back at me, did not recognize the desperate blue eyes. I felt silly in the new summer uniform the upperclassmen had called the "gray nasties." The uniform exuded the nauseating odor of new clothing. My hands smelled of Brasso and Kiwi polish. The heat was fierce and sweat stains spread beneath my arms, along my collar, and down my back. I spoke to my image in the mirror, "You stupid asshole, McLean. You poor dumb fucker. How did you get yourself in this mess?"

"Give me a shirt tuck, what's-your-name?" my new roommate said behind me. "Hurry up, will you? We've got to get to evening formation."

His name was Harvey Clearwater and he was from Memphis, Tennessee. "*The* Clearwaters of Memphis," he had been careful to explain.

"My name's Will, Harvey," I said. "Will. It's a simple

133

little name. Four letters. Starts with a capital *W*. Ends with a little bitty word synonymous with 'sick.' I like being called Will. It's a habit I got into in childhood."

"Just give me a shirt tuck, will you? They'll kill us if we're late."

"They'll kill us if we're early."

"My mother certainly didn't tell me this school would be anything like this," Harvey said. I cannot tell you how I detested Harvey.

"Well, *The* Clearwaters of Memphis have always been a tight-lipped crew."

"How do you like this place so far, tell me?" he said as I was giving him a shirt tuck.

"Oh me, Harvey," I answered, unable to keep myself from lashing out at my roommate every time he spoke. "I've found myself a home. This is a fabulous place. There's not many colleges in the country where you get to see seven of your classmates pass out from heat exhaustion the very first day of school."

Ignoring me, he said, "I'd be big stuff in a fraternity if I'd gone to the University of Tennessee. Clearwater is a big name in Tennessee."

"Yeh, you've only told me that a couple of thousand times today, Harvey, and I've only seen you alone for ten minutes."

"You've got a bad attitude, what's-your-name."

"I'm only beginning to have a bad attitude. I'm just getting started. In a month, I plan to have the shittiest goddam attitude in the United States."

"I don't want you to hurt my chances to make rank, you hear?" he said.

"What?" I could barely believe my rotten luck in getting this boy for a roommate.

"I plan to be a company commander. That's the least I can do for Mother. What are you shooting for, whatchama-callit?"

"If my mother will let me, Harvey, I'm shooting to be a civilian by tomorrow morning."

"They won't let you near a telephone for two weeks. And you can't write a letter, send up smoke signals, or pound on a tom-tom. Your mama won't even know if you're alive for two weeks. They lose twenty percent of the class in the first month."

"I hope I can make up part of that twenty percent," I said.

"You'll know if you can take it or not after tomorrow night," Harvey said, checking his watch.

"What happens tomorrow night that could be worse than what happened today?" I asked in alarm.

"Tomorrow is Hell Night."

"What happens on Hell Night?"

"Let your imagination run wild," he said, rolling his eyes. "And tell me your name just one more time. I'm terrible on names. I'll get it this time."

"Lee Vercingetorix. My mother was from Virginia and my father was from Gaul."

"Bad attitude, Lee," Harvey said, shaking his head back and forth. "Say, I've been having a tough time with those pushups and that constant running. I hope they let up some after Hell Night."

"We've got two minutes to get to formation," I said, turning my head sideways to read his watch.

"Will you support me, Lee?" he asked.

"Support you for what?"

"For company commander. You have to get the support of your classmates early."

"Harvey," I said. "If you want to be mayor of Charleston or Yertle the Turtle you have my solemn support. But you're not listening to me. I'm not going to be around. I don't belong here. I'm getting out in the next couple of days. I've just got to get to a phone."

"One more question, Lee."

"Shoot, Harvey."

"What's a douchebag?"

"I don't know," I said. "I've never heard of one, but a lot of people sure think I have a strong family resemblance to one."

* * *

All was prelude. The first day was a dress rehearsal, for the most severe test of the plebe system did not officially begin until the second evening. They ran and taunted and hustled us through the second day. We had no time to ourselves, no time to think, no time to rest, no time to familiarize ourselves with the cramped, austere cells where we slept at night. We changed uniforms four times during the second day. They screamed at us, abused us, beat on our chests with their fists. They ran us from one end of campus to the other.

In the late afternoon, the fatigue had entered my bloodstream and my legs glowed with pain. The blood seemed to collect around my brain. I felt a strange giddiness in the heat as though at any time I might faint and my skull would break against the scorched concrete of the quadrangle. Plebes fainted often during the first week. It was a sign to the cadre that they were performing their duties well. The prestige of sergeants increased when one of their knobs hit the planet unconscious. The sun seemed to be in collusion with the cadre. The heat had a man-eating quality about it. With each uniform change, I could squeeze cupfuls of perspiration into the small sink by the door. There was a ubiquitous stink to the platoons of freshmen, and it was the first time I had ever prayed for rain.

At 1700 hours, we stood at attention on the quadrangle at the end of a forty-five-minute segment of practicing rifle manual. Blasingame, the company commander, shouted out a final command to us, a surprise one, when he said, "At ease, dumbheads."

He continued to talk to us in a relaxed, intimate voice, friendly and void of menace. "Now, dumbheads. I know it's been a long, hot, upsetting day for all of you. I want to give all of you a chance to rest before mess tonight. When I order you to your rooms, I'd like you to put on your bathrobes and just relax in your rooms. Write a letter home to your parents if you want to. Take a nap. Or go down to the shower room and take a nice refreshing shower. You gentlemen have put out for big R today and to show you my appreciation, I'm going to let you have this time to yourselves."

His manner was so kindly and so brotherly that I felt like weeping out of pure human gratitude. This was the first time since I had entered the Gates of Legrand that an upperclassman had been anything but bestial to a group of freshmen. It was the first time a member of the cadre had spoken to us as though we had some standing, no matter how low, in the human community.

He continued in the same soothing voice, "Now go to your rooms, dumbheads. The cadre won't bother you. We need time to rest, too. Just relax, turn on your radios, and take it easy."

Then with a shout that echoed off the enclosed cement walls of the barracks, he screamed, "And you fucking scumbags better be back down on this quadrangle in thirty seconds. Now move it, waste-wads. Change your smelly uniforms and get back here on the double. We're going for more PT."

The sixty of us thundered off the quadrangle, yelling as we went. I made it quickly to my room on the first division.

Harvey came in right behind me as we began stripping off our wet uniforms and hurling them anywhere in our frantic haste to beat the thirty-second mark when they would begin chanting for us again. As I put on my Institute T-shirt and PT shorts, I noticed that a change had taken place in Harvey's eyes; the confidence that had gleamed in his shining gray eyes the day before was under siege. He had not spoken a word since before breakfast that morning. As he stood naked before me looking for his gym shoes, I saw how painfully underdeveloped his body was and realized that the strenuous physical exertion of these first days was taking an inestimable toll on the Clearwater boy from Memphis.

"Are you all right, Harvey?" I asked as I tied the laces of my shoes.

"They're not letting me eat at mess," he said. "I've got to eat or I can't stand this."

"Whose mess are you on?"

"Mr. Fox's."

I reached into my press where my one suit of civilian clothes hung limply among the uniforms and pulled out a package of M&M Peanuts.

"I'm a fanatic about M&M Peanuts. Eat all you want, Harvey."

He shoved a handful in his mouth.

"Five seconds, dumbheads," a voice shouted from the gallery.

"Two seconds, scumbags."

"My mother didn't tell me it was going to be like this at all," Harvey said.

"Neither did mine."

"Where are you, maggot-shits? Get down here, people. Now, people. I don't care if you run PT naked, dumbheads. I want you out of those rooms."

Doors slammed all over the R Company area as freshmen sprinted down the stairs.

"Thanks for the M&M's, Bill," Harvey said, laying an exhausted head on my shoulder. "They've got to let me eat. I've always needed regular meals."

"Harvey, you've got to pace yourself better. You look all washed out."

"I'm dying," he replied. "I've never done a pushup."

"Get down here, scumbags."

They took us on a two-mile run. We lapped the parade ground twice, circled the armory, passed the yacht basin, crossed the baseball field, and halted finally at the farthest

137

perimeter of the campus by the edge of the salt marsh, which separated the grounds of the Institute from the Ashley River. On the run, some of my classmates had stumbled, faltered, dropped out from exhaustion, and lay moaning on the grass or on the pavement, surrounded by the flushed, hostile faces of several cadre members screaming for them to rise. They were being forced to rise, to run again, to catch up to the chanting, driven platoon, and to rejoin their classmates. To drop out was to betray your fellows, and the central theme of those first hours of plebe week was that no one had the right "to shit on his classmates." It was the first and most basic law of the Corps.

The cadre broke off from us and drove the platoon of freshmen into the marsh itself. The long blades of Spartina grass sliced our bare legs, and the marsh was undermined by the immensity of our herded, desperate weight. We began to sink into the mud, first to our ankles, then to our knees. When we had gone far enough, they stood us at rigid attention and told us they would beat our asses bloody with their swords if we moved a single muscle. My shoes filled with water. I did not know why they had brought us to the marsh or why they watched us with such amused attention from their vantage points on dry land.

As I stood there, I realized that except for Harvey, I did not know the face of another classmate. They all looked the same to me, a race of bald, timorous zombies chanting a debased, newly minted language in a country alive with cruelty. As I waited in the marsh grass, the other plebes seemed repugnant to me, odious and contemptible. They looked too much like me, and their faces, like mine, were in pain. In their humiliation, they reminded me of what I had become.

The cadre began to cover each other with spray from aerosol cans. The hiss of the spray sounded like a colloquy of snakes in the parched summer grass. My tongue was swollen and I needed water. With the sun declining, in the stillness of the late afternoon in the Carolina lowcountry, we suddenly knew why we had ended the long run by being forced into the marsh. The first mosquito bit into my thigh. Instinctively, I made a move to kill it.

"Don't you move, maggot," Fox screamed at me.

Clouds of gnats and mosquitoes began to swarm before my eyes. I counted eight mosquitoes on the neck of the boy in front of me. Our coming had stirred an invisible empire of insects, and we had come as food for that empire. Soon I felt the insects biting me in a dozen places. It seemed as though the entire motionless platoon disappeared beneath an awful living drapery of tiny wings and feathery black legs. Around me, I began to hear the moans of freshmen about to break from the ordeal by insect. The mosquitoes fed deeply and leisurely, as though they had come upon a freshly slaughtered battalion with the blood still warm and fragrant in the quiet veins. Some of the upperclassmen were laughing so hard they were on their knees in the grass.

When I thought I could not endure another moment, Blasingame ordered us to hit the ground and we obeyed his order gratefully. My body entered the mud with a feeling of exquisite relief. We snaked our way back to the dry land on our bellies, fingering our way through the mud and marsh grass and destroying a large colony of fiddler crabs in our passage. The mud felt delicious and cool.

When we reached solid land again, they lined us up in long squads, laughing at our appearance. Now we were ludicrous, like actors in blackface. They assured us again and again that this ceremony in the marsh was simply an amusing preliminary, that the plebe system had not even begun. A freshman behind me began crying. Two of the cadre cut him out of the platoon and began racking him somewhere behind us. He was still crying when they ran us back to the barracks to face Hell Night. They wanted us showered and fresh for the real test. And as we ran, I could no longer control my terror. I could no longer pretend I was brave or calm or anything but afraid. Of the sixty mud-stained plebes who quick-timed back to fourth battalion, ten of us would be leaving the Institute the next morning. I was not the only freshman suffering from a severe crisis of nerves.

At 2000 hours Hell Night began. They herded us into the large alcove room on the first division, dressed in our bathrobes, underwear, fatigue caps, and flip-flops. They had turned on the radiators in the room that morning and locked the windows. Outside in an airless, humid Charleston night, the temperature was ninety-eight degrees Fahrenheit. We could hear the hammering of the radiators furiously working out of season, and the heat in the room dazzled and staggered us simultaneously. Our collective stink after a minute in the room repelled even us. There was something tropical and malarial in the corrupt fragrance in the room.

As I entered, I heard a radio somewhere in the barracks loudly playing "I Want to Hold Your Hand." I would never hear that song again without feeling the urgent movement of plebes being driven into that dark cell of heat and violence. I

139

would never be able to appreciate the music of the Beatles, never be able to define my coming of age through their joyous lyrics, because of that one radio playing that one song as I moved into the alcove room for the opening ceremonies of Hell Night. The Beatles died for me at that very moment, long before they ripened into the definitive voice of my generation. For in some far more essential way, I was abandoning my membership in that generation by the mere act of entering that room.

Only two members of the cadre, both sophomore corporals, were responsible for herding us into that room, but they packed us in with remarkable economy. It was as though some cynical modern theologian had challenged them to stand sixty freshmen on the head of a pin.

"Tighter. Tighter, dumbheads," they shouted. "Stick your dick into the asshole of the knob in front of you. Keep your eyes straight ahead. Tighter, people. Tighter."

We stood in a moist, trembling rectangle of flesh. An immense psychological pressure, palpable and inchoate, was loose in that room. Panic blossomed in grotesque and lurid forms among the freshmen in the sinking half-light of a luminous and mysterious dusk. In the shimmering greenhouse of the alcove, we sweated and waited in melancholy silence for the entrance of the full cadre.

After fifteen minutes, they marched into the room in an immaculate single file, moving with such precision that they seemed otherworldly, superhuman. They were elite and slim and malignant. Their presence was an articulate tribute to the force and puissance of men united by indivisible will, by absolute conviction. They were dressed in freshly starched cotton uniforms. Their grooming was impeccable. They were what we aspired to be. Circling us, they stood at attention, wincing as they caught the smell of us.

I heard someone else enter the room. His footsteps echoed loudly as though he were goose-stepping into the alcove. There was malice in his approach. He mounted a table directly in front of the plebes. Behind me, a freshman breathed hotly on my neck. I could feel the buttocks of the boy in front of me pressed flat against my groin. My arms were pinned to my side by the pressure of arms on my right and my left. Sweat poured down my body, and my eyes burned with salt and fatigue. The atmosphere was so thick and overheated it was like breathing underwater.

The figure on the table was R Company's first sergeant,

Maccabee. He eyed us with contempt for several moments, then screamed out, "Sit down, dumbheads."

In the crash that followed in blind obedience to that single command, I do not understand why bones were not broken or why someone was not seriously hurt. We landed together in a massive, disarranged pile. My right leg was draped over someone's shoulder. Someone sat on my left arm. I was sitting astride another boy's leg. But they let us writhe and maneuver like worms in a can until at last all of us could see the speaker, who stood rigidly on the table slapping his open palm with a swagger stick.

Then Maccabee began to speak in a deep, pitiless voice: "Gentlemen, I am your first sergeant and I want you to prepare for the ram."

He slapped his swagger stick loudly against his open palm.

"It is my responsibility, gentlemen, to turn this pile of maggot-sperm into Institute men. From what I have seen already from this putrid mound of dogshit, I think I have been assigned a hopeless task. But with the help of this cadre and this swagger stick I'm going to do my best to make sure that Romeo Company remains the best goddam company in the Corps. To accomplish this, gentlemen, I'm going to jack this swagger stick up your foul assholes every time I get near you this year. I'm going to be a monster who screams at you during every waking moment. I'm going to be watching every single move you make this year, gentlemen. For tonight we begin the long agonizing journey that will transform you from worthless scumbags into full-fledged Institute men. The cadre has an awesome responsibility to uphold. We are responsible to all the men who wear the ring not to allow any diarrhea to survive the plebe system. No diarrhea, I repeat, gentlemen. No diarrhea will wear the ring. That is my personal vow to you.

"There are sixty of you in this room tonight. When your class graduates in four years, there will be only twenty survivors from this room. Most of you will leave the first year. Some of you will not measure up academically; some of you will leave for honor violations; and some of you"—he paused dramatically—"will leave tonight.

"I will tell you what we, the cadre, expect from you. We expect—as you were—we demand absolute unquestioning obedience from you at all times. If you hesitate, if you question, if you refuse, then the full fury of this cadre will descend upon you in terrible force, and together we will drive you out of this school in forty-eight hours. No knob can withstand the power and the fury of the brotherhood when it is directed at him alone. Your only chance for survival is to band together in a tight, impregnable brotherhood of your own, to protect each other, to care for each other, and to lean on each other from this day forward until the day you graduate.

"As for myself," he continued, his cold eyes loathing us, "I would like to see every single one of you abortions pack your bags tonight and run home to your mother's skirts. This is the worst looking bunch of knobs that has entered the Institute in twenty years. But, gentlemen, I assure you that if you make it through the plebe system of Romeo Company, you could walk through the Gates of Hell and think you were entering Paradise instead. When you scumbags return to your rooms tonight, if you have enough strength left in your puny bodies to pick up a pen, I want you to write a letter to your mother and give her your love. Then I want you to write a letter to your girl friend and give her your heart. Then I want you to get down on your knees, say a prayer to God, and give him your soul."

Then he screamed, "Because, shitheads, as of this very moment, your asses belong to Maccabee!" Saliva ran from his mouth to his chin. He was beating the swagger stick furiously into his palm as though his left hand was boneless, nerveless tissue.

"Look up, dumbheads!" he commanded, his voice breaking with anger. Our necks moved simultaneously and we stared at the ceiling of the room. The sweat changed directions and began to flow into our ears.

"Do you see the hand of God coming down from heaven to help you, scumbags? Do you see the heavenly host coming to your rescue? No, dumbheads. You don't see anything. Because there's nothing to see, maggot-shits. No power on heaven or earth can help you now. You are beyond all help. You belong to me and me alone and I want each one of you to know that I'm a fucking maniac. I am stark raving mad and if it were up to me, if the fucking Commandant's Department would let me have my way, I'd pump this room full of DDT and let all of you die like the roach turds you really are. I've been insane for so long, criminally insane, douchebags, psychotically out of my fucking tree, that it gives me kind of a warm feeling all over when I think about sticking my swagger stick up your fucking asses and have it

142

come out all slick with your blood and intestines. But the reason you don't see the hand of God coming out of the heavens to help deliver you from this fucking madman first sergeant who's in control of your destiny is that God has ceased to exist for any of you. He doesn't care a fucking thing for a single one of you. He's dead for you all. Your new God is your first sergeant, the great god Maccabee. Look at me now, dumbheads. Stare into the crazy wild eyeballs of your new God. I am your God and you will obey my commandments or I'll jack it up your filthy asses.

"Here is your new bible," he said, holding aloft a copy of the Blue Book, which contained the rules and regulations of the Institute. "And here is what your new, insane, knob-destroying God thinks of your old Bible."

He threw his swagger stick to the floor and drew his long sword from his shining scabbard. Upon the wooden table by his feet lay a thick black Bible. He plunged his sword into the Bible with a deep, savage thrust, then lifted the skewered book aloft and held it high above his head. The Bible had been soaked in lighter fluid. With his free hand he lit a match, touched it to the book, which exploded into flames. The pure bright sacrilegious fire illuminated the grinning faces of the cadre, who had turned their faces toward the macabre light. The first sergeant moaned as he watched the thin leaves burn in sequence from Genesis to Kings, from Revelations toward Mark. Ash floated up to the ceiling in glowing black fragments. The freshmen watched. We had come to a place where a twenty-year-old boy roared out his own divinity, and the Bible was put to the sword and the torch to illustrate the preeminence of discipline. We were entering into the dark country of the plebe system now, and we were entering it afraid.

Then with extraordinary swiftness and efficiency, they were pushing and kicking and shoving us out the door toward the quadrangle. No lights were on in the barracks. The intense heat of the night air was deliciously cool after the steaming alcove room. The other three companies in the battalion had already completed their preliminary ceremonies, and their freshmen were already lined up in braced squads on the quadrangle. Our cadre divided us into squads of ten and put us into the plebe brace for the first time since we had arrived, with our chins rammed painfully against our necks and our spines rigid. The brace was the symbol that the plebe system had officially begun.

After aligning us, the cadre slipped quietly out of sight.

The barracks was completely dark. There was not a single sound in fourth battalion. The silence roared in our ears. Screaming had become a natural part of our environment. Without it, something was not right. There was something wicked in the air. Nothing had alarmed me quite so much since I had come to the Institute as the volatile dissonance of that exquisite soundlessness. There was not a single upper-classman on the quadrangle. My neck was already sore from the effort of pulling my chin hard against the upper vertebrae. The mosquitoes found us and began stinging the back of my legs, bringing back memories of the marsh. Somewhere in the barracks, the cadre watched and bided their time. I seized the opportunity to gather my wits with the acrid smell of the burning Bible still in my nostrils.

At the front sally port, the Officer of the Guard, with deliberate clumsiness, performed an elaborate ceremony locking the front gate. We heard it clang shut, the heavy key twist, and the lock slam into place. Now, the outside world could not enter fourth battalion to witness the second phase of Hell Night. Nor could any of us leave.

The loudspeaker switched on and an unseen musician played "Home, Sweet Home" on a harmonica. The harmonica whined and quavered. Normally I would have thought this touch very amusing, but I had noticed a serious diminishment of my sense of humor in the past two days.

When the music stopped there was a brief pause. Someone tapped on the microphone three times. Then he cleared his throat. A voice, pure and dutiful, spoke with resolution.

"Gentlemen," the voice said, as I tensed, "this is your regimental commander."

"It's coming," I thought, "it's coming now."

I looked to the right and left without moving my head. I wanted to prepare myself. I wanted to make sure the cadre was not stealing up on us from the side. I saw nothing. I did not know what was going to happen but I could feel the amazing tension in the barracks. I could sense the invisible readiness of the cadre.

Then the voice continued: "The plebe system for the class of 1967 is *now* in effect."

And they were on us.

The cadres of the four companies exploded out from their hiding places beneath the stairwells. They came in one violent full-throated roar of havoc. The lights were thrown on simultaneously. The light, so sudden, entered our retinas like acid. They fell on us in a crazed venomous pack. They seemed to be everywhere at once. Light and sound, light and fear, they boiled out onto the quadrangle in rabid, delirious bands. First the dark, then the light, then the screams, then their hot breath against our necks and ears, then the cry of them, the terrible roar of them abusing us, loathing us, hitting us, violating us, breaking us down to creatures less than human, less than they were. Disorder reigned in the bitter heat. I lost all control, and in that first moment, something began to die in me while something new and extraordinary began to live.

I jumped when I heard that first collective scream, the terrorism of their ruthless charge among the plebes. I braced hard and waited for them, I prepared myself for the ordeal. I planned on my survival in the assault of light and voices. I called out for the athlete within me to take over, for pure instinct to take control, and guide me safely through this night.

One of them almost knocked me over in his first sortie against me. I felt his mouth on my ear. His saliva flecked against my earlobe. He didn't say anything. He simply screamed into my ear. I reeled sideways but fell into the cunning, waiting shout of another, and he screamed me back to the other one. It was the pain that caused me to jerk violently back and forth; the eardrum could not endure the trauma of the sustained scream.

Then the voice on my right commanded, "Rack your fucking chin into your goddam fucking neck, scumbag. Rack it in, knob. I want to see the blood vessels break inside that ugly fucking skull of yours. Get it in, dumbhead. Rack it in. Put out for me, asswipe."

And simultaneously from the left I heard, "Shoulders back, abortion. Arms straight to your side. Get your fucking chin in. Rack it in. Rack it in, fuckstick. You better put out, scumbag. Maggot-sperm. Wad-waste."

A voice behind me began a softer, more menacing chant, strangely rhythmic, like a litany. "I'm going to kill you, douchebag. I'm going to be all over your fucking ass from now until the end of school. Rack that fucking chin in, waste-product. I said rack it in, screwbrain. Did you hear me, boy? Did you hear what I fucking said to you? I said grind that ugly fucking chin in or I'm going to rip your guts out with my hand and spread them all over this fucking quadrangle. Now rack it in, dumbhead."

Then the voices changed as they moved from freshman

to freshman, as they weaved through the stunned, disoriented files of plebes, as their voices became strained and raspy in the first moments of the attack. It was impossible to distinguish one voice from another, one upperclassman from another. They advanced against us in a single collectively malevolent voice. One voice, one scream, in light, in fury, without end, coming at us from all sides, from all angles, compassionless and out of control. Fists struck against my chest and spine. I did sixty pushups in the first ten minutes after the lights had come on. I ran in place. I answered them, screaming back my answers. I obeyed them. The chaos was fathomless. The barracks was inundated in an ocean of sound, a maelstrom of the human voice straining toward absolute limits, toward nullity, toward inconceivable thresholds of derangement. All was madness, screaming, light, cadre, obscenity. The plebe system burned the air of September. Voices rained down from all sides. Voices. Voices.

"What's your I.D. number, scumbag?"

"Recite the guard orders, prick."

"What's your name, maggot?"

"Does your mother fuck, douchebag?"

"Your mother should have stuck a coat hanger up her cunt to kill a maggot like you."

"What are you, boy?" a voice behind me asked. "Pop off."

"Pardon me, sir?" I asked, not recognizing my own voice.

"Repeat after me, dumbhead. I'm going to tell you what you are," the voice said. "You are an abortion."

"I'm an abortion, sir!" I screamed.

"A maggot."

"I'm a maggot, sir!"

"A douchebag."

"I am a douchebag, sir!"

"A used Kotex."

"I am a used Kotex, sir!"

"You are shit."

"I am shit, sir!"

"The shit that comes from a woman when she's on the rag."

"I am the shit that comes from a woman when she's on the rag!"

"A pubic hair on a nigger."

"I am a pubic hair on a nigger, sir!"

"Do you love this place, fuckstick? Pop off," a voice in

front of me screamed. My vision was blurred with sweat and I could not make out his face.

"Yes, sir!"

"Louder, fuckstick."

"Yes, sir!" I yelled.

"Louder. Say it like a man, shit maggot."

"Yes, sir!" I screamed.

"Did you hear me, boy? I said to sound off like a man."

"Yes, sir!" I screamed until my voice broke.

"You glad you came to this place, pussy? Pop off."

"Yes, sir!"

"I'm gonna make you sorry you were ever born, vagina-face."

"You're gonna die, McLean. You're gonna die, asswipe," said another voice.

"We got you for nine months, diarrhea. Every night for nine months it's going to be just like this. Every night the same. Nine months of this, McLean."

My brain swarmed with the images of hoarse sergeants navigating between the staggered lines of plebes. They seemed to increase in number as the night wore on. At times, they surrounded me and I could not calculate if there were two of them or ten of them. They screamed out their questions simultaneously. I did not know if I had been on the quadrangle for ten minutes or two hours. At some time during that night, my mind and body began a slow betrayal of me. The world transformed into a gauzy overcast fog empire, and my eyes could no longer focus on the overwrought faces that attacked me from all sides. My body took asylum in a mental and physical paralysis. My responses slowed; my answers became unintelligible and I could not control the responses of my tongue. I answered "yes" when a squad sergeant wanted to know if I was a woman, and "no" when asked if I'd ever been in the state of South Carolina. In the light and heat and noise, I was dizzy, shaken, and losing my slender hold on reality. I concentrated on not crying and not fainting.

At the same time, I was aware of a terrible coming apart in the ranks of the plebes. I heard the bodies of freshmen as they collapsed against the cement. The two boys on either side of me went down hard. The one on my left fell into me, knocked me out of line and into the arms of a cadre member who threw me onto the prostrate body of the boy who fell. Then he jerked me up and began pounding my chest with his fist, shouting, "You touched me, scumbag. You touched me with your putrid, stinking body. I'm going to remember you, scumbag. You're going to bleed for this. Give me fifty pushups, maggot-shit."

I hit the cement and began counting aloud to him, "One, sir, two, sir, three, sir." It was not long before I knew that I would never reach fifty. My arms began to spasm and he leaned far over to shout contemptuously in my ear, "Pussy, pussy, pussy, pussy." My arms began to spasm uncontrollably. I could no longer support my own weight and collapsed against the concrete.

"Get up, dumbhead," another voice spoke above me, a familiar one.

I rose to my feet, braced again, and found myself staring into the face of the first sergeant, Maccabee. He looked dry and cold and undefilable through the sweat which poured down my face.

"How are you feeling, Mr. McLean?" he asked seriously in a voice that contained no threat, no intimation of cruelty.

I could not believe the stupidity of the question. I wanted to say something like, "Fabulous, you fucking asshole. Terrific. Wonderful. Top of the day to you too, sir." But instead, I shouted, "Fine, sir."

"Bend your knees, Mr. McLean," he said kindly, "or you'll faint like some of your classmates. Your posture needs improvement. Get your shoulders back a little bit. That's fine. Now relax your mouth. Arms straight down by your sides. Very good. And remember this, Mr. McLean. Two years ago I was standing where you're standing tonight. Hell Night was the worst night I ever spent. I tried to quit the next day. If you stick this out, it will be worth all the pain. I promise you that. It's the system. That's all. Remember that. The system. None of this is personal. If you make it, then you and I will go out and drink some beer together in June."

The first sergeant drifted out of my angle of vision. Three others instantly replaced him, screaming, screaming, screaming. Their voices seemed to come from everywhere, from nowhere, disembodied, disengaged. Every voice screamed and every voice was the same. I could barely distinguish my screams from theirs.

Suddenly, a tall figure appeared in front of me. He was smiling broadly and I judged him to be at least six feet eight inches tall.

"Hi, Will. How's college?" he said.

Puzzled, I answered, "Fine, sir."

"Isn't this fun? Isn't this a nifty way to spend your second night in college?"

"Yes, sir."

"I'm Lancey Hemphill, Will. Center on the basketball team. Our coach wanted me to check on you during Hell Night."

"Tell him thanks a lot, sir."

"You don't call me 'sir.' We're jocks, Will. We try to stay apart from this bullshit as much as possible."

"Why didn't Coach Byrum tell me about this?" I asked in a whisper.

"It's very simple, Will. Because you and all the other numb-nuts would have signed scholarships with other schools. Believe me, Will, he screwed every one of us just like he screwed you. Just remember, this is all bullshit. Pure bullshit. It doesn't mean a thing. Try to take it as a big joke. You pissed God off and he's getting even by making you go to the Institute. If it gets too hot for you this year, you give me the names and weights of the heat-givers. I like to use dead corporals when I lift weights. Nighty-night," he said.

"Lancey," I said.

"Yeh, Will."

"It's too hot for me right now."

He laughed. "Oh, a funny guy, huh. Look, smackhead, it's supposed to be too hot tonight. This here is official heat," he said walking toward T Company area.

The freshmen kept falling like grotesque fruit to the quadrangle. They lay where they fell until a cadreman reached them, revived them, then stood them up until they fell again. After the third fall, orderlies strapped them to litters and rushed them to the infirmary, where the Institute had hired four extra nurses for the night. A boy in front of me toppled over as though both his legs had broken suddenly. They dragged him off the quadrangle by his arms.

The screaming was beginning to let up, not because of any benevolence on the part of the cadre, but because some of the upperclassmen had already lost their voices. Those that now filled the air were cracked and strained. There was a quality of sameness to the noise in the barracks as though the novelty of perversion was wearing off. Hell Night was winding down when Fox and Newman materialized before me. Fox grabbed my bathrobe and jerked me forward until our noses touched.

"Thought I'd forgotten about you, douchebag? Pop off."

"No, sir."

"I've been saving you for dessert, you scum-sucking jock. I saw you talking to that waste, Hemphill. Do you think he can save you, dumbhead? Nothing can save you, douchebag. Nothing in the world. I wanted you to know that you're going to be one of my special projects this year. I'm gonna rack your ass every day until you beg me to walk you out of these gates."

Newman pulled me away from Fox and I stood with my eyes an inch from his. Newman had the thin, cunning face of a mongrel with a complexion so white and sallow that his skin looked like the crust of a Camembert. His freckles were large and the color of blood samples viewed through a child's microscope.

"I hate jocks. I don't want to see a single jock in R Company, McLean. We're a military company, you see. So me and Mr. Fox have made a vow to run you out of here before graduation. Do you think we can do it, maggot-shit? Pop off."

"No, sir."

Trembling, I stood before them, drenched in sweat and ruin, spiritually plundered, fearing them and loathing myself for my stink, my helplessness, my total lack of power.

Fox began to whisper, breathing wet obscenities in my ear. "Rack your fucking chin in, douchebag. Harder, douchebag. I said rack it in, asswipe. You're not doing what I say, McLean. I want you to rack that chin into your beady, ugly neck, dumbfuck."

His face was so close to mine, I could smell his dinner. His nose was long, hooked, and elementary, like a Bronze Age cutting tool. As he whispered his lips curled back in a sneer, exposing the pink, shining sill of his upper gums.

"You don't belong here, maggot. You aren't man enough to make it through this school. I'm gonna cut your dick off and shove it into your mouth if you stay here over a week, douchebag. I'm gonna fuck you slow and easy with my swagger stick, scumbag."

His lips touched against my ear in a malignant parody of a kiss. The pleasure of discipline to Fox, I realized as I felt his tongue close to my ear, was related to a ruthless sexuality. There was something nightmarishly erotic in his brutality as I listened to his ugly whispers burning into my ears. I thought of the taking of beleaguered cities, the fury of plunder, and the forcing open of feminine mouths to receive the conqueror's semen. That's what it is, I thought. That's what it is, as I surveyed the images before me. This was the rape of boys. Hell Night had the feel and texture of a psychic rape. Throughout the barracks, a malignant virility was born in the hearts of plebes. A year from this night, many of us would be cadre abusing scared boys on this same quadrangle.

One hour and fifteen minutes after the plebe system officially began, a bugle reverberated through the barracks. It carried in its melody the authority of our release. The bugle ended what the regimental commander's voice had begun.

The cadre screamed at us, "Get to your rooms, dumbheads. Run, run, you scumbags. Get to your rooms, people."

I took one step toward my room and fell to my knees. My legs would not function. I could not rise. There was not a freshman in the barracks standing. The legs of our entire class had failed us.

Fox kicked me in the ass and screamed, "Crawl, maggot. Crawl, abortion. Crawl, Kotex."

He mounted me like a horse and rode me as I crawled across the cement. He beat my ass with sharp, stinging slaps. My knees began to bleed against the bathrobe. Fox jumped off me when I reached the gallery and joined the other crawlers as we braved a gauntlet of feet and the voices of the cadremen screaming out of the void above us. They kicked us and insulted us all the way to our rooms.

A boy dropped down in front of me and was crawled over by some of his classmates. I tried to rise to my feet, was kicked down by an unseen assailant, rose again, and helped the boy stumble into my room where we both collapsed on the floor in the darkness.

We lay there in absolute silence listening to the havoc outside on the galleries. He began crying and I began crying. We lay there weeping for several minutes until we heard the cadre ordering us out for showers. I couldn't lift myself off the floor. My arms rebelled when I tried to get to my feet. Rolling onto my side, I faced the stranger beside me.

"Are you all right?" I asked. I was still crying.

"Yes. I think so," he answered. "Thanks for helping me."

"I can't believe this is happening to me," I said.

"It's awful. It's simply awful."

"Where's my roommate?" I asked, looking around the room.

"I don't know your roommate. I don't even know you."

"My name's Will."

"Thanks again, Will."

"What's your name?"

We lay face to face, tears on our cheeks.

"My name is Tradd," he said. "I'm from Charleston."

"We've got to get up, Tradd. The animals are calling again."

Again, I tried to lift myself up off the floor, but I still could not summon enough strength to support my own weight. Tradd got slowly to his feet and began helping me rise. Elements of both our friendship and our survival were mysteriously contained in those tender, solicitous moments, as I put my arm around his shoulder and we leaned against each other. Through the long tyranny of that night, something had begun to stir and kick inside us. We were crying, but we were not quitting. Invisibly contained in both of us were the seeds that would insure the propagation of the system.

"To the showers, people!" a voice commanded outside on the galleries. "Clean your loathsome bodies, dumbwads."

The sound of the enemy's voice again brought me erect and ready to face them again. Tradd and I stared at each other with a sense of impending loss.

"Can we be friends, Tradd?" I asked. "I don't have any friends here."

"We already are," he answered.

Then we exited the room and joined the long line of plebes being driven in single file to the shower room.

In the shower room, we stripped naked and ran through two lines of jeering upperclassmen, who shoved us roughly into the cold water that sprayed from the six nozzles. They permitted us to remain under the water for only a few seconds, then forced us out of the shower, handed us bars of soap, and ordered us to lather up. They sent us sprinting back to our rooms with the soap caked all over our glistening bodies. The sweat and the soap and the stench combined to make our skin feel lizard-like. I stumbled back into the room and began trying to clean off the soap in the small sink by the door.

I was completely naked when the first sergeant and the company commander burst into my room.

"Room, attention!" I cried out, and went into a brace.

"Where's your roommate, McLean?" Blasingame asked. "Pop off."

"I don't know, sir," I answered. "I haven't seen him since after mess, sir."

"Did you see him anytime tonight?" Maccabee asked. "Pop off."

"I didn't see anybody tonight, sir."

"No one saw Clearwater on the quadrangle, McLean. And he's not at the hospital."

"Do you know where he is, Mr. McLean? Pop off," Blasingame said. "Pop off loud and clear, scumbag."

"No, sir."

The first sergeant went down on one knee and peered into the shadows beneath the lower bunk bed. Then he walked to my roommate's clothes press and opened it suddenly. It was empty. When he opened my press, I saw the frightened eyes of my roommate, Harvey Clearwater, blazing with something that went beyond even terror, looking past the first sergeant directly at me. He was asking me to help him, to deliver him in some way from the wrath of the cadre and the fury of the system. But I knew something about the system now and I dropped my eyes and did nothing.

"Sir, I don't belong here, sir. I just don't belong here," Harvey pleaded.

"You fucking worm," Blasingame said disgustedly. "You hid in a press while your classmates were on the quad."

"You shit on your classmates, Clearwater," the first sergeant said. "That's the only unforgivable sin at the Institute. Get out of there, scumbag. We're going to give you your own personal Hell Night."

Harvey climbed out of the press trembling violently. They shoved him out of the room and into the darkness on the gallery.

I finished washing the soap from my body. When I was done I put on a fresh pair of underwear and fell into the bottom rack without pulling down the covers. I was not the same boy who had awakened to reveille that morning. That boy was a stranger to me now and he could never be recalled. The system had transformed me into an original astonished creature. I had learned things about myself and others out there on the quadrangle that I had never known before. The cadre had ripped civilization from my back as though it were nothing more than strips of skin. They were going to change all of us into men by reducing us to children again, by breaking down every single vestige of civilization and society that we had brought to protect and sustain us. They would tame us like beasts of the field before they remade us in their own fierce image.

All through the four battalions, hurt and confused and

frightened and exhausted freshmen were thinking similar thoughts. Some of them were already planning to leave; some of them would last a month; others would leave at the Christmas break. But the extraordinary power of the plebe system was demonstrated most remarkably by the fact that there were four hundred boys who arrived at the exact same decision as I did that night in their own time and for their own reasons. Four hundred terrified boys vowed to themselves that no matter what happened, they would not quit.

"I will not quit. I will not quit," I said over and over to myself.

The last thing I remember before falling into a deep, dreamless sleep was the screaming of my roommate, Harvey Clearwater.

I never saw him again.

My college education had begun.

17

The rebel within was also born on Hell Night. On that night he took to the hills and began his long patient war of attrition against the man I was in danger of becoming. From the moment I crawled off the fourth battalion quadrangle, this lean anonymous guerrilla began a fierce and insistent rear guard action against my acceptance of the Institute's scheme of forging men out of boys.

I tried to join the flow. I wanted to participate in the plebe system as a believer, to become inflamed with the zealotry and esprit that sustained my classmates during those first dispiriting months. But the guerrilla within asserted his presence if not his primacy from the very beginning, and a small bloodless war, without strategies or anthems, began to rage for the control of my interior. This lonely, unconsenting rebel battled against the patriarchal influences that had shaped my childhood: the American South and the Catholic Church. These were the two pillars of authority upon which my life had been built, and I had learned their rituals well—their worship of order and tradition, their strict codes, their punishment of anarchy, and contempt for the man or woman who stood alone. They had not prepared me for a time in my life when I would stand alone. Yet the malnourished hill fighter, chalking slogans on the rocks and carrying on his isolated, unseen war, grew in stature during that first week. In the aftershock of Hell Night, the urgency of his protest brought reinforcements sprinting into the hills carrying news of my disaffection. Slowly, he began to threaten the whole rigidly structured, tight-assed fabric of my civilization. In the melancholy city within, the boulevards were wide and laid out in symmetrical grids, the bells of cathedrals rang on time, the cops never smiled, and the jails overflowed with silent, abused separatists. But the presence of the guerrilla, the single voice in my sad country who said "no," gave me hope that the plebe system would not mark me darkly, irretrievably. During sweat parties in that first month, losing my voice and surrounded by the cadre, I would feel him stealing up to an overhang to watch me with patient intensity. I shivered with gratitude when I heard him deep in the forests singing of my liberation, celebrating my passionate difference from the rest of them. I knew nothing about the duality of man's nature when I was eighteen, but I knew about the presence of my guerrilla, and as the months wore on, I knew that I would have to deal with his ascendancy. And I was certain that one day he would feel strong enough to storm the city and liberate it.

For the first month I made my own way and kept my mouth shut. I learned what was expected of me and I performed it with ardor and enthusiasm. I did the pushups, held out my rifle, ran the stairs, endured their screaming, suffered at mess, returned for the sweat parties after mess, memorized my plebe knowledge, and secretly began to study the system in order to learn its effect on me. I wanted to unlearn the system while I was still a part of it. Something in my character made it impossible for me to accept the validity of this long trial by humiliation. If this was an efficacious process for the training of men, I wanted no part of manhood, I was perfectly content with being a boy. I conducted my survey in private, and I learned some things that would be of value my whole life. There was an amazingly limitless capacity for ruthlessness at the heart of the family of man. Nothing I learned that year or in the years that followed made me doubt the absolute truth of that natural law I discovered during the first month of the plebe system. I saw enough cruelty in that month to last a lifetime, but I was to see a lot more.

If the cadre had been aware of my skepticism they

would have run me out of the barracks within twenty-four hours. There was no toleration of dissenters in "the system." "The system" was a phrase we heard from the time we rose at reveille until we fell exhausted into our beds at night. The plebe system. The Fourth Class system. Through the system, we would learn of our inner reserves of strength, our innate capacity to resist violence. This was the sacred text of our orthodoxy. Since I did not have the courage to quit, my time in the system became an inquest into the nature of aggrieved innocence.

I had come to the Institute to pay homage to the career of my father and my promise to him on his deathbed. Like most sons of domineering men, I had a compulsive need to test the quality of my manhood by marching resolutely into the territory he had carefully marked out as his own. I had to test myself in the military environment before I could strike out independently. But my father would have laughed his way through the plebe system and laughed at the son who took it so seriously. He would have mocked the son who cried secretly into his pillow each night. My tears would have shamed him.

When I called my mother after the second week I wept as soon as I heard her voice. She sounded kind and gentle and I had forgotten what it was like to talk to someone who loved me. I told her that it was dreadful, that I had made a terrible mistake, that I wanted to quit and come home, and that the Institute was a monstrous, unspeakable place. My mother knew me well and she uttered the exact words that would make me stay. She was sure, she told me softly, that I was more of a man than any of the cadre who were mistreating me and that I would certainly want to prove that to them and to myself. I think I could have faced my own doubts about my masculinity, but under no circumstances could I face my mother's. Early on, I had contracted that dread affliction of oldest or only children—I lived for the absolute approval of my parents.

Slowly, as the days passed, the plebes in R Company began to recognize each other. We began to make the friendships and form the alliances that would ease the passage through that difficult year. The real terror of Hell Night was that we had suffered in such complete solitude. That we suffered so friendlessly, exiled among complete strangers. Only when we began to make cautious overtures to each other did any of the system's mystique accrue to us. Our survival lay in our solidarity. We began to study each other's faces and transmit unseen signals as we gave each other shirt tucks or passed on the galleries. When classes started, we spoke in whispers before chemistry professors cleared their throats or while math professors copied algebraic formulae on blackboards. When we got the opportunity to talk in those first weeks, we did not talk about where we came from or what our sisters were like or how our fathers earned their bread; no, that was the world we had forsaken, that was the free zone outside the Gates of Legrand. We talked of survival and strategy. We were learning the art of being victims, studying the craft of endurance. In those early conversations were the first intimations that we were becoming a class.

I tried to find out who these boys were, and what had drawn them to the Institute. I discovered that the Institute drew its sons from every state in the Union but it was primarily a Southern school, dedicated to the task of making Southerners. Southerners possess a simple yet magnificent obsession with all things military, and they love authority in all forms, masculine or feminine. They love to wear uniforms, shoot guns, wage war, march in parades, salute flags, and hold fast to traditions that should have died centuries before. Southerners have much in common with the rest of mankind. Even the Yankees, most of whom had been rejected by the military academies, spent their years at the Institute perfecting the unctuous skills of Southern gentlemen.

All of us were white Caucasians in the class of 1967. Six hundred Protestants, one hundred Catholics, three Jews, two Greeks, one Puerto Rican. We came from the Carolinas, the green hill country of the Blue Ridge, from cruciform towns with a single intersection, from the blue dusted mountains of Tennessee and the Gold Coast of Florida, from lowcountry towns set like elegant tables upon the green linen of marsh. Six from California, eight from Texas, and one from Idaho. Nine came from New York, three from New Jersey, twelve from the Virginias; but most came from the southeast empire, most from the Carolinas.

All of us had gathered to become Institute men. There was only one task of the fourth class system—to turn us into the exact images of the cadre who abused us—to make us want to be like them.

I did not want to be like them.

That was what made me different from my classmates, and I soon began to feel isolated from them and some of them to be wary of me. Most of them had been fully aware of the severity of the plebe system when they chose the Institute,

157

and they welcomed its testing of their fortitude. Many of them planned to make the military their life's work. They had enrolled willingly at the Institute because of the system, not in spite of it. Their genuine enthusiasm contrasted starkly to my rejection of every indignity we suffered at the hands of the upperclassmen. To them, the excesses of the plebe system were salutary and character-building. Torture was simply an effective test of their bloom and vitality. It was the system and we had all agreed to abide by its laws. So I quit talking, even to my classmates, about my grievances against the system. I just kept my eyes open and tried to figure things out alone.

I saw that the plebe system was destroying the ability or the desire of the freshmen to use the word *I*. *I* was the one unforgivable obscenity, and the boys intrepid enough to hold fast to this extraordinary blasphemy found themselves excised from the body of the Corps with incredible swiftness. The Institute was a universe in love with the first person plural, the shout of the uniformed mob, which gave the school its fundamental identity, the source of its strength and invulnerability. The plebe system, then, infinitely reduced, was a grammarian's war between two pronouns and, infinitely extended, contained the elements of the major war of the twentieth century. The person who could survive the plebe year and still use the word *I* was the most seasoned and indefatigable breed of survivor. He was a man to be reckoned with, perhaps a dangerous one. No doubt, he was a lonely one. I wanted to be that man in my class. I made that pact with myself and broke it time and time again, for I was a son of the South and I had grown up using the word *we* when I was referring only to myself. It takes a lot more effort to unlearn things than to learn them.

By October the plebe system had changed because the freshmen had changed. They had become inured—or accustomed, at least—to the shouts of the cadre. But when the harassment of the plebe system became familiar, it also became tedious. I thought that even I had become accustomed to being afraid, and I had learned enough about the psychology of the cadre to be immune to their cruelty. It would not be the last time I would be completely wrong about my relationship to the Institute.

My task was fear. Some freshmen lost their fear very quickly; others lost their fear when it was subsumed by their total, passionate faith in the system. But I want to tell you that I never lost any of my fear. I told myself I had, but I was lying to myself. I was humiliated by the discovery of my limitless capacity for terror, for nightmare.

The Coward, though I did not know it before I came to the Institute, had a long and honorable residence in my psyche. I say honorable because I learned to pay homage to this fearful resident within. At times I could overwhelm the Coward and beat him cringing back into the dark interior, but there were other times, when the cadre was in full cry, that he took full possession of the frontier behind my eyes. He occupied me often. He was a guest of the purest fire. Each time during my freshman year that I acted bravely, I was paying ultimate homage to my cowardice. I knew I had to hide my fear. If the cadre discovered it or sensed its undermining presence, then they would come for me and they would come united. Each week the cadre selected one or two freshmen they would run out in the next forty-eight hours. They had chosen twelve boys since Hell Night and all twelve had left school soon afterward. The process was called "The Taming."

Few boys survived the Taming. It was the sport of breaking down plebes absolutely—to discover how much the boy could take before he was reduced to begging and to crawling, before he came completely apart. They broke you in their own time and their own way and they studied you carefully before they made their move. They usually chose the very weak. The boys selected to endure the most pressure of the system were always the most vulnerable and the least equipped to handle it. I was not one of the victims, at least not at first. I was not ugly or thin or obese or pimply. I did not limp or stutter or cry in front of them or lose my temper or pass out after doing twenty pushups. The victims were the very weakest and most sensitive among us, and each cadre member had his own particular victim whom he singled out as his own special project. My life appeared perfectly miserable to me, but what these boys suffered was worthy of epic poetry. And as those early days passed, the plebe system produced moments of magnificent courage among the victims. Some of them even survived the Taming.

I studied my masters with as much thoroughness as the system afforded. From observation and experience I knew which of them to avoid at all costs. Some of the cadre were basically harmless; some were even gentle, affable guys when you met them alone on campus. Some simply held the impartial, impersonal belief that the plebe system was a proven and effective method of turning boys into Institute men. But all of them required that we play the game. I had to learn the delicate and obsequious art form of being a plebe. The cadre was vigilant for the slightest sign of a bad attitude, of unchecked anger or frustration, or that sudden, desperate glazing in a freshman's eyes just before he was ready to crack. They studied us as carefully as we studied them, but with more patience. Slowly, as the year progressed, they discovered what our severest weak points were, and they profited by their diligent attention. They would introduce the marked freshman to horrible situations outside of the framework of the system, and by watching him, they would learn what he was truly afraid of. Then they would use that knowledge callously, and with deadly intent. If they could not discover some central fear, they had a final trick: The whole cadre would come at you alone. Very few indeed could withstand the onslaught of twenty determined men.

The Taming took different forms. In the second week they discovered quite by accident that Graham Craig was afraid of heights. He was a hot-tempered boy from Greensboro who had won the undivided attention of the cadre by quitting the Institute and then returning two days later. The Taming began. Maccabee noticed that Craig could not bring himself to look at the quadrangle from the fourth division. Craig admitted to vertigo. They put him inside a mattress cover, threw it over the side of the fourth division, and tied it to the railing on the gallery, one hundred ten feet above the concrete. Disoriented, Craig struggled until his head popped out of the mattress cover. He fainted when he saw where he was, an act highly amusing to the upperclassmen. They let him spend the night hanging over the railing. He never looked out again. The bag never moved and Craig resigned the next day.

Jeff Lieckweg feared snakes. He was from Cleveland and had never seen a snake alive until his squad sergeant, Muller, brought his pet boa constrictor with him when he inspected Lieckweg's room one morning. The snake terrified him. Lieckweg could not keep his mouth shut, could not bring himself to stop answering the upperclassmen insolently. He always looked angry and he always was. That night they tied his hands behind his back and lowered him by a rope tied to his feet into an open elevator pit. As they lowered him into the shaft, they told him they had dropped twelve copperheads into the shaft that day. They suggested he lie prefectly still when he reached the bottom of the shaft and perhaps the

160

snakes would not strike at him, perhaps they would not notice him. But it would be a shame if they lowered him on top of one or two of the snakes. That would be very bad, the cadre agreed. There were no snakes in the pit and Lieckweg never reached the bottom. He was screaming so loud halfway down that there was no need for any further taming and he left the barracks that night.

Masturbation was forbidden by the Blue Book. It may have been the most often violated law in history. But the cadre amused themselves by catching freshmen in the act of masturbating. Bill Agee, a fat, miserable boy from Fort Lauderdale, was caught masturbating every single night for two weeks. "I can't help it. I can't help it," he would cry out to the upperclassmen. The cadre made him walk around the campus wearing one white glove. You could see Agee clear across campus, spot him instantly among five hundred other freshmen, and keep careful watch on his comings and goings. It was a very public humiliation and everyone on campus, including the faculty and the President's wife, knew what the single white glove signified. Agee was degraded slowly, in degrees, and finally, long after he became the campus joke, he left R Company in tears. He was wearing one white glove when he walked out of the Gates of Legrand.

Rodney Aimar was a painfully thin, fragile boy from Anderson, South Carolina. He could not perform a single pushup when he arrived at the Institute. He could only do ten after a month of sustained harassment. Everyone knew it was just a matter of time before they broke Rodney, but he proved surprisingly resilient. He seemed absolutely impervious to their screaming, and he showed no inclination to leave. In fact, he confessed to his classmates that there was nothing they could do to run him out. He had planned to come to the Institute since he was a little tyke. That was his phrase, "a little tyke." He fully intended to stay. He also said you didn't have to be able to do pushups to be tough. If you had it inside, you could take anything the cadre could dish out. That was before the cadre found out about Rodney Aimar and bugs. They let his classmates watch his Taming. They tied him naked to his rack, which they had pulled out onto the gallery where we were braced in a straight line to watch him. His frail body struggled against the ropes. None of us knew what they were going to do. Fox had gone to a bait farm and bought a thousand crickets. They emptied box after box of the crickets over the body of Rodney Aimar. They gagged him so his screams would not attract a tac officer or the Bear.

On his face, on his genitals, on his chest, until his body almost disappeared beneath the swarm. We did not see Rodney Aimar after that night.

* * *

I am not sure when I first heard the name of Bobby Bentley of Ocilla, Georgia, or when I became aware that the cadre had vowed to run him out of R Company by Thanksgiving. I heard his name often during plebe week, echoing along the galleries, a name shouted contemptuously by beardless corporals. Before I ever saw him I knew that they had selected him for the Taming. But Bobby Bentley was different from the rest. He refused to quit the Institute even under the most monstrous pressure. He was a study in courage I will never forget.

Later I would learn that many of the same boys who suffered most grievously in the plebe system became the most brutal and sadistic of upperclassmen. The Institute had allowed them to find the courage that was hidden within them. Beneath the fat and bone, beneath the terror, the blade of the system had hit upon an undiscovered vein of iron. The system had surprised and honored them by alerting them to the existence of an enormous interior strength and capacity for survival. I witnessed the magnificent courage of the weak and then watched them turn into the defiled images of their tormentors. But that happened to others; it did not happen to Bobby Bentley.

He was thin to the point of emaciation and looked as though his body had been assembled from the discarded produce of a vegetable garden: arms of celery, legs of asparagus, and spine of broccoli. But Bobby was not a physical weakling like Rodney Aimar. Bobby could do pushups all night long and hold his rifle straight out in front of him as long as any of us. His sin was a weakness of another variety. He had the unfortunate tendency during the height of sweat parties to urinate in his pants. This had happened once during plebe week, twice the next week, four times the next, until finally, he pissed in his pants every time an upperclassman screamed at him. Within a week he was the prime target for removal in R Company. The cadre swarmed all over him. They went to work on Bobby Bentley from Ocilla, Georgia, with a savagery that passed swiftly into legend. Even the most tolerant and easy-going members of the cadre recognized the fact that Bentley was an embarrassment to the integrity and efficacy of the system. He rapidly became a symbol to them, and it soon became a joke among the other companies that the R Company cadre could not run out a boy who pissed in his pants during every formation. It became a point of honor during the month of October that Bobby Bentley be removed from the Corps. The level of cruelty directed at this frail plebe was extraordinary, and there were boys who left our class because they could not stand to watch what the cadre was doing to him.

But there was something in Bentley the cadre had not reckoned with, something that we, his classmates, had not guessed. At some point during that first month, after pissing all over himself at each formation, after being humiliated beyond the limits of human decency and having drawn packs of upperclassmen who made it a sport to scream at Bobby Bentley and watch him foul himself—this plebe, in the middle of a most intense agony, made a simple, awesome decision. Bobby Bentley decided he was going to stay.

But the cadre could not allow someone afflicted in the manner of Bobby Bentley to survive the plebe system. If they could not run out someone like him, a boy who could not even control his bladder, then how could they strike fear in the hearts and minds of other marginal plebes? For Bobby was not only surviving the plebe system, he was surviving the Taming.

Beginning in September, there was a sweat party every night in that despised hour after dinner and before evening study period. Each night they made Bobby Bentley piss in his uniform pants. They put a bucket beside him in formation. They made him wear his raincoat on sunny days. They forced him to wear diapers and rubber pants, made him come to formation in a bathing suit, made him speak in baby talk, suck on a pacifier, and drink his milk from a baby bottle. He stimulated the cadre's creative powers as they conjured up new and inexorable methods to assault the human spirit. He became their obsession, their failure.

When all else failed, they turned his classmates against him, the plebes who were his brothers and protectors under the system. They encouraged us to show contempt for him, to abandon him. They rewarded us for betraying him.

And it was easy to hate him in those first months. I needed someone whom I could visibly and openly hate, so I joined my classmates in vilifying Bobby Bentley and soon the freshmen despised him as much as the upperclassmen did. We hated him for his weakness, his frailty, his stained pants, and the smell that was always on him. He was unclean and he wore the odor of urine like some debased cologne. Often they would not let him change his pants for days. His stench belied the silence or anonymity of his approach. In a line of plebes, you could always smell the presence of Bobby Bentley.

So the freshmen began refusing to give him shirt tucks or help him get ready for parade. We neglected to tell him of meetings with the cadre or the time of required formations. When we left the campus for general leave on Saturday night, we left him behind in the barracks. We assumed the roles of his torturers, his tamers, and heaped all our repressed fury at the cadre on him. We abandoned Bobby Bentley because we saw ourselves in his affliction and did not like to be reminded that he was one of us, that he, too, represented our class, our virility, our sad, abused history. In a school where your only solace comes from the support and friendship of your classmates, the solitude of Bobby Bentley became awe-inspiring, mythic, and unbearable. At first we thought we had created an island, an unclean one, an untouchable; but that was not true. We had become a cadre in reserve, a platoon of Iscariots. My classmates and I, with our zealous endorsement of the cadre's contempt for Bentley, had indeed helped create something unseen in the class of 1967.

We had created the first man in our class.

On a rainy night in October, they lined up all his classmates facing him. There were thirty-eight of us who had survived through the first month. They ordered us to spit in the face of Bobby Bentley. We all did it; all thirty-seven of us. When it was my turn, his face was covered with spit and his eyes were tightly closed. I spat. I spat into his face and went back to the end of the line.

By the middle of October the cadre was getting desperate. They ordered all the plebes to talk individually with Bentley. The Taming had failed. They wanted us to talk some sense into his head, to tell him that he was hurting the image of our class, that his presence was bringing the additional wrath of the cadre on all our heads. Ten of my classmates had preceded me before I entered his room on the third division to encourage him to quit the Institute. He was writing a letter home when I entered his room. Looking up, he smiled at me and asked me to sit down.

"Where's your roommate, Bobby?" I asked. There was a strong stench of urine in the room. He noticed that I noticed it.

"I haven't had a roommate since plebe week. No one wants to room with a guy who pisses in his pants," he answered. "They won't let me send my uniforms to the laundry anymore. Except for the two I wear to class."

"They told me to talk to you, Bobby."

"I know, Will."

"Why don't you just get the hell out of here, Bobby? I mean, you're just causing trouble for the rest of us. They're starting to give sweat parties in your name, man. And it's perfectly obvious you don't belong here. Three-year-old kids don't do what you do, Bobby. You ought to have more pride than to stick around wetting your pants in front of them."

"I'm sorry about that," he said. "I really am. But I just can't help it, Will. It's embarrassing. I feel terrible about it. The doctors say it's nerves. Nerves. Every night I tell myself that tomorrow will be different, that I won't do it tomorrow. But every day's the same. I'm as disgusted with myself as the cadre is. I don't blame you or them for wanting me out."

"Then why don't you go?"

"Because it's my choice to stay. It's not yours and it's not theirs."

"You don't belong here, Bobby."

"My daddy paid his money just like everybody else's daddy."

"That's not what I mean and you know it."

"The other freshmen scream at me when they come up to talk to me, Will. At least most of them do. They come up to my room and treat me like they were the first sergeant. They call me pussy and dumbhead. Alexander even slapped me when I told him I was staying. But they don't know what it's like to be me. I don't blame them, you see. I'd do the same thing and say the same thing if I were them. I just can't help my nerves. It's just so embarrassing. I get this feeling in my stomach every time I hear the bugle blow at reveille. I know it's going to start again. I keep telling myself to take it one day at a time, not to let them get me down, that I can take anything for nine months. I need to prove to myself that I'm as tough as they are. Do you understand that, Will?"

"No."

"Then why are you here, Will?"

"Because I'm an asshole. And I'm sorry I came up here to bother you, Bobby. I would never have done something like this last year. I wasn't like this last year. I'm sorry. I'm really sorry."

"Does your roommate St. Croix want me to leave?"

"No, I don't think so, Bobby. He's afraid that if you leave, they'll start concentrating on him."

Bobby Bentley laughed, and I realized that I had never seen him laugh before, never seen most of my classmates laugh or even smile. I left that room feeling an excruciating shame for having willingly embraced my role as an inquisitor representing the cadre. I vowed that from that night on I was not going to be one of Bobby Bentley's problems. I certainly had enough of my own.

Three days later the entire freshman class of R Company met in the first division alcove room to discuss the problem of Bobby Bentley. It was the first official meeting we were allowed to conduct without the supervision of the cadre. It was our first moment of institutional democracy and the first time I had seen many of the faces of my classmates relaxed and unbraced.

John Alexander, by far the sharpest knob militarily, conducted the meeting with brisk efficiency. In the very first month, he had emerged as the natural leader of our class, and the cadre was already saying that he was excellent material for regimental commander. He began the meeting with a voice indicating a high seriousness of purpose: "At ease, men. We all know why we're here tonight. I've talked with several members of the cadre and they want us to help figure a way to run Bentley out of the Corps. He's hurting the image of our class and specifically he's hurting the image of R Company. Now I know all of us are in agreement that we want to prove that the class of 1967 is the best class ever to come through the Institute. In order to prove that, men, we just can't have a freshman peeing in his damn pants like a baby every time he comes to formation. I have a suggestion and I'd like to run it by you. I suggest we go up to his room right after this meeting. We go up there as a class and tell him that we voted unanimously that he's not worthy to be in our class. Then let's pack his bags and escort him bodily to the front gate. If he tries to resist, then we might have to become a little physical."

"Good, idea, John," a voice rang out.

"All right," three others agreed.

"Are there any objections?" Alexander asked.

I tried to speak, but I remained silent. In silence, I had long ago decided, was my deliverance. I wanted to walk through the plebe year unnoticed, drawing no controversy, and making no enemies. I had seen what the cadre did to plebes who made themselves too visible. The freshmen in that room were working themselves up into a mob. We were about to break out of the room when a voice objected.

"I object."

We turned toward the voice, and I got my first view of Mark Santoro, sitting in a chair beside the window. Behind me stood the musclebound freshman I had heard some of my classmates call "Pig." They were the only two Yankees left among the freshmen in R Company.

Mark slowly turned around in his chair, pointed a large finger at John Alexander, and said, motioning fiercely, "Get off the desk, motherfucker. I get nervous when people try to tell me things standing on that desk."

It was the first time I had noticed that Alexander was addressing us while standing on the same desk on which Maccabee had delivered his Hell Night speech.

"What's eating you, Santoro?" Alexander said, though some of the command had gone out of his voice.

"You're eating me, you Southern chicken shit. You and the rest of these king cocks from below the Mason-Dixon line."

Rising to his feet, Mark folded his arms as Pig moved around to his side to demonstrate his support of what his roommate was about to say.

"Pig and I have talked it over. We think Bobby Bentley has more guts than any other knob in this company."

"He's a waste, Santoro," Alexander said.

"When did you make corporal, Alexander?" Mark sneered. "When did you become a member of the cadre? How come you appointed yourself the guy who shits all over one of his classmates?"

"I've been talking to Mr. Maccabee and Mr. Blasingame about the problem of Bentley. I don't know why they chose to talk to me, but I think they felt like I knew what the rest of you guys were thinking. I'm only trying to help this class as a whole. They're giving the R Company knobs a chance to exercise a little leadership. They're leaving this to us. We've got a chance to earn their respect."

"It's their job to run freshmen out of school," Mark said. "It's our job to protect our classmates."

"He doesn't belong in this school," Jim Massengale said.

"He makes our class look like shit," Webb Stockton agreed.

"We've got to get rid of the Gerber baby."

"If we don't get his ass out of here, they'll take it out on us."

I said nothing but got up from the floor and motioned to Tradd. We started to walk out of the room.

"Where are you going, fellow?" Alexander asked sharply. It was a measure of my success at anonymity that Alexander, that most ambitious of freshmen, did not know my name.

"To my room," I said.

"The meeting's not over," Alexander said.

"It is for me."

"For me, too," Tradd said. "That boy's got enough problems without having to worry about his classmates. We've done enough to him already, and I think this meeting is ludicrous."

"You do, eh, St. Croix?" Alexander said. "Well, some people think you don't belong in this school any more than Bentley does. We ought to run both of you out of here tonight."

"Alexander, tell me something," I said.

"What do you want?"

"I'd like a piece of information from you. And you're the only person in this room who can give it."

"Well, hurry up and ask it," he said, looking at his watch. "We've got to decide what to do before taps."

"The question is this: Is it very hard to breathe when you have your nose stuck up the first sergeant's asshole?"

Tradd and I walked out with the laughter cascading behind us as the meeting broke up.

There were some significant results of that evening: Bentley would not be run out by his own classmates; a friendship began among Mark and Pig and me; and I had made my first open enemy in John Alexander.

After the meeting of the freshmen, the fury of the cadre rose against Bobby Bentley almost daily. And the laughter of the other upperclassmen grew more shrill and derisive as they came from the other three battalions to witness the frenzied efforts of the R Company cadre to run him out of the Corps. It grew deadly serious and assumed dimensions of insensate cruelty that broke the bounds of the plebe system as we had known it until that time.

Yet as the pressure on Bentley became more agonizing and grotesque, something also began to happen to the attitude of the R Company freshmen in general. In our collective unconscious, by slow accretions of awareness, we grew proud that Bobby Bentley was taking everything they could dish out, everything imaginable. They were beating him with their fists and standing on his spine as he did pushups. They flogged his ass with brooms and swords until it bled. They would not let him eat or sleep. Each night he would pass out in the shower room after they had their way with him. Often there were five or ten upperclassmen concentrating all their perverted energies on Bobby Bentley while the others took care of the rest of us.

An awareness was born among his classmates in those weeks that he was one of us, that Bobby Bentley, our classmate, was a gentle guy, much too gentle for the Institute, that he was showing a quality of courage beyond the strongest of us, and that in his own quiet, determined way, he may just have been the toughest freshman ever to walk through the Gates of Legrand. We began to be ashamed of ourselves for how we had treated him and to talk openly of our admiration for him. Soon he had become a symbol to all of us. He was braver than any of us. He was the best of us. He had endured over thirty days of the Taming, and it was the cadre who was showing signs of breaking.

The beauty of the plebe system, the one awesome virtue of that corrupt rite of passage, was made manifest as we began to gather around him and protect him. The brotherhood was taking effect. When they called for Bobby Bentley, it was as though they were calling to all of us, and our commitment to him deepened as we witnessed his debasement and his loneliness.

He made it past the Thanksgiving break. And the Taming went on. In December they called him out of the rack line, separating him as they always did from the main body of plebes to illustrate the extent of his abnormality. We watched as Bobby left our line and followed Fox and Newman into the shadows of the stairwell. But this night when they called for Bentley, Mark left the line without permission and followed right behind him, followed by Pig, by Tradd, by John Kinnell, by Webb Stockton, by Jim Massengale, by me, by all of us. And when they told him to hit the cement and pump out fifty pushups, all thirty-eight of us hit the cement simultaneously. The cadre went berserk. They quelled that small inconsequential revolt with ease as they dispersed us into smaller groups, shivering along the gallery. But it was our first indication of the strength, the formidable, irrefutable strength that comes from solidarity.

That night after taps, Bobby Bentley sneaked into the room of every freshman and thanked us for what we had done and begged us not to do it again. It would only cause trouble for us, he said. He wept when he came to our room and began thanking Tradd and me for the meaningless gesture. As I listened to him cry, his head against my

169

mattress, I wanted to embrace him in the darkness and beg his forgiveness for having spit in his face. But as usual, I did nothing. Many times I would think of the proper thing to do but only rarely could I do it.

It was on December 16, five days before the Christmas break, as they herded us under the stairwell, we remembered hearing rumors that this was the night they were going to make sure that he did not return to the Institute after Christmas. But the cadre did not know that we, the freshmen, were ready for them. We had spent the whole day passing secret communiqués among each other. We had planned to divert the attention of the cadre from Bentley to the rest of us, and it was surprising how quickly we adapted ourselves to strategies that disrupted and infuriated and sabotaged the designs and conspiracies of the cadre even if they were only temporary victories.

Again they forced Bobby Bentley out of the long line of plebes, stationing themselves at intervals along the line to make sure we did not follow him again. They made him face us, the thirty-seven against the one. His eyes were luminous with resignation, with the accumulated, embittering humiliation that was forced on him every single night of his life at the Institute. He met the helplessness of our collective gaze with the helplessness of his singular one.

Fox and Newman walked unhurriedly up to him. Silently they stood on each side of him, their mouths pressed close to his ears. When Blasingame gave the signal, they cut loose with screams that made all of us jump in the line. As always, urine poured out of Bobby Bentley's pants, made a pool between his legs. We could hear the piss running on the cement.

Fox and Newman kept screaming, "Piss, piss, piss, piss, you fucking pussy."

Then they stopped. They stopped when they heard it, when they heard us. You could tell the sound puzzled the cadre as the gallery went quiet. The sound they heard was the sound of the other thirty-seven freshmen pissing in their own pants, in affirmation of our allegiance to Bobby Bentley of Ocilla, Georgia. They heard the sound of urine running all along the gallery. I pissed for all I was worth. The urine was warm on my leg. It was the grandest piss I would ever piss in my life, the prince of pisses. All along the line of freshmen, puddles of urine formed by our shoes as we pissed together, in unison, an indivisible tribe, as brothers, as a class. It was a joyous piss, a sacramental piss, a transcendent one.

170

When Bobby Bentley saw what we were doing he began crying, no, not crying, he was screaming, he was coming apart, astonished and moved by our embracing of him, our championing of him. He raised his hands to us in thanks. Some of us cried to hear him; some of us cried when we saw him lift his hands in that melancholy inconsolable gesture of gratitude for the impure, overdue mercy of the formerly merciless.

The cadre recovered quickly and forced us to lie face down in our own urine. They rubbed our noses in it, made us roll in it, soak it into our uniforms, rub it into our hair and faces until they were nauseated and repulsed by the stink of us all. We did pushups until we dropped exhausted against the cement and could not rise and felt their kicks and punches land on our backs and necks. Some of us were vomiting, then all of us were vomiting. And I tell you there was a shimmering beauty and an inexorable nobility to those thirty-seven boys who rolled in piss and vomit as an act of contrition toward Bobby Bentley.

The cadre was all over us, but in those moments we had stepped out of their range of control. As we rolled in urine and vomit, in that hideous, stinking baptism, we rolled together as a class for the first time, as though controlled by a single, invincible will, and on that night, they could not hurt us, could not touch us, could not even approach us in the ecstasy and amplitude of our solidarity.

On this night we had ceased being plebes and had united together into an inseparable, undefeatable band. My joy was the joy of the tribe; my love was the love of the group, roaring and brawling and singing out in a single defiant voice. It was the first night we had defeated the fourth class system. We were no longer plebes on that gallery. We had become brothers, we had become men, revolutionaries, and there was nothing on that night they could do to stop us. The victory belonged to the class of 1967 and to Bobby Bentley of Ocilla, Georgia.

But at formation the next evening, the second battalion commander and the regimental executive officer walked up behind Bobby Bentley, whispered something to him, and led him out of the barracks in the darkness. He did not return for evening study period and was marked absent at the all-in check at taps. Nor did he appear the next day at reveille or at lunch. When we checked his room after mess that night, we found that someone had packed his luggage and taken his uniforms. The upperclassmen did not know exactly what

171

happened, but they said he had required special attention. Two days before the Christmas break he withdrew from school and never came back to say good-bye. Some said he left because he felt ashamed that he had implicated his classmates in his predicament. But there was another rumor that sounded far more sinister. The senior next door intimated to Tradd and me that he suspected Bentley had become a project of a secret organization called The Ten. Since the R Company cadre had failed to remove Bentley from the Corps, The Ten had decided to move. No one could survive the attention of The Ten. That was the rumor, that was the legend, although the senior was quick to admit that no one really knew if The Ten existed or not.

There were thirty-seven of us from R Company who had survived until Christmas. Six of us would decide not to return after the holidays. We began the cold season with thirty-one plebes and the worst of the system behind us.

18

These, then, are the memories of my nine long months as a plebe. In the barracks I learned much of what there was to know about my times, my unconscionable century. I grew accustomed to a climate of outrage and atrocity. I knew well the vernacular of suffering, and all the language and canons of the Institute had dissolved in my bloodstream. I understood the system by January, and I acquiesced to its laws by remaining. I was beginning to feel I had lived my whole life in enemy country. I felt they were killing off all that was good about me, but I didn't know what to do about it. I would do anything but quit.

So I retreated within myself. I tried to measure the magnitude of the felonies committed in the name of discipline and tradition, but I could not assign a value to the ruin of boys. I knew about the terrorism of the human spirit and understood that ruthless, immoral forces had planted alien flags in my soul. The plebe system gave cruelty a good name, disguised sadism in the severe raiment of duty. There was a field of energy to the cadre's meanness. I felt the puissance and evil of their thoughtless, callow maggotry. I would never forgive them. At the Institute, you had one year of terror and three of recovery, but I never recovered. I only learned the utter fatuity of resistance. Something in the eyes of plebes changed from the month of September to the month of June. Something in my eyes changed for all time.

All these crimes and dismemberments my friends and classmates find diminished and neutralized in memory. There is merit in forgetfulness. It is one of the gentlest forms of healing—and one of the most dangerous. But I am a prisoner of memory, and I have needed to clear out the debris of that year for many years. The year had too much to do with the kind of men my classmates and I became and the kind we did not become. Not one of my classmates will agree with many of my observations or conclusions about the system. They will say I was embittered, and I was. They will say that I did not belong there, and they will be right. They will say that I am trying to hurt the Institute, and they will be right again. But they are not prisoners of these memories as I am. I am describing the apprenticeship of a passionate dissenter. I am describing my education and the path that led me to manhood.

* * *

What was monstrous in September was normal by January. I returned to winter darkness, to icy winds along the gallery, to basketball games, and midterm exams. There were sweat parties every night after mess, abuse when we ate our food, hazing, sadness. Once again we endured the humiliations of the system, only by now we were veterans. Each time we walked into the barracks it was an act of singular courage. Each time we left our rooms we chanced an unpleasant encounter on the galleries. Some of us made it; some of us did not. It made very little difference which in the long run, but I was curious about the nature of both the survivors and the quitters.

Three more R Company freshmen left in January. They discovered at mess one morning that Lawrence Masters was allergic to tomato juice. At mess, you never made the mistake of admitting you did not like a certain food. I had refused to take any spinach when it was passed to me during the first month of school. I ate four plates of spinach when the cadre realized I loathed it. I developed a canny appetite for all food after that, but an allergy was a different thing. No plebe had yet offered that excuse. Fox forced Masters to drink eleven glasses of tomato juice. Masters was at Roper Hospital for two days in intensive care. For a time, they thought he might die. He did not, but he never returned to R Company.

Albie Boles was ranked fifth in the class on the first semester rank sheets. He performed well militarily and academically and seemed to be one of those kids who navigated through the plebe system unscathed. At three in the morning one Thursday, Albie woke the entire barracks screaming, "Help me! Help me! Please help me!" He was dreaming, but he began to have the same dream every night. In the dream, the cadre members would surround him, armed with icepicks and butcher knives, then move toward him, smiling as they came. Each night he woke up screaming out the same words. During the day, he was an exemplary freshman, but each night, the cadre approached closer and closer and his appeals for help became more desperate and unhinged. His screams were unnerving, and they finally forced him to take a medical discharge.

I witnessed the breaking of Howie Snyders. He was standing across from me during a sweat party after church one Sunday. We were forced to hold our M-1 rifles out at arm's length while the cadre kept watch and threatened us if we dropped the rifles. Eventually, if you held the rifle out long enough, you lost control of the muscles in your upper arms no matter how strong you were. The weak boys could not hold the rifle out very long, just as they could not do pushups very long or run very far. Howie Snyders was always dropping his M-1 to the pavement and always receiving demerits for gross abuse of government property.

Howie also wore his fear too openly. He had a luckless, timorous face like a hamster's. The upperclassmen could smell his fear. It was as pungent to them as the smell of fish about to turn. They were attracted to this terror; it stimulated their own cruelty. On this particular Sunday, Howie had dropped his rifle five consecutive times and he had drawn the company of three upperclassmen. When he put out the rifle the sixth time, something terrible happened to Howie Snyders. I had seen freshmen come apart before, but I had never seen anything like this. Something attacked his nervous system like a virulent toxin. His entire body went into convulsions and he lay moaning on the gallery as though he was having an epileptic fit. His eyes rolled back in his head, saliva ran from his mouth, tears streamed from his eyes, and he bounced across the concrete like a beached fish. The cadre began chanting above him, "Die, die, die, die." But one of them—Wentworth, the company exec, I think, but it really doesn't matter—put a broomstick in his mouth to make sure he would not swallow his tongue. It was not epilepsy and the doctors insisted that there was no physical dysfunction responsible for those symptoms. But Howie started to display the same symptoms during every sweat party on the galleries, until one night he was honorably discharged after biting off a piece of his tongue. Newman claimed the piece of Howie's tongue as a souvenir and preserved it in formaldehyde and displayed it proudly on his desk.

In February, Tradd and I moved into the fourth division alcove room with Mark Santoro and Dante Pignetti. It was an arrangement I had considered for a long time. I had noticed that during sweat parties the upperclassmen treated Pig and Mark differently than they treated the rest of us. I wanted to align my destiny and that of Tradd with the two strongest boys in our class, the only two whom the cadre feared physically. In the company boxing competition, Pig and Mark had destroyed several members of the senior class before Captain Mudge issued a memorandum declaring freshmen ineligible for the competition. Still, the point had been made, and I heard the cadre's voices change as they approached Pig and Mark on the galleries. If I could not frighten men physically myself, I wanted to establish solid allegiances with those who could. Pig and Mark were having trouble academically and I suggested that Tradd and I could help them in their course work. They could help us by keeping people like Fox and Newman out of our rooms during evening study period. We met at Big John's bar down on East Bay Street and agreed to the arrangement. We sat at the bar and told each other about ourselves and drank a pitcher of cold beer. It was my first beer on tap and I always associate the taste of draught beer with the faces of my three roommates. We talked about the plebe system and about the cadre. I had not laughed so hard since I had come to the Institute. Nor had I felt so safe.

I began to feel easier in the tenor and pace of those winter days. I played on the best freshman basketball team in the history of the Institute. There were seven of us in September, but by March only two of us remained, Reuben Clapsaddle and I. The others were victims of the plebe system and had left to display their talents at other colleges. I had begun to enjoy my classes and the silence of the library, with its dusty stacks and the smiling, perfumed woman who checked out books. On weekends, I explored the superb handsome streets of Charleston and watched the great freighters unloading their fragrant cargoes along the wharves. I decided that even though I had chosen the wrong school I had chosen the right city. I had no doubts then, and none now, that I spent four years in the loveliest city on the continent and that some indelible mark of civilization, some passionate intimacy with form and beauty, would remain with me always if only I were vigilant enough, if only I were resolute in my intention to assimilate the resonances and intimations of that exquisite city. I hungered for culture, yet had no idea what culture was or how to go about obtaining it or how I would know it once I had it in my grasp. I joined the Ballet Society and the Dock Street Theater. I attended performances with Tradd and his mother, Abigail, and afterward would listen to them discuss the performances. I would memorize what they had said and write letters to my mother telling her exactly the same thing, knowing that she would be pleased that her son was not only becoming a man but a cultured man as well. During intermission at the Dock Street Theater, Abigail, Tradd, and I would sit on the jostling board in the moon-brindled courtyard and Abigail would tell us about plays she had acted in at the same theater before she had married Commerce. Afterward we would walk back to the St. Croix mansion, the city unbearably lovely in the moonlight, and sometimes we would drink coffee at her sister's house on the curve of Church Street. Tradd and I would walk on each side of her, each of us holding one of Abigail's hands, and she would tell us stories of her childhood, of her trips to Europe, and her voice was shy in the darkness. There would be the smell of crushed narcissus on the sidewalk and lights shining from the night tables of second-story windows. We would pass by Catfish Row and the shop of Elizabeth O'Neill Verner, with her soft watercolors of her native city framed in the windows. We would walk in the cold, the collars of our uniform overcoats pulled high against our necks, and pass Terrell's dress shop and the house where Washington slept and the one where Dubose Hayward wrote and the one where Ed and Kitty Holt, Tradd's cousins, lived. It was the way I wanted college to be and I knew that I was absorbing something valuable though I did not know quite how. The refinement and dignity of those nights sustained me through the long nights in the barracks. I thought this was the education I desired and that in Tradd's mother I had found a woman who embodied every quality of grace and intelligence and virtue that I would look for in a wife. In Tradd, I thought I had found the gentleness and integrity that

176

I always required in my best friends and seldom displayed myself. And by enlisting Pig and Mark, I was adding strength and virility to the composition of the room. And though I did not know it then, I was gaining two of the finest, most loyal friends I would ever have.

By March, I had learned to live with the plebe system. My attitude had become one of almost Zen-like acceptance and resignation. Though I was still afraid, I had adjusted myself to nine months of misery. And I felt I was leading a lucky life in the barracks. I was not a victim and the cadre had not selected me for the Taming. I got the same as any other ordinary cadet, no more, no less. They didn't like me very much, but that bothered me little, since I liked them not at all.

Periodically, I worried about the effect of the plebe system on Tradd. He had already picked up the nickname "The Honey Prince" from the cadre, and not a single day went by without their referring to his effeminate manner and his high-pitched, aristocratic accent. They had toughened him during the year, but there were nights when he would be close to tears as he studied. "Faggot, faggot," they would scream at him. "You want to suck me off, faggot?" they would shout, unbuttoning their pants for him. When I voiced my concerns to Tradd about the cadre running him out, he calmed me by saying with extraordinary frankness, "Will, they know they'd be in trouble if they ran me out. They loathe me, I'm sure, but they also know I'm from an old Charleston family. That's something you don't understand, but it is true. If I told them I was going to leave, the cadre would beg me to stay. But I need to prove I can take everything. I need that for myself. It has nothing to do with them. I don't consider them gentlemen and they are all beneath our contempt."

Tradd was right. Though his passage through the system was brutal, the cadre only went so far with him, and then, as if they had signed a secret concordance, they would pull back from him in common recognition of their limits.

In the first week of March, however, it was not Tradd's survival that was in question. It was mine. I had tried hard for anonymity in R Company and had achieved it. I had perfected a bland personality, a bland appearance, and a bland record. Most upperclassmen outside the cadre did not even know my name and did not recognize me if they passed me on their way to class. Soon, all of them would know both my name and face, and all of them would concur that I had no place in R Company or the Corps of Cadets. I had made

177

my first egregious error of judgment as a plebe, and I would pay dearly for that error. I had published a poem in *The Guidon*, the school's literary magazine.

The Guidon had more to do with the death of literature than its propagation. Cadets at the Institute mishandled the English language with a heroic facility. I had written several poems for *The Guidon* in the first semester and they had not attracted the attention of a single upperclassman. Among them was a rhapsodic ode to Thomas Wolfe commemorating a pilgrimage I had made to Asheville the previous summer. The poem did no harm to Wolfe, but it was not helpful to the language. The second poem was an evocation of spring, a highly original topic, rare among young poets, and the conclusion any fair-minded reader might draw from scanning those twelve meager lines was that if I had really appreciated springtime I would never have debased its memory with that poem. But the two poems gave me great pleasure and compared to the other poems in the first issue of *The Guidon*, I suppose they looked downright Miltonic. I saw myself in a wholly new light. The jock-poet, I would whisper reverentially, or the poet-jock when my mood changed.

But when the second issue was going to press, I decided to show off my heretofore carefully concealed gift of humor. I had written the new poem after a particularly harsh sweat party in January and shown it to Mark, Pig, and Tradd. They were unanimous in their praise, and Pig said I did not have a hair on my ass if I didn't publish it in *The Guidon*. I had very few hairs on my ass but wanted to disguise that fact for as long as possible. I thought the poem was funny and thought the upperclassmen would think so too.

I did not even know *The Guidon* had come out until noon formation on Wednesday in the first week of March. I was bracing, standing in my squad, and waiting for my sergeant to inspect me. He was screaming at Jim Massengale, who stood directly on my right. A senior private named Bill Toons walked up holding the magazine. He looked at my nametag. Then he looked at a page in the open magazine. He looked at my nametag again, then back to the magazine. "I ain't believing you wrote this, McLean. I ain't fucking believing you wrote this and you're still alive."

Quigley, my squad sergeant, moved over and started reading from the magazine. He read it as quickly as he could. I calculated about one word every ten seconds. He looked up at my nametag. Maccabee walked up behind me holding a rolled-up copy of the magazine. He hit me in the head with it, a stinging blow that knocked my cap into the next squad of plebes.

"We don't let knobs run this kind of shit, McLean," Maccabee said. "Are you trying to run some shit on Big R? Pop off, boy."

"No, sir."

Wentworth, the company exec, walking up with his copy of *The Guidon*, shook his head sadly and said, "Mr. McLean, my classmates from some other companies read this to me when I was in my accounting class. They don't think the knobs in R Company have the proper respect for their superiors. Do you have respect for me, Mr. McLean? Pop off."

"Yes, sir."

"How much, dumbhead? Pop off."

"Oh, a tremendous amount, sir."

"I ain't believing he wrote this," Toons repeated. "He wouldn't have lasted five minutes in the old corps. Our first sergeant would have eaten this gauldy knob for breakfast, Maccabee."

"What's the meaning of this, McLean? Pop off," Maccabee said.

"Sir, it was a little joke, sir."

"You think this is funny, wad-waste? Pop off."

"Yes, sir. No, sir. I don't know, sir," I answered.

"Would you read it for the benefit of all of R Company, Mr. McLean?" Maccabee said. "I'd like you to go up to the front of the company and read this loud and clear."

He took me by the arm and led me to the front of the company, where I stood braced beside Blasingame, facing the three platoons of R Company. He handed me a copy of the magazine and made an announcement to R Company. "Gentlemen, we just discovered that we have a cadet recruit Shakespeare in Romeo Company and I've invited him to give a poetry reading before we march to mess."

My voice broke three times during the recitation. But Maccabee made me begin again until I recited the poem without a flaw. The entire barracks was silent, and the cadets of the other three companies listened intently as I read.

"Dedicated to the Cadre of Romeo Company

*"The dreams of youth are pleasant dreams
of women, whiskey, and the sea.
Last night I dreamt I was a dog
who found an upperclassman tree.*

179

*"The dreams of youth are silly dreams
of toads and other lowly species.
My cadre is a special breed
of strutting, screaming, human feces."*

I do not think the reaction of the cadre against me would have been so severe except for a couple of factors. First, the other three companies cracked up. The barracks filled with laughter as the upperclassmen in the other companies shouted derisively at R Company. Then Lancey Hemphill, the center on the basketball team, loped up behind me, put his arm around my shoulders, and shouted, "That's my man, Will. Piss all over these tight-assed dicks. Fuck Big R."

He shot the finger at R Company as he stood there with his arm around my shoulder.

But worst of all, the R Company plebes fell apart laughing. Pig was laughing uncontrollably, and cadre members were racking his ass to no avail. Pig's laughter infected Mark, who exploded with laughter in the first squad of the last platoon. One whole squad of freshmen lost control in the second platoon, and they passed it along to their entire platoon. The entire population of fourth battalion was laughing and mocking the R Company cadre. The cadre, in turn, was looking at me as if I were a reincarnation of Bobby Bentley. I could not imagine a more untenable situation. All this, I thought, to prove that my ass was not hairless.

Fox and Newman pushed me off the quadrangle and shoved me along the gallery until we reached the stairwell. About twelve curious upperclassmen from R Company followed. Fox, aware of his audience, jerked me by the collar and slammed my head against the stone pillar. He then punched me in the sternum and slapped me twice across the face. My anger flared and he caught it in my eyes.

"Come on, motherfucker. Throw a punch. You're gone anyway and I'd like to see it happen now as later. Throw a punch. Hit me, you fucking pussy," he said.

"A fucking jock," Newman said. "A fucking waste of a jock. Shits on his classmates by going to practice when we go to parade."

"Jocks shouldn't be allowed in this school," a voice added.

"I bet McLean doesn't even know his plebe knowledge," a voice said.

"He better know it," Fox said, punching my chest again.

"Rack that fucking chin in, waste-product. And tell me. How's the cow?"

"Sir, she walks, she talks, she's full of chalk, the lacteal fluid extracted from the female of the bovine species is highly prolific to the nth degree, sir," I answered by rote one of the formulae that passes for scholarship at military colleges.

"What is vomit, douchebag?" Fox whispered. "You better know it, fuckstick. You better know every piece of plebe knowledge or I'm going to beat the shit out of you right now."

"Sir, vomit is a putrescent liquid of a greenish yellow color often projected from the noble stomachs of dauntless upperclassmen when they discern the nauseous, repulsive, and monstrously assembled faces of plebes such as Will McLean, sir. Vomit is composed of three parts gross slime, four parts rotted meat, one part curdled acid, and ten parts from the diarrhea cans of West Point, sir."

"Would a plebe eat vomit, dumbhead? Pop off," Newman sneered.

"Not without salt and pepper and full bottle of catsup, sir," I responded.

"What would a plebe not eat, McLean?" a voice I did not recognize asked.

"Sir, a plebe would not eat a hemorrhoid out of the asshole of a naval admiral, a wart off the pecker of an army general, the first sergeant's mother, or any food prepared at the Institute mess hall."

The last bugle blew and I heard the battalion commander issue the order to commence to the mess hall.

Fox hit me again in the chest and raised his hand to slap my face again.

Newman interfered with the blow and said, "Not now, Gardiner. Wait."

"Wait for what? I want this fucker now."

"Wait for tonight," Newman said with a sneer, "for the Taming."

19

They broke me that night and they broke me quickly. It did not take them long to find my point of vulnerability. I did not fear heights or insects or open spaces. I feared them; I feared the cadre. My terror was in facing them alone, without my friends and classmates around me. I could not bear the isolation and their rabid, singular attention. When the system was impersonal and inclusive, I could bear it; but as soon as they specified me, I came apart at the seams. I would rather be called knob or dumbhead or shitface than McLean. I do not want my enemies ever to know my name again. That knowledge is in itself a violation of your sovereignty. When they call for you by name, then the system has changed and the vendetta has begun.

They called me out of the line of plebes when I returned from mess that night. All during the day I concentrated on being brave before them. I broke much quicker than any of my classmates before me. I broke, and I carry that night with me.

There were fourteen of them in the shower room when I entered. Fox pushed me to the center of the room. They rushed at me suddenly. It was as though a piece of meat had been thrown into a kennel of underfed dogs. I thought of dogs all evening. The cruel insensate faces of dogs near mine, the stench of their breath, the movement of their tongues, the quickness of their lean, precipitate movements against me. I had entered a country of dogs, with all their hunger and training and instinct turned murderously on me alone.

Fox and Newman were smoking cigarettes and put them out on my arms. I stifled a cry and felt the first implacable surge of the cadre as they surrounded me, each man screaming as he came, each man with his own obscenity and his own demands, with his own questions, his own needs and appeasements. The sound overwhelmed me. Two of them were screaming in my ears, four of them in front of my face, four or five of them behind me, all screaming.

"Right face," someone would scream.

"Left face," another would scream simultaneously.

"About face," also simultaneously.

"Give me fifty pushups."

"Recite the guard orders."

Hands were ripping my shirt. Punches were coming in from all sides. I was hurled down in the pushup position. The lights were too bright and I was disoriented. I was having trouble thinking. I did a hundred pushups. I did another hundred. Four of them lay down beside me, screaming in my ears even as I counted out the pushups. Their faces lay on the floor beside mine, and I could see their mouths and tongues and feel their saliva on my skin. Newman knelt on my back with his knees, leaned over and screamed for me to do another hundred pushups with him on top of me. I tried to rise, feeling his knees dig into my spine, listening to the amazing noise that centered around my head, angry at the lights, groaning now, trying to rise, the lights, the shouts, the unyielding pressures, the derangement, the unraveling. They jerked me up. I was put against the wall bracing, all fourteen of them still with me, all fourteen of their mouths pressing in upon me, all of them within inches of my eyes. I was handed a rifle, which I held out stiff-armed in front of me. They forced me into a deep knee bend and one of them slid a broomstick behind my knees as I went down. I held the broomstick between my thighs and calves at the joint behind the knees. It cut off the flow of blood to the legs, and in thirty seconds I fainted for the first time in my life. They threw water on me, revived me, stood me up with the rifle again, forced me to squat again, the pressure of the stick, blackness again. The second time I fainted, my face hit the shower room floor and I rose with blood in my mouth. Again the rifle and the broomstick and the shouts. Again I fainted. Five times I fainted. The screams again. The blood in my mouth. The light-killing swell of noise and I thought someone had turned off the lights, but then the lights came again in a blaze, a terrible migraine of light. And then I thought there was silence but the cadre was still around me, still screaming. I could not breathe and thought I was being strangled slowly, as though someone had covered my face with some deadly silk. I gasped for air and with the gasp came the first sob. And with the first sob came an absolute shattering, the death of my own small inconsequential civilization on that shower room floor.

The cadre was ready for the breakdown. It renewed their appetite and rewarded their forbearance. It signaled that the end was approaching.

"Cry, you pussy."

"Cry, you fucking baby."

"Aww, little baby wants his mama."

"Poor little baby boy."

"Cry, cry, cry, cry."

I broke down completely. I fell apart in front of them, beyond grief, beyond humiliation.

Then they came at me again. The rifle held straight out and the pressure of wood behind my knees. I fainted again. The flood of water over my face. Rising. Falling again.

The rifle and the confusion of the faces and the room and no asylum. The images of dogs and the fury of the pack as they shed the blood of the nineteen-year-old, as they assassinated the boy in me in one last savage feeding. I was sobbing uncontrollably now and begging them. I heard my voice and it was pleading with them. It was a voice asking for mercy.

"Please. Please don't. Not any more. I can't take any more."

Fox threw me on the floor and demanded that I lick his shoes. I licked them. I grasped his ankles and licked his shoes and licked my tears that fell on his shoes and begged him to stop. I would leave school that minute. But please, stop. I can't take any more. You've won. You've won.

I was kicked in the stomach and rolled over to Newman's shoes. I licked his shoes and other shoes and every shoe that was put beneath my mouth.

Then I heard more shouts, but I had heard shouting all night. The shoe I was licking was withdrawn and I heard a violent argument break out. The shower room was filling up with other men from other companies. I could not recognize them through the tears. I could not see or focus. I could not breathe, and the sobs still racked my body. I looked up again into the bright lights as the argument grew fiercer.

The varsity basketball team was there. They looked large on the basketball court, but in the tight confines of that shower room, they were huge, mythical.

Lancey Hemphill had Fox by the throat. The team and the cadre were screaming at each other now. Lancey saw me on the floor. He turned back to Fox and backhanded him like he was hitting a doll. There was movement among the R Company cadre toward Hemphill but not much. Lancey came over and lifted me into his arms. I put my arms around his neck and hid my eyes against his chest. I could not bear to let my teammates see me like this. I could not bear the pain on their faces as they looked at me.

Lancey stopped at the door and said to the cadre, "Anybody says a fucking word to McLean from now until the end of the year, I'm going to the Bear and tell him what went on in here tonight. Fuck R Company and fuck the Taming. I'll also beat the living shit out of every one of you duckbutts and my teammates will help me. You don't ever fuck with a basketball jock. What a bunch of chicken shits. What fucking chickens."

And Lancey Hemphill carried me like a child to my room.

I did not feel my roommates undress me. I felt the cold cloths on my face. I felt Mark's hands rubbing the tense muscles in my back and neck. I lay in my bed sweating and sobbing, but the sobs were tearless. I had no more to give that night. Tradd wrung out my uniform in the sink and Pig gave me a long, slow sponge bath, then rubbed me down with alcohol. I wanted to thank them. I remember that distinctly, but my lips could not form a single word. For three hours, I did not move but lay with my eyes open and unfocused on the ceiling. I was aware of people approaching me to look at me, to touch me, to whisper fervent words of support. My classmates came into the room one at a time to check in on me, to touch base, to tell me they understood: John Kinnell and Jim Massengale and Harvey Peak and Webb Stockton and John Alexander and all the rest. I heard them whispering to my roommates, and I heard Pig vowing revenge. All during evening study period I heard the hushed voices of angry boys, but they seemed to belong to another country that did not affect me.

Before taps, I began crying again, and the tears were real and flowing once more. I forced myself to stop, then began again. Each time I closed my eyes I saw them on me. I could not escape their voices, and my mouth tasted of the sweetish, nauseating oils of shoe polish. My tongue was discolored.

Pig came up and wiped my face with a washcloth. I fell asleep with him saying, "We'll get them back, paisan. We'll get them back."

"All this for a fucking poem," Mark said.

I did not hear the bugle play taps nor feel Mark cover me up with a blanket, nor Tradd remove my shirt and shoes. I did not see Pig set the clock for three in the morning. I did not hear the last conversation of my roommates before they went to sleep.

I awoke at half-past two and walked over to the sink for a glass of water. My whole body ached. I washed my face and examined the bruises on my body. I put an ointment on the two cigarette burns. I drank two more glasses of water.

I saw my face in the mirror, and it surprised me. I examined that grim, melancholy look. What has happened to me and will I ever be the same? I thought. They had transfigured my face in a single night. I had survived a day that would make me into a person I was never meant to be, because of what they had done to me, what they had said to me, what they had made me do. A new human was born in those two violent hours in the shower room. They had debased me, lessened me, and I had left something of irreplaceable value out there with the pack. I had lost something of inestimable worth, but I had finally learned all there was to know about the plebe system and my role in it. I had learned much of what I would need to know when I left the Gates of Legrand.

They had taught me about power and the abuse of power. Evil would always come to me disguised in systems and dignified by law. There would always be cadres and shower rooms, and they would always have dominion over me. They had taught me to hate them, but more significantly, they taught me that I was probably just like them, that I would abuse power whenever I had it, that I was the enemy of anyone who found himself beneath my boot.

They had promised to make a man out of me and they were doing it. They were making a mean and angry man. They had taken an eighteen-year-old boy. They had shaved his head, humiliated him, exhausted him. They had screamed at him for six months, starved him, made him afraid, obedient, humble, made him cry, made him sorry he was born. They castigated him, spat on him, beat him with their fists, waited for him in packs, sweated the youth out of him, ran him until he dropped, made him hate them and was hated in return, made him weep in front of them, lick their shoes, and beg them to let him leave.

Through all this they had left me a poisonous gift. They had made me want to belong to the brotherhood. They made me want to be one of them. And at the end of nine months, I would shake their hands during the recognition ceremony. They would call me by my first name and I would call them by their first names. And at that moment, even Fox, the worst of them all, the most cowardly and the most damaged by the system, would approach me and, with the benediction of history and tradition, call me his brother, his friend and comrade. He would call me himself. He would pass the fire and the dark eyes on to me, as I would pass it ruthlessly on to others. That was the way it worked.

I began crying again by the sink and the alarm went off. It was three o'clock in the morning. Pig and Mark were up at the sound of the alarm. They woke Tradd and began to dress silently. Pig told me to get dressed. I washed my face in the sink and got control of myself again. I put on a clean pair of pants and a T-shirt. Mark came up to me and squeezed my shoulder.

"We'll get him now," he said to me, but I didn't know what he meant.

They left the room and stepped onto a dark and noiseless gallery. I followed the three of them. The barracks slept. Mark carried a blanket under his arm. We padded softly in our bare feet down to the third division. We moved like commandoes, listening and watching for movement along the galleries.

We stopped at Fox's room.

Mark put his fingers to his lips when he saw the look of fear and astonishment cross my face. Pig carefully opened the door. Fox's roommate had mononucleosis and had been in the hospital since February. Fox slept soundly and alone in the bottom bunk. Pig signaled for us to follow him.

Fox slept on his back. His mouth was open and his head was tilted to his left. His breathing was deep and regular. We surrounded him and Pig gave the signal.

Mark threw the blanket over Fox's head and Pig began savagely punching the figure beneath the blanket. His fists battered Fox's face, and Mark's hand was clasped firmly against his mouth. Tradd and I began to beat against Fox's body with our fists, and Mark was flailing at him with his free hand. Fox struggled fiercely, but there were too many blows coming at once. Pig's arms were moving in short brutal punches as if he was working out on a speed bag. The blanket wrapping Fox's face became covered with blood. All of us kept striking and beating until the movement stopped almost completely. I moved up higher and began punching the face, going wild, hoping I was breaking bones.

Mark touched my shoulder, motioned toward the door, and the four of us broke out of that room and ran undetected and unobserved to our alcove on fourth division. We were laughing as we crawled back into our beds. Pig washed the blood off his hands before he climbed into his upper bunk.

Fox did not make it to morning formation the next day and was marked absent. When they found him after breakfast, his face was completely torn up. His face was swollen beyond recognition. The Corps blamed it on Lancey Hemphill and the basketball team, and the word went out to all the cadres to ease up on the jocks.

20

By the first of May the plebe system was winding down. We were one month away from being sophomores. The days were long again, and we sweated in our cotton uniforms as we sat in classes with all the windows open and the sweet fragrance of the Charleston spring hanging like an invisible canopy over the city. There were pigeons nesting in the eaves of the fourth division and regattas in the harbor on the weekends.

In the barracks, the grand forgetfulness had begun among the freshmen as we recognized the imminence of our apotheosis from plebes to upperclassmen. We began to stir with the arrogance of survivors and felt, at last, that we were legitimate citizens of that gray stone realm. The plebe system had relaxed to such a degree that we were beginning to leave the gutters and walk across the parade ground after dark when we were certain there were no upperclassmen around to intercept us. The barracks had lost its aura of terror and had begun to feel like a place where we belonged, a place that we had earned the right to call our own. Certainly, Fox and Newman and a few others had not relaxed at all, but most of their classmates had eased up to the point that they sometimes walked into our rooms during evening study period just to talk. They were not yet friendly, but they were preparing the ground for future alliances. During formation, you could begin selecting the sophomores and juniors who would be your friends the next year.

Yet there were still the occasional sweat parties, the room inspections, and the de rigueur harassment at mess. There was still the residue of the system and the halfhearted compliance to the system, which was in effect until the last week of school and the recognition ceremony. But the plebes stirred with impatience, and slowly in our own way, we began to act like cadets instead of knobs.

On Pig's birthday, his girl friend, Theresa, sent him a large package, which he unwrapped in the post office on Friday afternoon after parade. The package was filled to overflowing with Italian sausages, thick, aromatic cheeses, and a red-checkered tablecloth. There was also a large chocolate cake with fat pecans buttoned into the icing.

"A feast, paisans," Pig crowed with delight, "an Italian feast like we have on the feast of St. Joseph."

"St. Joseph wasn't Italian," Tradd said.

"He doesn't know what he was missing," Pig said, biting into a piece of provolone. "We'll eat like Nero tonight. We'll pretend we're watching lions eating a couple of fat Christians while we're doing some serious scoff on a couple of pounds of sausage and cheese."

"Let's pretend we're watching the lions eat a couple of fat upperclassmen."

"Oh gross," Tradd said. "Y'all are spoiling my appetite. It's bad enough thinking about eating all this greasy meat. Did they cook it thoroughly? What's in that sausage?"

"Meat," Pig said simply.

"The finest meat available, geek," Mark said.

"Italians make their sausage out of pig embryos and Vitalis, Tradd," I said seriously. "It's considered a delicacy by flies and maggots."

"Don't say anything about the food Theresa sent. You know how I feel about anything connected to Theresa."

"Theresa could send canned shit and Pig would eat it like caviar," Mark said.

"I'll eat the cake," Tradd said.

"Let's get back to the barracks," Pig said, putting the package under his arm. "Let's be real quiet though. I don't want the upperclassmen taking this stuff away and feeding their own ugly mugs."

* * *

We made the right-angle turn into the barracks and ran along the galleries toward the R Company area without much concern for interception. Most cadets were out in Charleston on general leave, and the barracks had the appearance of an abandoned fort. We were mounting the steps leading to second division when we heard a voice cry out from third division, "Halt, dumbheads."

Blasingame and Maccabee, dressed in salt-and-pepper, were coming down the stairs from third division on the way out to the parking lot beside the barracks.

"What have we here, Mr. Pignetti?" Blasingame said. "It looks like a care package from home. Am I correct?"

"Sir?" Pig said, clutching the package tighter under his arm.

"Surely, you understood me, Mr. Pignetti," Blasingame said, rubbing his hands together. "I think it is my duty to check this out thoroughly. We have a responsibility to the Institute to make sure our knobs don't get fat eating the goodies from their mothers' kitchens. Fat knobs make sloppy knobs, I've always said. And sloppy knobs are bad for Big R."

Blasingame removed the package from Pig's arm and opened it up beneath the bulletin board.

"What have we here?" he asked delightedly. "Wop food. Sausage. Pepperoni. Cheese."

"Great pepperoni, Mr. Pignetti," Maccabee said, biting off a piece and chewing with exaggerated relish.

"Permission to make a statement, sir," Pig said.

"Pop off, dumbhead," Maccabee answered.

"That's for my birthday, sir. My girl sent it."

"Well, thank her for us, dumb squat. Tell her it was awfully sweet of her to send us some wop food in honor of your birthday. We may even write her a thank-you note ourselves. Now, all of you hit the deck for fifty pushups and have a nice evening," Maccabee said.

"I love chocolate cake, dumbhead," Blasingame said, dipping his finger into the icing. "Come on, Mr. Maccabee. We'll take this contraband out to the party at the beachhouse. How lucky we were running late."

When we reached our room, Pig began beating his fists against the metal press, breaking the skin on two of his knuckles. It was like the sound of a bison crossing the hood of a car. Mark grabbed him from behind and restrained him. Pig's knuckles bled from raw wounds and small flowerets of blood marked the green metal. A vein the size of a pipe cleaner throbbed from his hairline to the bridge of his nose.

"Easy, Pig. Easy, paisan," Mark whispered, keeping Pig wrapped in a bear hug.

"I'll treat you to a pizza, Pig," Tradd said. "We can go down to Labrasca's."

"It was from Theresa. They had no right to steal something that Theresa sent. I'll get them for that. I'll beat the shit out of both of them at the company party next month."

"Be patient, Pig," Mark cautioned. "That's only a couple of weeks away."

"Why don't we get them now?" Tradd said.

We looked at him expectantly.

"Have y'all noticed that every time a knob brings cookies, cakes, sandwiches, or candy into the barracks, the upperclassmen take it and eat it all?"

"No, we haven't noticed that," Pig said, studying his hands.

"Even if we manage to smuggle it into our rooms, we have to hide it in our laundry bags, and whatever it is ends up tasting like dirty socks," Tradd continued.

"What do you plan on doing, Tradd?" I asked. "Lecture the upperclassmen on the rights of property?"

"I plan to smuggle some food into the barracks."

"So what?" Mark said.

"It's going to be something delicious," he said.

"So what?"

"It's going to be something we make."

"So what?" Pig asked.

"It's going to be something we want them to eat."

All of us screamed the same word at the same time.

"Yes!" we screamed.

* * *

On Saturday morning after inspection, all the freshmen in R Company drove to the St. Croix mansion on East Bay Street. Tradd and I drove to the Meeting Street Piggly Wiggly to buy the ingredients for the food we would prepare for the upperclassmen. Commerce had a keg of beer delivered to his home and set it up on the first story verandah. Ten of our classmates were drinking beer and sitting on the railing, looking out at the garden and listening to Commerce tell stories of the old Corps. Abigail was waiting for us in the kitchen with a puzzled though richly amused look on her face. Pig and Mark were drinking beer at the kitchen table along with John Kinnell and Jim Massengale.

"Since when did my plebes become enchanted with the culinary arts?" she asked.

"I'm sure we will need your expertise, Mother," Tradd said, removing the packages from the brown shopping bags.

"I've never cooked anything that didn't have tomato sauce in it," Mark said.

"I've never eaten anything I cooked, and I sure ain't gonna eat this slop we're going to cook up," Pig added.

"What are you going to cook?" Abigail asked.

"Fudge," we all answered, exploding with laughter.

191

"Fudge?" she asked. "I see nothing intrinsically humorous in fudge."

"It's got to look like the real stuff, Mrs. St. Croix," Mark said. "You can't let us make it look like something out of a peat bog."

"May I ask whom it's for?" she said.

"We want to show our appreciation to the cadre who trained us, Abigail," I said. "Those responsible for turning us into men."

"I'll get my *Charleston Receipts* and we'll begin," Abigail said.

"We don't need canceled checks, Mrs. St. Croix," Mark said. "We need to know how to cook."

"Poor Italians, Mother," Tradd said, smiling at Mark. "I'm beginning to understand Mussolini's rise to power. 'Receipts' is the way our Charleston ancestors used to say 'recipe,' Mark. 'Recipe' is a modern derivation."

"Yeh, stupid," Jim Massengale said cheerfully.

"Poor Charlestonians," Mark answered. "They don't know the difference between a recipe and a receipt."

"Let's get cooking," Pig suggested.

"Why are all of you so enamored of those frightful beasts that you want to feed them?"

"You've got to show some appreciation, Mrs. St. Croix," John Kinnell said shyly. "The world wouldn't be a very nice place without appreciation."

Mrs. St. Croix began reading aloud the recipe for fudge from her worn and food-spattered copy of *Charleston Receipts*. You can learn more about the society of Charleston from reading the recipes of her finest and most aristocratic cooks than from any history book ever written about the city. We melted thirty-two squares of Dutch bitter chocolate over a low fire. Then for fifteen minutes we took turns with the eggbeater until the mixture thickened into a creamy smoothness. We added sugar and salt and tasted it with our fingers.

"Now, how much of the other stuff should we add?" I asked.

"We don't want to kill them," answered Tradd.

"Speak for yourself, Tradd," Mark said. "I say we put it all in."

"What stuff?" Mrs. St. Croix asked.

"This," Pig said, emptying twenty packages of a chocolate laxative onto the kitchen table.

"You can't do that. You boys simply cannot put that into the fudge. It's criminal," she said.

We began opening the packages of Ex–Lax and emptying the contents of each box into the fudge.

"You'll make someone very sick," Abigail said. "Very sick. Perhaps we should consult a physician."

"We're not going to *make* them eat this, Mrs. St. Croix," Mark said, furiously handling the eggbeater. "In fact, we're going to beg them not to eat it."

"We want to help them," Pig said. "A couple of them just don't seem regular. This is purely for medicinal purposes."

"Let's sprinkle it with rat poison," Jim said.

"We don't want them to die," Mark said. "We only want them to suffer."

"Suffering is too good for them," Tradd said. "I want agony."

"What has this school done to my sweet boy?" Abigail asked. "To all my sweet boys."

* * *

We calculated our entry into the barracks precisely. We eschewed the obligatory silence of plebes and entered noisily, screaming, drunk, out of control. Fifteen of us made the right-angle turn at T Company and immediately spotted ten or twelve upperclassmen loitering beneath the light beside the R Company stairwell. Pig was in the lead. As he passed the garbage can on first division, he kicked it clattering into the quadrangle. The upperclassmen fanned out to intercept us. The first five of us were carrying beautifully wrapped boxes laden with chocolate fudge.

"Halt, dumbheads," a voice commanded. It was Fox.

"Where do you think you're going, afterbirths?" Newman asked.

"Apologize to that garbage can, Mr. Pignetti," Wentworth said to Pig.

Pig moved out on the quadrangle, replaced the garbage can, then climbed inside it, bracing. "Sir, Mr. Garbage Can, sir. Cadet Recruit Pignetti apologizes for bumping into you and causing you undue agitation, sir."

"I asked you a question, dumbheads," Newman said angrily. "Where are you waste-products going?"

"To our rooms, sir," Mark answered.

"What are in those boxes, nurds?" Fox asked.

"Nothing, sir," Tradd answered.

"It looks like it might be something good to eat, nurds. Right, nurds?" Wentworth said, his voice friendly and intimate.

"No, sir," all fifteen of us answered joyfully.

"Is that an official statement, dumbheads?" Fox asked.

"No, sir," we answered again.

"Aha!" Wentworth said. "So when we invoke the honor system you finally tell the truth. I'd hate to haul all of you before the honor court before you can enjoy the pleasures and privileges of being upperclassmen, dumbheads. I can't believe the good knobs of Big R would try to deny their cadre their rightful privilege to partake of your food."

"Sir. Permission to make a statement, sir," Tradd asked.

"Pop off, faggot," Newman barked.

"Sir, my mother made something for me and my classmates to eat while we started studying for exams. She would be glad to make some more for the upperclassmen next week, sir. I'm perfectly sure of that, sir."

"That's nice, faggot. That's sweet. It really is," Newman said. "But we upperclassmen have a responsibility to you fucking nurds. We have to make sure that the food in those boxes is not poison. You need some brave men to taste what's in those boxes. So why don't you gentlemen hand those six boxes over to the customs inspectors and do fifty pushups while we inspect the contents."

The fifteen of us hit the gallery and began pumping out the fifty pushups in unison, matching our voices and cadences. We could barely keep from laughing when we heard Fox exclaim, "It's goddam chocolate fudge."

He took a thick piece and began eating it. "With pecans in it. It's a goddam bonanza."

Upperclassmen surged toward the six boxes of chocolate, tearing off the wrapping, and grabbing as much fudge for themselves as they could. As the cry of "Fudge" went aloft in R Company, upperclassmen from the upper three divisions hurried down the stairs to claim their portions. The rush turned into a moderate, jostling stampede as we freshmen performed the happiest pushups of our plebe year. When we rose to our feet again, there was not a single piece of fudge remaining. The six boxes lay crumpled and empty on the gallery.

Newman said, licking the chocolate from his fingers, "Because you didn't want to generously share your good fortune with your superiors, dumbheads, you don't get anything. Now get to your rooms, asswipes. The all-in check has already begun."

We waited until forty-five minutes after midnight before we crept out into the shadowy, deserted galleries. I could see

Jim Massengale and Murray Seivers moving cautiously along the railing on fourth division. John Kinnell and Webb Stockton had already entered the latrine on third division. R Company freshmen were entering into the O and N Company areas, moving in the shadows. Tradd and I were responsible for the second division latrine. Mark and Pig headed for the first.

We entered the brightly lit latrine on the run. Tradd gathered every single roll of toilet paper and threw them into the utility sink which he had filled with water and ammonia. Working quickly, I covered the toilet seats with thick coats of black shoe polish. Tradd unscrewed the light bulbs in the ceiling, plunging the room into total darkness, and placed the bulbs in the pocket of his bathrobe. I turned the hot water nozzles in the shower on full blast. It was a hot night and the steam rising from the shower room floor made it impossible to breathe. Then I clogged the drain. Before we left, Tradd removed the eight light bulbs from his pocket and shattered them on the tile floor near the entrance.

"It's gross the way the upperclassmen go around barefooted in the galleries all the time," Tradd whispered. "This will discourage them."

"You're going to make a great upperclassman, St. Croix."

We heard Pig and Mark come back up the stairs.

"Finished?" Pig asked softly as he approached.

"Finished," Tradd responded.

"Good. Let me wire the door shut. You get to the room."

Working with speed and efficiency, Pig twisted four feet of barbed wire around the handles of the latrine door and then the screen door with a large pair of pliers. He could not have locked the door more effectively with a deadbolt.

"Let's get to our room quick. They'll be flying all over the barracks in a couple of minutes," Pig said.

Mark spotted a coke bottle atop some refuse in the garbage can. He took it to the room and, upon reaching the alcove, threw the bottle half the length of the gallery, shattering glass across the cement in front of the latrine door.

"It's going to be like crossing a mine field getting in there."

We lay in our racks, waiting and talking to each other in the darkness. Mark lit a cigarette. I asked for one and he threw me the pack. Inexpertly, I lit one and choked as I tried to inhale. I had never smoked a cigarette, and I tried to imitate Mark's brooding, sorrowful insouciance as he blew symmetrical plumes of smoke toward the ceiling.

"This has been one of the best days of my life," Tradd said from above me.

"There are some really good guys in our class. All paisans. All brothers," said Pig.

"Do you think our class will be as bad as the cadre of this year?" I asked. "Do you think we'll treat freshmen the same way?"

There was a moment of silence in the room.

"Yes," Mark said.

"Yes," said Pig and Tradd.

"So we haven't really learned anything at all," I said.

"That's not true, paisan," Pig said, laughing. "We learned how to rack ass."

"And to make fudge," Mark said, as we heard a door open suddenly on the first division.

It was followed quickly by two doors opening on third division. We heard the sound of flip-flops slapping against the galleries as someone sprinted toward the latrine. Another door opened and once again we heard the desperate feet passing our door. Screams and profanity resounded through the barracks as feet were cut by the glass and barbed wire punctured the flesh of hands. Doors were opening all over R Company. The sound of an M–1 stock beating against the barbed wire on third division echoed around the barracks. On the galleries, it was beginning to sound like a track meet. We heard a loud scream on second division.

"You should always wear shoes when you go to the latrine," Mark said. "You can never tell when there might be a broken coke bottle on the gallery."

One voice began chanting, "Toilet paper. Toilet paper. Toilet paper."

"Watch out for this glass."

"The water's hot as hell."

We left our beds and crept to the door, looking out on the gallery. Sitting astride the four garbage cans on fourth division were four R Company upperclassmen with expressions of consummate suffering on their faces. We saw Newman walking back to his room, naked except for his flip-flops. He was carrying his rifle by its sling. As he passed the room, we saw a large circle of polish on his buttocks. He was limping as though he was in great pain. He got halfway to his room, then, due to some urgent message delivered by nature, sprinted back to the latrine.

Blasingame, who had been asleep when we had come into the barracks, came up the stairs from third division with a quizzical, obdurate look on his face. Amazed, he studied the upperclassmen sitting naked on the garbage cans, as motionless as statuary.

"Boys," he called out. "Boys. Boys. What's happening to Big R? All my boys are shitting in cans. Goddam, boys. Use the latrines. Jesus Christ, all my boys are shitting in cans."

Pig had stuffed a towel in his mouth to keep from laughing out loud. I ran back to my rack and muffled my laughter in my pillow. Tradd and Mark were rolling on the floor. Tears were streaming down Mark's face.

When we could finally speak, Tradd said, "Do you think they'll have a sweat party tonight? How long will it take them before they figure it out?"

"They'll have to finish their business before they can figure it out," Pig said. "And, paisan, they're gonna be too weak to think about giving any sweat parties. Some of them will be on the commode for the rest of the night."

The sweat party the next day was the longest and toughest of the year, but we laughed our way through it. They knew and we knew that we were a scant two weeks away from being upperclassmen. We had made it.

21

Then it was June week, with tanned cadets walking by the storefronts of King Street in their white summer uniforms and the parents and relatives of seniors filling up all the hotels in the city and the suburbs. We had a full-dress parade each day and checked for our final grades taped on classroom doors in the academic buildings. Tradd surprised everyone and won the Star of the East medal as best-drilled cadet, in competition beneath the bright sweltering sun with cadets from every other company. Mark, Pig, and I cheered for him from the reviewing stand as Abigail and Commerce watched their son nervously sitting under an umbrella with General and Mrs. Durrell. When he was announced the winner, every member of R Company swarmed onto the field and carried him on their shoulders back to the barracks. By winning the

Star of the East, R Company had accumulated enough points to remain honor company for another year, and Maccabee received the Commandant's Cup from the General at parade the following day. Tradd had his picture taken with the General and Abigail and Commerce, and it appeared on the first page of the B section in the Charleston *News and Courier* on Wednesday of June week. He was the first Charleston boy to win the medal in twenty years, and as he said, smiling at his father, the first St. Croix to win it in history.

The rank sheets came out announcing the corporals among my classmates for the next year. Tradd, Mark, and Pig would be corporals and I would be a private, the highest military rank I would ever attain. I had been ranked in the bottom five of my class. The only reason I was not ranked lower was because Pig had rated me number one on his rank sheet. "Because of that poem, paisan," he exclaimed. "Because you've got hair on your ass." It was a ranking that I appreciated but which very few others understood.

The basketball team had a cookout at General Durrell's plantation house north of Charleston. Reuben Clapsaddle and I were the only survivors of the plebe system among the freshmen. Lancey Hemphill was named the most valuable player and Wig Bowman was named team captain for the next year by Coach Byrum. It had been another long, losing season for the varsity, and most of the team ate their steaks quickly and escaped the melancholy accusatory eyes of our coach. The General delivered a rather grumpy speech on the invaluable lessons to be derived from losing. Mrs. Durrell poured lemonade and apologized for not having attended a single game. She was every inch the General's wife and moved with the taut, tensile grace common to high-born Southern women.

Pig's girl friend, Theresa, flew down from New York and stayed for the entire week at the Francis Marion Hotel. She was a shy, frail-boned girl with long, shining hair like a blackbird's wing. She was as delicate as Pig was not, and it was obvious that they loved each other very much. It was good to be around them, and I studied how people were required to act when they were in love so I would know the forms and nuances of that sweet delirium if and when it happened to me. Pig let me dance with her at the graduation hop. I was the only other boy she had ever danced with since she met Pig when she was fourteen.

"Don't get too close, paisan," he warned gently. "He's

198

like a brother to me, Theresa, but I can't let him get too close."

I did not get too close. I had never danced a slow dance with a girl without touching her, but I did with Theresa as Mark and Tradd laughed at me from their table.

I attended that hop with the sister of my squad sergeant, Quigley. Her name was Susan and I didn't like her very much. She was a fine girl, but her face was suggestive of a variety of memories, all of them bad and all of them permanent. Her face was her brother's face and as I danced with her, her mouth reminded me of his mouth, her eyes became his eyes, and her breath was her brother's, not her own. She could not help who her brother was and neither could I. But a Quigley with breasts was still a Quigley. In the backwaters of consciousness, I looked upon her as linked in secret, obscene ways to the cadre, a soft breeder of cadremen and plebe systems. Her brother had not been the worst, but he had been one of them. I had licked and kissed his shoes during my Taming and could not bring myself to kiss his sister no matter how many times she pressed against me or how many times she turned her face toward mine as we walked along the Battery after the hop.

Every day after parade, Mark, Tradd, and I went fishing for sea bass with Commerce in the tidal rivers around Kiowah and Seabrook Island. On Tuesday, I was badly sunburned and Abigail rubbed vinegar on my back and shoulders when we returned. She cooked the fish in a white wine and cream sauce after we had cleaned them on the back porch. We had drinks on the verandah after dinner, and Commerce told long stories of spearfishing in the Virgin Islands and fishing for piranha on the Amazon River. Abigail and I would swing on the porch swing, Mark would sit on the bannister, and Tradd and Commerce would rock in the white wicker chairs as Commerce recounted in exact detail his memories of lost voyages away from Charleston. We drank our gin and tonics slowly and listened to the insects in the gardens and Commerce's voice as it navigated the seas of the world.

In our room after taps, the four of us began lying awake and telling each other the stories of our lives. We spoke of our fears and ambitions, our insecurities and disappointments. We were no longer in class, no longer exhausted by the plebe system, and for the first time we began to share the intimacies that come with long, leisurely hours of reminiscence. We vowed that our brotherhood, our four-sided union, would be sacred and eternal, and that ours was a friendship that would be stronger and more inviolate even than our allegiance to our class.

On the night before we were recognized, Pig took a pocket knife and we cut the veins of our wrists. We mingled our blood and made those awkward vows of friendship that, with boys, always come easier in symbolic sentimental gestures than in language. Our room shimmered in those last sweltering days with the joy of companionship.

"Now we're like Indians," Pig said, pressing a handkerchief to his wrist. "Now we're like fucking Indians, and we'll hunt buffalo together for the rest of our lives, paisans. For the rest of our lives."

Tradd told us that he had never had three close friends in his whole life, that he had always found it difficult and painful to make friends. He thanked us again and again in darkness when we could not see his face. Haltingly and movingly, he thanked us every night of our last memorable week as knobs.

On Thursday before graduation, the freshmen were bracing loosely on the quadrangle during noon formation. For weeks there had been little malice or threat on the faces of the upperclassmen, and we no longer feared the barracks. Final exams had milked the last drops of venom from the plebe system.

But on this day, they came at us again. They were swarming for a last time, screaming, pounding our chests, making us hit the quadrangle for pushups, forcing us to run in place, shouting the old familiar obscenities in our ears. For a half-hour, we sweated and recited plebe knowledge on the quadrangle until Blasingame issued an order to halt.

I rose up sweating, and Maccabee was in front of me.

"At ease, dumbhead," he said. "Let your chin out."

"Pardon me, sir?"

"I'm not a 'sir' anymore. My name's Frank," he said, smiling and extending his hand.

I shook his hand and said, "My name is Will, Frank."

"You and I are going over to Gene's Lounge tonight, Will. You and I are going to do some serious drinking."

"Sure, Mr. Maccabee, I mean, Frank," I said. "Sure. I'd like that."

And I tell you that at that moment, they had me. I almost wept. I don't know to this day if it was gratitude or relief or pride, but I know that they had me, and I almost broke down and cried in front of Frank Maccabee.

Soon upperclassmen began coming up, smiling at me, slapping me on the back, and calling me by my name for the first time. I learned the importance of naming that day, how a name can change your perception of both yourself and the universe.

"Hello, George. My name's Will."

"Hello, Larry. Will."

"Hello, Dan. Call me Will."

"Hello, D. J. My first name is Will."

Blasingame walked up to me and recited, laughing, " 'The dreams of youth are pleasant dreams of women, whiskey, and the sea.' You gauldy knob, my name's Philip."

"Hi, Philip," I said, shaking his hand. "My name's Will."

Then Fox came up to me.

He was not smiling and his approach still intimidated me. He looked at me, sneering insolently with his cruel mouth. He knew he walked among freshmen who despised him with only the gift of his first name to offer.

"My name's Gardiner, dumbhead," he said, extending his hand to me.

I did not take his hand. I slapped it away.

Then I looked into his narrow eyes and said coldly, "My name's Mr. McLean to you, Fox. And it's going to be Mr. McLean for your whole life."

"It was just the system, McLean, you little baby," he said angrily. "It wasn't anything personal. It was just the system and I was just doing my job."

"Let's just say I don't like your system and I didn't like the way you did your job."

"You just remember that I'll be a senior next year, you little shoe-licker. I'll jack it up your ass every time there's a room inspection. I'll get my classmates to shit on you so many times, you won't know what hit you. We'll run you out of here on excess demerits in a month."

"I'll see you at the company party, Fox," I answered. "If you have the guts to show, which I seriously doubt."

"I'll beat the living shit out of you, McLean," he said loudly.

"There's going to be twenty-eight guys to beat, Fox."

"I'll see you on the beach, McLean. What a pussy! I should have run you out the first week of school."

"You're going to wish you did when I'm sitting on top of that ugly nose of yours."

"Rack your goddam chin in, dumbhead," he ordered. "If

201

you won't let me recognize you, then you're still a knob to me. Rack that beady chin in, scumbag."

"Go fuck yourself, Fox."

* * *

The genius of the Institute lay in its complete mastery of all rites of passage, both great and small. They set aside one day at the very end of the year for all the companies to throw a beer party on the beach for a day of swimming and drinking, when the freshmen could challenge the upperclassmen to fights, thus allowing them to expend any unresolved frustrations and antagonisms of the year. Usually, these were good-natured wrestling matches in the sand, the freshmen testing their new-won manhood against the cadre who had conducted that severe nine-month test. It marked the first time the two groups fraternized together under official sanction. It was the first public occasion when the freshmen gathered together as first-class citizens of the realm, with all their rights intact and all their papers in order.

R Company assembled on the north end of the Isle of Palms. A keg of beer was set up between the beach and the stunted, wind-tortured vegetation that grew on the low sand dunes near the road.

The plebes huddled together in their bathing suits, drinking the cold beer and appraising the much larger group of upperclassmen. I looked at my classmates with admiration. Our bodies were hard and tempered. We could do pushups all night long and there was a healthy, vigorous glow to our group, an essential vitality as we prepared ourselves for the fracas. Twenty-eight had survived the long march of the plebe year. Thirty-two of our classmates had dropped out along the way and we, the survivors, considered them our inferiors. We had filled out in a year, but we still carried aggrieved mementoes of the journey. We whispered to each other as we began making our choices for when we would rush the upperclassmen.

Not that the upperclassmen were worried by our aggressive presence. They were veterans of company parties and their strategies. They had nothing to fear from us. There were more of them. They were older and stronger and more wily. But we had the bitter residue of humiliation and anger on our side. And I had my eye on Fox as he hung back in a crowd of classmates.

I lit a cigarette and began puffing on it as I drank one quick beer after another. I was neither a drinker nor a smoker nor a fighter, but I had planned to be all three on this day. I had awaited the company party the way an azalea awaited the spring. I watched as Fox broke loose from his group and ambled over to the beer keg to replenish his beer.

I walked up behind him slowly, making no overt or hostile movement, moving easily as though I simply wanted another beer. Fox did not see me coming though I saw the other upperclassmen noting my approach. The fight would begin soon and we all felt its imminence in the air.

I put my cigarette out on Fox's bare back. I ground it into his spine.

He screamed and turned. "What the fuck do you think you're doing, McLean?"

"Sorry, Fox," I apologized. "I mistook you for an ashtray. Everyone makes mistakes."

"I'm not going to forget this next year, maggot," he said, his hand gingerly touching the wound on his back.

"Next year," I said, "there ain't gonna be enough of you left next year to feed a Venus fly trap."

And I lowered my head and charged Fox, taking him down hard into the sand. I was punching as we hit the ground. Fox was kicking and grabbing at my hair. And the melee was on.

The two opposing groups charged at each other in a reckless, heedless assault, and there were no holds barred. There were fist fights and eye-gougings and ear-pullings. There were gang tackles, kicks to the groin, and hair-pullings. Four of them knocked me off Fox in the first furious charge. I found myself buried under a moving, grunting, angry pile of flesh.

I could not move. Maccabee and Wentworth had pinned my arms and someone was punching my stomach. I saw Pig and Mark working together, methodically cutting down anyone who moved within their range of operation. Tradd charged the group who had rendered me immobile and knocked off the guy who was hitting me in the stomach. It was Newman.

Newman took a swing at Tradd. It missed, but it was also a serious error of judgment. Pig and Mark both slammed into Newman from behind. Newman whirled, keeping his balance, and without looking threw a wild punch that landed on Mark's nose. There was a sudden violent flurry of punches and Newman was on his knees, the blood dripping from his face, slowly discoloring the sand.

The brawl lasted an hour. It was exhausting and enervating and deliciously pleasurable. I fought with every single person I despised and I licked most of them. I felt powerful and liberated on that beach. Pig, Mark, Tradd, and I began fighting as a team, moving from fracas to fracas, as the combatants spread out across the beach. We poured beer over Maccabee's head, stole Blasingame's bathing suit, and watched his naked behind sprint toward the cover of the sand dunes. Maccabee counterattacked with his classmates, spread-eagled me in the sand, and poured beer over my head and face until Pig could break through their line of defense. I had a wonderful time.

Then I saw Fox sitting astride Jim Massengale near the ocean's edge. I broke loose and was in a full sprint when I hit the miserable son of a bitch. I was on him before he got up. Every freshman in the class had challenged him and he could barely lift his arms to ward me off. I dragged him by the foot to the water's edge. When we reached the surf up to my knees, I dropped down and held his head under water. At intervals, I let him up to breathe. The space between the intervals grew longer and it gave me immense and furious pleasure to see his mouth open in a terrified quest for oxygen. He was desperate and afraid beneath me, and his body began to kick and flounder in panic. I heard a shout from the beach, and eight of Fox's classmates ran toward us. Pig threw a body block that felled two of them. Mark tackled one of them from behind, but the others knocked me off Fox and began dunking me under the water. They did it playfully. None of them realized I had been planning to murder Fox in the Atlantic Ocean.

The fighting grew sporadic and passionless. Upperclassmen and freshmen were walking arm in arm down the beach and singing songs up by the beer keg. Boys were shaking hands all over the beach. Maccabee put his arm around my neck and kissed me drunkenly on the cheek.

"I'm going to pour you a beer, Will," he said, "if I've got the fucking strength, which I doubt."

Frank Maccabee was drawing me a beer when Fox tapped me on the shoulder.

"I'm going to buy you a beer later on, Will. It's time that we recognized each other. My name is Gardiner and you gave me some licking today," he said, extending his hand in a gesture of reconciliation and the burying of hatchets.

I smiled, took his hand, and said very sweetly, "Don't you ever call me Will again, you cocksucker."

I shook his hand firmly with my right hand and hit him in the mouth with a punch I had readied since September. His teeth broke through his lower lip. The second punch caught him in the cheekbone. I went down with a shot to the left temple delivered by Quigley who was standing on my blind side. Mark crumpled Quigley with a punch to the back of his head and the afternoon had turned ugly again.

On the ground Fox looked up at me and said, "I'm going to run you out on demerits next year, McLean. Me and my classmates are going to get you out by first semester. I promise you that."

"Hey, Fox," I said, rubbing my temple as I got another beer. "I know how the system works now. You try to run me out of school and I'm going to take a little stroll over to the Bear's office and tell him that you're married. We'll leave hand in hand."

"You can't do that, Will," Maccabee said.

"Oh, I won't, Frank." I smiled. "Unless I have to. And I'm sure I won't. I'm absolutely positive I won't."

And I threw my beer into Fox's face as I left to join my classmates.

The freshmen built a fire on that beach and we sat around it telling stories about our plebe year. Already it was becoming history and even beginning to assume the fantastic shapes and distortions of mythology. It was memory now and memory was different for each one of us. I listened as Pig described how the four of us had gone down to Fox's room and beaten him senseless beneath the blanket at three o'clock in the morning. I listened as Alexander told how he couldn't wait for the new class of freshmen to arrive so he could make their lives as miserable as ours had been. Jim Massengale described Hell Night, and all of us laughed until we were rolling in the sand. Tradd imitated Maccabee delivering the speech on Hell Night.

I grabbed a bottle of bourbon from Murray Seivers and filled my paper cup with it.

"Easy, tiger," Mark warned. "Some things don't mix."

* * *

I left the fire and walked out to where the waves were breaking over my feet. I took a drink of the bourbon and stared out toward the ocean and remembered a chemistry class from first semester. The professor had given me an unknown chemical during a lab and told me to perform a series of set experiments to discover the identity of the chemical. Instead, I began to pour chemicals at random into the test tube the professor had set before me. The mixture changed colors twice and the changes were radical, extraordinary. Then I added another chemical, which was not marked, which itself was an unknown, though it was a colorless liquid without any volatile characteristics of its own. But when I began putting this liquid into the test tube drop by drop, I had created something terrible and violent. Smoke poured from the tube and the mixture began to spurt volcanically and crawl over the lip of the tube and spill onto the marble desk. The teacher ran up to me and with a long clamp angrily poured my creation down the drain and flunked me on that day's lab assignment. I remembered that moment often and wondered what mystery or metaphor of chemistry I had stumbled upon, what fierce, accidental power I had unleashed. As I stood on the beach with the noise of my classmates behind me, I thought that I must always search for the remarkable combinations, add unknowns, mix things that were clearly marked with things beyond marking. I would leave the simulated test and enter into forbidden territory. I would look for that moment when I would begin to pour alone and in wonder. I would always try to seize that moment and to accept its challenge. I wanted to become the seeker, the aroused and passionate explorer, and it was better to go at it knowing nothing at all, always choosing the unmarked bottle, always choosing your own unproven method, armed with nothing but faith and a belief in astonishment. And if by accident, I could make a volcano in a single test tube, then what could I do with all the strange, magnificent elements of the world with its infinity of unknowns, with the swarm of man, with civilization, with language?

Mark was right, I said to myself, drinking the bourbon. Some things don't mix. Some things don't mix at all, but sometimes in life you have to take the risk.

Before I walked back to my friends and classmates, before I returned to the fires as an upperclassman, as a sophomore, I made a vow to myself, a vow to the guerrilla in the hills, a vow to the poet who was about to enter the confused and dazzling city of memory.

I said this to myself and I meant it:

I will not be like them. I will not be like them.

I shall bear witness against them.

PART III

THE
WEARING
OF THE
RING

September 1966–January 1967

22

It did not rain during the month of September. The trees of the city took on a desperate, haunted look; the bitter sunlight of Charleston tortured the groves and drained the secret gardens, and the city itself seemed to resonate with a silent vegetable terror during that long dry season. Outside the barracks windows, the leaves when wind-blown crackled like thousands of errant wasps colliding in midair. The scorched lawn of autumn took on a look of savage thirst, and even the parade ground, that most tended and pampered of meadows, had an undermined greenness about it. The automatic sprinklers worked through the day and almost never ceased working through the night. The drought seemed an appropriate symbol for how I felt after the suicide of Poteete. Or perhaps I only noticed weather then, when my spirit was dry and brittle, and like the land itself was in terrible need of storm and change and deliverance.

I was famous among my roommates for my mercurial mood-swings. But they accepted my melancholy as some distorted mirror image of my overwrought flights of euphoria. Among themselves, they whispered that it had something to do with being Irish. Even the laughter of Irishmen was sad, they said, shrugging their shoulders as though they had invoked some immutable law of nature. I never seemed to learn from joy; I earned my portion of wisdom through sadness.

I lost something in that month but I gained a lot more. There was a general slowdown; it was a time of patience, of hard yet productive reflection, and a vast torpor that ate away at the part of me that was excessive, cynical, life-affirming, and curious to a fault.

Annie Kate liked me much better during this period when my guard was down. So did Tradd. Both of them found in my vulnerability an essential softness I lacked when my heels were clicking against the pavement just right and every word I uttered was a joke or the beginning of a joke. That was it. I had quit joking completely; the lines of endless banter ceased when there was nothing funny to say, nothing at all. I pretended to study during these long periods of self-exile, these joyless voyages to the interior, but it was study that could not come from books. I would sit at my desk, my eyes sightlessly focused on a text, and let my mind drift over the words like a cork taken by a current. I would not hear anything going on in the room around me. I would not hear Pig lifting weights or Tradd ordering supplies for R Company on the company phone or Mark humming Italian lullabies as he obsessively prepared his desk for his studies. I would not hear the sound of the bugles or companies marching to drill or Mark turning the radio to WTMA. I did not even hear the lion roaring at night in the Hampton Park Zoo or the whistle of the 11:42 train, the Lowcountry Zephyr, speeding across the trestle on the river at the exact same time that it had every single night I had been on campus. It was the sound of the lion and the train that I missed the most.

But when you are thinking and thinking deeply, familiar sounds go unheard and only startling or unfamiliar sounds can break you out of your thoughts. I had listened for that train and that lion every night after taps since my plebe year and I had found comfort in their regularity. They were often the last sounds I heard before I fell asleep and they would register in my subconscious.

It was a requirement of the plebe system that each freshman must piss on the lion before the beginning of the sophomore year. The lion had been pissed on so often by drunk cadets that he no longer moved or protested when boys unzipped their flies and approached his cage. He was old and humiliated and smelled strongly of human urine. Only at night was there some dignity and sense of dread to his roar.

Every night, the campus of the Institute would reverberate with the lion's roaring. If it was early enough, the cadets would sometimes roar back at him, beginning a strange exchange of messages between prisoners, two thousand captive boys sending greetings to the lonely beast surrounded by pigeons and flowers and raccoons in the park. But usually the lion would only sound his alarums in the deep of night.

The lion moved me deeply, but I loved the train. It passed through my dreams at 11:42 every night and at different times it had passed through malarial jungles, arguments with my mother, the slopes of mountains, the gardens of Annie Kate, the glooms beneath the Atlantic—it rumbled through my dreams each night at the exact same time and I am sure I would have known it if some accident had derailed it somewhere along the desolate tracks that cut through the marshes of the lowcountry and it had failed to come. It was always on time and that made it a good train to run through the campus of a military college.

Throughout the dry season of September, I missed the sounds of the lion and the train and never once remembered them forcing their way into my consciousness. I was trying to think things out alone. Poteete's name was never mentioned in the barracks. Like a cadet expelled for an honor violation, he became anathema and his memory was erased as though he had never existed, as though he had never stepped outside the rail on fourth division, as though he had not hung from his belt as we lay sleeping in the barracks. I thought about him constantly and tried to bury him in my own mind, tried to speak with him and ask his forgiveness for something neither one of us could help. It was part of my blazing egomania that I felt personally responsible for all the injustices of the Institute. Later, I would feel the same sort of impotent outrage when I studied the monstrous injustices of the world toward its meekest and most helpless citizens. I was young then, and my youth permitted me to believe that I could change the world if only I could devise a cunning enough strategy.

In those dry and cloudless days, solitude was a sweet water running through the fields of me, and I spoke with Poteete without the help of my roommates, my train, or my lion in the park. Alone, I was learning to think in my own way and growing confident in my ability to discriminate between an idea that was for me and one for all the rest. I had my own system of justice that sprang from the center of me. I felt I had a power—or a weakness, I could not be sure—given to very few human beings. I could put myself in the place of others and ask myself how I would feel if I were in their place. I could go out on the rail with Poteete and feel the pull of the concrete beneath me, the liberation that the leap through the air could bring. He lived in my memory and he hung there from his belt, his shadow moving back and forth like an accusation.

There was a time when I thought that I was all green coast and fertile marsh, that my interior lands were bounded by the Appalachian mountains, the skyline of Savannah, the citrus country of central Florida, and the eroded beaches on barrier islands threatened by the moon-swollen tides of the Atlantic. But as I grew older and explored my own starker regions more assiduously, I kept stumbling across pyramids, Mayan campfires, the rubble of Huns—civilizations that had no right of access to the terrain of a Southern boy's soul. I wanted desperately to find out why I felt different from the other boys at the Institute, why I felt more like Poteete than the rest of them. I wanted to find out why I was lonely and why I never felt lonelier than when I marched with the regiment, in step with the two thousand. When I picked up the yearbook on my desk, flipped through the pages, and looked at the faces of my friends, I thought I was looking at a field guide to ruined boys. That was not true. The Institute had helped many of those boys to find themselves. But as I turned to my own photograph and stared at the immobile smiling stranger who shared my features and my name, I realized that only one boy had been ruined. My task for the year was clear: I had to discover why the boy in that photograph loathed himself so completely and so violently.

On the twelfth day after Poteete died, I heard the lion in the park again. A half-hour later I heard the train rush through the windless Carolina night at 11:42. My senior year began for the second time.

* * *

It was my habit each evening after mess to walk to the library to check for messages that the black freshman, Pearce, might have slipped into the pages of *The Decline of the West*. On Wednesday night over two weeks after plebe week had ended, I received my first communiqué from Pearce. Bo Maybank had told me that Pearce had taken the best the E Company cadre could throw at him but the pressure on him was immense and his volatile temper was working against him. If the cadre could get him to throw a single punch at an upperclassman, he would be gone by the next morning. His note was brief and to the point: "Room 2426, after taps. Corporal Turpin and Sergeant Siddons."

At the library desk, I put in a call to the Bear's house. The Colonel was inspecting the barracks. Mrs. Berrineau told me she would tell him I had called when he returned.

I walked back across the parade ground beneath the shadows of the massive oak trees on the southern fringe of the parade ground and the two howitzer cannons, Barnwell and Freeman, named for the two Institute cadets who fired the first shots on Fort Sumter to begin the Civil War. The barracks swelled with the violent noise of seventeen cadres in full cry answered by the strained and desperate voices of the six hundred plebes. The noise was official and precisely the same every night. The sweat parties between the evening meal and evening study period had not changed since I was a freshman, and my classmates had proven as gifted in the arts of travail as our cadre had been.

When I entered my room, Reuben Clapsaddle, the six-foot-ten center on the basketball team, was sitting on my desk, talking to Mark and Pig and Tradd about the upcoming basketball season.

"It lives," Reuben said as I waved at him.

"Sir," I answered, dropping into my rack and kicking my shoes off onto the floor, "do you have a thyroid condition? You seem awfully tall to me."

"It even speaks," Mark said, turning in his chair to face me. "You've had a personality like a cup of yogurt for the last couple of weeks. It's about time you snapped out of it."

"That's what I'm here for, Will," Reuben explained. "Coach Byrum sent me over here to talk to you. He wants to know what happened to the old pep, the old spirit. He thinks you might be going through the change of life."

"I'm feeling fine, boys," I said staring at the top bunk. "Give the kid a few days and he'll come up dancing and singing again."

"You owe it to the team to snap out of it, Will. If we're going to go all the way, we've got to have you to bring it up the court. That's what Coach Byrum says."

"Reuben, thanks for your concern," I said. "No kidding, I appreciate your coming over here, but this is the fourth year that I haven't cared about what Coach Byrum thought or said."

"What a lousy attitude, Will," Reuben scolded, wagging a giant index finger at me. "Coach is afraid that your negativism will affect the team. If he was so worried about your goddam negativism then why in the hell did he make you captain of the fucking team?"

"Don't use that word in front of my girl, Clapsaddle," Pig said, solemnly pointing to the photograph on his desk. "You didn't know she was listening, but don't let it happen again."

Pig's eyes had glazed over with that feral, gauzy look he assumed whenever he invoked the image of Theresa in front of sacrilegious strangers in the room.

"What word?" Reuben exclaimed. "What are you talking about, Pig? That's why you're depressed, Will. You room with the honey prince and two muscle-bound Yankees with funny ideas and funny last names."

"Do you think my last name is funny, Reuben?" Mark said, rising to his feet. "You mean someone named Clapsaddle thinks that Santoro sounds funny?"

"Clapsaddle," Pig said. "It sounds like a donkey with gonorrhea."

"Reuben was joking, Mark," I said. "He didn't mean anything by it."

"Santoro is a beautiful name," Mark said to Reuben, ignoring me. "Don't you think so, Reuben?"

Reuben felt the climate of menace in the room, and I saw him look to me with luminous, fearful eyes for help. Reuben was one of those huge athletes who take their physical superiority for granted and often find themselves astonished and afraid when challenged by smaller, more violent men. When a man is six feet ten inches tall, he never has to learn the skills of self-defense. Being among the largest men on the planet, Reuben had never had to throw a punch in anger. Pig and Mark knew this instinctively the first time they met him.

"Santoro is one of the prettiest names I ever heard, Mark," Reuben said, slapping him playfully on the back. "Goddam, boy, that name is pure poetry."

Tradd was sitting at his desk in the alcove with his back toward the rest of us, filling a fountain pen with ink. The pen made squeaking respiratory noises. Without turning around, he asked in a voice that shivered with hurt, "Why do people call me the honey prince, Reuben?"

All of us turned to look at Tradd. In his corner and with that sad question hovering in the air, he was a portrait of solitude. It was one of those times when I realized that Tradd was one of the most isolated people I had ever known, a boy of such deep essential silences and unvoiced questions I almost felt I had never met or touched him, but only observed him from a distance. I tried to think of a way to answer his question with a joke, but once again humor had lost its adequacy to defuse and mollify.

"It's because you're rich, Tradd," I said finally. "People are always jealous of rich people."

"You don't lie very well," said Tradd.

"Folks think you act funny, Tradd," Reuben explained. "You ain't exactly the typical cadet now, are you, boy? You talk funny. You act funny. You walk funny and ya just don't seem like one of the boys. I've never known exactly what it means but it seems to fit you, boy."

"Only people who don't know you think it fits you, Tradd," Mark said, scowling again at Reuben.

"It's not my fault they think Tradd's a faggot," Reuben blustered. "I just heard the name, boys; I didn't make it up."

"He didn't mean that, Tradd," I said, rolling out of the bed and walking over to Tradd's desk. "Jocks aren't known for their overwhelming sensitivity."

Mark said, "You didn't make it up, Reuben, and I suggest you don't let me hear you use that phrase in this room again."

"We're brothers in this room, man," Pig added. "And when you hurt one brother, you hurt all of us."

"Are you hurt?" Mark asked Tradd gently.

"No, of course not," Tradd lied.

"Good," Pig said heartily. "Because if my roommate was hurt, Clapsaddle, I would have to find out why he was hurt, and I would have to hurt the thing that was hurting him, only I'd have to be sure that I hurt that thing much worse than Tradd was hurting. Do you dig, Clapsaddle?"

"Easy, ol' Pig. Why don't you use those big muscles to fight that white-haired creep they're bringing in with the county fair next week? He issued a challenge that no one at the Institute could stay in the ring for five minutes with him. I came over here to talk to Will, to pep the boy up, not to duke it out with my classmates. But I see what the problem is now, Will. Goddam, boy. No wonder you're depressed. You're rooming in a goddam insane asylum."

As he got up to leave Reuben stopped by Pig's desk near the door and tapped Theresa's picture frame with a huge lascivious finger. "Nice tits, Pig. Really nice tits," he said admiringly.

Mark reached Pig before I did, and it was his quickness and presence of mind that saved Reuben from an encounter with Pig that he would not soon have forgotten.

I rushed Reuben out the door, and it was clear from his bewildered expression that he had no idea what law he had broken or rule he had violated in the odd system of jurisprudence practiced in our room.

"It's a fucking zoo in there, Will," he said as I hustled him to the stairs. "Why don't you transfer down to first battalion?"

"Run, Reuben," I yelled, "do me a favor and run a very fast wind-sprint back to your room and brick yourself in for a week. Pig's funny about people talking about his girl."

And Reuben ran, taking the steps leading down to third division four at a time. I watched him as he crossed the quadrangle sally port; he loped along with the graceful, startled gait of a two-legged giraffe.

When I returned to the room, Mark had calmed Pig down. Tradd was studying in the alcove, and Mark was brushing his teeth in the sink by the door.

"Is that giant fruit fly gone?" Mark said, spitting into the sink.

"You basketball jocks are the strangest creatures in this school," Tradd announced. "The very strangest and that's the gospel according to the honey prince."

"You know better than to listen to nicknames, Tradd," I said. "Good God, we spent our whole freshman year being called douchebags and asswipes."

"That's different and you know it, Will. They called *all* of us douchebags."

"Listen, y'all," I said, "I've caused a lot of pressure in this room in the past two weeks. I was feeling real bad after what happened out there on the division, and I needed time to sort it out in my head."

Tradd spoke first. "You never have to apologize to your friends, Will. And you should know that. At least those friends who love you even though you're as peculiar as peculiar can be sometimes."

"Apologize to me," Mark demanded. "I think you've been a pain in the ass in the past two weeks. I'd rather room with the lion in the park. I want to see the ol' wise-cracking Will back and running his motor-mouth. I can't relate to you when you're not hurting someone's feelings."

"I'm back, Mark," I laughed. "I promise."

"You'll feel better after you take those vitamins I left on your desk. Depression is an absence of vitamins, boy. It's purely physical. I've never been depressed in my life."

"Pig," I said quietly so the others could study.

"Yeh, paisan," he whispered back affectionately. There was a vast artlessness to Pig's open, unlined face, as though he had never suffered the effects of a troubling thought in his life.

"I've got to talk to you, Pig."

"You can always talk to me, Will. We're brothers, right?" he said, reaching out for my neck and smiling when I drew back quickly. He was the only person I had ever met who did grueling exercises to build up the muscles in his fingers.

"You've got to promise me one thing," I asked. "You've got to promise that you won't beat me up when we talk."

"I could never lay a hand on you. It'd be like hitting my own brother. Or Theresa."

"Why did you get mad when Reuben cussed in front of Theresa's picture? It's stupid to get mad like that."

Pig made a gesture of dismissal with his hand like he was brushing flies away from his face. "I can't let guys cuss when my girl's around, Will. You know that."

"Your girl's not around, Pig. That's a picture of your girl. It's not the same thing."

"It is to me, paisan. If you cuss around my girl's picture, it's like you're spitting in my face. That's how I feel about it. I may be wrong, Will. I'm sorry. I'd never forgive myself if you forced me to kill you."

I nodded and said, "That would be terrible, Pig. But let me ask you this question. How does a person talk at all? How does one communicate in the barracks at all without using profanity? It's the only language that anyone understands. It's the natural language for this environment."

"If you feel like expressing a disgusting thought around Theresa, Will, I suggest that you use the real word. The proper word that a gentleman would use. Like instead of saying 'dick' or 'prick' or 'talleywhacker,' I suggest you use the word *penis*."

Mark slammed his chemistry book shut and buried his face in his hands.

I said, "Oh, penis. I get it. That does sound much better."

"And the word *fuck*," he said, whispering the forbidden word, "Theresa hates that word very much. So I'd like to respectfully ask that you not use it in her presence."

"Has Theresa ever heard the word, uh, that particular vulgarity that we beasts use for sexual intercourse?"

"Of course not, Will," he responded. "I'd be serving out a life sentence in Sing Sing if she had."

"You can't live in the barracks without using that word, Pig," I explained. "No cadet can live without that word."

217

"Use the real word instead," Pig sighed. "The proper word."

"You mean like 'Dante Pignetti is really intercoursed up.' Or 'Please pass the intercoursing salt.' What about fart, Pig? Can I use the word *fart*?"

"Don't do it, Will," he said sadly. "Don't push me to the absolute limit. No, of course you can't use that word. Common sense should have told you that. If you want to say that you have to rid yourself of a big smelly one then I suggest you say something like this: 'Pig, I think that in a few moments I will expel much flatus.' "

"Expel much flatus?" I said.

"That wouldn't offend Theresa," he continued. "She would appreciate your concern for her sensitivity."

"She wouldn't even know what I meant," I protested. "Heck, *I* wouldn't even know what I meant."

Mark growled again in exasperation. He had remained silently attentive to the dialogue, though all of us knew his silences often conveyed strong and unshakable opinions.

He walked over to Pig's desk and looked directly into Theresa's eyes and screamed at her: "I'm farting like a motherfucking bastard, Theresa, you flapping twat. So I'm fucking going out the fucking door to the fucking shit house to shit my fucking brains out. Do you hear me, Theresa? Do you hear me?"

"Crude, Mark. Very crude," Tradd said at his desk.

Pig stiffened but made no move, and Mark walked out of the door without any visible haste or worry.

When Mark had gone, I said, "We've got a double standard in this room, Pig. You didn't say a word when Mark was saying all that. You'd have fed me and Tradd to the crabs."

"He's trying to provoke me," Pig answered.

"That's very keen," I agreed. "Do you always have a sixth sense about these things?"

"There will be a proper moment. When Mark and I start fighting each other, it will be a classic duel. Only one of us will walk away from that fight. It's been coming for a long time."

"You guys are too close ever to fight, so quit talking that nonsense," I said. The mere thought of the two of them squaring off for combat filled me with a nameless dread. "And I haven't finished talking to you, Pig. I want to get this resolved here and now. I can't have my friends afraid to come up to this room. Reuben is going to tell everyone on the team

218

that I'm rooming with a homicidal maniac. Half of R Company is already afraid to come into the room. Hell, I'm afraid to come into the room sometimes. So let's just talk about you and Theresa. OK?"

His face colored suddenly, the thick bifurcated vein stood out on his forehead, and you could check his pulse by watching the silent drum beat delicately at his temple.

"It better be nice, McLean," he warned.

"What if it isn't, Pig? We're adults now, and what if I've got something to say that isn't nice?"

"Don't you say nothin' about my girl, man," he said. "What's the matter with her anyway? You think she's ugly or something? I'll break your ass if you think she's ugly. You think she's screwin' around on me? You think she's a whore? That's it. You think she's giving it away free to every guy in Brooklyn. What've you heard, Will? Who told you? I'll break his ass. I'll throw him off the fourth division."

He grabbed me suddenly by the collar and shoved me up against the wall by his desk.

"You stop that, Pig," Tradd cried out, spinning around in his chair and running toward us. "You are so tacky sometimes. So violent and tacky."

"Pig," I said quietly as Tradd vainly tried to remove one of Pig's hands from my collar. "This has been going on for four years now. You've got to quit worrying about Theresa. She's one of the sweetest, kindest, most gentle people on this earth, and she'd be appalled to know that for four years you've been beating up people who just look at her picture and comment on how pretty she is."

Pig grimaced as though he was experiencing unbearable physical pain. "I just don't like guys looking at my girl friend, Will. I've never been able to stand that. It's so dirty. When they say she's pretty, what they're really saying is that they'd like to fuck her. They're looking at her picture thinking what she looks like without clothes and then they think about spreading her legs and jumping up and down on her."

"That's not what they think, Pig," I said.

"No one in the world except animals like you would think of such a thing," Tradd said.

"How do you know, Will?" Pig asked with childlike earnestness.

"Because I look at her picture a lot and that's not what I think," I explained.

"What *do* you think?" he asked suspiciously.

"I've never had a single lusty thought about Theresa," I

assured him quickly. "I like the little things in life like not having my kidneys kicked in."

"You don't think she's good looking?" Pig said. "You think my girl's a dog. You're not attracted to her when you see her picture. I'll break your ass."

"This has got to stop, Pig," I said, feeling his hands tighten on my collar. "It's immature and you're too sweet a guy to be paranoid about Theresa. She loves you and that's it. You don't have to worry about anything. You don't have to stomp every poor squirrel who walks in here and says something about her picture."

"I want them to have respect," he muttered.

"They have respect, Pig," I said. "You're just afraid of something and I don't understand what it is."

"Will, I know you're not calling me chicken. Tell me you're not calling me chicken."

Tradd began talking softly into Pig's ear. "No, of course he's not calling you a chicken. But you are deathly afraid of some things you have no reason to fear, Pig. You are fighting phantoms and shapes that do not exist. You invent them. Will's right, and he's right to talk to you about it. All of us should have talked to you about it a long time ago. But we were afraid it might hurt your feelings or that you wouldn't understand it."

"I thought we were brothers." He spoke sadly, his eyes downcast. "I thought we shared everything."

"I'm sure that there's a lot we don't tell each other," Tradd said.

"You're an adult now, Pig," I said. "You're going to be an Army officer next year. You won't be able to pound everybody who makes some innocuous remark about your wife. There are going to be generals who'll pat her sweet behind at parties and colonels who'll snicker and make allusions about golden nights you spend in the sack with Theresa."

"Dead generals. Deceased colonels," Pig said curtly.

"It's time to grow up, Pig. It's no longer a cute, interesting form of human behavior. It's starting to look sick," I continued.

Tradd added with a certain measure of finality, "And it's always looked tacky."

"It's effective," Pig protested stubbornly. "No one puts the bad mouth on my girl."

"I grant you that, Pig," I agreed with rising exasperation. "From a strategic point of view you have successfully eliminated free and open discussion of Theresa's body. I would like you just to practice a little tolerance. Violence upsets me, Pig. I like to live in rooms where the screams of strangers being executed are not heard two or three times a day. Just try it for a while, Pig. For the sake of your beloved roommates."

"You know I'd do anything for my beloved roommates," Pig said.

"And we would do the same for you. You know that," Tradd answered, ducking beneath Pig's arm when Pig tried to embrace him.

"I couldn't have made it through this school without you guys. You guys knew my family was poor as hell and you guys have gone down to the wire giving me money and things. I'll never forget that. Never."

"We're not allowed to discuss money in this room," Tradd said, moving back to his desk. "Now you are violating a rule."

"Why don't we practice, Will?" Pig said brightly after Tradd had gone back to his studies. "Why don't you pretend that you're coming into the room for the first time and you say something dirty about Theresa. I won't do anything. I'll be tolerant. I won't even be tacky like Tradd says I am."

"I said you're tacky only when you act like a beast," Tradd amended from his corner. "It's impossible to explain to a Yankee what 'tacky' is. They simply have no word for it up north, but my God, do they ever need one."

"You won't go out of your Italian head and mop the floor with me?" I asked.

"I promise," Pig said. "And you know when I give my word I'd rather die than break it."

"OK," I said, staring with licentious abandon at Theresa's photograph. I licked my lips and began panting. Then I licked the breasts in the photograph, sliding my tongue along the glass and moaning orgasmically. Standing back, I said, "Hey Pig, ol' buddy. Some honey. Wooooo—Eeeee. She's got a set on her that could feed the city of Tokyo. Stacked like a brick shit house."

I studied his face closely, looking for some outward signs of his coming apart.

"You're doing okay, Pig?" I asked.

"Yeh," he said.

"You sure, Pig?"

"Yeh."

"Should I go on?"

221

"Yeh." He spoke through grimly tightened lips.

"I'd love to stick a big, hot, hairy banana in that sweet piece of Italian poon-tang. Yes sir. I'd love to play hide the sausage with that hot madonna. Should I go on?" I said, looking down at Pig.

"I'm going to have to hurt you for that, Will," he explained calmly. "You went too far. There has to be punishment. I wanted to practice tolerance, but you forced me to take action. Theresa wouldn't respect me if she knew what you said."

"I was pretending to be someone else," I screamed, backing away from Pig's desk. "It was a goddam game."

"I'll pretend I'm hitting someone else. I couldn't hit you because you're like my brother. So I'll pretend you're someone slimy I hate."

But before Pig could rise out of his desk, Mark entered the room swiftly and whispered a single word that made all of us dive for our desks and open our books.

"Bear," he said.

The door crashed open and Bear strode into the center of the room, his cigar blazing, his keen brown eyes surveying the room in one rapid sweep. His entries were always dramatic, and he always conducted his inspections with the flair and panache of a benevolent conquistador.

"Room, attention," Pig ordered.

"Why the big surprise, lambs?" He grinned through his cigar smoke. "All of you knew I was coming."

"Good evening, Colonel," Tradd said. "What an unexpected pleasure."

"What are you bums hiding from the Bear tonight?" he growled. "Is there liquor in Lamb Pignetti's press?" he said, flinging open Pig's steel locker, and lifting up the stacks of folded laundry, he searched for contraband material. "Does Lamb Santoro have pep pills he's selling to innocent dumbhead lambs hidden in a false drawer?" he said, running his hand beneath Mark's desk. "And is Mr. McLean writing seditious poetry telling the world that the Commandant in Charge of Discipline has no hair on his nuts? Is Lamb St. Croix making illegal plans to buy up the rest of South Carolina now that he and his family own Charleston?"

"Sir, my family is not as wealthy as you seem to think," Tradd protested.

"Yeh, Bubba, and my piss don't stink after I eat asparagus. Bolshevik," the Bear said, turning to me and examining the brass on my belt, "the only time we allow cadets to grow

222

penicillin mold on their brass is when they have a certified case of the clap."

"Haven't I told you about the girl I've been dating, Colonel?" I said, still standing at rigid attention. "I thought she was a nice girl even though she came from a low-class disreputable family. Her father was a brute with a single-digit IQ. But she had a nice personality even though she weighed three hundred pounds and had a handlebar moustache. I was very surprised, indeed, Colonel, when I contracted a social disease from this girl. And that is the reason for the mold on my brass."

"Who was this girl, Bubba? This poor woman so hard up she had to take you on as a boy friend?"

"It was your daughter, sir."

The roar of the Bear was difficult to describe adequately. Cadets often compared it to howitzers at parade, to Phantom jets exceeding the sound barrier, to the lion in the park. Some insisted that it matched all three simultaneously. But the howl he let loose in that room exceeded anything that I had ever heard issue from a human throat. I left my feet when he screamed.

"Bum! I got the best-looking daughter you've ever seen in your life and if you want to get crucified without nails or burn in hell before the Creator calls you or if you want me to set your eyeballs on fire with this cigar, then let me hear you say another single word about my daughter."

"I've been trying to teach Mr. McLean respect for women all evening, sir," Pig said triumphantly.

"Colonel," I whispered, "I didn't know you had a daughter. I would never have said that."

"She wouldn't be caught living or dead with a miserable excuse for a man like you, bum. But let me give you a couple of demerits to remind you of my daughter's honor the next time I come into this room."

"That won't be necessary, sir," I said. "Demerits only tend to make me forgetful."

"I've found that demerits have the opposite effect, Mr. McLean. I've found that they stimulate the memories of my lambs," he said, handing me a white slip.

"Colonel, don't you think the little epigram on these white slips is the silliest misuse of the English language you've ever heard? 'Discipline is training which makes punishment unnecessary.' That symbolizes the whole logic of the Institute to me."

"Then transfer to Clemson, lamb. I'll pack your bags,

223

drive you to the bus station, and kiss you on the lips good-bye. I happen to agree with that motto. Your parents pay good money to have me watch out for you and to remind you when you displease the Bear. Demerits are part of your education, lamb, like textbooks or grades or slide rules. The more demerits I give you, the more benefits you derive from an Institute education, the more returns your parents have on their original investment. Demerits are probably the only thing that reminds you this is a milary school, Mr. McLean."

"Amen," Tradd said.

When I had completed filling out the white slip, I surreptitiously removed Pearce's note from my pocket, folded it twice, and handed it with the white slip to the Bear. He placed them beneath his clipboard and as a farewell gesture blew a giant plume of cigar smoke in my face. The smoke could have eliminated a colony of termites. The Bear could have gotten a job with Orkin.

"Colonel, I like talking to you except when I have to breathe."

The Bear grinned his brown-toothed grin and said, "Thanks for the white slip, Bubba. Ninety-eight more demerits and I get to ship you to Clemson before you're allowed to disgrace the ring."

"Major Mudge gave me five demerits at the first Saturday morning inspection, sir," I said. "But I know you're too good-hearted to run a senior out for excess demerits."

"I'd do it with pleasure," he said. "I ran three out in May last year. Good lambs, too. But slobs, like you. I told them that I had no hard feelings toward them. I was just performing my duty and they were caught not performing theirs."

"Colonel, before you go. I want to apologize again for your daughter. But I would like to know one thing. Does your daughter take after you or your wife?"

"My wife, Bubba. Why?" he asked, glowering.

"The Lord is good after all," I said.

He laughed, looked around the room, and before he departed, said, "Two Italians, an Old Charlestonian, and a sloppy shanty Irishman from Georgia. You ought to set up a branch of the United Nations in this room. As you were, gentlemen, and good night."

* * *

Ten minutes before taps, Tradd and I walked down the gallery to take a shower. We were alone in the shower room.

The battalion was slowing up and the cadets shuffled along the galleries like tired cells in an artery. There was always a slight tension in the neurotic anticipation of taps.

Tradd spoke through water as he washed shampoo from his short-cropped hair.

"Mother would like you to come over for dinner after the football game on Saturday. You can spend the night if you can get the Bear to give you a weekend leave."

"I can't this Saturday, Tradd," I answered. "I've got something else I have to do." I let the hot stinging spray flow over my eyes and face. For three years I had gone to Tradd's house every single weekend simply because I had no other place to go. Suddenly I found myself invited to Annie Kate's house almost every weekend, and there was the growing, exhilarating, and unmentionable involvement with her.

"Mother will be disappointed," he said. "What are you doing, Will, if you don't mind me asking?"

"Don't tell Pig and Mark about this, but I've met a girl I really like."

"You!" Tradd said, genuinely surprised. "Does she like you too?"

"Not that much," I confessed.

"Is she a local girl? I may know her," he said.

"No," I lied. "She's from way off. Some nonexistent place like North Dakota. Her father's in the Navy."

"When will I get to meet her?"

"Not for a while, Tradd. She's very shy about meeting people. I can't tell you everything now, but I will someday, I promise. And you'll be the first one to meet her."

"Why don't you want Pig and Mark to know? They've been wanting you to have a girl friend for a long time."

"For about the same amount of time as they've wanted you to have a girl friend." I laughed. "I just don't want to get teased by them, Tradd. I've never been able to take teasing about girls."

"I've never had to," Tradd said, smiling to himself.

"I feel so awkward around girls. I never seem to think of the right thing to say. I can't seem to make them feel comfortable, and I always think they wish they were with someone else. They make me feel terminally shy, Tradd. Even ugly. I think I'm so aware of my face and how I look and how I appear to them that I can't even really see them or talk to them. How do you feel around girls, Tradd? I mean really. What goes on in your head when you're around a girl you really like?"

"I feel threatened, Will," he said seriously. "I feel like I'm about to be invaded, smothered completely. I'm rarely comfortable around them. But that's not surprising. I'm rarely comfortable around anybody."

"Except me," I corrected.

"Except you," he agreed.

"What about Mark and Pig?" I asked. "Why aren't you comfortable around them?"

"It's different with them, Will, and it's a difference hard to explain. I have great affection for them, and I know they feel the same about me. But the only time it really works for us is when all four of us are together. They're my friends and roommates only because of you. I didn't earn their friendship on my own. I think they would do anything for me. I've never met people with such a strong sense of loyalty and we've shared so much together. But we're such different types and it's such a strange accident that all of us are together. Still, it's a happy accident and I'm glad we all found each other."

"A great accident," I said.

"Especially for the honey prince," he said bitterly.

"Forget that shit, Tradd. The Corps has this nasty way of pinning damaging nicknames on people."

"It hurts only because it strikes so close to home, Will. One of the reasons I came to the Institute was because certain people, including my father, have always considered me effeminate. I thought if I survived the plebe system, it would quell all doubts about my masculinity. No one feared the plebe system as much as I did. I wasn't like you, Will. I knew all about the brutality and the excesses and I knew the cadre would despise me from the moment I walked into the Gates of Legrand. But I needed to prove to myself that I could take everything they could dish out. I loved it when I heard that football players quit because they couldn't take the system. I couldn't help it, Will. I loved it. I thought since I stayed when stronger boys left I would no longer have to put up with taunts about my voice or my manner. But that's not how it works at all. Not in the Corps of Cadets. It's a good nickname for me, Will. It's perfect. That's why I hate it so much. You've no idea how much a perfect nickname can hurt. I can't walk anywhere on campus without hearing it. Even if no one says it, I can still hear it."

Taps sounded through the barracks with all the old infinite sadness of finality. All cadets were one day closer to being whole men.

We dried ourselves quickly and returned down the

226

gallery to our alcove room in time for the all-in check. Mark and Pig were already in their racks and the lights were out. Tradd dressed in his modest striped pajamas while I fell into the bottom bunk in my shorts, my uniform crumpled in a heap beside my desk.

I loved this time of day best. It was my favorite time anywhere. I liked the approach of sleep as much as I liked sleep itself. The sheets were clean and the windows were open and the cicadas screamed in the dry oak branches outside the windows. The odor of the marsh was so urgent and strong, so evocative of the Atlantic and infinite fertility, that the breeze that lifted the sheets from my body smelled of trout and shad and mullet and flowed in a secret renegade creek through our room. Far off in that city of light and water the bells of St. Michael's tolled high over Broad Street, freighters moved through dark water, and the nightwalkers began their solitary and uncontested rule of the brick alleys. Tradd shifted in his bed above me. Lightning flashed in the distance and the earth began to think of rain.

"Hey, Will," Mark asked, "did you finish your paper for Edward the Great's class?"

"Not yet," I answered, turning toward the voice in the darkness. "I'm going to the library in the morning."

"How can you guys stand to look at that fat blivet?" Pig asked, rising up on one elbow. "He weighs three hundred pounds if he weighs an inch. His body is disgusting. He doesn't even need to go on a diet, man. He needs an operation to sew up his esophagus for about three months."

"He's a great teacher, Pig," Mark countered. "The best I've ever had."

"I'm not saying he's not, paisan. I'm just saying I couldn't sit and look at that body all day without getting sick to my stomach."

"Maybe he has glandular problems, Piglet," Tradd said. "Some fat people can't help being fat."

"That's what they all say," Pig explained. "Every fat blivet I've ever met told me he had bad glands. Not one of them ever told me about stuffing too much chow into their fat blivet faces. Reynolds ought to do himself a favor and take a vacation to some country having a famine."

Then Mark changed the subject suddenly by asking, "Will, did you ever get laid this summer?"

"No," I answered, rolling over to go to sleep and hoping that the gesture would end the conversation.

"Did you try?" Mark insisted.

227

"Sure," I said. "I'm in a perpetual state of trying. I came close, though. One girl let me walk her home after a movie, and we shook hands at the front door."

"Why can't you score, Will?" Pig asked. "You'd think you were an amputee or a homo, with the luck you have with women. Hell, there are broads with wide-ons all over the place waiting for a guy like you to come along."

"I got laid so many times this summer that I thought I was the only white man in South Philly," Mark boasted.

"You *are* the only white man in South Philly," Pig giggled.

Tradd's voice came from above me after a moment of silence. "Why didn't you ask me if I made love to a woman this summer, Mark?" Tradd said.

"You don't even look at women, Tradd," Mark explained. "Much less get laid by them."

"I met a girl this summer. I even made love to her. At least twice," he declared with stiff formality. "It happened when I was traveling in England."

Pig and Mark screamed simultaneously, and I heard their bare feet hit the floor as they made their way through the darkness to Tradd's rack. They began slapping his shoulders roughly and tickling his sides until he was breathless with laughter.

"You ol' stud horse," Mark said. "You've been keeping secrets from your roomies. Out there getting it and not saying anything."

"It's those quiet ones you can't trust. My daughters are always gonna date guys with the biggest mouths in Brooklyn. If they're talking then they can't be fucking," Pig crowed.

"Who was it, Tradd?" I said, rising up on the other side of the rack. "And was it human?"

"It's no one's personal beeswax except my own. And the young lady's in question, of course," Tradd said demurely, but it was obvious that he had never been the central figure in any discussion of sexual prowess and was enjoying the experience in his own baffled manner.

"Was she a nice girl?" I asked.

"She was a wonderful person," he replied. "But not really my type."

"How many times did you say you blew her socks off?" Pig asked, his tongue tracing his upper lip.

"Did she scream and claw your back and beg for the banana?" Mark asked.

228

"As you can see, Tradd," I said, "sex is a sacrament to our Italian roommates."

"It has Extreme Unction beat all to hell," Mark said.

"I want to hear about every disgusting, stinky detail," Pig said in a tone that eloquently expressed all the wildness and animalism of sex.

"I'm surprised at you, Pig," Tradd scolded. "You are forever thrashing innocent boys who come in this room and even look at Theresa in an untoward way, yet you insult my friend and my relationship with her by asking me to describe our acts of love together. I find your behavior very inconsistent."

"Hey, you're right, paisan. I'm sorry. I just didn't think," Pig said apologetically.

"I'm the last virgin left in the room," I groaned. "Hell, I'm probably the last one left in the world."

"You won't ever have any more pimples," Pig said with authority. "Pimples can't survive regular sex."

"I have regular sex," I said, "only I have it with myself."

"Oh, gross," Tradd said. "I'm sorry I brought up this repulsive subject."

"I think it's great," Mark said. "I'm proud of you, Tradd. I'm really proud. You're a man now, boy."

"Do you know one reason I did it?" Tradd said, and his voice was edged with that remote aristocratic sadness that was his trademark in serious conversation.

"It doesn't matter, Tradd," I said. "You didn't do anything wrong."

"It *was* wrong," he said sharply. "It was very wrong, and I did it for all the wrong reasons. I didn't enjoy it very much. I suffered tremendous guilt over the entire affair."

"You've got to get used to it, Tradd," Mark said gently. "Nobody likes it the first couple of times."

"I've loved it since I was eleven," Pig said dreamily. "I felt like the Lone Ranger when I first shot silver bullets into a broad."

"You're so gross, Pig," Tradd said, "but I want to tell you all the reason. I did it because I wanted people to stop calling me the honey prince. I thought that after it was over people would look at me differently. I thought people would intuitively know. But nothing happened. Nothing changed. People still think I'm a queer, and there's nothing I can do about it."

"Tradd," I sighed, "forget about that nickname. That's all you've talked about since Reuben called you that. He didn't mean anything by it."

"Hey, paisan," Pig said in a whisper, "if anyone calls you that name again, it will be like someone calling Theresa a cunt. I'll break his mouth. I'll wax the quadrangle with the bastard. I promise."

"You know how I feel about you guys," Tradd said, and the room was suddenly electric with the tension of inarticulate boys.

"We feel the same about you," Mark said. "All of you guys know what's in Mark's heart."

"Hey, we're brothers, paisans," Pig said. "I'd kick ass for all of you. Just point to a guy and ol' Piglet will kick his ass."

"I've never liked any of you assholes," I said.

It began to rain and I could see lightning embroidering the sky with a violent, jagged silver. "It's Satan setting the table," my grandmother used to tell me. I was overcome with the power of the feelings that hovered in the room, mingling with the smell of ozone and marsh grass. There could be storm warnings even in the most delicate and banal of conversations. I heard the thunder, then the whistle of the Lowcountry Zephyr as it approached the trestle that crossed the Ashley River.

Then I heard the lion.

I had never heard the lion and the train at the same time. I had never heard the lion roar at 11:42 when the train passed over the river bearing its freight and passengers and mail. I had never heard the lion, the train, the thunder, and the sound of rain piercing through the parched oak leaves outside my window. At the time I thought it was a good omen, but I was wrong. I was very wrong, and the lesson made me understand why the Greeks employed mysterious oracles, humans with dazzling and miraculous powers, to divine the complex signals and messages given off by an implacable and bewildering universe. But I was young then and every omen was a good one. I fell asleep that night thinking of Tradd's ineffable sadness, of Mark's gruff gentleness, of Pig's volatility and blind loyalty, of my virginity, of my pleasure in talking in bed at night, of secrets between roommates, of my inability to tell boys who loved me that I loved them. I went to sleep, deeply, silently, fully; and I never once thought about Bucky Poteete.

But from that night on, the year was marked with a

curious inevitability, as though we were all engaged in an amazing and irresistible game. All the secrets of the year were contained in that one night's conversation, so innocent and serious and natural, when the place settings were laid out by brisk, wicked hands. The storm embraced Charleston in a gale from the Atlantic. The drought of September ended, and all of us accepted invitations to a banquet of storm and ruin and evil. I had forgotten the rest of my grandmother's story. She had told me that Satan could set his table anywhere he wanted; he didn't need to wait for a storm.

23

When Annie Kate began to show through the raincoat, Mrs. Gervais moved her out to the family beach house on Sullivan's Island, a gray Victorian structure on the south end of the island, directly across from Fort Sumter, with an uncommonly beautiful view of the harbor and the city. Mrs. Gervais lived in mortal dread that someone who mattered, someone prominent in the thinly oxygenated heights of Charleston society, would spot Annie Kate during one of her nocturnal promenades through the quiet streets or while she distractedly picked flowers and nervously paced the brick pathways of their desultory garden. If Annie Kate had been a prisoner in the house of Church Street, she became both a prisoner and expatriate on the island, even though the beach was practically deserted during the winter and her freedom of movement was far greater, as we took three- and four-mile walks on the sand, collecting shells, and watching the ships enter and leave the harbor. She would wave vigorously to the freighters coming to Charleston to unload their cargo; she would ignore the ships embarking from the city as though she could not understand why anyone or anything would want to leave a place so perfect and desirable. In the completeness of her loneliness, she was growing more petulant and irrational. She spoke of Charleston as though it were a prize that exacted an awesome tithe of spirit from those who loved it. She was obsessed with regaining the city for herself, with reclaiming her inherent right to its privileges and charms. The pregnancy had deepened her, she said, and had made her wiser as she faced the lights of the city directly across from her porch on Sullivan's Island. I never forgot what she said about Charleston in those slow wonderful days when we talked for hours and hours about the uncertain future. Charleston was not just a city, she said. Charleston was a gift and the gift must be earned. She would then stare longingly at those enchanted lights, strung like a brilliant necklace along the curved neck of the peninsula, and swear that one day she would earn back her rightful place in the city she had lost as a girl before she even realized how passionately she loved it or knew how desperately she would miss it when it was so cruelly taken from her.

I visited Annie Kate on the island every weekend and on four occasions had wheedled Charleston passes from the Bear so I could eat dinner with her during the week. I do not know when I fell in love with Annie Kate, but that does not matter. Nor do I know why I fell in love with her, though that matters a great deal. All I know is that there came a point when I did not feel alive when I was not with her or talking to her on the phone or writing her a letter. She became part of every thought, citizen of every dream. I did not tell her of my love and barely even admitted it to myself. But I lived for those long casual walks down the beach and the sight of her small footprints in the glistening wet sand, and I prized each shell she lifted from the beach and examined in her delicate white hands. In those late months of autumn and in the first chill of that benign Carolina winter, I knew one thing for certain: It was not Charleston I was trying to earn.

I watched the changes in her body as her whole exterior ripened with child; the thing alive inside her had added its heartbeat to her bloodstream, its hunger to her hunger, its movement and needs to her own urgent desires. I observed her unconscious flowering, the effortless rosy bloom of her complexion, which seemed so vital and basic and life-affirming in that period of gestation in which I had no legitimate part. Her mother and I were the only witnesses to her shame and we alternately received both her gratitude and her scorn. She would cry often; her sorrow was of that black, despairing quality whose only cure she carried as flesh and baggage within her own flesh.

We were hunting sand dollars on the beach late on a Saturday afternoon in October. Annie Kate and I had explored the whole littoral for a mile, surveying the terrain left exposed at low tide with trained and patient eyes. This had become one of our rituals together, and though she would search for other varieties of shells when I was out of town or unable to see her, she would wait until I appeared on her front porch before setting off to extract these mute delicate coins from their settings in the sand. At first, we had collected only the larger specimens, but gradually as we learned what was rare and to be truly prized, we began to gather only the smallest sand dollars for our collection. Our trophies were sometimes as small as thumbnails and as fragile as contact lenses. Annie Kate collected the tiniest relics, round and cruciform and white as bone china when dried of sea water, and placed them in a glass-and-copper cricket box in her bedroom. Often we would sit together and admire the modest splendor of our accumulation. At times it looked like the coinage of a shy, diminutive species of angel. The sand dollar in its center bore the mark of a feathery cross, and it was this sign of the cross that we searched for in those leisurely hunts by the sea's edge. Our quest to find the smallest sand dollar became a competition between us, and as the months passed and Annie Kate grew larger with the child, the brittle, desiccated animals we unearthed from the sand became smaller and smaller. It was all a matter of training the eye to expect less.

But on that cold Saturday, I lifted out of the hard wet sand the largest sand dollar either of us had ever seen. It was the size of an ashtray, and I was about to skip it across the waves of an angry, wind-roiled sea when Annie Kate stopped me.

"Have you ever opened a sand dollar?" she asked, taking it from my hand and breaking it carefully in half as though she were dividing a slice of bread. "It has religious significance like the dogwood tree. You know about the true cross on the outside of the shell, but I bet you didn't know that the Holy Ghost made a home in the sand dollar on Good Friday. He had to find a quiet place to hide in the world during those hours Christ hung on the cross. Do you remember how the Holy Ghost always appeared in the form of a dove? Here are four doves, which commemorate the visit of the Holy Ghost. The cross, of course, represents Good Friday and the Crucifixion."

Annie Kate carefully picked four birdlike shells from the dried-out insides of the sand dollar, small and perishable as the wing bones of a hummingbird, each identical to the other, and each a perfectly wrought image of a grieving, secluded Paraclete. I did not know if the dovelike cartilage was part of the sand dollar's circulatory system or not and I never tried to find out. Southerners had a long tradition of looking for religious significance in even the most humble forms of nature, and I always preferred the explanations of folklore to the icy interpretations of science.

As I was looking at the four doves, Annie Kate said, "Mother doesn't want me to walk on the beach during the day anymore. She says that anyone can tell I'm pregnant from half a mile away and I can't take a chance on anyone in town accidentally seeing me."

"Why has she just started worrying now, Annie Kate? I've been surprised she's let you walk around on Sullivan's Island the way she has. It's not like you've gone to Tahiti. You can see the whole city from here."

"But you don't know Charleston," she insisted. "Nobody who is anybody ever comes to Sullivan's Island after Labor Day. Everyone knows that."

"I can't believe your mother owns two houses," I said, changing the subject.

"She owns two houses and can't afford to keep either one of them up."

"Why doesn't she rent this one out on the beach?" I asked.

"That would be admitting to the world that she doesn't have any money. It's true that she doesn't have a single dime, but she's far too proud to admit that. She thought I was going to marry a filthy rich boy who would restore our family to wealth and splendor. But then this happened," said Annie Kate distractedly, as she patted her stomach and we began to walk back toward her house.

"Annie Kate," I said, "can I ask you a personal question?"

I could feel her stiffen as we moved along the beach, our arms touching slightly. "It depends on how personal, Will."

"I wouldn't hurt your feelings for the world, I really wouldn't," I stammered. "But why did you decide to have this baby? Why didn't you get an abortion when you realized you were pregnant? Why did you decide to put yourself through this incredible trauma? No one had to know. It would have made your life so much simpler. And you'd be so much happier now. Every time I see you it makes me sad to see you so sad. I can't wait until the baby is born so I can see you smile every once in a while."

She turned on me angrily. "Never mention the baby to me again, Will. There is no baby. There is no baby at all. There are just nine horrible months of my life that never happened. There are nine horrible months when time stood absolutely still."

"What are you going to do with the baby, Annie Kate?" I said, looking away from her. "You've got to at least think about what you're going to do."

"You have no right to force me to think of anything, Will. I think too much as it is," she said bitterly, then softened when she saw the pained expression on my face. "Before I met you, Will, I used to smile all the time. And I know when this is over, I'll smile again. I'm really a very happy person. When I first realized I was pregnant, I hoped that I was just late with my period. I've always been irregular. I just drove the thought out of my mind. Even when I got morning sickness I pretended it was the flu. Meanwhile, I think I subconsciously knew what was happening. I was doing everything possible to get the boy to marry me before I told him. I didn't want to force him. I couldn't imagine telling my mother I was pregnant and had ruined all her plans for me. But I was even more embarrassed to tell her my boy friend said he never wanted to see me again. Finally, I was beginning to show a little bit, and I had to tell somebody. So I told him. I'll never forget how he looked at me, Will. He told me he would pay for an abortion, but by then I was so hurt and angry and shocked that I couldn't agree or disagree to anything. I was numb all over. Completely numb and humiliated. So for the next week I thought of ways to kill myself. I bought razor blades and collected sleeping pills. I called his house every single day and begged him to marry me. I went to his house once and begged him on my knees. It was horrible. I cried and cried until his mother brought me home. She was very kind and talked to my mother. They both cried for a long time. They cried for each other and cried for themselves but not for me and not for the baby. The boy left town the next day and went somewhere, up north to college, I think, but no one ever said. My mother and his mother concocted this plan: I was to tell everyone that I was changing my plans for college. Instead of going to Hollins, I was going to the University of California at Santa Barbara. Then I would hide out in my house until my time was up. There's a doctor in Charleston, an old friend of my mother's, who has agreed to deliver the baby. But I don't want to think of that. You see, Will, I was alone, completely alone, until I saw you get into your car on East Bay Street at the end of August."

"Do you wish you'd gone ahead and had the abortion?" I asked.

"Yes."

"I'm glad you didn't," I said, staring at the cramped brick enclosure of Fort Sumter at the entrance to the harbor.

"Why?"

"Because I'd never have met you, Annie Kate. You'd be away at some snob college dating rich Virginia boys or rich Charleston boys, and I'd have never gotten a chance to know you or be your friend."

"I haven't been very nice to you, Will," she said, adjusting the angle of my cap. "I've taken a lot of anger out on you that should be going toward someone else."

"I haven't minded. I just like being with you. I can't wait for weekends to come, Annie Kate. I hate it when we play games away and I can't see you. I can't do anything without thinking about you."

"How do you think about me, Will?" she asked coyly, a glint of renewed coquetry in her eyes. "Tell me everything you think about me."

"You won't get mad?"

"I'll be furious if you don't tell me."

"First I've got to describe my fantasy life to you, Annie Kate. My fantasy life has always been a lot richer than my real life. These incredible scenes run on in my head like a movie that can never stop. Sometimes I'm a basketball player who cannot be guarded by anyone in the world. I'm superhuman. I mean that I can do things with a basketball that have never been done before, never been thought about. It's all so vivid, Annie Kate. I can see every detail. I've been the lover of a hundred women who didn't even know I was attracted to them. Most of them I had never talked to. I followed one woman down King Street one day. She was one of the most beautiful women I had ever seen. I not only became her lover; I became her husband, the father of her children. I never met her and she never saw me. But in my mind she was absolutely crazy about me."

"Do you think about me like that?" she asked.

"Like what?"

"Do you think about making love to me? Is that one of your fantasies?"

"No, of course not, Annie Kate," I lied, and blushed.

"Is that because I'm pregnant?"

"No, not at all. That has nothing to do with it."

236

"Then you find me unattractive," she said sadly.

"You're beautiful, Annie Kate. Much too beautiful for me. I can't even look at you for too long. You're that pretty to me. When you stare at me I always have to turn away. It always makes me feel ugly."

"Poor boys and their pitiful egos. Will, why do you always talk about yourself as if you were the ugliest boy in the whole world? Why, I've seen at least one or two uglier boys, at least. Now don't you go looking like that. I was only kidding. See how your horrible humor is infectious? I bet everyone who is around you for any length of time jokes the same way you do. I was horrid and spoiled enough when I met you. Now I'm getting your sharp tongue, and no one is ever going to want me."

"I don't know of any man alive who wouldn't want you," I said.

"I know of at least one."

"I want you to know this, Annie Kate," I said, stopping on the beach and turning her toward me. "I don't know who he is or what he does or why he decided not to marry you or at least stick by you during all of this, but I personally think the guy's out of his mind to desert you. I think that anybody who walks away from you or walks away from your child has something bad wrong with him, that something is dead inside him that nothing can bring to life again. And I don't think he'll ever do any better with a woman as long as he lives."

"That's sweet, Will," she said, taking my arm and smiling warmly to herself, as we began to walk toward her house again. "That's beautiful and sweet and I appreciate it. Now let's talk some about you. What are you looking for in a wife? Have you ever thought about that?"

"I'd like her to be female," I said. "I've narrowed it down to that."

"There you go again," she scolded. "If someone tries to be serious and conduct an adult conversation then you start that horrible joking again."

"I'm sorry. I don't know why I do that, Annie Kate, but I do it to everybody, not just you. If something gets too close or too personal, then I can tell a joke or say something sarcastic and redirect the conversation. It's an old trick of mine, but I'll try not to use it on you."

"I have my little tricks, too," she admitted.

"What are they?"

"That's for you to find out and not for me to tell. It's foolish for a woman to tell all her secrets. But I will tell you one, Will"—her voice dropped into a deeper, sadder tone— "I'm not going to be very good for you. I promise you that."

"You're the best thing that's happened to me since I've been to the Institute."

"You're certainly not the best thing that's ever happened to me," she said bitterly.

We had reached the seawall, which ran for half a mile along the southwest beach. We were walking on the huge black boulders from which the wall was constructed. I removed her hand from my arm, sprang down from the rocks, and began walking swiftly to my car.

"Will," I heard her call from behind me. "Where are you going, Will? I didn't mean to say that. I was trying to be funny: like you do. It wasn't funny and I apologize."

"You don't make mean jokes like that to your friends, Annie Kate."

"And I'm your friend who just said something stupid. And I'm your friend who just couldn't bear it if you walked out of my life right now. Will, I'm begging you to come back."

"You don't have to beg," I said. "I didn't have anywhere to go except back to the barracks and that's nowhere to go at all."

"Come back here and sit down beside me. Let's sit on the rocks and watch the sunset, Will. I'm alone too much, and I look forward so much to your coming over every week. The loneliness is killing me, Will. It's absolutely killing me. If you didn't call me every day and write me every day, I think I would have killed myself by now."

My back was still turned away from her when I said, "When I write you or call you or even when I'm with you, Annie Kate, I keep wishing one thing—I wish that it was my child inside you. I wish that I had put the child inside you. I wish I was calling you to see how our child was doing, how my wife was doing, how the mother of my child was doing. I keep wishing it was our child, Annie Kate. That's the only fantasy I've had for months. It won't leave me, and I can't get rid of it. It's much too powerful."

I felt my face coloring deeply. I was always so stiff and formal whenever I took to the floor to stumble out the elemental steps in my awkward dance of love. I felt as shy as a sand dollar. There was no confident flow or rhythm to my words; it was a panicked, frightened spillage of deeply felt, long-suppressed emotion. I had a twenty-two-year-old need to tell some woman that I was in love with her. And I needed a woman who was in no position to refuse my advances, to dishonor and rebuff my initial fervent confession of love. Later, I would think that it was not an accident that I chose an unmarried mother half-crazy from loneliness and abandonment; there was enormous safety in loving such a woman.

"Come back here, Will," she said softly, "and sit beside me."

I turned and went back to her, standing on the rocks. The tide was beginning to roll in again, and those great black slabs of granite had the formidable task of inhibiting the erosion along the beach, of impeding the flow and will of the Atlantic Ocean with its immeasurable tonnage and its mindless habit, centuries old, of taking or giving or regaining whatever it damn well pleased. The whole Atlantic coast was littered with groins and jetties designed to keep a portion of the continent from plunging into the sea. The tide poured through the cracks and crevices of those boulders as easily as light filtered through stained glass.

A school of porpoises broke the surface of the water twenty feet from where we had sat down. Their air holes flared explosively like carburetors opening for fuel. Each individual porpoise made a sound slightly different from that of any other, so that the school, all twelve of them, flaring and sliding and dancing so near us, formed a kind of woodwind section on the sea's surface or even a single instrument, something unknown and astonishing to man, a celebration of breath itself, of oxygen and sea water and sunlight. They had the eyes of large dogs and their skin was the loveliest, silkiest green imaginable.

But even the porpoises could not distract us from the dazzling, soul-altering, brilliant sun as it sank below the horizon out by Tennessee and Alabama. Fort Sumter was behind us now, and its history changed for me as I saw it through the thickets of Annie Kate's blond hair, as I smelled it through the perfume behind her ears and on her neck. The waters of Charleston gleamed like a newly struck medallion in the last exhausted dissolution of light over water. The light filtered through the steeples of the city, and a faultless linen of the purest and most sensuous gold spread toward us on the water, like a glass of Chablis spilled across a light-stained table. The clouds above the city were filled with subtle shades of pink, magenta, pearl, mauve, and vermilion, but it changed slightly, imperceptibly, permanently with each passing moment, as though the colors were wrought from movable glass as in a kaleidoscope. The pressure of her hand changed as the sun changed and the world around Charleston darkened and the porpoises moved into deeper water and we could no longer hear the primitive music of their breathing. A huge white freighter with its interior lights turned on moved out toward the ocean, bright and celebratory, like a floating birthday cake. Annie Kate did not wave to ships that abandoned her city, but I waved vigorously and with a genuine sense of loss. I wanted the moment to last forever. I would have stopped the freighter near the buoy to Fort Sumter, turned it about, and presented its constant immutable approach to the city as a gift to Annie Kate, a ship that would never leave her. I cannot express how lordly and transfigured I felt at that moment. I was a prince of that harbor, a porpoise king—slim among the buoys and the water traffic. I was aware of the blood rushing in my ears, my heartbeat, the tiny pulse in my wrist, the veins as they stood out on my forearms. It was with a keen, famished regret that I watched the last inanimate light of the sun feather the edges of the horizon. But my hand still held tightly to the hand of Annie Kate, and I felt her body press closely to mine, and I knew that I was living out one of the most important days of my life.

We rose up from the rocks in half darkness with stars beginning to appear in the sky like pale, ethereal jewelry. Looking up at me she took my face in her hands. She studied me with the fine dancing eyes of a girl who has been well trained in the art of looking at a boy. I turned away and watched the waves break against the rocks where we stood. There was a pulse and rhythm to the tide's aggression against the beach, the harmony and fearfulness of an irresistible force. The sun refused to die out on the horizon. She turned my face back toward hers. There was surprising strength in her small hands. I could barely see myself reflected in her pupils, a diminutive boy smiling foolishly back at myself in that tiny black cell that sang my name on those rocks. It is a precious, world-transfiguring stare when a girl looks at you with love in her eyes for the first time. Pulling my neck toward her face, she kissed me softly. Her lips brushed mine lightly, tenderly, and I felt her mouth open and her tongue slip easily between my teeth. Our tongues met and we kissed with a formal, comical chasteness. We spoke to each other with those searching, silent tongues, at the exact moment when language was not enough. I kissed her as though I was trying to drink her into me. I passed dreams into her and received hers on the black rocks beside the Atlantic.

I did not know a human mouth could taste so sweet or that a human body could feel so fine as it memorized my shape. In her kisses were the hint of berries, of ripeness and salt, all the happy taste of fruit harvested near oceans. For years my own tongue had ripened for this moment. The wind blew through our hair and the spray dampened our faces. The smell of salt and Annie Kate filled my nostrils. She licked the sea water from my face and the sea was ebony and silver through the blond shining flag of her hair. She kissed my eyes and both sides of my throat, taking her time, moving slowly as she memorized the shape of my face and throat. I wanted to make myself handsome for her; I wanted my face to transform into something irresistible, something so outwardly dazzling that she would never want to leave my side again. But most of all, I just wanted to be handsome enough, handsome enough to be the man loved by Annie Kate Gervais.

24

Beautiful cities have a treacherous nature, and they dispense inferiority to the suburbs that grow up around them with the self-congratulatory piety of a queen distributing mint among lepers. A suburb is simply a form of homage to a city's vitality, but it rarely receives even the slightest consideration for that homage. Charleston had the democratic good will to look down on all of its suburbs, but it reserved a very special contempt for the industrial city of North Charleston, which not only had the temerity to be extraordinarily common and depressing but had also borrowed the sacred name. To live in North Charleston was an admission of defeat. Industry huddled within its boundaries and a thick miasmic smoke hovered over the tract houses and the trailer parks, infecting each breath of the working class. It was a fine city in which to develop emphysema or lung cancer, and it was a hated city. The jokes of the aristocracy were usually about Jews, niggers, and North Charleston. There was an incontestable sadness to this unpraised, homely suburb, and there was never any reason for us to pass through its ordinary streets. That is, unless we needed to drive to Columbia or the county fair set up its midway on a dusty, unused field at the edge of town.

I loved county fairs in the South. It was hard to believe that anything could be so consistently cheap and showy and vulgar year after year. Each year I thought that at least one class act would force its way into a booth or sideshow, but I was always mistaken. The lure of the fair was the perfect harmony of its joyous decadence, its burned-out dishonored vulgarity, its riot of colors and smells, its jangling, tawdry music, and its wicked glimpse into the outlaw life of hucksters, tattoo parlors, monstrous freaks, and strippers.

It was the presence of the strippers that emptied the barracks of cadets. In the desperately horny climate of the Institute, it was a rare cadet, indeed, who would pass up the chance to glimpse a human vagina, no matter how debased or unpalatable. The General had granted us late leave so we could enjoy the fair. He thought it would do the troops a world of good to ride the Ferris wheel.

The smell of the phosphorous plant hung over the fairgrounds as we bought our tickets for the next burlesque show. A carousel circled nearby, the voices of small children calling to their parents above the loud, voluptuous music as they kicked their small heels against the wooden flanks of their garish, silent beasts. A barker exhorted the crowd to enter a tent fifty feet away to glimpse the ugliest woman in the world.

"I'll buy you a ticket to that, Will," Mark teased, nudging me with his elbow. "She may be the only woman in America who'll go with you to the Ring Hop."

"I didn't know your mother was moonlighting with the fair, Mark," I replied.

"It's dangerous to talk about a guy's mother," Pig cautioned. "They'd kill you on the block I come from for saying something like that."

"North Charleston has such an odor," Tradd said, wrinkling his handsome nose, testing the rancid air as if it were infected.

"It's like driving up the asshole of an elephant," Mark said. "The whole South smells like this."

We were eating cotton candy and drinking cheap, watered-down beer out of paper cups when the tent opened and we moved forward with the eager crowd to press close to a flimsy, makeshift stage. Well over half the crowd consisted of cadets from the Institute, and we were dressed neatly in the same salt-and-pepper uniforms we had worn to a Greater

Issues Speech delivered by former President Truman the previous week.

The strippers gyrated into view, accompanied by jarring, quasi-sensual music and the aroused, incontinent applause of the crowd. It was not a dance we had paid money to see, for their movements were irreligious parodies of the province and spirit of dance. What we observed was a debasement of the copulatory act, a grinding, panting, anti-erotic mime of fucking itself. It took a while longer to figure out that we were watching a mother-daughter team perform in their first full season together. By then, the crowd was chanting for both of them to remove their G-strings and a flurry of silver coins thrown from every corner of the tent was bouncing across the stage. The mother and daughter exchanged glances, and both decided to postpone the moment of golden unveiling until more money littered the stage. Pulling at their G-strings, they taunted the crowd for their stinginess and the air was streaked with flying coins.

The mother had the sneering hauteur and debased professionalism of a woman who had known the more bestial instincts of men for too long. She was overweight and sweated profusely in the tent, which itself had become a greenhouse of prurient fantasy. She looked at us and smiled obscenely, and I had never seen a smile convey such unadulterated contempt; she looked at us with absolute hatred, as though she were staring into a toilet bowl filled with used condoms. I felt as though I were made of nothing but semen as I watched her and her daughter with a combination of repulsion and desire. I could hardly take my eyes off the mother and the long, thin Caesarian scar etched into her abdomen.

The daughter was a pretty girl with a ripe sensuous body, but her movements across the stage were amateurish imitations of her mother's. She and her mother had identical brown eyes, with a dull, exhausted opacity about them. They glared sorrowfully in the brightness of the tent. Their hair was peroxided a deadly white and looked like grain planted on ruined, untended soil.

The music increased in volume and the bodies of the two women glistened as they moved and swayed in graceless ecstasies back and forth across the stage, passing each other again and again, playing to different sections of the crowd. The music itself sounded as though a convicted lecher had composed it. When they slowly and meticulously removed their G-strings and threw them into the crowd, I realized that I was seeing the first two mature female genitals of my life.

Nor was I overwhelmed by the beauty of the sight. It was with something akin to genuine horror that I saw the mother snatch a cigarette out of a cadet's mouth, stick the filter end deep inside her, moan dramatically, then replace it between the startled cadet's lips. The other cadets roared out their approval.

"Oh gross," Tradd moaned beside me. "I have never seen such sickness, Will. What can possibly be attractive about those two sorrowful women?"

"Pretend to be filled with lust," I said to Tradd. "We're part of the act."

"Wet beavers." Pig sighed happily as the two strippers parted their legs and began moving toward the mob in short, limbo-like hops. "This fair is so low-class that strippers show you wet beavers."

"I sure hope my daughters can grow up and land great jobs like this," Mark said, laughing and whistling and slapping the despondent Tradd on the back.

"I feel like a gynecologist looking at this mess," Tradd said as the act continued toward its wild, concupiscent finale.

When the act was over the mother embraced her daughter and announced to the crowd, "She came out of my pussy naked and I knew I had a new stripper for the show. Give Sally a big hand."

Sally. Why did she have to have a name like Sally? I thought. Why did she have to be granted so sweet and guileless a name? The Sallys of the world were gentle and innocent and shy; the Sallys I had known did not even suspect the existence of such sleazy demimondes as this one beneath a tent in North Charleston. How did this Sally get here and how did her mother get here? Where do these women come from? What circumstances brought them to this point, beneath this tent, to be cheapened by the impiety and violence of boys' eyes, to be cheapened by Will McLean's eyes? And why had Will McLean come here and paid money and cheered with the others when the G-strings arced into the crowd? Why had I done this? I thought, as we filed out of the tent. And why does it make me sad? I had enjoyed it—or thought I had—until the mother had called her daughter Sally. By giving her a name, she had implicated me, made me responsible, guilty.

When we exited the tent, the air of North Charleston was positively exhilarating and we breathed the tangy, phosphorous-scented night air with relief. The crowd was moving down the midway toward the far end of the parade ground. As we moved with them, I could feel Pig tense up and begin talking to himself in a curt, unintelligible whisper. He began shadowboxing the air as we walked leisurely along, and cadets who walked near him began to shout encouragement and to lay bets with each other. We paid another dollar to a weasly, scrofulous man who announced the upcoming bout between Dante Pignetti and the Heavyweight Champion of the Southeast. Pig tried to get the three of us in free as his trainers, but the man cheerfully refused and cheerfully collected our money.

Pig undressed in the back of the tent, stripping down to a pair of white trunks, and put on his sweat socks and gym shoes. Over three hundred cadets had crowded into the tent to witness the main bout of the evening. On the night before, Otto the Facebreaker had knocked Grainger Sox, a defensive tackle on the football team, unconscious and he had been unable to play in that afternoon's game against William and Mary. The cadets were rowdy and boisterous and chanting for revenge. Heavy betting between townsmen and cadets was going on all over the tent. The high exaggerated flush of sexual energy still glowed in the crowd. We pressed forward, Mark, Tradd, and I bearing Pig on our shoulders as he blew kisses to his friends. Otto emerged from the other side of the tent and mounted the flimsily constructed ring and waited impassively in the corner, leaning his considerable weight against the rope. It was easy to see why Otto the Facebreaker had not been named Sally.

He had a fleshy, scarred face that looked like a target on an artillery range. His impassive black eyes had a slightly minted cast, but they registered more boredom than malevolence. He was a tall heavy-set man with an inordinately large chest and rather bunched, cream-colored muscles, and he gave the appearance of being too fat and sluggish and out of shape to give a good account of himself in a fair fight. But he also appeared to be a man who had never participated in a fair fight in his life. There was an immense power in his stillness; a strange, dispiriting confidence. He could have gotten a high-paying job scaring babies to death.

I watched him as he studied Pig, who was performing a series of calisthenics in his corner. It was as though Otto was reading a menu or looking at a plate of food. Otto ran his fingers through his long hair, which was peroxided in the same washed-out coloring as the strippers'.

"Everybody in this high-class operation has white hair except the midget with no arms and legs," I said, wiping the sweat from Pig's face and neck with a towel.

"That's because he couldn't reach for the bottle," Mark muttered, watching the motionless giant across the ring.

"That man is an absolute animal," Tradd whispered to Pig, who had sat down on the stool in his corner. "Don't you dare fight him, Pig, I forbid it. It's silly."

"You may have to use karate on him, Pig," I said, "and I'm not even sure that will stop him."

"I've told you, Will," Pig said, "it's forbidden to use karate except when I'm in mortal danger. This is sport. It may turn to street fighting, but it will never turn to karate."

"Then why do you waste two goddam hours of every day practicing the goddam worthless stuff?" Mark sneered.

"It's a discipline," Pig answered calmly. "It is the art form of self-defense. It's not to be wasted on losers who punch out farm boys at county fairs."

"I wouldn't get in that ring with a flame thrower and a division of Marines backing me up," I said.

Mark's eyes had narrowed into studious slits as he watched Otto perform a few half-hearted knee bends on the other side of the ring. "Get out of the ring, Pig," Mark suddenly ordered. "I'm not going to let you fight him."

"I'm already in the ring, Mark," Pig answered without surprise, as though he had anticipated Mark's reaction.

"I'm not letting you fight him," Mark insisted. "He'll kill you. I've seen guys like him before. They make their living by beating the shit out of college boys with nice bodies."

"Good, I agree with Mark," said Tradd, over the noise of the crowd. "Let's go back to my house. This fair is the tackiest thing I've ever been to. And the smell in here is vulgar."

The smell was overpowering, a combination of sawdust, human perspiration, and the crushed pulp of peanut shells and half-eaten cotton candy.

"Come on, Pig," Mark said. "Let's get the hell out of here."

"I'm fighting him," Pig said. "I need the money, Mark, and you know it. The hundred bucks could get me through the next couple of months."

"We'll chip in and get you the hundred, Pig," I said. "We've always got the money when you needed it, haven't we?"

"I'm sick of borrowing money from you guys. It's no fun begging nickels and dimes from your roommates."

"Get out of the ring," Mark shouted urgently in Pig's ear.

"Everyone in the school would know it," Pig responded wearily. "I'd lose face. I can take that creep. He doesn't keep himself in shape. I'm going to ride that turkey for five minutes."

The referee climbed into the center of the ring and announced the fight into a rusty, wheezing microphone. "Ladies and gentlemen," he crowed to the womanless crowd, "the challenger who has gallantly agreed to mortal combat with Otto the Facebreaker tonight is Cadet Dante Pignetti of Carolina Military Institute, weighing in at two hundred pounds. Give Pig a big hand."

The tent exploded with applause as Pig moved to the center of the ring, his feet dancing to the pulse of the crowd. Otto watched him as the cadets chanted deliriously, "Pig. Pig. Pig. Pig. Pig."

Pig's body was absolutely magnificent; he looked as though he had been carved by the hand of Michelangelo.

"It is a no-holds-barred match, ladies and gentlemen," the referee said.

"Keep away from him, Pig," Mark shouted as we left the ring. "Keep moving, keep low, and don't clinch with that bastard. He'll kill you in a clinch. Box him. Hammer his face and if he gets near you, move, move, move."

Pig nodded that he understood Mark while the tent boomed with jeers and hisses as Otto was introduced.

Pig moved toward the center of the ring and toward Otto the Facebreaker when the referee instructed, "Shake hands, gentlemen. And come out fighting."

"Don't," I heard Mark scream, but it was too late.

As Pig extended his arm to shake hands, Otto jammed two fingers directly into Pig's eyes. Pig let out a single cry of distress and surprise and pain, and his hands went instinctively to cover his eyes. Otto chopped him to the floor with a vicious rabbit punch to the back of the neck. The slow-moving, half-awake Otto was moving with the savage, awakened grace of a leopard as he landed a kick against the side of Pig's head. He lifted Pig's head off the floor by cruelly grabbing a knot of Pig's hair and was about to land a punch that easily could have broken Pig's jaw. He was about to land the final coup de grâce when a slim, frantic figure sprinted across the ring and wrapped himself around Otto's neck and back. Otto looked up with a slow-witted expression of both surprise and amusement, as though he had been attacked by a parakeet. He was no more surprised than I was. Or Mark. It was Tradd St. Croix.

"Oh, shit," Mark said, clambering into the ring.

There was an astonished and confused hum among the crowd as Otto tried to dislodge Tradd from his back. But Tradd was wrapped as tightly as a scarf, and he had shut his eyes as though he did not want to witness his own imminent execution. Otto finally reached over his back, grabbed Tradd's uniform, and removed him as though he was drawing an arrow from its quiver. Tradd landed on his back with a breathless thump. Otto studied Tradd with a rather detached and thoughtful curiosity as though he had never had to dispose of such a thin and fragile attacker. Pig had rolled away to a far corner trying to clear his eyes. Otto was still involved in the laborious process of deciding how to kill someone as small as Tradd when he had to reverse the process and decide how to deal with someone as large as Mark Santoro.

One problem Otto did not have was how to deal with Will McLean because ol' Willie had made a swift and instantaneous decision that Otto would only face three-fourths of the occupants of room 4428. I do not scuffle with people named Otto the Facebreaker.

Mark sent Otto reeling backward with a punch to the sternum. He then stepped between his roommates and the giant. I crawled into the ring, keeping a cold eye on Otto, grabbed Tradd by the collar, and jerked him beneath the ropes before Otto could make the terribly erroneous conclusion that I entertained any thoughts of violence toward him. I was feverish I was so afraid. The heat and noise and mayhem surrounding the ring had immobilized me and rendered me impotent, with that absurd helplessness of being a spectator to an event beyond my control.

"Have you gone apeshit?" I yelled to Tradd above the din of the crowd.

"I can't believe I did that," he said wondrously, jubilantly. "I just can't believe that I did that." He was screaming in disbelief and euphoria as cadets crowded around him, slapping him on the back and offering him drinks of whiskey. Bedlam was loose in that tent as Otto moved toward a midring reckoning with Mark.

Mark was crouched in a classic boxer's stance, watching

Otto's movements with that scowling and formidably embittered look that was a warning to strangers that he was not a man to be taken lightly. And Otto was not taking Mark lightly but was beginning to move easily, hugely and wickedly, relying on all the countless moments when he had roamed this roped, canvas province, stalking the strongest boys in hundreds of Southern counties, confident of his powers and his experience and his manhood. The hostility of the crowd, surreal and absurd when mingling with calliopes and the frenetic salesmanship of barkers, shimmered across the ring and Otto's broad back like something electric, ignited, and deadly. A hueless pallor dulled Mark's face, a proud untouchability so incongruent on a face that suddenly belonged to a boy. These moments were only seconds, instants of appraisal as Otto regained his bearings and moved in for the kill as though stalking some toothless cub for his own pleasure and entertainment.

But before Otto could close in on Mark, a new, strident sound entered the tent. It began low and steady like the hum of a high-tension wire, then increased in volume and shrillness, bestial and wild and unnamable, until we realized that it was coming from Pig. It ended in a kind of battle cry, a furious tattoo of combat and outrage. His eyes had cleared, and Pig was crouched in an oddly distorted, yet ceremonial, position as though he were offering prayers to a ruthless and malignant deity. His feet were planted widely apart, his knees were bent, and his hands were placed stiffly and formally in front of his face, like the forelegs of a praying mantis.

The cadets went wild.

"Karate!" they shouted in unison as Mark dove out of the ring beneath the bottom ropes.

Otto made another tour of the ring, watching Pig closely and waiting for him to make an aggressive opening move. But Pig was locked in his first position like a man in prayer or in pain. Again Pig's martial whine filled the tent. I had never seen him angrier. At that moment I wished I had brought Theresa's picture. I would have held it aloft and screamed, "Otto just called Theresa a gaping, flapping twat." But the one thing Pig did not require was motivation. Otto had done something no human being had ever done to Dante Pignetti; he had humiliated him physically and had done it before a tent full of witnesses. Every vein in Pig's body seemed to stand out in bold relief. Blood discolored his head in the place where Otto had yanked a snatch of his hair completely out.

Not that Otto appeared frightened or alarmed in the least. He simply looked bemused and interested in the novelty of Pig's stance. He was accustomed to twenty-second fights, brief and violent slaughters. He began laughing and as he laughed, he moved in with amazing speed and grace for the denouement.

He was still laughing when Pig kicked him across the ring.

Pig's kick caught Otto squarely in the forehead and with enormous force snapped the big man's head back savagely and sent him crashing into the far ropes. When Otto came off the ropes, his gait was drunken and staggered and the eyes that searched the lights for the opponent who had hurt him were unfocused and confused. Pig caught him on the rebound from the ropes and doubled him up with short, slashing punches to the midsection that sounded like an axe ruining soft wood. Grabbing a fistful of peroxided hair, Pig straightened Otto carefully, then drove the heel of his open palm into the center of the big man's face. Otto's nose exploded like an overripe berry, and he lay panting and semiconscious on the canvas deck. The blood spread evenly across his face with a terrible symmetry, like a rose fingerpainted by a child.

The cadets chanted, "Pig!"

And Pig answered, holding his arms victoriously above his head, "Oink."

"Pig!" the cadets repeated.

"Oink," he answered.

"Pig!"

"Oink."

Pig danced up to the referee, who was angrily tending to his hurt champion, and snatched the hundred-dollar bill from his pocket, waved it like a hankie to the crowd, then bent down on one knee to help minister to Otto the Facebreaker.

We drove away from the fairgrounds in my silver-gray 1959 Chevrolet with which my mother had bribed me when I threatened to drop out of the Institute in the spring of my sophomore year. We talked excitedly about the fight, each of us recounting the event in four separate and distorted narratives of the exact same events. By the time we had reached the city, the fight had become fiction, the truth divisible in four distinct incongruent ways. Three hundred unjoined versions would circulate through the barracks by midnight, gathered and appropriated by cadets who were not present but who would claim they were, until the fight would enter into the history of that academic year according to joyous laws of storytelling where the annexation of myth becomes a form of truth itself.

"I've got to stop for gas," I said, as we pulled into the Gulf station on Meeting Street, four blocks from Tradd's house. The old slave market with its glooms and arches cast its severe shadows on us. "Have any of you assholes been using my car lately? I've been getting shitty mileage."

"I used it last week, Will, when mine was in the garage," Mark said.

"How was the trip to Oregon?"

"I only went downtown. Goddam, let me pay you a buck," he answered.

"I probably need a tune-up."

Pig said from the back seat, "I'll check it out for you this week when I'm working on my clunker, Will."

"How's the fifty-dollar car coming along, Pig?" Tradd asked. "Do you think that sad machine will ever work?"

"It'll work," Pig said. "It may not work for long, but I'll get it working."

"By the way, Pig," I teased, "I thought you weren't supposed to use karate."

"I wasn't, paisan. I was wrong to use it."

"Was it because he poked his fingers in your eyes that you used it?" Tradd asked, turning around in the front seat to face Pig.

"Fill it up with regular," I said to the attendant, a wizened, elderly man who seemed in pain when he moved.

"Naw, the eyes didn't bother me," Pig said. "But when he started messing with the gorgeous curls, I knew that there'd be some heavy-duty chink-fighting going on in that ring."

Mark said, "You shouldn't have gotten into that ring, you dumb bastard. You could have gotten hurt real bad. And you could have gotten us all hurt."

"You couldn't have gotten Will hurt," Tradd said, smiling at me.

"I could have been seriously hurt if I'd been hit by one of your bodies flying out of the ring," I answered.

Pig turned serious for a moment. "Why didn't you come into the ring to help me, paisan? The whole room would have been in there duking it out for each other."

"I froze, Pig," I said, looking at him in the rearview mirror. "I was scared to death to get in that ring. Physical courage has never been my forte. I go in for moral courage, because with moral courage you don't get your face beat in or your eyes gouged out. By the way, Tradd, that was a brave thing you did."

"A stupid thing," Mark disagreed.

"It was wonderful," Tradd said dreamily. "Wonderful. That was the first courageous thing I've ever done in my whole life. I don't know what got into me. I simply cannot imagine what made me do it. Please don't tell Mother. She would disapprove, although I am equally sure that Father would love it."

"I got to tell her, paisan," Pig said, squeezing Tradd's frail neck affectionately. "You put it all on the line for me, Tradd. If it wasn't for you, Otto would be cleaning my nuts from between his toes. And you too, Mark."

"I went in there because of Tradd," Mark insisted. "You deserved to get your ass kicked for pulling off a dumb stunt like that. It would have done you good to get your ass kicked by that monkey. You got too much luck for your own good. You've always been able to step in manure and come out smelling like Chanel No. 5. But your time is coming, Pig. No one has luck all the time. You're using up too much of yours on stupid shit."

When the attendant approached the window to get paid, Pig thrust the hundred-dollar bill into his face.

"I can't cash this," the man sputtered.

"It's all we've got," Pig said sorrowfully.

"No, it isn't," I said, handing the man a ten-dollar bill.

"You don't have to pay for my gas, Pig," I said. "You'll be needing that money for other things, like tuition."

"I'm going to try to pay my own way this year, paisan," Pig announced. "I may need to borrow a little bit every once in a while, but I'm going to be hustling money all year. I've even got a job as a bartender on weekends down at the Merchant Seaman's club every other weekend."

"You'll get thrown out of school if they find out, Pig," Tradd warned. "That's too much of a chance for you to take. I won't hear of it."

"Just buy your own deodorant," Mark said. "I'm sick of finding your greasy armpit hairs on my deodorant stick."

"Oh gross," Tradd said. "How did I get stuck with such gross-talking creatures for roommates?"

"I'll never use your deodorant again, paisan."

"Good."

"Don't worry so much about money, Pig," I said.

"You're starting to get obsessive about the subject. We've always made it OK. We've made it just fine."

Pig looked at Mark and said with a vast unchristened hurt in his voice and a nakedness rare in the chronicles of our life together, "Mark, I can't help it that I was born poor. Do you think I like it? Do you think I like begging from guys I love?"

"Stop it," I demanded.

"Let's stop this silly talk of money," Tradd agreed.

"I want you to get your own deodorant, Pig. That's all," Mark said uneasily, examining the shadows of the slave market.

"We'll find out where Otto the Facebreaker buys his," I said. "Then we'll go shopping."

"Do you think I like it, Mark? Do you think I like it, Mark?" Pig said again.

"Yeh," Mark answered. "I think you like it."

25

If I had to say what I loved most about the city of Charleston, I would say that I loved the stillness and leisure of its early Sunday afternoons. There was a timelessness to those Sundays: a greenness to its parks and private arbors; the quiet hum of well-dressed crowds gathering beneath the columns of its churches; then the sudden bloom of sails and the gestures of small crews far out in the river; the abstraction of the walkers along the Battery; the pleasant symmetry of eighteenth-century houses clustered along the narrow feminine streets; bells over the city; the shrill robust games of happy children and the healthy glow of those children; the movement of freighters into the harbor after trans-Atlantic voyages. On Sundays, Charleston, without the dissonance of commerce or traffic, had the serene regularity of a city so magical in its harmony, so purified of stridency or disorder, so certain of its virtues, that it seemed a city separated from its century by an incorruptible cleanliness of spirit and image, a perfect environment for recreation and quiet pleasure. On Sundays, Charleston became a city of gardeners and strollers and fishermen and sailors cutting toward buoys. It was a city that could sit quietly observing itself, listening to the cooing of its pigeons in the colonnades, the purring of bees among the mint gardens, and the rumors of old people beneath the columns and belvederes.

I learned some things on those Sundays in Charleston, and my teacher was Abigail St. Croix. She taught me to see the city as she saw it and to measure all other cities by the standards of Charleston. Abigail would often take me for long walks after lunch at her house on Sunday. She would make me ache with love for the city. She would point out details I never would have noticed alone. Together, we studied the antiques in shop windows on lower King Street, and she would deliver small lectures on the histories of spoons, the travels of porcelain to the New World, or the elegance of the Queen Anne period. She would name each item that struck her fancy in the window and if I was not moved by its charm she would winsomely explain why I should be charmed and we would continue our walk. She would name things for me that previously existed only as parts of the undifferentiated landscape. She taught me the names of trees and flowers, styles of architecture, historical figures in the city, the names of mansions as they appeared in the National Register, the names of the families of harbor pilots, the various forms of Charleston brick—anything she thought of or needed to let me know as we walked off our lunches and enjoyed the languor of the city. Sometimes she took me to the houses of her friends, introduced me, and showed me formal interiors where each room was a work of art, where every corner had been created with the cautious, gifted eye of the miniaturist. Do everything well, Abigail said, and leave nothing to chance. There was no such thing as an insignificant detail, and everything had a name. She said many things on those walks and I remember most of them. Gardens, tended by quiet thoughtful people, make for pleasant cities, said Abigail St. Croix. And a century is a patient thing, she once observed, as we studied the delicate lattice-work of ficus attached to the south face of a carriage house on Legare Street. We would stop to listen to the songs of black women coming from kitchens, or conversations of men cleaning fish on their back porches, or the voice of the carriage driver describing the city to tourists as his horse moved through the narrow streets. Sometimes I would carry a shovel and a bag to scoop up the horse manure deposited on the streets for use in Abigail's own garden. Once we watched unseen as a woman arranged daffodils in a blue-flowered vase set on a table in a bay window curving out to the sidewalk. The woman's hands, with their length and thinness and their pale blue veins, looked exactly like Abigail's hands; and I wondered if Charleston women all came to have the same lovely hands, if a lifetime of handling flowers and linen aged their hands with a special softness and delicacy.

On those walks we talked about Tradd and Commerce, God, and politics, as well as the silliest, most fatuous, most inconsequential things. We talked about everything except those things that hurt or damaged or mattered most significantly in our lives. We never took each other to those intimate gardens hidden from the eyes of visitors. When I look back on those Sundays, I believe that Abigail and I each wanted to allow the other the privilege of entering those gardens at will, but we did not know where to find the gates and keys that would permit free and easy access. We knew about those gardens, but we did not know how to enter them.

On the second Sunday in November, I went to say good-bye to Commerce St. Croix, who was leaving the next week to meet a ship in Philadelphia. The dinner that afternoon consisted of those things that Commerce loved the best and would miss the most in his two-month absence. It began with a thick she-crab soup flavored mildly with an expensive dry sherry. The soup was followed by a superb coquille St. Jacques served in a spinach puree, which Abigail had imitated from a meal she and Commerce had enjoyed on a trip to the Dodin Bouffant in Paris years before. The meal ended with a homemade lime sherbet, followed by small demitasses of espresso, which we took in the living room.

The living room was not used, to my knowledge, except on Sundays. The room itself was, quite simply, an accumulation of precious objects. I sat rather stiffly in a Regency chair that had been pictured in a book celebrating the craftsmanship of Charleston antiques. A chandelier, the most famous in South Carolina, hung like a brilliant crystal stalactite from the ceiling, and the smell of furniture polish gave a permanent, opulent odor to the room, a perfume of endurance and nostalgia. Our conversation was rather muted and pleasant. Our voices were like prayers lifted up and offered as invocations to the house, and the house itself was an invocation to slower, more cautious days.

I was privileged to be a part of all this, I thought, as I listened to Commerce talk about his itinerary, and it seemed to me there were far worse strategies in life than to try to make each aspect of one's existence a minor work of art. But I was also beginning to notice something chilly and remote in an ambiance of such conscious perfection. There was no urgency in the effortless, classical preference for the simple over the ornate and showy. There was no personal statement in the house, no indelible signature of individuality; it was as though the collective unconscious of all Charlestonians, the living and the dead, had formed a committee of restrained equilibrists to design the interior of each room. There was nothing ugly or comical or beloved on the walls, no souvenir of travel, no bibelot or trinket to inspire memory. There was nothing hallucinatory or disturbing in the house, nothing to induce the white desperate blaze that had haunted the houses of my youth. Perhaps it was because my family had no nostalgia for the past, no sense of responsibility to uphold a proud and carefully wrought tradition. I had once bought the St. Croixs a hunting print from an antique shop in Charlottesville, Virginia. The print had cost twenty dollars, and it was the most expensive gift I had ever bought anyone. Abigail had seemed immensely pleased with the print, yet I never saw it hanging anywhere in the house. In fact, I never saw the print again. But something in me always looked for it, every time I entered the St. Croix mansion. Much later, on one of our Sunday walks, Abigail instructed me on the value of some English prints displayed in the windows of Schindler's. When she had finished I realized I had bought the St. Croixs a reproduction of a famous print, and even I knew that a reproduction would never hang in the house of St. Croix. All of this had something to do with why Pig and Mark seldom attended these dinners on Sunday afternoon. Unlike me, it bothered them to feel like reproductions.

Commerce looked over at me with a mischievous, excited expression. The sound of frail cups clicking into their saucers was the only other sound in the room when he announced, "I want to read something funny I found while re-reading one of my oldest journals last week. You and Tradd will really enjoy this, Will."

He left the room with his swift, birdlike gait and we heard his footsteps quick and light on the stairs.

"It's very rare for Father to read from his journals, Will," Tradd said, sipping the espresso with some slight distaste. "He treats them like Biblical texts."

"I've tried to keep journals, myself," I said. "Every time I buy a new journal, I write furiously in it for the first week or two. Then I put it away and never pick it up again. I've never had any staying power at all. Do you think that reflects badly on my personality?"

"Having roomed with you for four years, Will," Tradd said, "I think everything reflects badly on your personality."

"Slap your mouthy son, Abigail. He's trying to hurt my feelings."

"I'm glad you can't keep a journal, Will. I wish Commerce didn't keep one," said Abigail, listening to her husband's footsteps coming back down the stairs. "I'm sure he says dreadful, unforgivable things about me. It puts such pressure on me. Every time we fuss or have a fight, he races up to his study. I'm sure he records it all in such a way as to make me sound positively beastly. I do wish he would get another, more reputable hobby."

Commerce listened to her last sentences as he entered the room again, wearing his glasses, and leafing through the pages of a leather-bound journal.

"My journal is a record of my life, Abigail," he said defensively, "a complete record. I've been as diligent as a scientist in recording everything of significance that has happened to me since I was a cadet at the Institute. I mark down time and place. I note the weather conditions. If I have been fishing, I record the number and type of fish caught, what kind of bait I used, and where I caught them. When I die I'm leaving these journals to the Charleston museum. It might be interesting to some future historian who wants to follow an old Charlestonian through his daily life around the city and his tours around the globe."

"It sounds unimaginably dull to me, Father," Tradd said, staring into his cup as though examining it for flaws. "It sounds like a cookbook written by someone who doesn't like food."

"It is dull in many places. But it is accurate, and accuracy is all that really matters. The log of a ship is dull to anyone but a seaman, but a seaman finds it fascinating and filled with information. I record in my journal like the mariner I am."

"I would like to read your journals someday, Father," Tradd said. "I would learn a great deal about you, I suspect."

"You'll never read my journals," said Commerce sharply to his son. "A journal is the most private form of communication in the world, and it would be a violation of the form if I let you or Abigail or anybody read the journals. I will put a stipulation in my will that no one opens the journals until all of us are dead. Why do you think I have my door to the study padlocked when I'm at home? It's not that I don't trust you. It's that I don't wish to tempt you.

"I achieve accuracy. That is all. Now let me read Will and Tradd this rather interesting passage I found the other day. I think they will find this particular entry rather amusing. This scene took place on February 6, 1934, when I was a junior at the Institute. It reads as follows: 'Last night my roommate, Obie Kentsmith, and I, under the influence of Edgar Allan Poe and "The Cask of Amantillado," attempted to brick in our First Sergeant, one Bentley Durrell, who was not demonstrating the proper respect for his classmates. To wit, he was holding surprise room inspections whilst the rest of us were in class.' "

"Whilst?" Abigail said.

"I went through a very affected writing style while in college," Commerce explained.

"Whilst you were in college, Father," Tradd said without meeting Commerce's eyes.

" 'Obie and I,' " Commerce continued, " 'armed with trowels, brick, and mortar, waited until 0200 hours, then proceeded to build a brick wall in front of Durrell's door on second division. Alas, the mortar did not have time to set properly. . . .' "

"Alas?" Abigail interrupted again, highly amused.

" 'And Bentley managed to beat his way out to freedom using the butt of his rifle as a bludgeon at reveille,' " Commerce read, ignoring his wife. " 'All the talk in the barracks is speculation as to the identities of the perpetrators of this perfect crime. Obie and I do our best to keep from laughing right out loud during these discussions. Bentley came to our room all in a huff this morning and asked our help in finding the villains who had performed this dastardly deed. Obie and I gave our solemn word that we would help track down these odious criminals and bring them to justice.' "

"I can't believe you bricked the General into his room," I said.

"If the mortar had had another hour or two to set, Bentley would have been in real trouble," Commerce cackled. "They'd have had to call a demolition team in to get him out of there."

"That seems rather odd behavior for the scion of one of Charleston's oldest families, Father," Tradd said. "What

258

would you say if I went around the barracks bricking up every poor soul who tried to do his duty? Why, you wouldn't be able to open a single door in fourth battalion."

"I wouldn't say a word if you didn't get caught, and I didn't. No one suspected the scion of one of Charleston's oldest families to be capable of such shenanigans," Commerce said delightedly, still enjoying the success of his prank so many years after the fact.

"Well, I certainly don't think it's anything to be proud of," Abigail said. "Why don't you strike that passage so that future historian, whoever he is, does not think the St. Croix family was composed of men with absurd and childish senses of humor?"

"He will get the truth about the St. Croixs, Abigail, whatever that is."

"You mean, however you personally interpret the truth."

"Yes," Commerce said, immensely pleased with himself. "The truth, as I see it. But that's only fair. I'm the one who takes the time to keep journals. I deserve some reward. Now if y'all will please excuse me, I have some packing to finish. Don't leave without telling me good-bye, Will. I'll send you something nice from Europe."

He left the room and ascended the stairway again. For a few moments we sat in complete silence, the pleasant lassitude of Sunday overcoming us and a fragrant breeze pouring through the open first-floor windows. I looked about me again and said, "I want to catch what you've got, Abigail."

"Catch what, Will?" she asked.

"This thing that you've got. This Beauty Disease. I want to spend my entire life perfecting the art of making everything around me as beautiful as possible. I want my furniture to be beautiful, my house to be beautiful, my gardens, my children, my wife . . . everywhere I look I want to be stunned by the sheer absolute force of physical beauty."

"You're such a slob, Will," Tradd said with conviction. "You don't even shine your shoes or keep your part of the room clean."

"Please get your son to hush, Abigail," I appealed, with a gesture of dismissal toward Tradd. "I've already suggested once today that you slap his uppity mouth. The subject is beauty, Tradd, and I'm telling you how I'm going to go about getting it in my life. It's going to be very simple. I'm going to mold my life on the St. Croix family. I'm going to stop being excitable and flamboyant. I'm going to quit horsing around. From now on I'm going to be reserved and silently filled with wisdom. I'm not going for the cheap laugh anymore or make any attempt to amuse the herd. I'm going to dress impeccably. I'm going to shop for charming objects in antique shops and learn to prepare exquisite meals. I've got to make myself susceptible to the Beauty Disease. I want my whole life to be infected by beauty."

"Beauty Disease?" Tradd winced. "It sounds like some fungus Mother finds on her roses."

Folding her large bony hands on her lap, Abigail said reflectively, "I wouldn't call it a disease. I call it a search for quality. I've looked at my life carefully and I've made solicitous choices about what is truly important to me. I would recommend it to both of you as a way to improve your daily life in immeasurable ways."

"You have me for a roommate, Tradd," I said in a voice far too loud for the formal atmosphere of the room. "Your search for quality is over. You'll never be able to do any better."

"Oh, please, Will."

"I know," Abigail announced suddenly. "Let's perform a ceremony. It's one that I would love to share with the two favorite men in my life."

Abigail left the room as Tradd and I went into the dining room to clear the table and extinguish the candelabra. When she returned she was carrying a silver tray with a set of wine glasses and a crystal decanter filled with a pale liquid upon it. She filled three wine glasses with the fluid.

"What is this concoction, Mother?" Tradd asked, eyeing his glass suspiciously.

"When Commerce and I were first married, we went on a long honeymoon to Europe and both of us fell in love with Greece and especially the Greek islands. When I went to those islands I felt that I had come to a place where I was meant to be. I don't mean anything so prosaic as a sense of coming home. This was different, very different. It was like arriving at a place much safer than home. Something ancient and pure inside me responded to the life and spirit of those people. We brought back a jar of water from the Aegean sea, chilled it in a decanter, offered toasts to each other, and drank the water. Every time Commerce goes to the Aegean, he replenishes our supply. Each time he leaves to meet a ship, we drink some of the water for a bon voyage and a safe return. We'll drink our toast tonight together, but I don't think he would mind if I shared it with you two. I'm sure he'd be pleased."

"How romantic, Abigail."

"Mother," Tradd said, "Greeks urinate directly into the ocean, and that's the very least of what they do."

"My son, the antiromantic," she sighed, winking at me.

"Your son, the enlightened realist."

"Will will drink it with me," she said.

"So will Tradd," I said, raising my glass in a toast. "To the Beauty Disease."

"The disease," Tradd and Abigail echoed.

And another Sunday passed away in the St. Croix mansion. When I left the house, I could see by the look on Abigail's face that she was hurt that I did not have time for one of our walks around the city. I made an excuse about falling behind in my studies with the basketball season coming so close. But I embraced Commerce, told him I would write him, made my farewells, and walked to my car on East Bay Street.

Then I drove to Annie Kate's. I had already caught the Beauty Disease. It was a secret malady that I could share with none of my friends, but I was glad that at least this secret had a name.

26

We received our rings on the first truly cold day in November. The Carolina lowcountry did not have the spectacular autumns that were famous in the mountainous part of the state above Greenville; instead, there was a rather subtle transfiguration of the trees, a patient, almost invisible killing of the lush greens of summer and a reluctant, though inevitable, turning toward the coming winter months. The week before, the cadets had gone into their wool dress grays, a sign of winter's approach in Charleston more accurate than the discoloring of an oak leaf.

But it was in the marsh at the edge of the Institute that the winter could be most visibly seen and felt. Almost imperceptibly, at the beginning of November, the marsh began to change its color. Its marvelous fertility and brazen health, its deep, brilliant greenness altered and waned almost daily, as winter with its chilly nights and the slow cooling of the Atlantic started to settle into each stem and living thing in the marsh. The oystermen of Charleston began to haunt the banks and protected creeks around Folly Beach, and the shrimpboats anchored at Shem Creek were already dragging the shallows along the coast when the first light broke across the Eastern Seaboard. The entire marsh for two hundred miles began the lovely turn, the slow leisurely withdrawal into its vestments of gold, as the lowcountry prepared for the cycle of death and renewal. The marshes of Charleston had a different look when the weather was cold. And the Institute had a different look, and I felt like a different man the night I put on the ring.

The senior class gathered at 1900 hours on the parade ground to muster for the grand march to the South Carolina Hall on Meeting Street. We were arrayed in our full-dress uniforms, and we gathered in companies on the north end of the campus to begin the march by walking between two long lines of cadets composed of the boys from the three under classes. The cheering was deafening as the drums began to roll and the A Company seniors began the promenade of honor between the two immense files of underclassmen.

The ring march was the longest and most pleasant of a cadet's career. We left the Gates of Legrand with the regimental band playing fight songs of the Institute. We passed beside Hampton Park and the handsome residences of Moultrie Street before we turned south on Rutledge Street and began the long march to Broad. The city aged as we headed down the peninsula, the houses grew older and more distinguished, as though we were marching backward into history. Black children waved and danced to the music of the band, and old people watched our progress from sagging, unpainted verandahs. Policemen halted traffic at each intersection as our heels thundered on the asphalt, creating that strange alarming music of disciplined men moving according to a single will. The streetlights struck the brass insignias of our field caps as though someone was striking matches just above our eyes.

We passed Highway 17, Ashley Hall, and Charleston High School, crossed Calhoun Street, and neared the Charleston museum on our right, the oldest city museum in North America. The band quit playing as we approached the museum, and I heard Jeff Pomerantz prepare the seniors for the annual salute to the whale.

The baleen whale, whose skeleton hung like a graceful trellis from the ceiling in the main hall of the museum, was the unofficial mascot of the Institute. Plebes were required to make a special visit to the museum to salute the whale before they left for the Christmas holidays.

A Florida cadet had begun the tradition in 1910 when he had been denied entry into a debutante ball because of his questionable ancestry. The same week the cadet had learned the story of how the bones of a baleen whale, an extraordinary rarity in the coastal waters of South Carolina, had come to rest in the Charleston museum. In 1881, Charlestonians promenading along the Battery were more than mildly surprised to see the forty-foot whale entering the main channel of Charleston harbor. A long sea chase ensued, with Charlestonians, armed with harpoons, taking to the river in tugs and smaller boats to engage the disoriented mammal. For two days the harpoonists pursued the whale around the harbor until the beast died of its wounds and the exhaustion of the chase. It was dragged ashore, photographed, butchered, and its bones preserved and reassembled on the museum's ceiling. The cadet from Florida recognized in the epic of the baleen a perfect metaphor for Charleston's relationship to the outsider. He and every other cadet who came to the Institute from "away" knew some things the whale did not know: The city has never taken to visitors or uninvited strangers who tried to force an entry into the aristocratic milieu South of Broad. Many Charlestonians far preferred even whales to cadets, and the annual Salute to the Baleen was the Corps's recognition of this irrefutable truth.

When we reached the South Carolina Hall, we broke ranks and entered the main ballroom. The seniors of each company sat together at long tables that were covered with white damask and decorated with candelabra and carnations. We found our names printed on small place cards and sat primly, awaiting the arrival of the General. The band played light classical music, and most of the seniors stared at the small black box set beside each place card.

I looked around at the Romeo Company seniors and tried to relate the proud faces to the shivering, aghast initiates who had endured Hell Night on the fourth battalion quadrangle over three years before. We looked older and more mature, but we also looked the same. However, the difference was enormous and part of the bizarre and glorious alchemy that made us love the Institute more than anything we had ever loved before. That was the single most sublime and untranslatable mystery of the school. And I felt the immense weight and actuality of that mystery as I studied the small black box that was before me. Inside that box was an Institute ring. But this ring was different from all the other rings ever made. Engraved in a feathery script on the inside shank was the name: *William McLean*. Here, at last, was the symbol, the absolute proof, that I was part of all of this, that I had earned the right to love the school, and to criticize it.

As I looked around the Hall, I felt irrationally close to my classmates who had come to the auditorium for the most meaningful ceremony of our careers as cadets at the Institute. From the beginning of my plebe year, I could always articulate what I loathed about the school but never could find the adequate words or the proper voice to praise it. It was not a dilemma of language but of emotion and persona. I would always be a better hater of things and institutions than a lover of them.

But in this gathering, this coming together of the eldest members of the Corps, I was moved deeply and profoundly before the ceremony had even begun, before I had actually put on the ring. I was seized by the ineffable power of membership, of finally belonging to something. So long had I secretly thought of the day when I would wear the ring that not even my reflexive cynicism, not even my loneliness among the regiment, not even the profound differences that I insisted separated me from all the rest of them, could diminish my joy at wearing the ring. On this night I was adding my small inconsequential history to the history of the ring. It transformed you into something beyond the powers of men unseasoned by the Institute to comprehend. The ring would be our alterer, our connection to the bright circuit of immemorial fraternity.

The General walked through the center of the room followed by his usual cortege of aides. He acknowledged our cheers with an imperial wave of his arm. In his dress whites, he seemed a splendid figure of a man, one who could be elected emperor by acclamation in a crowd of boys. He made his way down the center aisle, calling many of the seniors by name as he passed by them. As he passed the R Company table, I saw his eyes focus on me, he smiled, and called out, "Congratulations, Will. Let's beat Auburn."

"Thank you, sir. We will, sir," said I, exhilarated that the General could recognize me on sight, that he chose to speak to me in front of my friends on the night I received the ring.

The General cleared his throat and adjusted the microphone at the head table. "Gentlemen," General Bentley Durrell said, "tonight it is my pleasure to welcome you to the brotherhood of the ring. On this night you enter into a realm of grandeur and distinction. On this night, you enter into the fellowship of the Line."

The auditorium was soundless. The fire-crowned candles flickered in white colonnades above the fresh linen, held in place by silver candelabra. The hall glowed like a cathedral nave at Eastertide.

"In the ancient days of empire," he continued, "when the words of emperors and kings were translated into law the moment they spoke, the ring of the emperor was the seal of his word and carried the imprimatur of his authority. When his subjects saw the imprint of the ring in the sealing wax of documents, they were certain of the legitimacy of those documents, and they knew that they came directly from the hand of their ruler. If the emperor was a weak man, the sight of his mark would evoke laughter and contempt, but if he was a stern and powerful ruler, his mark would instill fear and trembling and obedience.

"When people see the Institute ring on your hand, they will know that it represents power and discipline and the legitimacy of your passage through the system. With this ring you will be accepted by the entire fellowship of the Institute alumni. You will be welcome in their ranks no matter where you may meet them in your travels. Institute men are not merely emotional about the ring, they are religious about it. It is the sacred symbol of the ideals represented by the Institute. This circle binds you to the brotherhood, to the inviolable ranks. This ring encircles the world. He who wears the ring, the Great Seal of the Institute, wears it more proudly than any mere emperor or king.

He paused and with a voice almost undone by emotion and conviction said in a clear ringing pronouncement, "Gentlemen, at this moment, and according to the powers invested in me by the Board of Visitors, I command you now to wear the ring, the ring that you and you alone so gallantly and resolutely have earned."

Each of the four hundred seniors opened the small box in front of him, lifted the ring from its slot of black velvet, and placed the ring on his finger. Each of us felt the weight of the ring for the first time.

Then we heard the General's voice again as he intoned solemnly, "In the mystery of the circle, in the mystery of shape, of the shape without end, of the infinite form, the perfect form, I bind you to the brotherhood. I declare to the world that from this day forward you will walk as men of Carolina Military Institute. Gentlemen, by placing the ring on

265

your fingers, you have vowed to be true to the Line. I accept that vow and I shall hold you responsible to it."

An aide brought the General a glass of port.

We raised our glasses of port to the General.

He raised his glass to us.

"The ring," he said.

"The ring!" we roared back in one immense, passionate roar. Then we drank to the ring and to our vow.

"The Line," he said.

"The Line!" we roared, and we drank to the Line.

My hand felt different as I looked at my ring for the first time. I studied its adroit, inexorable images and translated the silent eloquence of its mythology and language so simply and unceasingly uttered in gold. Until this moment an essential part of me, some vital and unnamable center, had never felt that I was really part of the school. But now the cold gleam of the ring had enclosed me, bound me, and linked me to the Line, for as long as I lived. My hand had sprung suddenly alive as though I had taken its existence for granted. The ring on my finger made an articulate statement; it conveyed a piece of extraordinarily important information to me. It said—no, it shouted out—that Will McLean had added his weight and his story and his own bruised witness to the history of the ring, to the meaning of the ring, and its symbolism. I had encoded my own messages, scripts, and testimonies into the blazonry of the ring. I studied my new identity, my validation, and I felt changed, completely transfigured in the surprising grandeur of its gold. I was part of it. I had made it.

The General and the tactical officers and all the high-ranking members of the administration began moving through the hall congratulating each table of seniors. There was a forty-thousand-dollar investment on the hands of the four hundred seniors, and one element in the lore of the barracks was that the Institute ring contained more gold than any other college ring in the country. The room hummed with a euphoric, celebratory noise.

"Paisans," Pig said, taking our wine glasses and pouring all the remnants into his glass.

He made a toast to us.

"This is to brotherhood," he said. "The Brotherhood of the Room."

He took a sip of the wine and passed it to Tradd.

"Drinking out of the same glass! There's no telling what we'll all catch," Tradd said, wincing. But then he raised his ring to eye level and pointed the seal at all of us and said, "I propose a toast for all of us. To the four roommates who earned the ring together, who worked for the ring, who fought for the ring."

He drank and passed the glass to me.

I toasted: "To the best roommates in the world."

Mark did not or could not speak a word, he was so powerfully moved. He finished the wine and squeezed each of our shoulders with his hand. Tradd and I gave yelps of pain. Pig looked at Mark with an expression of naïve placid sentimentality. Pig's eyes had filled up with love of us, with the amazed, free-floating love of the world he always radiated when something touched his heart.

We came together, the four of us, with our arms locked around each other's shoulders, rocking slowly from side to side, in a close intimate huddle. Wordlessly we communicated the depth and primacy of our feelings. Then we placed our newly ringed hands together in the center of the circle, and we stared downward at the cluster of rings, the ring repeated four times; and the numeral of our class, 67, winked in the candlelight as our hands moved.

Pig laid his hand straight out, palm downward. I laid my hand on top of his, Tradd's on mine, Mark's on Tradd's. We looked at each other, but we could not hold each other's gaze for long. There was too much history in our eyes. No words were spoken until Pig spoke for all of us. "Paisans," he said simply, "for as long as we live. Paisans."

I remembered a line from my class on the origins of the English language. My professor had said something one day in class that I wasn't sure I heard correctly, but I never asked. Sometimes clarifications are undesirable, and this was such a time. I thought he said this: "The generic word for 'brother' is *brother*." I hope this is true, but I don't really care if it's not. I thought about that line after Pig had called us "paisans." No matter how brutal the Institute was in its rites of initiation and passage, there was always a heartbreaking romanticism in all the ceremonies and forms of the military. I shook hands with Mark and congratulated him. I shook hands with Pig and Tradd. We congratulated each other and honored each other with our eyes. The generic word for "brother" is *brother*.

As I looked around the hall at the rest of my classmates, as I shook hands and slapped the backs of the other R Company seniors, my mind flashed suddenly to plebe year, to a nightmarish vision of sweat parties under the stairwell, in

267

the shower room, on the quadrangle. I remembered the screaming at every meal, at every formation, relentless and without end. The pressure of that year again inhabited my thoughts like a migraine. That year could still hurt me when I least expected it. But I knew this on the night I received the ring: The reason I felt so genuinely transformed was because I had survived it with these classmates. There had been seven hundred of us present on the four quadrangles when our Hell Night ended, but only four hundred were destined to wear the ring. I had attached my fate to their fate, and they had attached theirs to mine. Each of us had made an individual decision not to be broken by the system. We had earned this moment. The Institute, with its genius for ceremony, had made us lust for this moment from the first day we had entered the Gates of Legrand.

I felt a tap on my shoulder. When I turned around I almost burned my nose on the end of a cigar.

"They didn't really give you a ring, did they, Bubba?" the Bear said plaintively in his rumbling basso profundo voice. "Let me buy it back from you and save the reputation of this school. How much will you take? A thousand dollars? Ten thousand? Just name the price, and I'll make an appointment with my banker."

"Can't have it, Colonel," I said, flashing it before him. "But it sure looks good, doesn't it, Colonel?"

"No, Bubba, it looks bad. Very bad," he said, as though he were sinking into some long-term spiritual malaise. "It's nauseating. Pure nauseating, that's what it is. When I see that ring on that grubby finger of yours, McLean, I feel like dynamiting the Gates of Legrand. I don't know whether to laugh or commit suicide. You may not believe this, but this school used to have high standards. You're living proof that we're going downhill fast. Quit now, Bubba, and I'll pay your way to Clemson. What's going to happen to the image of this school if we allow you to graduate?"

"I'll be one of the few demonstrably literate people ever to graduate from this school, Colonel."

He threw his head back and laughed, his cigar ash cascading to the floor. "I just wanted to come over here and congratulate you, Bubba. It's a great feeling to wear the ring, isn't it?"

"One of the best feelings I've ever had," I answered truthfully.

He glanced over my shoulder, his shrewd eyes appraising the activity in the hall. I looked behind me instinctively and saw Tradd studying us. The Bear always made Tradd nervous. The Bear began to talk to me in a slow controlled whisper.

"Have you heard from Oswald Spengler?" he asked.

"The West is still declining, Colonel."

"Is Africa declining?" he responded cryptically.

"Pearce is holding his own, Colonel. You must have taken care of that overaggressive sophomore corporal who was giving him grief down in E Company."

The Bear cackled and said, "He's now a gentle-as-a-lamb sophomore private walking eighty tours for hazing a dumbhead."

"You're a harsh man, Colonel."

"I'm a Girl Scout, Bubba," he answered, his eyes continuing to scan the crowd. "I've got the heart of Bambi."

"And if you'll be so kind as to permit me an observation, sir: You've also got the looks of Rin-Tin-Tin."

"Insulting a commissioned officer is good for forty tours, lamb," he said, bringing his hot cigar ash to within an inch of my left eye. I could feel the heat of the ash deep in the retina and I backed away from him. But he anticipated the retreat, and matched my step, following me with the cigar. His smile was brown and toothy and ironic.

"I like the way Rin-Tin-Tin looks, Colonel," I said, leaning out of the cigar's range. "But you're right. That statement might be misconstrued as an insult. I take it back, sir. You look a little better than Rin-Tin-Tin."

"I'm gonna look like a matinee idol, Bubba, when you're walking the quad with your M–1 rifle slung over your shoulder. By the way," he said, suddenly growing serious again, "when's the first road trip for you basketball bums?"

"The first week of December, Colonel. Why?"

"Because I'll need to read Spengler for a week if you're not on campus. Someone's got to watch out for Pearce when you're out proving that you're one of the worst athletes in the history of the Institute."

"Thanks, Colonel," I said. "But I've already taken care of that. My roommates will check on Pearce for me during those weeks the team is on the road."

"They know that you're bird-dogging Pearce for me?" he said angrily. "I told you not to tell a living soul, Bubba."

"They've known it from the beginning, Colonel Berrineau. I knew I'd be on the road a lot, and I tell them everything. There are no secrets in our room."

"If I'd wanted them, I'd have picked them myself," the

Bear said, his eyes hot and blazing like his cigar ash. "St. Croix is steady and harmless. But I don't know the other two very well. I've never trusted folks whose last names ended in an 'i' or an 'o' and I've never known a Yankee that can keep a secret."

"These two can. I promise, Colonel," I insisted.

"Do they like niggers?" the Bear asked.

"No, sir."

"Good," he said. "That makes me feel better. I trust people that hate niggers a lot more than I trust people like you. OK, Bubba. You made the new rules. Do they know to come see Papa Bear if there's trouble?"

"Yes, sir. They know the whole procedure."

"There's something you might be interested in knowing, Bubba," he said, catching Tradd in the act of watching us. He glowered back, forcing Tradd to drop his eyes as he resumed talking to Mark. "Did you ever hear of that knob Graubart, down in first battalion?"

"The kid from California," I answered. "Everybody's heard about the Western Waste, Colonel. I heard the cadre couldn't even make him do pushups. He was a legend by the time he quit."

"He resigned last week," the Bear explained. "Except he didn't resign in my office, not that he was a stickler for procedure. He resigned by telegram from San Francisco. When I went to inspect his room, I found something very interesting."

"What, Colonel?"

"Don't even tell this to your roommates, Bubba, and I mean that. I still don't know what it means, but I'm sure going to find out. I found a number painted on his door."

"So what, Colonel?"

"The number was a ten, Bubba."

"You think it was The Ten who ran him out?"

"I don't know who it was, Bubba. I just found the number on the door. It might just be a joke one of my lambs pulled off, but it sure did arouse my curiosity. If there is a Ten on this campus they're gonna wish they were a thousand when the Bear catches them farting downwind. This may be their first mistake or it may be nothing at all."

"How can we find out about The Ten?" I asked. "Where can we look?"

"Just keep your eyes and ears open, Bubba," he replied. "And keep your mouth shut."

270

"I'll start with Edward the Great," I said. "He knows everything that's ever happened on this campus."

"Colonel Reynolds will treat you differently the next time you talk to him," the Bear said, starting to move away from me.

"Why, Colonel?" I asked, puzzled.

"It's simple, Bubba," he said, moving out into the jubilant crowd again. "Now you wear the ring."

27

I chose my professors at the Institute with discrimination and care, on the basis of their legend in the Corps or the passion and neurosis they brought to the lectern, not on the subject they taught. Early on, I had discovered that I would rather take "Principles of Business Management" taught by an excellent teacher than suffer through "Shakespeare's Tragedies," a subject I normally would have enjoyed, with a mediocre one. Nothing bored me more than flaccid, humorless academicians punishing their students with limpid melancholy lectures while they polished up their deadly little monographs on vital subjects like "The Nose Hair of Grendel."

I developed The Great Teacher Theory late in my freshman year. It was a cornerstone of the theory that great teachers had great personalities and that the greatest teachers had outrageous personalities. I did not like decorum or rectitude in a classroom; I preferred a highly oxygenated atmosphere, a climate of intemperance, rhetoric, and feverish melodrama. And I wanted my teachers to make me smart.

A great teacher is my adversary, my conqueror, commissioned to chastise me. He leaves me tame and grateful for the new language he has purloined from other kings whose granaries are filled and whose libraries are famous. He tells me that teaching is the art of theft: of knowing what to steal and from whom.

Bad teachers do not touch me; the great ones never leave me. They ride with me during all my days, and I pass on to others what they have imparted to me. I exchange their handy gifts with strangers on trains, and I pretend the gifts are mine. I steal from the great teachers. And the truly wonderful thing about them is they would applaud my theft, laugh at the thought of it, realizing they had taught me their larcenous skills well.

I developed this theory in the classrooms of Colonel Edward T. Reynolds, whom the cadets called Edward the Great. Among the teachers in my life, and I had many good men and women, he belonged to the royal family.

But he was a difficult and temperamental man, and both Mark and I were nervous when we approached his class five minutes late the Monday afternoon after the Ring Ceremony. It took an act of courage to walk into Edward the Great's room after he had begun a lecture, but it was better to face his wrath than to incur a month's restriction to campus and twenty tours on the quadrangle.

"You do the talking, Will," Mark said, an agitated tremor in his voice. "It's your fault we're late."

"It's always my fault we're late," I agreed. "No problem, Mark. You just walk quickly to your seat and I'll take the grief from the Great."

Colonel Reynolds was deep into his lecture when we entered the room. He stopped in midsentence, colored furiously, and gave us a stare that could have frozen Montego Bay.

I smiled broadly and saluted him in a friendly, brotherly manner as Mark slipped to the rear of the classroom.

Because of his obesity, it was easy to forget that Reynolds was a remarkably handsome man. He was immaculately groomed; his black hair was always combed with obsessive neatness, and his nails were always manicured precisely. He was fine-featured, with expressive green eyes that could register violence or merriment with equal eloquence.

He weighed well over three hundred pounds and had no visible neck, just a monumental round head, proud and fierce and inscrutable, resting on an enormous body. His arms, though short, were stacked with muscles that carried an awesome authority.

He was both admired and dreaded on campus. He was as mercurial and unpredictable as the English history course he taught. His aroused green eyes and massive immovable dignity gave him the appearance of a deranged and overweight inquisitor. There were no quarrels with Edward the Great, only vendettas.

Yet he was a quintessential gentleman, courtly in the

finest sense, with a troubled, endangered civility rooted in the bruised mythology of the Old South. His classroom was his private domain, in which he approached the business of teaching with absolute gravity. When he lectured on the history of England, he was the most brilliant and passionate scholar I had ever heard, outrageously partisan, an immodest dispenser of inflamed rhetoric. He cherished language and its skillful use, and his own style was one of sustained floridity. Prose rolled off his tongue with both the sweetness and the sting of the hive about it. From him, the English language was a fine dancing thing, and you understood that, when properly used, it could bring about the fall of kings or the birth of gods or the death of kings and gods together.

But it was not his use of language that made him so controversial on campus; it was the extremity of his views. His colleagues on the faculty were mostly conservative but their conservatism possessed no fervor. It was not the fact that he was a racial supremacist that irritated his peers, it was that he seemed to loathe all the races and religions. He lacked the grace and acumen to despise only the blacks. He hated with equal gusto the French, the Jews, all Orientals, Slavs, Russians, Italians, Latin Americans, Turks, Arabs; in fact, he seemed to have a supreme, footnoted contempt for the entire family of man. The only races he did not hate were the races without history, without a chronicle of their crimes and atrocities. His field had not hardened him; it had made him narrow and paranoid, and his classroom was a forum for the astonishing bleakness of his creeds. But even though he was the most stunningly prejudiced man I had ever met, there was a sense of excitement and conflict and drama in his class that I had found nowhere else at the Institute. You learned much by disagreeing with everything that Edward T. Reynolds propounded.

He and I had become good friends in my sophomore year for the oddest of reasons. I had not known until I walked into his class that the group to be primarily blamed for the decline of Western civilization and culture was the Irish Catholics. I learned it when he called the roll in his survey course on European civilization, reached my name, and said as his eyes rested on my features:

"Mr. McLean, you are an Irish Catholic, are you not?"

"Yes, sir, I am."

"On your feet and stand at attention when you address an officer, swine," he bellowed as I sprang to my feet. "If I am not mistaken, this is still a military college. Now, Mr.

McLean, I would like to propose a serious question, and I would like a serious answer. Are you proud of being an Irish Catholic?"

"I've never thought about it one way or another, sir," I said nervously, as I spoke the truth.

"I suggest you do think about it with all your limited powers of ratiocination, Mr. McLean. You, of course, could not help the accident that selected you as a member of this contemptible race, but you must understand the significance of the fact and you must try to comprehend how the cards are stacked against you. Now, I have had many other Irishmen in my class, feisty devils all, and they would inevitably be ready to fight me after I pointed out several incontestable facts about the Irish. I am not a bigoted man, Mr. McLean, and I do believe that in a limited number of cases, it is possible for a single individual to rise above his racial origins and actually distinguish himself in ways uncommon to his stock. But I am a truthful man and I am an historian and feel that I would be remiss in my duties if I did not ringingly proclaim the truth no matter where I found it or in what shape. Do you not agree, Mr. McLean?"

"Absolutely, sir," I said, though I could feel my anger rising hotly to my throat.

"Good man." He nodded his black and leonine head affirmatively. "No, many poor simpletons at the Institute do not consider me a fair man. They actually consider me a contemptible bigot, Mr. McLean. I would like to know your honest views on that outrageous slander."

"I don't think you're a contemptible bigot, sir. I think you are a very simple bigot."

The class laughed nervously, but it was laughter instantly stifled by Reynolds's imperious glare. He was not amused.

"The Irish have a capacity for treacly gab and the humorous aside, Mr. McLean," he said sadly. "They are a merry race, though, God knows, they had very little to laugh about during the bloody tyrannous occupation of the English. Let there be no mistake, Mr. McLean, even though English blood flows in my veins I am not blind to the faults of the English; a more bloodthirsty, rapacious, and brutal people never existed on this planet. English blood comes from the sewer system of Western Europe, but their capacity for outrage is offset by their ability to govern. It has been left to the English to enforce a system of laws on inferiors like the Irish."

"And we Irish are eternally grateful, sir," I said.

"Sarcasm, of course, Mr. McLean, and I cannot blame you nor will I chastise you for your impudence. But if we had allowed the Irish to rule themselves, the race would be extinct by now, having bashed each other's brains out in drunken, mindless orgies and furious melees that only such degenerate races are capable of. Each Irishman is a nation unto himself, Mr. McLean. They are incapable either of self-rule or of accepting the hegemony of their superiors. But they are a freedom-loving people, of that there can be no question, though they lack the mental capacity to comprehend what the essence of freedom truly means. It is a nation of contradictions, sir. Consider this: Ireland is an island nation that has never developed a navy; a music-loving people who have produced only those harmless lilting ditties as their musical legacy; a bellicose people who have never known the sweet savor of victory in a single war; a Catholic country that has never produced a single doctor of the Church; a magnificently beautiful country, a country to inspire artists, but a country not yet immortalized in art; a philosophic people yet to produce a single philosopher of note; a sensual people who have never mastered the art of preparing food. What do you have to say for your tribe, Mr. McLean? Speak freely and without fear of retribution; this is an exchange of ideas."

"Your people look as though they've mastered the art of preparing food, sir. Great quantities of food."

The class shook with laughter but of the nervous, impermissible variety.

"Silence, swine," Reynolds commanded. "Witty. Triflingly witty, Mr. McLean, but I would like you to account for your people's history of ineptitude."

His stare withered me, and I heard my voice come out ineffectually, defensively. "But, sir, I was born in Georgia."

"And I was born in South Carolina, sir," he thundered. "But I am not talking about birthplace, I'm talking bloodline. I'm talking about origins. I am talking about racial patterns that have emerged in groups and have been catalogued and studied for centuries. Take a trout from a mountain stream, put him into an aquarium in the Gobi desert or in the sewers below Montparnasse, and you still have a trout. I could parachute you into County Limerick this very day, Mr. McLean, and it is very likely that within a single year you'd be cultivating potatoes, courting an ugly Irish wench, and running guns for the IRA. Now sit down, swine, forgive me for coming down so hard on you the first day, and I promise to teach you and the other simpletons some of the grandeur and sweep and horror of history as it spread into Western Europe."

Before he began his lecture, he warmed me with a buoyant, exhilarated smile. The smile was offered as a sign of friendship. When I saw the smile I realized verbal jousting was the only sport of Edward T. Reynolds, his only method of communication. But there was something else, something darker, subterranean, and inexpressible about the man, which caused me to pity him deeply and tenderly. He was a supremely lonely man, and Irish or not, I recognized a fellow countryman from that dreadful land on sight. Yet I did not know we would come to be friends until I took my first exam in his class and read the note he had written in the margin of the blue book: "You write well, Mr. McLean, but I am absolutely positive you have not mastered a single fact of European history. From this paper, I think you are full of merde. I will expect a great deal from you." He gave me a "D" on the paper and invited me for tea with him and his wife that afternoon. It was the beginning of many such afternoons, all of them stimulating, cordial, and memorable.

But the friendship did not extend to his classroom and tardiness was the one transgression he would not tolerate in any cadet.

"Halt, Santoro-swine," he ordered. "You know that I do not tolerate lateness. I was told when I came to this decaying institution twenty-three years ago that this was a school where discipline was a feminine deity and where cadets were worshipers at her sacred shrine. Do you have even the flimsiest excuse for such flagrant tardiness?"

"Yes, sir, he does," I answered from the front of the class.

"I was speaking to the Senate of Rome, not to the rabble of Dublin, sir," Colonel Reynolds said to me without a trace of humor in his voice.

"That is the root of our problem, sir," I said. "That is precisely why we are late."

"Explain yourself, Mr. McLean. Already, you may consider yourself under report."

"Sir, as we were dressing for this class, talking excitedly about the prospect of increasing our knowledge of English history and of listening spellbound to one of the superb lectures by our brilliant professor . . ."

"Mr. McLean," he said impatiently. "I have an extremely low tolerance for drivel."

"Yes, sir. My apologies, sir, and I will be brief. But as we were discussing today's class, I made an unfortunate and ill-considered remark about our professor's weight."

"And?"

"And Mr. Santoro told me that he would not allow an Irishman to speak critically about his favorite professor's girth."

"What did Mr. Santoro do, Mr. McLean?"

"He beat me soundly about the head and shoulders, sir. He abused me physically. The fracas made us lose track of time and thus, we were five minutes late, sir. There are no limits to our shame for interrupting your lecture, sir. So please continue."

I walked briskly to my seat, but before I could set my books down, Colonel Reynolds said, "Halt, swine. You are excused from class for the day. You will write me an official apology and an appeal for reinstatement to this class. You, Mr. Santoro," he said, grinning broadly at Mark, "are a fine, swart, Mediterranean fellow and I would like you to sit in a place of honor in this front desk beside me. I love any man who would throttle an impudent Irishman. Good day, Mr. McLean."

As I left the room, I paused beside his lectern and whispered, "I'd like to see you about something important after class, sir. I need your help."

"I will be in my office for the rest of the afternoon, Mr. McLean."

When he entered his office after class, I was sitting in a student's chair facing his desk.

"Attention, swine," he roared cheerfully. "A better man is entering the room. An Anglo-Saxon, I believe."

He threw his lecture notes on his cluttered desk and sank heavily into the huge leather chair behind it. He folded his hands, his fingers bunched like fat white bananas, and laid them on his extraordinary stomach, appraising me with civil, intuitive eyes.

"We were born during the wrong eras, Mr. McLean. We are both anachronisms. You should have been an Irish priest in the twelfth century with a shillelagh in your hand and a cause in your heart, standing in the chill surf of the Irish Sea, braining and smashing the sternums of English invaders. And I—I, Mr. McLean, should have been an English king with all the wenches of England at my beck and call, with an army of bandy-legged knights imploring me to raise a fleet to cross the Channel and wreak havoc along the French coast. We are

277

sad, pathetic creatures, Mr. McLean, and there is little hope for us in this world. What may I do for you, sir?"

"I have a question for you, sir," I said. "It's a matter of history."

"I'm glad you are finally showing a glimmer of interest in the craft of Herodotus."

"When you wrote your book on the history of Carolina Military Institute, Colonel, did you ever come across in your research a reference to an organization known as The Ten?"

"Why do you ask, sir?" he said, bringing his hands up under his chin.

"Because you did not mention The Ten a single time in your history. I read the book when I was a sophomore, but I checked it today to make sure. That's why I was late to class. I wanted to be positive The Ten was not mentioned."

"What have you heard about The Ten, Mr. McLean?"

"Just rumors, sir."

"Precisely. Rumors were all I could find when I was writing my history. Rumors make for captivating speculation but questionable history, sir. I tracked down rumor after rumor, looking for some documentation, some specific, tangible proof that the organization existed. I came up with absolutely no concrete data that either proved or disproved that The Ten is a secret and powerful organization on this campus."

"So you don't believe The Ten exists at all, Colonel?" I asked.

"I did not say that, Mr. McLean," he said. "The Irish always impulsively jump to conclusions. I said that I could find no documented proof that The Ten existed, ergo, I could not state with absolute assurance that the group did exist. I am an historian, not a psychic or a Hollywood gossip columnist."

"Sir, when I was a freshman, the General himself told a newspaper reporter that no secret societies would be tolerated on campus, that it was strictly forbidden by the Blue Book. He denied ever hearing about The Ten."

"He was lying," Colonel Reynolds said. "But he is not to be censured for it. He could not have become a four-star general without mastering the governmental art of deception."

"Lying?" I said incredulously. The myth of the General's unimpeachable rectitude was so strong on campus that the very idea seemed sacrilegious. "Isn't that odd for a man who speaks so passionately in defense of the honor system? How do you know he's lying?"

"Because anyone who has been around this campus long enough has at least heard of The Ten's existence. It may only be a legend, but it is not a legend without mystique and power. He would have to be a deaf mute not to have heard of it, and an ignoramus besides. Let me tell you an interesting anecdote, Mr. McLean, and see what you think. When Colonel Adamson, the Registrar, died in 1958, there was a wreath with ten white carnations on his casket at his funeral. There was a cageful of white doves. Ten doves. I counted both the carnations and the filthy birds. An anonymous contribution of ten thousand dollars was bequeathed to the Institute in his name. None of this means anything by itself. But then there was another funeral."

"Whose funeral, Colonel?" I asked, leaning forward hungrily.

"Remove your vile digits from the furniture, Mr. McLean," he commanded. "And have more patience. An historian is required to have infinite patience. The second funeral took place in Atlanta, Georgia. General Homer Stone, the hero of the Bulge, had died in his sleep, and I was sent as a representative of the Institute faculty. It was a dull, excruciating affair with insufferable long-winded eulogies. But what did catch my eye that day was a cageful of doves, a wreath with ten white carnations, and a note in the service announcing a ten-thousand-dollar scholarship at the Institute in General Stone's memory."

"So it does exist."

"Please never write history, Mr. McLean. You would do far better with science fiction. Let me continue," he said, leaning back serenely and lifting his eyes until they came to rest on the ceiling. "I interviewed over three hundred alumni when I was compiling my history of the Institute and I asked each of them about any information they may have had about The Ten. Most of them gave me the usual hodge-podge of rumor, though some of our most illustrious graduates adamantly insisted that The Ten did not exist at all. The organization was much more discussed in the late thirties than it has been in recent years. I pieced together the various fragments of rumor, and this is the rather fanciful portrait of the organization as I imagine it. Now, remember, Mr. McLean, this portrait is crudely sketched in the crayons of innuendo. Supposedly, membership in The Ten is the highest honor a cadet can aspire to at the Institute. Much of its mystique lies in its total secrecy. There is a bond of honor among the members never to reveal their membership, not even to their wives and family. I myself used to hear this kind of idle chatter when I was a cadet at the Institute. I always expected that if there were, indeed, such an organization I, of course, would be chosen as a member. I waited for someone to inform me of my selection but, of course, no one ever did. I would have been a far better choice than the ten scoundrels they selected in my place, of that I can assure you."

"What are the qualifications for membership, sir? Did anyone tell you anything about that? Even rumors?"

"Now you are talking like an historian, Mr. McLean," he said, smacking his lips in approval. "There are various theories on selection. But if there is such an organization it has a governing board that oversees the election of ten members of the rising senior class. Some alumni told me they heard the inductees were enrolled at homecoming, others insisted on Corps Day. One poor idiot was sure it was a communist plot. A papist thought it was a plot to keep Catholics out of the Corps. I interviewed many sad men, Mr. McLean."

"What is the responsibility of The Ten?" I asked. "What is their purpose for existence, if they do exist?"

"May I remind you, Mr. McLean, that The Ten does not issue a yearbook highlighting their activities."

"I know, sir," I said impatiently. "But you interviewed three hundred people. Didn't somebody, at least one person, tell you something about the purpose of The Ten?"

"I did hear this," he said, enjoying his role as the carrier of secrets, feeding my interest by throwing me one scrap at a time. "The Ten are selected to preserve the purity and integrity of the Corps of Cadets. They take an oath to uphold the traditions of the Institute at any and all costs. I was told that The Ten has a powerful lobby in the state legislature, that they are influential in contributing money to any political candidate deemed favorable to the Institute's interests, and that they watch individual members of the Corps carefully to make sure that no one graduates who is unworthy to wear the ring."

"What are the qualifications for membership?"

"Rumor again, Mr. McLean. All rumor, all worthless. But it varied. Mostly the things you would expect. Outstanding leadership ability, high academic standing, loyalty to the Institute, and military aptitude."

280

"Colonel," I said solemnly, "I don't see how they had the gall to pass me up."

"I am sure that potential revolutionaries never fill up the ranks of The Ten. You have a better chance of joining the College of Cardinals, you Irish swine. But I was told of one qualification that struck me as rather odd, but odd in a way entirely consistent with the Institute."

"What's that, Colonel?"

"One rather bitter, limp-wristed grad who not only believed that The Ten existed but was still angry after thirty years that he had not been selected as a member insisted that one criterion for membership is physical strength. It is not an effete organization."

"Then why didn't they choose Muscles McLean?"

"There might have been some question about your loyalty to the Institute."

"Ha!" I laughed. "I hope there was a great deal of question."

"Hold your tongue, wastrel," he demanded, beating his fist on the wooden desk and scattering his lecture notes about the room. "I will not allow trench-mouthed swine to tarnish the good name of the Institute. Many men before you have talked bitterly about the school when they were cadets only to become among its most ardent champions. Some have even contributed vast sums to the Institute."

"I would contribute vast sums to the demolition team that would tear this campus down."

"And what would you replace this campus with, Mr. McLean?" he retorted hotly. "What institution of equivalent value would you put in its place? The Institute has produced statesmen, warriors, ambassadors, and captains of industry. Its record of service to America is unsurpassed for a school of its size. What would be your substitute? What would you place over the ruins of this great institution that would render equal service to mankind?"

"Oh, I don't know, Colonel," I said, my smile betraying my foreknowledge of his reaction. "How about a diaper cleaning service?"

"You are a scoundrel and a disgrace even to your whimpering breed. Out of my office, scalawag, and keep a civil tongue about the Institute or I will throttle you myself to an inch of your life."

"I'm not worried about you, Colonel," I teased. "At least, not anymore."

"Why, swine?" he said, narrowing his eyes.

"You didn't make The Ten."

"That is true, Mr. McLean. But let me hasten to assure you that I could take all ten members from my feckless, small-boned class and hurl them forthwith into the outgoing tide of the Ashley River."

"Sir, in your youth, and this might be a personal question, but were you ... ah ... were you, how shall I phrase it ...," I stammered.

"You mean to ask in your whining cowardly way, sir, whether or not in my youth I was the same fat swine who sits before you today. I am not a man to mince words, Mr. McLean, and if we are to speak as reasonable men together— thinking, intelligent men—then you must speak the words as they spring from your whimpering tongue."

"Very well, sir," I said. "Were you fat when you were a cadet? I would like to know."

"Do you think I am fat now?" he inquired.

"I think, sir, that you are incredibly fat. Remember, sir, I am speaking freely as the words spring from my whimpering tongue."

"Does my weight disgust you, Mr. McLean?"

"Yes, sir, it disgusts me beyond all powers of description."

He rose suddenly and with surprising speed and grace made a lunge toward me across the desk. I stepped back toward the door, just barely avoiding his grasp. Breathing heavily and with a competitive glint in his eye, he growled, "If we had a fist fight this very moment, Mr. McLean, who do you think would emerge victorious?"

"I would, sir, because I would engage in a footrace before we began fighting. You would have a massive coronary after the fourth or fifth step, whereupon I would return and at my leisure strike you again and again in your left ventricle."

Laughter spilled out of his prodigious frame like gravel being unloaded from a dump truck. He was one of those large, dour men whose laughter was surprising in its infectiousness.

"I should have known better than to engage the Irish swine in a battle of words. But I would like to remind you of one indisputable fact, Mr. McLean. If you study history long enough with the diligence and passion it requires, you will come to recognize that the truly great men in history have been men of girth. Greatness does not often come in puny, fashionably slim packages. A great mind cannot be served by

282

anything other than a massive body. Mark my words well. Only a fool would dispute such an assertion."

"I believe it, sir," I said. "And I can only assume from that theory that you must be among the greatest men in history."

"A perspicacious lad, Mr. MacLean. A perspicacious swine, indeed. Not that I enjoy being overweight, mind you, and not that your insensitive jokes don't hurt. I have suffered greatly because of my size, you can make no mistake about that. It has altered my perception of the world; it has even altered my perception of God."

"How, sir?" I asked, puzzled.

"If there was a just and merciful God, Mr. McLean, then a dry martini would have a single calorie and a rye crisp would have four thousand. If there were truly a just and merciful God a banana split would have no calories and a bean sprout or a raw carrot would contain ten thousand calories. I have spent a great amount of time studying the cruelty of the universe."

I made a gesture of departure by picking up my books from the floor. "Thanks for your help, Colonel," I said. "By the way, if you were actually a member of The Ten, would you have told me what you just did about the organization?"

"I would not have told you a single word. I would have denied the existence of The Ten under torture. At least under the first phases of torture. I think it is a simple ass indeed who claims that he would not break down completely under the dominion of the torturer's grim art. I know myself well enough to realize that I would eventually crack after enough fingernails were removed by pliers or enough electric shock was applied to my genitalia."

"One last thing, sir," I said. "If I had been writing the history of the Institute I would have included all that you picked up about The Ten. I would have presented it as a rather intriguing rumor even if I had no documentary proof."

He looked hurt when I said this, deeply hurt, and he said soberly, "That is why you will never be an historian, Mr. McLean. I have greater documentation for the existence of Atlantis than I do for The Ten. History is not a higher form of astrology. I don't know if a single thing I told you is true or not."

"How do they decide who is worthy to wear the ring? That sounds strange, Colonel, especially since the plebe system takes care of that problem."

"I neglected to tell you that part. This rumor came from a rather hypocritical liberal who graduated in the midfifties and is presently a bureaucrat in Washington. He claimed that The Ten, if there is such a thing, and again, he had no more proof than any of the others, had vowed that the Institute would never graduate a woman or any man who would bring discredit on the school because of gross mental or physical peculiarities, which is rather humorous in the light of recent history."

"What's that?"

"The Ten supposedly has vowed that the Institute will never graduate a Negro. There are times, Mr. McLean, when I hope with all my heart that The Ten does exist, and . . ."

"And, sir?"

"And that they are true to their ideals. Good day, sir."

28

The next evening, I sat in the mess hall eating supper with the din of the Corps at rest about me. The seniors were displaying their rings to the other members of their mess, even allowing the freshmen to examine the bright, newly minted emblem that marked them as blood members of the tribe. I had visited the library that morning to check for messages from Pearce and had then visited the ring display in the Institute museum. Whenever an alumnus was killed in battle, it was traditional for his next of kin to return his ring to the museum for enshrinement upon black velvet in the macabre trophy case where these rings were proudly mounted. The alumni who had fallen at Bull Run, at Antietam, in the Argonne Forest, at Guadalcanal, at the Bulge, at Pork Chop Hill—all, all had willed that their rings be returned to the Institute. Looking into that case, it was difficult to realize that each ring represented the life of a man and also a death by fire. Each time I viewed the display, I was moved by the silence and the gravity of those squads of rings, so carefully and lovingly spaced. Like all other cadets who visited this room, I could not help but wonder if one day my own ring would take its place in those chill accumulations of gold.

I handed my ring down to the freshman, Beasley, who had braced and asked permission to see it. Pig refused to take his ring off to show anyone and vowed that he would never take it off. Beasley handled the ring as though I had gifted him with a small bone of a saint. He turned it over and over again; his fingers studied its contours, his eyes strained to read the Latin inscription in the South Carolina seal.

"It's beautiful, sir," he said.

"It's expensive, dumbhead," I answered.

"It's worth it, sir. That's why all of us are here."

The speakers of the intercom crackled at that moment. Beasley reached for my cup and filled it with coffee. Pig was hunched over his plate, protecting his food with his massive round shoulders. But our ears tensed for the announcement. It was extremely rare that an announcement was made before the completion of a meal. The adjutant's voice, clear and precise, filled the hall. The two thousand listened.

"Gentlemen," he said, "we have just received word that General Durrell's son, Alfred, Class of 1964, has been killed by a land mine in the Que Noc Province of Vietnam. There will be a memorial service for Lieutenant Durrell at 1300 hours tomorrow in the chapel. All cadets are urged to attend."

A silence fell on the mess hall, a long, embittered silence. The Corps did not move; the Corps did not speak.

Most of the seniors had known Al Durrell in some way. It was impossible to be the son of the General and escape notice in the Corps. But Al Durrell was not the typical son of a General. He never took advantage of his father's position while in the Corps. His plebe year was frightening to watch, I was told, because the cadre went to extraordinary lengths to prove there was no favoritism on their part, and he went to equally absurd lengths to prove he was no different from any other plebe. He took the worst they had to offer; he endured the most brutal excesses of the system. He kept his own counsel, in his solemn, patient acceptance of each outrage and humiliation, and won the respect of the Corps by never complaining to the Commandant's Department, or worse, reporting the hazing to his father. It was said that he even won the respect of his father, but this point was disputed. The General had stated publicly that he believed Al's ability to lead men was minimal. Al had inherited his father's nose and height but not the genes of greatness. He became a second lieutenant in the Corps, an unspectacular rank, and was a fair student and a game but mediocre intramural athlete. He was admired for his humility, his self-deprecating humor, and a certain quality of gentle detachment rarely prized in the barracks. I was bothered by a single thought when I tried to resuscitate my images of Al Durrell: It was easy to imagine him dead. I could not even recall the sound of his voice.

But outrage bloomed in the poisonous, oceanic silence that followed the announcement. No one was eating. A dead boy stuck in our throats.

"He was a nice guy. That's all he was. A nice guy," someone said behind me.

For several stunned moments the transfixion was complete as we rekindled the memory of Al Durrell in our minds and revived his shy, unaspiring grace. We had to kill him off in our memories, let the shrapnel have him, let the severing and the dying take place in our heads.

Then we were lifted out of our chairs as if an indiscernible cadre had begun barking orders, and I found myself walking with the Corps, the entire Corps, moving without cadence and in silence, with an awesome, unspeakable purpose. Many had grabbed the lighted candles from the mess tables, and we moved by the candlelight toward the mansion where the General, an inhuman figure to most of us, a man we thought of as immune from the travesties of history, sat with his wife and the now eternal absence of a son who had died in Asia.

We walked in a shifting sea of fire, each flame a small column in the chapel of our sorrow. The Corps stood on his front lawn, the light of the candles surreal and trembling as we fidgeted diffidently before the shadows on his verandah. We stood there numbly, not knowing what to do or say, not knowing how to express the feelings that thickened our tongues, not knowing how to cry or what to say to a mother who had lost her one son for all time and a warrior who had lost his one son to war.

But even though there was no order to our spontaneous assembly at the General's house, there was a ceremonial correctness to the gathering. The Corps had come together to honor Al Durrell, wearer of the ring, one of us, a boy who would always be a boy, a comrade who would always be a comrade, and to honor the father of this son, to ease the pain of his mother, to share their pain, and to show our own.

As we saw General Durrell and his wife appear at their front door, we realized we had caught them unawares: They had had no time to prepare for our reception. It was the first time I had ever seen General Durrell in civilian clothes. We were moved by Mrs. Durrell's tears; we were moved by his lack of tears. They stared into the light where we stood on the lawn. I could hear the breathing of the Corps around me, the suppressed fury of loss in the roar of our inhale. In that crowd of two thousand, twenty-eight of us would die in Vietnam. Twenty-eight rings would return to the glass case of the museum. I would think of those twenty-eight later, each of them, one at a time when I heard the news, and I would wonder if in this visitation to the General's house, the death of those twenty-eight was assured. But on that night, we breathed slowly, simultaneously, for it was one of those times when the Corps had become one. Our silence was fearful and magnificent as we faced the Durrells. The tide was out in the river and the smell of the marsh was a fertile, powerful musk. That night the smell of the ebb tide and the smell of death seemed one.

Our faces glowed above the candlelight. The General stepped forward to say something. He cleared his throat and looked down, his fingers moving as though he were shuffling imaginary notes on a podium. Then he stepped back when he heard his wife sob. She began to weep uncontrollably. Her weeping had the timbre of imponderable loss, even of despair. The General put his arm around his wife and stared back at us with eyes that had suddenly become institutional. It was difficult to interpret his actions. There was both a strain and a theatricality to his movements. He stood above us at attention, his bearing both stiff and formal as always, but the words of loss and endings were loose upon his tongue. He could not pull them together. He could not speak.

I wanted to embrace the man. I wanted to let his wife cry on my shoulder. I wanted to bring his quiet son back to life. Grief lined the General's face in an easily traceable fretwork. His eyes were drained of light.

Suddenly Mrs. Durrell stepped forward. In a voice that trembled with agony and hatred, and once again with despair, the frail and self-effacing woman shouted out to us: "Get them, boys. Get them. Get them and kill them. For Alfred. For me. For me." Then she broke again and returned to her husband.

I do not know where the chant started, but it was somewhere behind me. At first it was a single voice, low and primal. The others picked it up until it spread through the crowd. Then it was the Corps in a single voice thundering a message of violent condolence, of inchoate vengeance. In the language of the barracks, the Corps howled out its note of condolence to Alice Durrell.

> *"I want to go to Vietnam.*
> *I want to kill some Vietcong.*
> *I want to go to Vietnam.*
> *I want to kill some Vietcong."*

The chant passed over the campus. It was fearful and terrible and sublime; it came from the great violent heart of us. The power of evil burned through the conscience of the regiment, and it was the same as the power of love and grief.

Then Mrs. Durrell silenced the crowd by uplifting her hand.

"This is the most beautiful thing that has ever happened to me. Thank you, boys. Thank you so much for everything." Then she turned and walked into her house, her husband with her.

I spoke to no one on the walk back to the barracks. The Institute had affected me in strange ways, I knew, but I was not prepared for this proof of its authority. I had participated in the chant. I had screamed it out with the others. My voice and the voice of the barracks had merged as one. They were the same thing. It was the first time I knew it for certain.

29

In the middle of December, before the team's first long road trip around the South, I drove out to Annie Kate's house to give her a Christmas present. She was not in the house when I arrived, and I found her sitting alone on the rocks watching the sun set behind the Charleston skyline again. Behind us, the moon, a shimmering bright disc of winter chrome, was rising over the island, attended by the first pale stars of evening. She was wrapped in a blanket and I could see the vapor of her breath as I approached.

I had not known what to buy a girl I loved. In my lifetime, I had never brought any skill or imagination to the art of gift-giving. I could never match a gift with how I really felt. I had written my mother and told her I was in love with a girl. I told her everything about Annie Kate except that she was pregnant with another man's child. That was my guilty secret and one that I would not share, not even with my mother. I told her that Annie Kate reminded me of her and that was true. All women I admired reminded me of my mother. I wanted her advice on what a son should give to the first girl he had ever loved. My mother wrote back with a list of suggestions: White Shoulders perfume, a good book (preferably a classic), a leather purse, or a gold chain. She preferred the gold chain and assured me it would make a lovely Christmas present for any girl, even a girl from an old Charleston family. My mother also told me I could invite Annie Kate home for Christmas and that she would be glad to write Annie Kate's mother extending an invitation. Anyone that I loved, my mother assured me, she would love. Anyone that I loved, she already loved.

It was a gold chain I brought wrapped to Annie Kate on the rocks, to Annie Kate by the sea.

I handed her the gift and sat down beside her, pulling my overcoat collar high over my dress grays. She removed the wrapping and lifted the chain from the box. She held the chain up to the last light of the sun and the first hard blaze of moonlight, gold on gold and gold on silver. Then she put it around her neck and kissed me.

She smiled at me as she ran her finger around the chain, then darkened suddenly as though some switch had been thrown in her consciousness due to a failure of power and nerve. "You're not doing this just because you feel sorry for me, are you, Will? You're not loving me because you pity me? Because I'm pregnant?"

"I've told you before, Annie Kate," I answered. "I would never have met you if you hadn't been pregnant. Answer this truthfully. Would I have had any chance with you at all if you hadn't been in trouble?"

"No," she said, staring down at the rocks. "You're right. I've been programmed since birth to marry in my own class. I got pregnant with someone from my own class and look where it got me. I don't have one friend in the world who knows where I really am. Do you know, Will, that I have Charleston friends who write me in Santa Barbara? They send me letters to the house of my mother's cousin, who sends them back to Charleston. I write back telling about college and all the new friends I've made. I tell of cute charming

289

boys I go out with. I describe the mountains around Santa Barbara and tell of weekend trips to Big Sur and San Francisco. I send the letters back to my mother's cousin and she mails them out to my friends. I've never been to California in my life. Everything I write and say is a complete and total lie. My whole life is one huge ugly lie."

"You're much too hard on yourself, Annie Kate," I said. "You don't come from a society where you can cheerfully and honestly admit that you got knocked up. You and your mother are simply protecting your future. If your boy friend keeps his mouth shut, no one will ever know. Why didn't you just go to Santa Barbara and live with this woman, this mysterious cousin? Did y'all ever consider that?"

"My mother wouldn't have gotten the satisfaction of looking down her nose at me, telling me daily that I had ruined her life and everything she'd tried to do for me, if I'd gone to California. She wouldn't have been able to play her favorite role of the complete martyr. This way she gets to punish me a little bit each day. We both get to watch my betrayal of her grow a little bit each day. And we get to hurt each other a little bit each day. I sometimes go to bed at night and pray to God that I won't wake up. I think my mother would secretly bury me at sea rather than explain why I was in Charleston."

"Aren't you being a little hard on your mother, too? I think she's just trying to handle this in the best way she knows how."

"All she can talk about is how this affects her life and reputation. She never stops to think how it's affected me, how it's killing me one day at a time."

"What will you do with the baby, Annie Kate?" I said.

She turned on me furiously, screaming and out of control. "There is no baby. I've already told you that."

"You can pretend there's no baby and I can pretend there's no baby, but at the end of nine months, you're going to have to decide what to do with this phantom child who's going to be feeding at your breast."

"I would never breast-feed a child even if it were a normal child and not a bastard. I've always thought that women who breast-fed their children had horrid breasts. I bet the women in your family always breast-fed children. In my family, never! I had a colored wet nurse feed me."

"I grew up with this strange idea that a woman's breast

was made for feeding children," I said. "You pick up all kinds of weird ideas growing up outside of Charleston."

"You're trying to pick a fight with me, Will. You're trying to make me feel squalid and low again."

"No, I'm not," I protested. "I'm trying to get you to face reality. To make some plans. I'm trying to get you to think about what you're going to do with the child, Annie Kate. I've been trying since I first met you to get you to talk about it, and all you do is change the subject or pretend that I didn't really ask the question."

"It's not a child to me, Will," she said. "Can you understand that? I can't let it be. It's not alive inside me. If I thought about it as my child, I would start to love it. I have to protect myself. I have to think about it as something inanimate, something growing in me like a tumor or a plant, something that should have been cut out but wasn't. You see, I can't let this baby interfere with my life. I plan to have a wonderful life full of gay and happy times. Full of charming people."

"What about the baby?" I whispered. "Are you going to put it up for adoption?"

"Yes," she finally answered. "They're going to take it from me as soon as it's born. Does that satisfy you, Will? Does that answer your question? They'll give it to a nice family. They've promised me that."

"Jesus Christ," I said.

"What do you want me to do with it, Will? Put it in a perambulator, dress it in pink or blue, and parade it up and down the Battery, waving to my friends?"

"I don't know what to do," I said. "I've never been faced with a decision like that, and I don't know what I would do in your place. I'm sorry if I've upset you. It's none of my business."

"I sometimes pretend this is all happening to someone else, Will. Someone odious and despicable. I can't believe that God would let something like this happen to someone He didn't hate. I know that I sinned, but God knows that I've paid for that sin. I didn't do anything to deserve this kind of punishment. Yet it's so odd to have this thing growing inside me. Sometimes I hate it with all my heart. At other times I'm so full of love for it I could burst. It needs me so completely. It's so trusting and absolutely dependent on me. It can't help what I did. It's happy inside me. I know that; I can feel that. It doesn't even know that it's going to come into the world as a bastard. A bastard descended from some of the oldest families in Charleston."

"I wish there was something I could do, Annie Kate," I said, taking her hands into mine again. "I'd do anything to help you."

"Be my friend, Will McLean. Don't leave me during all this, no matter how cruel or horrid I am to you, no matter what mean things I say. Be my friend, but remember to keep your distance. I feel vile and unclean, and I don't want to infect you."

"Infect me, Annie Kate? I want to take it all. I want to feel every hurt you have, and I want us to beat them down together."

We kissed again, a harder, more urgent kiss. I pressed her body against mine and felt her small breasts flatten against my chest and the pressure and weight of her pregnancy coming between us. Her child came between us, a symbol of both what divided us and what had brought us inextricably together. But touching the place where the child was made it no longer symbolic; it was real and palpable and material.

I had dreamed often of this child of Annie Kate's. I had seen it run along the shore of Sullivan's Island chasing migrating birds and suddenly released balloons. I could see this child clearly; it had no discernible sex, but it was a blond and airy thing, a sea-child who stood knee-deep in the surf and laughed at the flight of pelicans and the sprints of sandcrabs to their lairs. I could see it lifting from the beach stranded jellyfish, which would hang off its fingers like translucent laundry, and the child would not be stung. It would lift stingrays from the shallows without fear of harm. This would be a magic child, inspirited with the wisdom and cunning of sea life—and none of the old silent rancor of Charleston.

As we returned toward her house, stepping carefully over the rocks, I wondered about that child moving in the mysterious inland sea of Annie Kate's body. I held her hand and realized that the blood I felt rushing through her wrist would soon be rushing through the brain of the fetus, that her body had become an aquarium and that her child was a swimmer in its lightless pool. We were three human hearts on that walk down the beach, three different views of the universe, three sets of aligned yet separate dreams. I wondered if I had dreamed in my mother's womb. What would be the first dream in a newly created brain—perhaps some ancient common dream of the species, an image of fire or the first shuddering memory of stars or bison on the walls of caverns? Or do the dreams of mothers become the dreams of the half-children? Did I dream my mother's dreams? Did I learn of roses and aircraft and snowfall because my mother's dreams had traveled her body with their images intact and electric and full of messages from the outside world?

* * *

The beach house was a three-story Victorian structure painted a dark and depressing gray and set thirty yards back from the groin protecting the undermined beach. During very high tides, sea water made large pools in the grass. A third of the lawn was desiccated and whitened with deposits of salt and the skeletons of small fish that had come in with the tide through the rocks and escaped the patient investigations of the seabirds patrolling that sector of the island.

But there was something unique and extraordinary about this summer home of Annie Kate's. It was the kind of house that invited the curiosity and the dread of the neighborhood's imaginative children. Its rooms were tall and narrow, but each one had a different shape, giving the house an odd imbalance yet, at the same time, an odd symmetry.

There were two high porches with excellent views of the harbor. The lower porch had French doors that connected to the living room; the upper porch led to the master bedroom. The furniture could only be described compassionately as beach furniture, but it reflected an eclectic, practical consciousness at work over the years.

As we approached the house we could smell oak burning in the fireplace and caught an unobstructed view of Annie Kate's mother rocking vigorously in front of the fire. Annie Kate dropped my hand quickly, and I moved laterally away from her.

"Mother!" she whispered unnecessarily.

"Oh, shit," I said. "Do you mind if I have a heart attack?"

"Don't you dare," she commanded. "We didn't do anything wrong. Do you think she might have seen us before the sun went down?"

"I'm going to tell her that you attacked me sexually while I was saying the rosary out there on the rocks."

"She's drunk," Annie Kate said.

"How can you tell?"

"By the way she's rocking. And because it's after sunset. And because I've lived with her for twenty years."

When we entered through the French doors, Mrs. Ger-

293

vais turned her head and said, "Well, well. The two love-birds."

Annie Kate fired back, "Mother, you have absoultely no right to spy on me."

"I wasn't spying, darling. I just drove out to visit my daughter."

"You don't want to visit with me," Annie Kate yelled. "You got drunk and wanted to come out here and tell me just one more time how I ruined your life and all your plans for me."

"Every goddam one of them," Mrs. Gervais hissed at the same time as she caught me staring rather pensively at her. I have a naturally pious stare and don't mean a thing by it, as I could have told her, but it was not the proper moment for explanations. "What are you looking at, cadet? I can drink in my own home without some callow-faced merchant's brat looking at me like I was dirt. Can't I? Don't I have that right?"

"I'm not looking at you, Mrs. Gervais," I said foolishly, since I had not taken my eyes off her since I had entered the room.

"What do you want from my daughter, Will?" Mrs. Gervais asked, appraising me coldly with drunken, hostile eyes. This was the first time I had ever seen her drinking heavily, though Annie Kate had commonly made vague references to this weakness of her mother. I had only known her as a rather perfect specimen of Charleston society on the downward slide.

"I want to be her friend, Mrs. Gervais," I said.

"That was a very affectionate way you have of express-ing friendship."

"I'm sorry," I stammered, blushing and looking for a mildly graceful way to leave.

"You *were* spying on us, Mother," said Annie Kate, bristling and outraged. "I refuse to let you spy on me or to interfere any further with my life."

"Well, at least with this one, I don't have to worry about your getting pregnant," she said, staring morosely at her daughter.

"You drunken, filthy slut," Annie Kate screamed, lung-ing for the bottle of vodka, which Mrs. Gervais had tucked carefully in the crook of her arm.

"Oh, so now it's me that's the slut. I would like to remind you, dear, and for the information of your pimply cadet, that your father and I were duly married in the eyes of the Lord a full three years before I brought you squalling into Charleston society. Calling your own mother a slut. After what you've done to me—after what you've done to the family name. To disgrace me and your dead father. He's lucky to be dead. He's lucky he didn't have to face this."

Annie Kate sobbed, turned away, and swiftly ran to the stairs.

When she was gone I said, "I'm glad you dropped by, Mrs. Gervais."

"Don't be impertinent with me, cadet," she said. "Not with me, Cadet Will McLean. Poor stupid Will McLean. Did you know, Will, that God planned that the world was to be a vast orb of disillusionment and pain? He planned it that way and it pleased him to see that the plan was letter perfect," she said, pouring herself a tall glassful of vodka.

"Why don't you quit drinking that stuff, Mrs. Gervais," I said.

"I own this house, cadet," she snapped. "You have no right to issue orders or even make suggestions in my own house. I issue orders here. I order you out of my house. I order you not to touch my daughter again. I order you not to look at my daughter with those pitying, self-righteous eyes of yours. Get back to the barracks where you belong, Will."

I turned to leave the house when she called my name with a despairing, disconsolate voice. "Will. It's no one's goddam fault. It's not your fault. It's not my fault. It's not Annie Kate's fault. I just don't want any of us to get hurt any more. I've been hurting so long now, it seems natural to me."

"It seems natural to me, too, Mrs. Gervais," I answered, with my back still turned away from her. "I think I'm going to find out that you're right. I hope you're wrong, but I don't think so."

"Come back here and look at me," she commanded, as she took a huge swallow of vodka. "Look at my face, Will. Look at it closely, cadet," she croaked as I approached her. "This face was once beautiful. I mean beautiful and not just pretty. Do you see what's happened to it? Do you see how it's been lined and ruined? It was so quick, Will, so quick. I was beautiful; then, suddenly, I was old. I don't know how it happened or why it happened or what any of it means, but I want you to memorize my face and watch how cruelly the years will scratch and claw away at your own. And remember this moment, Will, remember it when you're looking at your face in the mirror thirty years from now and seeing an ugly old man instead of a smooth-skinned cadet. It's the quickness of it all that will surprise you. The incredible swiftness. It's as if I've pulled down a shade on twenty years of my life," she said, taking another enormous swallow of her drink. "I couldn't stop it. I couldn't slow it down. And I've worried about it every single day of my life since my twenty-eighth birthday. Isn't that sad and stupid? Isn't that human?"

I knelt down beside her and whispered, "I think you're a fine looking woman, Mrs. Gervais."

She looked at me with furious skeptical eyes and said in a slow, measured voice meant to wound, "Go to hell, cadet. I don't need your condescension or your pity. I just need you to listen to my liquor talk and keep your mouth shut. I'm from Charleston, cadet, did you hear me? Charleston! And you aren't from anywhere. I'm from Charleston and my family was on the second ship that arrived in this city. Do you know what that means? Do you have any idea what that means?"

"Yeh, Mrs. Gervais," I shouted. "It means nothing. It doesn't mean a goddam thing. You still get old and Annie Kate still gets pregnant just like any other poor bastard on earth."

"If it means so little to you, cadet, then why do you hang around it so much? Why do you room with Tradd St. Croix? Why do you waste your time with Annie Kate? Can't you find a girl to like you who isn't pregnant and who isn't desperate for friendship? Can't you find a normal relationship? Or isn't it true that you know a Charleston girl would never look at a cadet from the lower classes unless she found herself absolutely and completely alone? But I want to tell you a truth about this society you're toadying up to—you wouldn't be worthy of Annie Kate if she had twenty-five bastards and four of them were fathered by blue-gum niggers."

"You're a sweetheart when you're drinking, Mrs. Gervais," I said, my upper lip trembling, out of control, and I had to make a concentrated effort to make my words understood. "But I want to tell you about my lower-class family. You've never asked, of course, but I have this need to tell you about this family I come from."

"I can't think of anything more boring," she said and yawned drunkenly.

"Tough shit," I answered. "I'm going to tell you about them anyway and you're going to listen because you're too drunk to get up from that rocking chair."

She answered me with a gesture of overstated eloquence;

she emptied the vodka bottle into her glass and began downing it defiantly.

"My father was from Savannah, Mrs. Gervais, the oldest child in a family of nine that caught hell in the Depression. His father worked for the Southern Railroad, had little education, was dirt poor, and sent every one of his kids through high school. My father entered the Marine Corps when he was twenty, and he fought the Japanese to make the world safe for Charleston snobs to look down their noses at him and his family. My mother's family came from the hills of Georgia. They were poor farmers and laborers, as poor as anyone I've ever known, yet there was a humility and simplicity about them that made them among the most remarkable people I have ever met. My mother never went to college, never had that chance, but she is beautiful and intelligent and possesses a natural class so innate that when I bring her to Charleston and introduce her to Commerce and to Abigail and to Tradd, it's as though she had lived in this city for a hundred years. It's like she invented this city and I get so proud I could burst. And then there's me, Mrs. Gervais. Me. Ol' Will."

I was pacing back and forth across the room behind her rocking chair, gesticulating fiercely, and shouting at the motionless, defeated woman who sat in her rocking chair staring directly into the fire. Her glass was empty now.

"I'm halfway between my mother and father. My father wouldn't have been interested in this city at all. He wouldn't have given a flying crap about this city. If he'd even have known about South of Broad society, I'd have probably found him drunk in front of St. Michael's one night shouting that he was going to beat the hell out of every male between twenty and fifty that he found cowering beneath verandahs clutching their genealogy charts. And I lack my mother's natural social grace and her effortless tact at dealing with aristocracies that nature and circumstance prevented her from joining. Ever since I came to this city, I've been made painfully aware of my origins. There were times when I was actually ashamed of who I was and where I came from. But I looked around and I studied the terrain and I figured out some things, Mrs. Gervais. I'm the second generation up from the lowest classes. I'm an immigrant among the classes. I have more than my parents had and my children will have more than I. And we have one advantage over you and people like you. We never look back. Our eyes are straight ahead and we're tough and we're street smart and we're still hungry and on the move. And we have the goddam tide of human destiny on our side."

Mrs. Gervais had passed out. The rocking chair had not moved in five minutes and she had not heard a single word I had said. From the stairway leading up to the second floor of the house, I heard the sound of mocking, fraudulent applause. Looking up, I saw Annie Kate at the top of the stairs, dressed in her bathrobe and slippers and clapping vigorously for my performance.

"Hurrah for the goddam tide of human destiny," she shouted.

I covered my face with my hands, leaned down, and rested my head against the bannister of the stairway. A moment later, I felt Annie Kate's hand on my shoulder but I did not uncover my eyes.

"I'm so ashamed that you heard that," I said. "I'm so ashamed that I said all that to your mother when she was drunk."

"Mother has a way of getting to people when she's been drinking," Annie Kate said, stroking my hair. "She's a nice person when she's not."

"I'm a nice person when I'm not making a horse's ass out of myself. Jesus Christ, I was just delivering a Horatio Alger lecture to a woman who had passed out."

"You'd have probably thrown her off the porch if she hadn't passed out," Annie Kate chided me, her finger tracing the stiffly barbered hairline at the back of my neck. "I've never seen you so mad."

"Why do I care if your mother thinks I was born in the steerage section of a ship on the way to Ellis Island? What's wrong with me? Why do I give a damn?"

"Because there's a mystique and confidence that comes from being an old Charlestonian that you'll never know, Will. That's what you're looking for. You're right to be proud about who you are and what you said about your family was beautiful. It's just that you'll never have what we have or understand what we have."

"I'm going to work hard not to want what you have. If what your mother said is true then I've been poisoned in this city. I've been poisoned by hanging around Tradd, these fine people and their fine houses, and you."

"I don't feel very poisonous right now," she said. "Please carry my mother to the couch, Will. I'd do it. She's very light, you know. But in my oh so delicate condition . . ."

I lifted Mrs. Gervais from the chair without the slightest strain; I calculated that she weighed less than ninety pounds. Her hair was feathery and disarranged. And as I laid her on the couch, I realized how wrong she was. She had not lost her beauty, though she was losing her youth.

Annie Kate covered her mother with a quilt.

Then we faced each other. Neither of us knew what to do or say. We had said and insinuated too much that evening for me to leave without further discussion or to stay without our destiny, our goddam human destiny, being further and irretrievably complicated.

My time in her gaze was a fine yet troubled thing. I could feel the fear of what the world had done to her rise up between us. She could sense my hurt, the inconceivable magnitude of my bruised vanity, and my need to allay the monstrously insistent fiats and injunctions of a male ego. I ached with a feverish, selfish, and awful need for her. I wanted to touch, to own, to have her. The room shimmered with my wanting her. Yet I could make no move, felt that I did not have the right to touch her or even think about touching her. The touch of a man had already harmed her enough.

Then she reached out for me. She led me up the stairs and I followed her, memorizing the lines of her body, the allure of roundness and the surprise of fullness and ripeness and youth. It was as though her entire body was filled up with milk.

When we entered her dark room, she turned and faced me. She untied her bathrobe and stepped out of her slippers in a shy clumsy movement. I drew her toward me and felt the nakedness of her back and shoulders, and the firmness of her buttocks. I kissed her eyes, her lips, her neck, her breasts. I had never touched a woman's breast before. She undressed me and we lay down on the bed together.

We stared at each other for a long time. She took my hand and placed it on her stomach and I felt the child kicking inside her.

"I'm sorry I'm pregnant, Will," she said. "I'm so sorry I'm pregnant."

"It's all right, Annie Kate. That doesn't matter to me."

"It should matter, Will."

"No."

We began to touch each other. We marveled at the warmth and youth and need of each other. Her tongue found my ear. My finger entered her. I kissed her breasts and began to circle her nipples with my tongue. I entered her and came almost at once. I was a terrible lover; humiliated, I apologized; I wanted to run away from that house and hide in the swells of the ocean that I could hear assaulting the rocks on the beach outside.

But she laughed and was kind and said it didn't matter, that she liked the touching and the closeness and the intimacy. So we talked of intimate things and we kissed again and I forgot about my ineptitude. I grew hard again, went into her again, and we began to move together. I began to say things to her that I had wanted to say to a woman since I was fifteen. We began to rock together, and moan together. I heard the sounds of the Atlantic and the sound of us loving each other and felt the child that lay between us and the easy, tender movement between us and her heels on the back of my thighs, her willingness, her openness to me, the completeness of the moment, the smell of her hair, then the fire, the fire again, and my spilling out inside her, and the cry that flowered in the room was my own cry.

And I lay there thinking, in all the new arrogance of lost virginity, "Now I know what it is like to love a woman, now I have touched the magic source, now I know why it is like nothing else in the world." I was not thinking of Annie Kate at all, in fact, I had forgotten she was in the room. Abstractedly, I began to rub her swollen stomach and did not become aware of her presence again until I felt the sudden untroubled kick of her child. I wanted the child to feel the pulse of my wrist as though I were its father. I looked at Annie Kate, surprised that I had forgotten that she was in the room. Her face was hurt; she had acknowledged my betrayal.

"Annie Katie," I said to her as she rolled away from me. "If you want to keep the child, I'll be glad to marry you."

"Aren't you the noble one," she said, and she was crying.

She cried for several minutes as I sat there naked on the bed, wondering whether I should try to comfort her or simply get dressed and return to the barracks. Both the truth and the cruelty of her remark had stunned me into a kind of dreamlike immobility. When I finally touched her shoulder, she grabbed my hand and said through tears, "Will. I'm so sorry, Will. No matter what I say to you, don't leave me now. I don't know what I'd do if you left me. I don't know why I have to hurt you, but I don't mean it. I can't help how I act now. But I can't afford to lose you. You're the only thing that's keeping me alive."

"You won't be able to lose me, Annie Kate," I whispered in her ear, kissing her neck and shoulders and spine.

I began massaging her back and soon she fell asleep and her breathing became calm again. I rose silently and checked my watch, the old ingrained nervous habit of the cadet. It was a law of the barracks that if you were having a good time it was fast approaching midnight. It was twenty minutes to twelve.

I put on my uniform hurriedly, kissed Annie Kate on the cheek, and raced downstairs. When I retrieved my field cap from the dining-room table, I glanced toward Mrs. Gervais. Her eyes were open and she was staring at me with a look ineffably grieving. Grief, her face said with a sad, wordless rhetoric: grief. I walked over and kissed her and pulled the blanket up around her.

I was going eighty when I crossed the Cooper River Bridge, high over the city, with the decks of ships below me in the river, going eighty and screaming with the joy and triumph and intoxication felt when a boy tenderly buries that shy, exhausted priest of his virginity and takes the first delicious step into the mansion of sex.

I made it inside the front gate of fourth battalion ten seconds before they locked the gates for the night. I danced across the quadrangle, and for the first time I did not care that there was nothing green in the barracks. I danced my way toward the stairwell of R Company, and I wanted to shout at the top of my lungs, "I am not a virgin! I am not a virgin!" I felt fertile and leafy and earthily fragrant with the odors of sex.

As I reached the steps leading up to first division I heard a voice call out from the darkness under the stairwell.

"Halt, Bubba."

I saw the cigar blazing like a lone, abandoned eye in the alcove.

"Bear," I said, surprised. "What are you doing here at this time of the night?"

"I'm the good shepherd and I've got to watch over my wayward lambs. What are you so happy about? I get nervous when I see you smile, McLean. You moved across that quad like you were trying out for Tinker Bell."

"A girl, Colonel," I said.

"When did you switch preferences, Bubba?"

"Tonight. Tonight, sir."

"McLean," the Bear said gently, his cigar blazing. "You're acting like it was the first time, Bubba."

301

"It was, Colonel."

He reached into his uniform pocket and brought out a Thompson cigar from Tampa, Florida. "Congratulations, Bubba. That's like inventing the wheel."

I still have that cigar.

30

I remember the winter of my senior year as one of the happiest times of my life. My walk was springy and I seemed to be in perfect step with the universe. I was playing good ball; I was in love with Annie Kate Gervais; I was taking Sunday afternoon walks with Abigail; my grades were good and my classes stimulating; there was an extraordinary harmony and contentment among my roommates. Those were magic times in Charleston; the days were cold and short, the city awoke to ice, and I arose each morning at the first bugle, refreshed and eager and golden in the darkness of 6:15 in the morning, vigorous and ready for the gifts the day would bring. In January during a game with George Washington, I had thrown a pass to Johnny DuBruhl who had cut toward the basket. He had not seen the pass and it had careened off the top of his head, hit the high part of the backboard, and fallen softly through the net. The scorekeeper awarded me a basket and Johnny an assist. That's how it was in that radiant season.

Every small act became a celebration of sorts for me. I could be seen running to class and running to practice and running to my car. I did not want to miss anything. I wanted to taste it all, savor every experience, register every sight, smell, and taste of those months. Before each game, a high school girl, a basketball fan, would call me up in the barracks and tell me where on campus she had left a single red rose for me to find. I never met this girl even though I tried earnestly to arrange a meeting. But I would follow her directions and find a rose in the chapel before the Furman game, a rose carefully placed on a shelf in the library before we played Clemson, a rose floating in a fountain in the General's front yard before we played William and Mary, a rose pinned on the climbing rope of the obstacle course before the Auburn

302

game. The roses were a symbol of my good fortune and I knew when the season ended there would be no more roses hidden for my pleasure by an enchanted, invisible stranger. But I wanted there always to be accidents and mysteries and roses in my life.

Since that time I have come to distrust periods of extreme happiness and now when I discover myself in the middle of one, I glance nervously around me, examine all locks, cut back all the shrubbery around my house, avoid introductions to strangers, and do not travel on airplanes. Happiness is an accident of nature, a beautiful and flawless aberration, like an albino. Like the albino it has no protective coloration. White. That is the color. Those placid, untroubled winter months are different shades of white in my memory, unsullied, and pure. But nature in the temperate zones is bitter toward all things white.

I know the day when things began to change. But the change was so slight, so imperceptible, I did not sense the shift. On the day we played the final game of the season, against Virginia Military Institute, the call from the mystery girl came just before noon formation. She had placed the final rose on the windshield wiper of my car along with a note. In the note she wished me all the luck in the world and was sorry that she was not pretty enough to meet me or to get to know me. The note was incredibly poignant. It shimmered with the solitude of a damaged and imaginative girl. She spoke the truth. It was the last rose of that winter, and I never did hear from her again. I hoped she would find a good man whom she could meet face to face. The one thing I knew for certain is that he would find her pretty enough. Of that, I had no doubt. There was only one thing different in her final gift. Her last rose was white.

I was up before the bugle that morning, splashing cold water on my face at the sink when reveille sounded across the campus. Often, I arose early on the days of games, all eagerness and drive and nervous energy. But I was always at my best in the morning anyhow. I had the metabolism of a canary at reveille, bright and chirpy and preening before the mirror. I was talkative in the morning, alive and glowing, one of those dreadful people who were the scourge of the cadets who relished silence and time and vast quantities of caffeine before their bodies could adapt to the shock of marching through a sunless world. But I drew energy and sustenance from the surge of the Corps around me. I felt like whistling and singing and joking as soon as my feet hit the floor.

When the bugle sounded, Mark shouted, "Fuck."

Pig shouted, "Fuck."

Tradd said wearily, "Oh, God. Already?"

"Up and at 'em, boys and girls," I said gleefully. "Another big day at Disneyland."

"Shut up, asshole." Mark sighed, pulling a pillow over his head.

It was dangerous strategy to joke with Mark before noon formation. He had made it a law of the room that I was not to speak to him or even look at him in the morning. He was the only person I've ever known who could navigate four flights of winding stairs, march to the mess hall, and eat breakfast without ever once opening his eyes.

Before I could go over and shake my roommates into a state of semi-consciousness, Beasley, the knob, burst into the room to announce that the Bear had entered the barracks to check on seniors late for morning formation.

"Good lad, Beasley," I said. "Pass the word among the freshmen that I'll be down in a second and that I want them loud this morning. All right, beloved roommates, get out of the rack and onto the floor."

"Fuck you, asshole," Mark grumbled from beneath the pillow. Mark had never been on time to a formation since we had become seniors as far as I knew.

When I reached the quadrangle I looked around, trying to spot where the Bear was hiding. I did not see him, so I began to tease the R Company freshmen who were already lined like bottles in their respective squads. I was part of an early warning system that alerted sleeping seniors in the battalion when the Bear or a tactical officer slipped into the barracks to write up delinquency reports on tardy upperclassmen.

I walked to the front of the company area and faced the freshmen.

"Good morning, dumbheads," I shouted.

"Good morning, sir," they answered in unison.

"Isn't it great to be alive and a member of the Corps of Cadets?" I asked.

"Yes, sir," they roared.

"I love this place, dumbheads. I think I've found myself a home. Isn't it great to wake up on a freezing winter morning in pitch darkness? Don't you just love it, douchebags?"

"Yes, sir."

"All over America, dumbheads, on lesser college campuses, campuses that do not specialize in producing whole men, boys exactly your age are turning over in their sleep and touching the huge, succulent boobs of their girl friends and moaning that they have to get up for their first class at two o'clock in the afternoon. They're hung over from a frat party and an all-night sexual orgy that started while you were engaged in a sweat party on third division. Doesn't that sound disgusting, dumbheads? Can you imagine going to college to have fun? Pop off!"

"No, sir!" they shouted.

I smelled the cigar smoke in the dark morning air. I had been waiting for it.

"Do you know why I came to the Institute, scumbags? Pop off!"

"No, sir!" they replied.

"I wanted to model myself after a great man. I wanted to model myself after that paragon of military virtue, that officer who was wounded in the behind while fleeing the German advance in the Battle of the Bulge, that fighting man of such superlative qualities that he has returned to his alma mater as commandant in charge of discipline. I came to the Institute, dumbheads, because I wanted to be exactly like Colonel Thomas Berrineau, affectionately known as the Bear. Please give him a big round of applause, wad-wastes. This man is like a father to me."

The freshmen applauded loudly and stiffly. It is hard to be cheerful when you are bracing in twenty-degree weather.

"Good morning, Bubba," Colonel Berrineau said, stepping up beside me and examining the R Company freshmen.

"Good morning, Colonel," I said. "How can you smoke that thing at six-fifteen in the morning, sir?"

"It helps me get rid of the sickly sweet taste of toothpaste, lamb, and it helps young lambs like you to smell the Bear sneaking up behind you. I got to give you bums some kind of break."

Then in a loud, commanding voice he addressed the plebes in Romeo Company. If the Bear's voice did not wake the seniors, they were probably dead.

"Is this bum McLean spreading sedition among my lamblets? Pop off!"

"Yes, sir!" they roared.

"Just why are you down here so early, Mr. McLean?" the Bear asked me knowingly.

"Sir," I said, turning toward the plebes. "I'm down here

305

because of my concern for these young dumbheads. Just look at them, sir. No pride, no spirit, no command presence to any of them. Now you and I are from the Old Corps, Colonel, and we are accustomed to a certain quality of douchebag that we are just not attracting to the Institute in these sad, decadent times. For instance, Jones. Where's my man Jones?"

An emaciated, bespectacled freshman from Atlanta stepped quickly forward from the second platoon. "Now, Colonel, when Mr. Jones was a young man he contracted polio of the face and had to wear a brace on his nose and upper lip for the first five years of his life. You'll notice that his nose still has a limp. Show the Colonel that painful limp in your left nostril, Jones."

Jones wrinkled his nose, rabbitlike, several times for effect.

"A terrible affliction, you will agree, Colonel," I continued. "But Jones has overcome it, much to his credit. He has to sleep with his nose suspended from a pulley but otherwise he's a model cadet, as I was when I was a freshman. What disturbed me about Jones, though, was when he told me he had applied for a job at the zoo shoveling elephant manure and was turned down. Finally, in desperation, he applied to the Institute and they gave him a four-year academic scholarship. Colonel, I tell you these are trying times."

"Young lamb," the Bear said to Jones, inspecting the freshman's twitchy nose more carefully. "Is that job at the zoo still open? We in the Commandant's Department have been worried about a career for Mr. McLean for quite some time."

The plebes shook with repressed, uncontainable laughter. The laughter of freshmen was a rare commodity on the quadrangle of the regiment.

Seniors were racing from their rooms from all over the barracks, tucking in their shirts as they came, shoes untied, hats askew, and eyes trained on their watches as they tried to outrun the final bugle that would make them late on the Bear's clipboard.

"You've got a good early warning system, Bubba," the Bear said, watching the harried movement of seniors.

"Are you going to the last game tonight?" I asked the Colonel.

"Sure, Bubba, I never miss a VMI game. I like to see what cadets from a good military college look like. How do you think our chances are?"

"They'll probably stomp us, Colonel," I answered. "The

one thing the Institute has taught me is how to lose gracefully and often. Sir, I must bid you adieu. My squad is incomplete and anxious without me to bring up the rear on the march to mess."

"I'll see you at parade next Friday, McLean," he warned. "You'll be off orders then, and I'll be checking to make sure your squad is complete with a senior private who walks like a duck and carries an M–1 like it was radioactive."

"M–1," I said, puzzled. "Isn't that a sauce you put on a steak?"

"No, it's something I'll put up your behind if you're not at that parade, Bubba."

"I can hardly wait to hear the drums roll and the guidons snap in the wind, Colonel. I've also hired a plane to seed the clouds and make it rain like hell that day so the damn thing will be canceled. I think it's a crime to make a jock go to parade for any occasion. We look silly out there, and people laugh at us and hurt our feelings."

The last bugle sounded. "By the way, Bubba," he whispered, walking to my platoon with me, "do you remember that ten I found painted on that freshman's door?"

"Vaguely," I said. "That was a long time ago."

"It looks like a coincidence," he said. "Some platoon sergeant painted that because it was the tenth knob that had been sent packing out of that company. I ended his career as an artist, but I wanted you to know that it looks like a false alarm."

"Colonel, I don't think we have anything to worry about anymore. Pearce has made it through the worst part of the year. It's getting toward the end of February, and I haven't even received a note from him in two months."

"We're just staying vigilant, Bubba. We're just getting Pearce through this school one day at a time. This is going to be the Year of the Nigger in the history of the Institute. Now get in line, Bubba. All the seniors made it to formation because of your big mouth. I won't report you for unshined shoes if we beat VMI tonight."

"We'll try, Colonel," I said, saluting him as he left the barracks.

* * *

That evening I walked through the front door of the Armory to play the last game I would ever play for Carolina Military Institute. I had come to the day when I would face the world without a sport. The Armory smelled of loss and

307

passage and absent crowds; it shimmered with memories of old forgotten games and the death of athletes. Something vital in me would die on this night. I had come to my absolute limits as an athlete, and they were not very great.

Athlete. The very word was beautiful to me. I looked up at the scoreboard and thought, Has there ever been a boy who loved this game as much as I have loved it? I had known the praise of crowds and knew nothing else on earth to equal it. When I played basketball, I was possessed by a nakedness of spirit, an absolute purity, a divine madness when I was let loose to ramble between the lines. Always, I was reckless and moving at full speed, and I never learned the potency of stillness, the craft of subtlety. I had moved about the court for four years without control, as though I were racing from basket to basket putting out fires or hurling myself on live grenades. I had played the game the best I could but was beaten time and time again. But I had willed myself to be, if not gifted, at least someone to be watched closely, and at times when the ball came my way and I came at my opponents in full flight, an athlete to be feared. I could hurt them only with recklessness. There were times when they knew I was a burning boy, a dancing, roaring, skipping, brawling boy—moments of pure empyrean magic when the demon of sport was born in the howl of my bloodstream, when my body and the flow of the game commingled in a wild and accidental mating and I turned into something I was never meant to be: an athlete who could not be stopped, a dreaded and respected gamesman loose and rambling on the court. I remembered those moments because there were so few of them and because the sport had tamed me with the knowledge of my own limitations, my earnest mediocrity. Yet, while controlling the flow of games with the unstealable dribble, I had been more truly alive than I would ever be again. I had learned that my grace came only in the full abandoned divinity of flight. I had known the joy, the pure orgasmic joy of the dance. It was a day of last roses, last dances.

As I walked toward the locker room, I thought about how I feared things being irrevocably finished. Had it been that long ago that I first entered this gymnasium as a freshman? Its size had startled me, its aura of seriousness and the big time. Had it been that long ago that I was eighteen? How could a human being deal with such swiftness, with such unrecallability?

I entered the dressing room, steamy from the overworked radiators, noisy with the nervous banter of the team dressing.

"Big Bo," I said, acknowledging Bo Maybank, who was wrapping the ankles of Doug Cumming on the training table.

"Will," he said, pleased to see me. "I won five bucks from Doug a half-hour ago. I made ten straight set shots from the top of the key."

"Never bet with midgets, Will," Doug said, slapping at my behind as I passed them on the way to my locker. Athletes have a strange but genuine compulsion to touch each other's asses.

I paused by Reuben Clapsaddle, who was lacing up his size eighteen shoes.

"My, what big feet you have, Grandma," I said.

"All the better to stomp little guards with, my dear," Reuben answered.

Johnny DuBruhl, the other starting guard and an inch shorter than I was, came up behind me and gave me a stinging slap on the rump. "Hurry up, little man, we've got a ball game to play and I've got a date after the game."

"You ought to see the girl, Will," Doug Cumming shouted from the training table.

"Don't move 'til I finish taping your ankles, Doug," Bo commanded.

Doug continued, "There's been a breakout at the zoo, man."

"Eat me, Cumming," Johnny shouted across the locker room.

"Hey, Doug," Dave Dunbar, a second string forward who was from the same Ohio town as Johnny, said, "do you know what Johnny's girl does for a living? She's got a real good job, man. They test new treads on tanks by running over her face before they send them out to the field."

"At least I've got a date," Johnny said. "That's more than I can say for the rest of you horny bastards."

"I thought I saw Johnny with a girl after the last game," Dave said. "But then I looked again and saw that I was mistaken."

"How'd you know you were wrong, Dave?" I asked.

"I drove past them in my Volkswagen and she chased after the car barking," he answered.

"I know you guys are just jealous," Johnny said. "I'm out there getting it while you guys are back in the barracks wearing one white glove."

Reuben changed the subject by saying, "Did you hear that Johnson of '65 got killed in Vietnam, Will?"

"No," I answered, with real shock.

"Both co-captains of the '65 football team were killed within a week of each other. You knew that McBride was killed in a firefight near Da Nang last week," Johnny continued, twirling a basketball expertly on his index finger. "Those were two really good guys. It's funny. It's kind of normal when I hear about regular Joes from the Corps getting zapped, but it always sort of surprises me when a jock has his brains blown out."

"Maybe basketball players just don't give a damn about this country," a high-pitched voice said from near the equipment room. It was Bo Maybank, and his tiny rodent's face was flushed with anger and the emotion of speaking something he had wanted to say to us for a long time.

"Oh, oh," Johnny said, laughing, "I got the Midget started on Vietnam."

"Speak for yourself, Bo," Reuben said, staring at the manager. "The Big Fella ain't playing no hide and seek with the little yellow people. That's a war for military dicks and Lilliputians."

"You don't mind other people getting killed for you, I guess, Reuben?" Bo muttered in a trembling, barely audible voice, nervously searching the room for allies.

"Just shut up and wrap ankles like a good little duck-butt," Doug said.

"I don't mind other people getting killed for Big Reuben," said Reuben. "Shit, I was so happy when I found out that I was too tall to get drafted that I almost went out and bought me a new record. Can you see me in Nam, Bo? I'd be dead in a fucking week. It's hard to be quiet in the jungle when you're six foot ten, man. The Vietcong would hear my big feet coming ten miles away. I could just see me on my tippy-toes trying to keep quiet. Crunch—Crunch—Crunch. They'd see me coming, stop eating rice for a sec, go blow fucking Reuben's legs off, then go back and make up a new batch of soy sauce. No sir, I'm happy to be six-ten and leave the fighting to you little poots."

"Let's think about VMI, boys," I said, amazed at my own sanctimonious tone.

"That's right, guys," Bo said penitently. "I shouldn't have started that before a game. The important thing now is the game. Will's right. I'm sorry. No kidding. I'm really sorry."

"It's OK, Midget," Johnny said. "We were all upset when we heard about those two."

"I'm sorry, everybody," Bo said.

"No problem, Bo," I said.

"We're living in fucked times," Doug said, doing knee bends to loosen his legs.

Bo Maybank walked up to me and began massaging the dense constricted muscles in my neck and shoulders. He massaged my face and neck with one of his towels. The towels, as always, were hot and slightly damp from the dryer. "Score a basket for me tonight, Will," he whispered so Reuben could not hear.

"I'll score one for you and one for Vietnam," I chided him.

"I hope I didn't upset the team, Will," he said. "I don't know what got into me."

"Light stuff, Bo," I said, pulling several hairs out of his almost hairless legs.

Bo stood barely five feet two in his stocking feet and weighed slightly less than a hundred pounds. He looked like a species of mankind not yet fully evolved. His skin was flushed a pale blue, as though his thinness would allow you to study his entire circulatory system without cutting into his body. His hands were thin and spidery and when stretched out over the hide of a basketball had the delicacy and fragile beauty of a fish skeleton.

He was also the best shooter on the team, of that there was no doubt whatsoever. He had the pure artistry of the natural. Each night as we left the gym we could see Bo shooting at the glass backboard with a Wilson Special that looked like a beachball in his hands. His wrist, thin as wire, would shoot the ball toward the rim and we would hear the pure sharp song of leather snapping through the net that was the signature of our trade. Once he had made eighteen straight set shots from the top of the circle and Coach Byrum admitted aloud that Bo was one of the best shooters he had ever seen. Then, in an indifferent aside, he winked at us and said, "But who cares about a five-foot midget who shoots good?" I had found Bo sobbing in the equipment room after he did not show up in the mess hall for dinner.

I looked up at Bo and smiled. I had never understood why Bo Maybank liked me so much better than I liked myself. I knew it had something to do with my being his vicarious counterpart in the game he was too small to play. When I had a bad game, he suffered more than I did, and when I did well, his entire face radiated joy. I was often embarrassed by how much Bo preferred me to my teammates, but I also needed his gentle and uncritical advocacy of me—I would always need people like Bo in my life. He had simply chosen me from the rest and sometimes a choice is explanation enough and requires no further study or elaboration. His hands were still on my shoulder when Coach Byrum entered the room.

It was painful to watch Byrum's face as he pleaded with us to win the final game of the season. It was an exhausted face, one full of absurd dignity and the jowly looseness that often comes to men who face an uncertain future and who drink too much because of that uncertainty. He knew and we knew that his days as basketball coach at the Institute were over. Byrum was not a great coach, that I had decided long ago, but he was a humane one; and I learned more from his frailties, his terrors, and his flawed vulnerable humanity than I would have learned from a great coach's strength.

After each pre-game speech during that long, losing season, there was a terrifying moment when we thought Coach Byrum would break down in front of us and cry out of frustration and humiliation before the whole team. His voice was raspy and eroded, as though he were breaking up from inside. He held his stomach with his left hand as he spoke and he kept a cup full of Maalox by his seat during games. Several times during the season I wanted to embrace his large, tragic frame and beg his forgiveness for not being a better athlete. Whenever he looked at me with his haunted frightened eyes, he broke my heart.

I stood in the front of the line by the locker room door with my teammates behind me. Bo handed me a new Wilson Special to dribble while leading the team onto the court for warm-ups. Reverently, I took the ball and inhaled its newness. It smelled like an expensive pair of men's shoes. I bounced it on the cement floor for luck, the feel of the leather so pleasant to my fingertips, so natural in my hands.

We could hear the deep-throated hum of the Corps waiting for the teams to emerge. Then we heard the partisan outcry as the VMI players appeared on the opposite side of the field house. The Corps greeted them with a volley of boos and hisses that reverberated across the campus. When the noise subsided, we waited for Bo to swing open the door to our locker room. Glazed with sweat, we tensed for the moment of entry, the butterflies swarming in their familiar, nervous dance in our stomachs; we listened closely to the

Corps's hymn of loathing directed at VMI, felt the eyes of the Corps turning toward us. Bo wiped my forehead with a towel. I winked at him. Then he flung the door open and we burst into the Armory, princes of the sudden light, flawed but game champions of the Corps of Cadets.

The Corps rose to its feet and greeted us in its cyclonic voice. It exploded in the wild, exhilarated language of a tribe screaming out its oneness with us. Nothing has ever affected me in that same profoundly visceral way as the salutation of the Corps when I broke free from the steamy enclave of the locker room into the blue-hazed, cavernous, light-filtered center of the Armory. The band struck up "Dixie." The screams entered my brain like some enormously powerful insulin, like gusts of pure oxygen, and I glided across the deeply polished mirror of the gymnasium floor, a boy in my prime who could run windsprints all day, a boy who could bring the ball up court against anybody on earth.

The team fanned out in two disciplined squads as I drove to the right side of the court and put the first warm-up shot high against the backboard and heard its sweet rippling sound as it fell through the nylon net. I was moving now and my motor was running. I fed off the applause. God, how I love this game, I thought, rebounding a missed shot and throwing a bounce pass to Doug Cumming as he broke toward the basket. God, how I love this game and how I wish I had been better at it. The happiest days of my boyhood were spent above the woodshine of oak and below the gaze of both friendly and hostile crowds. And I never loved the game better than when we played at home and sprinted directly into the fierce embrace of the Corps. It was a memorable thing to play a game with the Corps in all its virile wildness behind you. If a team played us in the Armory, we were ten points better than we were on the road and not because we automatically played better at home but because our skills merged with the fury of the Corps in full cry. Strangers could garner some glimpse of the plebe system's violent nature by sitting in the Armory and listening to the Corps's voice. The applause of the Corps, charged with repressed sexuality, was feral and imprisoned and out of control.

There was also an extra dimension of rivalry and fraternity when we played Virginia Military Institute. We were the last two state military colleges of any significance in the nation. Cadets were a rare and vanishing species of American fauna, and our contests were like duels between well-groomed gentlemen. Our hair was closely cropped, we said "sir" to the referees, we stood at attention during the National Anthem, and we were two of the last all-white basketball teams in the country. If the Institute was something from the Old South, then VMI was something from Old Virginia, and that was very different and very important indeed. I also liked the individual VMI players better than any other team in the Southern Conference. They were the only ones who did not laugh at our uniforms on road trips, did not call cadence as we walked to the locker room, and did not blame us for every death in the Vietnam War. The first stirrings of the antiwar movement were beginning on American college campuses, and the Institute became a highly visible symbol of that war to other student bodies.

The first antiwar demonstration I ever witnessed had stopped a game at George Washington University when fifty students staged a sit-down in center court. Reuben and I watched in amazement from the sidelines as campus police forcibly removed them from the gym. We were both disturbed and amused. As we watched, a pretty, brown-haired girl walked quietly up to us and said hello. When we looked around, she threw a bucket of human blood into our faces. Then she screamed at us, "How many kids did Institute graduates kill today, you bastards?" The crowd was booing loudly. Later, I realized they were jeering at the demonstrators but at that moment, I thought they were voicing some indefinable but universal loathing of me personally as I stood there wiping blood from my eyes and spitting it out of my mouth.

"Captain McLean," the referee said, tapping me on the shoulder.

"Just call me 'Cap,' Big George," I said, shaking hands with the referee I had seen three times a year for four years. "I don't like to stand on formality. Just call the fouls on them. I swear I'm not going to touch human flesh tonight."

"With you guarding Mance, I figure you'll foul out in this first half, Cap." Big George laughed, as we walked toward center court.

"Do you know any gamblers, George?" I whispered. "I can be bought cheap."

Jimmy Mance was watching me as we approached midcourt.

"Captain Mance," George said, nodding toward me, "Captain McLean."

"How you doing, Will?" Mance said, grinning and extending his hand. We shook hands warmly.

314

"It's my last game, Jimmy. Don't make me look like a complete jerk in front of the home crowd."

"I'll be lucky to score ten against you, Will," he said. "You know that."

The only way I could hold Mance to ten points would be to cut off one of his feet.

"George, I would like to file an official report," I said seriously.

"Will, would you please shut up and let me tell you the rules so we can get on with the game?"

"No, this is important, George. I have information from an impeccable source that Mr. Mance here is a Russian woman who had an operation so she could play ball for VMI."

Jimmy laughed loudly, for Jimmy Mance thought I was a hoot. It was the only thing about playing against him that was not personally humiliating. It had become an integral part of my strategy in defending him that I get him laughing at the opening tips and keep him giggling to the final whistle. I had once got him laughing so hard I had held him to twenty-two points. Another time I had made a joke about his mother, and he had ripped me for thirty-eight, fuming and choleric for the rest of the game. Even his sense of humor was a sensitive, high-strung instrument, and I had learned to play it delicately.

Jimmy Mance had played a far more important role in my life than he would ever realize. By observing this brilliant athlete, with his classical moves and his effortless grace, I could judge the depth and tenor of my own mediocrity. He was six feet four inches tall and built in that free-flowing, loose-muscled dignity of the natural. Every time I went against him I was unconscionably overmatched. He could jump higher, run faster, shoot better, pass more accurately ... it was as though God had deliberately set out to make a basketball player when he designed the body of Jimmy Mance. He had given me only the desire to be a great athlete, not the body. Mance had proven that to me each time I guarded him. My desire to stop him emphasized the extent of his gifts and the limits of my own. It was an honor to be on the same court with him, and I would tell my children of the nights I challenged him, guarded him, of the times I was beaten by him.

I left Mance and the referees and joined my teammates, who had encircled Coach Byrum, listening to him exhort us

315

to win in an endless string of clichés that made up the impoverished language of sport. Bo Maybank stroked my face with a warm towel.

The buzzer sounded and we took to the court for my last game at the Institute. And, oh, the feeling as the voice of the Corps greeted us. I burned with the majesty of my sport; I burned with the joy of living life at that moment. In the stands I saw Pig and Mark and Tradd standing with their arms raised in gestures of support for me, caught the eyes of Commerce and Abigail, saluted the General, saw the Bear and Edward the Great, noticed Pearce sitting in a crowd of plebes, heard Cain Gilbreath call my name in the first row of the stands, waved to the boys in R Company, and felt inalienable gratitude to this sport—this sport that had allowed me to become the showman, permitted the shy boy to strut and mug and preen for the approval of the crowd. I knew that Annie Kate would be listening to the game on radio, that my name would come to her through invisible waves as she sat in her isolation on Sullivan's Island. On the court, in the middle of games, I was completely happy. I felt cleansed of all sin, inflated with the grace of the planet, and free.

The centers rose toward the ball and I lost consciousness of the crowd, lost consciousness of myself, and entered into the high country of sport. Down the court I pursued Jimmy Mance. I watched a VMI forward pump in a beautiful jumper from the corner. I retrieved the ball out of bounds, flipped it to Johnny, moved up court, and saw the first play break down as Doug found himself trapped and surrounded in the corner as I ran toward him. He shoveled the ball to me just as I saw Reuben make a move on the VMI center and I shot the ball to him, as he went toward the rim for the ball and dunked it savagely through the basket. And I turned into the applause, exalted, running, wild on the court. I burned. I burned with the joy of the game. I tell you I was a burning boy that night in Charleston.

But burning alone could not stop or interfere with the brilliance of Jimmy Mance. He began to control the tempo and flow of the game with the sheer immensity of his gifts. He scored on his first five jumps shots. Down the court he would lope toward me, directly toward me, looking at me with those blazing predator's eyes, his body moving with a cold fluency, his dribble confident. He was the monarch of this brief season, and he knew the responsibilities of his reign. When he dribbled toward me maneuvering for his sixth shot,

I shouted to him above the din of the crowd, "You're humiliating me, Mance. You're making me look like shit in front of all my friends."

He smiled, then wheeled suddenly around a pic, and I watched the ball arc high into the air, barely above my outstretched hand. It hit the rim and fell into the hands of a leaping, fully extended Doug Cumming.

"You're human, Mance. You're actually a human being," I screamed, breaking to the center of the court where I received a perfect pass over my shoulder from Doug and broke toward our basket with Johnny DuBruhl's shout entering my left ear as he filled the lane. Driving toward Mance, who had fallen back to defend against the fast break, I cut toward his right side, went up into the air with him, waited until I saw both of his arms above my head, and hit Johnny with a behind-the-back pass he caught on the dead run. He scored without a man around him and the Corps went berserk. I danced back up the court, a thing of beauty, receiving the shouted praise as my just due.

But Mance came toward me again. And he came toward me every time VMI had the ball, every time we scored or missed a shot. His presence and the nobility of his skills excited me. He humbled me. He defeated me time and time again as he moved in my direction. I battled him with all my strength and canniness about the game. Every trick I knew I used against him. But he countered them with the simplicity of his art. I would drive the lane past him and score. He would answer me with a long jump shot from the top of the key. Then Reuben would break loose in the middle and score in one of his long sweeping hooks or Johnny would come off a pic and score on a lovely jump shot, tying the score.

Again, all eyes turned toward Mance, toward me guarding Mance, and he would break off a double pic with me scrambling to catch up to him and another shot would sting the net with astounding accuracy. His art was pure; his defender was only earnest. His team led by three at half-time. In those first twenty minutes, Mance had scored twenty-four points.

But he also had three fouls, and during the half-time talk Coach Byrum gave me license to drive the middle against Mance to get him to foul out. Byrum shouted the instructions at me as Bo wiped the sweat from my face with a towel.

As the centers faced off for the beginning of the second half, the cadets of R Company rose and gave me a standing ovation. Pig, Tradd, and Mark held aloft a banner that read,

"ROMEO LOVES McLEAN." I had to turn away from that banner and my company to avoid crying in front of three thousand people.

"I heard a joke in the barracks today, Jimmy," I said, laughing to myself. "It's the funniest goddam joke I've ever heard."

"What's the joke?" he asked as the referee moved between the centers.

"I'm not going to tell you," I said, grinning at him, "but I swear I laughed for an hour."

VMI's center controlled the jump. Mance received the ball and slowly began bringing it up the court. "What's the joke?" he repeated above the noise of the crowd.

"It's the funniest joke I've ever heard," I answered as he turned his back to me and began backing me toward the basket. He failed to see Johnny DuBruhl leave the man he was guarding and sweep around Mance's blind side, tipping the ball toward the scorer's table. I broke for our basket and called for the ball.

The pass was too long and I sprinted for it as hard as I could run. It hit the floor in front of me and bounced high above the basket. I reached it in midair and shot the ball at the same instant, laying it against the painted white square of the glass backboard. I knew the shot was good before I saw it go in. When you are playing as well as you can play, there are times when you do not have to watch your shots strike the cords of the net. Experience and touch and instinct tell you that the shot is good as soon as it leaves your hand.

When I reached Mance, I taunted him, "On that last play, All-American candidate Jimmy Mance looked like horseshit. Everybody's laughing at you, Jimmy."

"Tell me the joke, McLean," he threatened, keeping a wary eye on Johnny, "or I'm going to score every single time I come down the court. And you know I can come damn close to doing it."

After issuing this statement, he pumped in a perfect twenty-five-foot jump shot that robbed the crowd of its exultancy and confidence. I quickly told him the only joke I could remember on the spur of the moment. "A cadet's definition of an intellectual is anyone who can listen to the William Tell Overture without thinking of the Lone Ranger."

"That's not funny, McLean," he said, glowering angrily at me. "That's the worst joke I ever heard."

"You had to be there, Jimmy," I answered, receiving the in-bounds pass from Johnny and bringing it up the court.

When I reached the front court, Reuben and the forwards cleared out of the middle; Johnny moved to the left of the court and stood directly in front of our bench.

"Drive him, Will," Johnny called. "Drive his ass off."

The right side of the court was left open for me to maneuver Mance.

"You've got three fouls, Jimmy," I said, eyeing the big men of VMI dropping off their men to protect their star. "Be careful. The pro scouts want to know if you can play defense. If you can't guard me there's a chance you won't be able to handle Jerry West and Oscar Robertson."

"Come on, Will," Mance challenged, sweat dropping off him in clean, hot drops.

I broke hard for the basket, beating Mance in a quick first step, put my body between him and the ball, and drove past him with all the speed and skill earned in a ten-year apprenticeship in the sport. But I felt him recover, match me step for step, straining to retrieve the last essential angle, which I refused to surrender. When I left my feet, I felt his breath and hovering presence and knew that he foolishly was going to try to block the shot. I showed him the ball and saw his long, muscled arm slap at it. He slapped my wrist instead as I pump faked, and with my eyes still on the basket and traveling full speed I was in the midst of doing what I did the best in my game. I laid the ball in softly, perfectly, with an underhand sweep that barely eluded a leaping VMI forward who had sloughed off Doug to help Mance.

I made the foul shot and the score was tied. For the next fifteen minutes, the play was spirited and furious, but with three minutes to play Johnny hit a jump shot that tied the score for the thirteenth time in the game.

Mance came down the court with his eye fixed to the clock. Picking him up at half court, I tried to make him surrender the ball or give up his dribble. But he was too good and quick, and he taught me some lessons about ball handling as he moved me toward the key.

I could sense that the other VMI players were setting up a series of screens behind me.

"Pic right, Will," I heard Johnny cry out.

"Pic left," I heard Doug's voice and I knew that Mance was making his choices and taking his time.

I moved to my left, overplaying his right hand, his best

hand. With a beautiful crossover dribble he drove to his left past the first pic, but kept his eye on me for a second too long. He did not see Johnny anticipate his move and jump into his path, establishing a solid defensive position. He did not see Johnny until he ran right over him, his shoulder catching Johnny in the midsection. It sounded like the collision of steers, and Johnny somersaulted across the court. The referee put his palm behind his head and signaled a charging violation. There was bedlam in the crowd as the buzzer sounded and the official scorekeeper indicated that the great Jimmy Mance had fouled out of the game.

With his head down, Mance loped toward his bench. I followed him and near midcourt I laid my hand on his shoulder. He stopped, and we faced each other wordlessly. He put his arm around my shoulder, and we walked toward his bench together. The Corps rose and paid him homage in a thunderous, rousing ovation. Before he sat down, we embraced, embraced hard, and we held it for several moments. It would be the last time we would ever play against each other, the last time we would ever duel beneath the lights. He had scored forty points; I had scored twelve.

"If I guarded you every night, you'd be an All-American for sure, Jimmy," I said.

"If I played as well against everyone else, I'd deserve to be. Good luck, Will."

"You're the best I ever saw, Jimmy. The best I ever saw in my life."

Mance walked to his seat by his coach and out of my life forever.

Without Mance, the VMI team was not nearly as good a team as we were. But there are times in athletics when that does not matter. There are times when average ballplayers transform themselves by an immense spiritual effort into athletes they were never meant to be. When we returned to the court to face the disadvantaged VMI squad for the final minutes, we figured we would win the game easily. But we had not reckoned on the possibility of these splendid transformations. The VMI team came at us with hunger and spirit and élan. They surprised us with their hunger, the fierce terror of their want, as they scrapped us from line to line. The boardplay beneath the rim was fearful and savage. Only a last-second shot by Reuben tied the game and brought us into the first overtime. VMI had found heroes in three mediocre players, and it was beautiful to watch.

Though we did not know it then, we were engaged in

one of those games that would become legendary in the barracks. On this night, these two average college basketball teams would honor their sport with the irrepressible intensity of their will to win and the radiant chivalry of their gamesmanship. Each team scored nine points in the first five-minute overtime. Each team scored six in the second overtime. Each team scored seven in the third overtime. We were playing in the longest game in the history of the Institute.

As we prepared to take to the court, exhausted and feverish below the passionate crowd, we could not hear Coach Byrum's shouted instructions for our strategy in the fourth overtime. He was losing his voice and the noise of the crowd precluded any chance or need of hearing him. Bo Maybank stroked my arms and neck with a clean towel, and the pressure of his small hands felt almost sexual as I closed my eyes and listened to the masculine chant of the Corps in all its primitiveness and lawless carnality.

I could barely move as the horn sounded to end the fourth overtime. My feet and legs ached, and my knees felt as though someone had poured lead shot into them. I winked at Abigail, nodded to the General, and knelt on the floor to tie my shoes. Johnny DuBruhl came over, put a hand on my shoulder, and said, "Let's end it, Will. I'm tired as shit. If we have to go through one more overtime, I'm going to ask Byrum to forfeit."

"I'm dying, boy," I replied.

VMI scored two quick baskets in that first minute of play, but Doug hit a fall-away jumper in the corner and Johnny scored on a fast break. With three minutes left, VMI went into their freeze pattern and decided to gamble on taking the last shot of the game. The seconds fell slowly off the clock. I tried to pressure the sophomore guard who had taken Mance's place, but he was a fine and cautious ball handler. I dropped back off him as he fed a pass to a forward, who had come out to the back court to take the pressure off the VMI guards. When I looked at the clock again, there was only a minute left to play, and I edged out toward the sophomore again and tried to bother him into a mistake of inexperience.

With twenty-two seconds left, the sophomore passed to the VMI center, who had broken up to the foul line. The center shoveled a pass to the forward on my side of the court. The forward's eyes were nervous with the pressure, and I saw that he was desperately looking to get rid of the ball as soon as he could find an open man. My man moved to his right to receive an outlet pass. Doug, with his hands held high and his body taut and glistening, moved in quickly to pressure the forward. The forward pivoted cleanly away from Doug and glanced at the clock. Eighteen seconds. Seventeen. My body tensed as I felt the critical moment arrive as the game died on us. I saw the forward's eyes search for the man I was guarding. I pulled back and let my man slide out unmolested to receive the pass. But I carefully preserved an angle between my man and the passer. I crouched and waited and I knew I was going to make a move, knew I was going to gamble, that I was going to spring into the center of action, knew that I was going to, knew I was, knew I... fourteen seconds, thirteen... and I saw the ball coming through the air as I lunged outward, my hand extended, as I tipped the ball away and chased it to the side of the court, controlled it, went behind my back with the dribble, and broke for the center, with players from both teams exploding toward the far court. Then I felt it.

I felt the Corps. They had broken with me; they had risen to their feet and I was swept forward by the immensity of their sound. They carried me forward with their noise and the power of their advocacy. I heard their thunder, their storm, the whole prodigious solidarity of the brotherhood accompanying my charge down the court.

I watched two of the VMI players, blurred images of scrambling gold racing ahead of me, trying to position themselves to contain the fast break that was forming in perfect order as I approached them, coming faster than I had ever come before, the seconds spilling off the clock. I heard Johnny filling the lane to the right and Doug calling to me from the left and Reuben trailing four steps behind me. The ball was part of me and I was confident and exultant as I swept past center court and faced the two nameless VMI players who awaited my coming.

The first player came out to meet me. It was the sophomore guard, and he came too quickly, an error of inexperience. I slowed, faked a change to my right, and switched to my left hand, passing him in a blur. He had not recognized the old trick of hesitation, the small betrayal of speed that was the essence of the change of pace.

I heard Johnny screaming for the ball to my right. I turned my head toward him, but my eye fastened on the last defender. The VMI man moved out to cut off the pass to Johnny. But there would be no pass to Johnny. I left the floor, rising into the air, into the light and smoke, into the history of that night, into the death of time and the last game I would ever play. I rose up into the happiest, most glorious moment in my life, to take the shot I had awaited since I was a boy of ten. Realizing his mistake too late, the VMI forward lunged wildly toward me, but I moved my left shoulder between him and the ball, braced myself for his impact, and spun the ball softly, gently against the backboard. I did not see the ball go into the basket, but I did not need to. The marvelous noise of the Corps had turned the Armory into a vessel of unimaginable tumult.

I lay on my back, out of bounds, where the collision with the VMI forward had knocked me and stared straight up into the ceiling lights. But I was not seeing anything; I was taking in the praise of the crowd, accepting the homage of its brawling, rowdy lyrics. I heard the chant of my name. At that moment, the Corps and I were one body, one substance, one passionate, untamable force.

Then Johnny fell on me, locked me into a jubilant embrace, and we rolled on the gym floor, laughing hysterically. Rising, we began leaping up and down in a delirious, primitive dance of triumph. Doug and Reuben and Dave joined us, and I was slapped, pummeled, and hugged. All five VMI players had bowed their heads in that gesture of shame and failure I had known so many times in my career at the Institute. Their faces were dispirited, beaten, and exhausted.

Going to the foul line, I lifted both arms to the crowd and the noise carried me again, entered each cell of my dazzled, inflamed consciousness, and I let it take me, seduce me. . . . I wanted my life to freeze at that exact moment, with my arms raised above me, the crowd on its feet, those thousands of human voices screaming out my name.

The referees handed me the ball and I shot my free throw, watched the net shiver with the ball's entry, saw the long desperate pass of the VMI guard fall harmlessly into the far court, and heard the buzzer signal the end of the game.

Then the Corps was on me. I was in the center of an uproarious surge of gray uniforms; I was lifted toward the lights and found myself on the shoulders of Mark and Pig, felt hands reaching me, touching me, and I thought I would remember those hands more than anything else that night. I tried to preserve every memory of that delirious charge of the Corps onto center court. But you cannot preserve the memory of applause; it is too volatile, too perishable. Later it would astonish me that I could not satisfactorily summon back that moment. I remembered the ride to the locker room, the hands trying to reach me, the movement of the gray uniforms trying to get close to me. But it was my destiny and my character not to be able to recall the exact feeling, the exact one, of those brief seconds in the adoration of the Corps.

No, I would remember the towel . . . Bo Maybank's towel. Precisely and completely and for the rest of my life. I do not know how he got to me, but I felt his light leaps up to my face and felt the towel warm against my brow. And his face, I would remember his face as he wiped the sweat from mine, transfigured with joy for me—his face vulnerable and febrile and anonymous—as he danced on the floor below me, as he tried to reach me, as he tried to be a part of the finest moment of my life.

I would lose Bo after that night, as I would lose Jimmy Mance, Coach Byrum, Johnny, Doug, and Reuben. I would lose basketball and the fine camaraderie of athletics. But it was Bo I would miss the most, the little boy-child with his useless, lonely set shot and his towels fresh and warm from the dryers. His mother would call me three years later, grieving and proud, to tell me about the death of her son, the helicopter pilot, Lieutenant Bo Maybank. How can I say how splendid it must have been for him to come winged and ominous from the heights, dwarfing the tall men who had once teased him and stuffed him struggling and outraged into towel carts full of soiled laundry? How can I tell you that Bo never learned that height is not always the important thing? But he had learned all that he would ever need to learn about other small men with good eyes, good hands, instinctive cunning, and set shots far deadlier than his. A small man shot Bo Maybank out of the skies of Vietnam. The bullet entered his eye and blew out the back of his head.

His mother wept and I wept. I cried all night for that smallest of men who had loved me with his towels, who loved the game but never scored a single point or took a single shot except in empty gyms after the crowds had gone home. I remembered his tiny leaps up toward me after the VMI game and I regretted I had not looked down from the shoulders of my roommates, from the accolades of the crowd, looked down and done the right thing for once in my life, the grand and perfect gesture. I should have lifted Bo Maybank up with me, and together we should have taken that last frantic ride to the locker room. But I didn't; I wanted it all, all for myself.

* * *

When I finished dressing that evening, I walked out to the center court and stood, silent, in the middle of the gymnasium floor. I was one of the last to dress and the Armory was massive and lonely. I saw a basketball beneath the bench that Bo had not seen when he collected the equipment after the game. My footsteps echoed through the gym as I walked over to retrieve it. I dribbled the ball to the top of the key. I could measure my life in the number of jump shots and layups I had aimed at the steel rims of baskets. I had played the game because I felt ugly as a kid and painfully shy. People sought me out in my guise as an athlete. I did not have confidence they would seek me out or like me if I faced them nakedly, without the aura of my sport to recommend me. To masquerade my fear and insecurity I had found a sport to hide behind, and now I would have to perfect other disguises and join other masquerades. My time in gymnasiums was finished.

In the darkness of a gymnasium lit only by a winter moon, I shot a jump shot that hit the rim and bounced back toward me. I did not retrieve it. It bounced past the half-court line, the bounces getting smaller until the ball began rolling. I watched it roll past the other foul line, slowly now, until it crossed the out-of-bounds line and stopped. Out of bounds and out of my life. Like most other ballplayers I had a superstition. I could never leave the gym until I had made my last shot. But not tonight. I turned and began walking out of the gym. I had missed the shot and somewhere along the line, I had missed the point. But it was over now. I had gone to my limits as an athlete and I knew the secrets all athletes knew. I walked out of the gymnasium and never once did it occur to me to look back. I was free.

* * *

But as I passed through the dark corridor behind the stands, a voice called out to me from beneath the bleachers. I was startled and turned toward the voice, both angry and afraid.

"Mr. McLean," the voice said desperately, "I've got to see you, sir."

It was Pearce. I looked back toward the locker room and saw Doug Cumming saying good night to Bo.

"You scared the living shit out of me, Pearce," I said.

"I need your help, sir," he answered. "Could you come down to the yacht basin and talk to me? There's no one around there at this time of night. We can talk alone."

"Go on down there, Pearce. I'll walk around first battalion and cut across the baseball field."

He departed silently and I walked out the front door.

The boats of the marina were silvery with moonlight. Pearce's face was black and silver. He was handsome and frightened, and the moon highlighted his face like a coin recovered from pitch.

As I approached him, I realized I did not know this somber boy at all. In a real sense, you could never know a freshman at the Institute, no matter how resolutely you tried to remove the social barriers that separated you. A plebe could never fully trust an upperclassman, could not afford to relax his guard around anyone except his classmates, who shared his station and his exile. Pearce tensed as I neared him. When I called his name, he came to attention and braced.

"This isn't a sweat party, Pearce," I said. "I didn't come down here to rack ass. At ease."

Not until I said, "At ease," did he quit bracing. I was a senior and he was a freshman, and only the passage of time could free us from the recognition of our enmity. And there was a part of me that liked it very much, that Pearce snapped to attention when I entered his field of vision. I needed the silent ritualistic acknowledgment of my superiority.

Also, with Pearce, there was something atavistically Southern at work between us. I wanted his gratitude for my being a white Southerner who had changed. I wanted to be his deliverer, and I expected the same measure of servility from him that I demanded from all the other humans who were the victims of my deliverance. From his eyes I could tell that Pearce recognized the subtlety and tenuousness of both our connection and our enmity. Among the masts and with the hulls of boats reflecting in the waters of the incoming tide, we faced each other uncertainly, as allies, but most inimically and essentially, as white boy and nigger.

His eyes were dark and troubled as they moved past me toward the huge, illuminated silhouettes of the barracks, toward the baseball field, toward the Armory. He was looking to see if I'd been followed.

"Do you want to go water skiing, Pearce?" I said, glancing at my watch.

"Pardon me, sir?" he responded, puzzled and still looking over my shoulder.

"Why else did you call me down to the marina?" I asked. "Every time I see you I feel like I'm working for the CIA and you're going to pass me top secret plans for the destruction of Miami."

"You haven't been answering my notes, Mr. McLean," he said, and his tone was accusatory and angry.

"What?"

"I've left you four notes and you haven't answered a single one. You haven't tried to contact me."

"That's bullshit, dumbhead. I check that book every single day, and there hasn't been one communication from you in months. Are you sure you haven't been putting the notes in the wrong book?"

"*Decline of the West.* Between pages three hundred eight and nine, sir." There was irony in the way he emphasized the word *sir*.

"Pearce," I said, "has anyone seen you put those notes in there?"

"I don't think so, sir."

"Then I wonder if anyone has seen me check the book," I thought aloud, "or seen my roommates check it when the team's been on the road. Hell, Pearce, I've done it so much and it's such a habit, I don't even look to see if anyone's watching me anymore."

"The four notes I left you have all been removed from the book, sir," Pearce said. "I thought you had taken them but just didn't care to do anything about them. But someone has taken them, and someone obviously knows how I contact you."

"What did you say in the notes?" I asked, as I looked back over my shoulder, back toward the lights of the barracks.

"Mr. McLean, last week at retreat formation, someone came up behind me and said I had two weeks to leave the Institute of my own accord. He said if I didn't leave I'd get special treatment far worse than anything I had gotten until now. He said I would go on a long ride I'd never forget."

"Who was it, Pearce?" I asked. "If you knew who was talking to you then maybe I could find out what's going on."

"He came up from behind me, Mr. McLean," Pearce explained. "I'm on the quadrangle and I'm a knob and I'm bracing my ass off, sir. It's dark and I'm not allowed to move a muscle. Suddenly there's this strange mean voice telling me to get my black nigger ass out of this school or I'm going to take a ride in two weeks."

"There's no place they can take you without being seen or heard."

"Maybe they'll take me off campus," he said. "Once they get me out of those gates, America is a mighty big place, Mr. McLean."

"Don't piss me off, dumbhead," I said, irritated at his scornful tone. "I was just wondering how they'd get you off campus. They can't just tool through the front gates unless they have permission. They can't just drive right by the guard and the Officer in Charge. And they can't just take the only black smackhead in the history of the school without everybody on campus knowing it."

Then I remembered something, and it hit me with a blazing force and clarity. I was no longer standing with Pearce beneath the shadows of boats. Suddenly I was high in the air, dizzy with fear and the vision of the quadrangle far below me, and I was listening again to the crazed, unbalanced voice of a fat boy who would be dead in eight hours, hanged by his own belt. Poteete's voice roared out in my memory. He came to me now furious, wronged, and vengeful.

"Wait. I know where they'll take you, Pearce," I said.

"Where, sir?" he answered. "How do you know?"

"They'll take you to the 'house,' " I said, and my mind shimmered with this bright and singular connection to the past.

"What house?"

"I don't know, Pearce. I honestly don't know. But I'm positive that's where they'll take you, and I promise you one other thing."

"What's that, sir?"

"If they get you to the house, they'll run you out of this school," I said, and we stared at each other.

"There's one thing I forgot to tell you, sir," Pearce said. "Before this voice left me at retreat formation, he put his finger on my back. He made a mark on my back. He drew something with his finger."

"What did he draw, Pearce?"

"The number ten, sir."

"Jesus Christ," I said. "I don't understand any of this, Pearce. Every time I think The Ten is a figment of the collective imagination of the Corps and the alumni, something happens to make me feel they're as real and actual as the Gates of Legrand. Just when I think that you and the Bear are paranoid, these small events occur and I think we're

328

being watched and studied by people who anticipate our every move. Then I start to wonder if I'm paranoid."

"Sir, someone is taking the notes from the book. We know that for sure. And someone came to talk to me at retreat formation. And someone drew a ten on my back."

"Why have they waited so long to make their move? Why haven't they tried to get you out of here before now?" I asked.

"I don't know, sir," he replied coldly. "I'm not a member of their organization."

"Don't be a wiseass, Pearce. I was just starting to like you."

"I'm scared, Mr. McLean," he said. "I've been scared ever since that guy came and talked to me. He sounded mean."

"I'm scared for you," I said, putting my arm around his shoulder and walking him to the floating dock, where we sat and stared out into the dark waters that surged toward us from the Ashley River. The tide lifted and moved the dock gently beneath us.

"But we might both be scared for nothing. This could be some elaborate prank someone is playing on both of us. Nothing has really happened that's bad or sinister. It's just that we're talking like something has to happen, like we're waiting for a storm that doesn't even exist."

"It exists, sir," he said. "I can feel it happening all around me and now I'm sure it's going to happen. I thought you weren't answering my notes, that you just didn't give a shit. But I thought you were at least receiving them, Mr. McLean. That means someone intercepted them before you got there. That means someone knows everything between us."

"How's your roommate, Pearce?" I asked.

"A nice guy," he responded. "From Connecticut or New Jersey or one of those New England states up there. It's all just north to me. But Chuck's been great this year, and he takes a lot because he rooms with me. They make him wear white gloves at mess because he rooms with a nigger and they don't want him to get nigger germs on their food."

"Nice world, the planet Earth, eh, Pearce?" I said, taking off my shoes and socks. "Have you ever seen a basketball player's feet? We've got the ugliest feet in the world. Blood blisters, peeling flesh, and dead yellow skin all over. After a game, my feet burn all night, Pearce. Sometimes

329

I come down to this dock and soak my feet in the water."

"It's freezing, sir," he said as I lowered my feet into the water, grimaced, then pulled them back onto the dock and wiped them dry with a handkerchief.

"I don't know whether it hurts or feels good, Pearce, but I do it when the pain in my feet is real bad. I think it helps me but I'm not sure. That's the way I feel about this school sometimes. I think it's doing me a lot of good because so many people tell me it's good for me. But it hurts. It hurts all the time. Are you glad you came here, Pearce?"

"Yes, sir," he said without a trace of hesitation.

"I mean really, Pearce."

"I like it here, Mr. McLean," he said. "I don't like it when they call me nigger or coon or spear-chucker, but I knew that was going to happen. I like the military and I want to make a career out of the Army when I graduate. I've wanted to do that since I was a little kid, and this is the best preparation in the world."

"You're looking good, Pearce," I said, studying him with admiration. "A very sharp young knob. You're only about four months away from being a sophomore."

"I'm going to make it through this school, Mr. McLean," he said with sudden, absolute fervor. "I'm going to do what I have to do to make it because I'm going to wear one of those one day."

He pointed to my ring.

"Here," I said, removing my ring. "Try it on for size."

He placed the ring carefully, reverently on his left hand. It fit perfectly.

"The reason I asked about your roommate is this: Does he know you send me messages? Does he know how you send them?"

"Yes, sir," Pearce said in an embarrassed, sheepish voice.

"I told you not to tell anybody, didn't I?" I said harshly, becoming an upperclassman again.

"You've got to talk to somebody, Mr. McLean. And you told your roommates, too."

"I've known my roommates for four years. You've known yours for five months. Maybe he's the one feeding out information to our unknown friends."

"No, sir," Pearce said. "He's not that kind."

"Who is that kind?" I asked.

"I've thought of one or two people," he said. "It might be the Bear, sir."

"Bullshit, Pearce!" I shouted. "The Bear was the one who set this whole thing up. He was the one who was worried about you getting run out in the first place. He first mentioned the rumor about The Ten. He's the one who assigned me the job of making sure you stayed in school. He busted the corporal who was hazing you. He receives every note I pick up in the library."

"That's what I mean, sir," Pearce said when I had finished ranting. "He's the one who knows everything. Except for one other person, sir."

"Who's that, Pearce?"

"You, sir."

"You think it could be me, Pearce?" I said furiously. "That's just nigger talk. That's dumbass nigger talk."

He glowered at me in the darkness, an impotent sullenness to his anger.

"Yes, sir," he said, taking off my ring. "That's all I am. A dumbass nigger. A scared dumbass nigger surrounded by two thousand white boys. I don't know who to trust, Mr. McLean. I don't trust anybody. I don't mean to offend you, but you've got to know that you're just one of them to me. Just another white boy who's called people 'nigger' all his life."

"I didn't mean to say that, Pearce," I said. "I shouldn't have said that to you. I apologize. I hate that word with all my heart, and I'd do anything not to have said that to you. I had no right."

We stood up and faced each other.

"I could have gone to the Bear," he said. "I thought about that but I chose you. I had to tell someone who could help me. My roommate's as scared as I am."

"I promise you this, Pearce. I am not your enemy. I'm your friend and I'll help you in any way that I can. If there are people who are working against you in secret then I'll try to find out who they are and stop them."

"I believe you, sir," he answered.

"We'll get a new system of communication. I won't even tell the Bear about it. It'll be between you and me. And your roommate if you want. I won't even tell my roommates. But we're going to beat these bastards, and we're going to do it together."

"Thank you, sir," he said, and I saw that he was standing at attention again.

"We're usually allowed to recognize knobs only at the end of the year. But I want to recognize you tonight, Pearce."

I extended my hand for him to shake. He took it, and I felt the strength of the boy who stood before me.

"My name is Will," I said.

"My name is Tom, Will," he answered.

And Tom Pearce began crying on the dock, in the darkness, as though he would never stop.

PART IV

THE TEN

February–June 1967

31

I drove to the beach house on Sullivan's Island on the third weekend in February. Annie Kate's child was due in a week. A more profound alienation and solitude gripped her during those final days. She was very large now, and we never left the house even after dark. The child within had become her jailer. She still wore her raincoat, out of habit, I suppose, or because it granted her some irrational protection against the movement of the universe that had enveloped her in its rhythm of change and time and inevitability. She had become a season unto herself, and we could measure the passage from September to February by the growth of the child within her. Though she was unaware of it, Annie Kate had become the archetype of maternity and there was immense power and authority in her presence as she walked restlessly around the house, gazing out toward the city, or adding a log to the fire to cut the bitter island cold. The child may have been illegitimate, but the process was still magnificent and one could only observe it with amazement and humility. I felt that ancient inconsequentiality of being a male as I witnessed the rosy elaboration of her body. Here, then, at last, was divinity, the limitless mystery, the infinite strength of women. Was this why I had always been afraid of them? I did not know, and it did not matter. Annie Kate despised the way she looked and thought my ravings about mystery and infinity were only so much bullshit. She wanted it over with and asked for nothing more.

Before I went to the house, I walked along the stretch of beach between the lighthouse and Fort Moultrie. The tide was out. The sea was breathing in small, halfhearted waves. The water was flat and gray, almost mouse-colored. I was hunting for a sand dollar to add to Annie Kate's collection. She missed the walks on the beach, and I could always lift her spirit when I found one of those small, alluring shells impressed in the sands, still glistening from the withdrawn tide. I passed a dead seagull that the crabs had mutilated. There were dead she-crabs, with their white bellies showing and claws rigid. Pelicans, four of them, flew low over the waves, skimming the water like brown Frisbees. I walked for a half-hour before I discovered a sand dollar small enough to be included in the cricket box on the mantel in her bedroom. It was the smallest one I had found all year. The cross in its center could have fit inside a human tear. If smallness was fortune, then I had come across a treasure, infinitesimal and beyond value. I felt lucky. You had to decide what was estimable and precious in your life and set out to find it. The objects you valued defined you. So did this quest. This sand dollar would join the others in the cricket box, the accumulated relics of our long walks together as the child grew within her. I did not need any proof that our system of currency was special, extraordinary, and rare. I was in love for the first time in my life, and that was proof enough to me.

I drove to her house, parked in the back yard, and walked through the back door without knocking.

"Yoo-hoo, it's me, Paul Newman," I said, calling up the stairs.

Annie Kate came down the stairs and I kissed her on the cheek. Sometimes she let me kiss her on the mouth, but not often. She said she did not feel like kissing very much, and we had only made love twice since December. I remained an enthusiastic but pitifully inept lover, and she received little pleasure from my carryings on. I always let her make the decision to kiss me or not, to make love to me or not. Her rejection of me hurt more than she ever knew or I would admit, so I would rather let her make the overtures than have mine refused. I still retained the Catholic boy's belief that sex was some grotesque and beastly urge of men that women endured as part of the misery of their station. Annie Kate's condition was proof of the wages of sin and the horrors God visited on the impure. I think both of us looked upon her pregnancy that way sometimes.

"I brought you some flowers," I said. "They're white roses and they cost ten bucks a dozen."

"They're daisies, and they cost fifty cents a dozen," she said, going to the kitchen for a vase. I brought her flowers each time I came to see her. She would place them in water but never look at them, and I'm sure they brought her no joy.

"Thank you for the flowers," she said when she returned.

"And a final gift," I said, proferring the sand dollar in my palm.

"Oh, it's exquisite, Will. It might be the smallest yet."

"I ordered it out of the Sears Roebuck catalogue."

"Look, it's so thin you can see the light through it," she said, holding it up to the window.

"I passed by it the first time. I didn't see it until I was coming back to the car."

She took my hand and squeezed it and kissed me again on the cheek.

"Your hands are freezing," I said, rubbing one of them between mine.

"You ought to feel my feet," she said. Annie Kate was one of those people who never seemed to get enough blood in their extremities. Even on warm days her hands and feet were cool to the touch. On cold days, I would jump when she touched my neck.

"Sit over by the fireplace and I'll rub them down with alcohol before I go. Do your legs ache, too?"

"Where are you going?" she asked.

"Commerce and Abigail are giving their annual Mardi Gras party."

"Well, la-di-da. Are you one of the token cadets? Of course, I imagine you can have a lot more fun at her house than you can have with me."

"I've refused almost every dinner and party at their house this year, Annie Kate. I promised Abigail I'd come to this party. What have you got against the St. Croixs?"

"A lot! They've always considered themselves far superior to my family, who just happened to have come to Charleston before theirs did."

"I'm not invited because of my family," I said.

"No, Will. I'm sure you're not. Quite the opposite, I would say. Despite your family, I would say."

"What's eating you, Annie Kate?"

"They didn't invite my mother to their silly party."

"She couldn't go anyway. She has to stay with you."

"That's not the point. They never invite her. And I was snubbed so many times by Abigail I can't even count them. She just takes what she likes from people and gives nothing in return."

337

"I think you're as wrong as a person can be," I said defensively.

"Wrong?" she answered. "I know damn well I'm right. I know a lot more about her than you do. What costume will you wear?"

"Costume?" I asked.

"It's a Mardi Gras party. I'm sure they're going to wear costumes," she said.

"I think I'll go as a cadet from Carolina Military Institute since the General and the Bear will be there and I'll walk tours for the rest of the year if I'm caught in Charleston out of uniform."

"I still wish they'd invited Mother."

"Where is your mother?" I asked.

"She ran down to Ogletree's to pick up some food. She'll be back in a second. Will you rub my feet now, Will? I don't want to fight today."

"I'll get the alcohol."

"I already got it. It's here on the table."

I removed her shoes and socks and took one of her feet in my hands. Her feet were always cold and aching, especially during these last months of her pregnancy. I would rub them until they felt warm and they glowed in my hands with health and blood and vigor. Her feet were small and delicately shaped. Her toenails were immaculately trimmed and pale as shells. They were lovely in the firelight, mother-of-pearl and translucent. She kept her hands over her stomach as I stroked her feet.

Her mother walked in the back door carrying a single bag. Mrs. Gervais had come to like me very much, of that I have no doubt whatsoever. I assuaged her loneliness, and she had become accustomed to my professionally good-natured presence. And unlike her daughter, she took pleasure in my sense of humor.

"What are you doing to my daughter's feet?" Mrs. Gervais asked as she entered the room and sat beside Annie Kate on the couch. She touched Annie Kate's cheek affectionately and blew me a kiss as she wearily lit a cigarette. She wore defeat like a piece of cheap jewelry.

"Worshiping them. Anointing them with oil, Mrs. Gervais," I said. "When I'm finished, I'll dry them with my hair."

"Mary Magdalen had longer hair, I believe," said Mrs. Gervais.

"She didn't go to the Institute. It just takes me an hour

338

longer to dry feet than it took her. But you've got to make do."

"You ought to try it, Mother. Your feet get every bit as cold and sore as mine. In fact, I inherited your frigid little feet."

"No, thank you," Mrs. Gervais replied, watching me pour alcohol into my hands and work it into Annie Kate's feet.

"C'mon, Mrs. Gervais. It's one of the great pleasures in the world. And it gives me pleasure. I'm not attracted to women at all, but I become fiendish when I get hold of a foot."

I held Annie Kate's foot aloft in my hand.

"Look at this perfect foot. I dream about this foot. I would walk to the ends of the earth for a glimpse of these delicious toesies. After I'm finished I take these delicate toes and suck the alcohol off them."

I took Annie Kate's smallest toe gently between my teeth and began moaning and slurping.

"Stop it," Annie Kate said with a giggle. "It tickles."

Mrs. Gervais laughed her rich, affecting laugh.

I moved over beside her and took off her loafers. She protested but it was a protest without conviction. I removed her wool socks. She was the first woman I ever knew who wore slacks on a regular basis, and it was one of those idiosyncrasies that separated her from her neighbors South of Broad.

"My, what gorgeous feet you have, my dear," I said to her, putting her left foot on my knee and rubbing the alcohol into her instep. Her foot was cold and white and threaded with slightly swollen blue veins. The veins on the top of her foot had the same fine shape and extraordinary delicacy as her daughter's.

For five minutes, I squeezed and stroked her feet until I felt them warm and pulsing in my hands.

"Do the toes again, please," Mrs. Gervais said, her head resting against the couch and her eyes closed.

"Ah, the toes," I said, "where true pleasure resides. May I bite your toes when I'm finished, Mrs. Gervais? As a reward for my services?"

"You will do no such thing."

"Mother will think you are sick, Will," Annie Kate said, putting her socks back on.

Mrs. Gervais agreed. "You do sound disturbed when you talk like that, Will."

"Your mind tells you no, but your feet tell you yes, right, Mrs. Gervais?" I said, pretending to bite her big toe. She jerked her foot away from me, laughing.

"Will's going to a party tonight, Mother," Annie Kate said.

"How nice. Whose party?"

"The St. Croixs are having their annual Mardi Gras fête," Annie Kate said.

"I used to go to those," Mrs. Gervais said. "But that was before I met your father. Sometimes they were not unpleasant."

"I think it's disgusting that they quit inviting you," Annie Kate said bitterly.

"They're certainly not the only ones, dear."

"You want to go with me, Mrs. Gervais?" I offered. It was the natural reflex of Will McLean, the patron saint of piety. "The St. Croixs always try to get me to bring a date."

"No, thank you, Will. Someone has to be with Annie Kate."

"I'm not due for a week, Mother. If you want to go, I'll be fine. I can always call you."

"I don't think the St. Croixs would ever recover from the shock. No thanks."

"Well, I have to be going, ladies," I said, rising. "Call me if anything happens and I'll see y'all after chapel tomorrow morning."

I kissed both of them on the cheek. Annie Kate turned my face and kissed me on the mouth.

Mrs. Gervais said as I was leaving, "Thanks for massaging my feet, Will. They feel young right now and nothing has felt like that for a long time."

* * *

The party at the St. Croix house was part of the winter season in Charleston. Pig, Mark, and I went to the party together, and all of us were nervous about being the only cadets among the two hundred invited guests. None of us was comfortable around the St. Croixs' friends.

Commerce and Abigail answered the door together.

"My three favorite men in the world," Abigail said extravagantly.

"Good evening, gentlemen," Commerce said hospitably. "Get George to fix you a drink and make yourselves at home. I want you to enjoy yourselves tonight."

340

A string quartet, penguinesque in their tuxedoes and correct as finger bowls, played Mozart and Bach in the living room. The partygoers ignored the music. It was an extravagant adornment for the evening. I waved to Tradd across the room as we made our way through the crowd toward the bar. George, the black bartender, was dispensing drinks with all the self-effacing joviality required of his station. There was a feast spread out on the dining-room table, artfully arranged in silver. The faces of the guests, confident, urbane, and relaxed, were illuminated by a dozen candelabra and the soft liquid light of the downstairs chandeliers. The conversation was loud and spirited, and I felt like a visitor from another planet.

Abigail's dress was black, low-cut, and fashionably severe. Her hair was short and the color of new honey, and she smelled like perfume and soap. She steered me through the crowd, through the dense alliances of intermingled families where each face was a chronicle of privilege and subordination to the genealogy of great houses and proud names.

I got my drink and pulled back with Pig and Mark to a neutral corner. Pig attracted attention because of his build and because his head bumped into the chandelier in the dining room when he leaned over to spear a shrimp with a toothpick. He was mortified to find himself the center of attention, when a hundred eyes turned on him as the chandelier swung like a pendulum and tinkled prettily, with a sound like glass dominoes falling. But there was nothing for us to say to anyone and very few people approached us to talk.

"A lot of duckbutts among the ritzy, huh, Will?" Pig said, leaning down to whisper in my ear. "I bet there isn't a guy here who could bench press two hundred pounds."

"Yeh, but we couldn't lift their bank accounts."

"Boy, that's the truth," he said, taking another large swallow from his drink. Both of us were drinking too much, but in Charleston society that was customary if not required.

Mark had stopped to talk with an amiable, blue-haired woman who looked two hundred years old and gave every indication of monopolizing his company all night. Tradd was playing host to a small entourage of women in the living room. Occasionally he would catch our eyes and wink.

The Bear and his wife found us in our exile.

"Good evening, Colonel," I said as they approached. "Good evening, Mrs. Berrineau."

"Good evening, Will," she said. "Dante, how are you?"

"Fine, Mrs. Bear. Just fine," Pig answered.

"That's Mrs. Berrineau, Bubba," the Colonel amended, then turning to me, he said, "I didn't recognize you with your shoes shined, lamb. You're not a total disgrace to your alma mater tonight. I'd say you were only a ninety percent disgrace."

"You look lovely tonight, Mrs. Berrineau," I said, ignoring the Colonel's jibes.

"Thank you, Will. You look very nice yourself."

"What office are you running for, Bubba?" the Bear said. "Keep your eyes on him, darling. I'll watch his hands."

"I've never seen you in civilian clothes before, Colonel," I said, grinning. "I understand now why you stick to uniforms."

"You don't like that suit, Will? I picked it out for the Colonel," Mrs. Berrineau said.

"Oh, it's beautiful, Mrs. Berrineau. Pig and I were just talking about how good the Colonel looked before you walked up."

The Bear's eyes danced with joy. "Almost caught you on that one, huh, Bubba?" Then as he and Mrs. Berrineau walked away, he said, "I don't get to hang around the cheese in Charleston very often, Bubba, and if they see me pretending to enjoy talking with you, then I'll never get to see the cheese again. You lambs have a good time and don't drink too much."

The party was very painful to me, as parties usually were, and I felt the familiar loneliness of crowds. I watched the General as he received friends and admirers who wanted to brush against the immensity of his myth. I wondered if he ever grew weary of playing the role of the Great Man. I talked with Abigail and Commerce, but I was uncomfortable meeting them in their other life. I did not like to share them with two hundred other people. I did not want them to be part of this extraordinary fantasy. I preferred them in the comfortable informality of their own milieu, with Abigail arranging flowers, Tradd playing the piano, and Commerce descending the stairs after working long hours on his journals. After they left us, Pig and I got ready to make our departure.

I was trying to rescue Mark from his elderly admirer when George, the bartender, came up to me and said I had a phone call.

Excusing myself, I went to the hallway. There was a crowd in the hallway and I had trouble hearing who was on the phone.

It was Annie Kate.

"Will, the baby's coming."

"Are you at the hospital?"

"Mother's drunk, Will. Will you come drive me, please?"

"Have you called the doctor?"

"Not yet."

"I'm on my way. Don't worry, Annie Kate. I'll be there in a minute. Call the doctor. I'm coming."

I ran back into the living room and looked for the Bear. I bumped into a queenly, gray-haired woman and almost knocked her to the floor. I had met her before and disliked her on sight. She had three or four unpronounceable Huguenot names and she played the role of grande dame murderously. I excused myself and felt her stare withering the hairs on my neck.

Colonel and Mrs. Berrineau were talking to a group of men and women unknown to me. Some of the men wore Institute rings. It was a reflex of mine to check men's hands to see if they wore the ring.

"Colonel, may I see you for a minute? It's urgent, sir."

"Of course, Bubba," he said as he turned toward the group with whom he had been speaking. "Pardon me, sir. Pardon me, madam."

I hurried him to the verandah, and looking toward the door to make sure no one was listening, I said, "Colonel, I need a favor. I've never asked you for one, but I need one now."

"What is it, Bubba? I can't grant it or refuse it until I know what it is."

"Colonel, I'm not coming in tonight. I've got to break barracks."

"Sorry, Bubba, I have to cut you on that one."

"Bear, listen, please. There's a girl I know. She just went into labor. I just received a phone call. Her mother's drunk and can't drive her to the hospital. I know it sounds ridiculous, but I swear it's true."

"You swear by the Code, Bubba?" he said, fixing me with his large, serious eyes.

"I swear it, Colonel."

"Then get going, Bubba. That little girl needs you. I'll cover for you."

"Thanks, Colonel."

"Hurry, Bubba," he ordered. "Move it, boy. Move it. But remember. You'll have to pay the Bear."

"I know, Colonel. I knew that when I asked," I said, already running toward my car.

32

I have driven a car faster than I drove that night, but not in a city. I was going a hundred as I crossed the Cooper River Bridge. I passed through Mount Pleasant at eighty and did not even slow down for the stop sign at Middle Street when I reached Sullivan's Island.

She was waiting for me on the back porch in her raincoat. She walked toward the car, and I leaped out and helped her through the other door.

"Is it bad?" I asked.

"Bad," she said. "Will you get my suitcase, Will? The doctor will meet us at the emergency room at Roper."

"You won't believe how quick we'll be there," I assured her.

Running up to the back porch, I retrieved the small yellow suitcase and saw Mrs. Gervais unconscious, her head lying against the kitchen table, her mouth open.

Then I was in the car again, moving swiftly down the center of the island, slowing for the turn, and flooring it as I headed across the causeway between Sullivan's Island and Mount Pleasant. Annie Kate leaned against me, holding my arm tightly. I knew when the contractions came because her fingers dug into my arm and I could judge both the intervals and duration of the contractions by the pressure of her hands. I went through two red lights and was doing ninety as I passed Shem Creek and glimpsed the lights of Charleston to my left.

"Where are all the cops?" I said. "I'm breaking the law. I want a cop and I can't find one."

"Hurry, Will," she said, and I felt her fingers digging in again. Her head was against my shoulder and I was in love with her.

"Annie Kate," I said as we sped to the heights of the Cooper River Bridge, "everything's going to be all right. It's going to be over in just a little while. But I want you to know that I love you and I meant everything I said. If you decide to keep the baby, you and I can get married secretly. If you decide to give it up for adoption, I still love you and still want to marry you."

She did not answer but stiffened convulsively as one of the contractions hit her.

The doctor was waiting for us at the emergency room. He was an old, distinguished man. He had the proud, melancholy face one associated with Confederate veterans and looked old enough to have fired on Fort Sumter.

An attendant put Annie Kate into a wheelchair and I did not have time to say good-bye to her. The doctor looked at me with contempt and refused to shake my hand. I was confused until I realized he must have thought I was the one who had gotten Annie Kate pregnant.

The doctor took the suitcase and disappeared into the swinging doors that led to the emergency room. By the time I parked the car, there was only the attendant in the room, reading a magazine beneath a small, inadequate lamp.

"Where's the delivery room?" I asked.

"Third floor," he said without looking up.

"Can I go into the waiting room?"

"If you've got something to wait for."

"That girl. That woman that you just got out of the car. She's my wife. She's having my baby. I figured there must be a waiting room somewhere," I said.

"This must be your first."

"Yes, sir."

"Turn to your right when you get off the elevator. You'll see the signs, Daddy," the man said. "Bring me a cigar after the baby's born."

I sat in the empty, depressing waiting room with its torn calendars, Coke machines, and vinyl furniture for over an hour. I saw no one, not even a nurse. Once I thought I heard a baby's cry, but I was not certain and it could have been my imagination. There were things I had wanted to say to Annie Kate that I had not said. I relived the drive from the beach house to Roper in my mind. I said loving, wonderful things to Annie Kate. I acted like a man instead of a scared boy. My strength gave her strength. She whispered that she would marry me and that we would keep the child. I would be a father, at last. And I thought as I sat there that I could explain much of my conduct by referring to my enormous desire to protect, to nurture, and to father. To father. I loved that infinitive. I loved it.

The two green doors opened suddenly, and the doctor,

dressed now in white, walked out. His eyes were down but his face was grim and judgmental. He walked toward me and the walk seemed endless and dreamlike.

"The baby?" I asked.

"The baby is dead," the doctor answered. "The umbilical cord wrapped three times around its throat. It was as if the child was hung from a tree and strangled a little bit at a time. You not only don't have to worry about marrying the mother, son, you don't even have to worry about the guilt of putting the child up for adoption."

And the doctor, an old friend of the family, well known in Charleston for his discretion, turned and walked back through the green doors.

I do not know how long I stood there or how I got back to the barracks.

33

The next week I paid the Bear. "Paying the Bear" was an underground term in the Corps of Cadets. Whenever the Colonel did a cadet a favor by circumventing the rules of the Blue Book, that cadet would receive demerits in a punishment order for acts he did not commit. It was a private matter between the cadet and the Bear, and no one else in the Commandant's Department or the administration knew anything about it. It was an imperfect system of reparation and indemnity, but it was a secret and highly venerated law of the Corps. Because he covered for me when I missed the all-in check in the barracks, I had to pay the Bear. He restricted me to campus for a week and made me walk five tours on the second battalion quadrangle.

I tried to call Annie Kate at the hospital, but there was no one by that name among the maternity patients. For a week I tried to call Mrs. Gervais to tell her that I was restricted and could not go to see Annie Kate. No one answered the phone at the beach house or the house in town. I wrote four letters and received no replies to any of them. Each night, I waited in my room for someone to call me in the guardroom, but no one ever did.

It was seven days before I could leave the campus again. I drove out to Sullivan's Island, but the house was locked up and deserted. I returned to the city and drove to their house South of Broad. I knocked at the front door and Annie Kate answered it. She looked surprised to see me.

"Hi," I said. "I haven't heard from you in a while."

She was dressed in a sweater and skirt and looked perfectly lovely framed in the light by the door. I felt threatened that she was no longer pregnant and no longer needed me. I was shy before her beauty and her leanness.

"I've been busy packing and seeing some of my Charleston friends," she answered.

"Don't they think you're in California?"

"I'm on spring break. Everyone knows that California colleges have their vacations at odd times."

"I didn't know that," I said, noticing that she had not invited me inside.

"Now you do, Will," she said coldly.

"I almost didn't recognize you without your raincoat," I said, trying to make a joke.

"Ha. Ha. Ha," she said.

"How are you feeling?"

"Very well, thank you," she answered politely. "How are you feeling?"

"My feet are a little sore. I was restricted for a while after that night. I had to walk tours," I said.

"That's what you get for going to a silly military school."

"Yeh, I know."

"What else is new?" she asked.

"Nothing," I answered. "How about with you?"

"I'm going to California for real tomorrow," she said. "I'll be taking some courses this last quarter and an overload during the summer session to help catch up."

"No kidding," I said, trying to think of some way to knock down the terrible barriers that had sprung up between us. "Maybe I'll get out that way this summer and come see you."

"No, I don't think that would be such a good idea."

"Why? I've always wanted to see California," I said.

"You can see California without seeing me."

"It would be more fun with you," I said.

"That's just not a very good idea, Will. Maybe I'll see you when I get back for Christmas next year."

"That would really be nice, Annie Kate. What's your

347

address? I don't know where I'll be yet, but I'll write you some letters and let you know what's happening in the holy city!"

"Oh, that won't be necessary. Mother will tell me everything that's important. Next year will be a very big year for me. It's the start of my debutante season, you know. There will be hundreds of parties to attend before I'm presented at the St. Cecilia's ball."

"I'll bet you look beautiful that night," I said.

"I can assure you of that," she said, studying her nails. "Maybe I'll send you a picture."

"Maybe you'll need an escort," I said.

"Oh, that will be taken care of, Will. They've been doing these things for hundreds of years. It's the oldest, most prestigious ball in the country."

"It'll be something," I agreed. "I've never seen a debutante ball."

"Of course you haven't. Well, Will, it's been real nice seeing you again. I've got bunches of work to do before I leave tomorrow."

"Would you like me to drive you to the airport? I get out of classes at noon and I can possibly work out a Charleston pass with the Bear."

"Oh, no," she said, "I've got someone who'll be glad to drive me to the airport."

"You've got at least two people."

"That's sweet, Will. But I've made all the arrangements."

"Well," I said, trying to smile and keep my voice steady, "I guess this is good-bye, Annie Kate."

"Oh, I never, ever say good-bye. I detest farewells of any sort. They make me sad and make my skin break out."

"I wouldn't want to make your skin break out," I said sarcastically.

"Don't start your meanness now," she scolded. "You've been very sweet today and I want to remember you as an angel. You were my friend when I really needed a friend. I don't want to remember you with any negative feelings at all."

"The stuff I said the other night about getting married, Annie Kate. I meant that. Every word of it. I would still like to marry you and I'll be glad to wait for you to finish college or any time you like. I'm ready any time you are if you're still interested."

"Oh, that's so sweet," she said, touching my cheek. "But I think you should look for someone else, Will. Someone who could really appreciate your good qualities. You see, Will—and I don't want this to hurt your feelings—but I'm erasing all those bad thoughts out of my mind this year. All of them. I'm never going to think about this year at all. I'm going to pretend that none of it ever happened. I'm going to erase every single bad memory from my mind. You've been very sweet, Will, but you're a large part of the worst year of my life. When I see you, it reminds me of all that happened, of what I've been through."

"Meeting you was the best thing that ever happened to me, Annie Kate."

"Don't say that," she said shrilly. "Don't think it. Did you ever stop to think about me just once, Will? Can you imagine how humiliating the entire experience was for me? To get pregnant by a boy I loved from a fine family and have him tell me that he wouldn't marry me and that he felt no love for me at all? Can you imagine hiding for six months, terrified that your friends might see you, that you might be discovered or ridiculed and talked about at dinner parties? Only six people in the world know about my year of shame. Five of them will never say a word about what happened, Will. They are all Old Charlestonians and I can trust them with my life."

"But you're not sure about the ol' kid, huh, Annie Kate? You can't be sure what I'll say to my fat ugly wife when she's hanging out clothes at the trailer park."

"Don't get ugly. There's no need for that, Will. You must try to understand me. I can't ever love someone like you. We're too different. We want different things out of life. I want things that you can never give me. And you know too much about me that isn't really me."

"What are you talking about, Annie Kate?"

"I wasn't myself this past year. I was someone different, someone sad and lonely. Someone pitiful and afraid. I could never love anyone who loved me this past year, Will. I just couldn't. I don't even respect you very much for wanting to marry someone who was pregnant with another man's child."

"Who is going to love you, Annie Kate? Who will be worthy? Because the fact is that whoever marries you will be falling in love with a woman who was pregnant with another man's child at one time in her life."

"No, he won't, Will," she said simply. "He'll be marrying a virgin."

"What?"

"You'll figure it out, Will. In time, you'll understand."

"You won't tell the guy?"

"He'll never know. None of it ever happened. None of it. It was a terrible dream, but I'm awake now and everything is lovely again."

"Yeh, it's lovely."

"It's time for you to go, Will."

"I guess so. Well, I'll be seeing you around," I said.

"Thanks so much for dropping over, Will," she said, smiling at me and extending her hand. "It's so sweet of you to think of me."

I shook her hand and said, "I was in the neighborhood. Good-bye, Annie Kate."

"Hush. I already told you that I simply do not believe in saying good-bye."

"Hello, then. I hope you have a good life, Annie Kate. I really do. I'm sorry I'm not going to be a part of it. Let me hear from you. I'm sorry your baby died. I never got to tell you that."

"There was no baby, Will. There was only a bad dream and so much you didn't know or understand."

"I'm sorry your bad dream died," I said as I left her and walked toward the gate. "And I'm sorry I ever met you, Annie Kate."

The door closed behind me.

Two weeks later, I received a package in the mail from Santa Barbara. It was the cricket box full of sand dollars. Most of them had broken in transit. There was no note and no return address.

34

On Palm Sunday, I received an invitation to tea from Colonel Edward T. Reynolds. I met him and his wife on the steps of St. Philip's Church after the eleven o'clock service. Colonel Reynolds was easy to pick out of a crowd, and he made the other Anglican communicants look like an anemic, malnourished race indeed.

When he spotted me he said, "Remove thy carcass from the steps of the one true church, you papist swine."

His wife smiled and said, "Good morning, Cadet McLean." She was a small, delicately formed woman who weighed approximately as much as her husband's legs. There was an alarmed, nervous flutter to her eyelashes whenever she spoke in his presence, and I could not imagine the form and content of their conversations with each other when they were alone. She was the only one who had ever referred to me as "Cadet McLean." I had had tea at her house on several occasions and never once heard her express an idea of her own or disagree with one of Colonel Reynolds's.

"My dear," Colonel Reynolds said, turning respectfully to his wife, "while you are preparing tea, I would like your permission to take Mr. McLean on a brief stroll of the holy city."

"Of course, dear," she replied unhesitatingly, "but you and Cadet McLean will not be long?"

"Only long enough to digest that harmless drivel of a sermon we endured this morning."

"See you in a little while, Mrs. Reynolds. I won't let him play in any mud puddles," I said.

She looked at me, then at her husband, and slowly it dawned on her that I had made a joke. Her lips formed a nervous, unnatural smile as she excused herself and walked toward their house on State Street.

When she was out of earshot, Colonel Reynolds, sensing my slight discomfort, said, "Strict formality is the only thing that can save a marriage, Mr. McLean. It is a fearful institution. Although, of course, I am fond of my own spouse, I am acutely aware of my own shortcomings and realize that I am a demon to contend with, regardless of how she cherishes her marital vows. But enough of that, I have some things to tell you."

The azaleas were in full bloom and the gardens hummed with the gratitude of bees and the voices of lean, towheaded children playing spiritedly behind wrought-iron fences. We walked in the sunlight past the Dock Street Theater and the Huguenot Church, and it was like walking through the delicate pastels of a watercolor. The cold season had passed, and Charleston was celebrating the coming of spring with a thriftless, blazing eruption of flowers in its cemeteries and parks and gardens. The bells of St. Michael's solomnly rang at fifteen-minute intervals, dividing the lives of all the privileged citizens within hearing, fragmenting the day and the season with sound—a gentler, more civilized, bugling. The houses we passed began to exude the aromas of Sunday dinner: mulled shrimp, fried chicken, fish poaching in wine and cream sauces. At one house, I caught the smell of paprika; at the next, a hint of curry escaped from an open window. We walked the city, slowly, inhaling and appreciating its marvelous profusion of smells. Turning on Broad Street we moved toward the river and the Battery, past Rainbow Row and St. Michael's Alley. At first, we did not speak at all. The city had us, prisoners of its beauty and inertia. When we finally spoke, our voices seemed to violate the soundless scrimmage between the inaudible purr of the river and the green emergence of the gardens. No city could be more beautiful than Charleston during the brief reign of azaleas, no city on earth.

Colonel Reynolds walked as though his feet hurt, as though they had developed strategies to protest bearing the enormous weight they were not designed to carry. He carried himself with a strict absurd dignity; he was a heavy man who walked as though he was still a lean one, and he had the penetrating, confident eyes of one who seems to possess all that he sees. The sight of the Cooper River tranquilized him, as freighters navigated the channels, moving toward the sea lanes and away from azaleas.

"I have read too much history, Mr. McLean," he said, moving past Vanderhorst Row. "And it has depressed me about my fellow man."

"Why has it depressed you, sir?" I asked.

"Because the single theme of human existence is atrocity, sir. Even the most casual perusal of the subject would tell you that. Anything that man can do that will irreparably harm his fellow man, he will certainly do. I can close my eyes, Mr. McLean, close them this instant on this very pleasant walk, and my brain will come alive with horrendous, unspeakable images of heinous crimes men have performed against other men. Nothing surprises me anymore. Nothing shocks me. I have reached the point in my life when I am seized with an utter hopelessness about the human race. And you, sir," he said, fixing his gaze on me, "how do you feel about the race that violates this lovely planet?"

"I like human beings all right, Colonel," I said, "better than wart hogs or stingrays, anyway."

"I assure you, cad, that you would receive far more justice and mercy from a wart hog than from one of the monstrous chimps who wears a black robe and sits in judgment against his fellow man. The God that created man in his

352

own image, Mr. McLean, must be a vile, unconscionable being. Or he must be highly amused by depravity."

"Is that why you seem so unhappy, sir? Because of history?"

"On the contrary, Mr. McLean. History is my single pleasure. My unhappiness stems from the fact that I have contributed nothing to the study of history. My unhappiness is due to my mediocrity at the craft in which I once felt I was born to excel."

"But you wrote *The History of Carolina Military Institute,* sir."

"Yes, Mr. McLean, and Gibbon wrote *The Decline and Fall of the Roman Empire.* And Prescott wrote about the Conquest of Mexico. I chose a small insignificant topic because I had such pitiful gifts. Reynolds chose to write about an obscure military college located in an obscure Southern state. Do you know why I chose that subject, Mr. McLean? Do you have any idea why?"

"No, sir. Except that you love the school."

"I chose to write that book because I knew that no one else would want to. I would have the field completely to myself. I had to choose a subject small enough to fit my talents. I lacked the style, the vision, and the courage to undertake a grand project. . . . But this is not what I have come to talk to you about, Mr. McLean."

"I know I could do better in English history, Colonel. Now that basketball season is over, I promise to do better, to study a lot harder, and to make better grades."

He looked at me with complete bemusement.

"I give not a scat for your performance or lack thereof in the field of English history. You are an Irishman and a scoundrel, Mr. McLean, and I cannot expect you to master the sweep and scope of an alien and enemy culture. No, I have called you here today to make a confession to you."

"A confession, sir?" I said, puzzled.

"I do not stutter and I do not slur the King's English," he thundered imperiously. "A confession I said, and a confession I meant, Mr. McLean. Since when do I need to explain the meaning of the word to a sniveling papist? I have something to tell you that I should have told you that day you came to my office. But first, I want to make an inquiry of you."

"An inquiry, sir?"

"Yes, goddammit. I want to ask you a bloody question!"

"A question, sir?" I said, grinning up at his broad flustered face. Teasing Colonel Reynolds always afforded me enormous pleasure.

"Why did you come to my office to question me about my knowledge of The Ten?" he asked.

"Because I thought you'd be the one person who would answer me honestly if he knew anything at all. Also, I trust you and consider you a friend, even though you're not fond of the Irish."

"It's not that I am not *fond* of the Irish, Mr. McLean," he explained. "You have not fully comprehended my feelings for those godforsaken wretches. I absolutely loathe the Irish. It is an effort for me even to look at your face, so strongly do you bear the mark of your lowborn race. I only wish Cromwell had been less lenient and humane in his dealings with these pitiful, contemptible brutes. But I must apologize to you and tell you that I betrayed the trust you so ingenuously proffered me."

"How, sir?"

"I wrote a small section in my history book tracing the history of The Ten. It was almost pure speculation, and I had only one source."

"There was nothing in your book about The Ten, Colonel," I interrupted. "Not a single word."

"There was when I sent it to the Institute print shop, Mr. McLean," he said. "I mentioned only the barest facts that I could garner by piecing together the rumors and innuendoes that I had heard over a lifetime at the Institute. Do you remember my telling you that I attended the funeral of General Homer Stone, the hero of the Bulge?"

"Yes, sir," I said, "that's where you counted the ten carnations and the ten doves."

"Exactly," he said. "Well, the Widow Stone, a steely-eyed harridan of penurious Scottish stock, handed over to me her husband's correspondence of a lifetime. You would have thought she was entrusting me with the Rosetta Stone. The letters were boring and nearly illiterate. Literacy is the hallmark of neither generals nor heroes. But there was one letter of utmost interest to me. In it, General Stone was discussing the character and personality of a junior cadet who was about to be inducted into the ranks of an unnamed organization. The letter stated that the cadet met all the criteria for membership save one. He was an outstanding leader, an excellent student, was militarily sound, and had exhibited exemplary loyalty to the Institute. He lacked,

354

according to General Stone, the physical stamina that the organization deemed necessary."

"And you think General Stone was talking about The Ten."

"He was not talking, Mr. McLean," Colonel Reynolds stated with impatience. "He was writing a letter."

"Who was the letter addressed to, Colonel?"

"It was addressed to Colonel Adamson, at whose funeral I first noticed the carnations and doves in the year of our Lord 1958. It did not take a grand creative leap on my part to speculate that the organization of which he spoke was the elusive Ten. So with caution and restraint and citing the letter as a source, I wrote a rather jocular account of The Ten in my history, carefully stating that no one knew for sure whether The Ten existed or not, but that the rumor of its existence had always had a powerful hold on the imagination of the Corps and the alumni."

"What happened to that section, Colonel?"

"It disappeared," he answered. "It disappeared as though I had never written it."

"Did you ask the printer about it?"

"I asked the printer nothing, sir. I screamed at the printer and threatened to throttle him within an inch of his worthless life. But he told me that he printed the material that was handed to him, and indeed, upon investigation, he spoke the literal truth. Someone had removed that section. Not that it made any difference as to the quality of the work. The work is mediocre, though quite workmanlike. Not disgraceful, mind you, just mediocre." As he spoke, his face clouded over with a painful melancholy, as though he were uttering a truth that froze the very roots of his soul. "I complained to the head of the department who complained to the academic dean who complained to General Durrell. I received a note from the General saying that the printer had made an honest mistake, and perhaps that mistake had saved me from the embarrassment of being exposed for shoddy and inaccurate historical research. Imagine the nerve of Durrell, that up-country dandy, chiding me for shoddy scholarship. He even assured me that he himself had personally searched for some small clue about the existence of The Ten and had come up with nothing at all."

"Did you show him the letter, Colonel? That letter proves something."

"The letter proves nothing, Mr. McLean, because nothing is stated directly or resolutely. I was taking historical license, and I did not wish to confront a military man with a concept too difficult and complex for him to understand. But I wanted to clear this matter up with you, Mr. McLean. You scored a direct hit on an intellectual wound when you asked me why I had not mentioned The Ten in my history."

"Why didn't you tell me all of this when I asked you, Colonel?"

"Because of an incident that happened after my encounter with the printer. When I went back to study the letter from General Stone to Colonel Adamson, Mr. McLean, the letter was gone. The letter had been stolen out of my files."

"You could have told me that," I said. "That has nothing to do with you or with me."

He put a heavy arm around my shoulder and steered me against the railing of the seawall facing Sullivan's Island across the harbor. I could not look at Sullivan's Island.

"I believe The Ten exists, Mr. McLean," he said with sudden explosive passion. "I believe they exist and I am afraid of them."

"Even if it exists, Colonel, there's nothing to be afraid of. It's just a club."

"If it was just a club they would not censor history books. They would not enter a man's house to steal letters. Nothing else in my study was touched. Nothing else was moved or disturbed. One single letter disappeared. I wanted to suggest to you, Mr. McLean, that if you are looking for The Ten, you must proceed with restraint and caution. I also wanted to apologize for lying to you. By nature, I am a truthful man and the truth means a great deal to me. I have tried to develop a moral vision in my life and I have tried to live by it. I deceived you, and it has been sometimes difficult to sleep since we spoke in my office."

"Why didn't you tell somebody, Colonel? Breaking and entering is against the law. That's against *anybody's* moral vision."

"No, Mr. McLean"—he sighed—"there is no such thing as morality in these distressing times. What we are witnessing is the death of courtesy in Western civilization. I do not speak of the mincing, effete courtesy of these desperate times, but the virile, robust courtesy born in that most violent of times, the Middle Ages. I lament the passing of that form of chivalry which was the way that civilized men had agreed to treat each other during times of peace. It was a code and a hallmark of civilization, and men would rather have died by their

356

own hand than break the code. But enough of this, I have done my duty by warning you. If they will rob an historian of his sources, there is no telling what the scoundrels will do."

"We need another source," I said, half-speaking to myself.

"Pardon me?" the Colonel asked.

"We need one more source that The Ten really exists. That's one of the lessons I learned from your history class."

"I know of no other written source, Mr. McLean. And I had access to every letter and diary of every deceased alumnus and many of the living ones who played a significant role in the development of the Institute. That was the one hint, the single breakdown of secrecy I found."

"Did you interview any boys or men who were run out of the Institute?" I asked.

"Of course not, Mr. McLean," he said scornfully. "I was writing about the men who made the Institute great, not the swine who could not bear the stern test of her ministries. There is nothing, except venomous reprisals, that cravens who fled their freshman year could cast on the history of the Institute."

"Yes, sir," I said, thinking of my own freshman year. "But they might be able to reflect directly on the history of The Ten."

"Scoundrel!" he cried out, thumping me broadly on the shoulder. "There is a very minor historian beating his way out of that thick Irish skull of yours. Very, very minor but a presence nevertheless."

"I think I know who can tell me all about The Ten. If I can find him and if it exists and if it has the mandate to keep the Corps pure and undefiled that you say it has."

"I did not say I knew that for certain."

"Do you know anything for certain, Colonel?"

"That they are discourteous men. I think they are well-intentioned, but I know they are discourteous and uncivil."

"Is that all?"

"No, that is not all, Mr. McLean."

"What else, sir?"

"I know that I am afraid of them. That they stole the letter is unspeakable. That they eradicated their name from my historical account is unspeakable. They are scoundrels of the first order."

"And how should I find them, sir?" I asked, looking at him directly in the eyes.

"You need a primary source," he said, turning back toward Broad Street. "A primary source."

"I'm going to take off next weekend, Colonel. And I bet you a nickel I find one."

35

Columbia, South Carolina, is a difficult city to love once you have lived in Charleston. It is a functional city, located in the dead center of the state, a hundred miles from the mountains and a hundred miles from the sea. Its summers are merciless and its winters are bitter and it has all the homeliness of America's industrial midlands. But it is a vital, frisky city unburdened by the pretensions and the genealogical sinuosities of Charleston. Sherman had razed Columbia during the Civil War. It made you wonder how much the nature of Charleston depended on its deliverance from pillage and fire.

As we drove into the city, Mark said, "Columbia! What an armpit of a city. The whole place looks like it caught polio, then killed Doctor Salk."

We parked at Five Points, a busy district of student bars and small shops near the campus. The University of South Carolina had eighteen thousand more students than the Institute and fully half of them seemed to be staring at us as we walked down the street in our uniforms. Carolina was well-known around the state for its beautiful girls and its callow fraternity boys whose IQ's hovered around the cut-off point for morons. We passed by several college girls whom I would have married on the spot, without bloodtests or references.

"We're here, boys," I said, pointing to the entrance to a bar. "We're going to meet an old friend."

We walked upstairs to the Second Level, a tavern frequented by students and professors. It took a full twenty seconds for our eyes to adjust to the darkness. You needed a Seeing-Eye dog to find a seat even in midafternoon. Our uniforms attracted the curious and mildly hostile attention of the room as soon as we entered.

A young man approached me out of the darkness. He

was heavier than I had remembered him and his hair was full and luxuriantly swept back on his head. His clothes were stylish and well-kept. He wore a neatly trimmed moustache and in the terminology of the day could have been described as "collegiate."

"Hello, Will McLean," he said, standing in front of me.

We shook hands warmly.

I said, loud enough for Pig and Mark to hear, "Hello, Bobby Bentley, of Ocilla, Georgia."

"Bobby, is that you?" Pig said, sweeping around me and pummeling Bobby on the back.

"How did you find Bentley, Will?" Mark asked, clearly displeased.

"I called his house in Ocilla. I think there're only two or three houses in the whole town of Ocilla, Georgia, and there was only one Bentley in the phone book. His mother told me he was at Carolina."

"Come on over here, boys," Bobby said, gesturing with his arm. "I've got a pitcher of beer and some glasses. Where's Tradd, Will?"

"At some young lawyers' convention. Tradd's a big man on campus now," Pig said. "Wait 'til we tell him we saw you, Toecheese."

As we sat in the high-backed Naugahyde booth, I looked at Mark nervously. He had neither greeted Bobby nor said a single word to him. As always, Mark was measuring his response in his own good time. Bobby poured out the beers ceremoniously and as we clinked our glasses together, Pig called out a toast, "To life."

Mark called for another toast. He raised his glass to Bobby and said in a chilled, aggressive undertone, "To the Institute."

"Don't be a pain in the ass, Mark," I said. "Do you expect Bobby to love the goddam Institute after what they did to him there?"

"I'll be glad to drink to the Institute, Mark," Bobby responded graciously, clinking Mark's glass. "If that's what you really want."

Then he proposed another toast.

"To Carolina," he said, his eyes sparkling.

"Shit on Carolina," Mark growled.

"I can't drink to Carolina," Pig agreed.

"To friendship," I quickly interceded, and the four of us,

359

agreeing at last, drank to friendship. Pig and Mark would rather have drunk to the elimination of Italy than to the health of Carolina.

We drank in silence for a minute or two, feeling shy and alien in each other's company.

"How are you doing, Bobby?" I said at last. "You're looking good, boy."

"I'm doing fine, Will. I'm doing fine for a guy who never will be a Whole Man," he said with force and bitterness.

"How are your kidneys, Bentley?" Mark said.

"Shut up, Mark," I snapped. "What's got into you? I didn't bring you up here to rack Bobby's ass."

"My kidneys are fine, Mark," Bobby said coolly. "There was never any problem with my kidneys. I just wasn't cut out for the plebe system. My nerves wouldn't take it."

"We shouldn't be here, Will," Mark said.

"Why not, Mark?"

"Because we're not supposed to ever talk to anyone who finked out on his classmates during our knob year. As far as I'm concerned Bentley shit all over us. We stuck by him like brothers and he was gone the next fucking day. I don't forgive as easily as you do."

"The kid had bad nerves, Mark," Pig intervened. "If I'd known it was nerves I could have fortified ol' Bobby with some vitamins. The nerves need vitamins just like the muscles do."

"You haven't missed all that much, Bentley," Mark said. "Pig's still a dimwit."

"Mark," I said, "I asked Bobby to meet with us as a favor. If he had told me to go fuck myself, I wouldn't have blamed him a bit. This guy went through the worst plebe system any of us has ever seen. This is the guy, Mark, the goddam guy whose face you and I and Pig once spit into. Do you remember that, Mark? And you're trying to pretend we're bigger and tougher men than he is."

"They made you spit in my face," Bobby said, staring into his glass. "None of you guys is responsible for that. They were trying to run me out and they were using you guys as vehicles to do it."

"I'm sorry, Bentley," Mark said. "I forgot about the spitting. Will should have prepared us for this and I just wouldn't have come."

"Why did you come, Will?" Bobby said, turning to me. "You were very mysterious on the phone."

"I think you can tell me something, Bobby," I said. "I think you can clear something up for me. I didn't think of you at first and I should have. You had all the answers all the time, and it took me a long time to remember you. I've tried so hard and for so long to forget our freshman year that I've repressed almost everything that happened."

"So have I," Bobby answered. "I fill up with hatred every time I hear the name of that school mentioned. I get mad even when I see that the Institute wins a football game or when I see a car with an Institute sticker pass me on a Columbia street. I didn't sleep well for a year after I took off. I even went to a shrink for a while."

I leaned across the table and said, "Bobby, I want to ask you about your last days at the Institute. I want you to tell me everything that happened to you after that night all of us pissed in our pants under the R Company stairwell."

Bobby lit up. "Do you remember the looks on the upperclassmen's faces?"

"Why did you leave us after that, Bobby?" Mark asked. "We would have gone to the moon to keep you with us after that and you left the next goddam night."

"You disappeared after retreat formation the following evening," I said gently. "You withdrew from school without ever coming back to say good-bye to any of us."

"I didn't disappear from the barracks," Bobby said firmly.

"The hell you didn't," Mark countered.

"I was taken from the barracks," he said.

"Who took you, Bobby?" Pig asked.

"The gentlemen did not introduce themselves. Nor did they ask me if I wanted to go along for the ride."

"Where did they take you?" Mark asked, his voice tense and skeptical.

"It's hard to see things, Santoro, when you're blindfolded. I would have taken the blindfold off, but it's hard to move when your hands and feet are tied and you're put inside a mattress cover. I would have screamed but it's hard to scream with a rag stuck in your mouth. They put me into the trunk of a car. I must have been in that trunk for at least a half-hour," Bobby said.

"That's against the rules of the Blue Book, paisan," Pig exclaimed.

"No shit, Pig," Mark said. "If shit were napalm, they could drop your brains on Hanoi."

361

"Easy, Mark," I said. "Would you please relax? You're making everybody nervous. Why don't you wait out in the car if you don't want to hear this?"

"You can't make me wait out in the car, Will," Mark said defiantly.

"I can make him wait out in the car," Pig said, as my two roommates glared at each other across the table.

"Let's just let Bobby finish," I pleaded. "What happened, Bobby, when the car stopped? I know you don't know where the car stopped or who took you out of the car. But what happened when you got there, wherever it was?"

"That's when the fun and games began," he said, and the memory was obviously causing him great pain. "Two of them lifted me out of the trunk and carried me up the stairs of this big house where . . ."

"A house!" I cried out.

"Are you sure it was a house?" Pig said.

Mark began trembling with rage. His whole body tightened and his eyes widened with an immense, blistering anger. Then he said in a whisper, "Poteete. That poor fucking loser Poteete."

"Who's Poteete?" Bentley asked.

"Nobody, Bobby," I said quickly. "But what happened in the house? How do you know it was a big house?"

"Because after they carried me up these stairs, they opened the main door with a key, carried me through one room, then through three more rooms. Someone opened all the doors for the two guys carrying me. Finally, we got to a room that had a stone floor. You know, made out of flagstones or something. They dumped me out of the bag and tied me into a chair. Then they removed the blindfold."

"So you saw who they were," Pig said.

"I didn't say that. They had black hoods down over their faces with holes cut out for their eyes and noses and mouths. They had taken off their shirts. Some of them had swagger sticks. One of them had a M–1 with a fixed bayonet. He put the point of the bayonet against my balls and screamed he was going to castrate me before the night was over. It started just like a sweat party in the barracks only much worse."

"How was it worse, Bobby?" Mark asked, gentle now. "What did they do to you?"

"It's strange, Mark, how much more frightening it was outside the barracks. I knew there were no controls over them, none whatsoever. They didn't have to stop when the bugle blew. They didn't have to worry about the Bear discovering a sweat party. And they had all night to work on me, all of them at the same time. There were no limits to what they could do to me. They told me that they would kill me if I didn't leave the Institute. Then they told me they would make it look like an accident or a suicide."

"Were they after you because you pissed in your pants?" Pig asked.

"That's what they said, Pig," he answered. "They said I was a disgrace to the Corps of Cadets and a disgrace to my classmates. They started screaming as soon as we got there. It went on for hours. It was horrible. I got disoriented and dizzy. They untied me and made me hold an M–1 straight out until I dropped. You know the routine—pushups, deep knee bends, running in place. I pissed in my pants again and again until I was dry. They forced me to drink water until I almost strangled. I began vomiting and going into convulsions."

"Is that when you decided to leave?" Pig said, putting his hand on Bobby Bentley's arm.

"No," Bobby responded sadly. "Pig, I had made up my mind that no one in the world was going to run me out of that school. I had made that vow to myself just like you guys must have done during the year sometime. Then when all of you guys pissed on yourselves, I would rather have died then desert my classmates. That night you did that was one of the greatest things that ever happened to me. But I wasn't dealing just with the cadre of R Company. These people were just sick and brutal and dedicated totally to my leaving. They said they would take me to that house every night until I decided to leave, or they would take matters into their own hands."

"Nice guys," Mark said. "Nice bunch of fucking guys."

"The sweat party went on all night," Bobby continued, drawing in a deep breath. "I was covered with vomit and piss and I had begun hallucinating. Probably from fear and exhaustion. Then they did it.

"They doused me with gasoline. From head to foot. At first I thought they were cleaning off the smell of vomit. But then they all gathered at a place way across the room, staring at me behind those masks. I could see them smiling through the slit. One of them began passing boxes of matches around. They began lighting the matches and flicking them across the room at me. At first they were too far away for any danger. But then they started moving closer, cheering each time a match fell closer to the chair where I was sitting. I began begging for them to stop. But they kept throwing the matches nearer and nearer. I could see myself being set on fire and burning to death in that house. I was terrified because the whole thing looked so rehearsed. They were disciplined and trained to break me. Finally, I told them they had won, that I would quit that night, that I'd never go back to the Institute. Man, I was crying and dry heaving. My body had come completely apart. The smell of gasoline and vomit and piss was horrible. Then there was another smell."

"What smell, Bobby?" asked Mark.

"I'd shit in my pants, Mark," Bobby said, wincing. "I had shit in my pants and had to listen to them taunt me as they threw buckets of water on me and their laughter as they drove back to Charleston. You should have heard the cheer go up when I screamed that I would leave."

"Why didn't you tell anybody, Bobby?" I asked. "Why didn't you tell the Bear, or the tac officer, or even one of the nice guys in the R Company cadre?"

"Why don't you go fuck yourself, Will!" he shouted at me. "See, Will, when I was riding back in the trunk of that car that night, smelling my own shit and vomit and piss, I decided that I didn't want to be a part of that school. I didn't want any goddam part of it. I didn't want to wear the ring of that goddam school. See, boys, I still wake up some nights having nightmares in which these ghouls are coming toward me with matches. Laughing and with matches and gasoline all over the room. One thing I remember from that night. Every one of those bastards wore the ring. Every single one of them. They were all 'Whole Men.' All part of the system."

"That's not part of the system, Bobby," I said defensively. "You're describing something none of us ever heard about, that we didn't even know was part of the Institute. This is an outlaw group that doesn't have anything to do with the Corps, Bobby. It's mean in the barracks, Bobby. God knows, you know that better than anyone. But there are limits. These people exist outside the laws of the Corps. I swear the Corps doesn't even know about these guys."

"You got dealt some bad cards, paisan," Pig said, squeezing Bobby's arm. "Anybody would have quit."

"Where was the house, Bobby?" Mark asked, his face set in a deep, troubled scowl. "We've got to know where the house is or we can't do a thing."

"I don't know where the house is," Bobby said. "I've told you everything I know."

"Everything, Bobby?" I asked. "Have you told us everything that you can remember? I think this group might still be around the Institute and periodically take a kid out of the barracks and do to him what they did to you. We don't know how to find them or how to stop them. We don't know anything about them really. This is the first time we've been positive that they exist. Were any of them from R Company? Did you recognize any of their voices? Did any of them call each other by a first name? Or a nickname?"

He dropped his eyes and folded his hands around his glass of beer. His testimony had taken a fearful emotional toll, and I realized as I looked at him and awaited his answer that there still was a gentle frailty and vulnerability to Bobby Bentley that he would carry all his life.

"That night I didn't recognize a single voice," he said. "I'm sure none of them was from R Company. When you're a knob, you begin to recognize the voices of all the upperclassmen who work you over from day to day. I'm positive I didn't know a single one of them. Not until last year."

"Last year?" Mark said, puzzled.

"I was sitting here in this bar with my girl friend. Her name's Susie and she's from Greenville. Sometime when you're up I'd like to introduce her. She and I were sitting talking about things. You know, things like marriage, kids. Serious things. Nice things. I had just ordered another pitcher of beer when I heard the voice."

"Whose voice?" we asked simultaneously.

"I didn't know then, but it was a voice from that room. It was the voice of the meanest guy in that room. The most brutal voice from that night. It was a deep, cruel voice with a heavy Southern accent."

"How can you be sure it was the same voice?" Pig asked.

"Because I know," he said.

"How do you know?" Mark insisted.

Bobby's eyes filled up with rage and humiliation as he said, "I know because I pissed in my pants when I first heard the voice. Right here in this booth. Right in front of Susie."

There was a long silence among us. Mark, Pig, and I had all placed our hands beneath the table, a subconscious gesture, because we did not want to taunt or hurt Bobby with our rings.

"Who was it, Bobby?" Mark asked at last. "Who was the motherfucker?"

"I saw him when he got up. I didn't recognize him but Susie asked a friend of hers who's a bartender in here. The guy's name is Dan Molligen, and he's in his last year of law school at Carolina."

"He was the first battalion commander our knob year," Pig remembered. "A real first-class prick."

"No shit," Bobby said.

"He can tell us where the house is. We'll find out from Molligen."

"One more question, Bobby," I asked. "Just one more. I know this has been real hard for you. But how many of those guys were in the room that night? Do you remember the number?"

He drained a glass of beer and rose to leave. A light sweat covered his forehead. He said one brief, unequivocal word, "Ten," stood, and said good-bye.

"What do we do now?" I asked when he had gone. "We've got all weekend."

Mark slammed his fist down on the table and said, "Molligen."

36

We spent the rest of the day learning all there was to know about Dan Molligen. I was surprised by how quickly we adapted to the tactics of surveillance. Mark, in particular, displayed extraordinary—heretofore unperceived—skills in the craft of reconnaissance. In five phone calls to friends, he discovered that Molligen was unmarried and lived alone in a section of small brick duplexes on a hill above the University. He was in the top ten percent of his class, an assistant editor of the *Law Review*, and had a job waiting for him in the prestigious Columbia law firm of Sanders and Quackenbush when he graduated. He was engaged to a girl from Converse whose father owned a large department store in Spartanburg. Mark also discovered that Molligen was left-handed, smoked unfiltered Lucky Strikes, had worn braces until he was fourteen, and drove a late model XKE with the South Carolina license plate CL39–260. I found out that he was cordially disliked by most of his classmates at the law school, hung around mostly with Institute graduates, and still practiced sword manual in front of his bedroom mirror.

Pig found something more important still; he found Dan Molligen. He was studying in the law library, hunched over a set of massive brown books, and making careful notations in a small black book. Pig and I watched him for an hour, feeling ill-dressed and uncomfortable in the wrinkled civilian clothes we had brought with us. Mark left to go shopping. I kept reminding Pig that we didn't want to hurt Molligen; we just wanted him to reveal the location of the house where The Ten took those freshmen marked unworthy to wear the ring.

It grew dark, and still Molligen remained fixed at his desk, poring over his law books with remarkable powers of stillness and concentration, oblivious to our hostile presence. Mark returned with a shopping bag held tightly in his hand. We gathered outside the law school, and Mark whispered a plan.

"Will, you stay here and watch Molligen," he said. "When he gets up to leave, follow him to his car without being seen. You call this number and tell us he's on his way home."

"How will I know he's on his way home?" I asked. "What if he has a date or something?"

"He's different from you, Will," Mark said. "He'll probably do something odd like take a shower before he goes out. Anyway, we've got all night."

"What number is this?" I asked, staring at the piece of paper Mark had handed me.

"It's Molligen's number," Mark explained.

"You can't break into his fucking house, Mark!" I protested.

"You just call when he gets into his car," Mark answered.

"How are you going to make him talk?" I asked, growing more and more frightened.

"I wanted to kick his nuts in, but Pig had a better plan," Mark said.

"We used to catch guys in our neighborhood from rival gangs," Pig said delightedly. "We devised a sure-fire way to make 'em talk, and it's perfectly humane. That is, if they survive."

"Why are we doing all this?" I asked. "Let's stop now before we get into trouble we can't get out of."

"Now's the interesting part," Pig said, his excitement mounting. "What if the cavalry turned back to the fort when they heard the Indians attacking the wagon train, paisan? There wouldn't be nothing running around today but a bunch of bare-assed Indians hassling buffalo. Just think of it, no

367

pizza parlors, no Volkswagens, no weight rooms. See, we're the cavalry and this is like a movie. It's fun, man. Fun. Look here, Will."

From the large paper bag Mark held, Pig snatched a huge coil of thick rope.

"We came here because you brought us up here, Will," Mark said. "You dealt us into the game, and now we're going to finish it. You can help us if you want or you can pussy out on your roommates. It's your choice. But I want you to remember that Pig and I were the ones that grabbed Poteete off the railing that night. I know you think you're a lot more sensitive than us, but we'd like to find those guys as much as you would. Maybe more."

"We're not responsible for what The Ten does," I said desperately. "We're getting in too deep. We're not responsible for stopping it."

"I want to know what they did to Poteete," Mark said darkly, "and I want to know who did it. Pearce, I don't give a shit about. I've never even talked to Pearce, but Poteete was in my platoon."

"We've got to find out who the Indians are, paisan," Pig added. "We're the heroes, man. The fucking heroes. We can break The Ten just by getting Molligen in there to talk some good shit to us."

"Will," Mark said, cupping the back of my head with his large right hand and drawing me closer to him, "do you remember how scared we all were after Hell Night? Do you remember being so scared that none of the knobs would go down to the latrine because we thought we might meet an upperclassman? Do you remember us peeing in the sink and then cleaning the sink with Ajax? Do you remember being that scared? Well, how scared do you think you'd have been if someone had thrown gasoline on you and threatened to set your ass on fire? I'm not going to hurt Molligen, Will. I promise you that. But I'm going to scare him as bad as he scared Bentley. And I'm not going to lose one night's sleep over it."

"Don't pussy out on us now, paisan," said Pig.

I said, "I'll call you when Molligen leaves the library."

I came to admire my quarry's powers of concentration during the next two hours as I studied him from across the room. Once he looked up and saw me watching him, but I quickly diverted my eyes to a point above his gaze, as though I were engaged in some indissoluble dilemma of the law myself. I worried, fearing that he could recognize me later, but he did not seem the least bit suspicious of me. Why should he? I thought. There was no reason for him to believe that three seniors from the Institute were stalking him. It was hard enough for me to believe. He was a portrait of stillness for the most part. He studied in perfect silence with his small, narrow eyes . . . cadreman's eyes.

At ten o'clock he began collecting his legal pads, placing them carefully into his briefcase; then he returned the law books to their places on the shelves. He checked his watch. Then to my amusement, he gave himself a military shirt tuck, put on his sport coat, and walked briskly out the front door of the law school. I watched him from a library window as he made his way to the parking lot and unlocked his Jaguar. The phone was ringing at his house before he left the parking lot. It rang only once. Mark Santoro answered it.

"It's all set, Will," he said. "As soon as we get him in the trunk, we'll pick you up behind the gymnasium."

"The trunk?"

"It's the part of the automobile where the spare tire is usually found."

Mark was laughing as he hung up the phone.

* * *

It was over an hour before I saw my car pull into the parking lot behind the gymnasium. During my wait, my mind teemed with infinite dramas and innumerable possibilites of things that might have gone wrong at Molligen's house: suspicious neighbors, dogs, cruising patrol cars, a desperate struggle in the darkness that could have left my roommates badly injured, or even the simple bad luck of Molligen spending the night out with his fiancée. It also occurred to me that what we were doing could not only get us kicked out of the Institute; we could also be sent to prison. The law, unless it had changed significantly during the last unnerving hour, insisted on rather stern treatment for kidnapers. Pig was driving and barely slowed down as I climbed into the front seat. I was shaking.

"Did you get him?" I asked breathlessly, hoping they had not.

"It was a work of art," Pig said. "I wanted to take him down in my famous death hold but the number one paisan here"—he motioned with his thumb at Mark—"crumpled him without a fucking sound using his handkerchief."

"A handkerchief?" I said, puzzled.

"Soaked in chloroform by the master chemist," Mark

369

said. "Chemistry majors learn some useful shit, Will. You'd probably have tried to knock him out with a Norton anthology."

"When will he wake up?" I asked.

"He's probably awake now but he won't be too active for a while. Anyway, he's tied up, gagged, and stuffed in his mattress cover," Mark said, as we passed through Cayce, nervous about cops.

"Where are we taking him?" I asked.

"Do you remember when we went hunting with Commerce and Tradd in the Congaree swamp? That was Thanksgiving break of our sophomore year," Mark answered.

"That's where we're going," Pig said. "Me and Mark figured out a little scenario to get Molligen to talk."

"Are we going to bury him up to his neck in quicksand?" I asked nervously. "No kidding, boys, why don't we let him go now before this thing gets any more serious? We've already stepped into some deep shit and if anything goes wrong . . ."

"I just wish we were near the ocean," Pig said, ignoring me completely. "Did you ever see that movie where they buried Blackbeard up to his neck in the sand and watched the tide come in and drown his ass? I bet we could get Molligen to talk then."

"He'll talk and he'll talk fast," Mark assured us.

My hands were trembling against the dashboard and my eyes followed the sweep of the headlights as we moved along the soft rolling hill country of the South Carolina Piedmont and inhaled the resin smells of dense pine forests. We were streaking down back roads and sparsely traveled highways that cut through a wilder, more primitive South Carolina. We were twenty miles outside the Columbia city limits when I spoke in a voice I barely recognized. "Pig, Mark," I said, "I want us to stop this right now. I'm asking you to stop it. Before we do something we can never undo. I know I was the one that got you to come up here, but I thought we were just going to talk to Bentley. I didn't know it would lead us to Molligen. I didn't know it would lead us to all this. I thought it would just prove how goddam smart I am. I didn't mean for it to go this far. I swear I didn't and I'm scared. I'm scared worse than I've ever been in my life."

Mark reached under the seat and pulled out a bottle of Jack Daniels he had stolen from Molligen's house. He took a long deep swallow, tilting his head back against the seat. Passing the bottle to me, he said, "Shut up, Will. I don't want to hear you whining for the rest of the night. It makes me nervous."

Angrily I snatched the bottle from him and said, "This is what I get for rooming with the fucking Mafia."

"Drink some bourbon," Mark muttered. "It'll help kill that bird who lives in your stomach."

"What bird?" I asked.

"That chicken," he said.

I took a long swallow, too long. I gagged and spit the bourbon onto the floorboards. I took another drink and another.

"What's the plan?" I said, wiping my chin with my sleeve, calmer now. "I've got to know the plan so I can help."

We were entering the deep swamp country of the Carolinas, an ominous unsteady land threaded with ink-black creeks and covered with virgin groves of cypress and water oak. The sharp, pure blaze of starshine illuminated the swamp. Far from cities, we moved into the heart of the Congaree. The liquor was making me brave, and I faced the world with a strange, exhilarating wildness unknown to me, known only to those who have stepped into the realm of lawlessness and found an unnatural strength and power in the taste of its forbidden fruits. We could hear Molligen begin to thump around in the trunk like a large fish we had thrown in alive and fresh from the sea.

"Do you remember the railroad tracks that ran by the place where we camped with Commerce?" Mark asked.

"Sure," I answered. "We put pennies on the tracks to let the train flatten them out."

"We're going to tie him on the tracks and wait 'til a train comes," Mark said calmly. "Then we'll find out about the house, about his sex life, and about how many warts his mother has on her fat ass."

"That's nuts," I screamed. Even liquor could not grant me that much courage in a single night. "That's fucking crazy and you and Pig have gone out of your goddam dago gourds."

"Shhh, Will," Mark warned, making a motion toward the trunk, "speak lower so that bastard doesn't hear."

"Hey, paisan," Pig whispered. "We're not going to really tie him to the tracks the train uses. Don't you remember that old set of tracks that hasn't been used for years that runs right beside the new tracks? We're going to tie him up on the old tracks. It's perfectly harmless, paisan."

"If he doesn't die of a heart attack," I said. "Why don't you guys get a summer job with the Inquisition?"

"I thought of it myself," Pig boasted. "We did it to a guy in my gang who broke the code up in The City. He cussed in front of my mother. I was just going to kill him, but I wanted him to suffer before he died and have time to repent. We hogtied him to a siding where the trains run out to Long Island. He fainted when the train came by. We thought he was deader than shit. But I revived him."

"How?" Mark asked.

"I pissed in his face."

"Jesus Christ," I said. "Give me a chance to kill myself if I ever cuss in front of your mother."

"That's an even greater crime than cussing in front of Theresa," Pig explained. "That's probably the greatest crime a man can commit."

"We're almost there," Mark said, peering out the window. "There. That's the dirt road. Turn, baby. It's almost show time."

We drove for over three miles on the dirt road. The railroad tracks ran out through the southern edge of the swamp and the road we were on went up to the tracks but did not cross them. Pig stopped the car and for a brief moment we listened to the innumerable sounds of the Congaree and the muffled thump of Dan Molligen beating rhythmically against the top of the car's trunk like a damaged heart.

"He could have a fife and bugle corps with him out here and no one would ever hear," Pig said. "When do you think we'll get a train, Mark?"

"We've got all night and you know they make the run from Charleston to Columbia pretty often," Mark answered, looking at his watch. "Let's get Bimbo tied to the track. We don't want to miss a train."

"Here," Pig said, reaching into a brown shopping bag in the back seat. "Ol' Mark thought of everything. Put one of these on, Will."

They were Halloween masks, grotesque and out of season, that fitted over the entire head. They smelled like decomposing inner tubes. We exited the car as three monstrously warted ghouls, a matched and awful trinity. As Pig opened the trunk I breathed in the rancid smell of cheap rubber. The smell and the liquor sickened me.

Lifting Molligen roughly, we carried him struggling and moaning to the old rusted tracks that ran parallel and three yards away from the new ones. The tracks still in use had the silvery health of steel polished by the weight and awesome friction of trains at full throttle hurtling through the Carolina darkness. Mark cut him out of the mattress cover with a butcher knife commandeered from Molligen's house. He was blindfolded, gagged, and trussed securely in what appeared to me to be a professional manner. Working with speed and efficiency, Pig and Mark laid Molligen across the tracks and tied him at the throat and thighs. Then Mark removed the gag and the blindfold to begin the interrogation.

The three of us crouched around him as his eyes adjusted to seeing again. We could measure the precise speed of the adjustment from the time the blindfold came off to the time we heard him gasp with a kind of desperate fear when he focused on our masks.

"Who are you?" he said. "What do you want from me?"

Then he quickly changed his tactics and said in a more controlled voice, "I'm a professional lawyer. There could be some serious consequences to your actions."

Pig giggled, enjoying himself immensely.

"You're going to be dead within an hour, Mr. Molligen," Mark said in a high-pitched voice that sounded like a blend between an adolescent girl and the death-screams of the rabbit I had killed on that long-ago Thanksgiving Day. He was disguising his voice so that Molligen would never recognize him in the same way that Bentley had recognized Molligen. Pig and I followed Mark's example instinctively and with a certain pride in the thoroughness of our roommate's canniness under pressure. We took on the unnatural voices.

Pig wailed, "You gonna be cut in half by a train, Toecheese motherfucker."

"You guys are crazy," Molligen answered in his deep lyrical drawl, still making a superhuman effort to control his panic. It was easy to understand why Bentley never forgot the timbre and quality of that voice. There was a contemptuousness and sonorous menace that must have made him particularly feared among the plebes.

"You've hurt a friend of ours," I said in the changeling voice.

"Who did I hurt?" he screamed, tensing against the ropes, lifting his neck toward us, veins extended in his throat and forehead. "I didn't hurt anybody."

"Answer our questions, Molligen, and we'll let you go," Mark said. "Fuck with us and we're going to feed you to the first train that comes along."

"I'll answer any question you want to know," Molligen said, his eyes peering into the darkness down the track toward Charleston. "Hurry up and ask it. Hurry up."

"Are you a member of an organization called The Ten?" Mark asked.

"No," Molligen answered. "I've never heard of that organization."

"If you don't want to tell us the truth, Molligen, then we're just going to leave you on the tracks."

But Molligen had seen something. He had seen Mark's ring.

"You're from the Institute," he shouted. "You're from the Institute. I wear the ring, you bastards. I wear the ring and you're doing this to one of your brothers."

"Good-bye, brother," Mark said, rising to leave. "Say hi to the big train when it cuts you into three big pieces."

Pig and I left with Mark, walking without haste, and we were almost at the car when Molligen screamed for us to come back.

"Yes, I'm in The Ten," he admitted when we returned. "Now please untie me. I've told you what you wanted to know."

"You only told us one thing we wanted to know, Toe-cheese," Pig said.

"Where's the house, Molligen?" I asked, leaning down in his face, the misshapen nose of the mask touching his face. "Where is the house you bastards take knobs when you're trying to get rid of them?"

"I don't know what you're talking about, you fucking prick," he said. "You must be crazy."

At that very moment I saw the dead, weary eyes of Poteete looking out over the quadrangle of the fourth battalion on the last night he spent on this earth. The crazy eyes of Poteete after they had taken and broken him at the house.

I backhanded Molligen's face as he lay with his head half-sunk in gravel. Then I slapped it again coming back the other way. I saw blood on his mouth and I felt Mark lifting me up by the shoulders.

"I'm a nice guy, Molligen," I said, breathing hard and stunned with the suddenness and violence of my attack. "A nice guy who just wants a simple answer to a simple question."

"Yeh. You're a peach," he said, glowering at me.

"Listen," Pig shouted cheerfully.

"The train," Mark said matter-of-factly. "We better get

out of here. We don't want to be anywhere around here when they find him."

Molligen's face came apart with a seizure of fear awesome in its completeness.

Leaning down, Mark replaced the blindfold over Molligen's eyes. His body strained against the ropes and a sickening, pitiful whine filled the air.

"It wouldn't be humane to let you watch it, Molligen. We really are nice guys," Mark explained. "We're thinking about you all the time."

The train was thundering through the Congaree swamp wide open. There were no crossings to slow for on this stretch of the run to Columbia, no worry about drunk farmers in their pickups, no concern for anything except the power of the diesel and the swift delivery of freight. The light of the train was small at first and miles away in the flat lowlands. But it grew swiftly, like something ravenous and all-seeing and demonic. It came bearing down on us, a raging, maniacal eye, out of the wilderness, out of the swamplands, above the black rivers; it came with fury and incalculable, terrifying immensity to the man who felt its approach in his spine.

The glinting rails nine feet from Molligen's head strained and braced for the passing of the train. His screams were despairing and unhinged.

"The house, Molligen?" Mark asked.

"The house is . . ." Molligen started.

"Yes?" said Mark, tapping the butcher knife against the rail by Molligen's ear. "The train's coming fast, Molligen. There's not much time."

"It's General Durrell's plantation house. The one on Pritchard Island. Now cut me loose. Please. Please cut me loose. Goddam it."

"Sorry, Molligen," Mark said. "You waited too long. There's just not enough time."

"Oh, Jesus," Molligen screamed above Pig's laughter. "Jesus, Jesus, Jesus."

The train roared past us, mythic and flying and huge. Gravel shot past us like cartridges and even Molligen's screams were drowned out by the passing train.

When the train had gone, Mark walked up to Molligen, who had fallen into a stunned silence. Mark removed the blindfold and stared down into Molligen's face.

"You bastards. You rotten fucking bastards. You bastards. You rotten fucking bastards."

"We made a mistake, Molligen," Mark said. "We thought the train was coming on this track. Now you better pretend all of this is a big joke. If you don't then we're going to blow The Ten sky high and you're going to be the stool pigeon. Then we're going to come back and get you, Molligen, and tie you on the right track."

Molligen lifted his head and said, "I'll see you again, you motherfuckers."

Mark cut the ropes that fastened him to the rails. Then he cut the ropes that bound his feet and legs. Walking twenty feet down the track, Mark stuck the butcher knife into a railroad tie.

"Cut yourself loose when you can walk again, Molligen. Follow the tracks to the next highway. Take a left, and in three miles you'll be at the Interstate. Forget this ever happened."

"Adios, Toecheese," Pig said, and all of us sprinted to the car as Molligen tried to regain the use of his legs. In less than twenty minutes we were out of the Congaree swamp and heading back to Charleston.

We had reached I–26 when I realized we were still wearing the masks. None of us had spoken since we had left Molligen; all of us were lost in our own private, turbulent thoughts about that evening and what it implied about the future. When we removed the masks we became ourselves again. Cruelty was an easy sport to master when practiced anonymously. I was shaking again, not from revulsion at what I had done, but from something more sinister. I was shaking because I had enjoyed it all so much, every bit of it. I had especially enjoyed slapping Molligen and making him bleed. It was as though I was striking out against everything that had ever hurt or frightened me. Finally all my invisible terrors had a face. I had struck that face and seen blood form on its lips. For three years I had resisted all temptations to engage in the services and rituals of the plebe system. I had not screamed at plebes or starved them at mess or humiliated them on shower-room floors, but I had learned those macabre arts secretly and well. While Pig drove us toward Charleston, I realized that I had, at last, fulfilled my destiny and had taken my place as a cadreman, as a breaker of men. Was I doing all this for Poteete and Pearce and Bentley, or was I doing this because of a runaway megalomania I could not control? The answer lay in the very question, and I stared at the mask as though I had unearthed an effigy of my own endangered soul.

Pig was the first to break the silence.

"The General. The goddam General," he said. "Wait'll we tell the Bear."

Mark disagreed. "We don't tell the Bear anything. We're not going to breathe a word to anyone about what happened tonight. Goddam, Will," he said, looking at me contemptuously. "You're heavyweight champ of the world against guys who are tied up. I bet you're hell on newborn babies and terminal cancer patients."

"Go suck on your chloroform rag, Mark," I snapped back. "I got carried away. That's all. I didn't like the look on his snotty face. He was so goddam superior."

"Well, boys," Mark said, ignoring me. "We've got a serious reason to keep our mouths shut now."

"Why, Mark?" Pig asked.

"Because if it's the General behind all this and he finds out it was us who took Molligen, then we won't graduate from the Institute in a million years."

"What if they make a move against Pearce?" I asked.

Mark looked at me and said, "Will, I say let's give them the nigger. Let's give them anybody they want. I don't give a shit if The Ten runs out every goddam knob in the Corps as long as I get my diploma. I say we don't say a single word to anyone, not even Tradd. If he doesn't know anything, then he can't be hurt by it. And I'll guarantee you, they'll be looking for the three of us."

"Yeh, fuck Pearce anyway," Pig agreed. "I don't like niggers any more than The Ten does. Let's let it drop, Will. OK, paisan?"

"What about Poteete and Bentley?" I asked. "Do we just forget we know all about that now? Do we just let The Ten keep terrorizing guys like that?"

"That's what the plebe system's all about," Mark said. "Terror. Pure human terror on a grand scale. It's like what we did to Molligen tonight. We terrorized him. Or at least, Pig and I terrorized him, Will. You beat him."

"Maybe I should go talk to the General," I said. "Man to man. Tell him what we found out. Maybe he doesn't even know they use his house."

"Yeh, Will," Mark sneered. "Explain to him how we happened to be walking down the railroad tracks wearing Halloween masks and stumbled upon the body of Dan Molligen."

"I vote we keep our asses out of it, paisan," Pig said. "Man, we had a great night. A fabulous, kick-ass night that we'll tell our children about. But we got to let them have the nigger. Agreed?"

"I agree," said Mark.

But I said nothing. There was always a grandeur and a nobility in my megalomania. And also something cheap and loathsome that I could not help.

37

They took Pearce from his room in second battalion on the first Monday in April, on a rainy overcast night with fog lifting off the rivers and the prediction of a cold front moving in from the Midwest. Tradd and I were studying together for a test in medieval drama, straining irritably to extract meaning from those lean, extinct words that had fallen unmourned from the language. Mark was studying a chemistry text, making tiny notations in the margin and smoking one cigarette after another. Pig claimed he had nothing to study and was lifting weights in his corner of the room.

A sophomore orderly of the guard knocked and entered the room.

"Will McLean?" he asked, and brought a message to my desk. "It's from second battalion, Will. A knob just ran it over and said it was urgent. A few guys were racking his ass for being in the wrong battalion. That's why it took so long to get to you."

As he left the room, taps sounded high over the campus. I opened the note and read these words: *Two cadets took my roommate Tom Pearce from our room tonight. They said his grandmother was very sick and that he was authorized to go on special leave. He told me to contact you, Mr. McLean, if he was ever taken out of the barracks for any reason.*

"Pig, Mark," I said, sitting down in my chair, trying to think clearly, trying to formulate some kind of strategy. After our interrogation of Molligen, I had thought that he would issue a warning that someone was on the trail of The Ten and the organization would lie low. I had thought our secret foray against them had rendered The Ten impotent because we were as invisible and undetected as they were. "They took

378

Pearce from the barracks. This is a note from his roommate. Two guys came and said his grandmother was sick."

"Maybe his grandmother is sick," Mark said, unconcerned.

"Then the Bear would have come to tell him," I answered. "You know how it works around here."

"You think it's The Ten?" Pig asked.

"What are y'all squawking about now?" Tradd asked. "I think everyone in the room has lost his mind except me and I'm losing mine because I continue to live in this insane asylum."

"It's something you don't need to know about or want to know about, Tradd," Mark said. "Don't ask any more questions. It's just Will thinking he lives in Sherwood Forest."

"I'm going to the house," I said, rising. "You know that's where they've taken him."

"You aren't going anywhere, Will," Mark said, moving over to block the door. "You aren't going to fuck this room up any more than you already have for a nigger. There's some bad shit going on that we don't need to stir up."

"Has everybody in this room taken complete leave of his senses?" Tradd said, looking at each one of us, sensing our complicity and his exclusion. "I have a right to know what's going on."

"If Tradd doesn't know anything, then he can't get hurt by what we already know," Mark insisted. "We owe it to him to keep him out of it."

"We've never had secrets in this room, paisan. I don't see any reason to keep secrets from Tradd. I haven't liked it from the beginning," Pig argued. "He's a paisan like the rest of us and paisans tell each other their deepest thoughts."

"He didn't fuck up like the rest of us," Mark said. "He didn't hear what Molligen told us on the tracks. The General's in this, Will. Don't you see, if the nigger really is at that house, then they're doing this with the General's permission?"

"The General?" Tradd said.

"Mark," I said, moving toward him slowly. "I'm going to that house. I've got to do it."

"Why, Will?" Mark shouted. "Tell me the real reason why you've got to go. Is it because of your overwhelming love of niggers or is it something else, something we don't know about? There's not a single goddam reason you should stick your neck out for Pearce. If it was just your ass I

379

wouldn't care, but you could bring us all down with you. Even Tradd."

I tried to answer Mark firmly, but my voice quavered as I said, "Pearce doesn't have anyone to help him, Mark. He's going through the line all alone."

"Well, aren't you the sweetest guy in the world?" Mark said. "Aren't you a prince among men? Look, Will, there are a hundred billion niggers living outside the Gates of Legrand. Let them help him. They're the ones who sent him here. He's no concern of this room. We've got studying to do just to graduate. We've got senior essays to write. And you don't even know for certain that they've taken him to the General's house or that it's The Ten that's got him."

"What on earth are you talking about?" Tradd said furiously. "Would someone in this room please tell me the exact hour when all my roommates had complete psychotic breaks with reality? And what is all this talk about a house and a general? Or is it ten houses or ten generals?"

"Let's keep Tradd out of it," Mark repeated.

"If it can hurt you guys, then I have a right to know," Tradd said. "If it's harmful to you it should be equally harmful to me. It's condescending to protect me. It's as though I'm less of man than any of you."

"They'll tell you after I leave, Tradd," I said. "You're right, we should have told you, but there's no time now."

"Get away from the door, Mark," Pig warned. "Will can go to the house if he wants to go to the house. He can't help it that he loves niggers. I didn't like oysters when I first came south. But I acquired a taste for the little boogers and that's the same thing that happened to Will with niggers."

Mark stared at Pig incredulously. "What a fucking idjit," he said, shaking his large head sadly from side to side. "Let Will love them all he wants after graduation. He's sleeping here tonight."

"Mark," I said. "I promised Pearce that I'd help him if those guys ever took him. Remember what they did to Bentley? Remember how they tied him up and threw him into the trunk of a car? Can you imagine how scared Pearce must be with ten white boys taking him out into the country? I just want to go to the house to find out who's in The Ten. If we can just get one or two names, we've got them. We can neutralize them and make sure that Pearce survives the year. I want to find out who they are, Mark. I want to find out for me, not for Pearce. I need to know their names. Then they won't be able to hurt anybody. I'm curious, Mark. I want to know why they exist and why they operate out of the framework of the Corps."

Tradd spoke up from behind me. "Mark's right, Will. You're overwrought and sticking your nose in a place it shouldn't be. I don't even know what you're talking about, but it's obvious you shouldn't break barracks and go gallivanting about. Why don't you just take a Sominex and get some valuable shut-eye? If something's bothering you this much, just forget that it exists and eventually it'll disappear."

"That's what I'm afraid of, Tradd. That Pearce will simply disappear," I said, then turning to Mark I said gently, "I'll need your help getting out of the barracks, Mark."

"Fuck you," Mark said. "You aren't even getting out of this door."

"Mark," I said. "Just this once. That's all I'll ever ask of you. Just this one time and I'll never ask you for another favor. I'll need your help to get out of the barracks. A diversion."

"Did you find a note in *The Decline of the West*?" Tradd asked. "Did Pearce try to warn you in any way before tonight?"

"We changed the system of communication," I said.

"What?" Mark said. "You didn't tell us that, Will. I thought we had no secrets in this room."

"That's obviously a falsehood," Tradd said, miffed.

"Someone was intercepting the notes, Mark," I explained. "Pearce thought it might be the Bear."

"And you thought it might be one of us," Tradd said.

"I just didn't think it was important, Tradd," I explained. "There were no more basketball trips and no reason for any of you to check for messages anymore."

"That's a breach of trust, paisan," Pig said, shaking his head sadly, "you didn't trust us."

"This room is a veritable hotbox of secrets," Tradd said. "I still don't know the big secret you're hiding from me."

"We stepped in some powerful shit when we went up to Columbia a while back, Tradd," Mark said.

"Tell me," Tradd begged. "I have a right to know and I'm nearly perishing from curiosity."

"Tell him after I get out of the barracks," I said, listening as I heard the far-off whistle of the northbound train as it mounted the trestle on the far side of the Ashley River.

"My God, it's already eleven forty-two," I said, checking my watch.

"Right on time. Like always," Pig said.

"You and Tradd take care of the diversion," Mark said, leading me by the elbow out into the galley. "I'll get Robin Hood out of the barracks."

Escape from the barracks after taps required caution and artistry. Over the years, cadets, like other kinds of prisoners, spent much of their time devising routes and rituals of escape if the need arose to make their way to the real world during the hours between taps and reveille. On the first division of each barracks, small trap doors pocked the floors of the rooms; these doors led to a honeycomb of passages among the water pipes and electrical wires beneath the barracks. But since the Bear had returned as Commandant of Cadets, he had eliminated these avenues of escape by sealing up the existing trapdoors and severely punishing cadets who constructed new ones. Cadets in the Airborne Ranger Program had been known to rappel down the side of the barracks like rock climbers in a matter of seconds. Rope ladders, grappling hooks, and hacksaws to remove bars from the gates of rarely used sally ports had served in emergencies since the early days of the Institute. I had never left the barracks illegally, but I knew that Pig and Mark would insure my successful escape and re-entry. They had mastered the intricate stratagems for leaving the barracks at will and had often left in darkness to drink all night in the waterfront bars. As I followed Mark along the shadows of the first division, I reflected upon my irresistible attraction to the strong and the lawless. I did things because of Mark and Pig that I never would have done alone. Tradd and I were naturally timorous good citizens. Yet I wanted to acquire the militant courage of Mark and Pig more than anything, to taste the black and fearless life, to rush at things, to seize each moment and live it as though it were my last. If I could not live like that, at least I wanted them to think I could.

We slipped into the room of two O Company freshmen, a room next to the guardroom. One freshman snored loudly, like an engine in need of tuning, and his snoring emphasized the immense stony silence of fourth battalion. As we waited for Pig to make his move, I became aware of my wrist pulse against Mark's shoulder. I could feel my heart beat and the fiery, enlivening flow of adrenalin in the blood. Aware of my blood, of the heat in my body, of the unstillable activity in my cells, I braced as we saw a match flare high on fourth division where we lived. I was living again in the inspirited zone of pure instinct. I was an athlete again, a gamesman.

The first cherry bomb arced across the barracks in a flaming parabola.

"He's using his slingshot," Mark whispered.

It exploded on the second division of N Company, directly opposite from Pig. Since the barracks were completely enclosed, the explosion reverberated with the power and terrifying plangency of an artillery shell.

The OG rushed out of the guardroom, strapping on his sword and awkwardly positioning his field cap. Any disturbance in the barracks was his responsibility, and his eyes scanned the galleries for movement. The second cherry bomb landed on T Company's third division. Cadets began stirring in the barracks and moving sleepily out on the galleries to inspect the disturbance. The guard ordered everyone back into their rooms on the double. But the barracks were alive now, and the cadets, anonymous and sleep-dazed, began taunting and cursing the guard. In the confusion, Mark and I entered the guardroom on the run. Mark grabbed the set of heavy steel keys, slipped out the side door of the sally port, opened the gates soundlessly, quickly, and whispered, "Good luck and be careful," as I made my way in darkness toward the barbed-wire fence behind the faculty housing. I was sprinting when I heard the third cherry bomb explode. Pig had shot that one directly at the OG, who dove to the concrete to avoid losing an eye.

Soon I was entering my car, which I had parked off campus in the parking lot behind the football field. I drove quickly through the city toward the eastern side of the Charleston peninsula. When I mounted the Cooper River Bridge, crossing over the first of its high massive arcs, I could see the city shimmering and spired behind me and smell the virile harbor beneath me. I rolled down my window and felt the cold luxuriant air rush past me in great stinging gallons. I tried to relax; I tried to pretend I was not afraid. I imagined I was Pig or Mark. They would not be afraid.

But my hands trembled on the steering wheel, and I could feel the fear begin its business with me. I could feel it nervously moving within me like a thin silky gauze. There were stirrings all over my body and in different forms. Fear was a citizen of the stomach, a thin man at the knees. I should have asked Mark to come with me, I thought. All I had to do was ask and he would have come. So would Pig. So would Tradd. "What in the hell have I done to myself now?" I shouted aloud as I reached the highway 17 by-pass around Mount Pleasant.

Once I had thought the plebe system would make me fearless. By submitting myself to the canons of a merciless discipline, I had imagined that I would never again be physically afraid in the world. But the plebe system had had an opposite effect: It taught me that the world was indeed a place to fear. I had always wanted to be brave and strove desperately to hide the indisputable fact that I was a coward. Because I was ashamed of my cowardice, I had mastered the subtle art of appearing brave. What had been essential to my vanity in the barracks was not that I actually came to the aid of Pearce but that I demonstrated the sincere appearance of wanting to help him. The appearance would have been enough for me. I was certain of that. But they had trusted the sincerity of my wishes, and once again I had become a victim of my own fraudulent, pathetic bravado. Once I had ensnared myself in its ingenious trap, there was no way I could turn back. I could not turn back and face the contempt and derision of my roommates. But more significantly, I could not turn back because I knew I was afraid. By continuing to drive north toward the old rice and indigo plantations of the Wando River, I was paying ultimate homage to that fear and my inability to surrender to its tyranny over me. The only way I could endure being a coward was if I was the only one who knew it. I comforted myself by saying that my only duty on this night was to gather information. I promised myself that I would not be seen by a single living soul.

38

Extinguishing the lights of the car, I crossed the wooden bridge that spanned the tidal creek leading to General Durrell's plantation. Driving slowly down the dirt road that led to the main house, I came to a locked gate. I hid my car behind a palmetto grove beside a small family cemetery and started down the road on foot. There is always a lurid sense of menace to Southern forests at night, especially when the oak trees are centenarians and their branches, braceleted with thick vines and draped with their scarves of moss, bend low to the earth to make the darkness darker. There have always been too many live things in these forests for me. I would probably not have feared them—or The Ten—if I could identify them or their calls and shrieks. I was glad it was unseasonably cold as I walked, for I never liked walking the backwoods of the Carolinas during the high season of the Eastern diamondback. Soon, I was running and running swiftly; the flashy guard was running and afraid.

Suddenly, in full flight, I rounded a curve in the road and the plantation house came into view. It was fully lighted but there was not a car or human being in sight. Pausing, I drifted along the edge of the woods and began planning my approach to the house. I began speaking to myself in a low, unnerved whisper. The sound of my own voice reassured me, called me, as though my voice was the only absolute proof I had of the reality of the moment. "Easy, Will. Careful, Will. Find out who they are, then get the fuck out of this place."

Keeping to the forest, I circumnavigated the house, which gleamed like a white ship in the center of a perfectly trimmed lawn. In some outbuildings behind the house, I found three automobiles. All of them had Institute parking stickers, and I wrote the numbers of the stickers and the makes of the cars on a piece of paper in my wallet. I also recognized one of the cars, and I wrote down the name of the first of The Ten in my class: John Alexander.

But I still did not know for certain if Pearce was in the house. Unless I saw him with my own eyes there would be no value to my witness or testimony. Searching for the safest approach to the house, I crossed a road behind it that led to the ocean a quarter of a mile away. I had once had a footrace with Johnny DuBruhl down that road at a cookout the General gave for the basketball team in my junior year. I could just hear the breakers rippling along the beach.

A colonnade of oak trees led from the rear of the plantation house to the formal gardens enclosed by a lichen-covered brick wall. Crawling along the wall, I made it to the first tree, surveyed the house, then ran to the next tree. By keeping in the protection of those trees, I arrived unchallenged at the thick hedge of azaleas that encircled the entire house. The azaleas were perfect cover for my reconnaissance; they were trimmed precisely to my height and I could crouch unseen, moving from window to window, at my own slow pace.

The living room in the front of the house was empty and still, but there were uniforms scattered on coffee tables and

385

chairs and slung insouciantly across a baby grand piano. There was no light on in the dining room, but there was a door open and I could see a light on in the hallway. I moved through the azaleas cautiously, silently; and for a moment a delicious, almost palpable curiosity had replaced the fear.

Then I heard the strangest voices I had ever heard in my life: human voices I was sure, but they sounded more like the witless chorales of insects in the forest than anything readily attributable to the family of man. I had to cross into the light of the front portico and dash past the entry steps to get to the western wing of the house where I heard the voices. My ears registered each sound in the night. I looked around me and studied the terrain again before I continued my secret approach. I felt as if I could hear the flight of owls or the death of leaves in the garden. So alive was I, so burning with the intoxicants of this exact moment, that I felt as if I could count each cell of my body with my index finger. My body seemed enlarged, tingling, electric, and somehow invulnerable as I crept unseen beneath the covering azaleas. From the human shadows moving grotesquely on the lawn in front of me, I knew that whatever the activity taking place in the house it was occurring in the multiwindowed room on the far western wing. I was ten feet from the room when I heard the first scream.

Yes, Tom Pearce and I had indeed come to the same place on the same chilly April night.

Cautiously, I peered into the bottom pane of the first window in that room. The scene was exactly as Bobby Bentley had described it except for one significant and disturbing difference. When the members of The Ten screamed at Pearce they did so in high-pitched, effeminate voices, which collectively had the sound of a choir of possessed and maniacal castrati.

Pearce was tied up in a wooden chair in the middle of a room with no other piece of furniture in it. They had stripped him naked and sweat poured in dark streams from his brown, well-muscled body. A look of supreme agony and inexhaustible suffering shone in his eyes. His mouth had dropped open and saliva hung from his lips in obscene strings. Anger began to take the place of fear as I watched.

They worked on him in squads of three, screaming at him in those other-worldly, disembodied voices. On the brick floor I could see the sweaty imprint of Pearce's body and imagined their beginning the evening by breaking Pearce physically with three or four hundred pushups.

"You gonna leave my school, nigger?" one of the masks asked.

"No, sir," Pearce answered, though his voice was barely audible.

"We're gonna kill us a nigger tonight, Pearce. I always wanted to kill me a nigger," a voice said from a part of the room I could not see. There was so much movement in the room I could not count them accurately without being seen. But I was sure I knew how many of them were in the room.

"It's gonna be like this every night for the rest of the year, nigger. When you gonna sleep, nigger?"

"How does it feel to be a nigger, boy?" another mask screamed. "To wake up knowing you're a black cocksucker every day of your life. You're an ugly nigger boy. But you're going to be a dead nigger soon. We might even kill you tonight if you're lucky."

"I'm gonna make you suck my cock, nigger. That's the only thing niggers are good for. To suck a white man's cock. To suck their master's dick. You want to suck my sweet white cock, nigger?"

"No, sir. Please, sir," Pearce cried out.

"Give him the juice again," one voice shouted as Pearce began screaming and struggling against the ropes that were cutting into his flesh. There was blood on his wrists.

The black masks surrounded him, all screaming, some of them laughing, but the insane, demented, and joyless laughter one would expect to hear in inaccessible wards of insane asylums. The masks and voices were hideous in the lovely light of a chandelier, incongruously placed in this bizarre room obviously not built for chandeliers. The room must have been an old kitchen, I thought, but the wing looked new and I wondered to myself if the room had been constructed especially for these grim rites. Four of them held Pearce as a fifth applied a small clamp to the head of Pearce's penis. Then he flicked a switch and an electric current flowed brutally into Pearce's body, and he convulsed as he screamed. The screams carried over the entire island.

We had learned about counterinsurgency techniques in military science classes in our four years at the Institute. Experts in the field informed us that electricity, properly applied, could break a man's resistance quicker than any other method of interrogation.

The guy controlling the switch was John Alexander. I don't know how I knew for certain, but his stiff carriage and the odd way he balanced his shoulders when he moved revealed his identity as certainly as a fingerprint. An asshole moves like an asshole even when he wears a mask.

Alexander adjusted the switch controlling the amount of current sent into Pearce's body. You could judge the force and duration of the current by the intensity of Pearce's screams. I was nauseated and thought I might vomit in the bushes. I did not know how long I could be a spectator to such outrage. Then Pearce lost consciousness and the masks cheered. One of them threw a bucket of water into Pearce's face to revive him. Another took off his shirt and began mopping his chest of perspiration. I noticed the long, ugly, centipede-shaped scar incised into his left shoulder and knew I had discerned the identity of a second member of The Ten: my friend and fellow athlete Cain Gilbreath.

But even without the scar I should have recognized Cain's massive shoulders and his thick, brutal neck. The masks had hypnotized me; the masks and the rings that proved that all the members of The Ten were my classmates. If I could have ripped the masks from their heads, I was sure I could identify each member of the organization.

As Pearce fought his way back to consciousness, the phone rang in a distant room in the house, a sound as incongruous and misplaced as the chandelier casting a delicate light on the masked figures surrounding the naked black boy strapped to the wooden chair. The masks turned to each other in featureless puzzlement. Then one of them left the room quickly. The phone rang five times before it was answered.

When he returned he whispered something to the group. Two of them came directly toward the window where I was positioned. I sank down into the green depths of the azaleas, and breathing hard, I watched through the foliage as they peered into the black night. One of them glanced downward to the exact spot where I was hidden. As they returned to the group, I lowcrawled on my hands and knees to the thickest, most impenetrable part of the hedge. I saw a light go on in the custodian's house two hundred yards away, then go out again. I wondered if he had seen me at the window, and I was angry that I had forgotten about the existence of the fucking custodian. As I burrowed into the brush cover, the front door of the plantation house swung open, and two of them, armed with M-1's with fixed bayonets, moved swiftly into the yard and began stabbing the bushes with their bayonets. They did not speak but moved with extreme deliberation around the house, stabbing viciously and at random into the dark yielding thicknesses of the azalea hedge. I flattened myself and did not draw a breath for a full minute as they passed above me. The blade of one bayonet passed two feet above my head and was delivered with such force and thrust it would have skewered my throat had its aim been truer. How would the General explain a bayoneted athlete in the azaleas, I wondered, as they continued to work their way patiently around the house. My heart beat against the earth and my lips bit into the rooted, sandy soil. I did not move for twenty minutes, and I thought I would not move again that night until I was sure I could make a clean, unobserved escape. But I wanted to get away from that house, and most of all, I wanted to return to the secure anchorage of my room, to the safety of roommates. I wanted to escape from all responsibility for Pearce. I didn't move or lift my head until I heard Pearce screaming again. Undone, I put my hands over my ears, but the screams cut through my fingers and my eardrums felt as if they were being lacerated with glass.

I rose to the window once again and saw one of them dousing Pearce with gasoline. He poured the gasoline over Pearce's head, into his face, and splashed it against his chest and groin. The high-pitched voices were in full cry again as the lunatic chorus sang out their imbecilic, vicious chant of loathing. They gathered in the far corner of the room and lit candles in a ritualistic and strangely beautiful ceremony. Bowing to each other and grinning beneath the cloth masks, they began a slow cadenced march toward Pearce, the candles held like swords in front of them as they made their long approach.

"Set the nigger on fire."

"You gonna leave, nigger?"

"Fire, nigger, fire."

Pearce, delirious and insensate with terror, began screaming out of exhaustion and terror.

"I'll leave, sir. Please, sir. I'll leave. I'll leave. Never come back, sir. Please, sir."

And still they came, the fire before them.

I almost vomited again; I went down on my knees and tried to keep from retching. Pearce's screams, nausea, the smell of gasoline through the open windows, the sweetness of the azaleas. My hand found a brick.

I came out of those azaleas with that brick, with that weapon.

I threw it high, lobbing it like a grenade through the

window, the glass shattering with a surreal cleanliness, and continuing its arc, almost in slow motion and somehow dreamlike, the brick exploded into the chandelier and the room, suddenly silent, burst into a dazzling shower of ruined glass.

I smashed another pane with my fist, felt the bite of glass in the heel of my palm, and shouted into the room, "Pearce, it's Will McLean and I've seen it all." And pointing to the shoulder with the scar, I yelled, "And I know you, Cain Gilbreath, you motherfucker. And you, John Alexander. I know you."

Then I was running. I saw them moving toward the doors and exits, and my brain, overpowered with the images and visions of this demonic night, turned toward escape. I sprinted around the side of the house, moving low and fast, using the cover of the hedge until I had to break into the open and be exposed to the light. Already, I had made my first mistake and had run in the opposite direction from my car.

"There he is. Get him," I heard someone yell from the back door.

But by that time I had reached the road to the beach and I headed toward the sound of the breakers like a sprinter fast out of the blocks. I was running blindly down the road in complete darkness. If there had been a tree planted in the middle of the road I would never have seen it and would have left my brain decomposing in its bark. I remembered the road being straight, and I had to trust the accuracy of that memory because I began to hear the footsteps in pursuit of me, footsteps matching me stride for stride. My hand was aching in the cold and I could feel the blood warm between my fingers and dripping off my damaged hand. I was afraid the loss of blood would weaken me, slow me down, and allow them to catch me. Already there was a lightness in my head.

But I broke suddenly out onto the open beach and sprinted to the left, through soft, difficult sand, until I hit the hard wet sand at the ocean's edge.

Then I took off. The sprinter in me, the dashman, the flashy guard trained under the lights, ignited on that fast sand and let loose for two hundred deliriously heady yards, until I thought my lungs would burst. A light fog dusted the beach and the air was completely still, as though the earth and the water were thickening around me, trapping me cunningly in the thickness.

Casting a quick glance over my shoulder, I saw three black masks following me in the fog. Cain Gilbreath, with his thick, formidable body, was pursuing me with a grim intensity that frightened me more than anything had all night. I thought that my friendship with Cain would have meant enough to make me immune from his pursuit, at least. The three of them were running easily, pacing themselves, intent on letting me run myself out, exhausting myself in the first mile. I pressed my palm against my heart and tried to stem the flow of blood.

Behind them, two others emerged from the road and took up the chase through the fog. The distance made them little more than ethereal, insubstantial creatures, and I knew they had little chance of catching me.

I tried to form a strategy as I ran. I tried to concentrate my energies and clear my thoughts. Slowing down, I decided that I was the master of this chase even though I was the pursued.

Let me set the pace, I thought, feeling the blood against my chest, let me decide how the race will be run. My pursuers knew I was fast, had watched me on the court, knew that I was not a distance man, knew that I would fade fast over long distances. My forte was the quick explosive burst of speed, the change of pace and direction, and an ability to run as much as I needed to run. And as far, I thought. And as far.

I was a basketball player, I told myself, a running, jiving, fast-talking, quick-handed guard, and I had taken to the courts when I was nine years old and had never stopped running, never stopped shooting, never stopped developing those leg muscles that would carry me away from them. I could bleed and still outrun them. I had bled before in the fury of games and had never asked to come out in my life. Bleeding was a sign of honor among athletes, and I had left my blood and my sweat on a dozen courts around the South and would have loved to leave them on a hundred more.

So I ran. I ran. I tried to forget the slow men behind me and tried to remember instead the hurting lessons of my game, the injured knees, the sprained ankles, the burning thirst of practice, the elbows in the mouth, the missing teeth of forwards. If they caught me, I reasoned, it would be because they had earned the capture and they wanted me more than I wanted to escape. But no one has wanted things more than I have, I thought. That was the gift and hunger I brought to my game. I did not have the talent to match the hunger, but, by God, I had the speed.

In the elixir of these thoughts, in the high velocity of these thoughts, I turned toward my enemies again, forty yards behind me now. But I noticed with alarm that the last two had closed the gap considerably and were only ten yards behind Gilbreath and his companions. The last two were sprinters and were going to make a run for me before this race was finished.

Then I saw Gilbreath look over his shoulder.

And I heard this sound:

"Oink, oink."

"Pig," I shouted and stopped.

I whirled around, started back down the beach, and braced myself for the charge of Cain Gilbreath.

He rushed at me, came hard and with a low center of gravity, and I stood waiting for the charge, loose and crouching, aware of the blood spilling down my hand again. He came at me with superb, deadly balance, handling his bulk well, and before the collision I realized Cain had spent long seasons coming out of the line at defensive back, coming straight ahead in bone-stirring downfield blocks, coming toward dummies held by taut, screaming coaches at practice, and at that moment I knew I would learn the difference between a pulling lineman and a flashy guard. He had been bred and honed for contact; I had been trained to avoid it. His shoulder caught me at the knees and his full weight upended me. I flipped in a wild somersault and landed on my back. I rolled away from him and felt the shock of the cold breakers sting my hand. I rolled to avoid him, but he was quicker off the ground and his fist slammed into my cheek and his second blow glanced off my eyebrow. I moved into a fetal position and tried to cover my face with my hands as waves broke over me. He left me suddenly, and opening my eyes, I knew the pulling guard was going to learn some swift lessons about hitting the roommate of Mark Santoro and Dante Pignetti.

Mark reached him first.

Cain rose to meet him like a linebacker crouching to intercept a halfback, but Mark knew little about organized athletics. He came at Gilbreath like a streetfighter with little time on his hands and kicked Gilbreath in the nuts, dropping him to his knees. The second kick was to the face; the third to the stomach.

Mark turned the prone and bleeding body of Cain

Gilbreath over on the sand, went down with his knees on Gilbreath's arms, and began hitting his face with deliberate, brutal punches. After the third, I grabbed Mark.

Behind us, Pig had cut down one member of The Ten with a left hook to the nose and dispatched the other with a karate kick to the chest. Both of them scrambled to their feet and wisely began running back toward the house.

"Let's get the fuck out of here," I shouted.

We left Gilbreath lying on the beach, in the cold, in the fog, with the tide going out in the Atlantic.

★ ★ ★

Tradd, nervous in the shadows of the south sally port, let us in the barracks an hour before reveille with keys purloined again from the sleeping guard. Pig returned the keys, slipping into the guardroom as silently as though he was under water. My left eye had swollen shut, and when we got to our room, Tradd, with great and ginger concern, cleaned the cut on my cheek, removing grains of sand and clots of blood. He applied a cold compress to my eye and disinfected the deep cut in my hand by pouring alcohol directly on the wound.

"You deserve pain," Tradd said when I screamed. "You deserve an award for stupidity and vanity. I wish I could stick your whole head in alcohol."

"You missed the big one, paisan," Pig said to Tradd as he danced and shadowboxed around the room, aglow with the fevers of combat and running and escape. "Will was the wagon train. The Ten was the Indians. And me and Mark was the fucking U.S. Calvary sweeping out of the hills in the nick of time."

"Someone had to let you fools in the barracks," Tradd said.

"Thanks for following me out there," I said to Pig and Mark. "I don't know what they would have done if they'd caught me."

"Catch you?" Pig scoffed. "You can't catch anything that scared. You were flying down that beach, boy."

"I didn't want to go," Mark grumbled, removing his wet shoes and socks and hurling them at his press. "Meatbrain over there talked me into it. He said you couldn't handle it alone. You had it made until you threw that brick. You should have just seen what was going on and drifted on back here. You promised us you'd be careful. Throwing that brick was just stupid."

"Will doing something stupid would surprise you?"

Tradd asked. "Stupidity's just a habit of his. The poor fool's fallen in love with stupidity, and who knows what troubles his shenanigans tonight will bring this room? I want everyone in this room to know that I deplore all of your actions tonight and I refuse to share complicity in them. Y'all are acting like criminals and ruffians and fools."

"We've got them, Tradd," I said, holding a wet cloth over my hurt eye, amused at Tradd's prissy discontent. "Gilbreath is one of them. So is Alexander. I've got three numbers from their car stickers. They've got to come to us now. They've got to make a deal with us."

"And we're going to take any deal they offer," Mark said, addressing me directly. "We don't have any bargaining power at all, Will. We know a couple of names. So what? We know they get their rocks off kidnaping knobs and niggers. So what? They got the General and we got our dicks in our hands. This is the last night we're going to play fuck around with that bunch. They're into some serious shit that we don't know about and understand. Gilbreath is one of your best friends, Will. You guys have been wisecracking for four years, and he was trying to kill you out on that beach. He was swinging from left field. I mean, serious punching. Why? He was afraid of something, man. Your being there scared the shit out of him. No, we're going to make peace with The Ten. If we've got to kiss their asses on the parade ground at high noon and give them an hour to draw a crowd, then we're going to do it."

"We don't kiss ass in this room," Pig said proudly. "Not unless we want to. We kick ass instead. We kick ass and take names and call muster. We stick together like brothers and go on secret missions for her majesty. We have adventures and great times. That was the most fun I've ever had in my life out there on the beach tonight. Man, you should have seen those bastards' faces when they looked back and saw it was me and Mark chasing them."

"I have no philosophical problem about kissing ass, as you so crudely call it," Tradd said to Mark. "I agree with you that the position of this room is vulnerable. I feel vulnerable and I haven't even gone on any of your silly, childish forays against The Ten. But I do believe that Will is responsible for all of our involvement. You must also be responsible for getting us safely out of this, Will. You owe all of us that much, at least."

"You guys don't understand," I said, appealing to Tradd and Mark. "We're smarter than they are. We'll win because we use our heads better and we'll take more chances than they will. They can't match the imagination of this room. The creativity. They don't know what we'll do next because we don't know. We're unpredictable."

Mark's voice was strained and febrile as he answered me. "I'm not creative, Will. And I'm not that smart. But I'm smart enough to know you can get us out of this. But barely. You can barely get us out of this safely. I want to finish out this year. I'm like Tradd and I just want to be safe, Will. Do you understand that? Safe! Be smart and creative as hell. But think about making this room feel safe again. You owe that to the three of us."

"I'll take care of The Ten today," I said. "They'll have to come to me with terms. I'll make a deal with them. We'll keep our mouths shut if they let Pearce finish out the year. We've got them by the short hairs, boys. They're absolutely powerless."

"I wonder what they'll tell the General about that broken window," Mark thought aloud. "I couldn't believe it when I saw you throw that brick."

"The window's cheap," I laughed. "I took down a chandelier with that brick."

"Will," Tradd shouted in alarm and disgust. "Those chandeliers at the General's home are priceless. They're famous in the lowcountry as being among the finest ever brought to the New World from England. They cannot be replaced."

"Let him replace it with a light bulb. That's what he gets for letting his house be used as a torture chamber."

"You don't destroy beautiful things to make a point," Tradd argued.

"It was an attention-getting device, Tradd," I said. "It worked. It got me more attention than I've ever gotten in my life."

"Listen to me and Tradd," Mark said earnestly. "And make us safe again, Will."

Pig came up to my bunk and whispered to me so the others couldn't hear, "They're chicken shit, Will. You and I are the only two men in the room."

"These guys are just getting cold feet, Pig," I said, proud to be included in the ranks of men by the strongest man I knew.

"They're not like us, Will. They don't like being out there on the high wire. That's when you and I are at our best, when we're on the high wire."

Two days later, Cain Gilbreath, representing The Ten, made the approach for terms after military science class. His face was more swollen than mine, even though we both looked like we had used our faces to chop wood. We greeted each other with elaborate formality, exchanging pleasantries about our families and the baseball team, and both of us assiduously avoided any acknowledgment of the scene on the beach. The bandages on our faces and our half-closed eyes were enough acknowledgment. We arranged to meet in his room before evening formation that night to discuss "certain subjects," as he put it.

He was sitting at his desk when I entered his room, his neck and shoulders dominating the alcove. He was barechested and I saw again the scar's angry engraving in his flesh. He smelled of soap and English Leather. He was shining his belt buckle with Brasso and an old shine cloth. Grinning ironically, he gestured to a seat in front of him, and I sat down to talk. He avoided my eyes, and I thought about the terrible sadness in the death of our friendship.

"Let's have a debate," he said, beginning the talk with an old strategy between us.

"What about?" I said, taking my cue.

"Let's debate Vietnam."

"You always beat me when we debate about Vietnam," I said. "Let's pick another subject."

"Current events," Cain said, looking at me.

"Name the event."

"It happened yesterday in Columbia. A guy named Bobby Bentley had an accident up at Carolina. He fell down a flight of very steep stairs and broke both his arms. It's a theory of mine that guys who wash out of the plebe system are clumsier than guys who stay in and take the heat."

"That's a fine group you belong to, Cain," I said, controlling my anger.

"I don't belong to any group, Will," he said.

I laughed and said, "The name of the group is The Ten

396

and I know the names of five or six members. And I might know the names of a lot more."

"I've never heard of that group, Will," he said, polishing his brass with renewed vigor. "It must be new on campus."

"Cain, I don't know why you wanted to talk to me today. But don't bullshit me anymore. I saw what went on at the General's house the other night."

"Nothing went on, Will," he said, holding the brass up to the light. "That's what I wanted to talk to you about. It's important that no one ever hear about what you saw the other night. Very important. And it's for your sake and not mine."

"I don't know, Cain," I said. "I've got this big mouth and I just love to hear it run."

"Bobby Bentley suffered a terrible accident," Cain said coldly. "It could have been worse."

"Get off it, Cain. Am I supposed to start trembling when you make your stupid little threats? Am I supposed to beg your forgiveness? You mess with me and I'll go to the newspapers faster than you can throw gasoline on a kid tied to a chair."

"Pearce has made it, Will," Cain said. "That's the only thing your interference accomplished. Pearce stays if you can keep your mouth shut. I'm authorized to tell you that."

"I thought you didn't belong to The Ten."

"Never heard of it," he answered. "It's obviously a product of your overworked imagination. But Pearce is going to breeze through the rest of the year. In fact, Pearce claims he never left his room the other night."

"I'll remind him of the honor system, then I'll ask him the same question. If he lies, court will be in session just the way it would be for any other cadet."

"Go ahead, Will. Be a star. But if Pearce does go up before the honor court, which I seriously doubt, he will be found innocent. Of that, there's absolutely no doubt."

"So you've got someone on the honor court, too."

"Bobby Bentley was very badly hurt, Will. Very badly," Cain replied.

"So if I promise to keep quiet and Pig and Mark also promise, then we've reached a stalemate. We haven't told Tradd anything," I lied.

"How do we know that, Will?"

"I give you my word," I answered. "Now do we have a deal?"

He rose from his desk and walked to the door. He looked out onto the gallery, making sure no one was listening to our conversation.

"I don't know, Will," he answered enigmatically. "You don't understand how angry you've made some very important people. I called you here today as a friend, not as a member of any club. I was told that if you keep quiet, everything will be all right. But I'm not so sure. I don't believe that."

"Why, Cain?" I asked, suddenly feeling both nervous and vulnerable.

"There's danger, Will," he whispered. "I don't know what kind. I don't know what anyone can or will do. But there's danger and I can't help you. I wouldn't help you if I could. If I were you or Mark or Pig, I would resign from school today. Today! I wouldn't wait another minute. Get the fuck out of here and take an extra semester to graduate from Carolina. They're going to be watching you, Will. They're going to try to get you."

"Who shall I look out for, Cain?"

"Everybody," he said desperately. "Get out of this school, Will. Please get out of here."

"They can't do anything, Cain. I know too much."

"Maybe you do know too much," he answered.

"I'm not worried about those assholes, Cain," I asserted. "I'm really not."

"I would worry, Will, if I were you. You think you know a lot, but I'm telling you that you really know very little."

"I'll go to the Bear. I'll see what he has to say about all of this."

When I mentioned the Bear I saw a change come into Cain's flat, disengaged expression. He went to his locker and retrieved from it a small, badly focused photograph. He handed me the photograph and again checked the door for uninvited listeners.

It was a picture of four masked cadets surrounding a bound and naked freshman. In the background was a figure estranged and disembodied from the others, the unmistakable figure of the Bear, smoking his cigar and overseeing the proceedings with a malevolently inappropriate grin. The chandelier I had ruined hung above the freshman. I was trembling as I studied the face of the naked prisoner bracing against the ropes. It was Poteete. I took the photograph and put it in my shirt pocket. At first, I could not unbutton the pocket.

"How do I get out of this, Cain?" I asked. "As my friend, tell me how I get out of this. Do I have to go to the newspapers?"

"If you go to them, Will, people will think you're crazy. Pearce will swear he never left the barracks. I'll swear I never left the barracks. Pig and Mark never saw Pearce. It will be ugly. You'll be kicked out of school for lying and for reflecting discredit on the Institute."

"I've got friends on the honor court," I said. "They'll believe me."

"You'll be kicked out for lying," he repeated.

"I need time to think. I need time to plan. I'll go see Pearce today and make him admit he was at the house."

"You won't know when they decide to move against you, Will."

"Thanks for warning me, Cain. At least, I know there's danger now," I said, getting ready to leave. "By the way, you haven't apologized for hitting me the other night."

"I didn't hit you, Will," he said seriously. "I was in my room all night. You must have dreamed that."

"I must have dreamed that Mark hit you, too. And you must have dreamed the same thing. Your face looks like shit."

"Being funny isn't enough anymore, Will," Cain said. "It's time to be serious. One last piece of advice."

"What's that, Cain?"

"Watch who's behind you when you go downstairs and keep away from the railing on fourth division."

"Good-bye, Cain."

"We're never going to talk again, Will," he said, shaking hands with me. "I've enjoyed knowing you, but it's over between us. It's gone too far and I can't help you anymore. I just feel sorry for you."

* * *

Pearce was asleep in his second battalion room when I found him in the late afternoon. His room was flooded with rays of direct sunlight in which numberless motes of dust rose and fell like colorless, microscopic balloons. I heard the lion roar in Hampton Park as his feeding time approached. As I studied Pearce's face before I woke him, I wondered about his mixed and untraceable bloodlines, wondered what abducted tribes had combined to produce such furious hand-someness. I was sure that Pearce had descended from men and women unafraid of lions. He had proven that to me by walking into second battalion and into history on that first day of plebe week earlier this year. I shook him awake and he stared at me through the dusty sunlight. His brown eyes fixed me with their strength. A knob was not supposed to have strength in his eyes, especially one doused with gasoline and hurt with electricity only a couple of days before. His eyes alarmed me.

"Last time I saw you, Pearce, you smelled like a Texaco station," I said.

"Pardon me, Mr. McLean," he answered, warily standing at attention and bracing before me.

"Hey, at ease, man," I said. "You know what I mean. When they threw gasoline on you the other night."

"No one threw gasoline on me the other night, Mr. McLean," he answered.

"So they got to you, Tom, my good man," I said.

"I've slept in my room every night this week. Just like always, sir," he said.

"You know I'm on the honor court, Pearce," I warned him.

"I've been right here in my room, Mr. McLean. You can ask my roommate."

"You can help me now, Tom," I whispered urgently. "You're home free. They won't bother you anymore. They won't hurt you, but I'm afraid they're going to try to hurt me and my friends. If you back me up about the other night, they won't be able to make a move against me. Without you, my roommates and I are out there all alone, Tom. And it's cold out there. You know how cold it is."

"It's warm in here, Mr. McLean," he said flatly. "I'm never going to let it be cold again."

"Will you just tell the truth if I need you?" I pleaded. "If it's absolutely necessary to call on you?"

"The truth is that I haven't left this room at night all week," he said. "I never went to any house and don't know what you're talking about, sir."

"I didn't mention any house," I said. "How did you know there was a house?"

"You mentioned a house when we met on the dock at the yacht basin," he replied quickly.

"Yeh, I did, Pearce," I said angrily. "Do you remember

how frightened you were that night? Do you remember the two guys who came up to you at formation? Who wrote the number ten on your back? Who tied you naked to a chair? Who sent electric current through your dick? Who threw gasoline on you? Do you remember breaking the other night, Pearce? It wasn't that long ago. They had you, my friend. You'd cracked and you were gone when that brick came through that window. You'd be sleeping at home right now if I hadn't followed you to that plantation. That was a lynch mob that had you, Pearce. That was rape, man. And they'll keep doing that to kids year after year. Just what they did to you. And they'll make liars out of people. And if you're not careful, Pearce, you'll become just like them. You'll wear the goddam ring and lose your soul in the process."

A voice from the gallery behind me said, "My, but that was a very pretty, highfalutin speech."

I turned and saw John Alexander and his Siamese twin, Braselton, entering the room. Their belt buckles gleamed like jewels above their groins; their shoes sparkled when they reached the sun in the middle of the room; their shirt tucks were impeccable. The crispness of their appearance was so flawless that they looked like something cultivated, vegetables grown for refinement instead of nutrition. At that moment I hated it that I was a slob, a gross senior private with grunge on his brass and lusterless shoes. With his overzealous grooming and relentless attention to every extraneous detail of military dress, Alexander had always made me feel that I did not bathe enough. I could feel dirt form under my fingernails whenever he came into view. Alexander's eyes performed a silent inspection of me. He looked at me like he wanted to holler for a can of Raid.

Then he looked at Pearce and smiled warmly.

"At ease, Tom," Alexander said to the freshman. "We just came in here to make sure Will wasn't hazing you or violating any of the rules of the fourth class system. A lot of cadets are afflicted with racial prejudice, Will, and we've had to take extra precautions to protect Pearce here."

"You've got some business with Pearce, Will?" Braselton asked me, grinning.

"Yeh, Braselton, me and Pearce are thinking about opening up a Kentucky Fried Chicken franchise outside the Gates of Legrand."

"Hey, that's good. That's really a good joke, isn't it, John?" Braselton said, turning to his friend for approval.

"No one ever said McLean wasn't a riot," Alexander said. "Do you think Mr. McLean is a funny guy, Tom?"

"Yes, sir," Pearce said.

"I think he's the funniest guy I ever met," Alexander said. "I laugh every time I think of Mr. McLean."

"Me, too," Braselton agreed. "He's hysterical."

"How have you been sleeping, Tom?" Alexander asked. "How did you sleep last Monday night, for instance?"

"Very well, sir. I didn't wake up once, sir."

"I wish I could say the same," he said with a laugh. "That damn train wakes me up every night as it crosses the campus. You'd think I'd be used to it after four years. Then that damn lion started his roaring about three and kept me up for an hour. Yep, that was on Monday night, all right."

"Man, I slept like a log," Braselton said. "How'd you sleep, Will?"

"Not so good," I said, turning away from them and facing Pearce directly. "I had bad dreams. I dreamed that I got a note that said a friend of mine had been taken off campus. I dreamed that I broke barracks and found my friend tied to a chair with men in black masks dousing him with gasoline. Two of the men are in this room now. I dreamed I checked the parking stickers of two cars, and these two men, wearing masks, started walking toward my friend with fire in their hands. My friend started screaming."

"Sounds like a terrible nightmare, Will," Pearce said, and the two cadets behind me exploded with laughter.

"It's Mr. McLean to you, dumbhead," I screamed, pounding my fist on his chest and throwing him against the wall. "Now rack your fucking chin in, knob."

"Oh, dear, it looks like a sweat party," Alexander said mockingly.

"McLean's bucking for rank," Braselton said, in the only amusing aside of his mediocre and emulative life.

"Hit it for fifty," I shouted at Pearce, who dropped instantly to the floor and began counting out the push-ups.

"One, sir, two, sir, three, sir . . ." he counted.

"Faster, dumbhead," I ordered.

"Five, sir, six, sir . . ."

"Where were you Monday night?" I screamed in his ear.

"In my room, sir."

"Is that an official statement, dumbhead?" I asked. "As a

402

member of the honor court, I'm asking you: Do you swear you never left the room on that night?"

Pearce looked up at Braselton and Alexander. Looking at them, not at me, he said resolutely, "Yes, sir, I swear it."

Rising, I faced the two cadets near the doorway. "So you can't even leave the honor system alone."

"I don't know what you're talking about, McLean," Alexander responded.

"You sound paranoid, McLean," Braselton added.

Pearce was still doing pushups when I knelt beside him and whispered into his ear, "Thanks, Tom. Thanks for everything. If I ever need you, I'll leave a note in *The Decline of the West* by Oswald Spengler, between pages three hundred eight and nine."

40

The meeting we held in the room that night was both dismal and funereal in tone. I had lost the aggressive cockiness I had brought back to the room from the General's house. I had begun the day all feisty, unconquerable, and eager for the fracas; I had ended it timorously, defeated by a superior strategy. There were six weeks before June week and graduation. I suggested to my roommates that we become invisible until that time. I told them of my visits to Gilbreath and Pearce, of my rising awareness that we were helpless before the inspired, solitary malignancy of the intrigue against us. Their conspiracy was vast and all-enveloping; it included generals and commandants; it controlled the honor court; it co-opted its victims; it was spectral, incorporeal, and evil.

I spoke distractedly in a nervous dispirited voice, which had an alarming effect on Tradd and Mark. They instantly perceived the vulnerability of our position and its maddening elements of uncertainty. But on Pig, it had no effect at all. He was immune to the terrors of the unforeseeable future. He lacked all capacity for sustained worry or the distraught vigilance that comes from paranoia. I told them my greatest fear was that I did not know for sure that there was danger.

We could not know until they either moved against us or did not.

"I thought I could beat them," I admitted to my roommates. "I thought I was smarter than they were, that I could outwit them and make them come to me, accept my terms. I wanted to make them crawl. I wanted to humiliate them. Because they were secret and special and elite, I wanted to prove to them I was just as special as they were. They beat me."

"They beat all of us," Mark said, trying to make me feel better.

"You're always nosing around in places and situations where you have no business at all," Tradd scolded. "This was silliness in the first place and it's pure silliness now. All of us should be studying for exams, but instead we have to waste our energies on this juvenile nonsense. I don't think this tacky club has either the power or the inclination to waste their good time thinking about the members of this room. I think we should ignore the events of the past week, mind our own business, and get over it. We must put our trust in the fact that those 'enemies,' as Will calls them, are also our classmates. I don't think we have anything to fear from classmates. But I think we owe this entire unfortunate turn of events, Will, to your gigantic ego."

"I thought I was rooming with Tradd St. Croix," Mark said. "I missed it when he turned into Sigmund Freud."

"Will knows that what I'm saying is true," Tradd said.

"They've got me scared, Tradd," I said, looking at the gentlest and most sensitive of my roommates and the one whose judgment I trusted most during times of crisis. "I feel responsible for Mark and Pig going out to the house the other night. I may have even dragged you into it. Now I want to get all of us out of it and I'm not sure how to do it. But I think we've got to fold our tents, keep our mouths shut, and be careful. I think we should stick close together, only go out together, protect each other, and keep our noses clean. If I can tell Cain that we're no threat to The Ten, that we'll never tell anyone what we saw out at the house, then maybe they'll forget about us, maybe they'll let us finish out the year without trying to get us."

"I'm sick of talking about these assholes," Mark said. "I'm sick and tired of it. If they try to pull anything, then let's worry about it. But there's enough hot air in this room to fill up the Goodyear Blimp."

"How will they know their secret is safe with us?"

Tradd asked me, ignoring Mark. "How do we assure them that they can trust us?"

"We don't," Pig said, speaking for the first time during the session. "That's the worst thing we can do. That and letting them know that we're afraid of them. I say fuck them and the horses they rode in on. If they try to hurt anybody in this room, then they'll have Dante Pignetti paying them a social visit. If they give us any shit I'll tie Cain Gilbreath up to the tracks and get the name of every fucking one of them. Then I'll pay lots of social visits. I'll wear white gloves and full dress and I'll kick ass so hard they'll think it was D-Day on this campus."

"We don't know what they might have planned, Pig," I protested. "It could be anything. They pushed Bobby Bentley down a flight of stairs in Columbia. I tried to call him but he's checked out of school, and his mom won't tell me anything."

"They try to push me down a flight of stairs, I'll make them eat those fucking stairs," Pig exploded, flexing the muscles in his arms. "Then I'll make them eat Columbia. Fuck them. Let them be afraid of us. We haven't done anything wrong, man. They have. We've got to act like we've got the world by the balls, like we're not afraid of anybody or anything on earth. We've got to do what they don't expect."

"In this rare case, I think Pig might be right," Mark said. "The one thing we've got is knowledge of what that group is like and what they do. If they try to fuck us, then we fuck them. If they let us alone, then we let them alone. We'll just wait to see what happens."

"This is no time for juvenile bravado," Tradd said. "I agree with Will."

"It don't matter what you and Will think, paisan," Pig said. "Because Mark and I can kick the shit out of both of you any time we want to."

"So what!" Tradd flared. "Do you think that can change the way I think a single iota?"

"Sure it can. People have a tendency to believe everything I say when I'm breaking their arm," Pig said affably and without belligerence, only stating facts according to his vision of the world. "Now I declare this chicken-shit meeting officially over."

"Cain said that you, Mark, and I ought to drop out of school, Pig," I said.

Both Mark and Pig laughed heartily over that one, and

the subject dropped after Pig said, "He doesn't understand that Pig loves life on the high wire. I told you that the other night. That's where I belong, man. That's how I want to live."

41

They did not make a move. We did not hear from them. We received no ironic messages in our mail slots nor any menacing communiqués slipped beneath the door to our room, and after a week of vigilance we concluded that our silence had appeased The Ten. We said nothing to anyone about the events at the General's house. Each day was a small victory in our war of attrition. Each day we moved closer to the day when we would graduate, when we could be invulnerable to the displeasure of The Ten.

But it was easy to forget about danger when lulled into a false consciousness of safety by rituals that had not changed in a hundred years. It was difficult to perceive the hazard of those days when the city was so serenely beautiful and the gardens so flawlessly tended. The earth ripened in extravagant, sunstruck greens, and there were thunderstorms late every afternoon. The water dried quickly on the parade ground, and the campus was lovely to walk across at dusk. The life of the Corps went on as always. There was drill on Tuesday and physical training on Thursday; there were intramural games on Wednesday and parade on Friday. There were eight o'clock classes, morning room inspection by the tac officers, and the food in the mess hall was plentiful and hot and very bad. The days grew warmer and the custodians had to cut down dandelions that grew up overnight on the parade ground. Cadets began lying naked on the rooftops of the barracks to get tanned for weekends on the beach. A sophomore fell asleep in third battalion while sunbathing and received first-degree burns on his genitals. Three freshmen were missing for a day when their Boston Whaler broke down while they were fishing in the Gulf Stream.

In Charleston, black vendors began to sell fresh tomatoes and okra in the city market. Fresh flowers beautified the windows of mansions along East Bay Street. Men in shirt sleeves contentedly pushed their power mowers along the lawns of the suburbs. April was the last month you could buy oysters in the city, and the restaurants began scratching them from their menus. The trawlers with their black, mended netting began moving out of Shem Creek before daylight to shrimp the fertile shorelines along the barrier islands.

We relaxed and began to think more of graduation than of The Ten. We worked on our senior essays, spent long hours taking notes in the library, flirted with the women who checked out books, sent out graduation notices, and prepared ourselves mentally for life outside the Gates of Legrand. We knew the pleasant fatigue that comes from long hours of study. At night, we ate cheese and sardines on crackers in our room and prepared for the last exams we would ever take at the Institute. We all but had it made.

On the first Wednesday in May, Pig came into the room with a letter he was waving in his hand.

"I got the letter," he said to me.

"What letter?" all of us asked simultaneously.

"The most important letter in my whole life, paisans. I'd like to make an announcement in this room. This is going to make you guys even happier than it's made me. I feel happy just thinking how happy all of you are going to be."

"Tell us, for godsakes, Pig," Tradd demanded. "We've still got exams coming up."

"I've been as busy as a one-legged man in an ass-kicking contest all week long," said Mark, who had already begun to study for the night. "If I don't do some serious studying I'm not going to graduate with my class."

Pig smiled and said, "Theresa and I are getting married next Saturday."

"What?" Tradd said, shocked and disbelieving.

"Have you lost your fucking mind, Pig?" I said.

Mark sneered. "What mind?"

"She's flying to Charleston on Saturday morning and Father Bridges is going to marry us secretly at St. Mary's downtown. Everything is set. And I'm going to have three best men instead of one. All three of you paisans are going to be up at that altar when the Pig says his vows."

"Why don't you just wait until graduation like everyone else, Pig?" I said. "Otherwise, you'll get kicked out of school if someone finds out."

"Just have patience, Pig," Tradd advised. "It's only a month away from graduation and then everything will be legal. Then there can be a nice formal ceremony in the chapel with all your friends attending and a reception at Durrell Hall."

"We don't have the money for a nice wedding, paisan," Pig said, his countenance darkening. "That's one of the problems. And we're tired of waiting and we're flat broke anyway. We finally talked her parents into it, and I want her to be my wife when I walk across that stage in June. I want her to be Mrs. Pignetti."

"I can't believe that we had that long conversation about being careful last week, Pig, and then you announce that you're getting fucking married," I said.

"Hell, Will," Mark said. "We all know at least ten seniors who're secretly married already. It's no big deal. If asshole-breath wants to get married, then let him get married."

"Isn't anyone going to congratulate me?" Pig asked in a wounded voice.

"Congratulations, Pig," I said quickly. "And it's not that we're not happy for you and Theresa, it's just that we're worried about this other thing. Also, you and Theresa have always been married in my mind. I've always thought of you together."

Tradd came over to Pig and shook his hand warmly. "You're marrying a wonderful woman, Pig. And you know that I mean that."

"Yeh, I can't believe a sweet thing like Theresa is going to have to watch you take a shit while she's brushing her teeth for the rest of her life," Mark said, grinning broadly and pummeling Pig's back. Then Mark embraced him joyfully and with a raw animal vitality that made the room spring to life again. Mark lifted Pig off his feet and the two strong boys spun in a slow, exuberant circle as Tradd and I reached up to slap Pig's large, grinning head.

When Mark let Pig down to the floor, Tradd jumped up into Pig's arms and shouted, "Practice carrying me across the threshold, married man."

Pig reverently bore the limp and sighing Tradd across the room, hurled him without ceremony into a lower bunk, fell on top of him, and began humping him with joyful ferocity.

"Get this beast off me," Tradd screamed.

"Be gentle, Pig," I cautioned through my laughter.

"I bet Theresa does that to Pig," Mark said.

"Hey, don't say that about my girl, man," Pig moaned. "My God, I'm almost ready to come."

"Don't you dare, Pig!" Tradd squealed, scrambling out from under those great powerful arms. "Gross," Tradd muttered, straightening the creases in his trousers. "The thought of your semen makes me ill, Pig."

"I'm gonna name my three sons after you bastards," Pig announced.

"Tradd Pignetti," I said. "That's the stupidest name I've ever heard of."

"Yeah, I thought about that," Pig said seriously. "I'll name my youngest kid that. He'll be too little to know how fucked up that name is."

Mark groaned and said, "Can you believe ol' asshole-breath is going to be married Saturday? It seems like only yesterday that he got his black belt."

"It often seems to me, Pig, that you're not even old enough to get your driver's license," said Tradd.

"That reminds me," Pig said, snapping his fingers, "I've got to work on my car tonight and tomorrow to get the ol' clinker ready for the honeymoon trip."

"You can't work on your car at night," I said.

"Who can't?" Pig answered. "I hang a light on the hood and give the ol' girl a tune-up. I've done it plenty of times before."

"During evening study period?" Tradd asked.

"It's the best time. It's cool and the tacs are sniffing around in the barracks then. They never check the parking lot. But I need to ask you guys a big favor."

"Ask and you shall receive, my son," said Tradd.

"Man, I hate to ask this, paisans. I really do. It hurts me worse than you'll ever know. But you guys have been so wonderful about sharing money with me."

"How much do you need, meatbrain?" Mark said, reaching for his wallet.

"No, let me finish, paisan," Pig said to Mark. "I've wanted to say this for a long time. All of you here know I didn't have enough money to go to college. None of you ever mentioned it to me once in four years. Yet anytime you had money, I had money. Anytime I needed it badly, you got it for me. I mean you guys have been so great it makes me want to cry to think about it. I've already talked this over with Theresa, and we want all of you to know that you've got a home and a place to stay anytime you need it."

"Goddam it," I said, embarrassed and moved at the same time, "shut up and tell us how much you need."

"No, let me finish. I couldn't have made it through this

school without you guys. I wanted you to know that I realize that. I didn't have anything when I came to this school. Now, I'm not saying nothing against my family, man, and all of you know it. I'm proud of them, so proud I can barely stand to think of it because they worked their tails off to send me all the money they could. I never wanted to ask you guys for money. It hurt every time, but you guys never made me feel small when I did it. That's why you're going to be my brothers for the rest of my life."

"Next time I'm rooming with all rich kids like Tradd," I said.

"Me, too," Tradd agreed. "No more poverty-stricken wops for me."

"How much do you need, asshole-breath?" Mark asked.

"I've got twenty," I said, counting out eleven bills on my desk.

"I'll take it," Pig said.

"Here's thirty and congratulations," Tradd offered.

"I've only got five, but I'll cash a check tomorrow," Mark said. "By the way, what's the uniform for the funeral?"

"Full-dress salt-and-pepper," Pig said. "With sash and swords."

I said, "I'll have to borrow a sword."

Pig explained. "That's for the arch."

"How can three people form an arch?" Mark asked.

"Improvise," Pig said exuberantly. "Hey, thanks, guys, and I'll be in the parking lot if you need me."

"Don't get caught, Pig," I warned. "Or you'll be serving restrictions on your wedding day."

"Just stay here tonight, Pig," Tradd said. "Let's talk about your wedding. I'll call Mother and see if she can't have a small reception for you and Theresa."

"Yeh, don't take a chance on some tac busting you while you're changing a sparkplug," Mark said.

"Pig lives on the edge of madness. On the fucking edge." He grinned wildly, saluted us, then kissed us all on the cheeks before he disappeared into the darkness.

As Tradd selected some books from his shelf and placed them in his briefcase, he said, "I'm going to go to the library, then call Mother about arranging a reception for Pig and Theresa. Pig really should have stayed in the room."

The room grew quiet after the departure of Tradd and Pig. Mark flicked on the radio to an FM station. The music was uninspired, but it did not intrude on my thoughts and had a calming effect on me. I went to my desk, put on the lamp, and tried to start a paper on *The Portrait of a Lady*. I had never liked Henry James before I read that novel, had never expected to, and had considered him one of those irritatingly voluble novelists who used the language as if he hated English-speaking people. But he had moved me deeply with the story of Isabel Archer.

I heard Mark turning the pages of his chemistry text. He cleared his throat and shifted irascibly in his chair. He turned the radio down, then turned it up again. All the windows in the room were open and there was a breeze off the Ashley River.

I began my paper but began it badly. I never began things well. The first sentence had too many adjectives. So did the second. Remembering that my professor in the modern novel, Colonel Masters, a shy and excellent teacher, had chided me gently about my irrepressible love of adjectives, I started again with clear simple sentences. Nouns and verbs, nouns and verbs, and occasionally, to satisfy my own simple lust, I would throw in a delicious, overwrought adjective or two. I wrote six sentences, six strong sentences, then I thought about Annie Kate. I was doing that less often now. When she first left me, I could think of nothing else. Her tyranny over my dreams and my daydreams was unshakable and complete. The memory of her filled me with sadness. Isabel Archer had reminded me of Annie Kate and that had made the book cut deeply. And still I could not tell anyone of Annie Kate. She was still my secret, my shame, my love. I had thought of a thousand reasons to hate Annie Kate, but I was not capable of hating her. I had been hurt my first time out, the first time I had ever given my love completely, without holding back and without reservation. I had been hurt and I would survive it. I had given her the whole banquet, the whole shy feast of boyhood, and Annie Kate, as was her right, had decided that she did not want it. I wrote some more about Isabel Archer, and I wrote simply again and in a way that would please Colonel Masters.

As I wrote, the radio played on the edge of my consciousness and I heard Mark stir again. I liked it when I could feel myself study, when I was serious about it, when I was thinking about subjects that had nothing at all to do with life in the barracks. I loved the ritual of my room during evening study period. I cherished the silence in the barracks. Ritual was safety. I would study for the rest of the year and only leave my room for classes and formation. An hour passed quickly. Then there was a disturbance in the barracks.

It sounded far off, remote as an explosion on a star observed by an astronomer. But the noise grew louder, and Mark clicked off the radio and strained to hear it.

In a few moments we heard feet running on the gallery. Mark left the room to investigate. I walked over to his desk and cut the radio back on and turned it up loud. I would investigate nothing for the rest of the year. My curiosity had burned out on the General's island. I was a theme writer again, I thought, as I began to hear the old familiar sound of cadets whispering outside the alcove, of messages being passed, and rumors being borne along the arches of the galleries. Rumor moved with astonishing swiftness in the barracks, a system of communication developed out of a prisoner's instinct for survival behind stone walls. Voices grew louder outside my door. I heard shouting. I walked to Mark's desk again and turned the radio even louder. On the quadrangle, far below me, I heard the OC and OG ordering cadets back to their rooms. The entire barracks was alive, and all the cadets were pressing along the railings, staring through the arches, listening for innuendo, making judgments in the darkness, passing time and whispering. The loudspeaker crackled into life, and a voice commanded, "All cadets in fourth battalion will return to their rooms immediately. I say again. All cadets in fourth battalion will return to their rooms immediately." I refused to hear the voice, the voices. I was panic-stricken for no reason. I wanted Mark to return. I wanted Pig and Tradd around me. Desperately, I began writing again, flipping through the pages of *The Portrait of a Lady*, copying passages I had marked in ink.

The barracks became quiet again, but still I could feel the cold undercurrents, the whispers of discord loose among the arches again. I could hear the demons astir in the sally port, and I could see them fixing their baleful, inexhaustibly evil stares up on fourth division. It was not a premonition; it was an unconscious form of knowledge. The eye of the beast was on my room again. I felt it; I knew it; I had summoned it. I turned the radio up louder and switched it to a rock station. I tried to write about Henry James again but instead kept writing Annie Kate's name over and over again and wished that she still loved me, would do anything if she still loved me.

There were voices outside my door. I recognized one of them. I loved one of them. The beast, lathered and exhausted, had climbed the long circling stairs to the fourth division. His hooves clattered in my brain, nervously, impatiently. I thought he would attack me as he had before, frontally, the assault from the sea. But not this time. The beast had watched me for too long and knew my weakest points. He had killed Annie Kate's child as a sign of his powers, a monstrous proof of his existence. He had caused Annie Kate not to love me because he knew that would hurt even more than the death of the child. I had created the beast out of my doubts and neuroses, had fattened him on my nightmare, had made him hideous with my self-loathing, had taught him my secrets of deception and manipulation, and had nurtured him on my loneliness. He came to me only when I was limping and damaged and vulnerable, when all defenses were down. He never arrived when I was healthy, glowing, and eager for the fray. No, he made his black overtures only when I gave off a scent of frailty and weakness. He would see me trembling and I would hear his loathsome, volatile approaches cutting off my exits. The galleries were silent again.

The door opened.

Pig was led into the room by Major Mudge and the Officer of the Guard.

"This man is under room arrest, Mr. McLean," Major Mudge said without looking at me. "He is not to leave this room except under guard. Mr. Pignetti, report to my office at 0800 tomorrow to inform me of your decision."

They left the room. Pig and I stared at each other.

"Will," he said, and his voice broke me.

"Will," Pig said again, as though my name were a cry of help.

"What happened, Pig?" I asked. "Tell me everything that happened. Is it bad?"

Outside the door I could hear the murmuring voices again as the high-velocity winds of rumor began their roaring along the gallery.

"You've got to help me, Will," he begged, and it was begging, not asking.

"I can't help you until I know what happened," I answered. "Please sit down and tell me what happened."

"You can get me out of it," he said desperately, clutching at my collar and ripping off my R Company insignia. "You know them. They're your friends. You can talk to them and make a deal with them. Tell them we'll do anything."

"What are you talking about? What happened, for godsakes? Talk to me, Pig."

"You sit on the honor court," he said. "You can convince them that I'm innocent."

413

"Honor court!" I shouted at him. "What the fuck did you do, Pig? Did they get you for a goddam honor violation?"

"It was a setup, Will," Pig said despairingly. "I've always been careful. I'm too good to be surprised. But they knew I was there. They were watching me. They were hidden. I didn't see them until it was too late."

"Tell me what you did, Pig," I said, trying to remain rational.

"Don't you see, Will? They knew I was going to be out there. I was followed. I was followed out of this room and they waited until they saw me do something wrong, then they caught me. You were right, Will, they're going to try to get all of us. One by one."

The door opened suddenly. Mark walked into the room, his face dark and surly, and without speaking to either Pig or me flung open Pig's locker and began throwing his uniforms onto the floor.

"Start packing, asshole-breath," Mark said fiercely to Pig. "Start packing and don't talk."

Pig went over to Mark with his hands held in the air in a supplicatory, defeated gesture and said, "Please, Mark, don't do this to me. I need you guys now more than I ever have. I need the help of the paisans. I have to have it. I'm dead without your help."

"Pig," Mark exploded. "You poor dumb bastard. You're dead anyway. You're dead, boy, and there's nothing anybody can do about it. Will, Mudge and the OG caught Pig out in the parking lot with a gas can and a siphoning hose, unscrewing the gas cap from a car that wasn't his. Pretty, huh? Isn't that a pretty little crime? It makes a lot of fucking sense after we just laid over fifty bananas on him right before he went down to steal gas in the parking lot."

"Oh, Jesus," I said. "Oh, Jesus, Pig. It's over. They caught you doing that?"

"I can't resign, Will," he said pleadingly. "I've got to beat the rap. You've got to help me beat the rap."

"There's no rap to beat, Pig," I said, my voice putting distance between us. "There's nothing to do. There's no case to fucking try. You got caught red-handed when you knew they were after you, after all of us. It was stealing, period. The only thing left for you to do is resign and move to some other college. You're out of this school, Pig. I can promise you that. You might as well take off your ring and throw it into the Ashley River. You're gone, Pig. You're out."

414

Pig grabbed me and shook me violently. I thought he was going to begin hitting me with his fist. He raised his fist but did not strike.

"You shut up, Will," he threatened. "You shut up now or I'll hurt you bad. I'll break bones and hurt you. There's got to be a way. You know all the members of the court. You could talk to them. You could get to one of them. You're one of them."

"You touch him and I'll kill you, Pig," Mark said, moving toward us.

"Do you want me to pay them off, Pig?" I said to him. "It isn't the fucking Mafia over there. I go around talking to guys on the court and they'll ship me out of here along with you. What do you want me to tell them, Pig? What do I say to them? Help me out, man? Do I say that my good friend, Dante Pignetti, was out for an evening stroll in the parking lot with a gas can and a siphoning hose? Pig, you've got to resign. I've been on the court. I know the game. You go before the court and the drums will roll for you, boy. All of us will be on the parade ground after dark with those drums beating and you walking the line between us. You just don't have the right to put us through that. We don't deserve that from you."

"I thought you were my friend," he said.

"I am your friend, Pig," I said softly, laying his head on my shoulder. "This is your friend talking. Your friend is telling you to resign."

"What about the Army?" he asked.

"That's over for now," I answered.

"What do I tell my father? My mother? How can I tell Theresa? We're getting married on Saturday. I can't call off the wedding. How can I tell my family and my fiancée that I'm getting kicked out of the Institute for an honor violation? I'll be disgraced."

"You are disgraced, meatbrain," Mark snarled, moving in between Pig and me. "Get it through your fat Italian head. It's finished."

Pig looked at me and said, "The honor court's my only chance, Will. Will you defend me before the court?"

"You'll lose, Pig," I said, dropping my eyes from his. "You'll lose and it'll be much worse for all of us."

"Will you defend me, paisan?" he insisted. "I'm begging you, paisan. I'll get on my fucking knees and beg you. I need you, paisan."

"You'll lose, Pig," I said again. "Do you hear me?

There's nothing to defend. There's nothing to say. There's only the mercy of the court, and I've been on that court. There's not that much mercy there. I'm not merciful when I'm on that court. You just sit in judgment and if a cadet lies, steals, or cheats, you kick him out. It's much better for you to resign with an honor violation pending against you, Pig, than to walk to the drums. You've seen people get drummed out of here, Pig. We must have seen twenty or thirty guys leave that way. There's nothing worse than can happen on this campus. Man, it's hard walking between those lines, walking the length of the regiment, with your friends turning their backs on you and swearing never to speak your name again."

In horror, Pig said, "Will you speak my name again, Will?"

I looked directly into his eyes and said, "Not if you leave on an honor violation, Pig."

"You won't even speak my *name*, paisan?" he asked disbelievingly, as though the reality, the untenability, of his position was reaching his consciousness at last. "You won't even say my name or be my friend or come to visit me and Theresa?"

"No," I answered.

"And you, Mark?" said Pig.

"You know the system, Pig," Mark said, turning away from him. "You've been a part of it. You leave on an honor violation and it's like you've died. No, it's like you never even existed."

"But we've been through too much," he protested vainly. "We beat the plebe system together and we made it all the way to the end of our senior year together. We fought them all the way, the four of us, together, as brothers, as close as any guys in the world can be, and now you're telling me that I'm not even going to be a name to you. I'm not even going to be a *name* to you? I'm not even going to be alive to you."

"Shut up, Pig," Mark said. "Be a man."

"You be a man, Santoro. It's my ass we're talking about. It's my life that's going to be ruined. It's my parents I'm going to have to tell. It's my fiancée who's going to be hurt. How can I look Theresa in the eyes and tell her I was dishonorable? She wouldn't believe it. She knows me too well."

"You *were* dishonorable," Mark said. "Now accept the consequences. There's nothing more to be said. I don't want Will to defend you before the court. I won't let Tradd do it either."

416

"Why not?" Pig asked. "Will you please tell me why the fuck not? I have a right to be tried."

"Because I don't want them defending someone who's guilty, someone who doesn't deserve to wear the ring."

"You son of a bitch," Pig said.

"You're a guy who siphons gas for nickles and dimes, meatbrain. You're a two-bit crook. You don't take it like a man when you get caught. You want to drag Will through the slime with you. You don't have the guts to go it alone."

"It ain't your ass, Mark. That's the difference." Pig was screaming now.

"Boy, you really are a big-time thief, Pig," Mark screamed back. "A real first-class operator with style written all over you. There's something you don't know, Will. Something that Pig isn't telling you that I heard down in the guardroom."

"Shut up, Mark," Pig pleaded.

"When they caught Mr. Big Time, he was opening up the gas tank of a certain car with cadet number 16407 on the sticker. It's all in Major Mudge's report."

"That's my car," I said, puzzled.

"That's right," Mark said, pointing an accusatory finger at Pig. "The ol' paisan, the ol' brother, the ol' meatbrain was getting ready to steal from his fucking roommate who'd just lent him twenty bills."

"I didn't want to ask you for any more money, Will," Pig explained in a desperately humiliated voice. "I've asked for too much already. I didn't want to bother you. I knew you wouldn't mind."

The door opened, but none of us looked up as Tradd came into the room. He walked over to Pig in his graceful, diffident stride ,and embraced him. He held him tightly for several moments, both of them close to tears.

"I'm sorry, Pig. I'm sorry for everything," Tradd said in a barely audible voice. "This is terrible."

"If I don't have you, paisans, I don't have nothing," Pig said.

"Have you seen the door?" Tradd said to me.

"What do you mean?" I asked.

"Open the door and see for yourself, Will," he replied.

I went to the door and opened it. There was no one in the alcove and the alcoves were deserted. Then I saw it on the door, freshly painted: the number 10.

All of us gathered around that number and studied it as

though it were one of those grotesque totems nailed to trees along perilous frontiers to warn visitors that they were entering a country where none of the natives were friendly. It was a sign that they were watching us, that they would come for us and did not mean to take prisoners. With the number they were claiming Pig as the first victim in their vendetta against us. They were stalking us and they wanted us to know it. We looked anxiously at each other, brothers again.

Finally, Pig spoke. "You've got to try to help me now. I deserve that much."

"You do, Pig," I said, transfixed by the crudely painted numeral on the door. "We better start preparing your case. The court will meet tomorrow night and we're going to have to sling shit all over that courtroom. Mark, will you go tell Gauldin Grace that Pig will stand trial and that the three of us will defend him? Tradd, will you go with him? None of us should go out of this room alone from now on."

"Tradd's not a part of this," Mark said. "Surely those pricks know that."

"We don't know what they think," I said. "Will you go tell Gauldin?"

"Yeh, I'll tell him."

But it was Tradd who seemed most unnerved by the sign of The Ten on the door. He shrank away from it as though it were a manifestation of virulent prophecies scribbled like obscene graffiti on the walls of holy places. He smeared the number with his hand as though erasing it would eliminate the terror and threat in our lives.

"You OK, Tradd?" I asked.

"Sad, Will," he answered. "Just very, very sad."

* * *

Convocations of the honor court on the top floor of Durrell Hall were always conducted with an inflexible and saturnine efficiency. There was absolutely no sense of felicity or horseplay in the dark official room, with its formal leather chairs, its immaculately polished mahogany table, and its deeply grained walnut paneling. The room looked as if it had been built by a melancholy carpenter whose specialty was coffins. I had seen the mere gravity of this room unnerve an accused cadet. I would always associate honor with dark wood because of my experience in that room.

Most cadets never saw the honor court, but no one who did ever forgot its relentless solemnity. For some cadets it was their final interior glimpse of the Institute. For others, the room represented the first time in their young lives that they were required to function as agents of vengeance, as factotums and enforcers of a strict, intransigent code of ethics.

I watched the entrance of the twelve members of the honor court who would hear the case against Dante Pignetti. I knew all of them well, had learned about their personalities, their flaws and weaknesses, their strengths and virtues, during the thirteen cases I had sat on through the year. We had weighed evidence together, argued frequently and sometimes bitterly, agreed and passionately disagreed, but eventually, we had passed judgment on the lives of our peers. I had come out of the experience respecting the integrity and honesty of all of them. There was a sense both of power and of suffering in rendering such irrevocably final decisions. I had seen some of them cry unashamedly after casting guilty verdicts. They had seen me do the same. The system was imperfect and it was brutal. But I had learned something during my tenure on the court: None of these boys received pleasure from hearing the drummers begin their slow dirge in front of second battalion. We did it because we believed in the system and its concept of honor. But belief alone did not prevent the court from making you older. That was the court's ineffable gift to you. They looked like twelve octogenarian children as they filed into their seats. They looked terribly old and distraught as they heard Gauldin Grace call the court to order and listened to the prosecuting counsel read the charges. This was the trial of a classmate and at the Institute that was the most serious thing of all.

After the charges were read, Gauldin addressed Dante Pignetti. "The accused will rise and face the honor court."

Pig lifted off his chair beside me and walked stiffly and unnaturally to the center of the room, equidistant from the prosecuting table, the defense table, and the highly polished table of the honor court. His shoes sparkled and his uniform was freshly pressed. Pig was impressive and handsome in his uniform, though this was the single room on campus where military bearing and proficiency meant nothing at all.

"How do you plead, Mr. Pignetti?" Gauldin asked officiously.

"Not guilty, your honor," he answered in a firm controlled voice.

"Would the prosecutor please present his opening statement."

The prosecutor was Jim Rowland from third battalion,

an extraordinarily bright and conscientious cadet who had been accepted at Harvard Law School. I knew he would not have undertaken the case unless he thought Pig was guilty beyond a doubt. It was not a propitious sign to see Jim in the desk opposite us. He had one of those refined discriminating intellects whose powers of logic were more than equal to my powers of obfuscation. He adjusted his glasses as he rose from his desk and ran a distracted hand through his short-cropped bristly hair. He studied his notes, which were written in a meticulously neat script on a yellow legal pad. I had never seen Jim Rowland smile once while performing his duty. The honor court had selected its sternest, most competent prosecutor to try Pig's case.

When Jim Rowland presented the facts it seemed to be the most open-and-shut case I had ever heard appear before the honor court. He simply recited the events and circumstances leading up to the moment when Mudge and the OG caught Pig unscrewing the gas cap of a car, with a siphoning hose draped around his neck and a gas can in one hand.

"So you see, gentlemen," Rowland concluded, "there is no case to try. There is nothing to be considered. No deliberation is necessary. Cadet Pignetti was caught in the very act of stealing. I will present the two witnesses who apprehended Cadet Pignetti. They will testify that this cadet," he said loudly, gesturing at Pig, whose neck stiffened, "is guilty, as charged, of the honor violation of stealing. There has never been such an open-and-shut case of stealing since I have been at the Institute," he concluded, echoing our own thoughts exactly.

"Your opening statement, Mr. McLean," Gauldin said.

Stepping to the center of the room, I saw out of the corner of my eye the figure of Mark massaging Pig's tense, formidable shoulders. Pig's whole body had tightened since we arrived in this room, and he was flushed with the effort to control his panic.

"I would like a ruling from the court, your honor," I said to Gauldin. "I do not understand the exact nature of those charges even after the opening statement by the prosecution."

Jim Rowland jumped to his feet and said, "I will be glad to clarify those charges, your honor. I will make them as simple as possible for Mr. McLean. He must have a serious problem if he does not understand the charges as presented."

Several members of the court snickered at this but were

420

silenced by an icy glance from Gauldin, who allowed no levity in his court.

"Cadet Pignetti is accused of stealing, Mr. McLean," Rowland continued. "Those are the charges. Do you understand them now?"

"What ruling do you wish the court to make, Mr. McLean?" Gauldin asked.

"What did Mr. Pignetti steal, sir?" I asked Gauldin. "I'm still rather confused."

A buzz of perturbation swept along the table of the honor court, but the rap of Gauldin's gavel silenced them.

"Why is Mr. McLean stalling?" Rowland asked the court. "Is he wasting our time because his case is so weak?"

"I don't understand your point, Will," Gauldin said. "Would you explain yourself to the court?"

"I want to know what Mr. Pignetti stole," I repeated.

"He stole gasoline from a car in the fourth battalion parking lot," Gauldin explained. "Is that not correct, Mr. Rowland?"

"That is correct, your honor."

"How much gasoline?" I asked.

"He was apprehended in the very act of stealing," Rowland said. "He had not completed the act."

"Then he stole no gasoline," I said.

"Technically, he stole no gasoline, but only because he was caught before he could complete the theft," Jim said, looking at me with complete exasperation.

"Then, Mr. Rowland, you are saying that Major Mudge caught Mr. Pignetti *before* he was able to commit an honor violation."

"That is not what I am saying at all, Mr. McLean," Rowland said, understanding the nature of my strategy at last. "I am saying that he caught Mr. Pignetti in the very act of committing an honor violation."

"But if he stole nothing, Mr. Rowland," I insisted, "then there is no honor violation. There is no stolen property in this case."

"Will, I see absolutely no merit in your line of reasoning," Gauldin said, rapping the table again even though he made no ruling.

"Mr. Grace," I said, turning away from Jim Rowland, "may I remind you and the other members of the court that the code says that a cadet will not lie, steal, cheat, or tolerate any cadet who does. The code says nothing about a cadet thinking of lying, contemplating cheating, or planning to steal. The code punishes those who do, not those who think about doing. Mr. Pignetti stole nothing. There was no gas in the can when he was apprehended. If there was no gas, then I suggest there was no theft. You are punishing Mr. Pignetti for what he might have done, not what he did. The honor code does not cover such cases."

"The court rules that you are playing with words, Mr. McLean," Gauldin said, looking to his right and left to catch glances of approval from other members of the court. Eleven such glances were forthcoming.

"I'm discussing proof, Mr. Chairman," I argued. "There was nothing stolen. There is no evidence to present to this court. There was no property taken."

"It's obvious that Mr. Pignetti was planning to steal. The only reason there is no evidence is that Major Mudge interrupted the theft," Gauldin countered.

"Then we should be grateful that Major Mudge prevented Mr. Pignetti from committing an honor violation. It is irrelevant to discuss what Mr. Pignetti might have stolen. Unless he actually stole some gasoline, there is no theft. None. He has been accused of stealing. The code unequivocally states that stealing will not be tolerated. Show me what Mr. Pignetti stole. How much did he steal? This court has no right to kick a man out of school for something he might have done."

"The court has already ruled that you are just playing with words, Mr. McLean." Gauldin spoke sharply. "We do not have time to play with words. We need to resolve this case expeditiously."

"Let me remind you, Mr. Chairman," I responded, "that the honor code is made up only of words, that every time the court convenes it is only to 'play with words,' that you open and close every session with words, and that you condemn and expel cadets from the Institute with words. We would like the court to alter the charges. We would like you to say that Mr. Pignetti was apprehended in the parking lot the moment before it looked like he was going to steal. That is not playing with language. That is being precise with language."

"I am not at all convinced by your line of reasoning, Mr. McLean," Gauldin said impatiently.

"I am not trying to convince only you, Gauldin," I said, my eyes moving to the other members of the court. "I am

422

trying to convince a single member of this court that since there was no theft, there was no honor violation. If I can convince just one of my friends on the court that my roommate does not deserve to be kicked out of school for something he was about to do, then my roommate will graduate with us in June."

"Objection, your honor," Jim Rowland said, rising. "I object to Mr. McLean's involving his friendship with members of the honor court. This is irrelevant to the case."

"Sustained," Gauldin agreed, nodding his head.

"I do not mean to belabor this point of language, your honor," I continued, "but I would like to cite a precedent case for the benefit of the court. In 1928, when the Institute was still located at its old site in downtown Charleston, there was a vegetable stand frequented by cadets directly across the street from the school. The owner of the store complained to Institute authorities that cadets were stealing quantities of vegetables from his store. The Commandant of Cadets at that time amended the honor code and made it a specific violation to steal vegetables from this particular shop. A Cadet Kersey from Roanoke, Virginia, was brought to trial for stealing an onion. He was brought before the honor court and accused of stealing vegetables. Does anyone on the court wish to make a conjecture on how this case was resolved?"

"Objection, your honor," Jim Rowland said, an expression of pain and annoyance on his face. "This is irrelevant and a complete waste of the court's time."

"How is this relevant, Mr. McLean?" the chairman asked.

"Because of words, Mr. Chairman," I said earnestly. "Because of the way we are trained to think by the Institute when we are members of the honor court. We are trained to ignore nuances. When I told that story, all of you made a note that Cadet Kersey was obviously guilty of stealing a vegetable. They found that onion in his pocket and the storekeeper had seen him take it. I thought he was guilty too when I studied the history of that case today in the library. But the honor court of 1928 found Cadet Kersey innocent. They found him innocent because of words, gentlemen. Cadet Kersey had not stolen a *vegetable;* he had stolen an *herb*. The honor code did not cover the stealing of herbs and because of that case the honor code was amended and improved to cover the theft of anything, be it animal, vegetable, or mineral. But it was not amended in such a way that it covers cases such as this present one. When Mr. Pignetti was

423

apprehended, he had no vegetables and no herbs and no gasoline. He had not yet stolen anything."

"I rule that your line of reasoning has absolutely no merit, Mr. McLean," Gauldin said, hammering the table once again. "And I think you are hurting your case much more than helping it."

Before I could respond, Pig angrily muttered a slurred, barely audible word that caused every eye in the room to fix on him in amazement. The word did not register with the court, but it registered instantly with Tradd, Mark, and me. Pig had called Gauldin Grace a motherfucker in Italian.

"I would like to request a brief recess before Mr. Rowland calls his first witness, your honor."

"Granted," Gauldin said, looking at Pig.

I walked to the table where Pig sat, red-faced, anxious, and sweating profusely. Sweat was pouring off his face, and Tradd was wiping him dry with a white linen handkerchief monogrammed with his initials. The gesture moved me and reminded me of Bo Maybank massaging me with his towels.

We gathered around Pig solicitously. Mark tenderly rubbed Pig's thick, taut shoulders, trying to get him to uncoil and relax; his entire body was flexed and his breathing came hard.

"Pig," I whispered to him, "it won't help your case to call the chairman of the honor committee a motherfucker. I know you're under enormous pressure, but we can't afford any more outbursts. We've got to keep the faith, paisan. That bullshit I just slung all over the court probably didn't work, but all we've got to do is convince one of those guys. Just one of them, Pig. It has to be unanimous to throw you out of here. You just concentrate on staying cool. We're not going to call you to testify so you don't have to worry about blowing up on the witness stand. But don't piss these guys off by muttering under your breath every time a ruling goes against us."

"Be cool, meatbrain," Mark said softly.

"They're going to kick me out of here," Pig said, staring wildly at us. "They're going to kick me out of this school. I can feel it. I can feel it in this room, man. It's like I'm attending my own funeral."

"We haven't finished blowing smoke," Mark said, his mouth close to Pig's ear.

"It's just disgusting how copiously Italians perspire," Tradd said, wrinkling his nose and continuing to wipe the sweat from Pig's forehead. "American bodies are simply incapable of producing such moisture."

It was the first time Pig had smiled since the night before. It loosened all of us, and we went back to our chairs and awaited the moment when Jim Rowland would call his first witness. As we listened to the testimony of the OG, I placed my right hand on Pig's shoulder and squeezed it, as we endured the flat, monotonous testimony, which damaged Pig grievously with its assuredness and its utter simplicity. Mark continued to massage Pig's neck and shoulders while Tradd dried the sweat on his face. All of us were holding on to Pig, protecting him; by touching Pig, we were touching each other, felt the connection of our time together, the depth and awful brevity of our common history, and the dazzling intensity of our friendship. We had gathered in an indissoluble band around our endangered friend, and we touched him because it was the only form of speech or communication available, our only way of telling him that we were with him at the lowest and most vulnerable hours of his life. A transcendent feeling of superhuman, perfect solidarity with my friends overwhelmed me at that moment. I was dizzy with love and dread. I was connected to the heartbeats and pulses of my roommates by a benign, vital symbiosis, and I felt that I depended on them for blood and oxygen, and if one of them had abandoned the rest of us at that very instant, my spirit and my body could not have absorbed such trauma, such loss.

The OG's testimony was brief and flawless. Jim Rowland led him through his lines with admirable economy. The defense table did not object once to the testimony nor did we cross-examine the witness when Jim had finished.

Major Mudge entered the courtroom with an imperious leanness and stride. He was sworn in and repeated the exact testimony of the OG. Only the phraseology and the emphasis differed at all. Mudge had a surprisingly dramatic flair as he spoke, stabbing the air in front of him with a perfectly manicured index finger, which moved as thoughtlessly and precisely as a metronome. To be fair, his testimony pained him deeply. Though as the tactical officer of R Company he had always cheerfully loathed me, he had liked Pig a great deal.

When he finished speaking, Mark rose for the cross-

425

examination. He approached Mudge with brio and hunger, stealthy and quick-limbed.

"Major Mudge," he said, "I have no problems with your testimony at all. But I would like you to describe the automobile from which Mr. Pignetti was about to steal the gas."

"Certainly, Mr. Santoro," Mudge answered, consulting his notes. "It was a gray 1959 Chevrolet badly in need of a wash."

"Whose automobile was it, sir?" Mark asked.

"I don't know who the car belonged to, Mr. Santoro. I considered that irrelevant. But the sticker number on the car was 16407."

Mark removed a sheaf of papers from the clipboard he was carrying. "Would you please look up that number, Major, and tell the court the name of the car's owner?"

"Objection, your honor," Jim Rowland protested. "I also find this line of questioning completely irrelevant, but that should come as no surprise to the court, since the entire defense we have heard tonight has been completely irrelevant."

"I assure you, your honor," Mark said quickly, "the ownership of the car is extremely relevant."

"It can't hurt anything to know who owned the car," Gauldin ruled. "If you would be so kind as to enlighten the court, Major."

"The vehicle is owned by . . ." Mudge said, going down the numerical listing of all the automobiles registered on campus. Then he stopped, confused, and looked over at me. "The car is owned by Cadet McLean," he said. "I should have known. It was really in need of a wash."

There was a bewildered murmur among the members of the honor court. The faces of the individual members registered surprise and even anger. They looked at Pig, at me, and each other as it occurred to them that if Pig was, indeed, the thief, then I was the victim.

The victim kept his hand on the thief's shoulder and the thief in a natural, unconscious gesture placed his hand over mine.

"I have no more questions for the Major," Mark said.

"Then call your first witness," Gauldin ordered as Major Mudge made his exit.

"I would like to call as my first witness Mr. Will McLean, your honor," Mark said.

"Objection, your honor," Jim Rowland shouted. "Mr.

McLean is a member of the defense. He cannot be both a member of the defense and a chief witness."

"There's nothing in the honor code that says that, your honor," Mark shot back.

"Overruled," Gauldin said wearily. "Swear the witness in and let's get on with this."

It was a lesson in perspective for me to take the witness stand and face the same honor court on which I had served my entire senior year. These were all my good friends; yet, on this night, their collective gaze was harsh and malevolent. The members looked at me as they were required to do, as a witness and not as a friend.

As I waited for Mark to question, an abstract, disjointed thought began troubling me. Pig's dilemma had demonstrated that the concept of honor meant very little to me at all or at least not when it involved my friends and their security. If I could help Pig get out of this room unharmed and safe, I would tell any lie I could and I would tell it under oath. I would commit an honor violation as easily and simply as I adjusted my uniform belt in the morning. But the realization was troubling only because it was worthless. We had reached a critical juncture where not the wildest, most egregious falsehood could help Pig. Our only chance was to confuse the honor court. That was the strategy we had evolved in an all-night vigil in our room as Pig's last and only chance. But we had also decided, the four of us in a secret vote, that a lie might help Pig and I was the one selected to tell it under oath. The honor committee would never question the veracity of one of its own members. Anything I swore to would be above suspicion. I had voted guilty on three separate occasions during the year in cases involving lying. I had felt no sense of remorse whatsoever when I heard the drums echoing across the campus for those three cadets. Now I was going to lie and I had premeditated that lie for several hours. I tried not to think about lying as I faced the blameless countenance of Gauldin Grace; I tried not to think about hypocrisy. I tried to concentrate on looking as if I were telling the truth. Only three other people would ever know I was lying, and according to the honor code they too would be implicated in the lie by their toleration of it. Our entire room was entering into the dark country of honor and there were no maps to guide us, no stars on which to fix our sextants, no bells to alert us to the dangers of cities overrun by our enemies. In this country, there were only drums and the drums were waiting, hostile and silent.

"When did you discover that Mr. Pignetti was apprehended while taking the gas cap off your car?" Mark asked me.

"Last night after Major Mudge brought Pig back to the room."

"Were you disturbed when you heard it was your car, Mr. McLean?" he asked.

"Irrelevant," Jim Rowland said. "Irrelevant and a complete waste of time."

"Overruled, Mr. Rowland," Gauldin said. "I am curious about what they are trying to prove by this line of questioning. I've been curious the whole evening about the nature of the defense."

"No, it did not disturb me," I answered. "It relieved me."

"Would you tell the court why it relieved you, Mr. McLean?" Mark said, fixing me with his expressive dark eyes.

"Because if it was my car, there could be no question of its being an honor violation. If it had been any other cadet besides one of his roommates, then it was probable that Pig was about to commit an honor violation. But because of the code that exists in our room, Pig could not commit an honor violation against me even if he had taken every drop of gas in my car."

"Objection, objection, objection, your honor." Jim rose, shouting above the attendant murmuring that ran through the court. "That is the most preposterous suggestion I have ever heard delivered between these four walls. To suggest that the honor system does not exist among roommates is preposterous."

"I don't understand what you're driving at, Mr. Santoro," Gauldin agreed.

"We are trying to explain how a code developed in our room, your honor. It was a code among the four of us. It was as important to us as the honor code and we have lived by it."

"This is the honor court, Mr. Santoro." Gauldin spoke, his voice an accurate gauge of the court's rising exasperation with our line of defense. "We did not come here to discuss the code that happened to have developed in your room. I'm very happy that y'all developed a code, but it has nothing to do with this trial."

"If Mr. Pignetti did not break the code of the room then

we can prove he did not break the honor code of the Institute, Mr. Grace," Mark said, and he raised his hands in a sign of entreaty, of subordination.

"Get on with it," Gauldin said with a sigh.

Mark turned back to me and said, "Why do you say that it was impossible for Mr. Pignetti to commit an honor violation against you, Mr. McLean?"

"Because the four of us had made a pact together. It began in our freshman year. The pact worked like this: If I had money, then they had money. If they had food or clothing, then I had food or clothing. If I was in trouble, then they were in trouble. It was an imperfect system, but we worked on it for four years. We helped each other out and supported each other with the system. Pig could not steal gas from my car because it was his gas, too. He could not steal the car because it was his car. He could not steal money from my wallet because it was his money. If he needed gas from my car, then it was his for the taking and he did not have to ask my permission."

The court groaned in a collectively annoyed chorus and Jim Rowland jumped to his feet with a vociferous objection.

"This is madness, Mr. Chairman," Jim said amidst the hubbub. "This has nothing to do with the honor system of this school. This is a pitiful attempt to subvert the system and make this court forget what brought us here tonight. Cadet Pignetti was caught in the parking lot of fourth battalion with a gas can and a siphoning hose, unscrewing a gas cap from an automobile. Those are the facts and that is why Mr. Pignetti is up before the honor court. To suggest that Mr. Pignetti is immune from the honor system if he is lucky enough to be caught stealing from his roommate is absolutely ridiculous. These arguments are not worthy to be heard by this court."

"If it was my car, then it was his gas," I said.

"I have not ruled on that last objection," Gauldin snapped at me, flustered.

"And I strongly suggest that you rule in my favor," Jim said peremptorily. "I think the honor court has had enough of this."

"Overruled," said Gauldin feverishly. It was not a smart strategy to suggest too strongly how Gauldin should rule on an objection. He was a man of resolute will, and Jim Rowland knew he had made a critical error by the vehemence with which Gauldin ruled and then gavelled the other members of the court into silence. Gauldin, though serene in appearance, had an inflammable temper, which the application of too much pressure could quickly ignite.

"When did you last fill your car with gasoline, Mr. McLean?" Mark asked.

"Last Sunday at the Gulf station by the Ashley River Bridge," I answered.

"Who was with you when you filled the car up?"

"Mr. Pignetti was with me."

"Who paid for the gasoline?" Mark asked.

"I had left my wallet in the barracks. Pig gave me the money to pay for the gas," I lied.

"Mr. Pignetti paid for you to fill up your gas tank?"

"Yes," I lied again.

"So even if Mr. Pignetti had actually taken gas out of your tank, which he did not, and even if you insist that the gas belongs to him since he is your friend and roommate, it is also true that he paid for the gas in your car anyway."

"Yes. He paid for the gas."

"But even if he had not paid for the gas, you insist it still would belong to Mr. Pignetti."

"And to you and Tradd. It would belong to all of us," I said.

"I will not even honor this line of reasoning with an objection, Mr. Grace," Jim Rowland said from his chair.

"Then I suggest you keep quiet, Mr. Prosecutor," Gauldin answered, still miffed.

"Your witness, Mr. Prosecutor," Mark said.

"I do not have a single thing to ask Mr. McLean," Jim Rowland said, coming up from behind me, grabbing the back of my chair, and looking over my head at the members of the committee. "Except this: Why didn't Mr. Pignetti just tell you he was going down to the parking lot to siphon off a couple of gallons of your gas, Will? I mean really. Even though you had this beautiful relationship in this room, please explain to me and the members of this court why Mr. Pignetti just didn't tell you that he needed a couple of gallons worth of gas and was going down to take them from your car, which, of course, as we all know by now, in this beautiful and socialistic room, was also his car."

"I don't know why he didn't tell me," I answered, grateful to be telling the truth again. "I think he might have been embarrassed to tell me."

"Embarrassed?" Jim said sarcastically. "Embarrassed? How could anyone be embarrassed in this beautiful room? All were comrades in this room. All was common property. How could there possibly be embarrassment in fantasyland, in this fourth battalion utopia?"

"I had just lent Pig twenty dollars. Tradd had lent him thirty. Mark had lent him five. I don't think Pig wanted to waste any of that money on gasoline."

"And why not, Mr. McLean?" Jim said, leaning down close to my ear. "I think fifty-five dollars is more than sufficient to buy a tank of gasoline."

"Pig was getting married this Saturday in St. Mary's Church downtown," I said. "I'm sure he wanted to use all that money for his honeymoon. I'm sure he didn't want to waste any of it on gasoline."

"You are aware, Mr. McLean, that this is a military college and that we sign statements at the beginning of the year saying we are not married," Jim stated officiously.

"Yes, I have heard this is a military college," I answered, irritated by his tone of voice, but I caught an admonishing gesture from Tradd warning me that this was an inappropriate time to practice the craft of my wiseass humor. "But I only said that Mr. Pignetti was planning to get married. The ceremony was set, his fiancée was flying down, the papers were being readied, they had both taken blood tests, but unless Mr. Pignetti had actually gone through the entire wedding ceremony, he would not have been married. It's just like the gasoline."

"Nonsense," Rowland said.

"Possibly," I answered. "But you also realize that being married while you're a cadet is not an honor violation. It's an expellable offense but only through the Commandant's Department. All of us know seniors who are married. Some of us have even met the children of our classmates."

"But flouting the rules of the Institute seems to have been common in this beautiful room."

"If you would like, Mr. Rowland, I can introduce you to a cadet sitting on this honor court tonight who is married. It's not a common practice in the Corps of Cadets but it's not all that uncommon either."

I had made an irrevocable tactical error and regretted it as soon as I had spoken. My rigid competitiveness made me want to win every single verbal joust with Jim Rowland. When I saw Fuzzy Swanson blush deeply and begin to write notes furiously on the yellow pad in front of him, I knew I had probably lost Pig one crucial vote on the committee. I had no right to forfeit any votes for my roommate because of

431

some perverse psychic hunger to illustrate the cunning of my wit.

"I hope the committee will forgive me that indiscretion. I had no right to say that and I apologize," I said, but I had lost Fuzzy Swanson forever.

"You certainly didn't, Mr. McLean," Gauldin agreed.

"So you are testifying to the court that you believe Mr. Pignetti was stealing gas because he was embarrassed to ask his roommates for any more money," Jim Rowland said.

"I did not testify that Mr. Pignetti was stealing gas," I corrected. "I testified that he stole absolutely nothing."

"No further questions, your honor," Jim Rowland said, returning to his seat.

"Do members of the honor court have any further questions?" Gauldin asked. Then he granted a twenty-minute recess while we prepared final arguments.

Jim Rowland pulled no surprises in his summation; he was not given to verbal legerdemain or tricks of logic. He had a mind that worked in cogent and predictable ways but he brought to his argument a profound integrity, a total commitment to his belief in Pig's guilt. When he finished, I knew from the silence in the room, the quality and menace and duration of the silence, that Jim Rowland had convinced at least some of the members of the court of that guilt.

Tradd lifted himself up from his seat and walked to the center of the room in his shy, unhurried gait. His voice quavered as he began to speak. The words he spoke were fragile and delicate. Jim Rowland's summation had the strength of his integrity behind it; Tradd St. Croix's summation would be a cry from his heart.

"I know the court has been angered by our defense of our roommate, Dante Pignetti. This is because we love our roommate and would do almost anything to save him from a conviction by the honor court. But there is one thing I personally would like the court to consider when you make this decision. It's something that has nothing to do with the honor code but has everything to do with why Pig was out in the parking lot that night. It's because Pig's poor. I don't mean just that he comes from a family that doesn't have enough money. I mean poor in ways that the rest of us will never be able to understand. I have always had money, plenty of money, and it never occurred to me how I would act if I had no money at all. Pig is the first person I ever knew well who is without money. You act differently when you're poor. It affects the way you view the world, and you worry

432

irrationally about how you're going to pay your tuition or buy your uniforms or borrow enough money to pay for your ring. It makes you different from everyone around you."

Tradd paused and looked at Pig. But Pig was looking at the floor and a deep crimson flush of humiliation and shame colored his face. Tradd continued, and his voice gained power and conviction as he turned back to face the members of the committee. "I would like for the court to consider carefully what Will said, what Mark said, and what I am saying to you now. The system *was* different in our room. We never talked about it because it embarrassed all of us to talk about it. But our room had to be different because of the simple yet crucial fact that Pig was poor. Will didn't have much money and neither did Mark. I was the rich kid in the room, and they had to protect me just as they had to protect Pig. If any of us received any extra money from our parents, we kept what we needed and put the rest of it into the room kitty. We pooled the money we did not need. I was not allowed to put in more money than Mark or Will. That was their rule because I was rich. If Mark, Will, and I had been rooming together we would not have had to work out that system. The system developed because Pig was in that room, and we had to figure out a way to get him money without humiliating him. Whenever he could, Pig would put money in the kitty, and those were the happiest days in the room. Normally, he would only take money from the kitty and he would always do it when we were not in the room, when we were not witnesses to him accepting our charity. But he knew it was for him. You see, we felt sorry for Pig, and guilty that he was poor and we were not.

"I think something terrible happened with our system. I think we put Pig on the dole. He was the poor kid, and we decided we would get him through college whether he asked for it or not. We turned him into a welfare case.

"I believe Pig when he tells me he took gas only from Will's car or Mark's car or my car. I believe he felt he had asked for too much already. He knew that what was ours was his for the asking. He knew that we would have gotten him more money if he needed more money, that we would have bought him gas for his car if he had only asked. I believe that Pig took the gas only because it would be one less thing he would have to ask for.

"We believe that there is nothing Pig could steal from us. If it was ours, then it was his, too. If he had been caught trying to siphon gas from another cadet's car, then there

433

would not have been a trial tonight. None of us would have defended him. But it was Will McLean's car, gentlemen, and Will McLean's gas. Pig could not steal from Will McLean and he could not steal from Mark Santoro and he could not steal from me. If there were a theft or an attempted theft, then I would like this court to show me the victim. You have heard the so-called victim testify that there was no theft. You cannot steal what belongs to you, what you know is yours. When the court deliberates, it will have to decide about the efficacy of the way our room worked.

"There has been an incredible courage in Pig's career at the Institute. He has been an exemplary cadet, a platoon leader. He finished second in his platoon during ROTC summer camp. He has studied hard and performed well for the Institute wrestling team. You must decide tonight whether Dante Pignetti will wear the ring or not. You must decide whether you are going to punish him for being poor. We trust you will think about these things, gentlemen, and render a verdict of innocent."

Gauldin Grace hit the table once with his gavel. "The court will be cleared for the deliberation of the honor committee."

For one hour the court remained locked behind the huge oak doors that led to their inner chambers. We awaited the verdict in the small anteroom across the hall where witnesses were sequestered before being called in to testify. Tradd went down to the first floor and bought a package of Marlboros from a machine in the knob canteen. None of us smoked on anything like a regular basis, but all of us smoked that night. At first, we did not talk about the case at all. Instead, we reminisced about our plebe year, about Hell Night, about the time we put laxative in the fudge, about our first weekend leave, about Christmas furloughs, rank sheets—we talked about anything that would not remind us why we were gathered together in that room. We laughed too much but the laughter felt good. It was a sweet time together and it made the waiting go faster. At times, Pig would lose the drift of the conversation, and his mind would float out alone to a place where we could not follow. His eyes never left the floor. But before the hour was up, he finally had to speak to us about what had happened in court.

"What are our chances, Will?" he asked. "You know those guys and I don't. They all looked like they would stomp babies to me."

"I honestly don't know, Pig," I answered. "I don't even

know how I would vote if I didn't know you. The case is a little strange."

"They won't kick me out," Pig said, but his words sounded more like prayer than conviction. "They won't kick me out because I'm a senior and I wear the ring and I've come so far. It's only a little more than a month before we graduate. I wasn't thinking good, with Theresa coming down on Saturday."

"When was your thinking ever good, asshole-breath?" Mark said, scowling beneath blue smoke.

"You didn't have any right telling them that my family was poor, Tradd," Pig said, more to himself than to Tradd. "They looked at me like I was shit when you were saying all that. You said it like I didn't pull my weight in the room, like I was some kind of freeloader. Hell, I always put in my fair share, paisan. You should have told them that. When you guys caught cold, who pumped you up with Vitamin C? Pig, that's who. And when you looked anemic last year, Tradd, who was right there with the old iron tablets? Pig, that's who. They should know all that. And you should have told them that my family may not have all the money in the world, but that the Pignettis are proud and don't bow their heads for no man. Those assholes don't have any respect for me. They think I'm shit. And look at them. They're all in lousy shape. I mean really poor health. I'm going to write out a weight program for each one of them, Will. No matter how it comes out, I want these creeps to take better care of their bodies. They think I don't have any pride or self-respect. I got more pride than all them motherfuckers put together. You should have told them that, Paisan."

"I'm sorry, Pig," Tradd said. "I thought they could see that. I didn't think there was any need to say something that is so obvious to everyone."

"And, Pig," I cautioned, "no matter what the outcome. I mean, I pray it's going to be good, but if it isn't, you've got to take it like a man. Do you understand? You can't kick the door of the honor court shut and beat the living shit out of everything that moves in the room."

Pig raised his hand calmly and said, "I told you that I have more pride than anyone in that room. They think I'm just a poor Italian slob. After they find me innocent, I'll go to each of their rooms in the barracks, and I'll explain to them that Tradd forgot to tell them about the pride of the Pignetti family."

There was a knock at the door.

Paul Vacendak, the secretary of the honor court, opened the door and told us the court had reached a verdict.

We knelt together in the center of that small room, held hands, and Mark led us in reciting the Lord's Prayer. Pig's hand was slick with sweat when I grasped it.

Entering the room, we took our seats and tried to interpret the expressions on the members' faces. But these boys were now seasoned veterans of judging their peers, and they gave no overt signals of how they had voted.

Gauldin Grace's voice rang out in the room. "The accused will rise and face the honor court."

Pig rose to attention and faced them with a rigid, implacable courage.

"The members of this court find you guilty as charged."

Pig's knees buckled at the sound of the word *guilty*. He staggered forward a single unconscious step as though he had not clearly heard the verdict, as though he needed clarification. Then he turned back toward us and put his arms out to us like a child asking his mother for protection.

Then he let out a cry of pain I will carry with me every single day of my life. The cry was so unexpected, so high-pitched and despairing. It was the cry of a small animal, a tiny nocturnal creature, a herbivore that depended on stealth and speed for survival. There was no strength in the cry, and it reduced my roommate to the level of prey.

We caught him in mid-stagger. Mark pulled his arm around his shoulder and took his whole weight.

"Gauldin, could we have a few minutes before we go to the parade ground?" I asked.

"Hurry, Will," he answered. "He can call his parents from the witness room. You know the procedure. And Will."

"Yeh, Gauldin," I said, unable to look at him.

"We're all sorry. It was horrible. But we voted the way we had to. The guys want you to know that they're thinking about you."

"Tell them thanks, Gauldin."

When we returned to the witness room, we sat him down in one of the wing-backed leather chairs near the door. We did not know how to look at him or how to speak to him. Already, we were putting distance between ourselves and him. We were beginning the merciless process of turning him into a stranger, someone we had never known, someone we would never know again, someone so untouchable and unclean of spirit that we would not acknowledge him on the streets if we passed him ten years hence. That was the process

Mark, Tradd, and I had begun as we fought for last words to say to him, as we struggled toward a humane and brotherly farewell.

As we sat there, we heard the drummers begin their cold tattoo of banishment on the parade ground, heard its sinister echo as it pulsed along the galleries of the four battalions, as it summoned the regiment for the drumming out.

"Just remember this," I said desperately. "This isn't the end of the world. There are other colleges and they won't even know what this fucking honor system is. They won't even know what a military school is. You can start over. The General will write you a good letter of recommendation. He'll just say you couldn't adjust to the military way of life. You've got to forget this as soon as you can."

"You've got to call your parents," Mark said. "They'll be waiting to hear what happened."

"I didn't tell them that I'd been accused of an honor violation," he said, breathing hard, as though he had just completed a long-distance run.

"What!" Mark shouted. "You didn't prepare them at all?"

He lifted his eyes as though he heard the drums for the first time. "How could I tell my parents that their son might get kicked out of the Institute? They would never have gotten over it," he whispered.

"What do you think this will do to them?" Mark said, but softened immediately. "I'm sorry. Jesus, I'm sorry."

"Do you want me to call them?" Tradd asked. "I could break it to them gently or even better, I could have Mother do it. She always knows what to say in situations like this."

"No, I'll tell them when the time is right," he said. "When it's right for me."

"Try not to think about what's happening on the parade ground tonight," Tradd advised. "Don't think about it and you'll get over it much more quickly."

I looked at Pig and said, "I've got to ask you to give me your ring."

"No," he said, furiously clenching his fist.

"You have no choice," I said, lowering my eyes. "I've got to give it to Gauldin when I leave the room."

"Let me keep the ring, Will," he begged, "I earned it. I earned the right to wear it. They're taking everything else away from me."

"Give me the ring," I said.

"It's mine, Will."

"Not anymore."

"Give him the fucking ring," Mark said savagely, turning toward the door. "You're making it too hard."

He removed the ring and threw it at my head. It missed by inches and struck the lampshade on the far side of the room.

"Be a man. Be a fucking man," Mark said. "Let's see some of that pride you bullshitted about."

"You'll see it, paisan," he said, but a light went out in his eyes and something deadly replaced that light. "You'll see it and you'll always remember Dante Pignetti for his pride. I promise you that."

"You can catch the train for New York if you hurry," Tradd said, checking his watch. "Or else you can catch a Trailways downtown. One leaves at three in the morning, I think."

I retrieved the ring, placed it in my breast pocket, and walked over to him. There was a knock on the door.

"It's time," I said.

He rose to his feet and turned toward the door with his back toward us.

"Good-bye, paisans," he said. "And thank you. Thank you from my heart. My heart, paisans."

We surrounded him and the three of us embraced him for the last time. He did not look at us and he did not return our embraces. He pulled away from us and left the room without looking back. I felt his ring in my breast pocket with my hand, and I felt my own heart beating against the gold band.

When we reached the parade ground the Corps was assembling for the drumming out. My body felt as if it had been shot full of Novocain. We did not walk; we staggered out of Durrell Hall and watched as the regiment divided into two parts, like a huge cell in the process of a grotesque, unnatural mitosis. The Corps split up into two enormous lines stretching from one end of the parade ground to the other, a thousand cadets staring at a thousand other cadets, with a corridor six feet wide between them. It was down this corridor that he would march for the last time in a ruthless parade of one. It was called The Walk of Shame by the Corps and it was the most dreaded and barbaric ceremony at the Institute. I had sent nine boys on The Walk of Shame. I had felt a perfect justification for it and had convinced myself it was the price of dishonor in a school in which honor was a sacred word. I had swelled with power at my ability to summon the sleeping regiment.

Listening to the shouts of the company commanders moving the sluggish platoons into position, dressing up to the right, I took my place at the end of the immense file, out of place, far away from R Company, but at the spot where he would take his last step on campus. There was a yellow cab parked at the north end of the parade ground. The light in the cab was on, its motor was running, and the cab driver was smoking a cigarette and reading a newspaper.

I stood between Mark and Tradd. I wanted to say something to them but there were no proper words. I wanted desperately to hold their hands, to touch them again, to make some human connection that would make the darkness right again. But I was a cadet who was well trained and I stood at attention, waiting.

The drums ceased and the parade ground was as silent as an inland sea. At the other end of the parade ground, I heard Gauldin Grace's harsh, overextended voice screaming out the findings of the honor court.

"Gentlemen, the honor court has met tonight and has found Pignetti, D. A., Company R, guilty of the honor violation of stealing. His name will never be spoken by any man from Carolina Military Institute. He will never return to this campus so long as he may live. His name and memory are anathema to anyone who aspires to wear the ring. Let him go from us and never be heard from again. Let him begin The Walk of Shame."

The drums resumed their pulse. He began his last slow walk a quarter of a mile from his roommates. As he walked between the first two cadets in the line, they performed a simultaneous about-face and turned their backs to him. The next two cadets repeated the maneuver and the next two and the next two and the next two, turning from him as he passed before them.

Nameless, he marched in step on the long unrepeatable promenade between the divided regiment. Nameless, he had become a disgraced regiment of one as he navigated the narrow green corridor of grass between the backs of boys.

There was a dark intimacy to this ceremony of excommunication. I could hear the breathing of the two thousand, but that was all. This was a ritual amazing because of its silence. I stood in the grass awaiting the moment I would renounce my roommate.

With a sidelong glance, I studied his proud approach

between the lines. I began to read the mysteries between those lines. As he walked he hurt me. As he walked, I could feel him changing me forever. As he came, I could feel my part in all of this. His face came into focus; it was set like statuary. He was marching like a creature with intimate associations with the depths, something eyeless and with a nervous system of such primitive simplicity that he was beyond pain, beyond touch. His face held a cold strange beauty as he approached, as his peers danced their about-faces in his passage, a rippling, exotically symmetrical maneuvering of the regiment, each in his own time, each a stunning duet of rejection.

I know now what I should have done. I always know it too late. Now I know what the code of friendship required of Tradd, Mark, and me. We should have left that line and made that walk with him. We should have lifted him up on our shoulders, and carried him through the lines. We should have stripped off our uniforms and hurled them at the honor committee, ripped off our insignia and epaulets and flung them at all those who dared turn from us. We should have walked together, arm in arm, the four of us, laughing and mocking, inseparable, and shouting "fuck you" to all who turned their backs on us, kicking their asses, and daring anyone to make a move toward any of us. We should have swaggered down those disciplined ranks, drunken and out of control, delirious with the powerful insulin of our shared history. We should have walked with the bright shimmer of murderous, unrepentant angels and accepted the banishment from the Corps together. We should have set the barracks on fire, salted the parade ground, and spat on the great seal of the Institute. Together, we should have gone out there in a blaze of obscenity and sacrilege. We should have become monstrous men and our salvation would have lain in the very nature of our monstrousness. We should have abandoned that campus with outrage and rebellion and wildness. We should have vomited out the bile of those four years in the barracks and walked as four against the two thousand, four against the regiment, shouting, "No, no, no, no."

But we did nothing; we were boys.

He saw us when we heard Mark sobbing. None of us had ever heard Mark cry before. It was a new sound in the universe. Mark must have held that first sob for a full half-minute; it burst out of his lungs in an explosion of grief. When Mark broke, I felt permission to break and I passed that permission to Tradd. It was a simple weeping he saw as he passed us, three boys crying and crying hard as we stood on the trimmed greensward listening to the drums that dishonored our roommate.

He stopped as he passed us by and spoke to all of us. His voice was stern and peremptory. "Turn," he commanded.

Mark had not executed an about-face when he passed in front of him, nor had I, nor had Tradd.

"Turn, paisans," he said, returning to Mark. "That's how it's played. Now turn, or they'll get you."

"Get laid, asshole-breath," Mark said through tears.

"Turn," he shouted as he slapped Mark slightly, lovingly, on the cheek, and placing one hand on Mark's shoulder and another on his hip, he kissed Mark and turned him. He kissed me and turned me. He kissed Tradd and turned him. The entire regiment now faced away from the nameless one. He entered the running cab and it pulled away from the curb and drove slowly toward the Gates of Legrand. The Walk of Shame was over.

Immediately the parade ground reverberated with the shouted commands of seventeen company commanders assembling their companies for the march back to the barracks. We walked the length of the parade ground to join R Company, passing behind the other three battalions and saying nothing to each other. I watched the slow solitary progress of the cab as it moved down the Avenue of Remembrance. I was surprised to see it stop, turn around, and come back in the opposite direction, pass us by, then drive past the military science building and disappear behind the Armory. Even in his removal from the Corps, he would refuse to honor tradition.

"Where's he going?" I heard Tradd say behind me. "He's going to miss his train if he doesn't hurry."

I glanced at the clock high atop the parapets of second battalion. It was nearly time for the 11:42 train to cross the Ashley River.

"Maybe he'll try to flag the train down as it goes through campus," Mark said. "Can you imagine how his parents are going to take it?"

Then we heard the whistle of the train as it approached the Ashley River, the old comfortable sound, as much a part of the interior life of cadets as the single note of steel, as the ritual locking of the gates at night.

It did not hit me until we had reached our platoons in R Company and then it hit me in a killing blaze of light. It hit me and I was running, sprinting again. "The train," I screamed.

I do not remember that run very well, only the strangeness of it, the odd perception of time being both motionless and frantically rushing by at the same time. I remember the battalions beginning to move out, the call of cadence, the shape of the dark chapel, the fecund smell of the Corps's trampled grass, the shadows of missiles and tanks, the flag illuminated high above second battalion, above the clock, the pavement, the sound of my footsteps on the pavement; but I do not remember the act of running. I know that I ran but the run was a dream. I ran as though I were obese and exhausted and beaten.

I saw the train hurtling across the trestle and I heard the screams of the cab driver. I saw my roommate marching resolutely toward the train, dazed, in the same resigned, unequivocal walk that had carried him through the regiment. The drums had not stopped for him nor would they ever stop. His walk was stiffly military, unbearably proud; it was not faltering or hesitant. He had gone as far as he would go. He had done all the things he would do. He had lived all the life he wanted to live. He needed one last moment of pride and honor. He was taking his powerful body toward the train. That body, which we all feared, had fears of its own and could not face a father's hurt eyes, a mother's disappointment, or the canceled wedding trip of a black-haired girl. He feared a life where friends could not speak his name. He could not think of the deeper hurt and it was not in him to think of it. As always, he was ruled by the tyranny of instinct, by passion and the instant legislation of a simple heart. We had turned our backs on him, but now he was walking to a place where there would be no turning away, no loss of contact, no refusal to acknowledge or touch. He would make a last insane connection. The train would not turn for him. There would be no about-faces.

"No!" I screamed while the terrible squeal of the brakes cut through the night air as the engineer spotted the boy on the tracks.

He turned toward me and smiled. I swear he smiled and said a single word I could not hear because of the noise of the brakes.

But I knew the word.

"Paisan," he said, and turned to meet the train.

* * *

That night the Corps learned something about a different, harsher code of honor. They found him in sections and pieces along the marsh that bordered the trestle. Those few of us who saw his body after his death still become horrified when we try to describe what the train did to him. What the train undid.

I turned away from him for a second time. I turned away and vomited, but kept walking, putting distance between me and the trestle and the marsh. People were running past me now, cadets shouting, "My God," behind me. I heard the Bear ordering everyone back to the barracks, and felt a numbness overcome me and I could not speak or cry or think. I just knew that I needed to put distance between myself and that torn, lifeless thing I had loved for four years. As I walked and as I heard the noise and tumult and confusion behind me, I understood for the first time why the punishment for Lot's wife was so severe. There were times when it was unforgivable to look back.

It was an hour later when I returned to the barracks. I do not remember where I went during that hour. The OG in fourth battalion unlocked the gate and let me pass without reporting me. I climbed the dark silent steps to the fourth division. The light in our room was on and Mark and Tradd were waiting up for me. We looked at each other but there was nothing to say.

I did not tell Tradd and Mark what I had seen by the tracks. They had already heard and asked no questions. In the mirror I saw my face. It was the face of a boy who had seen too much. Getting into bed, I began listening to the voice inside me. At first, I didn't think it was my voice. It sounded so warlike, so vengeful, so invincible. It sounded cold and evil, but it was a comfort to me in the following days when I would not leave my bed, when I only wanted to listen to the voice. "I will get them," the voice said. "I will get them."

42

For three days after the death of Dante Pignetti, I lay in my bed. Mark and Tradd thought I was mourning Pig's loss but that was not it. I was studying what special gifts I could bring to the subject of vengeance. I was biding my time and waiting for the cold black fury to pass over me.

For three days I slept over eighteen hours a day, gathering my strength and dreaming of The Ten. I tried to interpret the nature of their secret agenda against us. They had moved against cadets before and had always succeeded in their mission. Their table of organization included the President and the Commandant of the Institute. But I had knowledge of them; I would watch how they operated against the enemies who had broken their membrane of secrecy.

On the bed I was a lone, absurd figure in the history of my times, a sleeper in the century of ruthless law, of bombers over suburbs, of artillery barrages destroying the gaily painted walls of kindergartens. In my bed, I dreamed of military science classes, imaginary troop movements, and the portraits of boys slain in Vietnam hanging from the library walls. In these dreams I satisfied my own sick and overextended need to be my own greatest hero. I had a passion for the undefiled virtuous stand and a need to sacrifice myself for some immaculate cause. I knew this and hated myself for it and could do nothing about it. Ah, Annie Kate, I will marry you and adopt your child because I'm so good. Ah, Bo Maybank, of course I'll be your friend and accept your soft towels because I'm so kind. Ah, Tom Pearce, of course I will ease your journey through the plebe system because I am so saintly. Ah, Pig, of course I will defend you before the honor court even though you have been dishonorable because I am so noble. Who else would I take as prisoners of my high sanctity before my life was over?

I tried to think of Pig during this time but it was hard. I can seldom judge how I feel about an important event in my life as it happens. There is always a time lapse before I am sure exactly what it is I feel. I did know that my refusal to rise from my bed upset my roommates and alarmed my classmates in R Company. They thought it was my finer sensibilities and my greater love of Pig that put me in the bed, that separated me from the rest of them. I secretly enjoyed my honorary role as chief mourner. They thought well of me because I was not like them, because I was unable to carry on and incapable of blocking the horror of that suicide on the tracks.

"Too sensitive," they would whisper as they conferred with each other in the alcove. They did not know I was Pig's avenger and cadreman, not his chief mourner. I would open my eyes and smile at my friends, then return to the business of sleeping. I kept my hatred secret behind that smile as I always did. The smile was the weapon to keep your eyes on. I should have warned my friends never to turn their backs on my smile. But I was not talking in those days; I was looking for something. In daydreams, I saw myself cut down by firing squads in sun-bleached courtyards as I screamed out the word *Libertad* to the small tyrant who watched from the palace window. I threw myself on hand grenades, and charged into the machine-gun fire aimed by impregnable gunners. But I was not looking for that so I slept some more and could not move very well in those days or participate in the life of the campus, which continued undisturbed as it always had and always would. Nothing could still the coming of reveille, the gathering of platoons, or the striking of flags at retreat.

But I did not get in trouble with the Commandant's Department during this period, and it was one of those times I loved the Corps of Cadets with all my heart. For the Corps conspired to protect me, to give me time for collecting myself, for surrendering myself up to whatever force took up residence within when my roommate died. There were times when the Corps could be a powerful protector of its own members, and if ever its love was turned on you for any reason, you were always surprised and ennobled by the heat and fire and passion of it. During those days, the Corps reminded me that I was one of them and that I had paid my dues to the Line. They fed me, protected me from the eyes of the OC, from the gaze of observant teachers, from the interrogations of the officers, from delinquency reports, white slips, demerits, or formation reports. The Corps kept the Institute at bay until I was ready to rejoin it. And word had gotten around the Line that something smelled about the way Dante Pignetti had been run out of school. It was not a rumor, but more a feeling, vague and ethereal, which settled into the collective consciousness of the Corps. The feeling ran so strong that it took the form of a joke.

At first I was shocked when I saw Pig's death becoming a subject for cadet humor. An unknown author had scratched this line into the paint above the urinal on fourth division: *Dante Pignetti was railroaded out of the Institute.* Since all cadets were honor-bound never to speak Pig's name aloud, his death became a natural subject for the school's graffiti writers. Angry, I took my belt buckle and scratched out Pig's name. But I thought more about it and what I knew about cadet psychology and how they dealt with tragedy. They had

445

laughed at Pig's death. That was the only way the Corps could deal with it or anything like it. There was a fierce and undeniable health in their response. And beneath the humor, on a much deeper level, was the sentiment that something was imbalanced and unanswered and unjust in the death on the tracks. The Corps was wondering what it was that had driven Pig to such a horrible death.

The Ten bided their time and the days passed without incident. I got better and stronger. I waited for them to move again. But this time would be different, I told myself. This time I would do everything I had to do.

I had discovered a power unknown to me and I would use it.

The Ten could match my strategies, but not my fury.

43

I had attended military science classes for four years, and frontal assaults obsessed me. When I read military history, the romance and desperation of charges attracted my attention and respect. Marines and their sons were comfortable only with fierce, contested landings on beachheads and the subsequent inland drive, moving in a straight undeviating line and killing everything that threatened to halt their advance. This was a legacy from my father. I would rather confront and be confronted directly. I wanted to see the swift charge of my enemy as he made his perilous approach to my zone of fire. My nature did not respond as well to envelopment movements, to the stealth of an enemy who trusted in more complicated operations. I did not want to hear the twigs break in the forest behind me or quail flush before the platoon advancing on their bellies to my rear. But frontal assaults lacked subtlety and grace. That was not how The Ten would come for me and Mark Santoro.

It was on Friday in the second week of May, with the hot damp weather stealing into the lowcountry, that Mark entered the room after evening mess and said, "Well now, at least, we know how they're going to fuck us."

"What are you talking about, Mark?"

"Have you seen the latest demerit list?" said Mark.

"No."

"Well, I suggest you take a good look at it," he said. "Your name takes up a full page. Mine takes up a little more than a page."

"How many demerits did I get?" I asked.

"Not many," Mark answered. "Only thirty-two. Thirty-two big ones, baby. Ol' Mark came in at thirty-five. They've torn our room apart on four occasions in the last four days when we were in class and burned us for everything from improperly folded socks to fart stains on our underwear. At least they're not going after Tradd. That's probably because his family founded America and then decided to buy South Carolina."

"They can't do that, Mark," I said. "They can't get away with giving seniors that many demerits. Everyone will know they're after us."

"They seem to be getting away with it to me," he said. "They shipped three seniors last year for excess demerits and five the year before. It's not that unusual."

Tradd entered the room and said in a worried voice, "Did y'all see the DL?"

"See it?" Mark replied. "I *was* the fucking DL. Me and Mr. Sensitive here."

"What are you going to do about it?" Tradd asked.

"Who gave us the demerits?" I said, ignoring Tradd's question because I had no immediate answer. "Who were the reporting officers?"

"There were four different ones," Mark said. "Asshole Butler. Asshole Wentworth. Asshole Davis. And flaming asshole Allison."

"All Institute grads," I said, thinking aloud.

"Bingo, Mr. Einstein," Mark said, pacing the room. "They're going to run us out of here on excess demerits. They're going to kick us out of here a couple of days before graduation. I bet those motherfuckers time it perfectly. I bet they hit us with our last demerits right before the General hands us our diplomas."

"How many demerits do you have so far this year, Will?" Tradd asked, going to his desk and tearing a sheet of paper from his notebook.

"Before this DL I had forty-five," I said.

Tradd figured quickly and said, "You now have seventy-seven demerits for the year, Will. Since a senior is allowed a hundred, you have only twenty-three to go before you're out."

"I had twenty-three for the year when I woke up this

447

morning and shaved my pretty face," Mark said. "Now I've got fifty-eight big pimples on my shiny Italian ass with plenty of time to plant forty-two more."

"We've got to think," I said.

"Think about what, Will?" Mark said. "There's nothing to think about except getting ready for Saturday-morning inspection tomorrow. I'm going to look like the Hope Diamond when Mudge inspects me and I'm going to get every knob in R Company up here to get this room ready for inspection. I'm going to blitz down my dick and dare Mudge to give me a single demerit. And this room is going to look like Betty Crocker's kitchen."

"That won't do any good, Mark," I said. "They'll get us even if I look good as God and you look like my son. So this is how they're going to do it."

"You've got to resign," Tradd said seriously. "That is your only chance to get out of this with any dignity."

"I'm graduating with my class, Tradd," Mark said with startling fervor. "I've sweated blood with this class and I'm walking out of this dump with them."

"That's how I feel about it, too, Tradd," I said. "Only if I go, I'm going to make The Ten a household word across this state."

"That's foolishness," Tradd said. "That's just nonsense and foolishness. You must act sensibly and do what you have to do. Threats can't help you now, Will. Now you've got to salvage what you can."

There was a loud shuffle of feet in the alcove and a knock on the door. John Kinnell, the R Company commander, came through the door first. He was followed by the other seventeen seniors in R Company.

"Supreme Commander," I said to John, "to what do we owe the pleasure of this visit?"

"We're having a meeting of the R Company seniors and we thought we would use your room."

"Thanks for asking, John," Tradd said.

There were twenty-one of us left of the sixty frightened boys who had entered R Company as freshmen in 1963. We were the veterans of a thousand formations together, a hundred parades, and countless hours of the easy camaraderie that is so simple and uncomplicated among boys bound by a common goal. They came into the room loosely, joking and slapping ass, and took their seats on the desks and floor and racks. But there was a seriousness to their visit belied by all the humor and banter.

"Hey, McLean," Jim Massengale said, "you can date my sister for the Graduation Hop if you buy a flea collar."

"Who's going to pay for the roach tablets to kill all those bugs crawling around the hair on her legs?" Henry Peak added, poking Jim in his fleshy stomach.

"OK, fellas," John Kinnell said, motioning for quiet with his hands. "Let's get this meeting started."

The room fell silent. It was always wonderful to me how John could control a group of cadets by virtue of his shyness and interior serenity. He was the antithesis of the prototypical cadet leader. He lacked aggressiveness, manipulation, and all those drives and instincts that marked the others in the Corps. We had selected him as company commander for his modesty, his quiet integrity, his simple goodness, and none of us had ever had a single regret.

"We wanted to have this meeting up here tonight because we're worried about you two," John said to me and Mark. "Something strange is going on in this room and none of us knows what it is. Now you don't have to tell us if you don't think it's any of our business. And I mean that, Will and Mark. You know that I mean it. But after what happened on the tracks and after seeing the DL tonight . . . well, the guys and I started putting things together and we'd like to know what's going on. If we can, we'd like to help you."

"Who ever heard of a senior getting thirty demos on a DL?" Murray Seivers said. "Knobs don't even rate thirty on one list. Maybe I can understand you racking up that many, Will. You're a fucking load militarily, but Mark is as sharp as anyone around."

"Something stinks in Big R, boys, and you're not letting your classmates in on it," Jim Massengale said.

"We've been through too much shit together, man, to let you guys get run out right before graduation."

John said, "We haven't heard anything from Will or Mark. Tradd, do you know what's going on?"

"Someone wants to run Will and Mark out of school," said Tradd simply.

"Why?" eighteen voices asked.

"Because we found something out," I said. "We can't tell you about it now, guys. Because that's the only thing we've got going for us, that no one else knows. But if it looks like we're not going to make it, we'll tell you everything."

"You've got Romeo Company going for you, Will," John said. "And if we can help you out, we will. We wanted you to know that."

449

"Thanks, John. Thanks to all of you guys," I said. "But we're not out of here yet. We've just got to make it through the next two weeks. And it seems like the smartest thing for us to do is keep our mouths shut and hope for the best."

"To keep your mouth shut, Will," Tradd said. "That might be too much for your nervous system."

"Let's tell them everything," Mark said suddenly. "Let's tell them that we've got some mean mothers out to get us."

"Who are they, Mark?" Webb asked.

"Don't, Mark," I said. "That will only make it worse. Then we won't even be able to bargain."

"We can't bargain now," Mark said, agitated and moving about. "You see anyone in this room trying to bargain with us? Show me the son of a bitch and I'll bargain my ass off."

"Sorry, Mark," Tradd said soothingly. "Will's right. If you keep quiet this might blow over. They might be bluffing."

"If you guys can't tell us what's happening," John said, maintaining his calm, "then there's no way we can help you. You'll have to go it alone. We don't even know if anyone's really after you or not."

"Someone is really after us," Mark said directly to John. "I'll prove that to you."

"How?"

"No matter how Will and I shine up for inspection tomorrow, no matter how many knobs help clean up this room tonight, I will bet good money that he and I get murdered."

"Forget getting knobs to help," Murray said, looking at his classmates. "We'll clean your room. Twenty-one seniors cleaning a room ought to make damn sure that you sloppy bastards don't get burned tomorrow."

"All right," several voices said as the seniors of R Company began picking up brooms and dustpans, pulling our shoes and brass out of our presses, singing the R Company song as they worked.

"We *will* clean this gross room, gentlemen," said Harry.

"We *will* receive a merit or two, gentlemen," said Eddie.

"Who's going to bathe McLean?" said Murray.

"Not me," said Jim. "I'm in charge of burning his uniforms and disinfecting his socks."

"If a fly shits in here, wipe his little ass for him," said Webb.

450

"Negative, put diapers on him before he shits," said Eddie Sheer.

Mark, Tradd, and I watched our classmates in silence. Then we began the long preparation for the most important inspection of our lives.

* * *

When I walked out onto the quadrangle for inspection the next morning, my shoes were astonishing things, all black dazzle, glittering in the bright sunlight like two small lakes seen from a plane. I felt as if I were wearing two pieces of furniture instead of shoes.

The seniors gathered around me and Mark, inspecting us with their trained and expert eyes. Henry Peak brought out his shine rag and removed a smudge from my breastplate. I felt hands straightening my webbing from behind, adjusting my cartridge box, and wiping the lint from my shako.

John Kinnell brought me my rifle as if he were delivering good news to the king. I took it from him gingerly.

"This rifle better be clean, dumbhead," I said to him. "Mudge better not find any oil on this deadly anachronism."

"I boiled it down last night," John replied, winking at me.

"That's illegal, son. That's against all the rules of the Institute. I feel it is my duty as an exemplary cadet to report you to the proper authorities."

"Go ahead and report me," John said. "The inside of that rifle is as clean as a new baby's asshole. You could perform surgery with that mother and not worry about infection. If Mudge gives you any demerits for that rifle, then I'm going to tell him after inspection that I was the one who cleaned it."

"Thanks, John. Thanks for everything."

"I'd like to see them give you a single demerit," he said. "You look good. You almost look as good as me."

"I feel like a jewel," I said. "A fucking jewel. I just love shining up. I think I'm turning into a military dick."

A cadet in full-dress salt-and-pepper looked like a baroque piece from a nineteenth-century chess set. The uniform blouse, with its shiny bronze buttons and its tight cut, emphasized the curve of the chest and shoulders and the strength of the young back. The starched white pants came up high against the crotch, and the emphasis again was boldly erotic as you felt the tightness around the buttocks and the pull against the groin. Inspection, like parade, was fraught with sexuality.

451

I never felt entirely comfortable in the everyday cotton fields we wore to class, but in full dress I felt like an absurd and fantastic hybrid. But on this morning I felt pure and untouchable. There was a snap and cleanliness in the air and I was soldierly. I was ready for the Major. I stood there, alert and frisky, the sharpest son of a bitch in the regiment.

I watched as the Major approached R Company in his familiar erect swagger. I did not hear the Bear approach me from the rear. I smelled his cigar and saw the smoke come over my left shoulder. I remembered the picture of the Bear watching the elimination of Poteete.

"I thought you were dead, Bubba," he said. "I haven't heard from you in a while and the Bear gets nervous when one of his lambs deserts the flock."

"I've been right here, Colonel," I whispered. "Shining my shoes and bucking for rank. You know how I am."

"Unfortunately, I do, Bubba," he said. "You are a bum, McLean. A blight on the reputation of the Institute, a living, breathing sacrilege against all the ideals for which this school stands. Why have you rolled over and played dead with me, Bubba?"

"I know everything now, Colonel," I said. "The game is over and you don't have to play it anymore. They should have told you that."

"Told me what, Bubba?" he said, coming around in front of me, his cigar blazing near my face. "Who should have told me what? Answer me, mister."

"You set me up, Colonel," I said in a flat, emotionless voice. "You set me up and I'll never forgive you as long as I live."

"Bubba, the Bear has never been good at riddles. That's because the Bear is slow sometimes and stupid at other times. I've checked on Pearce and he's riding high over in second battalion. They're treating him like he's setting up E Company with free black poontang. But I've just gone over last night's DL and someone sure does have a hard-on when they walk into your room."

"Big shock, huh, Colonel?"

"Bubba, if you get smart with me, I'm going to burn out both your eyes with this cigar and give you an extra nostril or two in the big Irish nose. Now I don't know what's going on, but you and I are going to have a heart-to-heart before this week is up."

"No, sir," I said firmly. "I have nothing to say to you, sir."

He reached in his pocket, pulled out a handful of white slips, and waved them in front of my eyes.

"Do you see these, Bubba?" he said. "Major Kleber handed me these slips this morning. He inspected your room yesterday and tore it apart. You picked up ten demerits and that somber dago you hang out with picked up sixteen. What's going on, Bubba?" the Bear said, speaking so low no one else in the platoon could hear. "There's talk in the Corps that something's up."

"You know what's going on, Colonel. You're part of what's going on. I'm finished with people like you. It's going to be over soon."

"You aren't kidding, Bubba," he said. "You'll be filling out applications to Clemson in a few days if you don't tell me what this is all about."

"I don't need your help, Colonel."

"Bubba, you come see me tomorrow. That's a direct order. You come to my quarters or to my office or so help me Jehovah I'll crucify you without nails. I'm giving you a direct order to report to me."

He left quickly, angrily. A plume of smoke hung in the air where he had been standing as Mudge approached my platoon for inspection.

He spent five minutes inspecting Mark and I could tell things were going badly for my roommate. Then he rapidly went down the lines of cadets. I would be the last cadet he inspected in R Company. I did not feel quite so splendid when he crossed into my field of vision. He squinted as though he was observing me through unadjusted field glasses.

I snapped the bolt of my rifle open for his inspection. He snatched it from me expertly, examined it, peered into the barrel, then presented it back to me.

"Gross rifle—SMI," he said to the guidon corporal, who marked down my infraction. I could see the look of astonishment on John Kinnell's face out of the corner of my eye.

Then the Major's eyes traveled from my shoes to my waistplate, to my breastplate, to my shako. He shook his head negatively, sadly, disgustedly.

"Gross Personal Appearance—SMI," he said. "Try to do something about your shoes, Mr. McLean. They're a disgrace."

"Why are you doing this, Major?" I said. "What did they promise you? You're a West Pointer, not one of them."

He did not answer me, but he looked both surprised and

amused. He turned again to the guidon corporal and said, "Improper Behavior at SMI."

He looked back at me and smiled.

Then he left the barracks.

Mark and I both had received fifteen demerits apiece. We were the only cadets in R Company to be burned. But it was the first error of judgment The Ten had made since they had taken Pearce out of the barracks. It alerted the seniors of R Company that two of their classmates were victims of a conspiracy, a conspiracy sanctioned by the only tactical officer any of us had ever had at Carolina Military Institue.

I did not pass one hundred demerits until the following Friday, when Major Mudge conducted a morning room inspection. Mark passed that watermark of expulsion later in the day. A sense of torpor and resignation had entered the room and infected us spiritually with that species of painless despair which comes when you have accepted the inevitable and know how things inexorably must end.

We dressed for Friday's parade in absolute silence until Mark said, "It's over, Will."

"It looks that way."

"I don't want you two to talk about it around me," Tradd said, close to tears. He turned toward the open window and stood there watching two faculty wives playing a game of tennis. "I can't bear that any of this is happening. All of this has been so upsetting and there's not a single thing anyone can do about it."

"We've got to take it like men," Mark said, looking very much like a boy. "We won't crawl before those motherfuckers, Will. OK? We'll go out of here like champs."

"I'm not going to give them my ring," I said.

"You've got to give it to them, Will," Tradd said. "You've got to play their game or they won't give you your records or transcripts or recommend that you be admitted to another college. And you can't blackmail the General with what you know about The Ten because he'll make sure you never graduate anywhere in this country."

"Fuck him," I said. "I earned this ring and I'm going to keep it. I paid for it. It's mine."

"Not if you don't graduate, Will," Tradd said. "You know how the game is played."

"I'm out of the game, Tradd," I answered. "I ain't playing the game no more."

"I'm going to kick the shit out of Cain Gilbreath, John

454

Alexander, and that pimp Braselton before I go," Mark grumbled, putting on his white gloves.

"You'll have to wait your turn," I said.

"You boys are talking pure nonsense," Tradd said. "Now get control of yourselves."

"Straighten my webbing, Tradd?" I asked. "It's all twisted in the back and I want to look sharp for my last parade."

"The last parade," Mark said. "I'll buy you a drink afterwards, Will. Why don't you and your parents come along, Tradd? We'll go to Henry's and get drunk."

"We're going down to Fort Benning to look for an apartment for me when I report in," Tradd said. "And besides, I haven't told Mother and Father any of these terrible things that have been happening to you. I haven't been able to bring myself to do it. Mother was so upset about . . ."

He stopped before he said Pig's name. "We're leaving right after parade."

"Have you told your mother, Will?" Mark asked.

"No," I answered. "I want her to be happy for at least a couple of more days in her life. I kept thinking that this really wouldn't happen, that they really wouldn't go through with it. Denial is a wonderful thing sometimes."

"I want to stop talking about it," Tradd insisted.

"See what I mean about denial?" I said, going up and putting my arm around his shoulders. He was embarrassed by the gesture and pulled back shyly.

"I haven't told my parents either," Mark said, adjusting his shako. "Every relative I've got from North Philly to southern Italy is planning to come for graduation next week. It's hard to get up the nerve to tell them there's not going to be a graduation."

"Room, attention!" Tradd suddenly shouted.

The Bear filled the doorway and he moved swiftly into the room, with angry eyes blazing. He let loose with a yell that caused all of us to jump.

"Out of here, Santoro. Move it, boy. Out of here, St. Croix. Move, move. Move. Stand fast, McLean. Get those shoulders back, mister, and stand tall like a cadet. Take those beady eyes off me. You want to buy this uniform, mister?"

"No, sir, I . . ." I began.

"Shut up," he roared.

It had been a long time since I had heard the Bear in top form, using his spectacular voice like a weapon requisitioned from ordnance. Mark and Tradd sprinted out the door, their swords slapping against their thighs as they ran.

His face was flushed and agitated. Placing his thick loose lips against my earlobe he began racking me like I was a knob again.

"Mister, I thought I told you to report to me after inspection last Saturday. I thought I gave you a direct order to get your fat ass over to see me on the double. Do you think I like wasting my time tracking all over this campus looking for my wayward lambs, boy?"

"Sir," I tried to say.

"Shut up. You'll answer me when I want you to, boy. Now, speak," he ordered.

"Sir, I . . ."

"Shut up," he yelled blowing cigar smoke into my face. "Now what do you have to say for yourself, boy? I want to hear your excuse."

"Sir, my excuse is . . ."

"Shut up," he yelled again. "I'm sick of playing your little games, McLean. I'm tired of it and you're in serious trouble, lamb."

"Sir."

"Shut up," screamed the Bear, shoving me against my desk. "Unless I'm mistaken, Mr. McLean, the Institute is still a military college and you're still a cadet and you're still subject to the rules of the Blue Book even though it looks like you're not going to be subject to those rules in a couple of days, Bubba. The Bear wants to know what's been going on over here in fourth battalion and why you've started to look at me like I was some kind of low-grade dogshit."

"Because I think you're some kind of low-grade dogshit, Colonel," I said.

I thought he was going to knock me on the floor; in fact, I braced myself to be struck by the Commandant of Cadets. I didn't know if the Bear was a powerful man physically but he had a craggy, massively roughhewn face that gave him the appearance of being a fighter of extraordinary gifts. At that moment, I both hated and feared the man.

But he said nothing and made no hostile advances toward me. Instead, his eyes softened and his voice sounded hurt as he turned away from me and said, "Why, Bubba? I don't understand it."

"It's no good to act any longer, Colonel. It's over."

"You're damn right it's over, lamb," he said, waving a memorandum in front of my eyes. "This is an order from the General, Will. He wants you to report to his office at 1300 on Monday. See the color of this paper, Bubba? That's a code. Anytime the General sends me an order typed on blue paper that cadet is long gone. Long gone, Bubba, and there's nothing that can bring him back. You go in at 1300. Santoro follows at 1330. Then I meet with you, process you, and drive you to the Gates of Legrand."

"We'll go peacefully, Colonel."

"Why didn't you come to me for help, Bubba? Why didn't you come and tell me what was going on? I don't understand it. I should have seen this coming but I was too busy with the other lambs. Two thousand cadets is too many for one man. If this was VMI, I'd only have twelve hundred lambs to watch after, and you boys couldn't take a crap without the Bear being there to hand you toilet paper. But it's hard to keep up with this big a flock."

"You're one of them, Colonel," I said, wanting to spit in his face.

"One of whom, Bubba?"

"The Ten, Colonel. I've known for a long time now. So you don't have to pretend any longer. I don't even care anymore. I'm getting where I don't even want to graduate from a school like this."

"This is a great school, Bubba, so don't talk about the school."

"Yeh, it's a fabulous school. I hear botulism's a nice disease, too."

"Who told you I was a member of The Ten?"

"Another member of The Ten."

"Names, Bubba. The Bear deals in names."

"I'm not going to give you any names. I'm not going to give you anything, Colonel."

"He's a goddam liar."

"One of you is, that's for sure."

"Put a 'sir' at the end of your sentences, mister. You may be gone but you're going out of here like a cadet."

"*Sir,*" I said mockingly.

"You found out that The Ten actually exists?" he asked, and I exploded.

"I don't deserve to be played with, *sir,*" I screamed at him. "I've been played with enough in the past couple of weeks, *sir.* Your bastards have put me and Mark on fishhooks, *sir,* and let us dangle from the lines, *sir.* I've had enough, *sir.*

457

Enough, do you hear me, *sir?* Do you hear me good, *sir?* Enough, goddammit. You set me up and I walked right into the trap. The liaison for Pearce. What bullshit! I got a roommate killed. My roommate's dead because you called me to your office at the beginning of the year. It's like I put a gun to his head and pulled the trigger, *sir.* That's horrible to live with for the rest of your life, *sir.*"

"Don't you see, Bubba," he said, "don't you understand I'm the only one who can help you and Santoro? And I'm not even sure I can help you now."

"You can help me by leaving me alone," I said.

He walked over to my desk. He removed his Institute ring and laid it in the center of the desk.

"Bubba, you take this ring. You know what it means to me. I'm giving you this ring as a pledge that I'm talking the truth. The ring is my word of honor. If you don't believe me then throw my ring away. Come to my quarters when you've figured some of this out. There's not much time. On Monday I'll have to sign an order of dismissal for excess demerits. That's twelve days before you graduate, Bubba."

The last call for parade sounded through the barracks.

"Don't be late to formation, Bubba," he said, leaving the room. "I'd hate to have to write you up."

44

I did not have time to analyze the meaning of the Bear's visit or the significance of the symbolic removing of his ring as proof of his word. The gesture had moved me powerfully and confused me deeply. But I was late to formation and R Company was leaving the barracks as I hit the quadrangle and I had to sprint to overtake them. I did not want to miss my last parade at the Institute.

I loved those Friday afternoon parades at the Institute. It was the one military ceremony that never failed to please me, to satisfy some instinctive human craving for ceremony within me. It was the Corps's grandest hour, the coming together of the four battalions in a stunningly beautiful and ritualistic dance of two thousand across the parade ground.

When R Company strutted on the field that day, I felt

closer to the Corps than I ever had, felt the old solidarity and oneness of the brotherhood as they marched in unison to the drums and bugles and bagpipes. The seniors of R Company had gathered around me in a protective phalanx, enveloped me in the heart of the company, bantered with me all the way out to the field, and, in the way of the Corps, tried to make me forget for a time the events that had led to my imminent expulsion.

A vast crowd had gathered in the reviewing stand, and the richly variegated colors in their summer garments made the stand look like an enormous impressionist painting in the sunlight. American flags snapped in the wind on top of every building contiguous to the parade ground. The General, in a snow-white dress uniform, watched as the companies moved out to their positions, following the sharp flowing movements of seventeen guidon corporals. I would gladly have left R Company, walked over to where the General was standing, and beat out his dentures with the stock of my M–1, but the astonishing power of the group had seized me again, and I marched as one with the Corps, congruent with the multi-limbed kinetics of the regiment, obedient to the cadence of drums as two thousand heels struck lowcountry dirt at the same time.

R Company moved into its position on the parade ground as smoothly as a ship gliding into its moorings. John Kinnell gave the command for the company to halt. I studied Jim Massengale's ample shoulders. As I did, a mosquito the size of a thumbnail landed on the back of his neck. Mosquitoes and gnats were put on earth to test the fortitude of cadets at parade.

"B–52, six o'clock, Jim," I whispered through clenched teeth.

"Fuck," Jim sore. "I got to kill the little cocksucker."

"Hell, Jim," Murray Seivers said, biting his chin strap, "you're almost a whole man. Oniy a pussy would slap that poor little mosquito."

"Little!" Jim protested. "He almost knocked me over when he landed. Oh, Jesus! He's already sucked a gallon of my blood."

"That's a smart mosquito," Murray whispered. "He picked the fattest blivet in the Corps."

"You ever seen Jim's dick?" Webb Stockton said, joining the secret colloquy among the seniors. "It's fourteen pounds of baby fat. When he's with a girl it doesn't get hard, it sweats."

"Hey, Santoro," Eddie Sheer whispered to Mark at the front of the company, "the sun's hot as hell. How about moving your nose an inch and darkening this side of the parade ground?"

"What's the difference between an Italian and a nigger?" Jim whispered through the ranks.

"I don't know, you fat fucking creep, but I better like the answer," Mark said as we presented arms by order of the Battalion Commander.

"The spelling," Jim said.

To the audience in the reviewing stand, the companies presented an image of absolute stillness, order, silence, and discipline. But all along the ranks the companies engaged in secret interior dialogues. Cadets at parade were masterful ventriloquists and adept at not getting caught unaware by the quiet approach of a tac officer from the rear. You developed an uncanny sixth sense about when it was safe to communicate and when it was not. Yet there were moments of absolute stillness among the ranks. When we presented arms for the national anthem, not a single word was spoken. When the General announced the names of alumni killed in Vietnam, there was not a single movement or sound in the ranks. Even in breaking the rules, an inviolable etiquette was at work. The Corps made its own rules and broke them all in the proper time. Many of the jokes at parade we had heard as freshmen from the senior privates. They were part of the legacy and tradition of R Company.

"Beaver shot. Ten o'clock. Yellow dress," Jim whispered.

"That's my mama," Eddie Sheer gasped in mock surprise.

"No, it isn't," Murray said, "that's my daddy. I told him never to come to parade dressed like that."

"I thought that beaver looked funny," Webb said.

"Beaver shot, twelve o'clock," Jim said again. Jim's whole sexual life was centered around carelessly seated women at parade.

"That woman's standing up," Webb complained.

"Use your imagination," said Henry Peak.

"Hey, Tradd," I said, my eyes scanning the crowd, "there's your folks."

"Where, Will?" he asked.

"Two o'clock."

"Which one's the mother?" Webb asked.

"Please leave my mother out of this grossness," Tradd pleaded.

"She looks like a real lady, Tradd," Jim said.

"Thank you for not being gross, James," Tradd said, a little too quickly.

"Do you think she would like to sit in my face?" Jim asked.

When the Regimental Commander gave the loud resonant command to pass in review and the bagpipers led the band across the entire length of the field, I had a long moment of resigned sadness when I realized that I would miss all of this, would miss the uncomplicated camaraderie of boys, would miss being a part of something so alien yet so magical to me.

I followed the drums, submitted myself to them, as R Company moved out in a simultaneous step, the first lovely movement of our dance across the green. It was that submission to a larger will that I secretly loved about the Institute, the complete subjugation of the ego to the grand scheme and the utter majesty of moving in step with two thousand men. The drums sounded in my ear and in my brain, as I instinctively obeyed the rhythm of the Corps. "Discipline, discipline, discipline," the drums said each time my foot struck the ground. We made the turn at the far end of the parade ground and began our exaggerated, formal strut past the eyes of tourists and alumni and generals.

As we neared the reviewing stand, I followed the movement of the guidon and when it fell my neck snapped to the right at the exact moment John Kinnell completed the command, "Eyes . . . right." Faces materialized out of the blurred crowd. I saw Coach Byrum, the General, Colonel Reynolds, Abigail and Commerce, and faces of men and women I would never know as long as I lived, people I would know only on this one march, who would die for me as soon as I passed them, whose anonymous faces represented the majority of the human race.

We turned again at the opposite end of the parade ground and headed toward fourth battalion, breaking into the Romeo song as soon as we left the grass. Girls waiting for their dates gathered in shy, giggling clusters around the front sally ports. Cadets whistled at the girls. Rifle butts slammed down on the concrete in the barracks. We passed beneath the main arch and crossed the checkerboard squares of the quadrangle on the way to the R Company area. The senior privates broke ranks and began to mount the stairs on their way to their rooms.

Tradd dressed quickly and left to join his parents for the long ride to Fort Benning. He was having trouble looking at me. Mark did not come into the room until after Tradd left. He was introspective and brooding when he entered the room. Undressing, he threw his uniform into the corner on the floor.

"Let's stay drunk this weekend, Mark," I said. "That will make Monday easier. The Bear told me they were kicking us out on Monday, big fella. He was acting funny, Mark," I said, fingering the Bear's ring on my desk.

"Will," Mark said, looking up at me with his large and infinitely sad eyes.

"What's wrong, Mark?"

"Do you know when you spotted Abigail and Commerce at parade today?"

"Yeh," I answered. "That was them. I saw them again when we passed in review."

"I know it was them," he said, "but did you see who was standing next to Commerce? Standing next to him and talking like they were old friends. I mean, arms on each other's shoulders and everything?"

"They were in a crowd, Mark," I said. "I was lucky enough to be able to spot them."

"I wasn't sure when we were way out on the field," he said. "But when we passed in review, I caught a good glimpse of the guy, Will. I almost dropped my sword."

"Who was it, Mark? Goddam, I'm dying of curiosity."

He walked up to me and took my shoulders into his large hands.

"Will," he said. "It was Dan Molligen. The guy we put on the tracks."

45

For the first time since I had received the gift from Abigail, I slipped my key into the gleaming oak door of the

St. Croix mansion. Mark stood watch in the shadows of the piazza, observing an elderly couple crossing Meeting Street. It was a sad and fragrant dusk in the starless city, and a mild rain was falling. I would be leaving Charleston soon, I thought, leaving the city of the two rivers, which had imparted a passionate sense of aesthetics within me, which had given me a love of antiquity and cloistered gardens. I would be leaving the city that had taught me to fear the world.

The door opened and I stepped into the entry hall. With that single step, I betrayed the spirit of the gift and the trust of Abigail St. Croix. I whispered to Mark to follow, and as I did my voice seemed to belong to a stranger. Was it because it was a man's voice at last? I wondered, but I doubted it. I did not feel the confidence I associated with manhood as I moved through the tenebrous gloom of the house. I was afraid again, but I had lived with fear a long time now and some vague presentiment that it would always be present. Fear was an old, familiar inhabitant by now, but I had developed strategies for hiding and suppressing it. Or at least, I thought I had. In those days I was coming to realize that everything I once believed about myself had no truth or validity at all. And I did not know how to reverse the habits and testimonies of a twenty-two-year lie.

"What are we looking for?" Mark demanded. "Why are we here? Do you think we'll find Molligen in the bathroom taking a whizz?"

"I know where we might find some kind of an answer to all this," I said, walking over to the credenza in the dining room where the liquor was kept. "If I'm wrong, then the St. Croixs never have to know we entered their house while they were away. Do you want a drink?"

"Scotch," he said, as I knew he would. My hand moved clumsily among the crystal decanters in the dark and I chose the Jack Daniels for myself, the Chivas Regal for Mark. Always there were divisions of geography and preference between us, rites we observed out of habit and affection.

"Scotch tastes like orangutan piss to me," I said.

"It tastes like Scotch to me," said Mark. "I've never tasted orangutan piss."

"Open your mouth wide and say, 'ah.'"

"How can we joke at a time like this?" he said wearily as he walked into the entrance hall and sat down on the first step of the spiral staircase. "We're going to be kicked out of school on Monday."

"It won't be so bad for you, Mark. You're Italian. No one can really expect an Italian boy to finish a four-year college. It defies all laws of genetics."

"It defies all laws of chance that I haven't beaten your brains out at least once in four years," he said as he laughed.

The jokes made us feel better. We drank slowly, listening to the rain. I studied a portrait of Abigail that hung above the mantel in the dining room. It was visible from where we sat on the stairway, illuminated by a soft, diffuse light from the street. Abigail's mother had commissioned the portrait the year Abigail and Commerce were married. It was a callow, boyish face in the portrait, with a forced and unconvincing smile. The portrait failed to capture any glimpses into Abigail's fragility and bruised loneliness. It did not hint of the delicately subtle charm of her awkwardness. The only essential quality of the woman it reflected was her awesome integrity, her unimpeachable correctness. Her stare was an accusation to me.

"Do you think you've ever had a relative who's had her portrait painted?" I asked Mark.

"Naw," he answered. "We take snapshots in my family."

"Do you think if Abigail had been our age she might have been attracted to us?" I asked. "Do you think she might have fallen in love with one of us?"

"Don't talk dirty about Abigail," Mark said, displeased.

"I'm not talking dirty," I protested. "I'm serious and I'm talking about falling in love."

Mark leaned forward, staring at the portrait for some clue or manifestation from the youthful, stiffly formal Abigail. In the portrait she was exactly our age.

"Naw," he said finally. "She wouldn't have given us a second look. You and I weren't born right to get one of these South of Broad chicks. They marry birth certificates and houses down here. That's why this city's so fucked up."

"Mark, I went out with a South of Broad girl this year."

"We knew it was somebody," he answered. "We didn't see your ass on weekends for the first six months of school. Thanks for introducing me. What's the matter; does she break out in hives when she meets Yankees or were you just ashamed of me?"

"No, it wasn't like that at all, Mark," I said. "She was pregnant."

"Congratulations, Daddy," he said, squeezing my shoulder lustily.

"It wasn't my child," I said. "I wanted it to be, Mark. I even started thinking of it as mine and thinking up names for it if it was a boy or a girl. I don't know what it was—it didn't make it."

"What happened to the broad?"

"She ditched me after the kid was born dead."

"The bitch finally came to her senses, huh?" Mark said, but he saw me wince with pain and memory. "Hey, I'm sorry, Will. I'm sorry I said that. I'm just glad you're interested in broads at all. You had us wondering for a long time. I thought you and Tradd might have had something going on the side."

"Did you really?"

"Not really. But you haven't exactly been murder on the broads since I've known you. And you're so goddam secretive about women."

"I've always been interested in girls, but that doesn't mean I can talk to them unless I know them really well. I've always thought girls would like me if they ever got to know me. You know, that wonderful, sensitive guy I'm convinced I am. I always thought that they would love me if they could get past my sarcasm and my fear of them. This girl got past it all. Her name was Annie Kate Gervais, Mark. Isn't that a beautiful name? I let down all the defenses for her. I thought about her every moment. I felt alive thinking about her, on fire. I was on fire when I was away from her, too, Mark, but it was a different kind of fire. I told Annie Kate things I had never told anybody. I felt handsome around her. For the first time in my whole life, I felt handsome. I'd look in the mirror and I'd feel good about the way I looked. She changed me completely, Mark, and I'll never be the same person I was before. I'll never be happy until I feel that way about someone again and she feels the same about me. But she left me and I'm sure I'll never see her or hear from her again. See, I was sure she loved me as much as I did her. I was sure she dreamed about me as much as I dreamed about her. But I was wrong, Mark. I was wrong about that just like I've been wrong about everything else this year. I can't even look at her house now. I can't go to the places where we walked. I hurt every time I think about her. I'm afraid I won't ever find that again. And I feel ugly again, so ugly that I can't stand it."

"You had it bad, son," Mark said softly. "But that's what

465

you get for going after one of these society dames. You should have known she was out of your league. And anyway, Will, if she didn't love you as much as you loved her, then she's not worth a shit. I mean that. She's not worth a shit."

I rose and began walking up the stairs.

"Let's get this over with," I said.

"Why don't we just leave, Will?" Mark said behind me. "I don't like the way this feels. It isn't right. It just isn't right."

"We've come to the point in our lives, Mark, when being right or wrong doesn't make much difference anymore. It's the only thing I know to do. If you're sure that you saw Commerce and Molligen together."

"I'm sure."

"Then we might find out how they know each other."

"How are we going to find that out?"

"We're going to read Commerce's journals, Mark," I said, turning to face my roommate on the dark stairs.

"Are you crazy, Will?" Mark said, holding my wrist. "Have you flipped your tree?"

"What do we have to lose, Mark?" I said. "Name me one goddam thing we've got to lose."

"Commerce, Abigail, and Tradd," he said.

"I've got to try everything, Mark. Everything. Do you understand that? I got us into this. All of this is my fault. Every time I look at you I feel guilty. I think that if you only had had another roommate, then you'd dance across that stage June Week without a hitch. I could take it if it was just me, Mark. I really could. But I hurt the whole room. Tradd can't look at either one of us without practically crying. You've got to start over as an academic junior at some lousy college in Pennsylvania and lose your Army contract in the process. And one guy eats a train because he couldn't stand it. I don't know if there's anything in Commerce's journals to help us. But if we can just get a clue, something, anything that I can bluff the General with."

"Let's go," Mark said.

We climbed to the third floor and came to the locked door where Commerce had his office. I went to the palm outside his door and moved it as I had seen him do in September. The key was beneath the planter. I took it and walked to the forbidden door, the one place in Charleston where I knew Commerce felt completely safe. I inserted the key into the lock, looked back at Mark, then pushed into the room.

The office reflected the concerns and passions of a mariner. It was furnished like a captain's cabin on a ship. There were nautical charts and sextants, rare shells, and immaculate small models of every ship on which Commerce had served during his life on the shipping lanes. His desk was made from a hatch cover of a derelict vessel.

We lit a small captain's lantern and pulled the thick black curtains on the windows. On bookshelves against the wall, we saw the three rows of the leather-bound journals of Commerce St. Croix, the personal literature of one man's voyage on the earth. The journals looked like a set of expensive encyclopedias.

"Great," Mark said. "This is only going to take three years to read all this shit."

"We'll work fast and only read references about the Institute," I answered, taking the first journal off the shelf. I opened it and read the first entry. "Christ, he wrote this on his fifteenth birthday. He wasn't even at the Institute then."

"I'll go through the last journal and work back," Mark suggested. "You go through his years at the Institute and work forward."

"Each journal represents a year in his life, Mark," I said, pointing to the first page of the second journal. "We are dealing with an organized man."

"Shut up," Mark said. "I'm reading about a hangover Commerce had on New Year's Day this year in Marseilles. Holy shit, Will, Commerce had a broad in bed with him."

"Don't read the personal stuff, Mark," I said disapprovingly. "That's prying into Commerce's private life."

Mark looked up at me scornfully and said, "Oh, I see. We're going to read Commerce's journals, but we want to make sure we don't pry into his private life. Excuse me for being born stupid."

"You know what I mean."

"I find it interesting that the upper classes like to play hide the banana when they get away from their wives. Could you imagine what Tradd would think of his father doing that?"

"Let's get to work, Mark."

"We're not going to find a thing," he said.

"Maybe, maybe not."

I began reading the journal of Commerce's freshman

year at the Institute. It was fascinating to compare the evolution of the plebe system from his time to the 1960s. His knob year lacked the brutality and harassment that had marked our initiation into the fraternity of Institute men. At that time, the Institute was more of a training ground for gentlemen of the manor than anything else. There were no sweat parties in the shower rooms and no tradition for breaking plebes. Commerce had enjoyed the rituals of military drill and had flourished in the environment of an austere and congenial discipline. It was a happy boy who kept this meticulous and rather banal account of his first year. I came across one name that caught my eye immediately. Bentley Durrell was in Commerce's physics class and they had met in the library to exchange notes before a test.

Mark was reading the most recent journal with keen attention. He read much more slowly than I did and reading was never a pleasure to him. He was frowning as he read. I decided to skip over to Commerce's junior year. I learned immediately that Commerce was the supply sergeant in H Company. On the second page, he mentioned Bentley Durrell again. Durrell was the regimental sergeant major and had pulled a surprise inspection on his classmates' rooms. He had given Commerce four demerits for an unmade bed.

"Ha!" I laughed. "Durrell shit all over his classmates. Wouldn't you know it?"

Mark did not answer and I began to grow bored with the reading. Commerce was a boring writer and his insights were uninspired. He observed with the eye of an accountant, with unassailable accuracy but no interest in the delicious, gossipy detail, or the incongruities or neuroses of the characters he so drily introduced. He used the language as he would a branch of mathematics.

I learned what grades he received on every test, how many merits or demerits he garnered each month, and how he spent his money.

I began to skip pages, glancing at them perfunctorily. I stopped to read about the Ring Ceremony, noting the small differences in emphasis and tradition. There was a long account of an inspection Commerce himself had conducted on the quadrangle, a description of a girl he had dated from Agnes Scott, a conversation he had with his father, an argument he had with his roommates, more test scores, and some quotations from Marcus Aurelius. I skipped more and more pages, pausing on an entry describing a debutante ball in South Carolina Hall and a parade on Corps Day. Corps

Day had not changed at all as I found in Commerce's earnest, lusterless prose. I turned the page.

I turned the page and found it.

I was dizzy as I read these words written in the same precise script:

> Later that evening after the Corps Day ceremonies had ended, I was inducted into a secret organization known as The Ten. I have heard rumors about The Ten since I was a freshman, but had become convinced that it did not exist. My roommate and I once even argued about it, a debate I recorded earlier in this journal. I cannot even tell Obie he was right. They took us to the President's house, blindfolded us, then drove us deep into the country for the induction ceremony. Over a hundred members of The Ten were in attendance, and the induction was very impressive indeed. We were told the history of the organization since its beginnings after the Federal occupation of the Institute during Reconstruction. We took an oath to uphold the purity and ideals of The Ten for as long as we shall live. The membership list reads like a Who's Who list of Institute graduates, and I felt both fortunate and honored to be selected. My uncle, William St. Croix, was my sponsor. . . .

At the bottom of the page, Commerce listed the nine other classmates selected with him. Bentley Durrell was the third name on the list.

"Turn to Corps Day, Mark," I said. "We've found it."

"Wait a minute, Will. I'm reading something very interesting."

I took down the next journal after Commerce's senior year and turned quickly to Corps Day. At the bottom of the page again, I found the names of the second ten men selected for membership in The Ten. I copied the names down carefully in a small notebook I had pulled from my back pocket. Mark was scowling and introspective as he read the Corps Day entry of 1967.

"These ten names are the new members of The Ten from this year's junior class, Mark. Copy those names. We might get out of this yet. We just might make it, boy," I said.

I was working fast now, taking down each journal,

turning quickly to the Corps Day description, copying the names and going to the next journal. Even when Commerce was overseas, he always carefully recorded the names of the new members on their date of election, not when he received the news.

Mark copied the names of the new inductees in 1967 on a sheet of paper but the troubled, deeply melancholy expression remained on his face. He looked puzzled and indecisive. He removed the second to the last journal from the bottom shelf.

"That's the year our class was inducted into The Ten. Now we'll know all the bastards who've been fucking with us."

Mark flipped through the journal. It took him a long time to find the Corps Day entry for 1966, an unconscionably long time. By this time I had listed eight sets of members in my notebook.

I saw Mark stiffen.

"What's wrong, Mark?" I asked, but he couldn't speak.

He pointed to something in the journal.

"Oh, my God," I gasped. "Oh, my God, Mark."

For five minutes we sat in that room without a word passing between us.

Then Mark spoke, "I've got some other things to tell you, Will."

"About what?"

"About Annie Kate."

46

At eleven o'clock, after we had carefully replaced the journals and eliminated all traces of our presence in the house, we left the St. Croix mansion and returned to the Institute. We had filled our notebooks with names and dates, with information that would alter, transform, and ruin utterly the fragile, tenuous network of destinies and alliances that had begun in innocence when I first talked to Cadet Recruit Pearce in September. That is how fate wounds you, I thought, as Mark steered down Rutledge Avenue. It sets you up with the banality of common events, camouflages the danger signals, positions you with kind and mothering hands, whispers graceful cadences and cunning lullabies, and leads you blithely to terrifying reckoning, perhaps to extinction, but always to banality again. If it was not fate, then I did not know what to call it, did not know its name. But I felt its malignant presence in that slow ride toward the barracks, through those charming streets of immense, enduring houses, through darkness and sadness and rain. I felt all the pain of growing older, the hazard of wisdom, and the death of beautiful illusions. There was a change in me, a violent shift in the sand, and I felt the cobra stir in the blood. I felt heat; I felt ice.

When we reached the parking lot beside fourth battalion, I embraced Mark tenderly and held him for over a minute, the big man limp and inert in my arms.

"I'll take care of the rest of it tonight, Mark. Try to get some sleep. I'll be back before taps. We're going to make it, son."

"Who gives a damn? I hate this school. I hate this city," he said.

"It's not the school or the city, Mark. We know that now. It's this other thing. It's this aberration. Now remember we don't tell anyone."

I left Mark and walked past the tennis courts, smelling the sweet aroma of wet clay. I glanced toward the General's house to my left as I came to the doorway of the Bear's quarters. His wife answered the doorbell and told me that the Colonel was upstairs in his bedroom watching television. She invited me inside and asked me if I wanted a cup of coffee. "Yes, ma'am," I said, and climbed the stairs to the Colonel's bedroom.

"Colonel," I called out at the top of the stairs.

"Drive in, Bubba," he said from the bedroom.

He was in his pajamas, smoking a cigar, reading a book, and there was gunfire on the television, although I did not notice what was playing. I saluted him out of habit even though he wasn't in uniform. Out of habit, he saluted back.

"What's wrong, Bubba?" he asked.

"Everything, Colonel," I said, unable to meet his gaze. "The whole goddam world is wrong."

"If you're just learning that, lamb, then you're on your way to being a man."

"I know who they are, Colonel. I know every goddam one of them."

"The Ten, Bubba?"

"Yes, sir. Here's why I thought you were one of them.

471

Cain Gilbreath gave me this photograph when I told him I was coming to you for help."

I handed him the photograph of Poteete being tortured with him in the background.

"It's a fake, Bubba. You should have been able to see that."

"I see it now, Colonel. I didn't see it then. I looked at your class, Colonel. I found the names of the ten men in your class who are members. Your name wasn't among them. You were telling the truth the whole time. They knew you would help me so they faked the picture."

"The ring is my word, Bubba. The ring means something."

"I shouldn't have come to this school, Colonel. I didn't belong here. I've hated all this. It's been bad for me."

"Some good, some bad, Bubba. It's your school for the rest of your life. No matter what happens."

"I mean that it's not my nature to live in a place like this. It's a cruel place, Colonel, a loveless place."

"Sometimes, Bubba. Just like any other place."

I took his ring out of my pocket and he placed it on his finger. He did not mention my tears and neither did Mrs. Berrineau when she brought the coffee. I was not the first cadet to come to the Berrineau house because of some grief or personal hurt, nor would I be the last. It was a law of the Corps I had learned in the first month of my freshman year, only I had ignored it: If you're in trouble, go to the Bear. I was one of a long line of cadets who had wept while sitting on the foot of his bed. He did not mind. He expected it of boys.

Then I spread out my notebook and told him the entire history of The Ten and the names of every single graduate who held membership in the secret order. Every so often, he would whistle as I named a former governor of the state, a United States Senator, ambassadors, presidents of large corporations, Army generals. As I spoke, I knew that Colonel Reynolds would be pleased. On this night I had become a historian and had finally discovered a primary source.

When I had finished, the Bear said, "In two days, Bubba, you go to the General's office to get your walking papers. We've got over forty-eight hours to prepare a surprise for him. You and Santoro report to my office at 0800 tomorow. We've got final exams, Bubba, final exams."

"Colonel, won't you get in trouble with the General when he finds out you know all this?"

"Sure, Bubba," the Bear said through his cigar smoke. "He'll fire me."

"But this is your career, Colonel."

"I don't mind, Bubba. The Army was my career, and I loved every minute of it. This is just icing on the cake. This is just playing shepherd to my flock of lambs. And there's one thing you never understood, McLean, you being a Bolshevik and everything. I love this school. That's a simple fact. And I love what this school and this ring are supposed to stand for. And I'll tell you something else, Bubba."

"Yes, sir."

"We're going to break The Ten on Monday. But we better be ready when Monday rolls around, Bubba, because the General's smarter than you and I are ever going to be. Now I'm going to call in some debts from some of the lambs who owe me big favors. I'll get all the dirt I can on The Ten in your class. And the Bear is going to have a heart-to-heart with Mr. Pearce. He's going to sign a full report about what happened at that house that night or I'm going to crucify him without wood or nails. Meanwhile, you give me a list of the names of cadets you would trust with your gonads. And I mean trust completely, Bubba."

"Right now, Colonel, you could take all the cadets I still trust and have a meeting in a kayak out on the Ashley River."

"Glad you can still laugh, lamb. But come growling and serious to my office tomorrow. You aren't out of the woods yet. The only thing you've done tonight is to lead the Bear into those woods with you. And, Bubba . . ."

"Yes, sir?"

"It's lonely in the god-blessed woods."

47

When I walked into his office on Monday afternoon, General Bentley Durrell looked like the last surviving member of an elite but critically endangered peerage. His manner was efficient; his demeanor pontifical. He studied me with the eyes of a hunter. His mouth tightened with bureaucratic indignation as he prepared to initiate the rites of excommunication from the Corps of Cadets. His face was lined with a cruel though delicate glaciation of years and a wrinkled bunching of the flesh beneath his chin. He was, at once, an old man and an incontestably handsome one. He stared at me dispassionately for an indeterminate amount of time. I had expected to be afraid but instead, there had been a restorative investiture of calm now that we had finally arrived at the hour of reckoning. For the first time, I was facing the specter and power and the incorporeal evil of The Ten with all my questions answered and all my fears allayed. For the first time I was walking the world unafraid of generals. For the first time I was approaching General Durrell as an adult; I was facing him as a man.

I saluted him and he returned my salute.

"I want to call a truce, sir," I said, surprising him by speaking first.

He was genuinely amused by my opening sally. "A truce?" he replied in his remarkable deep voice. "I wasn't aware there was a war between us."

"Yes, sir. There is a war between us."

"Who declared that war?" he asked.

"Circumstance declared it."

"What is this war all about, Mr. McLean? I've always preferred men who speak straight, who get directly to the point. Do you know why you've been summoned to my office today?"

"I'll be kicked out of school today, General. Nine days before I graduate."

"You're correct, Mr. McLean. This is one of the saddest duties of my office and one of the most necessary. It always grieves us to be forced to expel a senior, especially one who has come so far in the line. Now if you had been cautious, if you had shined up properly, if you had conducted yourself judiciously, if you had modified your behavior to blend in with the average cadet, then I think you would have had no problem in graduating with your class, Mr. McLean."

"The word was put out to run me and my roommate out of the Corps, General. Every clue comes back to you. You have decided to run me out, sir."

He laughed contemptuously and said, "I have more important matters to consider than the excess demerits of a senior private."

"Not since The Ten was discovered, sir."

"The Ten, Mr. McLean? What is The Ten? I've been hearing rumors about the existence of The Ten since I was a cadet. I can assure you that no such organization exists."

"Members are selected on Corps Day each year, General. You were selected with nine of your classmates in the spring of your junior year."

"We've known about the existence of cadet fraternities for years, Mr. McLean. I was in one and so was every other graduate who ever came through here. It's a frivolity we tolerate probably because there's nothing we could do to stop them anyhow."

"The Ten is no fraternity, sir. It's a gang and you're responsible for its excesses."

"Are you trying to blackmail me, Mr. McLean?" he said, smiling at his hands, in perfect control of the situation.

"Yes, sir, I sure am," I answered. "I want to make a deal with you. My roommate and I will remain quiet about The Ten if you allow us to graduate."

"I find that most amusing, Mr. McLean. I also find you insulting and impertinent. How should I react to these desperate charges of yours, Mr. McLean? Should I act afraid? Should I tremble before your unprovable accusations? I helped land the victorious Army of the Pacific during World War II, I was a roving ambassador for President Eisenhower, have met the crowned heads of Europe and half the leaders of the Iron Curtain countries, so you will excuse me if I'm not suitably impressed by your idle, cowardly threats. But you tell me, Mr. McLean. If you were I, how would you react?"

"I would act ashamed, sir."

"You are going to need this air of moral superiority to get you through the rest of what might prove to be a very trying day for you," the General answered, his anger measurable in the slow, burning floridity in the hollows of his cheeks. "Your case is cut and dried and there is no question of leniency. Major Mudge, your tactical officer, has recommended instant dismissal and I have concurred with his recommendation. I must ask you now for your ring."

"No," I said.

"Put a 'sir' on that, mister," the General said, pushing his chair back from his desk.

"No, sir," I said. "You don't get my ring until I'm officially withdrawn from the Institute. That is clearly stated in the Blue Book."

"That moment is but a signature away, Mr. McLean," said the General as he reached for a pen on his desk.

"Don't sign that paper, sir," I said, surprised at the confidence, no, the command, in my voice.

He looked up at me and we stared at each other for a moment. He looked at the door, then back at me.

"Mr. McLean, I want to make this as easy on you as possible. I cannot tell you how this action saddens me, but you know the rules of the Institute. It is my duty to sign these papers to expel you from the Institute. This action is irrevocable and I am doing it in the best interest of the school and yourself. I will write a letter of recommendation for you that will enable you to attend and graduate from any college in the country. All this will depend on your conducting yourself like a gentleman."

"I conduct myself like a gentleman when I'm in the presence of gentlemen."

"Your impudence will only jeopardize your future, sir," he said, preparing to write.

"What I know will also jeopardize yours, General," I answered. "What I know about The Ten."

"Who would believe you when you tried to slander the Institute? Who would believe the word of an expelled, embittered cadet from the Institute?"

There was a loud knock on the door.

The Bear entered the General's office in his dress uniform. He saluted the General and stood directly beside me facing him. The desk had become a point of division and demarcation. "I would believe that cadet, General."

"Colonel Berrineau, may I ask who ordered you to report to my office?" the General said, recovering from his initial astonishment.

"Mr. McLean asked me here, sir," the Bear answered. "He asked for my help. He said that you were running him out of school."

"Good day, Colonel," the General ordered coldly, rising out of his seat. *"I* am the only one who extends invitations to my office, not Mr. McLean. You will report back to your office and you will have a satisfactory excuse for your actions when I speak with you at 0800 tomorrow. And, for the record, I am not running Mr. McLean out of school. I am simply acting on a recommendation of his tactical officer and expelling him for excess demerits. This is not a pleasant task and I fail to understand why you are helping Mr. McLean in making it even more difficult."

"One moment, sir." The Bear spoke in a perfectly calm and respectful voice, but he seemed diminished and overshadowed in the presence of the General. "A new delinquency report has been issued from my office today."

"I don't see the point, Colonel," the General said. "Nor do I wish to see your face any longer. Good day, sir."

"Mr. McLean is prominently listed, sir."

"I'm quite aware of that, Colonel. I called you this morning to get the final tally of demerits."

"I didn't tell you that in the same list, Mr. McLean was awarded a total of fifty-seven merits. Thirty for outstanding performance of duty, five for outstanding personal appearance, five for outstanding room, five for reflecting outstanding credit on Carolina Military Institute. And so on, General. Subtracting merits from demerits, Mr. McLean only has forty-five demerits for the year. The same holds true for Santoro."

"I see, Colonel," the General whispered in a rage. "I understand perfectly well."

"Another thing, sir," the Bear said. "I heard everything said in this room just now."

"You eavesdropped, Colonel. You eavesdropped on your superior officer. For what reason, Colonel?"

"I needed to find out something, General. Something very important."

"What did you need to find out?"

"I needed to find out if you were a liar. I was sorry to find out that you were."

"So you are calling me a liar, Colonel?" the General said in a cool, detached tone.

"I am calling you a goddam liar," the Bear answered, equally cool, equally detached. "I am calling you a disgrace to the ring, a disgrace to the Line. I am calling you unworthy to be President of this great school. Mr. McLean has given me a list of names, General. The list contains all the names of alleged members of The Ten and the names of the boys they have run out of school for the past thirty years. He has provided me with a complete history of The Ten, a history that turns my stomach, General. I have contacted twelve of the boys who were kidnaped and taken to your plantation house on their last night as cadets. They all have volunteered to swear to the fact in a court of law."

"You will give the list to me, Colonel," the General said. "That is a direct order. You will mention this list to no one. You will report to your quarters to await further instructions."

"You'll get the list, General, when McLean and Santoro graduate. If they do not graduate, then I will go to the press and give the list to them."

477

"Your allegations will seem much less severe and trustworthy when they come from the mouth of a former Commandant of Cadets who was relieved of his command for incompetence. I was going to dismiss you when the school year was over, Colonel, but your insubordination leaves me no choice. You will submit your resignation when you report to my office tomorrow," the General declared, but then his voice softened, became conciliatory, ingratiating, as though he realized he was pushing too hard, too quickly. His strategy shifted in congruence with his voice. "But Colonel, we are both being far too hasty. We've been through far too much together to have our professional relationship end because of the lies of this one boy. And he is lying, Colonel. I assure you of that and his lies nearly cost you your job. I know how much the job means to you, Colonel. There is a chance for you to continue as Commandant and we can forget any of this happened. This can be a simple disagreement among men of good will. I still want you on my team, Colonel Berrineau, but only if you want to be, only if I'm assured of your absolute loyalty to me and my staff. It's up to you, Colonel, it's entirely your decision."

The Bear was silent for a moment, reflective, and his face was worried. I thought I'd lost him.

"General," the Bear said, "Mr. McLean got involved in all this because of a request I made at the beginning of the year. I feel personally responsible for his involvement in this affair. I didn't know anything until he came to my quarters two nights ago. Now I know everything."

"Your job is extremely important to you, is it not, Colonel?"

"Yes, sir, you know it's important to me."

"Very good, then. We have struck a deal, Colonel?" the General said.

"You can kiss my ass, General Durrell," the Bear replied.

"You would betray the Institute, Colonel?" the General whispered harshly.

"No, sir," the Bear answered without emotion. "I would never do that. Would you, sir?"

"There's not much loyalty in you, Colonel," the General replied. "Now get out of my office and you report to your quarters, sir. Colonel Lyall will be Acting Commandant until we can find your replacement."

"You're going to be amazed how much loyalty there is in me, General," the Bear answered. Then turning to me he said,

"I'm in it with you all the way, Will. You and I are going to show him what this school can produce, Bubba. We're going to show him what it really means to wear the ring." Before he departed, he whispered so only I could hear, "Now when I go, you play the last card. Play it, Bubba."

When the Bear left the room, I felt the full weight of my isolation and solitude as I faced the General's hostile, appraising eyes alone. But the mood in the room had changed since the Bear's declaration of support for me, and for the first time there was something uncertain, even endangered, in the General's expression.

"I'm signing the papers to expel you from the Institute, Mr. McLean. I wish to remind you that there is nothing personal in this action."

"What am I being expelled for?"

"Excess demerits, of course, Mr. McLean."

"I have forty-five demerits for the year, General. You'll have to come up with something else."

"I am protecting you and Mr. Santoro from a far greater charge, Mr. McLean. A certain Daniel Molligen, a '64 graduate, was going to bring criminal charges against you and Mr. Santoro for assault and kidnaping. It was only my personal intervention on your behalf which prevented him from going to the police. But the nature of the crime is grievous enough to require your expulsion. The Blue Book specifically states that any cadet accused of a felony will be subject to instant expulsion. I would like to do you and your roommate a favor by keeping this off your record. It would be wise for you to go along with excess demerits. Very wise, Mr. McLean, and very important. You see, I would be more than happy to intervene personally on your behalf with other college presidents. And I would hate to see you do something foolish and never be allowed to complete your college education."

"And how would you do that, General?"

"I will put on your record that you were expelled on a morals charge of the most heinous nature, Mr. McLean. I would not like to do that. But with your threats and unfounded accusations, you would leave me very little choice. But I'm certain we can work something out, Will. Don't you agree?"

"What do I have to do to graduate, General? That's all I want. For me and my roommate to graduate."

"You'll have no problem graduating, Will. It just won't be from the Institute. Things have gone a little too far for that. But it's not the end of the world. I might even be able to pull a few strings for you and Mr. Santoro and see that your

479

tuitions and educational expenses are provided for. You seem to think there's some plot against you, Will, and that's simply not true. You may have convinced Colonel Berrineau, but there are no secret organizations, nothing of that sort. There is only Mr. Molligen and his willingness to press charges against you. I'm trying to help you in every way that I can, but you're trying to make it so difficult for me. I just don't want to see a young man's life ruined."

"And what would I have to do, General?"

"Nothing, Will. Nothing at all. Many cadets who are expelled for excess demerits often write me after they graduate from other colleges and thank me for giving them such a valuable lesson so early in life. Discipline is both valuable and effective, Will. The only thing I ask of you is that you keep in touch. Drop me a letter when you get settled in your new school. Let me know how you're doing. I'm always going to be interested in your career. I mean that sincerely. And if I can ever help you in any way, I will do it gladly and you have my word of honor on it."

"Can I have your word of honor on another thing, sir?"

"Certainly, Will."

"Can I have your word of honor that The Ten does not exist?"

He leaned forward over his desk; his eyes met mine steadily.

"You have my word of honor, Will," he whispered.

"And all I have to do is to leave the Institute quietly."

"That and convince Colonel Berrineau that you were stretching the truth when you concocted that information about The Ten. That shouldn't be very difficult. Without you and your roommate, he would look a bit foolish going to the newspapers. Colonel Berrineau would never be able to find work again, and I know you wouldn't want to be responsible for that."

"So you want me to betray the Bear?"

"Not betray him, Will. Certainly not that. But bring him to his senses, son. Make him see the light as you're seeing it now."

"I do see the light, General."

"I knew you would, Will. The future is so important. So important, indeed."

"So is the present, General. Because you have to make a decision in the present. You have to make a very important decision right now, General."

"What do you mean, Will?"

"Look out the window, General. Look to your left. Standing by the mailbox across the street."

Calmly, the General looked out the window and saw Mark Santoro standing beside the mailbox holding a large stack of letters in his hand. I slid a thick letter across his desk.

"General," I said, "my roommate is across the street at the faculty mailbox. He is holding fifty letters in his hand. Some are addressed to twenty-five reporters across the state. Others are addressed to influential state senators and representatives who did not attend the Institute. In the letter before you is a brief description of The Ten, including the methods for eliminating freshmen from the ranks of the Corps. Words like kidnaping and torture are used quite frequently. There is also a separate list of every single member of The Ten. If I walk to the window and take off my ring, Mark will mail every single letter. Tonight, we will hand deliver a copy of the letter to every single member of the Corps of Cadets. At this very moment, you can decide whether The Ten remains a secret organization or becomes the most famous group in South Carolina."

The General rose from his seat and walked over to the window.

"Report back to the barracks immediately, Mr. Santoro," he shouted out to Mark from the open window. "I have called the Provost Marshal."

Mark Santoro smiled at General Bentley Durrell, war hero and four-star general, and shot him the finger.

I walked over beside the General and slowly began to remove my ring.

The General grabbed my wrist.

His hands were spidery, liver-spotted; their fragility moved me with their age. Their spent, exhausted weakness.

"Send your roommate back to the barracks, Mr. McLean. I think we can arrange something satisfactory to both sides."

He picked up the papers he had just signed expelling me from school and began tearing them up, deliberately and carefully.

I gave a thumbs up signal to Mark and he began walking toward the barracks. Then I turned again to face General Durrell alone.

He had returned to his seat; his eyes were closed and his face was loosened and unjoined as though all the salts and preservatives of unvanquishable authority had washed away in some sudden, unforeseeable monsoon. But he calmed himself as he sat there and I watched as the disciplined old veteran returned slowly, reviving himself as he mastered his environment again, as he realized once more who he was and who I was, the vast division of age and experience that separated us, as we faced each other in the nakedness of truth at last, without stratagems or mysteries or any more cards to play, in the hot afternoon sun of that sweltering Charleston day in 1967.

He began to speak to me in a fatigued, desiccated voice. "If I had gotten to you early enough, Mr. McLean," he began, "if I had recognized your potential, I could have made an outstanding cadet out of you, an outstanding soldier. You think well on your feet. Very rare for an athlete. What a shame you remained hidden from me until the very last. What a loss for both of us."

"I would make a terrible soldier, General," I said. "This school has proven that to me."

"Why, Mr. McLean?" he asked, his eyes still tightly closed.

"Because, sir," I answered, "I think I would willingly die for a man like Colonel Berrineau, but I could never follow a man like you."

His eyes opened, an angry flowering of yellow light.

"No cadet has ever talked to me like that, Mr. McLean," he said. "No cadet has ever dared. They tell me I'm greatly feared in the Corps of Cadets, and I've always taken that as a most extraordinary compliment. Imagine an old man like me being feared by two thousand bucks in the prime of their manhood."

"I've always been afraid you, sir," I admitted. "Scared to death of you. I never could speak to you even when you came back into the locker room to congratulate the team after a victory. I've never spoken to you without fear or a sense of inadequacy. I was required to read your book when I was a knob, required to memorize your battle campaigns, to read your biography. My father had wanted you to run for President instead of Eisenhower. I grew up hearing your name. I'll never forget seeing you on that first day of school four years ago when you talked to the incoming freshmen about duty, honor, and a moral commitment to serve mankind. One thing never occurred to me that day."

"What is that?" he asked wearily.

"It never occurred to me that I might be better man than

you ever were, General. And that I would meet many far better men here at the Institute."

He rose imperiously and began pacing the carpet behind his desk, every inch the General again, every inch the Great Man defending the sanctity of his myth.

"You!" he sneered. "You will never be one percent of the man I am or was, Mr. McLean. When I took the job as President of this college, I sensed this country was in imminent danger from within and without. I knew that it was going to take men of iron to turn this country around. I took this job because I wanted to fill this nation with patriots, with men who would die for this country rather than submit to tyrants. I wanted to turn out men unlike you in every way, Mr. McLean, men who could change the history of the world, who would take from the Institute a vision of America so great and so transcendent that nothing could damage that vision. I wanted to produce a new breed of valiant men, citizen warriors, who would continue to strive to make this country the greatest in the history of the world. And I have done it, Mr. McLean. And I will continue to do it even if one or two misfits like you and your roommate make it through the Institute. You will do me no harm, Mr. McLean, and you will make no mark."

"Yeh, yeh, yeh," I answered. "I've heard it all before, General. I've heard it in every speech you've ever delivered to the Corps. Now I just don't believe any of it when it comes from your lips."

"You will leave my office immediately, Mr. McLean. But first, I need a single piece of information from you. I need to know how you came in possession of that list. You and your roommate will graduate with your class. But I must know where you got the list."

"And if I don't tell you?"

"Then you will not graduate and I will have to fight against your slander in other ways. It would be difficult for the college but we could weather the storm, Mr. McLean. There is no doubt about that."

"I broke into Commerce St. Croix's house and copied the lists from his journals. He doesn't know I did it."

"You're a man of high moral integrity, McLean," the General answered. "I could expel you for that reprehensible act alone."

"You didn't exactly model your career after the life of Christ, General Durrell," I answered.

"You are free to go, Mr. McLean," he said, in control

again. "But I want your word of honor that you will destroy those letters. Every single copy of them."

"You have my word of honor, sir."

I saluted him and began walking to the door. Before I reached the door, I heard him say, "One last thing, McLean. Do you ever think about your place in history? What do you think will be your place in the history of the Institute? I already know my place. But what about yours? Tell me about your place in the history of the school."

He was laughing at me, mocking me, and I turned, loathing every single thing he stood for on earth.

"General," I said, "I want you to hear this and I want you to think about it."

"What do you have to say, McLean?"

"I plan to write that history, sir."

48

That night I sat alone in the St. Croix garden, listening as Tradd and Abigail played a duet for harp and piano in the music room. Far off in the city, I could hear the barking of dogs and the sound of traffic on Broad Street. Biding my time circumspectly among the roses, I watched them in secret, thinking the long, troubled thoughts of my last days as a cadet. In the supernatural light of chandeliers, their faces were clear and shining; they appeared so thoughtlessly unmarked, so charmingly innocent of all the furies and conspiracies and irreversible fragmentations that had brought me to their garden.

Abigail's arms moved with elegant grace along the shining gold strings of the harp. At the piano, Tradd's white fine-boned face was taut with rapt concentration as he read the notes of the score and instantly translated them into sound. The music infiltrated the garden like the movement of flowers. There was an unnamable loneliness to the harp and also a quiet, decorous lust in its accompaniment. I had learned about flowers and music in the St. Croix mansion. And I had learned much, much more.

The son and the mother looked at each other and smiled. Their eyes met in a gentle and satisfied concordance as the music danced from their fingertips. Tradd's piano would pose a delicate question and receive an answer from the harp with startling immediacy and with questions of its own. I felt the sharp sting of emptiness and solitude that you feel so acutely and with such internal sorrow and wonder whenever music is performed well. But my head was filled with nightmares featuring trains.

How different this garden was from Annie Kate's and her mother's, I thought. In this garden, nature was denied its capacity for accident. Abigail controlled too tyrannically the luxuriant vegetable flow that grew in such thriftless riot in the warm Carolina days. The alien quality of this garden was in the severe zealotry of its tending. Never cut back too radically, Abigail, I said to myself. Grant to nature and to climate some freedom, some vivacity of form, some of the ancient symmetry that comes from wildness.

I let them finish the piece. The music changed at the very end. The piano flowed through the garden like swift water and the harp replied with clean honey that poured into the water. I lifted up out of the roses and jasmine when they were done. Summoning my courage, I rapped the polished brass knocker at the front door. Once again, I was set loose to drift in the city beneath the palms and spires, a stranger among the gardens. Loneliness again, I thought, my native land.

Tradd answered the door and did not immediately recognize me in the shadows of the verandah.

"Will," he said at last. "I heard you made it. I heard you beat the General. Congratulations, you old thing."

He embraced me warmly. "This is a night to celebrate. Mother, it's Will. He's come home and he's going to graduate as an Institute man."

Abigail came to the vestibule, her clumsiness of gesture and movement somehow more eloquent and moving than they had ever been before. Her guileless eyes appraised me lovingly and I laid my head against her cheek and let her hands stroke the back of my head. "It's all over now, Will. We can now start the business of forgetting this dreadful year. Where's Mark? Is he coming over?"

"No, Abigail," I said. "He stayed in the barracks. He was too tired to come."

"What did you say to the General, Will?" Tradd asked. "I've had three cadets call to say that you and he went to war and that you won hands down. It's all over the campus. And I heard the Bear was fired as Commandant. I want to hear every word of it. Every single syllable, and I refuse to let you skip over any parts of it."

"Of course, he'll tell us everything, Tradd. Let the poor boy come inside and fix himself a drink and get comfortable. He'll catch a death of a cold standing in this draft."

"A cold, mother?" Tradd said. "Oh, really now, not at the end of May."

"That's the easiest time to catch a chill, when you're least expecting it. I've always caught the most horrid chills in summer."

"Where's Commerce?" I said, looking nervously toward the stairway.

"Father was rather a grouch when he came in, Will," Tradd said. "He's in one of his black humors."

"He's in his study," Abigail said crossly. "As usual he's agitated about something. He came home today muttering and incoherent and doing everything to make himself unpleasant. He's been in his room all afternoon and has refused to speak. I tried to get him to join us for dinner, but he wouldn't even answer my knocks. Men are the strangest of all God's creatures, at least the one I married. He did do a very singular thing though. When he returned from an alumni meeting at the Institute today, he changed the lock on his study. It's a combination lock and it looks extremely tacky. I told him that too, but of course, he simply ignored me."

"He'll get over it, Mother," Tradd said. "He always does."

"What's in the jar, Will?" Abigail inquired, noticing for the first time the container I held in my left hand.

"Water," I said. "It's chilled and fine. Vintage 1967. I want to begin a new tradition in the St. Croix family. One that you can remember me by. I want this occasion to be as memorable as when we drank the water from the Aegean."

"We don't need traditions to remember you by, Will," Abigail said. "You're a part of all this now. You're part of the traditions of this house. But the human soul can always use a new tradition. Sometimes we require them. It's been a hard year on both of you. A tragic year."

Abigail took the jar of water and poured it slowly into the Waterford decanter on her sideboard in the dining room. Tradd and I took our seats at the dining room table.

"Have we changed much since our knob year, Tradd?" I asked. "Do we look the same? Do we feel the same things? Do we think the same thoughts?"

"Goodness, no, Will," he said assuredly. "At least, I pray

that we've matured considerably since then. We were boys our knob year and all our thoughts were foolish, boyish thoughts. In a matter of days we'll officially be whole men. Then we'll think mature, noble thoughts for the rest of our lives. I'm just joking, of course, but we have earned our maturity, Will. We went through the system and that automatically changes you. It's what makes us different from our contemporaries in other colleges."

"Do you really believe that, Tradd? Or do you just want to believe it?" I asked.

"I sincerely believe it, Will. And I've believed it the whole time I've been at the Institute. Tradition has always held an important place in my life and I've believed in the system. I have never felt the need for rebellion the way you have. That's why I'm fairly astonished that you want to start a new tradition tonight."

"If Will wants to start one, then I want to participate in it," Abigail said, coming toward us with a tray, three wine glasses, and the decanter of water.

I poured the water into the three slender glasses.

"It looks filthy," Tradd exclaimed, grimacing at his mother. "Are you sure it's safe to drink, Will? I certainly don't want to contract rickets or typhoid fever or whatever it is you catch from drinking contaminated water."

"Heavens, Tradd," Abigail laughed. "We're not in Mexico."

"It's perfectly safe," I promised. "A toast."

"Let's all make toasts," Abigail suggested.

"A splendid idea, Mother."

"Here's to the success of my son in his career and to the success of my adopted son in his career," Abigail said, her eyes moving from Tradd to me.

Tradd raised his glass to me and said with feeling, "Here's to my roommate, Will McLean, who has been the best friend I ever had in my life."

"To friendship," I said, and there were tears in all of our eyes.

We clinked the glasses lightly together. Tradd and Abigail drank deeply. I did not drink any of the water. Instead, with great deliberation, I flung the glass of water in Tradd's face.

"Will!" Abigail cried. "I hope you don't think that's amusing. I'm surprised at you. In fact, I'm shocked."

I ignored her and fixed my eyes on my roommate. I watched his expression change from shock to indignation, then to the terrible awareness that he was facing me as an enemy for the first time in our lives.

"Tradd, you once told me that if you ever had a son you didn't want to name him Tradd St. Croix, that you didn't want that name to continue through another generation, that you thought one Tradd St. Croix was enough for the world. Well, I agree with you. One is more than enough. But I found a name for your son. You can name him Judas, Tradd."

"How long have you known?" Tradd asked, nervously wiping his face with a handkerchief.

"For three of the longest days in my life. But I didn't know how to confront you, Tradd. I didn't know how to tell you that I hated your guts. It's hard to quit loving someone when you've had only three days to do it. It's hard to believe that someone can hold your love and friendship so cheaply. You were one of them, Tradd. My God, you were with them all the time."

"It's not like you think, Will. I swear it's not like you think. I can explain everything. There's a perfectly logical explanation for everything. They promised me you'd never find out. They promised me that, Will. But you must listen to me," he said desperately, reaching out to touch me.

"Tell me what this is all about, Will," Abigail demanded. "Tell me this instant. What has happened to you?"

Spinning around to face her, I said, "Happened to me, Abigail? Happened to me? How can I begin to tell you what has happened to me? What can I say to you that would make you understand? All this beauty around you. This house, your flowers, your fine silver, your antiques, your music, your perfect life. Such beauty, such stunning beauty, but you missed it, Abigail, you missed seeing the corruption and the goddam evil that has grown up around you. See this face? See this rich kid's face?" I said, grasping Tradd's jaw and turning it in profile toward his mother. "He betrayed three people, Abigail, three people who loved him. One of them is dead because of this sad worthless son of yours. That water you drank, Abigail, the water you drank tonight is not from the Aegean Sea or the Bay of Siam or any other romantic place. The water is from the Ashley River. It's flavored with the bones and blood of our roommate, Tradd. Do you remember him? Do you, Abigail? Do you remember how poor he was? Do you remember how the other three of us got him through it all, gave him money, shared everything, and called him our brother? How did you feel when he killed himself on the trestle? How did you feel when you heard they found pieces of our roommate in the marsh, Tradd?"

"Stop it, Will," Tradd pleaded, cupping his hands over his ears. "Please stop it and give me a chance to explain. I have a right to defend myself. You haven't heard my side of it."

"Do you remember his name, Tradd?" I continued, enjoying his anguish. "I do. I remember it, but I can't say it. I can't say it because the Institute is that strong within me. It's in me so deep I'll never get it out, Tradd. It's strong, Tradd. It's so strong, Abigail. Far more powerful than I ever realized because I haven't been able to speak his name since he was voted guilty by the honor court. I can't even mention my goddamn roommate's name. Help me say it, Tradd. Please help me say it."

"Listen to Tradd, Will," Abigail said, and her voice was pitiful. "I don't understand any of this, but I'm sure Tradd has a reasonable explanation. Just listen to what he has to say and get control of yourself."

As Tradd approached me I turned my back toward him and found myself facing an antique mirror that reflected our three images in tarnished, distorted tones. He put his hands on my shoulders and leaned his head against my shoulders.

"Will," he said, and there was a cry in his voice, "you've always been strong and accepted. You could always be one of the boys if you chose to be. Often, you didn't want to be, but you still had the choice. You've never been the Honey Prince, Will. That's me. I'm the Honey Prince. I've been the Honey Prince for four years. You've always been an athlete and could win the approval of other men easily. I never had that. I was always considered weak and ineffectual until I came to the Institute. You've never understood my love for the school or anyone else's love for it. I'm grateful, Will, eternally grateful for the Institute's giving me the chance to prove that I could take everything they could dish out. The school gave me a chance to respect myself, to like myself. It was the first time I ever felt manly. I bet you think that's a joke, don't you, Will? The Honey Prince feeling manly. Well, I did, and when I was selected for The Ten, it was the greatest thing that ever happened to me. It's the Institute's highest honor, and her most distinguished alumni are members. It wasn't until later that I found out that it was because of my father's membership that I was inducted. I didn't know that my selection was automatic. How do you think I felt then? It was my heritage again, Will. I've never earned a single thing in my life on my own merits. Everything is because my name is Tradd St. Croix."

"You earned our friendship, Tradd," I answered him in the mirror. "You earned it because we thought you were wonderful and generous and kind, not because you were a St. Croix."

"I can't stand to see you boys do this to each other," Abigail whispered to us. "I simply can't bear it."

"Listen to me, Will," Tradd said. "I need you now more than I ever did. This is the time I really need you. This is the time you can prove your friendship to me, the first time it's really been tested. Everything got carried away from us, Will. We were all swept away by events beyond our control. Think about my situation. I was in the worst situation of anyone in the room. I had sworn a vow of secrecy to The Ten. I was proud to take that vow, Will. Prouder than anything I've ever done. Then you got involved with Pearce and they told me I had to watch you and report everything you did or said concerning Pearce. I wanted to tell you everything, Will. You have no idea how many times I wanted to go up to you and tell you every single thing. But there was never a chance, Will, and there was the vow. It just got worse and worse and you got into it deeper and deeper. Then our roommate was killed and it was all over. There was no way I could tell you after that, Will. But you must try to understand that my situation was untenable. No matter what I did it would look like I was betraying someone."

"You chose them, Tradd."

"It was not a choice, Will. I didn't like what The Ten did to freshmen any more than you did. I was trying to get them to stop that horrible practice of taking freshmen to the General's house. I was working from the inside, Will. I'm sorry about everything that happened. Oh God, Will. I'm so sorry and I'd do anything to rectify it. I'm sorry about Poteete. I'm sorry about our roommate. But they made their own choices. I did not make any choices for them. What Poteete did was the result of a personality disorder. What our roommate did was simply wrong. He committed an honor violation that had nothing to do with me or you or The Ten."

"What about what Tradd did?" I asked in a trembling voice. "I want to know about Tradd St. Croix. How did it feel to throw gasoline on Poteete, Tradd? Tell me about that. Did you feel like a big man? Did you feel powerful? I bet you didn't feel like the Honey Prince that night, did you, big fella? And our roommate? Our roommate, Tradd. You made the call to those bastards. You left the room as soon as he did. You went out and called them, didn't you? You even called them the night I went to the house. You told them about Bobby Bentley. You were the one intercepting the messages from Pearce. Because you were the key to running all of us out, the three guys who had accidentally interfered with the workings of The Ten. And all for what, Tradd? Because of the Honey Prince. Was that the monster that destroyed our room? The goddam Honey Prince."

"Listen to me, Will. Please listen to me and forget this other stuff. I'm begging you to forget it. It's over now and there's nothing we can do about it. When you went to the house and discovered the secret of The Ten, there was nothing I could do to warn you or protect you or help you. It became a matter of grave concern to people much older and much more important than me or you. They marked you, Will. The Board of Governors issued a decree that you guys were not to graduate under any circumstance. I pleaded your cases before them. It made me *sick,* Will. Physically ill. I told them I could keep you quiet, that I could use my friendship to insure your silence. I still feel I was right. I'm sorry I was part of everything that was hurting you. Do you hear me, Will? Please hear what I'm saying. Will. I need you now. I'll do whatever you want, Will. I'll resign from The Ten. I'll do anything. Anything at all, Will. There's nothing we can do now except start completely fresh and pretend that none of this ever happened. I'll be a better friend because of this. I've learned so much, Will. And I've suffered. You've no idea how I've suffered. We simply must get over it. We must, Will."

I removed the key to the St. Croix mansion from my back pocket and let it drop to the floor.

"When you went to Fort Benning on Friday, I entered the house and spent four of the worst hours of my life copying names and dates out of Commerce's journals. That's how I knew you were in The Ten, Tradd."

"That's unforgivable, Will," Abigail said angrily. "Commerce will never forgive a breach of trust like that. Those journals are sacred to him."

"The key's on the floor, Abigail. I'll never use it again. But there's one more thing in the journals I would like explained to me. One more thing that hurts and that I don't understand. Why did you two set me up with Annie Kate?"

Tradd's face in the mirror was both surprised and angry.

"What are you talking about, Will? How do you even know about Annie Kate? No one knows about her except . . . Those damn journals of Father's."

Abigail moved quickly to her son and laid her hands on his shoulders. Our faces shone darkly, sadly in the mirror, an aggrieved and hopeless trinity.

Abigail spoke. "I was the one responsible for your meeting Annie Kate, Will. I arranged that meeting last August. I knew she was waiting for you in that alley."

"Mother, what on earth are you talking about? Annie Kate went to California. Father paid for the trip. It was all arranged and all secret. You promised that it would remain a secret. Annie Kate swore to it."

"Annie Kate didn't tell me a thing, Tradd. You're right. It was the journal that told me you were the father of Annie Kate's child. But please explain to me all about Annie Kate, Abigail. Why was I selected to see her through her pregnancy? Why didn't you let me in on the secret? I wouldn't have told anyone. I wouldn't have fallen in love with her. I wouldn't have been left by her."

"You fell in *love* with Annie Kate, Will?" Tradd gasped. "Not really. Not with *her*. I'd like to hear that explanation myself, Mother. You lied to me and told me she was in California. You lied to me, Mother."

"We couldn't *make* her go to California, Tradd," Abigail replied, whispering into her son's ear. "We didn't want you to worry about her. She wanted her child to be born in Charleston even if she couldn't keep it."

"But the child died, Mother. Or were you lying about that too?"

"You're goddamn right it died, Tradd. The doctor came and told me your goddam child strangled as it was being born. That should have been you, not me, Tradd. It wasn't right for Annie Kate, or that child, or you, or me, that I was the one listening to the doctor explain in that cold, professional voice that these things sometimes happen. It wasn't fair that I was allowed to fall in love with a girl who was having my roommate's child."

"Tradd had nothing to do with that, Will," Abigail said, tightening her grip on her son's shoulders. "He believed she was in California because that's what I told him. But I didn't realize how lonely the girl would get. How isolated she would feel. She would call at night and cry for hours, Will. I didn't care for the girl and I would never have given my approval for Tradd to marry her, but her crying broke my

492

heart. I simply couldn't bear it, just as I couldn't even bring myself to admit that she was carrying my son's child. I knew you'd take care of Annie Kate, Will. I knew you'd feel sorry for her. I knew you couldn't resist helping someone with such a sad story. You have an awesome need to pity people, Will. I even think that's why you're so fond of me."

"It makes you feel infinitely superior to them, Will," Tradd said. "That's why I know you'll forgive me. I know all about you. You'll forgive me and expect my gratitude for the rest of our lives. By forgiving me, you'll own a part of me. Your kindness never comes free. There's always a terrible price to pay for the victims of that kindness. But you and I are closer friends than even we knew, Will. We balance out each other's weaknesses and insecurities."

"Remember this, too, Will," Abigail said. "You need Tradd more than he needs you. Tradd can help you now. He can help you in your life. He can use his name and his friends to get you ahead no matter what you do."

"I wouldn't let him unzip my fly."

Breaking away from Tradd, I walked to the window overlooking the back section of the garden.

Behind me, as he flung his mother's hands from his shoulders, Tradd said angrily, "How does it feel to need to be a saint, Will? That must be a terribly heavy burden to carry around. You saved me during our plebe year, Will. You really did. But you've got to be careful of the people you save. Some of us don't have the capacity for worship that you require. Adoration can be an exhausting thing."

"So can friendship, Tradd."

"I didn't mean that, Will. Forgive me for saying that. I just can't lose you. I can't afford to lose you. Do you hear me, Will? I'm begging you. I'll do anything to get your friendship back. You have no idea how important it is to me."

But I was no longer listening to Tradd. There was a fire in the southwestern corner of the garden in the trash barrel where Abigail burned leaves during the fall and I was watching the fire. The flames rose high above the garden wall and illuminated the taut, nervous figure of Commerce St. Croix. He was burning his journals one at a time, offering the history of his life to the flames. For several moments, I watched him. He was destroying his autobiography, his secret, modest legacy to the literature of his times, and he was crying as he did it.

"Tell Commerce I know that what I did with his journals was unforgivable, but it was the only way," I said, then turning back toward them. "I never felt happier in Charleston than when I was in this house. There was such peace here. Such safety. I felt completely safe here."

"You can still feel safe here," Abigail said.

"Please, Will," Tradd said, close to tears. "Please. I deserve one more chance. Please don't leave me like this. We love each other. You know we do, Will. Tell me you don't love me. Yes, tell me that. Tell me you don't love me, Will."

"I can't tell you that, Tradd," I said. And I left the St. Croix mansion forever.

49

On the last night I would ever be a cadet, I walked the old city of Charleston as an act of homage and gratitude. My time in the city was up and the long seasoning was complete. Tomorrow I would walk across the stage beneath the gaze of colonels for the last time. I could bear the tonnage of their gaze no longer. My education at the Institute was finished. I knew what I had to do now and what I had to watch out for and whom I had to fear. I could write my own Blue Book now and its rules and codicils would be my own. I would think my own thoughts, not theirs.

But I would not forget the lessons of the Institute. The Institute was my destiny, my character, and my metaphor. I would walk along the dark galleries, from arch to arch, from cadre to merciless cadre, from taming to taming, from system to unconscionable system for as long as I lived. The landscape would change, and the faces, and the names, but there would be no leaving of the barracks for me.

Slowly, I walked the entire Battery from Murray Boulevard to East Bay. It had rained in the afternoon and the rain was fresh in the alleyways. I walked the streets I loved the best: King and Legare, Tradd and Water, Meeting and South Battery, Church and Lamboll. I walked down Stoll's Alley and back to the water down Longitude Lane, then up Tradd Street again and through Bedon's Alley to Elliot Street.

Memory in these incomparable streets, in mosaics of pain and sweetness, was clear to me now, a unity at last. I remembered small and unimportant things from the past: the whispers of roommates during thunderstorms, the smell of brass polish on my fingertips, the first swim at Folly Beach in April, lightning over the Atlantic, shelling oysters at Bowen's Island during a rare Carolina snowstorm, pigeons strutting across the graveyard at St. Philip's, lawyers moving out of their offices to lunch on Broad Street, the darkness at reveille on cold winter mornings, regattas, the flash of bagpipers' tartans passing in review, blue herons in the marshes, the pressure of the chinstrap on my shako, brotherhood, shad roe at Henry's, camellias floating above water in a porcelain bowl, the scowl of Mark Santoro, and brotherhood again.

As I walked the streets I listened to the conversations and murmurings of families on verandahs. I walked slowly through the city of the four-year test, the city of exquisite, measureless beauty, smelling the wet flowers shimmering with aroma in the secret gardens behind high brick walls. All around me was the smell of sweetbay and jasmine, loquat and wisteria, and the stammering of insects among the daphne and tea olive.

I had come to Charleston as a young boy, a lonely visitor slouching through its well-tended streets, a young boy, lean and grassy, who grew fluent in his devotion and appreciation of that city's inestimable charm. I was a boy there and saw things through the eyes of a boy for the last time. The boy was dying and I wanted to leave him in the silent lanes South of Broad. I would leave him with no regrets except that I had not stopped to honor his passing. I had not thanked the boy for his capacity for astonishment, for curiosity, and for survival. I was indebted to that boy. I owed him my respect and my thanks. I owed him my remembrance of the lessons he learned so keenly and so ominously. He had issued me a challenge as he passed the baton to the man in me: He had challenged me to have the courage to become a gentle, harmless man. For so long, I had felt like the last boy in America and now, at last, it was time to leave him. Now it was the man. The man was the quest.

I stopped along the Battery, at the exact point where the Ashley and the Cooper rivers met; and I stared out toward the lights on Sullivan's Island. Beneath the streetlight, I pulled a letter from my back pocket and read it again. Since I had received it the previous day, I had read it over and over again, obsessively—the only letter I ever would receive from Annie Kate Gervais.

"Dear Will,

"Now you know everything. I cried when I heard you knew. And I felt bad about myself again. Abigail called and asked me to intercede with you on Tradd's behalf. After what she and Tradd had put me through, I never wanted to hear their names again. I told her that, too. But I'm sorry you had to be hurt by me again. I don't remember much about our time together, Will, but I remember you were sweet. And I remember that you loved me. I'm not sure I loved you back, but some of me did. I'm sure of that, Will. You'll make some girl a fine husband, but I was not right for you.

"I want to tell you why Tradd would not marry me. It's important for me to tell you. My father was from North Charleston. They called him white trash South of Broad, but he was a wonderful charming man who swept my mother right off her feet. Mother's family was very fine, but also poor, and they never forgave her. You know the rest, Will. There won't be any debutante parties for me, no St. Cecilia ball, no yacht club. Tradd was my only chance. But, of course, Abigail wouldn't have a St. Croix marrying a Gervais from North Charleston. It's a funny story, isn't it, Will? She thought I got pregnant intentionally and convinced Tradd of the same thing. Isn't it a funny story?

"I've got to go now. I'm getting good grades. California is nice. I just love to watch the surfers, and everyone out here thinks I'm a charming Southern belle from an aristocratic family. That's what I tell them. I never look for shells or sand dollars when I walk on the beach out here. Please don't answer this letter, Will. I hope you understand.

"Annie Kate."

I turned away from the seawall and walked across White Point Gardens. I tried to think of a summing up, a chronicle of things I had learned at the Institute; I wanted a list of the strengths and deficiencies I was bringing to the task of becoming a man. I knew this or thought I did: I wanted to live life passionately, in luxurious free form, without squads, without uniforms or ranks. Freedom was the only thing I had never known, and it was time to walk with abandon, immune from the battalions, answerable only to myself. I would make my own way now, conscious of my singularity, proud of it. I would run wild, out of step, and unrestrained. And though I had learned in the barracks that I would always be afraid, I had also learned that I was not for sale and could not be rented out for any price. I had found one thing—at last, at last—to like about myself.

I walked the beautiful city in uniform for the last time. I knew now it was possible to fall in love with a whole city. I stopped in Hampton Park to say good-bye to the lion. Then I returned to the barracks.

* * *

Mark and I dressed for graduation. It was a perfect June morning. I had just watched as Mark and hundreds of my classmates were sworn in as second lieutenants in the Army. In two years, eight of them would be dead in Vietnam. On returning to the barracks, I had thrown all my uniforms except my full dress into the garbage can in fourth division, doused them with gasoline, and lit them with a match. The blaze had been spectacular and infinitely satisfying.

It was lonely in the room with just the two of us.

"Hey, lieutenant," I said as I adjusted my suspenders. "I don't want to hear about you winning any medals in Vietnam. You hear me?"

Mark turned and grinned at me. "Yeh, I hear you, asshole-breath."

"Promise me, Mark," I said seriously, "promise me that you'll be careful. Promise me."

"I will. I'll be careful. I promise, Will. And I won't win any medals."

And he was careful. But sometimes being careful is not enough. It was not enough for my roommate, Mark Santoro. He lied about the medals. Mark won lots of medals and became the most decorated Institute graduate of the Vietnam era. His father had the medals mounted and framed and displayed them proudly to me on the day that Mark Santoro's portrait was unveiled on the wall of the library at the Institute.

We finished dressing for graduation and we embraced for a long time. Then we went down to the quadrangle and formed up with the seniors of R Company. We marched out of the barracks to join the rest of the four hundred.

Four thousand people sat beneath the trees on the south end of the parade ground to watch the graduation. I saw my family and waved to them. The campus was beautiful and leafy and the parade ground blazed in the deepest green of summer. There were brown-skinned girls in cotton print dresses and proud mothers and fathers applauding as their sons crossed the stage to receive their diplomas from the General.

When my name was called by the adjutant, I walked toward the General, received the diploma in my left hand, stepped back, and saluted him.

He returned the salute coldly and shook my hand.

"Do not disgrace the ring, Mr. McLean," he said.

"Dante Pignetti," I answered. "Dante Pignetti, my roommate, sir."

He stared at me, then turned away.

As I walked across that stage I felt something growing within me, something powerful, deeply committed, and unfathomable. I wondered if the crowd could see it in my walk. It was the witness, one afflicted with all the hurt and burden and grandeur of memory. I wondered if they could see the difference.

No, they saw only a boy who had joined the Line, a boy with a diploma, a smiling happy boy. They saw a boy who would be an Institute man for the rest of his life. A whole man.

They could not see the difference. They did not know their system had proffered me an inestimable gift: It had given me the chance to prove that, though I wore the ring, I was not one of them.

When the ceremony was over, I found the Bear and handed him my diploma along with a ballpoint pen.

"What's this for, lamb?"

"I want you to sign it, Colonel. I want you to make it official," I answered, and pointing to General Durrell's signature, I said, "I want the name of a man I can respect on my diploma, Colonel."

He handed me back the diploma without signing it. "There already is, Bubba," he answered. "There already is."

And he pointed to my name.

ABOUT THE AUTHOR

Pat Conroy's first three books were all made into major motion pictures: *The Water Is Wide* became *Conrack*, starring Jon Voight, *The Great Santini*, starring Robert Duvall and *The Lords of Discipline*, starring David Keith. A graduate of The Citadel, Mr. Conroy lives in his native Atlanta. His forthcoming novel is *The Prince of Tides*.

Special Offer
Buy a Bantam Book
for only 50¢.

Now you can have Bantam's catalog filled with hundreds of titles plus take advantage of our unique and exciting bonus book offer. A special offer which gives you the opportunity to purchase a Bantam book for only 50¢. Here's how!

By ordering any five books at the regular price per order, you can also choose any other single book listed (up to a $4.95 value) for just 50¢. Some restrictions do apply, but for further details why not send for Bantam's catalog of titles today!

Just send us your name and address and we will send you a catalog!
